HALLOWED BY THEIR NAME

THE UNOFFICIAL IRON MAIDEN BIBLE

MARTIN POPOFF

Hallowed By Their Name

The Unofficial Iron Maiden Bible

Martin Popoff

SCHIFFER PUBLISHING

4880 Lower Valley Road • Atglen, PA 19310

OTHER SCHIFFER BOOKS BY THE AUTHOR

*The Art of Metal: Five Decades of Heavy Metal Album Covers,
Posters, T-shirts, and More*
978-0-7643-6597-3

OTHER SCHIFFER BOOKS ON RELATED SUBJECTS

*The Who: Concert Memories from the Classic Years,
1964 to 1976*
Edoardo Genzolini
978-0-7643-6402-0

Copyright © 2025 by Martin Popoff

Library of Congress Control Number (Standard Edition): 2024932159
Library of Congress Control Number (Beast Edition): 2024937870

All rights reserved. No part of this work may be reproduced or used in any form or by any means—graphic, electronic, or mechanical, including photocopying or information storage and retrieval systems—without written permission from the publisher.
   The scanning, uploading, and distribution of this book or any part thereof via the Internet or any other means without the permission of the publisher is illegal and punishable by law. Please purchase only authorized editions and do not participate in or encourage the electronic piracy of copyrighted materials.
   "Schiffer," "Schiffer Publishing, Ltd.," and the pen and inkwell logo are registered trademarks of Schiffer Publishing, Ltd.

Red devil hands holding paper scroll for deal with devil concept, isolated on black
   background © by Elisanth Courtesy of www.bigstock.com.
Set of different grunge textures isolated on dark background. Vector. Abstract traced
   backgrounds for design. © by Vodoleyka Courtesy of www.bigstock.com
Inkwell bottle design vector image © by AStudio-1 Courtesy of www.vectorstock.com
Black ink bottle splash art illustration icon design. © by Martin Aleksov
Courtesy of www.shutterstock.com
Feather quill pen icon, classic stationery illustration. © by difugi creative
Courtesy of www.shutterstock.com

Designed by Christopher Bower and Jack Chappell
Cover design by Christopher Bower
Type set in Exocet OTCECY/Minion Pro

ISBN (Standard Edition): 978-0-7643-6816-5
Ebook: 978-1-5073-0391-7
ISBN (Beast Edition): 978-0-7643-6868-4

Printed in China

Published by Schiffer Publishing, Ltd.
4880 Lower Valley Road
Atglen, PA 19310
Phone: (610) 593-1777; Fax: (610) 593-2002
Email: Info@schifferbooks.com
Web: www.schifferbooks.com

For our complete selection of fine books on this and related subjects, please visit our website at www.schifferbooks.com. You may also write for a free catalog.
   Schiffer Publishing's titles are available at special discounts for bulk purchases for sales promotions or premiums. Special editions, including personalized covers, corporate imprints, and excerpts, can be created in large quantities for special needs. For more information, contact the publisher.
   We are always looking for people to write books on new and related subjects. If you have an idea for a book, please contact us at proposals@schifferbooks.com.

CONTENTS

Preface 6
Introduction: Early Days 10

Chapter 1	Iron Maiden	48
Chapter 2	Killers	84
Chapter 3	The Number of the Beast	106
Chapter 4	Piece of Mind	136
Chapter 5	Powerslave	162
Chapter 6	Live After Death	188
Chapter 7	Somewhere in Time	198
Chapter 8	Seventh Son of a Seventh Son	218
Chapter 9	Tattooed Millionaire and No Prayer for the Dying	236
Chapter 10	Fear of the Dark	258
Chapter 11	A Real Live One, A Real Dead One, and Live at Donington	272
Chapter 12	Balls to Picasso and Alive in Studio A	284
Chapter 13	The X Factor	292
Chapter 14	Skunkworks and Accident of Birth	318
Chapter 15	The Chemical Wedding and Scream for Me Brazil	342
Chapter 16	Virtual XI and the Return of Bruce	364
Chapter 17	Brave New World and Rock in Rio	394
Chapter 18	Dance of Death and Death on the Road	432
Chapter 19	The Best of Bruce Dickinson and Tyranny of Souls	454
Chapter 20	A Matter of Life and Death and Flight 666	466
Chapter 21	The Final Frontier and En Vivo!	498
Chapter 22	Primal Rock Rebellion and British Lion	526
Chapter 23	The Book of Souls and The Book of Souls: Live Chapter	540
Chapter 24	Senjutsu	578

Epilogue 602
Discography 612
Sources 638
Acknowledgments 644
Author Biography and Bibliography 645
Index 652

PREFACE

Well, folks, pull up your leg warmers, lace up the runners, and get set to join me on a trip through the legacy albums of the #1 band in heavy metal. It's pretty strange for an old-timer like me to say that, because I instantly think about the originators, Black Sabbath, and the very best of the 1970s and the bringers of leather and studs, Judas Priest, when I muse upon something like that. And then if I was a young whippersnapper, I'd probably say that Metallica was the number one heavy metal band of all time—you don't get much bigger than the Black Album. And what of *Back in Black*? It seems there are a few candidates.

Still, weirdly, by some measures, all positives and negatives included, I would have to say that Iron Maiden are the biggest, most iconic heavy metal band of all time. It is of no mind that they are from an era between the 1970s bands and Metallica (obviously, just barely in relation to the latter), but it is kind of cool that they occupy that space and also, pertinently, that they came right from the heart of the New Wave of British Heavy Metal (NWOBHM).

To focus on one matchup, there's always been a raging debate concerning where Maiden should fit vis-à-vis Priest. Nobody is debating that Black Sabbath are the godfathers, the originators. Keying in on Metallica, one would have to say that Iron Maiden's continuing and continual presence with new records and selling hundreds of thousands of tickets every tour—well, they simply have inched past Metallica by being firmly in pop consciousness more often and more intensely. But Priest is a funny one. Most ardent fans of this stuff would have put Priest ahead, at least until about 1986. For a moment later, at *Painkiller*, maybe the Priest legacy remained stronger. Both bands effectively went away for the 1990s, but when they returned, well, Maiden just kept growing and growing, not so much in record sales, but just communion with the whole goddamn world.

And yes, it's valid to make it more than about record sales. It's Derek Riggs and Eddie, it's the inspiration of Bruce as a cancer survivor, it's Bruce as a renaissance man, and it's Steve as the undying flame of the band and, to boot, how down to earth he is. As well, it's the personality of Nicko, it's Dave and his sunny disposition, it's Janick with his guitar slung 'round his back and back again, and then it's the secret songwriting skills with an extra layer of class on top from Adrian. It's all of that, plus a huge mountain of anthems. And then it's the fans singing those anthems louder than Dickinson ever could (because he's running around half the time).

And so here we are about to celebrate the band's legacy. I hope it's a headbanger of a trip down memory lane for you, because it certainly was fun for me, reliving these records that I've played hundreds of times, but also coming away really pleased with how good *Somewhere in Time* was, to bring up for you something specific.

And I gotta say, once you get to chapter 9 of this metal monster and into the midsection, the guts of 'er, what I enjoyed most was giving the Bruce Dickinson solo catalog a good hard look. Because, let's face it, we all know this was not the best decade for Maiden albums. When writing the first third, I was already eagerly looking forward to this. I've yet to meet a Maiden fan who did not readily celebrate Bruce's solo work, especially *The Chemical Wedding*. Goddamn it, if that panoramic masterpiece is not better than any Maiden record ever, it's surely the magical working that Bruce Dickinson should be most proud of across his entire career, with the solo dimension of it pushing it up above whatever Maiden album you feel might be a shade better, right? I mean in terms of something of which Bruce can personally be proud, accomplishment-wise, it's gotta be up there.

And okay, *Balls to Picasso* didn't get any better with the passing years, but I was joyously reminded how brilliant *Skunkworks* was. I do recall being fully on board at the time, but still, back then it came and went without dozens of spins. Flash forward thirty years, and I gotta say, the biggest bonus out of doing this section was rediscovering this hugely underrated gem. Again, it's a bit of an unspoken, but I swear, Bruce is going to go to his grave knowing damn well that the best art he put on this planet is his solo material.

Still, understandably, talking about Maiden in the 1990s was not as fun and poignant and nostalgic as dealing with what is pretty much considered the glory years, to keep it tight, say *Iron Maiden* through *Powerslave*. What sustained me through that was, like I say, the deep-tissue massage applied to the Bruce Dickinson catalog, a fine bank of records that needed its due. More of a struggle, however, was talking about a bunch of Iron Maiden albums that I'm not particularly fond of, even if the exercise of examining them so closely resulted in little jolts of headbanging admiration that otherwise might not have happened. But that is a distant memory, made even more remote and rosy-colored forgivable because I love the way that Iron Maiden came back strong in the first decade of the 2000s, with Bruce back at the helm, although not necessarily solely because of him.

I'm not one, particularly, to drink the Kool-Aid that the first record back, *Brave New World*, was all that great shakes. In fact, with the hindsight of twenty years, it's amazing that he stayed with the band. Because all those things he said that needed to have happen out of Steve, well, they didn't really happen, because it was more or less business as usual continuing on from *The X Factor* and *Virtual XI*. Sure, bringing in Kevin Shirley made the record sound better than the two Blaze albums, but it was no production triumph. And the songs were full up with the usual often very annoying Iron Maiden tropes, in particular those pointless mellow intros.

But I'm full-on warm in the belly to report that I liked *Dance of Death* a little bit better and then *A Matter of Life and Death* more again. And then, again, making this book quite the pleasure to write, well, my two favorite Iron Maiden albums of the whole catalog after *Powerslave* would be—wait for it—*The Final Frontier* and *The Book of Souls*.

But to reiterate, sensibly, you have to give me the fact that being as old as dirt, writing this introduction at sixty years of age it's inevitable that I would love *Iron Maiden*, *Killers*, *The Number of the Beast*, *Piece of Mind*, and *Powerslave* unequivocally, without reserve. Those records are sacrosanct. As I've always said, the first four are very different from each other and each super magical, and the last of that suite, *Powerslave*, well, sure, it's a bit *Piece of Mind* redux, but I still love it dearly.

But man, the band's recent material creates such a sense of inspiration and excitement for me that if ever I fell out of love with Iron Maiden, that love affair is renewed, and, to boot, in the right way, through a large clutch of their modern-era songs, rather than just the inanity of worshiping the band through their live shows, something I always found kind of stupid.

This is exactly the reason I loved writing that damn Ted Nugent book, *Epic Ted Nugent*. I think his last records are some of his best (excepting, unfortunately, *The Music Made Me Do It*, which came out later). Also in this camp, I would put the likes of Motörhead, Cheap Trick, Deep Purple, Uriah Heep, and even Kiss in the Tommy Thayer era. But no, the Ted Nugent story runs somewhat the same narrative arc as Maiden, where I'm really not on board for a bunch of the middle period but then am tickled to death that I could say without reservation that both of these bands were and are on a creative high deep into their senior citizen years.

Back to the current tome and wending our way into the final third of it: along the way, yes, we have a few diversions to talk about. There is another smart an' solid Bruce Dickinson solo album, there's Primal Rock Rebellion from Adrian Smith, and there are not one, but two, British Lion albums. As well, as with the previous two-thirds, I've given you at least the short goods on what ex-members of the band have been up to—in particular, Paul Di'Anno and Blaze Bayley—but I sort of deliberately decided that it is really only Bruce Dickinson, Primal Rock Rebellion, and British Lion that would get varying but, on balance, fairly serious examination.

I'm kind of ambivalent about the fact that I put the live albums in the chapter headings—I really don't talk about them that much because I simply don't care. Live albums matter to me little, as do live shows, which might sound like sacrilege when it comes to this firecracker of a live band, one that takes it to the world immensely. But like I say—and all of you who've read a lot of my books know this—to me, the most important thing is the original writing and recording of the songs, and their presence on the studio albums. That's what we go into detail here, and again, that's what I'm so damn happy about it, because as the 2000s march ever on, Maiden remain vitally and inspiringly both about records and concerts.

Disagree with me as you may; I know it's kind of a contrarian view (plug for our YouTube show, *The Contrarians!*), but that's truly the way I feel. Go tell me as much on Facebook and Twitter if you like, but here you go. I hope this book convinces you somewhat the importance of the modern-era records, but indeed I hope, in a wider sense, it keeps you focused on the fact that this band kept coming back to the trough in the 2000s and 2010s and 2020s, writing for us long records the whole way. In other words, it's not just about the old hits from the 1980s, which is the case for so many for Steve's weakening competitors. This is a vital, valid, substantial band who wants to keep in the game, and for that we salute them.

Anyway, yeah, before we go, let me give you a bit of background of why this book exists. Some of you may know that this is my sixth Iron Maiden book. I did a timeline and quotes book called *2 Minutes to Midnight*, which is now long out of print. Next came a self-published trio of books called *Where Eagles Dare: Iron Maiden in the '80s*, *Holy Smoke: Iron Maiden in the '90s*, and *Empire of the Clouds: Iron Maiden in the 2000s*, all of which are also long out of print. These books made use of that material, but I'd finally gotten the opportunity to write just regular narrative volumes, expanding out of that restrictive format greatly, putting in lots of my own analysis, putting things together and increasing the readability and flow versus that near oral history format, utilizing my usual, comfortable, album-by-album, song-by-song, walk-in-the-power-chord-park methodology. There's also lots of fresh interview footage not seen before, as well as some tapping of the available press I'd previously not used.

In the main, *Hallowed By Their Name: The Unofficial Iron Maiden Bible* is the gathered actualization of that trilogy in more than properly published form, put into motion by Bob Biondi and the great people of Schiffer Publishing, Ltd. However, there is much rewriting and additional interview material beyond the trilogy, not to mention an updating most crucially around a chapter concerning the album *Senjutsu*.

Let it also be known that this current tome has nothing to do with my second Iron Maiden book, *Iron Maiden: Album by Album*, which was part of a series of five books that I did where I talked to all manner of Iron Maiden expert and famous fans and we just went through the albums in a Q&A format, sorta like sitting around the kitchen table drinking beers and debating your favorite records. So yes, no overlap with that one at all.

Most satisfying about this book is the opportunity to see in the physical world the biggest, loudest Iron Maiden tome—yes, sure, a bible—ever assembled and of all time, featuring the most ever said about the band between two covers in a format supporting and celebrating that mountain of words, of substance, of muscle on the bone.

In any event, hope I have covered everything I should be saying in this introduction. These things can be kind of hard to do. Consider this one more of a "notes on process situation," an explanation for why the book exists rather than the ins and outs of my fond memories as a fan of Maiden right from the beginning. Well, not exactly the beginning—I must confess I never got *The Soundhouse Tapes*. But I did get—both pretty much immediately—an import copy of the first album and the first *Metal for Muthas*, and then everything very quickly as a new release after that. Is that enough street cred? To be sure, I'm not British, but I wish I was, if that helps.

But if I fretted over my credentials, I wouldn't have done any of these books, let alone all 110 or 120 of them, right? Sometimes you just gotta get on with it. And that, in fact, is a great lesson to learn from Rod Smallwood and the guys in Maiden. If anybody exemplified the can-do, stiff-upper-lip attitude of the British during and after the wars, it's those guys. I'm sure they would be loath to be called role models, but dammit, Rod, Steve, Bruce, Dave, Adrian, Janick, and, yes, even Nicko . . . they're friggin' role models, aren't they? I think so. They've offered value for money the whole time, and they've stuck to their guns, never bowing to trends, always fighting for metal, and then doing it with a balance of class and Who-like danger at the same time. So yeah, lots to admire about Maiden.

Anyway, over, and out—let's swing open the pub door and see what kind of good ol' hard and hearty rock 'n' roll we might have heard in the East End of London back in 1977.

MARTIN POPOFF
martinp@inforamp.net | martinpopoff.com

INTRODUCTION: EARLY DAYS

It may all look like some flourish of heavy metal magic—there was once no Iron Maiden and suddenly they were everywhere—but Steve Harris and his ragtag gang of merry men most certainly paid their dues, as they say. Some bands do this in public, making record after record that no one cares about, but the world's greatest New Wave of British Heavy Metal bands did it in the pubs. Not glamorous, to be sure, but then again, there's not the same wear and tear on body and mind when you can schlep home every night and rely on the lorry driver day job for food and rent.

'Arry, having been born Stephen Percy Harris in Leytonstone, London, on March 12, 1956, was good enough at football to get close to a training slot with West Ham United but then switched gears once he discovered the bass. Into his first band at sixteen, Steve was wielding a Fender Precision he had purchased for £40. School had gone by the wayside as well by this point, and soon would his first band, Influence. By November 1973, Steve is on to Gypsy's Kiss, which is of course Cockney slang for piss!

Harris and the various East End Londoners with whom he'd commune were growing up at a magical time in music, just after the birth proper of heavy metal, which happened to coincide with the birth of progressive rock, all by the British, all in 1970.

"All I knew is that I wanted to play hard, aggressive music with lots of melody, with lots of harmony guitars and lots of time changes," says Steve, beginning our journey with a solid bit of introspection that would come true and remain that way almost fifty years later. "I was influenced by heavy stuff like Sabbath and Deep Purple, Led Zeppelin. But I also loved stuff like Free and Wishbone Ash and the Who, and progressive bands like Jethro Tull, Yes, early Genesis. I wanted to incorporate all that stuff. Lizzy wasn't so much the influence on the guitars. I liked their stuff to a point, but it was mainly Wishbone Ash. I know they weren't as well known over there. If you listen to an old album called *Argus*, you can really hear it. I mean, it's more mellow than Maiden."

Argus hit the shelves on the author's ninth birthday, back in 1972. Wishbone Ash are considered one of the innovators of twin leads, and perhaps the earliest inspiration in that department to hail from the UK as well as demonstrate the technique regularly in clubs around London. The engineer on *Argus* was Martin Birch, who a decade later would produce many of Iron Maiden's milestone records.

"The *Argus* album was voted the best album of 1972," recalls Harris. "Quite rightly so, in my opinion. Absolute classic. I mean, I still listen to it now and it still sounds amazing to me. And as you say, Martin Birch was the engineer on the album, so that was a very influential album, I think. There were a lot of bands around playing Wishbone Ash covers at the time. Everybody in the pubs and clubs at that time started off playing covers same as we did, same as everybody did. The difference with us was we would always try and [*sic*] choose songs that weren't as well known. So, if we chose a Thin Lizzy song, it would be something that was not one of the hits. And everyone was doing 'All Right Now,' so we might do that, but we'd also do something like 'I'm a Mover,' which wasn't as well known.

"Montrose's first album was very much a cult album," continues Steve, citing an American classic fronted by none other than Sammy Hagar, "so we didn't really do much off that. We did something off the second album, *Paper Money*, which wasn't as well known. We did 'I Got the Fire,' which we ended up recording, and that was one of the main songs of our set at one point. But everyone thought it was an original because they'd not heard that album.

"So, we consciously went out of our way to choose songs that weren't as well known so that they would be refreshing. Because you could go every week to see a band playing 'All Right Now' and 'Stairway to Heaven,' but not everybody was playing the sort of songs we were choosing. So even though we were doing some originals and some covers, the covers seemed like they were originals as well. And then as soon as we got more originals, we'd bin the covers anyway."

Meanwhile, in early 1974, future Iron Maiden vocalist Dennis Wilcock is in a band called Front Room, with Paul Samson and Chris Aylmer, both future Samson members. Samson would of course feature a firecracker of a lead vocalist named Bruce Dickinson, born August 7, 1958, in Worksop, Nottinghamshire.

Initially raised by his grandparents, Bruce was moved from Worksop to Sheffield, where his parents had recently relocated. As an impressionable eight-year-old, Bruce Dickinson would meet the band Octopus, who were staying at the hotel his parents were managing. There are parallels here to how Maiden hero Phil Lynott first came under the spell of show business, with Lynott's mother, Philomena, running a hotel that catered to a steady stream of entertainers. By 1971, defiantly independent after having been shuffled among a series of schools, Dickinson is sent off on his own at age thirteen to attend a public school in Northamptonshire called Oundle. It is here that Bruce learns about heavy rock, Dickinson also seeing his first live concert, by hard-hitting progressive blues rockers Wild Turkey, which featured Jethro Tull guitarist Glen Cornick.

Back at the tree roots, in October 1974, Steve is now in a band called Smiler, along with Doug Sampson (drums), the aforementioned Dennis Wilcock singing, plus Mick Clee and Tony Clee on guitars.

"When we played together with Smiler," recalled Sampson, speaking with Jimmy Kay, "I knew Steve was a good bass player. Later, when I auditioned for Maiden, he'd gone ten levels higher. He had really, really changed his whole bass-playing style. It was like the beginning of what he is now. So, I actually jumped in and upped my game, really quickly. Because it really was another level."

On the subject of meeting Steve in the first place, Doug says, "I answered an ad—I think it was the *Melody Maker*—and it was after a drummer for a boogie band, like a bluesy boogie band. I was seventeen. All the guys were a little older. I rung up, got an audition, and turned up to the audition, and the bass player of this band was Steve Harris. We'd never met each other before. Done the audition, an old Savoy Brown song, I think, that kind of music. Me and Steve just hit it off from the first go. We just really played well together. And the whole band sounded all right. And so, I got the job. I think they were taking a bit of a chance on me because I was an unknown quantity. I'd never been in a proper band before. Just done stuff with schoolmates and stuff. So, it was a leap, a little bit further than I'd done before.

"We were quite successful, really, around the pubs and clubs of London," continues Sampson. "But Dennis decided he wanted to leave and try something else. I think he was after forming his own band. So, with that, we all sat down, thought about getting another singer and all that, and Steve at that point decided he was gonna go off and do something of his own. He was gonna form his own band. And he said to me, Are you interested, because I'm gonna go on to form a band. I said no, I'm gonna have to have a break from the rehearsing and all that and get myself sorted out financially, get a job, one thing and another. So, I said no, I'll pass on this. And that's what happened. Steve went off and, as you know, he formed Iron Maiden."

Sampson would later be back in the fold, but for now the only other connective to Maiden would be the song "Innocent Exile." "Yes, that's the only song that I can remember Steve coming up. I can't remember anything else that we actually played with Smiler. It was a very bluesy sort of boogie style of music; we'd done a couple of ZZ Top songs, that sort of thing."

Further on influences, Steve explains that "Sabbath had the riffs, and they had the dark element—the dark, dirgey, slow, heavy kind of vibe—but also they had great melodies and great songs. I mean the bottom line of any band, life span of any band, I've always said, it's the songs. You can have a great technically minded band, but if they're not playing good songs, then you're not really going to listen to them too much. So, it's great songwriting abilities. And they were a lot more melodic than people would give them credit for. And us also, later, because I think a lot of people pass us off as being some metal band with not a lot of melody. Well, that's obviously the people who didn't listen to it properly. But definitely, Sabbath had that kind of raw, earthy, very heavy and dark sound."

In the mid-1970s in London, although Sabbath was doing well, all the rage was glam, with the likes of Slade, Sweet, T. Rex, David Bowie, and Mud. Roxy Music also fit that mold somewhat, as did Queen and Mott the Hoople. Also causing trouble around town was Iggy Pop and his Stooges, recording *Raw Power* in London. Both glam and proto punk like the Stooges were the New York Dolls. Steve would be having none of this, especially punk, and into the future would champion progressive rock, despite it going out of fashion, albeit briefly, in the lurid light of punk circa the late 1970s. There was also something called pub rock, sort of old-timey rock 'n' roll with a shot of energy. But no one was more pub rock than Iron Maiden. Playing the likes of the Cart & Horses and the Ruskin Arms for years, Harris would eventually put a fully functioning pub in his house.

But Steve was not a big Deep Purple fan, surprisingly. "No, it was more Wishbone Ash and Free. I liked Deep Purple—we all did—but they weren't as much an influence. Bands like Jethro Tull were actually more of an influence, believe it or not, than Deep Purple. I had *Made in Japan* and ended up buying a few Purple albums, whatever, but they weren't a major influence. Black Sabbath were probably more an influence, and Led Zeppelin as well. Some people thought that we were doing the twin guitar thing version of Purple at times, but that certainly wasn't intentional. Free were definitely a bigger influence. If you listen to Dave's guitar playing, he was definitely influenced by Paul Kossoff a lot and also Hendrix; Free were a massive influence." The Dave that Steve is referring to is blond bomber Dave Murray, born in Edmonton, London, on December 23, 1956.

"Oh yeah, I loved Sabbath," says Dave, in agreement with Steve. "Always, pretty much all the way through, really. Always loved the Sabs, from the first album onwards. I actually saw them after the first album came out. And it was kind of neat. It was in London somewhere, kind of a theater, and I remember being up in the balcony and it was just this huge sound, and it was brilliant. And the audience was full of witches and stuff [laughs], witches and warlocks; it was just a vibe. It was a great thing. It's just that the songs were really big, and the riffs were kind of ominous and it was really fat sounding. There was something about Tony Iommi's guitar playing that was amazing. Because of course he would do the heavy stuff, but he would go into the acoustic-type stuff and the piano. It really wasn't one-dimensional; they were stretching out. And as I've said, the strongest thing about any band is their material, their songs. And Sabbath has definitely got it. I followed them right through, from the first album onwards. When the album came out, I went out and bought it [laughs], played it till the vinyl wore out.

"It was always a great thing to go buy the vinyl in the record store," continues Murray, "waiting for the album to come out, having the vinyl, that big thing. I've got it all put in storage somewhere, all my Deep Purple, Zeppelin, Sabbath, the Hendrix albums. If I liked a band, I just went out and bought everything available. And those were the days when most of the albums had eight tracks on them, and that was it. Today you get an album, it's got sixteen, twenty songs. But there was something about going out and getting the vinyl, just the artwork. And there were times I'd be waiting for the album to come out. You had to be a bit more of a detective back then. You'd get the magazines and stuff. But then again, it's a wonderful thing now how easily accessible everything is. But yes, Jethro Tull, Cream, all that. First album I ever bought was *Electric Warrior* by T. Rex, which came out, I think, in 1971. And I knew it was coming out, and I remember going down to the store and waiting for it to come in, and it was just a vibe. The artwork, with that silhouette with gold on the front of the album, and I still think it's one of my favorite albums. And the price was two quid or something [laughs].

"But yeah, personally, when I started out, I was listening to the blues guys, Hendrix and that sort of thing, Santana, Free, and then a band like Wishbone Ash and Thin Lizzy—I really dug the stuff they were doing. We didn't go out to try and emulate these guys, but it was there subconsciously, when the songs were being put together. There are those areas where you say, okay, that would be nice, there's a melody, and you put a harmony on top of that. It kind of sweetens things up a little bit when you've got a heavy driving sound. So basically, Wishbone Ash got us into that headset."

Dave would arrive in the ranks soon enough, although in 1975 he began his recording career by appearing on a single called "Cafe de Dance" with his "mad punk" band Secret. In parallel, though, on December 25, 1975, Steve was busy christening his band Iron Maiden. This is shortly after he leaves his former band, Smiler. The first Maiden lineup consists of Steve on bass, Paul Mario Day (later of More and Wildfire) on vocals, Dave Sullivan and Terry Rance (both formerly with the Tinted Aspex) on guitars, and Ron Matthews on drums. John Northfield would replace Dave Sullivan, resulting in the short-lived lineup #2. Paul Mario Day would soon be replaced by Dennis Wilcock, resulting in lineup #3, which also sees Dave Sullivan returning, replacing John Northfield.

According to Steve Harris's diary, May 1, 1976, at St. Nicholas Hall in Poplar, qualifies as Iron Maiden's first gig, although there is some dispute over whether this took place, or if it was in fact a Gypsy's Kiss gig. Conversely, June 9, 1976, at Cart & Horses, Stratford, is the gig that noted Maiden expert Garry Bushell considers the first show. Nonetheless, Steve says the gig happened, with payment for the show being £5.

"It was actually 1975 when we formed," notes Harris, "and then it took us four and a half years to get a record deal, and I think it was purely what was happening—or not happening, in our case—back in those days, in the music biz at the time. I think it was just the whole reaction . . . I mean, we were around for the punk thing; the punk thing happens around 1977, so it was difficult at first to work, and then the whole sort of backlash with that was really tough.

"I think it was a good thing in a way," continues Harris. "In retrospect I suppose it's easy to say that, but at the time it was being really annoyed at not getting attention and not getting gigs. But it was a good thing in a way, because it was four and a half years before we got the deal, and everything happened after that. Making the album, going on tour, consequently, tour after tour, the whole thing happened really quickly, from playing sort of pubs to playing big places. And we wouldn't have been prepared for that if we had got signed after a year or something. Going out and playing all those gigs, just kind of being together as a band for that amount of time, it stood us in good stead for later."

For the name of the band, Steve took inspiration from the 1939 film *The Man in the Iron Mask*. Possibly apropos, a British comedy called *The Iron Maiden* is issued in 1962— the film is released a year later in the US as *Swinging Maiden*. The "iron maiden" of the film was a traction engine, a type of train locomotive used for heavy haulage. But as the story goes, essentially *The Man in the Iron Mask* led Steve to thinking about the torture device called the iron maiden, essentially a tight body-shaped box lined with spikes on the inside.

Curiously, also in 1970, a band at this point six years old called Bum changes their name to Iron Maiden upon signing to Gemini Records in 1970. A debut album is recorded, but before the album comes out, the label folds. A duplicate set of master tapes owned by one of the band members is used to issue what would have been their first album, as *Maiden Voyage*, in 1998. Although completely unrelated to the famous Iron Maiden, the band's sound is nevertheless a form of doomy, psychedelic hard rock.

While Steve is establishing the Iron Maiden concept, future Maiden mainstay Adrian Smith, in 1974, is purchasing for £235 his first professional guitar, a Gibson Les Paul Goldtop, which he still uses to this day. Adrian Frederick Smith was born in Hackney, East London, on February 27, 1957. In terms of his influences, *Machine Head* is the first album he owns, Smith using it to break the ice with school chum Dave Murray. The two form their first band, Stone Free, shortly thereafter, with Dave soon moving on to a soft-rock band called Electric Gas. Further connecting these young musicians, "Smoke on the Water" becomes a staple of Steve's band Gypsy's Kiss, along with Black Sabbath's "Paranoid" and Free's "All Right Now."

"It's gotta be Black Sabbath, hasn't it?" muses Adrian, on where heavy metal starts. "I mean, 'Paranoid' was also quite a big hit in the UK, so you heard that on the radio. They were massively influential. But really, I never heard the expression heavy metal until the late 1970s / early 1980s. To me it was always hard rock or heavy rock, with Purple, Sabbath, even Free. And then the metal thing crept in at the end of the 1970s / early 1980s. But I suppose if you could call anything metal at the time, it was probably Sabbath.

"It was just the whole atmosphere they created, I suppose," reflects Smith. "But again, there's quite a lot of blues in the soloing side of it. But the sound of the guitar, some of the tunings, it was that very doomy kind of sound which you'd associate with metal rather than a happy poppy sound. I suppose Zeppelin touched on it with 'Whole Lotta Love' and some of the heavier stuff, but there was a lot more to Zeppelin, a lot of folks and loads of blues. They were before Sabbath, and maybe they touched on metal with 'Communication Breakdown' and that sort of rock 'n' roll metal. It's almost like the white man's blues, heavy metal."

On the subject of heavy metal evolving out of the blues, Smith figures, "There's a definite connection there. Dave's the same. He listened to Hendrix a lot. He was greatly influenced by blues. I think probably all of us are influenced a bit by Hendrix, but blues is a big influence on metal, and if you take AC/DC, I mean, what Angus plays is very blues; it's amped up, but a lot of it comes from blues.

"The first thing I listened to was *Free Live!*—classic album, with 'All Right Now' and all those great songs," continues Smith. "Just electrifying, and the guitar was really kind of raunchy and raw and loud. And I just had to, you know, get a guitar and plug it into a big amp and away you go. Of course, it's not that simple, but you know what I mean. So, it was the guy from Free, Paul Kossoff, all the Lizzy guitarists, Gary Moore, Scott Gorham . . . Pat Travers I already liked, and Johnny Winter. So, it was more kind of blues guys.

"I think I'd already been playing five or six years before Van Halen came out, so when he came out, he probably didn't have the influence on me that he did on the kids that started playing just after that. Then we're coming out with the finger tapping and all that. I was kind of entrenched in my own style before that, although Van Halen was incredible. He was like the late 1970s / early 1980s version of Hendrix. He took it up even further. But my early influences were more the second-generation rock blues guitarists. And I still play like that. People say Maiden are metal, and I suppose it is, but there's a lot of other influences. There's almost a folky influence in what Maiden does. In a convoluted way, there's a bit of blues in there, in the soloing, the scale patterns; you know, Maiden's pretty unique. It's kind of a mishmash. And there's a progressive influence—Steve loves all the progressive bands."

In August 1976, Adrian's band Evil Ways become Urchin and land a deal with DJM Records. Around this time, future Maiden singer Paul Di'Anno was mucking about, singing in bands, and working as a butcher and a chef. Paul Andrews (the Di'Anno wouldn't come until his days with the band Smiler) was born in Chingford, London, on May 17, 1958. If you ever wondered why in future years Paul would spend so much time in Brazil, it's because he held dual British and Brazilian citizenship, having been born to a Brazilian dad.

Meanwhile, unbeknown to the Maiden boys, another soon-to-be-important figure in their lives was getting together an infrastructure that would prove tantamount to the band's future success. In 1976, Rod Smallwood and Andy Taylor found Smallwood-Taylor Enterprises, later to become Sanctuary Group, named after the popular and punky early Iron Maiden track. "One of the best guys businesswise," says Di'Anno of Smallwood, "because you deal with some assholes in the business, obviously. But he's a Yorkshire man. He's from up north and he calls a spade a spade basically. And what you see is what you get. He's a pretty good guy. I haven't seen him for a lot of years."

Smallwood, born in Huddersfield on February 17, 1950, met Taylor when both were at Trinity College, Cambridge. His early interests were cricket and rugby, but when studying architecture at Trinity, beginning in 1968, he started to book bands for social functions at the school. Bruce Dickinson had done very much the same thing at his own school.

Also, on the subject of infrastructure of sorts, in 1975, UK rock DJ Neal Kay establishes the Soundhouse (or Bandwagon) in the backroom of the Prince of Wales pub in Kingsbury. The Soundhouse was called "London's Only Heavy Rock Disco." The nights that Kay commandeered—one night a week and then the key Sunday night slot—began to take off. Then it was five nights a week and "denim-clad" patrons became the norm, while Neal spun records by Sabbath, Zeppelin, Purple, Thin Lizzy, and Rush. It soon became known as the Heavy Metal Soundhouse. Eventually the club would start to book bands such as Praying Mantis, Nutz, Iron Maiden, Angel Witch, and Samson.

"I was out of work and there was no exposure for any up-and-coming bands," explains Kay. "There was hardly any exposure for the bands that everyone knew. Venues were not interested; no one was interested. The industry had suddenly decided that punk was the thing, and I was getting progressively more and more angry about the whole thing, and I was just an individual. I was a professional DJ, yeah?, but I was still very annoyed. And they took me to this pub one night. I was trucking; I was out of music; I just didn't want to work in it. And I was trucking for a living. And my driving buddy took me to a place one night after work on a Wednesday night near where we lived up in Kingsbury near Wembley. You know the football arena Wembley? It was near there, and it was called the Prince of Wales, and they had a once-a-week rock thing happening there, DJs playing rock music, and he said to me, 'You're going to like this. Come and have a beer.'

"I went in there and I was so impressed," continues Kay. "The sound system was fucking huge, man. It was really big. It wasn't a disco system; it was a fucking ginormous great band PA system. And I had a beer, and you know what? That night, they asked out over the PA if there were any DJs in the house that wanted to come up and work with them and present the rock show, because they were not really sort of rock DJs. I went up there and got the job on the spot, and that's how that happened. Remarkable.

"So, the war was on. It was really vital to try and let the industry know that finally there was a place that would give exposure to rock, and the Bandwagon kind of picked up from that moment on. It was like the pop music of the day five nights a week, rock one night a week, and it was something else for the seventh. And there were a lot of underage kids getting into the commercial music nights, and the license of the place was threatened soon after I joined. I remember going to court to fight the license, and you know the most bizarre twist of all? When it was discovered that there was no trouble on the heavy metal or hard rock night, and people came in couples and they were older, the judge, the silly old fucker, he did, he swung around and said, 'Well, I'll grant you your license on the condition that this form of music takes precedence at least five nights a week!' [laughs]."

Score one for metal, which would please the likes of "classic rock" Steve Harris to no end. Like Van Halen grinding away with a Jim Dandy look-alike for a singer, what Steve was trying to do was looking out of lockstep with the times. The odds of success would look even dimmer once punk picked up the pace, if not for the flag for hard rock being flown by Neal Kay and his growing following.

"Yeah, oh wow!" laughs Neal, remembering the judgment of the court. "So, by appointment to her majesty. Un-fucking-believable. Fucking right [laughs]. It was like I had a coat hanger in my mouth—I didn't stop grinning for a week. The old judge had just given me control of the old Soundhouse, as it became known. Where after that we worked hard, very, very hard indeed, contacting the various people, had all the seats thrown out, had new rules instilled. No one with a suit, shirt, and a tie was allowed in. I threw all the stripes out and had my own doormen put in. I was a member of a bike club at the time, and they became our door staff, actually.

"And finally, after an awful lot of work, Geoff Barton, the journalist from *Sounds*, came down to see what we were doing, and was absolutely amazed, and he wrote a double center-page spread in *Sounds* magazine, which was the magazine of the day. And he subtitled it on the front page of *Sounds*, and would you believe it, 'A Survivor's Report from a Heavy Metal Discothèque!,' exclamation mark, 'cause the thing had been unheard of. And we didn't play anything but rock; we played, as it's known now, classic rock. And by and by, tapes started arriving, cassettes from all over the world, and it became apparent very quickly that record companies just weren't listening to anybody.

"And bear in mind once again, the radio—or total lack of it—the DJ, the radio DJ, Tommy Vance, did a three-hour show once a week on Radio One and called it *The Friday Night Rock Show*. And that was the only outlet that rock had. That was it on radio, and we had the Soundhouse, because *Sounds* had decided to get behind it, and, in turn, other journalists came. Fuck me, I think the London *Times* or the London *Guardian* came to see what all the fuss was about on a Sunday night. We wiped them out; very funny actually.

"I thought of other ways of raising the profile," continues Kay. "I contacted CBS, Epic Records, and I got Ted Nugent and his band to come down and meet the kids on a personal appearance after a London Hammersmith Odeon show. He was the first. That had never happened before! But I had serious contacts up at the record companies by now, because I was playing all the rock and getting an awful lot of publicity for doing it, and I thought, well, what better than that, if Ted Nugent—he was big in those days—if Gonzo came. Then others would follow, and the press would follow too, and the profile of the club and the music would go sky high.

"Look, the structure of the Soundhouse, musically, was very, very, very wide. I said I'd play Styx, Journey, all this sort of stuff. We played prog; we played everything that was good music. What we didn't play was shit. If you couldn't play, write, or sing, then you weren't heard at the Soundhouse. That made the Soundhouse a very selective audience, and it gave live bands a hell of a hard time. By then I had something like a 10K PA in there just for playing records on. It was so loud that we had to fly the discotheque console from the rafters on chains to avoid the rest of the low-frequency feedback, which we did, and it was sort of like a ship's compass if you know what I mean, kind of nimble-mounted. So, if everyone jumped up and down and went bloody mad with their histrionics on the floor, the whole place shook. But if you're going to do it, that's how you do it. There's no point pussyfooting around.

"It was a reaction against the big bands, really," says Steve on the subject of punk, sounding uncommonly charitable. "I suppose bands like Zeppelin and things like that didn't play very often or anymore, and when they did, they played these massive venues, and the whole sort of business was geared towards that kind of stuff. It was a reaction against that, really. But I grew up listening to that stuff, the early 1970s stuff, rock, progressive rock, classic rock; that's the stuff I grew up on and really loved. So that's the stuff we wanted to emulate. Even when we did covers, it was those types of bands, and we sort of learned our trade like that. And once the punks came along, they couldn't really play very well. It's not like the punks now—they can play. But the ones at the time couldn't really play their instruments very well, so it didn't go down too well with bands like us."

Record executive Ashley Goodall, who would soon sign Iron Maiden to their EMI deal—Ashley had joined the label in 1978—expressed much the same sentiment with respect to the "dinosaurs" as it were.

"I think they'd been removed from access. Zeppelin hardly played the UK. They were all off around America doing stadiums and things. Actually, getting hold of Zeppelin, for example, in the UK was quite hard to do. But then you also had a lot of heavy rock bands like Sabbath coming through, Deep Purple, and they did really well at the beginning of the 1970s, but by 1975 they'd gone a bit boring. So, I think you look at it in five-year groups, age groups, and you get the next sixteen-year-olds, and what do they want to do? They want to have their own bands. Also, Radio One was like the most boring radio station in the world. The Pistols always talked about Captain and Tennille, the Carpenters, incredibly dull stuff on it, American and British pop culture, which wasn't very exciting. So, there wasn't really much you could get your hands on, and there was a bit of a vacancy for excitement."

Ashley also mirrors Steve's denigrating attitude toward the punk—at least from a musical standpoint. "Simplicity versus complexity, right? Punk is a really simple form of gut-driven attitude, emotion, like a child wailing, right? I love it, that raw kind of adolescence just screaming out. And therefore, in the music, you had a very low ability to play music to actually be a punk, because it's all about attitude and the ability to really short-punch a song. So, it was really democratized.

"Heavy metal, on the other hand, I think is quite complicated. People say there's a lot in common with heavy metal and classical music because the top end is often quite sophisticated. There's complex rhythms; you've got to be a pretty good keyboard player, great guitarist, amazing drummer. So, the musicianship level is quite different; the complexity at which it works is quite a different level. So, simplicity versus complexity is an interesting analogy just for starters. Let alone possibly age group, let alone whether you're a serious musician, whether you're trying to have a pot at it or whatever. Not to say some punk people weren't good musicians, but on the whole, they weren't amazing musicians."

On what the New Wave of British Heavy Metal might have learned from punk, Goodall figures, "Attitude and energy and live events. But it really didn't borrow much else from it, other than that it was we can get up and have a go ourselves. So that idea of encouraging young bands and people to start playing again, breathe new life into it, and probably a new load of bands came out as a consequence. And actually again, this generational thing—the next generation after the first wave of rock gods were saying we're doing it for ourselves. So, it was generational ownership, the fact you can get up and do it. It's DIY. Nothing's stopping you.

"So first you had this kind of tsunami of punk going on, underneath which was this continual substratum of heavy rock bands, some of which were newer, some of which weren't. And I guess since the middle of punk, people said, well, actually, I don't buy into punk, but actually I'm quite a good musician—I like heavy rock. Or I'd seen Zeppelin or Purple or Judas Priest before; I'm going to do my own version of that. It's the next generation down, down to these fifteen-, sixteen-, eighteen-year-olds saying I'm going to do it myself, I'm going to play live, I'm quite a good musician, and I'm going to play heavy rock. And what I found was I'd been going to gigs a lot and seeing punk bands and suddenly realized that actually the punk bands were not pulling so many people, but the heavy rock bands were. And so, whether they were just suddenly the new force for gravity or whether they'd always had these people there, the live scene was happy and lively, and everyone started going to live gigs, and therefore you had a bigger population watching heavy metal."

In 1976, fan Rob Loonhouse shows up at the Soundhouse with a wooden fake guitar, and air guitar is born.

"Okay, this is all about the spirit of rock 'n' roll for me," chuckles Kay. "I've seen it; I've been seeing it all my life. Joe Cocker, I will say, was the first, visually, ever to do this onstage at the Woodstock festival while they're playing the solo in 'With a Little Help from My Friends'; Joe Cocker's standing there playing his imaginary guitar. The hero of heroes. I think that's the first visually recorded episode. I didn't invent it; it was already there. It's what people do when they are really taken with the spirit of the thing.

"At the Bandwagon the Loonies went one further. Actually, it went three further. The first thing that happened was Rob Loonhouse, one Rob Yeatman, a professional photographer by trade by day, and a glorious leader of the lunatics at the time, walked into the Soundhouse one day with a hardboard Flying V. No strings, but a whammy bar. And everyone said, 'Rob, what are you going to do with that? There's no strings on it, man; you can't play it.' 'Don't need any.' Ah, interesting.

"Okay, get on with the show, play the show, lighting up, time, full lights, crack up the old sound system. The whole bar's shaking, fit to bust. Suddenly into the limelight steps one Loonhouse, picks up the Flying V, and whilst I'm playing the Judas Priest track, lo and behold Rob Loonhouse plays the solo! On the Flying V. And everyone saw him. And I thought that's novel. It's completely insane but it's novel. And afterwards I said to him, 'Why did you do that?' And he said, 'Well, I felt like doing it, mate.' All right. Sure. No problem, man.

"Next week there was five of them. The week after there was ten. Then there was fifteen. Then we started the triple-decker headbanging with them, and they'd stack up on each other's shoulders, three up. And there'd be a sea up there of air guitar players. At Christmas we ran Headbanger of the Year, or, as it became known, Air Guitarist of the Year. The year after, it got so crazy, I finished up inviting an all-star guest panel to judge the final, amongst which were members from Rainbow, Priest, Maiden; all manner of high-falutin' stars were there. What is it? It's headbanging band of the year.

"Rob Loonhouse by now had formed Willy Flasher and the Raincoats, and he had built himself a double-neck Flying V and cardboard keyboards, and he had a cardboard drum kit for a drummer, and he had a whole stage set made of cardboard. And he had road crew. And in the middle of the set, they arranged for the drum set to explode all over the place; the road crew come running out onstage and start plugging in all these cables and rebuilding the kit. And it's just sensational. Absolutely sensational.

"I would say this is a lot more to do with just the 'wagon rather than anything else, because you didn't see this so much elsewhere," explains Kay. "It's partially my fault for driving them crazy because I'd come from a showbiz side, and I'm kind of a showman. I'm never satisfied with just playing records—any fool can do that. That's not it; you have to do more. And what I realized in the end was I'd grown a whole culture of rock 'n' roll loonies. I mean, we used to do the craziest things. In the middle of a set of fast-moving rock, I'd suddenly put in a tiny little bit of country and western, just about thirty bars, hoe-down music, real rapid, and then go straight back into the metal again.

At Christmas show time, we'd do about thirty bars of 'Snow White and the Seven Dwarfs' hi-ho, and the metalers would be on their knees going around the Soundhouse like the dwarfs. We inspired and encouraged total over-the-top behavior."

Back to the pubs: in November 1976, Dave Murray and early Maiden vocalist Dennis Wilcock have a band called Warlock. Elsewhere, Iron Maiden's lineup keeps shifting through this period. Lineup #4 consists of the previous core of Steve, Dennis, and Ron, with two new guitarists replacing Dave and Terry; namely, Dave Murray and Rob Angelo (soon to be in Praying Mantis and then Weapon). On November 13, the band plays a battle of the bands at the Queen Elizabeth Public House in Chingford and finish second. Meanwhile on May 13, 1977, Urchin, featuring Adrian Smith, issue their "Black Leather Fantasy" / "Rock and Roll Woman" single. The A-side is written by Adrian. For a brief time, Dave Murray is also in the band. Of note, the "Charlotte the Harlot" / "22 Acacia Avenue" story line of Maiden's circa the early 1980s reaches back to these early Urchin days.

Explains Steve, "It was difficult because we tried to get Adrian and Dave to join before the first album, and he was still doing his thing with Urchin, his band Urchin, and he'd been with them for years, and he was fronting it and singing lead vocals for that, so he sort of had to see that through, really. And it's not like we were hoping and praying it wouldn't work for him, because we didn't think like that, really. We just went on ahead, got someone else, and carried on with it. But when it didn't work out with him, we just got straight back on it and said, 'Look, you're joining this time, no argument, that's it. You're in.' He was like, 'Okay then.' That was it, really. But they played together in sort of an early band before, young band writing together when they very first started learning. So, they had a good affinity anyway. And because they're such different styles of playing, they really complemented each other. Wishbone Ash, Thin Lizzy . . . there were elements of that in their playing, but the fact that we were a much more aggressive, heavier band lent itself to the fact they were able to play more aggressively, but melodically over the top also."

Prospects were starting to improve for hard-charging guitar rock at this point, thanks to the likes of Neal Kay, despite the spotlight being shone on punk. In 1977 both Samson and Angel Witch form, the latter under the name Lucifer. There's an Iron Maiden connection in that early Angel Witch member Steve Jones went on to form Speed, with Bruce Dickinson. As well, the band was always considered similar to Maiden and became Maiden's key competition for a brief period in 1980.

Spring 1977 and Iron Maiden's lineup #5 features quite an upheaval, with Steve and Dennis remaining, now with Terry Wapram on guitar and Ron "Rebel" Matthews on guitar.

"Dennis Wilcock came to the Marquee, because he did the photography for a band called Bearded Lady who were great friends of ours," explains Terry Wapram, to Jimmy Kay from the *Metal Voice*. "And I was down there with a band. I believe the band at the time would've been called Hooker, and I guested with them as well, and I was seen there. And at that point—I don't really remember the full story—there'd been some problem with Dave and Bob Sawyer, who I know as well. But there was some problem, and Dave was going out of the band at the time. I mean, obviously, Dave came back. But he approached me when, I think, things were a little shaky. But I was kind of busy at the time, so I didn't do anything about it straightaway. And then I think the band I was working with kind of slowed up a bit. So, I approached them, and I basically went down and played with them and got given the job. They didn't put me under any pressure or anything—basically just started rehearsing with them. It was quite a turbulent time, really. I feel it was a time when they were sort of finding their feet and working out what they really needed. Obviously, moving away from the two-guitar thing was not necessarily the right choice.

"But they wanted to try keyboards," continues Wapram. "And we know now [that] later on they got keyboards in the lineup, someone off to the side now. But I think when you took the other guitar out, it made it quite challenging. And obviously I was a very capable guitarist, because I'd been playing in three-pieces a lot of the time, where you really had to fill all the holes in. So that wasn't a problem. The problem was not being able to play the harmonies properly. I remember in the beginning, Steve Harris developed a kind of style where he was playing the bass, and then he would play some of the harmony with me and then jump back down on the bass. So, he'd go up the neck as well. But that obviously took some of the power out of it. So basically, they went back to a two-guitar lineup.

"But that's how I got in. They really didn't make it hard at all. I kind of showed interest and I approached them, and I went down, and he gave me the job. And at that point Ronnie Rebel was playing the drums, and we played a number of gigs just like the four of us. And then something went wrong with Ron. They appeared unhappy with Ron, and they put out the ad for a drummer and a keyboard player, and Thunderstick came in and got the gig. That's when he was working under his own name, Barry Graham Perkis. This is before he became Thunderstick. And Tony Moore came in. And it was funny, because I was talking to Tony on his radio show, and he asked a really funny question. It was quite embarrassing, really. He said, 'You know, when I came down and got the job straightaway,' he said, 'how many other people showed up to the audition?' And I had to start laughing. I mean, we were live on radio, and I said, 'You were the only one. But we did genuinely really like you.' But he's another close friend as well. Tony has had a very interesting career; same as Barry, Thunderstick, joining Samson."

Asked what material we know, and love was existing at that time, Terry says, "I mean, myself, I played all of the first album, obviously in rehearsals and sometimes live, plus a good chunk of the second album. And then some of the things like 'Killers' definitely came after me. Even 'Running Free.' 'Wrathchild' was being played for a long period of time. It didn't go in chronological order, really. I think they picked what their favorites were for the first album plus a few extras. But the whole kind of two albums, as I say, there are songs on there that definitely were outside of my time period.

"Some of the stuff was played slower initially before it was recorded," continued Wapram. Which is an interesting concept: Maiden as a 1970s band rather than an NWOBHM band or, specifically, an influence on speed metal or thrash. "Which actually didn't take it away from it. It kinda made it very powerful, or sort of a steady pace."

Terry gets more specific when talking about one of the songs he most definitely was present and accounted for, with respect to its genesis.

"Obviously I'd like to say categorically, before I make any comment like that, in my opinion, when you help with a song, you're not writing it. But yes, certain bits of the songs, and 'Phantom of the Opera' springs to mind. I was very impressed when I was first shown that riff. I really thought it crossed a barrier and went into a hole 'nother thing. It was like their version of 'Bohemian Rhapsody,' where there were so many pieces. But I was sitting down with Steve and looking at that, with Tony Moore as well. We would be looking at pieces and everyone would go, 'How about a bit of this, a bit of that?,' and he'd say yes or no and 'We can do this; we can do that.' So, there was a good involvement in that one and a few other bits and pieces. But that one in particular.

"It's funny, playing it now [Terry was playing in a sort of historical Iron Maiden tribute at the time called the Ides of March], I thought that would be the one I felt would be the most work to relearn. I've sat down and reexamined it. Because when I first started to replay it, I kind of played it more lumpy, kind of like it might've gone at the time. And then when I tried to play what I considered my version against the actual track, just to make sure everything was in line, I quickly fell out of line with the track. And I realized [that] the version that ended up on the album—just the main riff, the opening riff—was slightly tweaked, possibly, from what we were doing. But once I started playing it, it was no different in difficulty to play. It was just flipping through the notes quicker and maybe missing one. That stuff can be quite quick. So, if you miss a note it, it can sound like it, even though it's not right. But that would be the only one I would have any real comment on.

"I spent a lot of time rehearsing with them more than actually playing live," continues Terry, confirming his tenure. "It was sort of in flux. We'd done gigs with Ronnie, and then Ronnie went out. And then Tony Moore and Thunderstick came in. I think Tony had done the one gig with them, as far as I can remember. He lived in the same road as me at the time. And I remember him coming around to me and saying, 'I'm not really feeling quite right about this. I'm going to pull out.' And he actually used my pay phone, in my street, and rung them up, and came out. And so, at that point it all went a bit strange, and there were discussions what would go on. I didn't really show any interest in being in a two-guitar lineup, because at that point, as I say, I'd never really done it. So, when I showed no real interest in being in a two-guitar lineup, that's when they decided to kind of move on without me. But it was a very interesting period. I spent a massive amount of time sitting around at Steve's nan's, tinkering around with things with him. It was a very interesting time, really."

Some studio work as well. "Yeah, there was a program over here called *Metal Mickey*, and this particular studio owned this robot thing; when you went in the foyer, the robot was in there. We rehearsed quite a lot in there. But the lineup was changing all the time. You get one thing right, and then you have to start rehearsing with someone else. And then Tony went out, and that was a big thing—well, what are we going to do now? But what I like about it was, Steve never lost his vision of what he was trying to do. I think they came back stronger when they tried all these other things. They realized a two-guitar lineup was correct for them. Or [at] least the harmony lineup. And I obviously appreciate the three of them now."

Clarifying further, Terry says, "I played five, maybe six gigs with them. The funniest one I remember playing with them, we were on a fairground. I told this story in the early days' video. Dave Lights was doing the lights, but there was no real budget. They used to use half house bricks, take all the gunpowder out of the fireworks, and put two live wires through the mains in, and then plug the plug in and flick a switch, and obviously it ignited when the current went through the gunpowder. And we were at this fairground, and I had a big pedal board at the time, and I hadn't really paid attention to when the flashes were going to go off. And we were playing away, and in the distance you can see the Ferris wheel going around, people looking at it. I stepped forward to stand on something just exactly as Dave Lights set off one of these thunder flashes. It nearly took my eyebrows off. I mean, it completely shocked me. I stood back, and the weirdest thing is, all this molten gunpowder leaked out of the brick onto the stage, set fire to the corner of my pedal board, and also started to burn the PA cables. I mean, loads of people were running around and got it under control, but that just cracked me up. You had to stay like it was part of the show, so you couldn't crack up. It was mental, really funny. But they were always famous for their show at the time. Even as a sort of pub band, they put on the best show around, with smoke and lights.

"But I was in at about eight months, and Thunderstick came in after me, as I was already there playing with Ronnie, and we had already done gigs. I'd left in February 1978, and I think Thunderstick might've gone on to March or something. They've had some ridiculous amount of guitarists. But they deserve to be where they are. They're a really hardworking, very talented band. But it just feels nice to be part of something that big. At the time, when I went into them, they were the biggest thing on the pub circuit, and you could tell they were rising. But I couldn't tell at that point how far that they could go. And then when I came out and Dennis came out, slightly after me, to form V1 with me, that really knocked Steve back for a while. He was kind of considering at the time his options if he could pull it all back together. Because he was just like with Dave Murray, really, and the drummer. But obviously they've grown enormously. I know some people kind of don't like them to move on, and they just want more of the same. But the amount of albums they've done, the amount of years they've been on top of their game, it had to move from where they originally stood. I mean, the first two albums are utterly iconic, but they've done some great albums later on as well, and they're still producing great music and amazing live shows.

"I started out in recording, with a company called Pye," explains Thunderstick, also in conversation with Jimmy Kay from *The Metal Voice*. "I started out as a tape op, a sound engineer, so what happened was, I used to get so frustrated on being on the wrong side of the glass, and recording these guys as opposed to actually out there doing it for myself. And so I kind of gave that up and started really working hard at trying to play, in a band that was suitable. I started playing when I was nine years old. My parents bought me a drum kit because they really wanted to keep their furniture [laughs]. I had a pair of drumsticks that I was using to beat up on their furniture. So yeah, it was a frustrating time. But by the time that I was eighteen, I had been in several bands.

"So, I'd joined up with a little band that was local to me, and I was constantly trying and looking for, you know, *the* band, as it were. And in those days, you didn't have obviously anything like the internet. The way the bands communicated was through the back pages of a weekly music magazine called *Melody Maker*. And it was a religious thing, that if you were a musician looking for a gig, you'd always turned to the back pages and there would be all the different adverts from various bands. And sure enough, there was an advert in there for a keyboard player and a drummer, for this band called Iron Maiden.

"The ad read: 'The one & only original exciting, visual & metal Iron Maiden rock band requires serious, talented, tasteful & only the best drummer with big set up and style. Synth/keyboard Rainbow/Lonestar style.' And then there were two phone numbers for Dennis, followed by a threatening 'No Idiots.'

"And so, I answered the ad," continues Purkis. "I went along and auditioned much like many other drummers. I can remember sitting in a corridor with [laughs], just nonstop drummers all the way down this corridor—'Next, next!' And I got the gig. And they were advertising for a keyboard player at the same time, so that's when a guy called Tony Moore came on board."

Addressing the power structure of the band at that point, Thunderstick wonders, "Therein lies the story. Yes, who hired me? I thought that it was a joint effort of Steve Harris and Dennis Wilcock. Dennis, being the singer, he was also the man that was at the time responsible for the logos and stuff like that. I mean, the typeface that Iron Maiden still use to this day was formulated back in those days. Dennis had such a large import into the band at that time. But I really do think that the two of them were running it, as it were.

"But Steve Harris would make an effort to come up to my house. I owned a house in Southeast London, and the rest of the guys were all from the East End, very proud of their heritage, as Steve still is. For me, crossing over from South London to East London was almost like going into completely unknown territory [laughs]; it really was. They were all East Enders. But Steve would come to my house, and we would then go through bass and drum parts. I'd never done that before. I'd always rehearsed with bands, of course, but I've never actually sort of knocked it down to the point where you only had the bass and drums. So, you're building a rhythm section rather than building a band. And that's what we used to do. And then we'd rehearse with the whole band, back in the East End."

Iron Maiden lineup #6 is the same as lineup #5, sans the keyboardist. Lineup #7 finds Dave Murray rejoining. As Barry relates, the band's iconic logo font is already in use at this point, with gig notices also promising "You ain't seen nothing yet!" The logo was designed by Ray Hollingsworth and Dennis, with the type style formalized by Larabie Fonts as a true-type font in 1996 as "Metal Lord Heavy."

Fortunately for Maiden fans, Thunderstick managed to record one of the band's rehearsal sessions, consisting of "Burning Ambition," "Drifter," "Sanctuary," "Prowler," "Another Life," "Transylvania," "Strange World," "Floating" (which became "Purgatory"), "Charlotte the Harlot," "Rothchild" ("Wrathchild"), "Innocent Exile," and "Iron Maiden." The material sounds pretty much like the recorded versions, if in general a tad slower and with cleaner guitars. "Sanctuary" is notable for its jazzy verse chords. "Another World" is a little more rock 'n' rollsy here than the official take, but of interest is the fact that you can hear the fast eight-note high-hat work coming from Thunderstick that we so often attribute to Clive Burr as one of his signature moves.

"It was work in progress," continues Purkis. "I mean, we were all young, but they were professional. But they were not professional musicians at the time. They were professional in their outlook. And it was great. As I just said, we got together and went through bass and drum parts. The promotion stuff that they would work on, they had their own logo, etc. Up until then I'd never experienced that. But on joining them I thought, 'Yeah, they are focused.'"

After a particularly bad gig in November 1977 at the Bridge House in Canning Town, the accepted narrative is that Steve Harris rethinks Iron Maiden and fires the entire band.

"No, no, nothing like that," corrects Thunderstick. "What happened was, it started falling apart. Something happened between Steve and Dennis Wilcock, the singer, and

Dennis was like, oh, I've had enough of it and what have you, and it just petered out. There was no great big argument or anything. Steve was intimating that he would go back to doing what he was doing at the time, training to be a civil engineer or something like that. And he was doing tech drawing at the time. And he intimated that he would go back to learn that. I can remember, we got a gig in South London and the band turned up without Dennis, the singer, and we couldn't play. Plus, Steve had by that time realized that the keyboard player wasn't going to work at all, so he had gone. And another guitarist was coming in, and Terry, the original guitarist that was in the band with me, he didn't want another guitarist in, that other guitarist being Dave Murray, obviously. And it just sort of fell apart. We attended this gig, and we didn't get to play the gig. In fact, we only sat around just talking and it was like, 'Okay, see you,' and that was it. There was nothing official. We just didn't bother phoning each other."

But don't worry—Harris still hated punk, and so he wasn't about to change the name of the band to Steve Strange & the Iron Maidens. "Anything to do with punk, we didn't want to have anything to do with it—at all," explains Harris. "I remember going down to a gig somewhere in West London, and a band called Chelsea were playing, punk band, and we went in there; it was just people diving about all over the place, spitting over the band and all this, and we just said, well, there's no way we could play. Because if our audience came down here, and they start spitting on us, it's just all going to go off anyway. It'll kick off. So, we didn't bother to play there.

"It was just, I hated everything about it, absolutely everything. There was no respect with the punks. There was a brotherhood and respect going on with the rock community because I think everybody was feeling a bit hard done by, because they weren't getting the gigs anymore. The punk bands were getting the gigs. Anything that was more mainstream rock wasn't even looked at anymore. And so, it was really tough for bands at the time. I mean there were a lot of pubs and clubs around; there was just nowhere to play, because it was all locked out with all these Herberts diving about all over the place and spitting [laughs]."

But again, thanks to guys like Steve and Neal Kay, there was this other "new wave" of hard rock bands starting to assert themselves. Says Garry Bushell, "It was parallel to punk, and some of the reasons it happened were the same reasons punk happened. People had just got fed up with superstar bands, stadium bands being completely out of touch or living a playboy lifestyle and not relating to the sort of things the kids who were coming to see them were into. Someone like Iron Maiden came along and they were exactly the same as the kids in the audience. They were young, they were all working class, their music was wild, it was heavy, it was direct. They connected immediately with the crowd, and there was that instant rapport, and that's why Maiden's crowd was almost like a football crowd. They were almost like a terrorist crowd in the fact that they were boisterous, they were loud, they were just as blue collar as you can be. The atmosphere of those early Maiden gigs was very much like the working class that was at punk gigs."

"Yes, there were things happening," agrees NWOBHM journalist John Tucker, "but the big problem is they weren't getting reported because no one was interested. But all those bands were slugging away somewhere. I'd hate to think how many gigs Saxon played before they actually got signed, but that's how you honed it. You just keep going. You play for people like a dog, but you play your guts out and you learn the good bits and the bad bits.

"So yeah, these bands weren't manufactured; they didn't come from nowhere. They were already doing what they thought they were doing best. Being true to yourself, I suppose. Playing the music that . . . assuming this is what you were brought up on, this is what you listened to, maybe your older brother had it, whatever. But this is what you heard, and this is what you wanted to do.

"Speaking personally, I never ever got punk," continues Tucker. "I never bought a punk single. I got the vibe behind it, I couldn't stand the vocals, I didn't see the point of it. So, speaking personally, I just kept buying what I wanted to buy, what I wanted to listen to, and I presumed that these people who were brought up on the same things as I listened to just wanted to be true to themselves and just play what they wanted to do, even before they knew it was never, ever going to be fashionable again. I mean how long do you plug away is a whole question in itself. How long would Steve Harris have kept Iron Maiden going if by 1982, 1983, it was still completely unfashionable? You gotta pay the bills, after all, somehow. But be true to yourself. That's one of the things we can do. We can be true to ourselves."

Into 1978, and Dennis Wilcock and Terry Wapram, both former Iron Maiden (Dennis's last gig was April 9, gone the same day as Thunderstick), record a demo at Spaceward Studios as V1. Steve Harris likes the sound of it and decides to use the same studio for Maiden's demo. Dennis's next act is called Gibraltar, which he keeps through 1981. But then misfortune hits Maiden, when the band's equipment is stolen on February 3, 1978, prompting cancellation of a handful of pub gigs. As part of the above shuffle in personnel, Adrian joins up with Steve for a second time, leaving Urchin. In 1978, Urchin issue their second single, "She's a Roller" / "Long Time No Woman." The A-side is an Adrian Smith composition.

Steve's replacement for Thunderstick turns out to be Doug Sampson, returning to the fold from the Smiler days. This is happening simultaneously with the departure of Dennis. "Yes, they'd done a gig at the Bridge House, and that particular night it wasn't the greatest gig that they'd ever done. I realized afterwards the reason why was that Dennis was about to leave—he'd had enough. And it didn't go the way Steve really wanted to that night. So I was in the audience, and after the gig Steve came over to me and said, 'Dennis is going, and I'm not really happy the way it's going tonight. Are you interested in joining the band or collapse this one, and we'll restart, and it will just be you, myself, and Dave Murray?' I said, yeah, let's go for it. Yeah. No problem."

And the reason why Sampson jumped at it? "It was awesome. It had energy. Seeing what Dennis is like, blood everywhere and swords coming through his mouth and masks. It was very theatrical. It was fast; it was different to what was around the pubs at the time. And it was packing out the Carts & Horses week in and week out. I probably saw all the gigs down there, so I knew the set before I went for rehearsal; I knew the songs just from watching them so many times."

As for Dave, "He was just amazing," says Doug. "I didn't know him until I joined the band. I just used to go and see him. His style and his energy . . . he was just brilliant. I can't say enough about him. I mean, in all the time I've known him, I don't think I've ever heard him do a bum note. He used to do this thing at the end of the show where he'd play with his teeth. I enjoyed being onstage as much as or like a member of the audience, because I thought this was just phenomenal, brilliant."

As spring turns to summer, Iron Maiden, now consisting of Steve, Doug Sampson on drums, and Dave Murray on guitar, rehearse at Star Studios in Bow. Soon Steve meets Paul Di'Anno for the first time, and Di'Anno joins the band as replacement for the departed Dennis Wilcock.

Recalls Doug, "I met up with a chap down at the Red Lion, at Leytonstone High Road, and 'It's great, but we haven't got a vocalist.' 'Well, one of my friends is a vocalist,' and I said, 'Well we're rehearsing down at Scarf Studios, if you want to drag him along, feel free.' So, the next day on the Sunday, this chap called Paul Di'Anno came in. I don't remember what songs we'd done, but I knew we were knocked out by him. And from that minute he was the vocalist for Iron Maiden. We heard a phenomenal voice, and he really suited the band at that particular time. This just took it to a completely different level."

Original crew member Steve "Loopy" Newhouse, in conversation with Jimmy Kay from the *Metal Voice*, remembers the story this way. "Paul and I have known each other since we were 'round about ten years old. Originally, I was going to a different school about 5 miles away. But when I was eleven, we started going to the same schools, so we were together right from the age of eleven. There used to be a group of about twenty to thirty of us hanging around. We used to live on one estate, and we all got to know each other that way. And then me and Paul became really, really chummy and then went off and did our own thing. Yeah, we just stayed friends all the way through. He was always a funny guy. I knew his parents. His parents were funny as well. So, he's actually picked that up. I got my humor from my dad. I just expanded it [laughs]. But yeah, we went to school and just generally hung around together all the time.

"Whenever we went to each other's houses, you always went into the bedroom, right? He shared a bedroom with his brothers, and I used to share a bedroom with my brother. So we'd go to each other's bedrooms, and nine, ten, we were left alone. Paul used to sing along with whatever record was playing. We'd be listening to stuff like Bob Marley or Bob Dylan, and he'd always sing along. So, it was no surprise, really, when first Paul got a job with a band called Rock Candy. They were a sort of Essex-based band. And he started singing with them, and it was astonishing. I didn't realize he had such good range. And then it was through a mutual friend that he ended up getting a job with Maiden.

"They played a lot around the area," continues Loopy. "Obviously, being East London boys, we used to go all over the place. I didn't realize until after—good ol' diaries—when Maiden did their first-ever gig, with Paul Day at the Cart & Horses, I was there. Paul Di'Anno said, 'I'm not sure I can make the gig tonight' and as it turned out, I went with another friend of mine. We both went along to the Cart & Horses, and we had no money between us, so we actually only stayed for a pint, and we left. It was also quite a bit of a walk. But yeah, I actually saw Maiden do their very, very first gig, in the Cart & Horses.

"But around the East End of London they were well known. And we also knew that they were looking for a new singer. It was just like Paul being in the right place at the right time. We met up with his mutual friend, Trevor, who said, 'Steve Harris is here; go and have a word.' He was gone about five minutes, and he comes back and says, 'Steve wants to have a chat with you.' So, Paul goes, 'Oh, okay, hold me pint.' So, I'm standing there like a tit in a trance holding two pints [laughs]. Paul goes, he has his chat, comes back, and says, 'I've got an audition for Wednesday night.' And of course, Paul went off and has the audition. Whether I saw it coming, don't know. Because at that time, Maiden were really well known. To take Paul on, without even really knowing what he sounded like . . . but Trevor vouched for him and gave him high praise and all the rest of it."

Regarding Paul Mario Day, Steve says, "He didn't have a presence. When I saw them at the Cart & Horses, all Paul Day did, apart from the fact that he was singing, he would walk in circles around his mic stand. But that was about it. If I remember right, he also wore a top hat, which didn't do him any favors. I think it was just to hide the bald bit [laughs].

"It was quite astonishing," recalls Loopy, thinking back to the first show ever with his buddy fronting. "The first gig Maiden did with Di'Anno as singer was at the Bridge House in Canning Town, and there were a few fans there but not that many. Two or three nights later, on a Saturday night, we did the Ruskin Arms, Paul's first show there, and the place was absolutely packed. And it's been recorded that there were over 400 people in there. Now that place is comfortable with about 200–400 was squeezed together. There were no bad reviews. We had a great time."

And then from there, as Steve puts it, "Paul was just getting bored of going to the studio on his own. He asked me to go along. I went along and helped out and stayed. It's as simple as that—again, right place, right time."

"I had several punk bands," laughs Paul Di'Anno, on his checkered past. "Oh God, this is not going to help me at all, is it? We had a band called the Pedophiles [laughs]. How sick is that?! We were just little kids, fourteen, fifteen years old. I mean, I joined Iron Maiden when I was sixteen. Steve and all that, they were very single-minded. It was his band, and he wanted to get it going. And I had actually seen Iron Maiden play a few times with various singers, and we walked out on them about three times because we thought they were bloody hopeless [laughs]. How wrong was I? Then all of a sudden after that, we got together—well, Steve put us together. Steve was a couple of years older than me at school and all that. He was just leaving as I was joining high school. And they asked me to go down if I fancied auditioning. And I thought, well, I've got nothing better to do, so I went down there and sort of got the job, but I didn't really want it. I wasn't interested because I was into punk. I don't know; anyway, we sat down and started writing and something just clicked, and it was great."

In terms of his influences, Paul says, "I used to like Glenn Hughes when he was singing with Deep Purple. Obviously, the Pistols, Damned, Clash, Ramones, Misfits, most punk basically, Tubeway Army—it's not really heavy metal, is it? I liked Judas Priest, Slade, Led Zeppelin."

But Paul doesn't have any stories about meeting his punk heroes back in the day. "No, I wish there was. I was never that lucky. I went to see them and never got to meet any of them, although I met Steve Jones in 1991, 1992, in LA; it was great. He walked into a bar, and I went, blimey [laughs], one of my heroes! But I'm not really one to want to meet these people. I've loads and loads of rock people who are friends as well, from all around the world, but as I say, this normality thing, I really wouldn't go up and ask anybody for an autograph or try to hang out with them just for the fact that they were heroes of mine. Something sort of stops me from doing it. Because I've even been put in the same situation myself. I can't get me head around that.

"I mean, you want to see this out in Brazil," continues Di'Anno. "I go to sign records and it's unbelievable; the shopping malls, they get extra security in and stuff like that. I just can't get the grips of that. I'm like, what the hell is going on?! I'm supposed to be signing records for an hour, and you're there for something like four. Four hours, and you're going, Jesus, man, this is unbelievable. In a way I love it, but I'm scared of it as well because no one should have that much power! That could possibly be one of the reasons I didn't go for it, try to keep the dream life, I suppose [laughs]."

Paul never met any of his heroes moving through recording studios either. "No, I don't think so. I remember Martin Birch told us that David Coverdale was in a car accident when we were doing the album, turned his Porsche into a coffee table or something. But we had met Whitesnake—Jon Lord, Ian Paice—when we went over to America on our first tour supporting Judas Priest. They were supporting for a little while, and so was Steve Marriott from Humble Pie, who is one of my big heroes, because he is also an East London local boy, an absolutely brilliant guy. I was just so sad when he died a few years back. So, there you go. You don't get many from our area doing anything, you know, East London. It's pretty much like a ghetto area. So, it's kind of nice when that happens. And he was one big, huge star at one stage. And after he left Rod Stewart, he even adopted his hairstyle. And Kiss, they were brilliant, absolutely wonderful people, I must admit."

Asked whether the Maiden guys would sneer at his punk roots, Paul says, "I don't suppose we talked about it too often. We were just concentrating on what we were doing."

In any event, Paul and the guys together . . . it was working live, says Ashley Goodall. "It's natural, that natural kind of circle you get of refreshment and evolution and then decay, and then the new ones come up out of it; it's that cycle of music that happens all the time. So, it was natural these bands would play smaller venues, more-intimate venues. I didn't see people kind of diving in the crowd the way the punks did. There was a massive amount of headbanging going on and lots of stuff, participation, but actually with a kind of intimacy. But the physical 'Let's go jump in the crowd and spit on them,' none of that was happening. I didn't see Paul Di'Anno leap into the crowd, but he would engage with them, and it's that reengagement with the crowd rather than leaping in on all fours that worked."

In essence, Paul represented a merger between punk and metal, which was ever so lightly and slightly reflected in the crowd the band attracted. And then more so on the first album to come, through a vocal style out of Di'Anno that had a lot of shout and speak in it.

"Absolutely, absolutely," agrees Bushell. "That's exactly what it was like. Paul used to come onstage, and he'd wear a porkpie hat, which is what the skinheads and the two-tone bands had repopularized. It was very much that "rude boy" look. He'd come on and he'd have the leather jacket and the bullet belt and the porkpie hat. He would go out and he'd talk their language, absolutely the same.

"The difference between them and, say, a band like the Cockney Rejects, who were the more violent end of the punk scene, was the Rejects would come out and say, 'We're West Ham, and if you're not West Ham, we're gonna attack!' [laughs]. 'We'll see you outside,' sort of thing. Whereas Paul Di'Anno would come out and say, 'We're West Ham, you're Leicester, you're Liverpool; tonight we're gonna have a party.' And that was the difference in that issue. The aggression that was there was channeled into the music; it wasn't aimed at any of the people. So, it absolutely brought people together. Motörhead coexisted, and they were playing with bands like that. Certainly, between the upper-class punks, there wasn't a big rift between them and the rock bands. The Sex Pistols, Cook and Jones in particular, were huge, huge fans of Thin Lizzy, and there was a huge respect. And then they did the band called Greedy Bastards with Phil Lynott."

Before the end of the year, heavy metal history would finally be made by this improbable revolving door of a band out of fashion but soon to be all the rage. On December 30 and 31, Iron Maiden records "Prowler," "Invasion," "Strange World," and "Iron Maiden" at Spaceward Studios in Cambridge, later to be issued as *The Soundhouse Tapes* (minus "Strange World"). Viking tale "Invasion" is particularly interesting because of its very British punk melody at the "Muster the men" part, a knees-up spot of music that has Maiden sounding like Sham 69.

Notes Doug on the deletion of "Strange World": "I don't know if it was a matter of space, because it was only a 45 vinyl, or the fact that 'Strange World' was like a slow one. We wanted to showcase the power and the speed of what we normally do, and that we threw into the live show. There was another side to Iron Maiden, but it didn't reach the vinyl. But I don't actually know why. I wasn't part of that decision. But I think that's what it was about. They wanted to showcase what the band was about—speed, heaviness, and lots of energy."

Recalling the sessions, Sampson says, "We were rehearsing. I don't think we even did a gig at that point. And Steve said, 'I really need to get a demo tape together so I can take it around the clubs and pubs.' So, I said, well, we'll all pay and chip in, and we'll go to this place that Dennis had recorded at, Spaceward Studios, New Year's Eve—'Great.' And it's the first time Steve and I had been in a studio. Dave had done a bit of recording before, so it wasn't too daunting for him. But yeah, more than anything, I can remember doing 'Strange World.' My personal memory of that was like, it was just so haunting. The old studio just took on a different feel, quite eerie, really. When I hear it now, it still brings back memories of that recording session."

The band at this point consists of Steve Harris, Dave Murray, Paul Di'Anno, Doug Sampson, and Paul Cairns.

"He was there," confirms Loopy, concerning Paul Cairns, who is not credited on the EP. "The official story is that because he left the band, there was no point putting him on. But he obviously did it. Anybody that has a listen to it, especially through headphones, you've got Dave's distinctive sound, but on the other side, you've got somebody who sounds like Dave Gilmour, just not quite as good. It's two distinctive sounds. Plus the fact, when you listen to the opening of 'Prowler,' it was Paul Cairns who was playing guitar. It's funny, talk about Paul Cairns. I hadn't seen Doug Sampson for many, many years, probably about twenty years. We met up in hospitality, 2010, at an arena to see Maiden. I hadn't seen Maiden for ages up to that point. I'd been asked about Paul Cairns. I said to Doug, 'Do you remember Paul Cairns?' And he says no [laughs]. But yeah, Paul was there."

The extended single to be issued commercially would emerge on the band's own Rock Hard Records, and as the year comes to a close, suddenly quite a bit of very heavy metal is being tracked at studios about the UK, by newer, younger punters—as well as Lemmy, who is busy making what is arguably the heaviest record of the entire 1970s on either side of the pond, a little something called *Overkill*, issued on Bronze in March 1979.

Fact is that *The Soundhouse Tapes* songs represent a significant shift in heavy metal thought processes. Unlike other bands thus far, even the very heaviest such as Black

Sabbath and Judas Priest, who used heavy metal as a tool, Maiden somehow "were" metal, representing a visceral response to punk but also an answer to such things as the wimping out of Led Zeppelin and the disappearance of Deep Purple. These unknown survivors of the underground were angry about something, but there was also a positivity, as if they were angry about a type of music not being made, so we'd better roll up our sleeves and do it ourselves.

"We tried to do something different, really," explains Steve. "I suppose it was the aggression in music and playing faster maybe, but also incorporating things like twin guitars, melody, prog-type stuff as well, and time changes. But it was just a more aggressive attitude, and I think that's where a lot of people tried to liken us with the punk thing. I mean, we still play 'Iron Maiden' in the set now, and the song tends to get a lot of liking to the punky side of thing because it's fast. But it's got harmony guitars in it, so I don't think it's punk myself. But I think a lot of people lumped it in with that, because that's what was happening at the time.

"But we didn't want to be associated with it at all. It's not like we wanted to ride on the crest of the wave with punk—we didn't. We didn't want anything to do with it. We hated it; we absolutely hated it. We really didn't want to be part of any of it. To you living overseas, maybe you look at it a different way, but in England at the time, it was absolutely punk on one side . . . it was a bit like Mods and Rockers—it was like punk and rock, classic rock, whatever, and they didn't like each other at all."

Addressing the idea of why the New Wave of British Heavy Metal (henceforth called the NWOBHM) had to be willed into existence, future Maiden guitarist Dennis Stratton says, "That's a big question. Basically, I think that the original frontrunners like Deep Purple, Black Sabbath, and Led Zeppelin had been around for quite a long time in the late 1960s and 1970s. You've got to remember that we're England—it was a very small country, so the music influences, the music scene, it changes very quickly. It's nothing like America, where you have loads of radio stations.

"I think that what happened was bands were playing in and around England—I come from East London, so I can only talk for London—but most of the bands were from London or around the outer areas of London. Everyone was playing their own kind of music, but nothing was happening because there wasn't many bands touring at the time. UFO, they went to America. But you had all the bands like Maiden, Saxon, Def Leppard, and the Tygers of Pan Tang all rehearsing and trying to write songs to make it bigger.

"I remember about 1976–77," continues Stratton, "the band I was playing with, RDB, which was Remus Down Boulevard, we were signed to Quarry Management, who managed Status Quo. And the next minute, we were on tour with Status Quo, and we're going back in 1976, 1977, and we had to go abroad. It was Europe, Scandinavia, Germany, France, all over. No concerts in England, because I think, at the time, the music scene in England regarding heavy metal or heavy rock just seemed to disappear, so these bands had to go abroad to get audiences. I think when Maiden came along, they had been doing all the gigs for many, many years but not doing big concerts, like just clubs. I think, at the end of the day, after the punk scene happened, with Neal Kay and Maiden and Saxon, there was a new wave of heavy metal that had to happen because all the original frontrunners had gone asleep. Or they were in Japan or America."

"There's not a single point that you can actually look at," reflects Neal Kay, on the birth of a scene made for—and by—Iron Maiden. "It was a sort of progression. Basically, behind the closed doors of Bandwagon, the first thing I know we needed to do was get a name for the club. I saw an opportunity and felt strongly that here, if only I could get the media's attention—this was before punk by two years—I felt that we had an opportunity to present our case for some much-needed publicity. If only we could get the weight of the media behind us, then maybe the record companies would jump up and pay some attention. It wasn't just us. There were bands out there, new bands, young bands, sent me demo tapes, once Geoff Barton's exposé of what I then called the Bandwagon Heavy Metal Soundhouse—I hate the word 'discotheque' and did then—that's why I called it a Soundhouse, to get away from the term of discotheque.

"And also, I had this massive sound system there. It wasn't a discotheque club system. It was a band PA, and it could blow windows out, and it was the only place in the country that had one at discotheque level. In 1977 they used my picture onstage at the 'wagon as the front-page advert in *Melody Maker* for Sounds Expo at Earls Court that year. We had the biggest club sound system in the country, and you couldn't blow it up. Not with records. It was impossible.

"It was a really broad spectrum for a start," continues Kay, "because I personally have a love for all things rock, not just heavy metal. We hadn't heard that phrase. Let's get this sorted. We hadn't heard the phrase 'heavy metal' until it came from the States. We didn't know what that was. It was something new. Everybody had a different definition for it, and I think they still do today, depending on their angle. Musician, DJ, promoter, record company—no one knows exactly how to describe it. When I first heard the phrase whilst I was looking for a new name for the Soundhouse, I took it to mean high-energy rock. Which doesn't necessarily have to be as heavy as heavy metal. It doesn't have to be Black Sabbath moving at the speed of light. It doesn't have to be Motörhead thundering along at the speed of light. There were other bands out there that had high energy but may not have necessarily been a heavy metal band.

"But the point is, I guess the key thing is that (a) you believed in rock, and (b) you didn't believe in punk, and you wanted to play music that was musical for young people. That was rock. I already had an audience there. I mean I had a lot of help from the years I spent as a club DJ in London. The 1960s taught me how to be a professional disc jockey. How not to speak over records. How not to lose a floor. How to have a lot of respect for musicians, how to have a lot of respect for great music. I had all that behind me and a lot of years. I'd also worked outside the UK, so when I went to the Bandwagon, I brought all that with me, and of course my own family's stage legend with me, too, and that mattered."

Slowly, things started heating up, explains Kay, beginning in the media with print, all important in the UK due to the relentless weekly schedule of the music papers.

"As for sending these heavy metal charts to *Sounds*? Right, well that's easy enough, really. It's like this. For two years, from 1975 to 1977, I worked at building the 'wagon up. I had it five nights a week, including Friday and Saturday and Sunday nights. I had the best nights. Hell, I could do what I wanted, and because of that I could broaden everything. We tell this story of Floyd in quadraphonic. The company that supported me just rolled in another couple of PA towers, and we'd do the Floyd story, we'd do the Thin Lizzy, the Free / Bad Company story; we'd do all these things.

"And at the same time, I was cracking away at the media every day that I could," says Neal. "I kept phoning up *Sounds*, which was the big metal rock paper at the time. In the end, Geoff Barton took notice. I said to him if you come up, you will not be disappointed.

I will show you something you have never seen before, I promise you. And in the end, he came. And we deafened him. He was Deaf Barton after that. He couldn't believe it. And neither could I, because when we saw the results, it was astonishing. He put a center page, double spread, about us in *Sounds*, and he'd explained about the whacking great PA system we had. He became famous in the end, he really did.

"We kept punk outside—it never existed," explains Neal, who is in lockstep with Steve when it comes to proficiency as a musician equaling relevance and validity. "Nor was anybody even interested in listening to it. No one wanted to know. The cross section of the audience came from all different walks of life. They were not just working-class heroes. The odd thing was that they crossed into hierarchy as well. Hell, we had a rocket scientist. We had a geologist from the oil rigs used to come and see us. We had a total cross section of humanity that expressed a love and desire, a spirit, a total lifestyle given over to rock.

"It was his little piece of heaven. That's what Geoff said," continues Kay. "It was his little piece of heaven. He couldn't believe it. He wrote on the front page of *Sounds*, a survivor's report from—would you believe—a heavy metal disco. That was on the front page. His exposé took in everything. I mean as time went by, within a few months the popularity of the Soundhouse was unbelievable. They came from everywhere. From across the Irish Sea, from Scotland, from Wales, lunatics from Norway, maniacs from Europe. We were totally inundated with this unbelievable surge of young rock humanity.

"But it didn't stop there. In Geoff Barton I'd found a kind of a brother—a kindred spirit—and he was as passionate about it as I was. And I knew that he was going to be the man that was going to help me do what I must do. And Geoff came to me one day and said, 'Look, we've had a yak down here at *Sounds*. Would you be interested in doing a chart, a heavy metal chart, for the paper every week?' And I said, 'Well actually I'm thinking about doing a Soundhouse one; we'll collect the punters' requests each night, and I'll take them home at the end of the week and shuffle them into a kind of Top 20 or something, and when I've sorted it, you can have it for print if you want.' And he said, 'Yeah, that's a cool idea.' And it happened.

"But at the same time, I was getting hundreds of cassettes from bands all over Europe. Mainly of course from the UK, but they didn't stop there. There was no outlet for young bands. Record companies weren't interested. It was punk or nothing at the time, and these rock bands, these youngsters, some were only kids. They had nowhere to go, no one to listen to, no one to support them, no one to move the product higher, no one to press it, print it, release it, and get it there. And it began to get me really annoyed because I thought this is crazy. There's something happening here, but no one's listening again.

"Concerning this phrase 'New Wave of British Heavy Metal,' I mean that's a difficult one to actually define. Al Lewis, the editor of *Sounds* at the time, is the man who invented the term, the New Wave of British Heavy Metal. He came up with it. We had so many tapes coming in from all over the place, that by then I'd also started putting on bands, too, actually. I think a young band called Heroes possibly was the first to ever play the Soundhouse. I think Pete Townshend's cousin or nephew or someone like that was in the band. We did actually establish in the end a NWOBHM circuit of these bands, right? But it was early days because we weren't really equipped to put live bands on. And the other problem for them was that my PA was five times bigger than theirs.

"And it had another effect. Because we had such a superb system, my audience was used to listening to vinyl then, and cassettes, because there wasn't anything else, through an unbelievable PA. Plus I was playing a broad spectrum of music. It could be anything from Motörhead to Styx and back again through prog rock to AC/DC. The earlier stuff we included as well as a kind of feed and follow-on. But we didn't major in your first-generation bands, Sabbath, Purple, this sort of legacy from the legends at the end of the 1960s. Obviously Led Zeppelin, because I mean all these major bands had their first albums out by 1969. Hendrix, of course, who went very heavy. It was completely across the board.

"Once they'd done the article on the Soundhouse and started printing our chart, something else happened that we weren't actually expecting," continues Neal. "All these kids in these bands suddenly saw an outlet for their tapes. And whereupon they're all fed up sending them to big corporate record companies, the only thing . . . the most useful thing that punk actually gave was the independent track. It said that, well, you know, stuff the labels, who cares? You can do your own thing. Maybe this is an alternative route. I would listen. I did a lot of interviews back then with *Sounds*, and Geoff would phone up and say, 'What's happening this week?' And I'd say, 'Look, put it in print, ask the guys to send all their tapes in; I'll listen to them. And if I can, I'll pass them on.' Because at the same time I was real busy trying to get the attention of the record companies. Because I realized without them no one's going anywhere."

As Neal and Geoff continued to lay the groundwork for the new metal, February 15, 1979, Iron Maiden play the Bridge House, Canning Town, a show that Paul Di'Anno believes to be his first with the band. The famously punk-hating bass player and leader of Maiden now has a punk fan as his new front man.

"There was a period of time when we didn't have two guitars because we couldn't find a guitar player who fit in right at the time," says Steve, on the band's by-now-comical lineup disruptions. "We went out basically, like musically, a three-piece. So, I was playing on the bass the harmony figures a lot of the time that the second guitar would have been playing, and then going back to try and hold the riffing down. So even doing it like that, you know, we knew that we needed to get back to the two-guitar thing because we felt it was restricting us a little. And it felt right having two guitars.

"At one point we had second guitar players in and out like you wouldn't believe. God knows how many. It was really a trying time, to be honest, because it was just going back before the first album. But even with the first album, as well, people in and out. They'd join and they're in the band for like effectively a week after rehearsing or something, do a couple of gigs or something, and just, you know, girlfriend wouldn't let them come rehearse, things like that. So, it was a pretty frustrating time to try and get people worked back in again. It was a very trying time. But we knew what we wanted. We knew we wanted the two-guitar thing. We even had a keyboard player for a little while, but that didn't work. I think it would have worked if he was a rhythm guitar player as well. Some songs, songs like 'Wrathchild' or whatever, just didn't need keyboards."

Illustrative of Steve's guitarist woes, on April 9, 1979, Paul Cairns misses a gig due to his broken leg and never plays with Iron Maiden again. But the band didn't miss a step, when two weeks later, April 21, the *Sounds* magazine Heavy Metal Chart places Iron Maiden at #1 with "Prowler," while the band's anthemic badge-of-honor title song, "Iron Maiden," clocks in at #11. It was a week after this that Maiden play the Soundhouse for the first time.

No doubt the ardent budding headbanger with a bit of knowledge could tell by now that Iron Maiden as a concept (for who could ever tell who was actually in the band this week) was a remarkable thing. As early as 1977, the band had in their set the likes of "Prowler," "Transylvania," "Iron Maiden," "Drifter," "Another Life," "Purgatory," "Charlotte the Harlot," "Wrathchild," and "Innocent Exile." So like Van Halen again, this was a band brimming with front-edge original material, although it must be said that it isn't that these songs were particularly novel compared to the heaviest and the best out there at the time (most notably Judas Priest), it's just that they represented an astonishing clutch of flash compositions by a young band, one still far from their first record deal and record.

Notes Dennis Stratton of the slightly ill fit of Paul Di'Anno against the rest of the Iron Maiden at this juncture, "I just think he was a little bit lost in some kind of fashion or whatever. When I joined the band, he was totally with Maiden, and then when we did gigs, he would wear a porkpie hat, or he would dance around like a bit of a Mod or whatever. The band still stayed the same; there was no problem with the actual Maiden set and the Maiden outlook to the way we recorded the album. I just think Paul liked to be a bit different, and I can't really answer for that. Steve Harris was always a very big leader and still is, so he wouldn't stand for that. But I remember when we took Paul to Japan in 1995, he had dreadlocks put in, hair extensions. It was just an image thing, I think. But the punk scene was more messy, more—excuse me for saying—but more out of tune, more messy than anything else. It was nothing to do with the metal scene; it was different audiences.

"But I used to go down the pubs to watch different punk bands. I even used to hire out a PA, do PA hire for Siouxsie and the Banshees and things like that. But the two audiences would never be at the same gig. You would never have a punk band on with a metal band, although it has happened since. In them days, you had either a soft-rock band or a heavy rock band or a punk band, but they were different audiences."

After Maiden's first Bandwagon show on the author's sixteenth birthday, Paul Todd auditions for the open guitar slot in Maiden and wins the gig, but he decides against joining the band, soon signing on with More, another early purveyor of new hard rock realities, featuring as lead singer ex-Maiden man Paul Mario Day. As well, on May 4, 1979, "Iron Lady" Margaret Thatcher and the conservatives take over the governing of the UK, ousting Labour. Years of strife and confrontation ensue, with Maiden soon to get into the fray with an illustration on one of their 45 sleeves. A few days later, Maiden's gig at the Music Machine, Camden, London, gets a notice in *Sounds*.

The band soon were gigging regularly, says Paul. "Lots. Yes, I would reckon a good couple of hundred. We were all keeping day jobs down and stuff like that, and getting home at 5:00 in the morning from somewhere off in old sunny Scotland and get home and have just enough time for a shower and a cup of coffee and then go to work [laughs]. It was really good fun, that was. But it was worth it in the end, wasn't it?"

Two weeks later we get the issue of *Sounds*—dated May 19, 1979—that winds up giving this new metal movement its unwieldy name. Featuring Ted Nugent on the cover, this edition includes a detailed (and not particularly glowing) review of a three-NWOBHM-band live bill—Angel Witch, Iron Maiden, Samson—by Geoff Barton, called Deaf Barton. The editor of the newspaper, Alan Lewis (and soul and Motown fan, evidently), adds a few words of intro subtitle that includes the saying "New Wave of British Heavy Metal" for the first time. The full headline reads: "If You Want Blood (and flashbombs and dry ice and confetti) You've Got It / The New Wave of British Heavy Metal: First in an Occasional Series by Deaf Barton / The Page for Idiots Who Play Cardboard Guitars." The cover also includes a banner at the top that shouts, "HEAVY METAL . . . THE NEW BRITISH BANDS." Interestingly, the text for the Ted Nugent cover story reads "YEEEAAARGH!," which is a bit like "Kerrang!"

"I was invited by the manager of the Music Machine," recalls Neal Kay, on the fateful Music Machine gig that caused the NWOBHM. "It was the old BBC TV theater in Camden. It held about 1,500 people, which was a fair size for London then. It had two or three step-up platforms at the back, levels, floors. It had a whacking great stage bar. The stage was real high, and it was a big stage. And Mick phoned me up and said, 'Look, I've been reading all about you and what you've been doing, and your fans and followers and all this.'

"By then the Soundhouse was getting people coming in from all over the place. South London, North London, hell, they were flying in for weekends, and the locals were putting them up. It was just unbelievable. And Mick said, 'Look, how would you like to put on your own like three-band show during the week and compare it?' And I thought yeah, what a shot. It's going to enable me to present to the industry in London new bands, and they don't have to come out to Kingsbury to the 'wagon. Because back then the business was notorious for not wanting to go anywhere. Hell, you had to do the damn thing on their desktop, if you could have got it there. They didn't even like leaving their own office, you know? Go to Wembley? You must be joking! It's like darkest Africa back then. Back then they didn't want to do it.

"But I thought the Music Machine was a great expansion," figures Kay. "It was a big place, and it didn't bother me that much—it gave a stage to the bands. I put myself in the auditorium and on the floor somewhere, out of the light, just my discotheque console and me and my microphone to compare the evening, and I arranged and did everything, really, I suppose. Did the lot. But if it was that particular night, it could have been a mixture. If Iron Maiden didn't play that night, it could have been Praying Mantis, it could have been Toad the Wet Sprocket; I don't know because I don't remember, other than saying that if Maiden were there, then that was the night that they were obviously seen.

"You see, I still found myself very much on my own back then. Things were kind of getting out of hand in so many ways. I found myself having to drive all this on my own. The 'wagon, the Music Machine, the organizing of all this stuff and the staging of stuff, and it was like there was no one to help me do anything. There wasn't. I did all the business myself. I got into the Soundhouse in the early afternoons, I got on the phones, I went to the record companies, I did the whole lot. Because if there's no one else, you must do it. And you find out your mistakes and you do it properly, and then you do it professionally, and then you do it so that people respect you for doing it. And that's the only way to be, and if you're going to upset someone, you may as well upset someone but get on with it.

"By then, it was always an unofficial thing. I don't think they'd ever have liked to have thought of themselves as a movement, but what I would have called it was a brotherhood. I would have called it a band of brothers, if I can use that overblown phrase, because that, to me, is what it became. I actually called the members of Soundhouse the Soundhouse Nation. That's what they were to me, and that was in print all over the place. They weren't just punters, they weren't just people, they were the Soundhouse Nation, and for me they were the finest club audience in rock on earth. Because they could move mountains, and they did."

Says Steve of Neal, "Well, he was obviously very sort of evangelistic about the whole thing; he totally believed in it. And you know it was great. He was great to us, which is why we liked to repay him, later on, when we were doing headline tours and stuff—we took him out as a DJ, as a thank-you. Because he really did help us. But he helped us because he liked our music. He wouldn't have helped us for no reason. But he really loved the demos, and it just went from there. We did like two or three at the Music Machine, so not sure which one you mean. But they were all really quite key. Because it was like a real gathering of the hard-core fans. The Music Machine became this kind of thing, every now and again, and you know, Motörhead played there all the time as well. So, all of them were really good."

Reiterates journalist John Tucker on the NWOBHM, "It's always dated from the byline that Alan Lewis put to Geoff Barton's feature in May 1979. And the bands that were featured on that bill that he reviewed that night were Angel Witch, Samson, and Iron Maiden. Angel Witch had been noodling around London for some time as a four-piece. Samson, as you know, a lot more bluesy in their early incarnations. Maiden had always been pretty much straight down the line. So, these bands had been playing from about 1976, inspired by the old guard and taking a nod from the likes of Priest, who, yeah, maybe were the bridge between old, new, and punk, and looking to break out and do something new.

"But I think the one that everybody claims to be at was this one in Camden, in terms of standout gigs in the early days. As I say, you've got Samson, Iron Maiden, and Angel Witch. These are all London-based bands, and you've got this thing about territory. It's hard to break out of territory; they're all known in London, which is your big market. Three-band bill, coupled together, and *Sounds* is asked to review it, so Geoff Barton goes down and sees these three bands. And all of a sudden, you've got something quite, quite different. Samson is still fairly bluesy at this stage, but you've got Angel Witch, who . . . they're rough. At the end of the day, Angel Witch were never very polished. They make a hell of a racket and they do it very well.

"Then you've got Maiden, who must have been the first band to marry a metal band with a bit of an early punk singer. I saw Iron Maiden before I heard Iron Maiden. I saw them at a local gig, and I could not believe it when the vocalist walked in wearing a porkpie hat and had his hair cut really short, and the rest of them looked like what you'd expect a metal band to look like. Very odd. So that was a bit different. But yes, this was the one that was reviewed, this was the one that was given the byline of 'New Wave of British Heavy Metal,' and this is the one that everyone wishes they were there. That was one I'd like to have gone to. I'm sure like most of these things, it wasn't particularly brilliant or particularly different—it was just three bands doing their thing. But it was the combination and the culmination of a lot of people's hard work, and on the night, someone saw it, and someone reviewed it, and, face it, things were never quite the same again."

At the beginning of the summer of 1979, Rod Smallwood enters the picture. Like Bruce, having been involved with booking bands in college (at Cambridge, with his buddy Andy Taylor), Rod parlayed that experience into a position with the MAM agency, working with Be Bop Deluxe, Cockney Rebel, Judas Priest, and Dutch rockers Golden Earring. Rod also worked with Cockney Rebel directly, through Trigram Music, and later, just before his jump to Maiden, he worked for Silver Star Ltd. After nearly quitting the music business for good, Rod received a tape of Steve's Maiden demo. Rod sought the band out, first to set up a couple of showcase gigs, and then to chat about management.

"I was back in the music biz," explained Rod to *Brave Words & Bloody Knuckles* in 2005. "I was going back to college to read law. I was in the interim period, because being management there wasn't much happening. Punk, I didn't really get off on punk a lot. It was a bit too pop and a bit too fashion, really. Some things were great, like the Pistols, but so much was a fashion statement, and I wasn't really that into it. Nothing was happening for me. I thought I could be a good manager, but I had nothing to manage that I liked, so I thought I might as well go and do something else. So, I was going back to college when coincidentally my best friend at the rugby club said he had a friend at work that had a tape of this band Iron Maiden, and did I want to listen to it? I did, and when I saw the band, I thought they had very special qualities, the directness they had with the fans and the honesty that came out through their eyes. The vibe with the audience was terrific. I ditched going back to college and did Maiden, and that was it. I didn't do anything else from the word go."

Further building a base for the new heavy revolution, a memorable early NWOBHM battle royale takes place at the Music Machine, Camden Town, on September 30, 1979. Sledgehammer and Iron Maiden wind up supporting something called "Iron Fist & the Hordes from Hell," a.k.a. Motörhead. In the fall of 1979, Maiden's lineup is now Steve and Paul Di'Anno, with Dave Murray and Tony Parsons on guitars and Doug Sampson on drums, with Parsons leaving shortly thereafter and the band being relegated to a four-piece once again. It is this lineup that records, in October, tracks for the forthcoming *Metal for Muthas* compilation, in Manchester Square, London.

Also around this time, Rod Smallwood calls illustrator Derek Riggs (born February 13, 1958, in Portsmouth) 'round to his office for a look at his portfolio. Rod secures the Eddie image for use on the band's first album, even though a deal had yet to be signed with a label. The era of overtly heavy metal illustration is born. Later in the month, Iron Maiden make the cover of *Sounds*—specifically Paul and Eddie—further suggesting an excitement level for metal's new baby bands. Further evidence of the hype is illustrated by Maiden's first headline show at the legendary Marquee club, on October 19. Gigs throughout the month of October have various A&R men coming out to see the band, with Chrysalis, CBS, and Warner Bros. declining on signing.

Into November, while waiting to pen a proposed deal with EMI, Iron Maiden privately issue *The Soundhouse Tapes*. The back cover features testimonial from Neal Kay. The band presses five thousand copies of the short EP, of which three thousand are sold mail order in the first week.

Explains Kay, "Now the Iron Maiden *Soundhouse Tapes* EP, that was sold by the band from their gigs. It's before they were signed, and they called it *The Soundhouse Tapes* after the Soundhouse. The story goes that they only had five hundred initially pressed, and Steve did not have enough money to pay for the master tape of that recording session. And it was agreed that he'd get the money together and go back in a few days and get the tape. But when he went back, because it had been a few days longer than he had said, the engineers had reused the tape. It was gone. All they had was the pressings they made the first five hundred from. So, when they needed more, that's how they got them.

"I mean, look, there was a movement definitely. The movement was amongst the newer bands that released cassettes and tapes, and I started taking bands in, starting punting the tapes around the industry. And even the industry had its head up its ass most of the day. I had a lot of friends at record companies, very high-level heads of A&R, these sorts of people. Half of them didn't know what time of day it was. I mean if I tell you how many people turned down the Iron Maiden demo, and incidentally I'm more than happy to show you the original Iron Maiden demo cassette. There's only two in the world. Steve has one and I've got the other, and it still plays. That's real history. Oh yes.

"But when I took the cassette 'round to the record companies, I got laughed out of the offices of CBS, who just couldn't hear it. I went to A&M with it, and I knew a guy called Charlie up there; he was head of A&R. I mean over here, they had Styx and bands like this; they had a nice stable of not real rocking bands, but I was just interested in getting the name about anyway, you know? And Charlie just laughed at me. He just looked at me and said, 'What's this?' I think I retorted, 'Your future, Charlie.' But that didn't work."

Adds Steve, on the power of the demo tape, "We made a tape, a four-track demo tape basically, and we took it down to Neal Kay's Soundhouse, and it was like the other end of the earth for us, because we were in East London, and it was right 'round the other side north somewhere, London, in the darkest depths of Hinden way, that sort of way. So, we took the tape to him and left it with him. Just to try to get a gig, not for any other reason, really. We knew it was a good place for cool fans, rock fans.

"And he started playing the tracks off the tape. He had a set chart in *Sounds*, from the weekly *Sounds* magazine. Obviously, people like Rush were in there, and then all of a sudden, our track started going up the charts until #1, along with all this stuff. And so, me and Paul, actually, went down there one night just to see what would happen, you know, when they played one of our tracks. Of course, we weren't known then or anything like that, so we'd just stand at the bar watching what was going on. And the whole place just went crazy when the Maiden tracks come on. So, we went and saw Neal again and said, 'Look, you obviously really like the tape. Can we now get a gig?' and all that.

"He was like, yeah, definitely into taking us on. And so when we played there, straightaway, the first time we played there, it was sold out and everything. It was pretty amazing, really, to see . . . for us, you know, (a) being in the chart anywhere, Top 20, and to actually start moving up, and at one time we had two or three tracks all in the Top 20, and (b) for them to be freaking out over our songs, and they're not even released yet. It was really an exciting time.

"There were two main sources of these demo tapes, demo cassettes," continues Neal. "Either they arrived by post, or members of bands would bring them in and see me at the Soundhouse. Uninvited, they'd turn up in the evening show and cautiously come up to the stage and say, 'Hey, mate, here's our demo tape. Would you take it and give it a listen? And if you like it, do us a favor, give us a ring, will you?' I mean my heart used to go out to them. I was the only one it seemed at the time who had the guts and the bollocks to do anything about it. And it's the thing with me, and it always was. I don't like seeing people repressed in any way—I do not. And when it comes to music, it's the most important thing sought out in my working life. And this kind of music is absolute. And when no one cares and no one wants to know and no one wants to do anything, then someone has to stand up.

"I think it was Steve and Dave, actually, who came by. I seem to remember it was Steve and Dave, but you're asking a lot of me now. I'm sure it was Steve. Actually, I believe I was very rude at the time, I do remember. They came up to the stage and in their east-end Cockney voice, which is where they come from, they presented the tape, and I'm sure it was Steve said to me something like, 'Do us a favor, mate. Take it home and give it a listen, and if you like it, give us a ring.' And I probably swung around—I'm absolutely convinced I did—and said, 'Oh yeah, you and about five million others. When I get the chance, pal, I will do it. Thanks.'

"Oh no! I mean how can I have done that? But it was just another approach made by another small band, and you've got to remember all business took place in front of the Soundhouse audience. We did business, and it got so elevated at one stage that I had Peter Mensch on one side of me from Leber Krebs and Cliff Burnstein from Phonogram LA on the other side, trying to get me to convince Praying Mantis to sign a contract with them, while I'm working an audience at the Soundhouse."

Doug Sampson recalls the response from Neal in similar fashion. "Yes, so Steve gave a copy to Neal Kay, who was a DJ, at the Soundhouse in London. And I think he said, 'Well, have a listen.' And it was like, 'Yeah, you and about four hundred other people, Steve.' And he took a copy, and about three days later he got on the phone with Steve, saying this is brilliant. You know, this is one hell of a demo; he absolutely loved it. And then he just started playing it and playing it, the demo, at his heavy metal Soundhouse disco, at the time, and it was just taking off. And he actually had a chart at *Sounds*—the music magazine had asked him to do a chart on requests. And it was coming in that we were getting to #1 virtually every week, with one of the songs off *The Soundhouse Tapes*. So people began to notice. Especially record companies, who didn't know what the hell was going on here. We were up there with bands like Montrose and Judas Priest. Why is this happening? You know, so that's what really got us in the public eye, I think, thanks to Neal, really."

"I took the Maiden tape home that night with a bunch of others—went mad!" confirms Neal, with a slight difference in the details. "Went absolutely berserk. That's it. There it is. That's it. Fait accompli. Checkmate, for it's there. It was there. That's it! I couldn't sleep that night. I had to phone Steve. The next morning . . . well, I just couldn't stop playing that tape. It was fresh, powerful, key changes, great chord progressions, incredible flowing melody, speed, performance to the level, everything that all the others hadn't. And to top it, they went to a studio to do it as well. The quality of the tape was miles higher than anything else. The only other band that ever came up with anything as good was Praying Mantis, and they were actually five or six months before Iron Maiden. The dates on their demo tells me. But the Maiden tape was awe-inspiring. I don't know how else to put it. Here's a band waiting to smack the world, basically.

"And I feel the same about those guys today as I did over thirty-something years ago. I am delighted and pleased and happy that they have conquered the world, toured the world, and still are doing so to the *n*th degree. Though I knew they would back then, though. That's the thing. But they did not play the club. Not at first. Basically, what happened was this. I got this tape, I took it home; I listened to it. I was jumping around my lounge, swinging the old air guitar over me shoulders, and thinking this is really exciting. And it's about 3:00 in the morning, and my first wife's trying to get some sleep. And I can't calm down because there's no chance. All I know is I've got to get this out to the public, and I've got to get it to the industry.

"Now I'd made some serious contacts by then. The first thing that helped me on the way was a personal appearance arranged with CBS and Epic of Ted Nugent and his whole band. He came to play London Hammersmith Odeon; I went up to the record company and said I want to try something real unusual. I don't know how you're going to go for this, and they finished up talking about it. You know what? They gave me Ted Nugent and his band on a Tuesday night up at the Soundhouse for a guest appearance. After then no one could refuse me. How could they? I've had Ted there.

"So, the record companies wanted more. They wanted a lot more from me, and that was great because then I could get a lot more out of them. We exchanged white labels; they made sure I had the very latest stuff, transatlantic, anything I wanted within reason. And I got more personal appearances: Sammy Hagar came to the club, as well with his band, members of Rainbow did; I had loads of stuff happening. So, by the time I got the Iron Maiden demo tape, I had already made some very firm friends in reasonably high places in the record companies, and I could go up there and take tapes up and say listen to this, listen to that.

"As for the crowd reaction to Maiden," says Kay, "we had a system developed by then between me and the audience because they were a respected audience by then. It was known that if you were a shit band, don't play the Soundhouse, because the audience will give you the silent treatment. And I used to have this thing. I'd get on the mic and say, 'Look, evening Soundhouse, nice to see you here. We've got some new stuff to play tonight, and in the time-honored fashion and tradition, you tell me afterwards if it's thumbs up or not in the usual manner.' And they'd whistle and stamp their feet and go mad and make terrible noises if they loved it. If they didn't, you could hear a pin drop.

"And they didn't need that with Maiden. The floor was full. It was just happening. It was happening straightaway. It went straight in the charts; two or three of the tracks off there just went. And that told me even more what I needed to know. I knew anyway that you couldn't deny it. I said it on the back of the EP. I said here's something that must not be ignored. Of course, convincing the labels, that was a different story at first.

"The Maiden demo, they named it after the club, we knew that. And Rob Loonhouse did the pictures. It was an honor, I suppose. A thing to say thanks. I mean the Soundhouse was an amazing club. Because of all these antics, we had people who used to perform acts. I'd do certain numbers like 'Planet's on Fire,' Sammy Hagar. There's a chorus in it. A bunch of guys and girls got together and started doing this sort of doo-wop shit in the middle of it, just like the old stuff, and then go straight back to the air guitar again. You had to see it to believe it.

"Gradually the media cottoned onto this lunacy that was sort of growing. They came down, and even the *Times* sent a bloke down, poor man. He kind of came in a human being, but actually I think they melted him somewhere about the fifth number. We found his jacket and shoes, broke shoes, on the stage. Don't know what happened to him. We destroyed him. We used to take this old Focus track, 'Hocus Pocus,' and when you get to the little twiddly bit, I used to whack the faders down and everyone would scream, 'Fuck off!', and I'd whip them up again, and it was like the Soundhouse thing. And when we didn't like someone that was like invited to do an article on us or someone who had besmirched the fair name of the club, I'd play 'Hocus Pocus' and bellow, 'And one for . . .' and point to him. 'Fuck off!' they all screamed.

"We had a hell of an audience. And they were, I think, respected by the industry, because although they could play all these games . . . I used to take them to the coast, as well. I hired three coaches once and ran the Soundhouse down to the south coast for the day, and because I was a member of a bike club at the time, I also used to do bike runs for the Soundhouse members. I took 114 bikes one time, down to Hastings, and we finished up back at the Soundhouse. I ran it like a social club for heavy metalers. I wasn't interested in normal things. Anyone could do normal things. It's nothing.

"And they were rock fans. As I say, Rush, these sorts of people, Aerosmith, a lot of progressive stuff as well, but mainly sort of rock stuff, classic rock stuff. So, they were there. Well, they never went away; it's just that punk . . . the press weren't writing about these people, and because they weren't, it became more of an underground thing again, a real roots thing. And it was actually a really good feeling to be part of all that. It is just amazing, because we would go up to somewhere like, I don't know, North of England, Blackpool, or even up into Scotland, Aberdeen for the first time, and we would have three hundred people coming to the gigs without ever having seen us before, mainly because they had checked out . . . they couldn't get the EP or anything because it wasn't out yet, but they were checking out the tracks, and the fact that they've got the profile of being in the Top Ten, 'Who is this band?! Iron Maiden—never heard of 'em,' sort of thing. And they're top of the chart. So, people were coming to check us out, and I've always said, when you've got people in, then that's it. You're there to prove your point. And we did [laughs]."

Reiterates journalist John Tucker, "By 1978, the Soundhouse was well enough established for the young Steve Harris or the young Dave Murray, actually, to take the Iron Maiden demo in the tail end of 1978 and say, 'Give this a spin, will you?' When the revolution actually started is the interesting question. I mean it's sort of the name—we can date the name to a particular magazine. But when did things actually start happening? When did record companies actually start saying, hey, we need to have one of these on our books? It was a chicken-and-egg situation. What came first? Explosions of bands filling a void, or loads of people scouting around to find bands that were already doing their thing, but doing it very locally?

"I think one of the things about the NWOBHM was it was all over the country, but in isolation. Even now you have bands not knowing anything, really, about their peers. The guys in Bitches Sin up in Cambria knew nothing about Diamond Head—two big bands, two contemporary bands—and knew nothing about each other. Because even though it's a small country, there's not a lot of communication apart from *The Friday Rock Show*, no great radio play apart from two hours Friday night.

"So, a lot of bands think they're working in isolation and they're really doing something, and then they find out, oh, there's another band doing a similar thing. And those things come together at the same time, the likes of me sitting here, and you're reading about all these bands from an external point of view, a fan point of view. And you're seeing things happening and you are seeing a pattern, a network almost. It wasn't the easiest acronym or name to come up with that joined all those dots together."

Closing the decade, Maiden keep up the momentum, on November 25 and 26, the four-piece lineup of Steve, Paul, Dave, and Doug record a demo version of "Running Free" at Wessex Studios, which later shows up on the *Axe Attack* compilation. The producer on the session is Guy Edwards. The band also records "Burning Ambition," which will be serve as the B-side to their first single.

"The first version of 'Running Free,' we weren't particularly happy about it," recalls Doug Sampson. "But 'Burning Ambition' was all right. But I don't think that we were terribly happy with how it came out. So that's the one that's survived and is still around, that version of 'Running Free.' But after I left, they rerecorded it with Clive."

Sampson is not one to claim for himself uncredited writing services across a number of Maiden tracks, but he does think he had a hand in "Running Free."

"I would say 'Running Free' was the only one that I had a major input on. Because I was messing around in the studio in the rehearsal room, just messing around doing glam rock, Mud- and Sweet-style beats. And I was playing this beat and just generally just messing about. And Steve came in and started putting a bass line to it. It just started off as a joke; that's how I saw it. And then Dave came in and then 'Hang on a minute; I think we've got a song here. It's got possibilities.' We got the structure of the song down, and Paul went off, he had some ideas, and I remember him just sitting outside on some steps jotting some words down. And he came back, 'I think we've got a song here,' and it worked."

Indeed, the "Running Free" demo with Doug has much more of a straightened-out glam feel, which is underscored by two extra extended musical parts where the band just hammers that Chapman/Chinn-styled knees-up glam dance beat into the ground. Less tribal and shuffling than the version we know, the glam era is also evoked by the lack of high-hat and the snappy, hard-whacked snare.

Into the following month, a five-piece lineup (the band's twelfth!) of Steve, Paul, Dave, Doug, and now Dennis Stratton on guitar records a *Friday Rock Show* session, consisting of "Iron Maiden," "Running Free," "Transylvania," and "Sanctuary." Dennis Stratton is ex-Harvest, Wedgewood, and RDB, coming to the situation with experience, but not much of it heavy in nature.

"At the time, I was working with my band RDB, and we went out as a rock band," qualifies Stratton. "It was a lot of blues influence, just following the trend of Rory Gallagher, Status Quo, that sort of stuff. Joining Maiden was a bit of an eye-opener for me because Steve had written the songs for the first album. Dave Murray and Paul Di'Anno were the only ones in the band. There was no drama, there was no secondary power, there was just three of them. They'd been through different lineups and different guitarists or different drummers that just would collapse at pubs.

"But when they signed the deal with EMI, they had to start thinking serious, like, 'We're going somewhere.' Rod Smallwood would phone me; he sent me a telegram—'cause he knew I was working with the other band at the time—so I went in. But with Maiden, because they were a heavy metal riff band, they'd never really experimented with harmony guitars, where[as] I was brought up on Capability Brown and Wishbone Ash, all the old American bands with the harmony guitar stuff. Scott Gorham used to come and watch us play because he loved this harmony guitar thing.

"So, when I went into Maiden, I didn't know anything different; I never knew anything else but to put harmony to what Dave Murray was playing. So, the songs were already written, the album was ready to be recorded, but with my way of playing and my love of harmony guitars, it was the fact that 'Okay, we'll do "Phantom of the Opera," we'll do this, we'll do that.' But the harmony guitar has to go in there. It's more than a rhythm guitar and a lead guitar; it had to be two guitars. Basically, the album was written, the songs were ready to go, we just recorded the album, and that was it.

"I never knew any different by what the band sounded like before I joined them," continues Dennis. "I heard the demo tapes, I heard *The Soundhouse Tapes*, but they're just raw demos. I thought, I've been in the studio many, many times recording; when this album's recorded, the debut album's gotta be one of the best. The idea was to go in there and put these harmony guitars down, and it changed the sound of Maiden a little bit. They still had the rawness of the band—the heaviness was still there—but it just made it a little bit more interesting with the harmony guitars."

Concurrently in December, Iron Maiden finally see some success somewhere other than the underground and sign their deal with EMI, while Doug Sampson is still in the band. Ear to the ground, it seems that the majors might have an appetite for stronger stuff than Def Leppard; indeed, EMI would also soon figure prominently in laying the groundwork with a couple of *Metal for Muthas* compilations, while MCA chimes in with Quartz and Tygers of Pan Tang.

"Living in band land, as it were, you'd go to these events," explains EMI's Ashley Goodall, on hooking up with Neal Kay and then Maiden. "I think I saw him first at the Music Machine, where he was the dude, the DJ, putting on the records, where there were a lot of people, a thousand people, couple bands playing a night, three bands or whatever. You'd see that week after week, effectively. I'm not sure it was there I met him, and quite frankly, I'm not sure I was sober. But conversations happen and there was a lot going on, like, 'Hey, what are we going to do with this?'

"And I realized there was a lot happening, a lot of bands going on, and I was interested because with EMI I had access to a studio to do something. I was new; I was a new boy and hadn't really done much, so I was really interested in this whole area and could see that it had a ground roots thing. I would have been well aware of Maiden and one or two others, so it was a collaboration in the sense that he would have suggested try these guys, these guys, whatever. Ultimately, I probably would have had a selective mechanism in there, because you don't want everything. He would have helped me, and I would have pulled it together. I may have even suggested doing an album because that's where I came from. So, you know, seemed natural to me.

"It was at the Music Machine, pretty sure," affirms Ashley, on the subject of the first time he ever saw Iron Maiden live. "And it was full of people wearing red T-shirts with Iron Maiden on them, and they were supporting somebody. There was a lot of people there. I thought, hey, there's something happening here. They got onstage, whoa. Attitude. Energy. Intent. Great songs, great playing, pretty much it was there, and I was excited.

"And Ozzy Osbourne was there. I remember seeing him. He looked at the time a little bit worse for wear but interested in it. Obviously, kind of looking and thinking, hmm, new generation here. And I don't think he was doing too well at the time either, so you know, suddenly you saw the older generation looking on as well. I remember that particularly poignant moment. Obviously being supportive, but it's like, 'Have the baton, guys.' So that was the Music Machine. It was a big event; I can see it now in my mind quite clearly, big lights. It was actually used very much as a punk venue. I remember seeing X-Ray Spex there and a lot of other punk bands. I can't remember who the headliner was, but it might have been Motörhead, actually. I also saw them at the Swan in Hammersmith, which is a little pub which I think is still there, and it was probably about sixty fans, pretty hard core. It was like going to a kind of political rally. You had the kind of Marxists in their reds going, 'Oi, oi.' There was a little bit of weird political activism in the fanship. Not saying they're a political band, but that kind of attitude. There was a lot of that in Britain at the time. Striking, doing stuff, workers' revolutionary party, you know. So, there was a little bit of that mixed in with these red shirts of the dedicated.

"Firstly, they came from the East," continues Ashley, framing the fan base. "Interestingly, punk was a West London thing. It was Notting Hill. It was trendy kind of art-schoolish stuff—Siouxsie Sioux, Malcolm McLaren, art school, right? So, you had the kind of trendy kids. Metal was not art school. It was engineering, it was mechanics, it was people from the east where they did real jobs, where there was an earthiness about it, where they drank beer. Where they weren't prissy about how they looked, apart from T-shirts, or they had kind of denim on. So, there was a completely different look to the people. Perfectly sweet, nice, intelligent people, but just a different crowd. So, it's like a revolution had come in. Weird kind of characters would emerge; big, huge guys with long hair, sort of odd-looking, slightly oddball people, the misfits that didn't fit the funky punk. You could be ugly and interesting and different. It was much more permissive of weirdocity, you know?"

"I know why they signed us," muses Steve, recalling the merger slightly differently. "Because they'd come down to the Soundhouse and saw it was jam-packed, and they couldn't get in. In fact, they were stuck in the back. They couldn't see properly or anything like that. I think whether they liked the music or not, they thought bloody 'ell, what's going on here? We better sign these guys before someone else does. There was obviously something going on. There was a real buzz, and so whether they understood us musically, I suppose, is debatable, but I suppose it didn't really matter. They just knew that there was this thing going on, and they signed us on a three-album deal, which at the time was unheard of, really."

"Well, the thing was that Maiden wanted to put out an EP," explains Neal. "See, they didn't sign initially. I mean, I had a lot of trouble myself trying to get record companies to hear it. I suddenly realized amongst all this madness and cacophony that we were really comfortable in the Soundhouse, and that we understood our world very well, and that others that came to us did too. But you know the old bowler hat brigade of the 1940s and 1950s, and those that held the power in the industry, they had lost power when the Beatles actually happened.

"Up until that time you couldn't do a damn thing if you were an artist. You were told exactly what you'd record; you were told how to record it. In some cases, you didn't even play it; you just sang it. The industry had total control over your product, your output and how you did it. The Beatles happened and changed all that shit forever, thank Christ. And of course, stateside Buddy Holly must take the ticket for that as well, because he was one of the first to record, unofficially put down arrangements, and he worked in a very freelance way.

"So that all changed everything, but it hadn't changed stuff enough. That was all right for the concept of normal music, but when you're working outside of normal music, we were considered a counterculture, I feel, back then. My dream was to get it to mainstream. I didn't want it to be seen as counterculture or a fashion or anything else. The problem with the media is that I was afraid they would try and turn it into a fashion. And it's not—it's a way of life. You can't turn a way of life into a fashion. It's rubbish.

"And it worried me a lot at the time. But the big problem was that these guys high up in the record industry, the established ones, still couldn't hear it. I took Maiden's demo tape . . . I can remember clearly taking it to CBS, and I knew them all out there, at that time. I really did. And they were not bad guys. They'd helped me a huge amount before with the Soundhouse promotion and stuff. And they couldn't hear it. They wouldn't sign it. They didn't understand it. Well, first of all A&M passed, and that really surprised me. I knew Charlie real well up there, and he'd been the man who'd been feeding me Styx stuff and all sorts of stuff, and it was loved at the club. But A&M are not really a sort of a hard rock label.

"I actually fancied Phonogram, because at the time, with Cliff Burnstein operating in the UK on attachment, and Peter Mensch from Leber Krebs sniffing around for management . . . between the two of them they had 90 percent of the established acts anyway. They really did. All these bands were signed to Leber Krebs management at the time. And Burnstein had signed a hell of a lot to Phonogram. Of course, Atlantic was the other. And it seemed like the Americans were just miles ahead in understanding rock. The troubadours of the folk-rock era and the businessmen lead by David Geffen opened up everything into a more free, more cool, countercultural way of making things mainstream.

"But yes, EMI were the only ones that would bloody well listen," continues Kay. "And also, Rod Smallwood, by then, was on the scene. And Rod obviously signed Maiden to management. Actually, that critical gig did take place at the Soundhouse. Brian Shepherd was the name of the guy who came from EMI to check out Iron Maiden. I'd put the show on, and it was a sellout. You couldn't move. Sheppy came late. He was short, like me. He shoved his way into the Bandwagon, and he couldn't see anything. He couldn't see a bloody thing. And in front of him there was a bunch of kids holding up a big banner, Iron Maiden, so he couldn't even see the stage that night.

"And I think Ashley Goodall was with him, but Ash had been a friend of mine who'd asked me to help put together *Metal for Muthas*, which preceded the Maiden thing. So they came down to the 'wagon, they couldn't see the band, but the place was really jumping. It was rocking. And I understand at the end of it, Rod turned to Sheppy, Brian, and said, 'What do you think?' And Brian said, 'Well, I can't see anything, that's for sure. But everyone seems to love them, and I've heard it, so yeah, I like it. We'll have it.'

"And apparently it was signed that way," concludes Neal. "I'm delighted it was done at the Soundhouse. There's a lot of people actually accuse me of being a bit jingoistic where Iron Maiden are concerned, I suppose, and see it as a pet project. No, they're wrong. I didn't see it as a pet project, I saw it as a special project for the world. I never saw Maiden in any other way, and all the bands that I've ever listened to that I've looked at from these demos, I only ever consider them if I can shut my eyes and see them onstage at the Odeon or any of the big outdoor fests. I'm not looking for pub bands. There's no money. And that's what Mr. Businessman wants. Hell, we need the spirit. We need the rock 'n' roll, man."

"Oh yeah, very, very happy, with the initial signing, for sure," chuckles Di'Anno, who adds a tale of easy come, easy go. "But I sold out some of my songs to Iron Maiden a few years ago. I wasn't too happy about that deal, but the guy who was actually managing me at the time sort of did not hold out enough. So, I got a certain percentage, but I was also told by an insider that they would have offered me something up to about a million dollars for my stuff, and I'm like, oh shit! [laughs]. Never mind. Money's not everything, is it? But I'm still collecting royalties, yes, definitely. Rather lucrative at times, I would say [laughs]. But then again, it goes to me kids; I don't really care."

CHAPTER 1
Iron Maiden

"Bloody 'ell, what's that?!"

As the 1980s dawned, Iron Maiden were entering a decade seemingly tailor-made for what they had to offer, after five years of Steve going against the grain, celebrating in his heavied-up way all his love of fading legends from the blues to heavy metal to progressive rock.

The 1980s would be a golden age for heavy metal on both sides of the Atlantic. For the first few years, an igniting of sorts would take place through the New Wave of British Heavy Metal (NWOBHM). That spark would inflame an incubator of rockers in Los Angeles (and San Francisco, New York, and Toronto!), giving birth to the golden age of thrash in disparate locales, as well as massive commercial bounty for "hair" metal bands, all of that scene centered in LA. And where does Maiden preside through this heady heavy metal age? Well, first as a characteristic band from that magical UK phalanx and then later as an iconoclast, like Motörhead, like AC/DC, as a band that would never bow to the trending pressures of the age but keep on keeping on, crafting records using their hard-considered signature sound, and generally having a good time through the entire decade.

Iron Maiden's most milestoned year as a band would indeed be the tidy first from a decade in which heavy metal would never be far from the top of the charts in one form or another. The year of our Lord 1980 would mark no less than the appearance of the band's instantly successful debut EP, their appearance on the iconic NWOBHM compilation *Metal for Muthas*, the excited and exciting issuance of the band's first singles (within a scene that was loving the format), their first major touring work, and, most importantly, the release of the band's debut album, *Iron Maiden*.

But it wouldn't be Maiden if they didn't ring in the New Year with another lineup change, and this would be a significant one, with the band acquiring drummer Clive Burr, who in January replaces Doug Sampson.

"Devastated, but it was a mutual thing," recalls Loopy on the loss of Sampson. "Doug knew the band was getting bigger, and I don't think healthwise he could cope with it. And we were

The boss, Concert Hall, Toronto, Ontario, Canada, June 19, 1981. © Bill Baran

in the studio for probably a couple of weeks, and I'm sitting there twiddling my thumbs, but the rest of the band were playing. And then Dennis came in—he was with us for a couple of days—and he went, 'I know a drummer.' And I think within two days, Clive Burr had come in. He came in with his own kit and started joining in with what the band were doing, and they could see straightaway, you know, this guy's phenomenal. And yeah, it was a shock to see Dougie go, but then it was also great to see Clive come in. You've got to have the right members to go there. You've got to have the right people. And Maiden had the right people."

Asked by Jimmy what his first impressions were of Clive, and Loopy says, "I had no idea, no idea at all—never seen him play. Apparently, he had been in a couple bands that I had heard of. Samson was one of them. But yeah, never seen him play. And he came in and started thrashing around on this kit, and in a quiet moment I said, 'Geez, you hit those things hard.' And he said, 'That's what they're there for.' And he's absolutely right. It doesn't matter if you make a dent in your snare skin—that can be replaced. But it's there to be hit. And to prove a point, Paiste, in Switzerland, invented a cymbal specifically for drummers like Clive called Rude, and I think Nicko McBrain uses a Rude cymbal now, and they were developed specifically for hard hitters. We set the drum kit up in the studio, and Clive went, 'Right, let's try these out.' So, we fitted all these Rude cymbals, and Clive went around the kit, and he hit this cymbal so hard that a chunk of it flew across the studio. And Clive went, 'Well, that's going to have to go back.' So, we ended up sending all the cymbals back to Paiste and said, 'Very nice, but . . . ,' and they sort of redeveloped it and sent us back another batch which worked perfectly. But yeah, I think if it wasn't for Clive, you wouldn't have the Rude cymbal you've got now."

Clive Burr was born on March 8, 1957, in East Ham, London, and comes to the band after playing on Samson's first couple of singles. About to perform on a groundbreaking very early NWOBHM album, Burr had now also been featured on what are arguably two of the very first singles attributable to the genre, via Samson, although he turned out to be too early to experience the tenure of Bruce Dickinson in that band.

As Clive told *Rock Hard*, "I've always wanted to play the drums. At the time I wasn't playing in a regular band. I was playing pubs with various bands, even though I didn't have the legal age to get in. I've always been crazy about drumming, but I only could get through thanks to a succession of opportunities and meetings. One day I got a phone call from Dennis Stratton, who told me that Maiden were looking for a new drummer. Steve Harris and Rod Smallwood then came to see me in this tiny pub where I was playing at the time. Then they wanted to meet me, so they could see for themselves

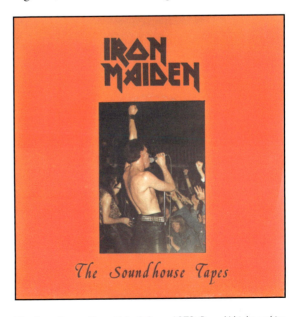

The Soundhouse Tapes 7-inch from 1979. *Dave Wright archive*

The compilation that announced the New Wave of British Heavy Metal. *Dave Wright archive*

Iron Maiden's first major label release, issued a week before the iconic *Metal for Muthas* grab bag of new metal goodies. *Dave Wright archive*

what my playing was like. After a few days I got another call from them, this time asking me to come down to rehearse with them. So, I met the whole band, and everything went so well that I got the job. I didn't write anything. I just brought in my style."

February would be a busy month. The *Metal for Muthas* tour was about to bring the new metal to the masses, headlined variously by Samson, Saxon, and Motörhead. The tour featured, at various times, twenty-two different NWOBHM bands, including Iron Maiden, who would bow out halfway through to work on their debut record.

Steve remembers all too well the excitement around this new movement, remarking of the phrase "New Wave of British Heavy Metal" that "I remember it was put in *Sounds* magazine, and it was all part to do with the Neal Kay thing, the whole tie-in, and all these bands; it was an underground movement going on, and it was just this term that had come up, the New Wave of British Heavy Metal, and it really stuck. It became this whole movement. And it was great to be part of that. We didn't think of that, we didn't come up with that, but it was nice to be lumped in with it all, because it was a whole vibe going on. The unification was, again, against the punk thing. The punk thing was a reaction against the big rock bands, and we were a reaction against that as well. Because we were trying to get gigs and the whole thing. It was just the whole feeling of a togetherness, of this. We've got this good music here, and we need to get out and sort of show it to people."

Ashley Goodall from EMI was liking what he was seeing. "Di'Anno was very good. He was very exciting, he had a leather jacket on, he looked pretty good, and he went for it. And Steve Harris was great, just up there exactly as he is today, giving it some. Energy, intent, attitude, driving, flipping piledriver. So that was great. Actually, the drummer, I think there was a bit of changing going on because he wasn't quite as solid as Clive Burr was. Dave Murray, of course, calm, gentlemanly, funny, and talented. Just quietly getting on with it, no ego, beautiful. So, you had a band that wasn't particularly egotistical but were really into what they were doing. When they were onstage, they were like demons going for it. Complete attitude."

"I mean, Maiden, Mantis, and meself toured *Muthas* in our own right," recalls Neal Kay, referring there to Praying Mantis. "Before then we did the 'heavy metal crusade.' That was—and I love the title of that—that was like taking it to the people. That was crusading for justice, for me. And people hate me talking like this. They always did when I was working in the industry, but fuck 'em. I don't care. I think that when you mean something, and it matters that much to you, if you're going to stand for it, then to hell with everything. Nothing can get in the way. Nothing. No part-timers, no stupidity, no people who don't understand. They don't belong, so just go around them or through them.

"And the crusade did all this. It took two, three bands at a time, with myself in the usual comparé/DJ role, out to a circuit of universities, colleges. It was arranged by Paul Samson's manager, Alistair Primrose. The only problem with that was Samson headlined all the shows, and by about the fourth or fifth it was clear that Iron Maiden, in the middle section, should have been the headline band. And I'm not being cruel, I'm not being rude, and I certainly wouldn't besmirch Paul Samson's name, because the guy died a couple years back, and he and his wife were very close friends of my first wife and I [sic] outside of music. We liked Paul very much, but Paul's idea of . . . to him there never was a New Wave of British Heavy Metal."

It's an interesting point. Paul Samson just never seemed to be wired the same way as Steve and the other guys. They would make some wallopingly good music in the coming years—in fact, better for Paul's blues grounding—but it wouldn't be so egregiously and happily metal, like Saxon, even like Priest, who were grasping how much of the bat that was left for them. Quite notably, Def Leppard would soon join Paul Samson in that sentiment, that they didn't want to be part of this, thank you very much.

Adds Dennis Stratton on the tour: "Praying Mantis had been in the same camp as Maiden and Tygers of Pan Tang and Saxon and everyone else. We were all mates, and the situation was that Praying Mantis would support Iron Maiden on the *Metal for Muthas* tour because that was put together with Neal Kay doing the DJing. So, it was just two bands touring around England—England, Scotland, and Wales—just doing the first tour because, sooner or later, very shortly, the Maiden album was gonna come out."

February 10 found Maiden billed along with another NWOBHM act with a whole lot of potential. "We only played one show with Iron Maiden, I think, at the Lyceum, which was terrible," recalls Diamond Head guitarist Brian Tatler. "They sound-checked all afternoon, until the doors opened, and then people come running in. And they said, "Okay, you can soundcheck now." And they wouldn't move their equipment and things, so Duncan had to set up at the side of the stage. They just seemed to have no room. And we had twenty minutes to do a set. So, we could only do four songs, because our songs were so long. And it just seemed like they were almost scared of the competition, so they just gave us a hard time. And we felt, well, we ain't gonna blow you off, are we? We just need the exposure. And they wouldn't speak to us either. We just didn't really get much of a feel with the Iron Maiden guys.

Dennis Stratton (*far right*). Olympiahalle, Munich, Germany, September 18, 1980. © *Wolfgang Guerster*

"But we were a little . . . we always thought Diamond Head were better. We had this protective thing, well, we're better than any of these bands. We had a little bit of ego, a little bit of bravado, and so really, we were looking to the people who had gone before us—Zeppelin, Sabbath—as our kind of yardstick. We wanted to be like that, rather than any of the new breed."

Wrote Malcolm Dome of Maiden's performance on the evening, "The East End titans didn't disappoint, the faithful either hurling themselves with great gusto into 'Running Free,' 'Sanctuary,' 'Wrathchild,' 'Iron Maiden,' and a whole host of other rabble-rousing earthshakers, which forced the denim-and-leather hordes to their knees in supplication. Technically speaking, new Maidens drummer Clive Burr (formerly with Samson) and second guitarist Dennis Stratton (ex-RDB and 140 Dice) looked to be shaping up nicely, giving the band a fuller and more balanced sound. Perhaps the most important point put across by Maiden was that, happily, they haven't lost their basic and uncomplicated approach to both the music and the fans; something which so many bands mistakenly discard during the transition period from local cult heroes to national rock fame. More power to their amps."

A show on February 8, says Dennis, marked the first appearance of Eddie onstage. "One of my very closest friends is Dave Lights, who quit Maiden before I joined them. He was the lighting designer, and he came up with Eddie the Head on a pole and on a backdrop. I think they took Eddie as far as they could, and then they had to make it something very clever, work the artistic side of it, so Eddie was sort of brought in halfway through, when we were recording the album. He was brought in, we looked at it and thought, 'Yeah, great,' and then that was it. Funny thing was that Rod Smallwood wanted to call him Bert or some other name, but we stuck with Eddie [laughs]."

That day also marked the band's debut single, "Running Free," backed with "Burning Ambition," which coincides with the release of the *Metal for Muthas* compilation, both releases being on EMI.

"Aah, now this is my baby," says Paul of the celebrated tribal heavy metal anthem, the first big song of the movement. "You see, Steve got a writing credit on that because he sort of put the bass line down. But I had the whole rough idea of how I wanted it to be. And I actually got the idea from one of me mum's records, Gary Glitter [laughs], would you believe, just the idea of that drumbeat, 'Rock and Roll Part 1' or whatever that hit was called. My mum was playing it, because she was a big Gary Glitter fan, although she's not too fond of him at the moment [laughs]. So, I listened to this and thought, 'Ooh, might get an idea out of that.' And the lyrics obviously represent me and my youth, sort of thing, and that was it. Once you actually have the idea, it normally fits around pretty easy, and that came together in less than a couple of hours, I reckon. But then Steve put the bass line down on it, so he got a credit on it."

Paul Di'Anno, Concert Hall, Toronto, Ontario, Canada, June 19, 1981. This is the band's first-ever show in Canada. © Bill Baran

This contradicts in a number of subtle ways Doug Sampson's story on how the song came about, and one would have to surmise, weighing both explanations, that Doug's seems most accurate.

Adds Paul, on the reference to a bar called the "Bottle Top," "Well, back in Australia, they're called bottle shops, which is like your liquor stores. So, what I did is I just used that. And described the top of the bottle, you know, when you take the cap off, basically, the bottle top. So, I just made up a club called the Bottle Top. I'm a genius sometimes [laughs]."

"If you think about 'Running Free,' it's pretty upbeat," says Goodall, now through EMI the proprietor of the physical manifestation of "Running Free"; namely, the picture sleeve 7-inch in the shops. "There was a lot of that kind of punk freedom in there, so that's an upbeat track. But the adrenaline level was higher than punk. It had the energy and impact that some of the punk did, but with a musical finesse, and that's the difference."

Continues Ashley, on the actual nuts and bolts of getting to this point: "My role was to identify talent, which is exactly what I was doing. I happened to home in on the areas that (a) I thought was growing, and (b) I liked. Simple as that. And so being out there, I saw this band, I thought right, they're happening, there's a lot of followers, they've put an independent single out in the first instance, which I think we held for a bit. So, I had got to the stage where I recognized they were breaking, at least locally. And knowing that rock was a big international thing, being part of EMI, with people like Deep Purple, you knew there was a global audience for it. What I learned at EMI was to think global—do not think UK. You had EMI around the world, and the pressing plants were ready to sell records in America, in Germany, in Japan, in Brazil.

"And that was the mindset with which I approached the signing of bands I wanted to sign. Did they have international ability? Yes. Heavy metal sells, end of story. Let's go for that. And then secondly, which are the bands you want to go for? Maiden were clearly the leaders; they clearly had a following. So, you could say that if you structured the deal well enough, you know you're going to have some sales, as opposed to just putting it out and hoping Radio One's going to play it. So, was there a quantum amount of people that would probably buy it? Yes. Was there a buzz about the band? Yes. Were they growing? Yes. Was management good? Yes. Could they play? Did you like them? Could you die for them? Yes. So, all these questions you had to kind of add up.

"So, once I made my mind up that I think these guys are hot, obviously I wanted to stick close to them. It was in the context of these other bands developing, and this idea of a bigger grouping of British heavy metal which seemed to be coming to the fore. They seemed to be the leaders of the pack, which is great—always go for the leader. And at this stage, things were moving quite fast. This would be like weeks, and things would move up a notch quite rapidly. Bands break and they suddenly become a buzz, and suddenly within six months you've got something really hot on your hands. It's not like you wait around waiting for things to happen. It was a fairly dynamic time.

"So independent single, interest in them, getting to know them, following them, seeing things moving fast, management moving them in the right direction, Neal Kay, *Sounds*, people getting behind them—all the signs were good. Doing the album, great, coming together. While we were doing it, it quite emerged that let's do two tracks, because you're the leaders, guys. And then it got to the stage when—I can't remember exactly when—then I convinced EMI they've got to sign them. So, the next job for me was to sell it into the company, get my boss down, Brian Shepherd, get the marketing guys on board: 'Could you sell this, guys?' 'Yes, positive.' Marketing guys said we love it, we need this kind of stuff, thank you. Brian was on board. He understood exactly what it was about.

"So, I had the support from the marketing and the A&R guys, and that's hugely important. So down to the gigs, get them there—I think we took him to the Swan—yes, it's happening; I knew Rod from before. I'm not going to talk about details, but Rod had had an issue with EMI before, so it was a bit of a kind of smoothing of the waters there. And all set to go, really."

But we aren't done yet.

"No, so suddenly then you've got a situation: 'Oh, EMI are interested,' and obviously as a manager you're hedging your bets and checking out other record labels, and so were other labels. So, you suddenly thought, uh oh, bit of a fight on here. I think Chrysalis were the other ones, actually, at the time, who were pretty interested. So, we started to have a kind of bidding auction going on.

"But by this time, we had *Metal for Muthas* sort of done and in the bag, so that was a good place to be. So, I kind of wonder whether Rod always thought EMI was the best. You'd have to ask him that. And whether he was just ensuring he got the best deal, or whether he was genuinely hedging his bets. But there was a fight with Chrysalis, and we did actually have to commit to two albums firm, which at the time was really unusual. EMI didn't do two albums firm, and a lot of tour support. As well as a recording. So, there was quite a big commitment from EMI to the band, and it had to go to board level. And Brian got that signed off, which is great.

"So, we eventually signed them, but we also had the plan to say we've got a sequence of events here. They've had the independent single, we're going to do *Metal for Muthas*, and as part of the platform to help break them, we're going to give you tour support. So, we put them on the Judas Priest tour as the support band, just as they were breaking beautifully, and followed by the single. So, you had a Top 20 *Metal for Muthas* platforming, the buzz was happening, *Sounds*, all the media were there, and it was happening. And we put the single out and it charted straight off. They wanted to do it live on *Top of the Pops*, which was unheard of, again. Actually, it sounded pretty awful, quite frankly. The sound was not set up for it, and if they'd actually put their record in, it might well have had more impact. But it still did well, they got on *Top of the Pops*, they were not compromised, they wanted to be a live credible band, not a kind of miming band, all power to them, and I think the decision was good in the end. But I wish we had better sound."

"We went on this silly English pop program," adds Rod Smallwood. "Well, not silly; it's actually quite a good chart pop program called *Top of the Pops*, which has been going for thirty years or something now. We actually went on there week one of our debut single—no one does that. No one releases a single and gets on *Top of the Pops* in the first week, not in those days. As a metal band we thought it was cool. We all went down and played live, the first time since the Who had done it about twelve years before. We took all our monitors, put them in there big and loud, and had a great time."

Iron Maiden's new cover artist, Derek Riggs, soon to be a mainstay of the band for decades, curiously had the "Running Free" single represent his debut piece of artwork to bear the Iron Maiden stamp, and not the landmark Eddie of the debut album.

Paul and Steve looking to conquer the world (but for now, supporting Kiss). Olympiahalle, Munich, Germany, September 18, 1980. © *Wolfgang Guerster*

"They wanted something sinister lurking in the background," says Derek, "but they didn't want to give the face away. So, it's a somewhat obscured Eddie. That was the trick with the single. The first single comes out before the album, so you want to do something that's related to the album, without giving away what's on the album. So that's what that was. They wanted something dark and sinister, without giving away what the album cover was. So, Eddie is pretty much in silhouette—you can see what's going on. That patch of white... it's a broken bottle, and I had to highlight it somehow because it didn't show up very well. That's why the white is on there. That was my idea to put those heavy metal band names in there—I just wanted some graffiti on the wall—but they suggested some of the more contemporary ones, like Scorpions and Judas Priest. The chap running isn't based on anyone; it's just a figure. And that extra hand there... well, it's running free, but he's not free, is he? He's running straight into trouble [laughs]."

Explaining how he got the job in the first place, Derek explains that "Maiden's manager asked to see my portfolio, and, well, the cover that was the first Iron Maiden album, that was already finished. I had done that a year and a half previous to Maiden forming, basically. They had only been together about six or eight months, and I had that picture in my portfolio for about a year and a half. And I did it, well, for various reasons. Anyway, I had an agent at the time, and they were supposed to be a good agent, although I never got any work out of them. And they gave it back to me and said, 'Look, we don't think this is very commercial' [laughs]. So, I went off and sold it for about twenty years [laughs]."

Adds Ashley: "At the time, also, we had to look at album sleeves and things, and we brought in the options for artwork. They wanted something like Frank Frazetta or Hipgnosis, like Yes sleeves. But actually, we came up with a guy, Derek Riggs, and I remember, I'd seen the artwork there with his Eddie character on it and we said, yeah, we like that one. So, we put the Iron Maiden logo over it, Eddie was born. But first there was first single, 'Running Free,' bang, off you go. I think they went Top 20 or something with 'Running Free,' which is amazing because it was about the first heavy metal record that had actually broken through for one hundred years in the UK [laughs]. So, the image or the concept of Eddie was fused with the whole brand idea, and the thing took off. And they gigged and gigged hard. They went to Europe; the album then went to #4 straight off, which was huge. Broke immediately, you know? And they went to #1 in Germany; it just broke massive straight off.

"I think we'd shown early interest," figures Ashley, on why he thinks Maiden went with EMI. "And we got to know them. Met the guys, made an effort with them. Relationships are really important in the record business. And if you feel you can have a relationship with a band, that's really important. If you can't, you're not going anywhere. So, I think

A couple of super-early-days notices of intent. *Martin Popoff archive*

there was an element of relationship. I think Rod was smart enough to recognize that EMI had the clout to deliver, and not just deliver in the UK but internationally. He's got a good marketing head on his shoulders. So, my guess is having reassurance from EMI that they would be a priority, that they had the backing from everyone at EMI and that the marketing clout will be there, that probably gave him a big swing.

"Plus, the fact that we gave them two albums firm, plus the fact that everyone was creaming themselves, right? They were genuinely up for Maiden, right? Charlie Webster, the marketing guy . . . it's the right kind of company for them because they had that good rock pedigree and had that big international system, and they were big in the market and made a difference. Just analytically, that would have swung it. The deal worked well, and I think hopefully we had a relationship, and we'd shown early interest, ahead of everyone else, helping break them, getting a plan in place, getting *Metal for Muthas* there and the whole company behind it. And when EMI in those days got behind you, it's a big punch. So, it worked."

The "Running Free" single would soon be working its magic, but even before that, the band's metal-enthusiastic live shows were holding up their end of the bargain.

"We had a following right from the start," agrees Steve, "literally from the first couple of gigs that we played. You know, we just got a following. They just started coming to the gigs and making their own shirts and stuff like that; we didn't have any shirts to sell or anything yet. It was just too-early days. And they started making their own things, and really following us about. I mean, it's not very far, but it's difficult to get from one part of London to another. It's the same just playing like Stratford and going to Ruskin or Harrow Road in Barking. It's quite a way, and difficult to get to, but yet they still used to turn up there, and it was amazing, really.

"Right from that early thing, we just had this hard-core following, which gave us an edge over a lot of the other bands. We would go play the Music Machine, where there were three or four or five bands on the bill, and we would get such a reaction because it was almost like a rent-a-crowd coming as well. We would pick up new people as well, but the hard-core fans followed us about. Just as they do now, but, you know, now it's a more massive scale.

"When we made the first album, or just before the first album, there was a lot of punk stuff at the time, which we were heavily against. But I think the difference between us, the newer bands, or the older bands at the time, is we were playing faster and also playing stuff with maybe more time changes in it. Probably more harmony guitars also. A lot of the bands only had one guitar player. A couple of them had two, bands like Thin Lizzy, who influenced us in a way, but a lot of the bands had one guitar, three-piece band, or one guitar with a keyboard player and stuff. So, what we were doing was a bit different with the twin-guitar thing, playing heavier twin guitars, and playing faster, more aggressive stuff, with a little bit of prog thrown in. So, there were those elements which made us a little different from what was going on before. That's what I like to think anyway."

For his part, Ashley saw in Steve somebody who was driven to make this thing work. Indeed, if you add up the people who had cycled through the band by this point, just mathematically, with Steve being the constant, one would have no doubt affirming that the man had paid his dues, that he had the bumps and scrapes to prove he had an uncommon set of survival skills.

"Steve Harris was focused, absolutely—it was his band. He was just determined. He had a view of what he wanted to deliver, he wrote the songs, he's delivered consistently all the way through. He's up there leading the cheerleader from behind, as it were, all the time. Very clear. And he transmitted that to Rod carefully, and Rod was very clear about transmitting it to us. So, I think him and Rod, actually, is the nexus of success. I'm not dismissing what the others have done, but if you're talking about the driving factors, they're a really big one because Rod really got Steve . . . 'We're a beer band, not a drug band, we play, we're real, we're gutsy, we like rugby, football, we are earthy.' He got what they were about, and he translated that really well. And you know, it's all about sales, all about live, he absolutely reads them dead right. No artifice. Just do it. And they could do it. I mean it gave the promotion people a complete nightmare at *Top of the Pops* because they were just not set up for it. But they got it through, and I guess when you're hot and you're running, people do stuff."

A week after the single, Maiden appears on record again when *Metal for Muthas* is issued, on EMI, on February 15 (this contradicts Ashley's timeline, but it's so close, one can almost debate the definition of release date here—may as well call it concurrent). Regarding the compilation, it might not seem like a big deal today, but it was a statement at the beginning, through that title, the metal guy on the cover, and the idea that it was presenting a bunch of baby bands, previously unheard of in hard rock, and, really, preceded demonstrably by and for punk bands only three years earlier. The album reached a surprising #12 on the UK charts and spawned the aforementioned NWOBHM tour (actual start date was February 1). Maiden's "Sanctuary" was a featured track on the album, the song inspiring the name of Maiden-associated company Sanctuary Records. Acts on the album were Iron Maiden (two songs), Sledgehammer, EF Band, Toad the Wet Sprocket, Praying Mantis, Ethel the Frog, Angel Witch, Samson, and Nutz.

"It was my first thing I did in the music business," begins Ashley, explaining the record. "It was something that I loved, what I was in there for—I dove in. I grew up on the previous generation of Deep Purple, Black Sabbath, and Led Zeppelin. I played in a band myself, so it was my chance to do it for myself. I had an EMI studio there which was sitting around the corner that they weren't using enough. And I thought, Great, we've got these bands; let's pull it together, put them in there, make some stuff. And we did. We recorded a lot of it in EMI Studios in Manchester Square. It was reasonably low cost, there was no risk to the company, we paid a bit of money to some people, and they probably got royalties and things. So, it was a good low-risk opportunity for me to prove what I did as an A&R guy. It was not going to cost them the earth, and it just kind of worked. Got lucky.

"There'd been compilations before of various things," continues Goodall, "and often they'd worked, but actually I just liked the idea of making a statement of something, and actually also using it as a platform for Maiden, because that was also the other agenda. I just persuaded them to do it. I thought, well, fuck it, go for it. Why not? Let them get on with it. Like I say, I didn't cost them a lot, I put them in the studio, there's no huge advances, pull it together. You could do that sort of thing in those days. It was low risk, it was fun, and suddenly it seemed to be happening as well. It's like something's going on. There's stuff in the papers, there are things going on, Maiden was starting to take off. 'Hey, there's something in this, guys.' So off we went."

As to the finer point of *Metal for Muthas* fitting the EMI scheme of things, Goodall figures, "Maybe I'm just the kind of bloke that likes that kind of music and I fitted EMI's ethos. But the funny thing about EMI was we put out a lot of junk as well. It's not like a massive kind of selection process of, oh, we only put one record out a week. There was a lot of stuff going out. So, you could sneak stuff in, actually. But if you had the passion for it . . . and usually what I like to do is build rapport and support from the marketing guys and the promotion guys. If you get a buzz going with them and get them on side, you're halfway there. We did it with Duran Duran and Toto. Same happened there. Get the buzz, get the company on board, and then the job's easy."

"It just woke everyone up," says Ashley, on the effect *Metal for Muthas* had on the industry. "No one expected it. It's like, what the fuck's that? And then having the radio people say *Metal for Muthas* on the radio was just funny in itself because you had this kind of rather straight British radio, and then having to say things like *Metal for Muthas*, which is a slightly risqué thing. And so, it took everyone by surprise. It was quite hilarious in that sense, but it also gave everyone a lot of confidence, and particularly Maiden. It was a great platform for them.

"I think you had to play to your audience, right?" continues Goodall, with respect to the press response. "If the *NME* is not interested in this kind of stuff, *Sounds* was. They got a kind of orgasm of excitement. So, it was *Sounds*' thing, and then of course you've got *Kerrang!* and other things developing around this whole genre. So, it became reestablished as quite a powerful genre in the end. *Melody Maker* would kind of go halfway house, as they typically do. And radio would be quite limited to Tommy Vance in the evenings on Radio One, and you've maybe got like a two-hour slot on a Thursday or something, where Tommy Vance would put out the odd record. But actually, it was quite hard to get heavy rock played on UK radio, so therefore it had to go underground or live. It became a live experience, which was its strength in the end."

"We had two tracks on there," explains an ever-competitive Steve, "and we were opening side A of the disc as well, so the profile for us was really good on there. And then after that we went out and did the *Metal for Muthas* tour with Praying Mantis supporting, and again, it was just this whole movement going on. It was really quite exciting to be part of this whole thing. Obviously, there were a lot of bands around, Toad the Wet Sprocket and people like that, strange name. But there were all these bands. So, if you were a fan going to the gigs, it was pretty obvious what was going on. It was this underground thing, but for someone outside coming in, they might not have realized straightaway what was going on. It was obviously there, and it was proved when he put that record together and it did really well."

Recalls Doug on the recording, "We went to the EMI Studios to do them. That was a different league as well because it's not a demo. This was like in a proper studio, quite a jump from what we'd been doing. I remember we stayed there; I think right till the early hours of the morning. Me and Paul and Dave were just crashed out in the corridor of the studio and slept on the floor. I don't think the executives that were stepping over us could actually believe what they were seeing. I think maybe too many lagers might've had an effect on us as well."

But very soon, Doug put himself out of the band, to be replaced by Clive Burr.

"Yeah, well, we'd done more and more gigs, and we were living at the back of a lorry, the Green Goddess, coming offstage soaking wet, into a lorry, freezing cold, into a sleeping bag, and this went on for a couple of months. In the end, it got to the stage where it was beginning to affect my health. I sort of had a virus building up through the whole time. The more gigs we played, the worse it was getting. And I got to the stage, just before Christmas, where I said to Steve, 'I don't know if I'm gonna be able to carry on doing this.' And Steve said, 'Just carry on till Christmas and then we'll have to have a chat.' So, we got all the gigs out of the way and then had a meeting, and I said, 'Look, I think it's time that I went.' So that's when I left."

As for whether he thinks the band could have waited for him to recover, Sampson says emphatically, "Oh, definitely not—no, no. No, it should've happened how it happened. Definitely. Because the window that they had to get that thing going . . . the timing was really, really needed to be right at that point."

Back to *Metal for Muthas* (soon to be followed by a second volume plus an EP): "I helped Ashley Goodall from the label put that together," says Neal. "It was like a sampler of the NWOBHM cassette bands, and it was put together just as a sampler in mind. It wasn't meant to be a ten-million-dollar production or anything like that, although I was absolutely fucked off to death with the artwork. I thought it was absolutely horrible, to be honest with you. It sold us down the river, man. Down in Mississippi. Without even a paddle. Awful, you know?

"The actual idea was Ashley's, not mine. He didn't have a name for it. I named it, and that caused a lot of trouble up north, which I will explain in a minute. His idea with EMI was to take all these demo tapes. I was to put them together and come up with stuff. So, he gave me some tapes to listen to that had been sent into EMI, because everyone knew by then that EMI was listening, because *Sounds* told them they were. Which is good.

"And Ashley represented the new, younger generation of A&R men. His attitude was different. I mean Sheppy, Brian Shepherd, was one of those as well. EMI had a pretty good A&R department actually, at the time, as opposed to some of the others that were just cloth-eared and weren't going to listen. They became the enemy as well, you know. But Ashley was good. He was very young at the time. He may only have been in his very early twenties—I'm sure he was—but he kind of believed in me and I believed in him.

"He phoned me up and said, 'I've got this idea for this compilation thing with all these new bands. Why don't you come up to Manchester Square and we'll talk about it?' And I did. I came into London, and by the end of the afternoon we had an idea that we were going to do it. He gave me a load of tapes, I took them away, I came up with some tracks and stuff I thought were good. Bands were encouraged to record their own stuff for the album, which I thought was a terrible idea, because the recordings were not all that, some of them. Maiden got two tracks on the *Muthas* thing, which everyone knows, and Praying Mantis were on there too."

"There were a number of compilations, but *Muthas* was the king," explains John Tucker. "The MCA one, *Brute Force*, had some lovely stuff on it. And again, I go into this in my book *Suzie Smiled* because there were bands on that that never went anywhere, and that's the only place you'll find them. And it's interesting because MCA tried to jump on the bandwagon and put out an album called *Precious Metal*, which is pretty much classic and American rock, and realized they completely missed the point. So, the second time around they got it dead right. But *Metal for Muthas*, February 1980, that was when things were happening. And that was a good showcase. That was a good way of getting all these bands from wherever in the UK to actually helping the likes of us who were spread out a bit find out what's new and what's happening.

"Nutz were on there, and Toad the Wet Sprocket, who were a kid's band—they were fourteen. Their moms and dads drove them everywhere, and they had such little combos when they played live at the 'wagon, they had to put their little amps on chairs. And their moms and dads were there. The lead singer was a milkman from Luton, I remember, but they were so damn good. And I'll tell you what, they could play 'Blues in A' better than anybody. I mean it was a great idea. It suddenly woke everyone up, both sides of the fence, to the fact that the record companies were suddenly listening. If they'd put out a compilation of all these unheard-of new bands, then something was finally moving. And it did inspire a lot of others to get more actively involved on different levels."

As mentioned, Iron Maiden scotched the second half of the *Metal for Muthas* tour to head into the studio, Kingsway, to work on a full album, with Will Malone producing.

Remarks Dennis on the subject of Malone: "Basically, I got on with him okay and I got on with the engineer as well. The funny thing was that because Dave Murray, Paul Di'Anno, and Steve Harris hadn't really recorded a proper album—it was their first album—and because I'd already recorded some stuff, I knew being in the studio was very, very important. So, I spent a lot of time in the studio doing a lot of the stuff in the background (i.e., harmony guitars, backing vocals, harmony vocals). I spent a lot more time in the studio than the rest of them because I was building the song up. Once Dave had done the rhythm guitar and the guitar solo, I was left to do my bits, and you can build the track up. Steve Harris's choice was Will Malone. Now I think it was the wrong choice, because I think he expected it to be better. But regarding Will Malone, that had nothing to do with us—Steve chose him. But I got on with him okay because I was in the studio quite a lot."

Adds Paul on Will: "Gee, who the hell was he?! I don't know where the hell we got him from. I think we're the only thing he's ever done, and you can tell [laughs]. I just turned up there that day. Oh, I remember one thing. I think he did some orchestration bits for Mike Oldfield. Wow, that's really heavy metal, isn't it? We just got on with that. I can't even remember what he looks like. It's Steve Harris's band, and it always will be. We just got on with it, and that was it. I suppose we looked at each other

A svelte Dave Murray, Germany 1980. © *Wolfgang Guerster*

for guidance. We had done a demo before, *The Soundhouse Tapes*, so we had actually been in studios before, just to sort of make demos that were never released or anything."

Even Loopy sort of regrets what went down with the debut. "Paul's voice was massive. It's a shame that the first album didn't do incredible. It was such a badly produced album. There was one particular evening when Dennis and Will Malone and the engineer stayed in the studio, trying to improve the vocals. When Dennis and Rod listened to the vocals the following day, Rod went—you can just imagine—'Oh, bloody 'ell, sounds like Queen!' And they actually scratched all of Dennis's backing vocals. That's where Lionheart comes in. He's doing what he wanted there, and he's getting it right all the time with Lionheart. He's a lovely, lovely guy."

"It was our first time in the studio to do an album, so we pretty much left the band to the producer at the time," reflects Dave. "We'd go and do the tracks and left it to his judgment as far as performances go. All in all, these were songs we'd actually been playing for the last three to four years. They'd been written about 1976. We were playing them live, so they were very well rehearsed. The first album we recorded in Kingsway Studio in London. We'd done *The Soundhouse Tapes* prior, but we hadn't done much recording, so there was a bit of naivety. We took the bus to the studio every day, did our work, then went home. Like I say, a lot of those tracks on the first album, we had been playing them for a couple of years, so it was nice to put them down. It was probably one of the worst-sounding albums—we weren't happy with the production. But for that time, it really captured the raw energy of the band."

While Maiden lay in wait to conquer the world, tragedy struck rock 'n' roll when on February 18, AC/DC's Bon Scott dies, in London, freezing to death in a car after a night of heavy drinking. On a happier note, in March, *Sounds* issues its 1979 reader's poll results, and metal dominates. Def Leppard wins best new band, with Iron Maiden, Samson, and Saxon making a showing. Rush, a major NWOBHM influence, wins best band. Geoff Barton, however, elsewhere in the issue, slags Def Leppard at length, for a second time in as many months.

As the *Metal for Muthas* tour winds up, March 7 would mark the first leg of Judas Priest's *British Steel* tour, the significance of which is that the support band was Iron Maiden, who apparently boldly bragged about blowing Priest off the stage and, according to witnesses, often did. There were nineteen shows up and down the UK, and although Priest was in fact about to fare better than Maiden ever did in terms of record sales, there was a contrast onstage between an old guard and the scruffier, faster, hungrier form of heavy metal coming from this band of East London pirates called Iron Maiden.

"Well, Paul didn't know very much, because he insulted Judas Priest before the tour started," scoffs Stratton. "Basically, they weren't very happy with what he said, and so they weren't very happy with the band. It was something like 'old-school, new school'; it was something like, 'We're not worried about supporting.' It was just something you don't say. When you're going on tour . . . I was on tour with Status Quo in 1976–1977, and, to me, they were gods and I have respect for my peers, and you look up to them and say, 'You've done it, you've been there and seen it, and I'm just learning.' I think you can get too big-headed and your mouth sort of runs away with things.

"Personally, I got on very well with Glenn Tipton. We used to have a drink, sit in the dressing room talking together, not a problem. But I think what happened with Priest is the same as what happened with Kiss in Europe. What they don't realize is when you've got a support band that have got a big following, who are angry for stardom and angry to get to the top of the ladder, then all I've got to say is they invited the wrong band to support them."

"What happened was, when Priest arrived at some of the venues that we were doing with them, 50 percent of the audience were Maiden. We had the same thing in Europe with Kiss, that when we used to arrive at the football stadiums, we used to see thousands of youngsters with Iron Maiden T-shirts on, which, for a support band, you don't expect to see that. Everyone follows the main band. So basically, what happened with the Priest tour, they weren't too happy with what Paul had said in the press, and also they didn't like the idea of us snapping at their heels, thinking, 'We're gonna be as good as you,' and 50 percent of the audience were followers of Iron Maiden. You know, for a main band, that's very worrying. We just all knew what we had to do. You build yourself up, 'cause every time you go out, you wanna blow them off the stage. There's no problem with a support band because you're under no pressure. So, we were laughing because we sat back and thought, 'If the audience is 50 percent Maiden and 50 percent Judas Priest, then we have a chance.' All we could do was go out and give it the best we could."

"Well, let's just say that a lot of our fans turned up," confirms Steve, "and we were a bit surprised, because obviously they were a British band, and nobody expected us to be . . . you know, I think a lot of people bought tickets that were Maiden fans, without a doubt. And so, it definitely showed in the reaction—it was fantastic. I still think they're a great band, but we did really make it hard work for them. They had to work really hard every night, and maybe they weren't used to that, I don't know."

Promo photo; *left to right*: Dave Murray, Clive Burr, Paul Di'Anno, Dennis Stratton, Steve Harris. *Dave Wright archive*

For his part, however, Di'Anno pleads innocent to the charges put upon him. "I don't know, somebody said from our camp, 'Oh, I can't wait until we get on tour with Judas Priest, because Paul says we're gonna blow 'em away' [laughs]. And they probably thought, Guess who's got the brains for that?—me. And it wasn't me. I never said anything of the sort. I had the utmost respect for Priest: they were awesome. So, I never said it. I don't think it was any of the band anyway. It might've been one of the crew or a guitar tech or somebody, somebody who was involved with us. So obviously the atmosphere was a bit strange when we went on the tour [laughs]. But the second time we went on tour with them, on the *Point of Entry* tour in the States, everything was all right by then. I got on really well with them all. It was great."

As Loopy recalls the debacle, "The real story is, Paul had done an interview with *Sounds* magazine—I think it was a week prior to the tour—saying that we were going to blow Priest off the stage. And K. K. [Downing] picked up on that, and K. K. wouldn't talk to any of the band or crew all the way through it. I was going to say that K. K. has issues. I will leave it there. But it's all under the bridge, isn't it? It's what we call old hat. I mean, the rest of the band were fine with us. I think it was Harris's birthday when we were on tour, and we were in Sheffield and we had a night off, and all the Priest guys turned up in this Volvo and tried to drive it through the hotel foyer. But it was Ian, Rob, and the rest of the band all turned up, and both the crews turned up. And course we got to know the crew really well, because they worked with us in our own tour. They went out and did Judas Priest, and then they came back out with us while we picked up the *Metal for Muthas* tour after the Judas Priest tour. So, we knew a lot of the crew, and it was a great tour.

"It was mad. Years later, Pete Bryant, who was one of the early roadies with me, the early Killer crew—he used to look after guitars, so he would look after Dave and Dennis—we met up to at the Clive Burr benefit. And Pete said to me, 'You realize, from our first gig at Ruskin Arms to our first headline show at the Rainbow Theatre was nine months.' He was like, 'Going from four hundred people squeezed into a small pub to playing in front of three thousand people at the Rainbow Theatre was nine months.' That kind of information is staggering; it blew me away. And I was there [laughs]."

"Maiden had already come through," figures journalist Garry Bushell. "They'd obviously been signed by EMI by then, and they'd had *The Soundhouse Tapes* and that, but that was a very important tour for Maiden. It was a chance to play to an audience who hadn't seen them before. And, of course, Priest have not got the pace—obviously very heavy—but they've not got the pace that Maiden had. Maiden were much faster, if I recall."

Dave in Toronto, 1981. © Bill Baran

"They may have been giving them a run for their money," reflects Neal, "but Iron Maiden went behind Judas Priest on their first major tour with the release of their album. I mean I knew them well; they were friends at the time. They'd come to the Soundhouse for me. We did a video for them, "Living After Midnight," in which I loaned them Rob Loonhouse and the Headbangers. And there's a scene in that video where they come to the solo and Rob Loonhouse replaced K. K. Downing and plays it on his hardboard guitar.

"I knew the Priest camp real good, and I went along to see some of those shows, and as good as Maiden were... look, you suddenly don't become a rock 'n' roll hero overnight. You need to learn the profession. You need to tread the boards, learn the ways of rock 'n' roll. Priest was brilliant and probably still are. They were a very experienced band back then. They'd replaced their drummer Les Binks—he'd gone. They had a new twin-guitar-driven fast feel. Their earlier stuff had been a little more stodgy, but well put down, well driven, well respected, but the newer stuff from Priest was dead heavy metal. You know, there's no question.

"So, they were the perfect band for Maiden to support on tour. They let Maiden on board without any tour fee. They trucked their stuff. I mean it was a nice relationship that was going on. I went to see them; I'd just come off tour with April Wine, I think, in Sheffield. I'd been with April Wine, the Canadian band, and some others, and I knew that Priest and Maiden were playing the city hall or somewhere, and I was there, and I went that night and saw all the boys and everybody. The thing was that Maiden were very good, but Priest, for me, were still the more polished because they had more time at it."

Guitarist Mick Tucker, from rough 'n' ready NWOBHMers Tank, offers his own unique view on the matchup. "I'd seen them at a club in Middlesborough, a tiny little club which holds about two hundred, and you had Eddie the Head behind that used to spew blood. That was with Dennis Stratton, the original lineup there, as the first album was released. Then I'd seen them at Newcastle supporting Judas Priest. They were actually getting their own gear off the stage. I think Paul Di'Anno said they're going to blow them off the stage, apparently, from what I read. And the Newcastle May Fest, pretty big stage, but obviously Priest had just said you've got 3 foot of stage across the front. They had no room at all, and no lights, nothing. I think they got a pretty rough day. But I thought they were great; it was loads of attitude, heavy, twin lead guitars—absolutely brilliant."

Amid all this, playing with Priest but without a record out, a couple of other new-era heavy metal hopefuls beat Maiden to the punch with their own debuts. On March 12, Angel Witch issue their classic self-titled album, on Bronze, a record widely heralded as a NWOBHM masterpiece every bit as good as the debut Iron Maiden album would be, if not better. But very rapidly, the dominance of Maiden in a live environment would help crown Maiden as the winner of this battle of the bands. "I quite liked the first Angel Witch album," says Harris. "I thought they could have made it. We actually did some gigs with them. Their problem is that they split up before they had a chance to evolve. I think what happens to too many young bands is they're forced to evolve too quickly, and they have to do it in the eyes of the press, which is not a good thing."

Two days later, Def Leppard issue, on Polygram, *On through the Night*, which peaks at #15. Def Leppard are soon to be credited with taking the NWOBHM stateside, even if only Saxon, Motörhead, and Maiden would subsequently benefit from the invitation.

The same day, April 14, Judas Priest issue *British Steel*. Although one might argue that musically speaking the record is a slight step away from a NWOBHM sound, the concept of "British steel" helps give shape to the reality of the NWOBHM. Plus, the album's anthems directly about metal help make the record a huge success for the band, Priest no doubt leading—as well as being swept along by—Britain's and North America's quickly growing appetite for all things metal. Iron Maiden will become the major beneficiary of this phenomenon; a bit ironic, given the friction.

And then, incredibly, not ten days later, Black Sabbath issue their classic *Heaven and Hell* album, which revives the band's career, due to the invigorating arrival of Ronnie James Dio to the fold. Another ten days would pass, and Saxon issue their seminal second album, *Wheels of Steel*. Iron Maiden, Motörhead, and now Saxon would become the flagship bands of the suddenly action-packed NWOBHM.

Record in the can but not in the shops yet, on April 1, Iron Maiden embark on their first headlining tour, beginning at the Rainbow, with Praying Mantis as support. As the record emerges, the band will be busy blanketing the UK, eventually, in August, getting to mainland Europe for the first time in support of Kiss. On April 3, Maiden play the Marquee, recordings from which producing versions of "Drifter" and "I Got the Fire" that will show up on the band's "Sanctuary" single from the following month. Two days later the band plays their first date outside the UK, at the Wheel Pop Festival in Belgium. Highlight of the show turns out to be the malfunction of the band's Eddie head, which, instead of spewing red smoke, explodes. On April 10, Maiden play an entirely instrumental set at the Central Hall in Grimsby after Paul Di'Anno begs off ill—the seed is sown.

And then it was time. On April 14, 1980, punters in Britain walked into their respective local record shops and were confronted with the ghoulish piercing eyes of Eddie, this leathery green thing of beauty only hinted at through the band's first single and through the band's live show.

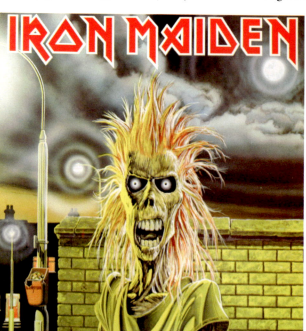

Dave Wright archive

"Heavy metal wasn't taking off at the time," explains the inventor of Eddie, Derek Riggs, on how this striking image came about. "Punk was big in England, and they were all walking around with their hair sticking up with grease and wearing leopard skins and shit like that. I was working on monsters. I was trying to do book covers, and there are versions of monsters with like a fucking monkey with wings [laughs]. It's a demon from hell, and the most hideous thing you can imagine is a fucking monkey with wings?! This isn't Kansas.

"So anyway, I just thought, well, I'll make it like a person, and I had this picture of this head stuck on a tank from somewhere, some war or the other. I think it might have been just a piece of propaganda, but it looked pretty cool, so I took this and kind of used it for anatomical reference, because you don't get many pictures of dried-up skulls. And the background of that is the streets where I used to live in London. So, I just kind of put the two together. I used to read H. P. Lovecraft, and I read an interview with him where he says anyone can make a horror story horrible in the wilds of Transylvania, with a hooting owl and all that, but what's it like if you shove it right on your doorstep? So, I stuck him right on your doorstep.

"And until I did that . . . it was such a departure from what people were doing. It's hard to spot when you look back, but at the time, demons were all monkeys with wings, fantasy, and horror, and it was just men hitting each other with swords, and the things were all happening within the picture frame. There was no contact between you and this fantasy world. And nobody ever really painted anything horrible. It was all fairies. But horror art, really, it hadn't really gotten anywhere; it stopped. It was uninteresting. So, I did this thing that was about twice as horrible as anything else that was around, and I made it look straight out at you. You know, he was looking into you, and you weren't getting away [laughs]. And it made a connection directly with the viewer. There was no barrier in the way; there was no little world. You were looking in on a picture of your world, and he was looking back out at you from it."

Remarks Goodall on why the *Iron Maiden* cover worked so well, "It had their logo on it, which is always good, and which they'd already established pretty well. And to make it even more alluring, you had a really stark, uncompromising character there, this slightly wild creature. I think if you'd just stuck the band on the front, they would have looked like a band of rock guys, actually. So what? But here you've created a brand, and that's the difference. Iron Maiden's actually a brand, and underneath that brand they've managed to change the people and maintain the brand. So, they created a brand without really knowing it, and that brand is Eddie, an enhanced element above and beyond what the music does."

"It was kind of unique," figures Adrian Smith, very soon to be in the band but, significantly, not on the debut album. "It translated great to the stage. It was a great visual tool to use, and to the album. It meant that we could get on with playing and writing music, and Eddie could be the outrageous visual side of the band. Although onstage we do our thing. Plus, it's just a very eye-catching kind of logo, and people seem to really get into it. They get a tattoo . . . the first time we'd come to America, we saw people with tattoos on their arms of Eddie and their car spray-painted with the monster all over it. I had one guy who'd built like a 20-foot Eddie on top of his house. I don't know how his parents let him get away with that.

"But it just inspired this sort of almost fanaticism. I think you have to have something to draw attention to music. I mean, that's a time-honored kind of thing, although if your music doesn't stand up, then it's all pointless. But that definitely draws attention to the band. But Eddie, he's got . . . you can see his brain and he's got green skin and his skin's falling off. I mean who wouldn't love him, really?"

"Adding the Eddie thing meant that we didn't have to be on the front covers," notes Steve, "which has always been a good thing. And it takes you to another element. A lot of people actually said to me—especially in the States and Canada, where we didn't even tour with the first album—they'd look through the album racks as people used to do in those days, and they'd see that front cover and go, 'Bloody 'ell, what's that?!' And then they'd turn it over and they'd see the live picture of the band on the back. And then they say, well, I've got to have this—before they've even heard what it is. Definitely made an impact."

"So, you've already captured people," continues Harris. "Although that's not really why we did it initially, the Eddie thing as such, because it started off as a bit of a joke, really, in the sense that we had . . . well it wasn't original, but the second singer we had, he used to do a bit of a Kiss thing where he used to put a sword through his mouth and the blood and guts and all this stuff. And when he left, we didn't want to incorporate that within the band itself, but we thought we'd try to incorporate it in some other way.

"So, we came up with this Kabuki-type mask, which eventually became Eddie, because we don't pronounce the H in London, so you just say Eddie the 'ed. And then it became this thing. And then we just had this real simple thing like a fish pump pumping blood through the mouth. So, you get it all over the drummer's head, because in the pubs it'd be sitting right above him. He used to love it, actually; he was in his element. He was like part of the show.

"And then we used to put lights around it, and the eyes lit up with smoke coming out, and sort of embellish it like that. We always wanted to put on a show, even in pubs. We would go into the change room and get changed, because we always felt you don't want to look like every other band that gets up there. You need to look around in a pub and think, who's in the band, then? Because everyone's wearing jeans and T-shirts or whatever. And then four guys or five guys will get up, and, okay, it's them then. So, we would go off and get changed and just think, well, we're going to put on a show, even in a pub. Even though it's a room probably not much bigger than this, we'd put on a show visually ourselves and add elements of theatrics within what we were doing.

Martin Popoff archive

"But Eddie meant that we didn't have to be that persona. We could have the Eddie thing, and it would be like outside of us as such. And we wanted to entertain people and not freak people out, because it wasn't that kind of thing. But it was just something different as well and made people take notice. Because we always felt that once you got people in, then you can prove what you can do, and they either like it or they don't, but you gotta get people in in the first place.

"And trying to fill up pubs in them days wasn't easy," continues Harris. "But right from the start we got a real good following happening, and word-of-mouth thing—you gotta go and check this band out. Because it's the music and the theatrics also. It was visually something to see as well as go and enjoy the music. You know, it was important. And those elements are still there now, obviously. You make it an event so people go away thinking, wow, I've just seen something a little bit different, a little bit special. I think people saw that it worked. I think people saw the Eddie thing was doing exactly what it was meant to do and entertain people. But also get people excited and talking and basically go see you. Once you've got people there, you can prove what you can do.

"But as I say, the hardest thing is getting them there in the first place. You just had to do everything you could. And you couldn't really afford big advertising campaigns. Yeah, you could go get a few posters together maybe and go slap them about. But if there wasn't the buzz about the name that was on those posters or some sort of striking image on there like Eddie or whatever, then it makes it that much more difficult. And I think anything that's going to make it easier to get people in to see you, you've just gotta get them there in the first place. Once they're there, I think you can hook them in. If you're good enough, you can hook them in, but it's very tough getting them there."

The back cover of *Iron Maiden* featured a live shot of the band looking as if they were part of a satanic ritual. An early but already evolved Eddie is up behind the drums doing his thing, and there's unspecified fire down on the crowd-obscured stage. Paul looks like he's conducting a sacrifice. EMI went the extra mile, allowing Iron Maiden the prestigious custom artwork for the round labels on the actual records. There's another Eddie there, but unfortunately (and maybe even unprofessionally) it doesn't really look like the same monster as depicted on the cover.

Once past the wrapper and inside the record, the dark yet fast-paced *Iron Maiden* album proved to be a squarely heavy metal record but intriguingly poked and prodded by both punk and prog. What the album exuded was atmosphere, chemistry, a sense of purpose, even oddity, with lyrics (and as discussed, a front cover) that reprised an idea brilliantly executed by Black Sabbath nearly exactly ten years earlier, of overtly using horror thematically to create a full-on package that refreshingly embraced what had often been subliminal tenets of heavy metal. In this respect, Maiden were establishing themselves as one of the most intense and intensely committed bands within a heavy metal movement whose central thrust was already the championing of metal.

Across the album, as exemplified by opening track, "Prowler," there's this sense of the chaotic, dotted here and there with still freshly painted forms of speed metal, laid down crudely but with confidence. And there's no doubt that some of this abstract magic came from Paul Di'Anno's happy-thug-punk influence and his attendant sometimes rapping style, as if committing wholesale to singing was just too uncool for him. In any event, the record is well paced, sequenced and varied, comprising a cogent mix of heavy and light, speedy bits against doom, the anthemic next to the opaque.

And again, the opening track, "Prowler," is in possession of many of these establishing and jelling tenets. The song is fast, but not to the point of speed metal. It's appointed with a novel riff on which wah-wah is applied. There are backing vocals, drama-inducing chord changes, little guitar licks here and there, and—trademark of all trademarks—chugging, articulated bass. The prog is represented by a break that sounds like a piece

Promo photo live shot, similar to the one used on the back cover of the debut album. *Dave Wright archive*

of a completely different song. Here twin leads are deftly stacked, in advance of a fast section that houses the guitar solo. Then we're back to the tale, not of a slasher, but merely a flasher.

"Lyrics is usually the last thing," muses Steve, who gets sole credit on this song. "It's kind of restricting at times if you get a strong melody line. If the melody line is that strong, you have to stick to it. You find that the syllables and certain words you might want to use don't fit there, and you have to find something else. And that can be a bit frustrating. I think it's most important that the melody is strong. I mean, that's the way we've always written anyway, since the first album."

Next up is "Remember Tomorrow," which establishes the NWOBHM ethic of ballads not about love and the loss of it, but rather dark subjects, accompanied by dark music. Here the softly picked but electric melody line is devilish, and the guys don't leave us hanging without a heavy part. When that comes—it's not exactly a chorus—it's panoramic and proggy, and then there's a second faster surprise, which also represents an establishment of a trope, one that would be carried forward into thrash. Already, through two tracks, Maiden has brought a considerable amount of substance, even if presented through the filter of somewhat bare-bones production values.

"I'm fond of 'Remember Tomorrow,'" says Di'Anno, "because I wrote that about my granddad, in a weird sort of roundabout way. 'Running Free,' 'Remember Tomorrow,' 'Killers,' and 'Sanctuary' are mine. That's about it. Like I say, it was mostly

Steve's band. That was another thing that was coming to a head. Because some of the songs I wrote were probably some of the better ones, if I don't mind saying so, not to be funny about it. In some ways, anyway. So, it worked out both ways; it was all right. But yes, you were only allowed to put a few in because most of the other songs were Steve Harris's. I mean Dave and Steve put their little bits together to make a tune, but 90 percent of it was Steve. I wasn't writing music with Iron Maiden; I was only doing a few lyrics."

Paul had recently had his grandfather, who was a diabetic, "give up" and die, after having had his toe and heel amputated, then his leg at the knee. He says that his grandfather would say, "Remember tomorrow," as a bit of optimistic advice, meaning that today things might not be going so well, but remember that there is always tomorrow.

As Paul told Jimmy Kay, "Yeah, yeah, my granddad would say that, just saying, 'It's gonna be all right.' Just sort of that, and it became a little bit more. And it's strange, actually, that 'unchain the colors' line. Must've been taking drugs or something at the time [laughs]. But no, no. It's like, things aren't really black and white, are they? So, you unchain the colors so you can see clearly. It's a bit complicated."

As Di'Anno indicates, credit-wise, on this record Steve and Paul share "Remember Tomorrow" and "Running Free." "Charlotte the Harlot" goes completely to Dave Murray, but all the rest are credited solely to Harris.

"Running Free" we've somewhat discussed, but it's worth noting how it fits now past the single issue amid the other songs on the first album. With much of the record aligning along themes of darkness, violence, and horror (rendered timeless; i.e., lacking in modern-day technology), this was one for the punters, even if the reference to being thrown in an LA jail for the night (and driving a pickup truck, for that matter) is jarring and incongruous. The particulars were instantly shoved aside by all of us who loved this greeting card from the band, with the chorus refrain taking beery position at the front of the stage. Paul says the song is somewhat autobiographical, referring to his knockabout days as a rebel and even a skinhead.

Although, speaking with *Rock Hard* magazine in 2004, Paul said, "I've never been a skinhead. I was more like a mod. It's true that I was a right bastard, and that I loved to go out on the piss and, whenever possible, get into a fight and ruin the evening for a maximum of people, and then do my utmost to pull some bird that was already with someone. That was my 'special,' the icing on the cake! I also remember Phil Collen of Def Leppard. We used to hang out together in the East End of London, the area where we were born. He was behaving exactly like me—he was even worse! I loved to be the center of attraction. And I was doing whatever I could to make people aware of who I was. As a teenager, I spent a huge amount of time wreaking havoc, pissing off as many people as possible in the neighborhood, just like Phil! I was such a bastard. Anyway, as a kid, I used to hang out with complete nutters, but it all changed when I joined Maiden and I converted to metal."

But music didn't come naturally to Di'Anno. "Let's say that there weren't any musicians in my family, but my parents loved music and there was always a record on at home. Anything. From Frank Sinatra to the Rolling Stones or Mantovani, and, of course, let's not forget the Sex Pistols. At our place, there was an old piano in the living room, and I was trying to play—not very well! I was making a bit of a racket, and even the neighbors were complaining! I was a fucking awful pianist, and one day I sprayed the poor piano with lighter fuel, and I set fire to it. All right, I'd been drinking a bit beforehand, and it seemed like a good idea at the time. My mom never forgave me. What a bad son, eh?"

In 1995, Steve curiously remarked that "I suppose 'Running Free' sounds a bit dated. But then it's about fifteen years old. But then again 'Iron Maiden' we still play, and it's more like seventeen years old, and it still sounds fairly fresh. But 'Running Free,' at this point, we've dropped from the set."

This reveals a bit of ambivalence toward the song on the part of Harris, which is somewhat justified, given that "Running Free" is about as crudely assembled as Maiden would get, bashed out atop a tribal rhythm not far off the postpunk of Killing Joke.

Last track on side 1 of the original vinyl is where Iron Maiden puts it all together for a sustained assault, the metal and the complication combined, the speed and the riffing high up the fret board working in white-knuckle concert. Steve says that "Phantom of the Opera" was one of his earliest attempts at a proggier style of heavy metal, and he is still proud of the song today, featuring it in Maiden set lists regularly over the years. He still enjoys playing the bass parts, listening to the guitar weaves, and anticipates the opportunities for crowd participation.

For the verses, a complex rhythm suddenly comes to a stop, and Paul sings in convoluted unison over twin guitars. Late in the sequence there are dark, moody passages that take the band timelessly into a sort of melding of the Renaissance with the medieval. Halfway through, Steve plays some solo bass triplets that evoke Budgie and, when the guitars join in, Priest. Later, we get the band's first truly classic twin lead, amid all manner of solo licks and quickly arriving and dissolving twinned situations. This takes place over another freshly established Maiden tenet, the gallop, this one measured and midpaced.

"That's another one of Steve's," says Paul of the lyric, based on French writer Gaston Leroux's story of the same name, published in 1910. "Now that one did take a bit of time because it's a bloody nightmare to sing. It's bad enough live, but to get it dead on for an actual recording, I think I had to do that one three times or so. If I said less, I'd probably be lying [laughs]."

On May 26, 1897, Archibald Constable and Company publishes Bram Stoker's *Dracula*, which inspires the dramatic and note-dense instrumental that kicks off side 2 of *Iron Maiden*. Cracks Paul, "I used to like 'Transylvania' because I used to get a rest in. That was all right. Oh God, I think I like every track on the first album."

"Transylvania" further proposes this idea that perhaps Maiden might be a link in the chain between Rush and Queensryche and then Fates Warning in the creation and establishment of what might be called progressive metal. Steve is too cognizant of headbanging norms to go full prog on us, but "Transylvania" is indeed thespian and dramatic and timeless, a bit toward pomp and circumstance, which in rock talk leads us to "pomp rock," with "Transylvania" evocative of certain heavy tendencies from Styx, most notably something like "The Grand Illusion."

Next up is "Strange World," a full-on "dirgey" ballad in the dark spirit of Black Sabbath. Credited solely to Steve, it's a remarkable yet brief tale or vignette about alien abduction, the protagonist seemingly happily trapped on a planet with "girls drinking plasma wine."

"Charlotte the Harlot" is loosely linked with "22 Acacia Avenue" and "From Here to Eternity," the three said to compose the Charlotte Saga. This one, which amounts to what is a pretty brutal admonishment of a hooker "friend," is entirely Dave's, but Steve is proud to call it a Maiden song and enjoys playing it live because it's not of a style he would write. It's a brisk heavy metal rocker, a bit on the traditional side but dressed up with enough stops and starts to make it Maiden. Rumor has it that it's about a real girl with whom old-days Maiden singer Dennis Wilcock had an acquaintance, and indeed the song goes back that far.

Iron Maiden closes in fine fashion with its title track, its "Black Sabbath" as it were. Except that Steve pens a heart attack of a heavy metal rocker, twin leads afire, punky rock 'n' roll rhythm, cool descending bass line behind the guitars. Musical surprises emerge as the tale progresses, one in which the protagonist invites his victim to his personal chamber of horrors, slamming him or her (but, let's face it, likely a her) into the "iron maiden," which results in a mess of blood upon the floor.

"I did like that one actually," remarks Paul. "That was one of the songs that actually got me to join up with Maiden. Because they had the song before me, when they had already worked with two other singers. I went to see them one night. I'd been offered the job, and I went to see them play, and me and my mate, actually the guy who became the drum tech for Maiden, we was best friends at school, we walked out on Maiden twice. We thought they were absolutely garbage. But that was the one song that I actually thought was any good [laughs]."

Once *Iron Maiden* was put out for public consumption, fans were intrigued and on board. There might have been more professional sounding heavy metal records to buy, certainly by the old guard but even by some of the newer bands—Angel Witch, Def Leppard, More, and, yes, most definitely Quartz with *Stand Up and Fight*—but there was a magic here in the songs that couldn't be denied. And then there was an album with a similar sense of magic but less sort of impressive playing and professionalism: Diamond Head's *Lightning to the Nations*. Quartz was seen as not photogenic enough and a bit old, and Angel Witch apparently couldn't cut it live and had too much internal drama to get past their first brilliant record intact. But in 1980, Maiden, Def Leppard, and Diamond Head all were seen as superstars in waiting.

As Steve says, EMI were clearly behind Maiden, quick to announce the band stateside. The label booked a full-color, full-page ad in *Billboard*, a vote of confidence in terms of telling the industry about a baby band. A big, lurid shot of the album cover is topped by a red headline reading "Rock 'n' roll isn't pretty!" Below the threatening Eddie, the text reads: "Iron Maiden have spearheaded the recent surge of headbangin' rock in the UK and have a proven smash LP that packs a starry-eyed punch! *Iron Maiden*—cast from heavy metal rock 'n' roll—is produced by Will Malone."

Di'Anno firmly places *Iron Maiden* near the apex of the best albums he's ever done, with his dislike for the follow-up *Killers* being one of many factors leading to his departure from the band. "I thought the first album had a really good raw feeling to it," says Paul of the debut, and yet, concerning *Killers* and its increased technical feel, "If I thought about it properly, I guess they probably always would have gone that way in the end. If you think about some of the stuff that went on on the first album, it's not surprising. It was always going to become a bit too complicated for what I wanted. I like more of a riff than this going off on tangents. But then again, there's no band that does it better than Iron Maiden, is there?"

"The first album was tremendous," says Rod. "It took off straightaway—we debuted at #4 in the UK chart." Adds Steve, "It was important the album came out at the time it did, because obviously you need to come out there before a lot of other bands get in there. We just came out before other bands came in. And the fact that we got the deal with EMI was a big thing as well, because it was worldwide distribution and all that, so that made a massive difference too. But the fact that we played, again, getting back to the four and a half years before getting signed, that came into play very much, so then, because the album came out and it went straight into #4, and it surprised everybody, including me.

"But it wasn't a total surprise. It was a surprise we went that high, but we thought that maybe, possibly, we'd chart, because we'd done the groundwork all over the UK, so many gigs all over the place, and built up this following. So we thought, well, even if half of them buy it, we're probably going to be doing all right. And it seemed like everyone bought it, so it went straight into the chart at #4, which was amazing. And so being the first band to do that and chart that heavily, it made a real statement; it really did. It stood out in a lot of ways."

At this point, all there was to do was keep hammering away from the lip of the stage, leg up on the monitors. From May 15 to July 1, 1980, the lion's share of the band's live dates found Praying Mantis (another hopeful, and, believe it or not, almost a signee to Leber Krebs) in the support slot, with Neal Kay on the bill as well, DJing.

On May 16, Iron Maiden issue "Sanctuary" / "Drifter" / "I Got the Fire" as a 7-inch single, with the controversial sleeve that featured Eddie murdering Margaret Thatcher. Not four days later, London's *Daily Mirror* reprints the "Sanctuary" sleeve along with the tag line "IT'S MURDER! Maggie gets rock mugging." The single rises to #29 in the UK charts.

"I actually thought of that idea," explains Derek Riggs, "and they said no, because we don't want any link with Margaret Thatcher or things like that, or iron women. And then he must've changed his mind and said make it Margaret Thatcher now. And then they put a sticker over the face. The lyric says in the song, 'I've never killed a woman before, but I know how it feels,' a bullshit lyric, you know, but I just took that and illustrated it; that's all. And then I got halfway through, and they said, 'Well, make it Margaret Thatcher,' so I did. I try to create a narrative in my pictures, because it gives the fans something to do [laughs]. They can look at it and say this is happening or that's happening."

"Sanctuary" has proven to be a lovable and enduring song in the Iron Maiden canon (it would be added to the North American issue of the debut), but it's pretty darn punky. As Steve explained to *Sounds* back in 1980, there was a point in time when the band was being advised to get with the program. "That punk tag was all the work of this bird at RCA, horny bird like, and she kept trying to make us 'go punk.' She tried to get us a gig at the Roxy. I think she even got our name printed on a poster, but we told her where to go. We didn't want nothing to do with it. She also got us included in a *Sounds* new wave roundup thing. We done our nuts when we saw it and wrote a letter in at the time."

"Drifter" is a capable enough non-LP original, but the important song here is "I Got the Fire." Just like the music on the first album—and indeed on the front cover—marked a shift toward the idea of defining and then championing heavy metal, picking songs to cover such as this heavy and relatively obscure Montrose number also marks a shift in metal consciousness. Maiden would go on to prove that it wasn't a fluke either, adding this idea of covering songs they *wished* were more metal and then making them so. Both

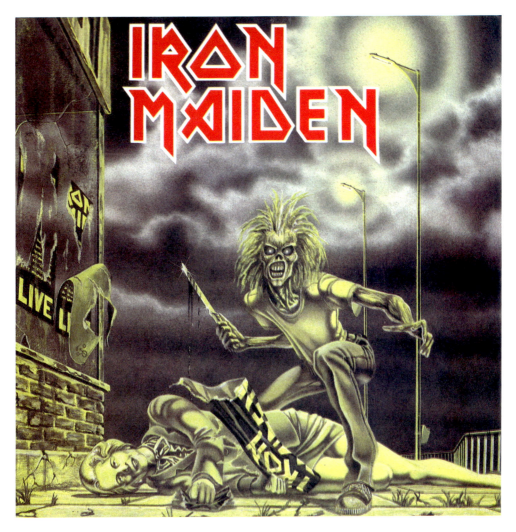

Dave Wright archive

desires match up with what the true, deep, and committed metal fans would do if they had their own bands—Maiden were us. In other words, it's not Free or Led Zeppelin or "Summertime Blues," it's Golden Earring, Jethro Tull, Montrose, and Skyhooks.

Around this time, *Metal for Muthas Volume II* is issued. The album is more independent heavy than the preceding *Metal for Muthas*, featuring Trespass (two songs), Eazy Money, Xero, White Spirit, Dark Star, Horsepower, Red Alert, Chevy, and the Raid. None of these bands would break, but then again, the first one isn't full of future rock stars either.

On July 3 through 5, Maiden make a three-date stand at the Marquee, after having sold out the Rainbow Theatre in London on June 20. Raven supports on the first night, with the gig being filmed for ITV. Fist supports on July 4 and 5.

The band was firing on all cylinders, including the business side of it, says Dennis. "There weren't any weaknesses. It was just Steve and Rod running the band, and whatever they said, that was it. It went that way. Steve has always been a good leader, and he's always had a name; he always knew what he wanted and, to be honest with you, if they had a disagreement and Rod Smallwood would have left, Maiden would still be as big as they are now, because Steve had this dream and this aim to do it. And he would have done it anyway, with Rod up there or not. It was great management and great organization, but Steve always . . . that's been his band and that's what he's done."

On August 10, Maiden play the Global Village in London. Support comes from Angel Witch, the band's main NWOBHM competitors from a recorded-output point of view, plus Adrian Smith's band Urchin. A week later, ITV screens the episode of *Twentieth Century Box* featuring Iron Maiden filmed live the past month at the Marquee. But more significantly, *Iron Maiden* is issued in North America, after the metal faithful got to live with their import copies for a good three months, informing all their friends what's around the corner (Eddie).

Indeed, as an indication of that, from August 22 to 24, England's venerable Reading Rock festival goes full-on heavy metal. The complete lineup (in order of performance) is as follows. Friday: Red Alert, O1 Band, Hellions, Praying Mantis, Fischer Z, Nine Below Zero, Krokus, Gillan, and Rory Gallagher. Saturday: Trimmer and Jenkins, Headboys, Writz, Broken Home, Samson, Q Tips, Pat Travers Band, Angel City (did not play), Iron Maiden, and UFO. Sunday: Pencils (did not play), Sledgehammer, Tygers of Pan Tang, Girl, Budgie, Magnum, Gary Moore's G Force (did not play), Ozzy Osbourne (replaced by Slade), Def Leppard, and Whitesnake. Maiden is said to have triumphed on the Saturday night, over Pat Travers, on just before them, and headliners UFO. Their set has come to be defined as the coming-out party for Maiden and indeed the NWOBHM in general, underscored by both Travers and UFO being part of the old guard.

"Well, that was great for us," reminisces Steve, "because obviously it was a big, fantastic festival. I'd been there in 1973 to see Genesis and loads of other bands, and so to actually play there was amazing, and UFO were playing, and so that was a really big thing for me as well, and just the whole vibe of it. And the reaction we got was incredible. I think everybody was just willing us to do well. You know, wherever we were playing, the crowd was growing with the band, effectively. Because they just wanted to see us go to the next stage and the next level. And whenever we went and did something that, it was a big thing, a turning point for us, a festival like that, for example, and then they were really behind it and wanted us to do well. It was like they were all willing us along. It was quite a fantastic time to be involved with the band, really."

Mirroring and then effectively underscoring their experience with Priest, from August 29 to October 13, 1980, Maiden support Kiss on the European leg of their *Unmasked* tour. The show on August 29 represents the band's first in Italy, now a longtime bastion of Iron Maiden support.

"Fantastic experience," recalls Rod. "Bill Aucoin, their manager at the time, had booked two shows in Paris at the Hippodrome, came in after the first night, and said what an incredible response we'd got in Paris, unbelievable. The kind of reaction a headliner would be proud to get. He came and said jokingly, 'From now on, we'll support you.' Kiss were just fantastic to tour with and we went down great, and of course so did they. They were the sort of band not to be threatened by us."

"Well, the Kiss tour came toward the end of 1980, as the record came out in February or March," explains Steve. "So, by the time we get on the tour it's toward the end of the year, and the album had been out for a while. And it had been selling well in England and these other places that we just didn't expect to be any sales, really. And we went on the Kiss tour, and all of a sudden we were playing from 8,000 to 10,000 people to 25,000 people in a couple open-air gigs, huge crowds. Again, there were a lot of fans turning up, getting right down in front early so they could see us, which was amazing, which gave us confidence and gave us the people to actually feed off of in front. And it just spread to the rest of the crowd. It was amazing."

Adds Dennis, "When they finalized the Kiss tour, we were told straightaway that we would not be playing any shows in England with Kiss. And that just proved the point straightaway that they were worried. So, they don't want us supporting them in England because the majority, I imagine, it would be 75/25 or 50/50 again, that the crowd would be Iron Maiden. But surely, they didn't want us supporting them in England at all.

"As I said earlier, we'd drive towards somewhere in Italy or France or wherever, and when you turn up in the afternoon . . . it's the middle of the afternoon and you're going towards a big venue like a football stadium or a big arena or wherever, and you get an idea what the crowd's gonna be like, 'cause as you're driving through the streets towards the big venue, you're seeing 50,000 to 60,000 fans walking around the streets or sitting outside on the grass or sitting outside bars. And, when you drive past in a bus, you can see that half of them have Kiss T-shirts on and the other half had Maiden T-shirts on. So, we got such a brilliant, great reception on the Kiss tour. And also, I got on really well with Gene Simmons and Paul Stanley because they took me out on my birthday, and we had a great time.

"But it was getting to the point where, as the tour went on, Maiden were getting bigger and bigger, and more fans were joining the fan base. Kiss have always been a huge band, but at the time, I think it was very, very good timing by EMI or Rod Smallwood or whatever, the fact that Kiss was trying to prove a point that they were still one of the frontrunners. Although they're still out there now, they were a little bit weak at times, so when we went on tour with them, as I said, we've got nothing to lose and everything to gain."

Recalls Paul, "The guys from Kiss were wonderful, especially Gene, who was looking after my money, which isn't exactly my strong point. In fact, he was keeping my dough and was giving me the strict minimum when I really needed it, which prevented me from blowing it on rubbish. Gene has treated me like a son. He taught me what to do and not to do. We started the tour as support for Kiss, and all of a sudden we became very popular. So, it was Kiss that looked like an opening act. It was also during this tour that Dennis Stratton's fate was sealed."

"Immediate explosion in Germany" is the first thing that comes to mind for Ashley Goodall, on how the band was doing on this very first European campaign. "So, they did the UK, UK prime, in at #4; EMI were creaming it for them in Germany, I think straight into #1. They did a tour with Kiss. Brought them on tour for that. I mean the fact that they'd done it with Judas Priest and Kiss, they had a lot of exposure in the UK, everyone was gagging for it, right? The next big thing. But it wasn't punk, which didn't translate. Heavy rock did. Germany had always been there, the land of metal. Northern Europe: it was still the land of Thor. So actually, you gave them a product that just walked straight in there, out of Valhalla, straight on the plate. Plus, you had EMI gagging for it, and it was beautifully set up, and bang, straight in. The tour, the lot was there."

September 11 marked the first-ever show for the band in Germany, and on the twenty-third the first ever in France, but October 13 would mark Dennis Stratton's last show with Maiden, at the band's first-ever stop in Norway. Stratton leaves the band after butting heads with Steve and Rod. He would be replaced by Adrian Smith, then currently with Broadway Brats (Girl's Phil Collen was also considered). This date also marks the end of the band's support of Kiss on their *Unmasked* tour.

Reflects Stratton, "Because I'd already toured with many bands, I think it's good to have a bit of freedom to mix with other people, listen to different music. And I think what happened was that Rod, being a young manager and wanting to keep the band together, he wanted all the band to stay together, and I just wanted a bit of space, and he thought I wasn't into the music. He thought I wasn't into the heavy metal bands; he thought I wasn't into Iron Maiden. Basically, I liked to listen to the Eagles, George Benson, all different types of music.

"I think what happened in the end was, near the end of the Kiss tour, he came to the hotel room and he said—I was having a shower; I was listening to David Coverdale sing 'Soldier of Fortune'—and he came and he said, 'Look, I just don't think you're into the band as much as you should be; I don't think you're committed to the heavy metal music.' And I just said, 'If I play Iron Maiden stuff all night and I come back to the hotel and listen to Motörhead for the rest of the night, by the end of the week my ears are gonna be shot.' So, I just said, 'I need to relax and just to chill out,' because I was a bit older than him and probably older than the band. I just had my own ways of relaxing. The funny thing is, when we got back to England, we had this big argument about my commitment to the band and all that, and he was saying, 'I can't fault the playing, I can't fault the singing; it's just you're out of tune towards the heavy metal music.'

"But you gotta remember, that was the first album. He was very nervous; he wanted the band to be as big as they are, but the funny thing is, after all them years, when I was in America, in Los Angeles in 1984 with Lionheart, we were recording for CBS and I met up with Rod at the Rainbow and he said, 'I'll buy you a beer.' And we sat down, and he said to me, 'Everything you said all came true.' He tried to keep the band together so much that they ended up . . . they don't want to be together; they want their own space. It was just one of them things.

"When we got back from the Kiss tour, we had this argument and I said, 'Okay, if you think I'm not into it . . . ,' and he said, 'We think your outlook towards heavy metal . . . ,' and I said, 'Well, is it me playing?' And he said no. 'Is it me singing?'; he said no. I said, 'Well, then, I can't change the way I am,' and he said, 'Well, you've got to,' and I said, 'Well, I can't. If I wanna listen to other music, I will.' And that was it. We ended up parting company."

As Paul explained to *Rock Hard*'s Philippe Lageat in 2004, "I don't want to show any disrespect to Den, 'cause I really like him. But I never thought he was a good guitarist. I even think that with such limited abilities, he's really been lucky to be in Maiden, mostly that he wasn't so keen on metal. By the way, I discovered a few years later that Dennis was more or less 'antimetal' and that he'd only joined Maiden because he felt that the band had a great potential. Adrian was—and still is—a brilliant guitarist and one of the major elements in Maiden. He's basically contributed to make the band what it is today. In fact, Dennis had a fantastic voice and should have become a pop/rock singer. He loved this soft style. Before he joined Maiden, I used to go often to the Cart & Horses and watch him play with his former band, Wedgewood. He was then an excellent singer and seemed to be more comfortable there than as a member of Iron Maiden. Dennis has never really been part of the metal world, and he's never accepted this universe, even if he maybe says the opposite now. He was really into pop, and he wanted to have three-voice harmonies in Maiden or crap like that.

"But Steve never gave in," continued Paul. "We even had to force Dennis to wear a leather jacket, which he hated, and we tried to get him to act 'metal'! On the other hand, Adrian never pretended. He had the right attitude; he really was into it, and he loved anything related to this genre. Steve and Dennis had a few ding-dongs because he didn't like the metal gear and was only listening to pop music. He really pissed Steve off during the Kiss tour when, in Spain, he started complaining that he had to wear denim and leather. Steve was doing his nut, and I think that this is when he realized that he had to get rid of Dennis. During the whole time he was in the band, we had to pretend that he was one of ours, which was an outright lie, because he only liked the Beach Boys and the Eagles. I hope that what I'm telling you here won't cause him any trouble, because I like him a lot, as well as his voice. But even now he spends his weekends playing covers of Oasis or Robbie Williams in pubs in the East End of London. Not really metal, is it?"

As Loopy frames it, "The decision to get rid of Dennis . . . I think that was one of the reasons behind Pete Bryant leaving. And so, when Adrian comes in, he ended up with a completely new roadie that Tony Wigens had found. But yeah, Dennis leaving was a massive

German-issue EP. *Dave Wright archive*

blow. But of course, everybody knew Adrian. So, him sort of joining was so natural. And of course, he was Dave's partner. He was asked several times and he kept turning it down. Eventually there wasn't much happening with Urchin, and so he saw a big chance and went for it."

On October 27, Iron Maiden issue "Women in Uniform," a Skyhooks cover, backed with "Invasion." The 12-inch version adds a live version of "Phantom of the Opera." Again, the whole package represents a new NWOBHM way of doing business. Back in the dreary 1970s, from a heavy band you'd get the ballad as an A-side and a heavier but not too heavy track from the album as the B-side, and you'd be lucky to see a picture sleeve. Maiden tangled with an obscure song from the other side of the world and interpreted it exactly the way the sweaty throngs at the lip of the stage would have wanted them to. Then they hit them with a non-LP original and, just to show they've been around the block, a live version of something off the record, all of it, of course, with image-matching picture sleeve.

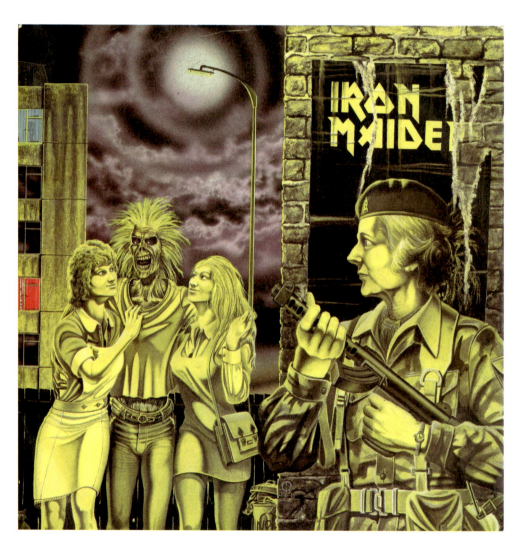

Dave Wright archive

Iron Maiden's version of "Women in Uniform," suggested to them by their new publishing company, Zomba, would be the last Maiden recording for guitarist Dennis Stratton. The song also served as the platform for Maiden's first professional music video, which helped send it to a #35 chart placement. The track was recorded—and not to the band's satisfaction—by Tony Platt at Battery Studios.

Remarks Derek Riggs, on bringing Margaret Thatcher back for a second sleeve, "Well, I think that was Rod's idea; he wanted to bring Margaret Thatcher back and have a machine gun Eddie. But I couldn't find a profile of Margaret Thatcher anywhere, so I had to make one up [laughs]. I have no clue whether it looks like her. A few people say that they recognize her, but I don't know. The girls, I just painted them. I can't remember where the idea came from. That's right, it's nurses, women in uniform, isn't it? So, I've got Eddie with a couple of women in uniform."

Before the year is out, EMI issues their *Mutha's Pride* EP compilation, featuring Quartz, Wildfire, White Spirit, and Baby Jane. Baby Jane was never heard from again, Wildfire made a couple of records on a small label, but Quartz and White Spirit would record for MCA, the only major who might have been even more active than EMI in the NWOBHM. White Spirit featured future Maiden guitarist Janick Gers.

In November 1980, Maiden see the release of *Live!!+One*, but in Japan only, featuring three Di'Anno-era live tracks plus the band's cover of "Women in Uniform." Despite the band having not visited yet, Japan quickly had learned much about Maiden, thanks to journalist Masa Ito, with that country being the first to award the band with a gold record, for the debut no less, which lagged behind its follow-ups in most territories.

November 8, 1980, marked new guitarist Adrian Smith's first show with Iron Maiden, a TV recording situation, for *Rock Pop* in Munich, Germany. Two weeks later he performs his first proper concert with the band, the first date of the band's next UK tour, at Brunel University in Uxbridge. The gig was close enough to London to have a number of EMI staffers in attendance. After ten UK shows to close out the month, the band would enter the studio to begin work on the second album.

Smith took to the band's patented twin-lead approach straightaway. "Yeah, it thickens out the sound, yeah. I've played in three-piece bands, and it's great fun, but you tend to play differently. Filling in all the gaps. Like I say, you've got more discipline between the two of you; otherwise, it'll sound just like a big mess. Funny enough, a lot of the songs I wrote—certainly in the 1980s—didn't have guitar harmonies. Ironically, Steve wrote a lot of the guitar harmonies in 'The Trooper' and 'Hallowed' and a lot of the classic Maiden stuff. Steve was really specific; he was really into the idea of two guitars. And he wrote a lot of that stuff, the two guitar parts. In the latest incarnation of the band, I started writing more for three guitars, you know? But yeah, a lot of the classic harmony lines you hear is the guitar stuff that Steve wrote."

A month later, on December 21, Maiden record their live set at a sort of Christmas party concert for what will be the seven-track *Live at the Rainbow* concert video, issued in May of '81. The prerelease version of "Killers" performed here includes different lyrics from the forthcoming album version.

Notes Paul, "I remember, with 'Killers,' the video, *Live at the Rainbow*, the lyrics on that are completely different from what was on the record because I had about five minutes to make it up; otherwise, it would have been instrumental. So, I had to make it up before we went onstage [laughs]. It's a bit stupid when you're playing in front of 3,500 people and it's the first time you're ever doing a live recording. I think it took me two takes to get it right. The only problem we ever used to have recording-wise was basically Steve and his clacky bass guitar sound, where he doesn't use a pick [laughs]. That was that, and it went through nearly every bloody song. He never used a pick. I don't know if he does now, but he never did then. And with a Fender, you get the most amazing, horrible clacky sound all the time. It was a nightmare."

Hmm . . . complaining about Steve's bass sound might not be the best career move in the world. Hope it all works out fine for Paul.

Martin Popoff archive

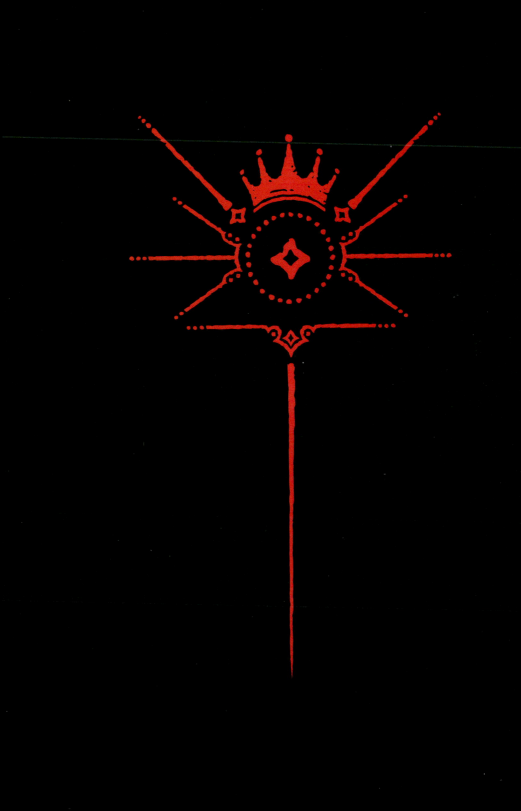

CHAPTER 2
Killers

"Martin turned everything full circle."

All eyes were on the now-one-year-old NWOBHM and, for all intents and purposes, the one-year-old Iron Maiden in terms of the public consciousness. As was the case with Van Halen and their second album, *II*, for their sophomore effort Iron Maiden would be mining their existing live favorites for potential anthems as well as penning new numbers.

From early December 1980 into January the following year, Maiden would work at Battery Studios, with Martin Birch presiding as producer. Birch had worked with Deep Purple, Rainbow, and Whitesnake, as well as on assorted Purple solo albums. He had also recently knob-twiddled Black Sabbath back into relevance through his masterful job on *Heaven and Hell*. Significant to Steve, Birch was also the engineer on the first three Wishbone Ash albums.

"All I remember was that he was pretty on the case," says Di'Anno, "what with his pedigree from Deep Purple and Whitesnake. I just remember that I never had to complain once about, oh, this is too low or whatever. It's always perfect every day. It was just so relaxed, so easy to go in and do. That was always my biggest regret. I wish Martin Birch had done the first Iron Maiden album. Because I think with that rawer sound we have, I think that would have really done it."

The *Killers* album was recorded in a very, very small single studio in the backstreets of Willesden, in London," explains Loopy. "There were metal doors that opened, you loaded your gear straight in, doors closed, everything soundproofed. That was it. The studio and the sound room and that was it. *Killers* was recorded really quickly. I think the studio time was less than two weeks. They'd been playing the songs live for long enough that it was easy. Backing vocals and guitar solos were done quick. Let's face it, Martin Birch had worked with Gillan and Dio, so he knew what he wanted to get out of them, and he had taken that experience to Di'Anno, and later even Bruce, to a certain extent."

"For *Killers*, we in fact did have a few ideas and songs sort of knocking around," explains Dave Murray. "But a lot of the stuff we were playing previously went on the first album. Some of those songs were there anyway, and we just kind of held back. *Killers* is when Martin came in, the first album, and that was just a whole . . . Martin turned everything full circle, 360, really. We'd been big fans of Martin because he'd worked with Deep Purple and Sabbath. It was like working with this guy who recorded albums that we grew up listening to. So that was a blast doing that in London as well—the studio had quite a good vibe to it.

"*Killers* is really raw, although there was a lot of complex stuff on there, playing-wise," continues Murray. "But it does have a rawer kind of edge to it. As we moved on, it was still heavy, but everything got a bit more polished, in a good way. It didn't really need the rough edges. But that's a sign of the times and our age and everything. As you get older, you want everything to be a bit cleaner and sweeter yet still have the intensity there. But some of the songs were around, and a lot of it was written specifically for it. And Paul, he was quite happy. I mean, he was cowriting some of the stuff there. What it is, I think, being in the studio as opposed to being on the road, two completely different worlds. In the studio, you can spend some time working on different bits of songs; you can overdub and fix things and make it right. So, everyone had a good chance, a couple of months working on the songs and stuff. But at the time, for the energy and stuff, he was singing great; he sounded great on that album. So he was into it then. It was after that [when] the wheels started coming off. But there's something special about *Killers*."

Noted Steve, speaking with *Sounds* in 1981, on the use of older material on *Killers*: "Because you've been playing them for some time doesn't mean that everybody else in the rest of the world has heard them. And not only that, if you didn't lay them down, you'd never record them, and they'd be lost forever. Because you're not always going to be playing them, and if you've got them on the album, at least people can always listen to them. If you've got a good song, you should put it on vinyl, really, and if you haven't got room on the first album, then you put it on the second one."

Killers was issued on February 2, 1981, and not for another five months in America—rewarded for the wait, the American fans would get "Twilight Zone" tacked on. As for the album cover, Eddie was on the lookout for new victims. Metalheads were exempt from his wrath, although not always—witness the "Running Free" single. Still, metal's favorite grinning cadaver was prowling the same dismal nightscapes, having of course missed the last train back after the gig.

Explains Derek on his thinking, "I had the idea for the *Killers* cover, and I mentioned it to Dave Lights [Maiden's lighting guy], and he had run off and talked to Rod about it, who had said they were doing another album and they wanted to use Eddie again because he was quite popular. So, I just went ahead and painted it. Communication-wise,

Fourth Golden Summernight Concert, Stuttgart, Germany, August 15, 1981. © *Wolfgang Guerster*

I was talking to Dave at about the same time I was talking to Rod. But Rod is often off with the band doing stuff. So often it was Dave, or whoever I thought could get a message to Rod. The band didn't take much notice at all. Occasionally when they came across the paintings, they would go, 'Oh, that's cool,' and they just went off.

"Those streets are where I used to live in London," notes Derek, who applies the same philosophy as the debut, in terms of placing the horror where we live. "It's not exactly the block of flats I used to live in, but it's close enough. That would have been my flat with my cat in the window. But I didn't have a black one. I had a tortoiseshell and a white tabby, and the tortoiseshell and white was called Cat Black the Wizard's Hat, and the tabby was called Magus Matter Guru Master of the Universe.

"The building is not quite right either, because where I lived, the one in the end only had two layers. It was a funny block of flats, but great, actually. It was in Finchley in North London, and it was an old decrepit block of flats, desperately in need of repair. And it was set back off the road in a gap, so nobody could ever find it because there were trees growing up all the way around. There were houses here, houses here, houses there, there was a road that went like that, and the block of flats was in the middle, trees all the way around it, so you couldn't see it from the road. There was just one long driveway that went in, and one long driveway that went out the back that nobody ever used. And all the trees had grown up and the grass had gone completely apeshit [laughs] because nobody had ever tended it.

"It had a caretaker, and he was fighting a losing battle, I think. They had what turned out to be allotments in the back, which had gone completely wild. And somebody had built a swing in a tree. So, it was like living in the countryside in the middle of London; it was great. Except the roof used to leak all the time. I used to put pots and pans of different sizes and you could play tunes. The woman upstairs, she had a hole in her roof, apparently. And snow used to settle on her floor, and it used to melt and drip through the ceiling. So winter, I would have quite a wet kitchen."

None of the figures in the window on the *Killers* picture are meant to be anyone specific, but Maiden did request that Derek add in the Ruskin Arms, down to the lower left, that being a pub in which Maiden had plied their ghoulish trade. "I kept the kinky sex shop and the Letraset," adds Derek, addressing the same wee corner of shops. "That's actually a joke. Rub-on letters, that crap people use, they got them from a company called Letraset— Letraset instant lettering—so I just took the logo off and used that. They blew this cover up in Virgin Records in London, about

Dave Wright archive

12-foot-square, and they stuck it in their window. They got some guys who projected it onto wood, and he painted it and it was bloody fierce actually, quite awesome. You would walk down the street and you had this 12-foot Eddie looking at you, which was like, 'Whoa.'"

Once into the record, Maiden opens the proceedings with an instrumental intro that is downright regal, yet also entirely heavy metal. Strange pedigree to this one. Maiden had been performing the song as far back as 1977. At that point, drummer Thunderstick was in the band. Thunderstick went on to Samson, who included a very similar song on their second album, *Head On*, calling it "Thunderburst" and crediting it to Dickinson, Samson, Aylmer, Thunderstick, and Steve Harris. "The Ides of March" is credited solely to Steve Harris.

"I'll tell you what happened," explains Thunderstick. "We went in and recorded *Head On*. Because it was going to be the first album that Bruce Dickinson was going to appear on, we had quite an intense writing period as soon as Bruce joined the band, because we had been a three-piece. So, when Bruce joined the band, it was really intense; it was great. It was just what we needed—a new injection of life and what have you. So, we went in and recorded *Head On*, and I brought 'Thunderburst' to the table. It's called 'Thunderburst' because it was my idea. I had this rolling drum pattern that went through the toms, and I explained that we had done this when I was a member of Iron Maiden. So, we recorded it.

"And Paul Samson and Clive Burr were quite good mates, because Clive had been in Samson before I joined Samson. We kind of literally swapped places. Clive went to Maiden, and I went to Samson, and there was a time [laughs] when Clive would have Samson stenciled on his drum cases and he would be with Iron Maiden, and vice versa for myself—I would have Iron Maiden on my drum cases when I was gigging with Samson. It was quite strange.

"Anyway, Clive Burr went over to Paul Samson's house, and they were sitting there, and Paul played the first side of the *Head On* album, and Clive was 'Great, yeah, that's really good.' So, they went to slap the second side on, on the B-side, and up came 'Thunderburst,' and Clive nearly fell off his chair. He said, 'Jesus, you can't put this on.' And he put on his finished recordings and up came 'Ides of March.'

"And then what happened after that was that my management at the time, the Samson management, didn't really want to have any involvement in this, and it was 'No, we don't want to get involved with this.' I was summoned to EMI, the EMI building, and in front of me was Steve Harris, Rod Smallwood, and a couple of representatives from the legal team, and also a couple of representatives of EMI. And I was told in no uncertain terms that Steve Harris would take half songwriting, 50 percent songwriting, on the "Thunderburst' track, and I would receive absolutely nothing on 'The Ides of March.' If I wanted to contest that, then we'll see you in court. And that was about it. That's about the sum of it, really. That's why Steve has 50 percent of the songwriting on 'Thunderburst,' and I have absolutely nothing on 'The Ides of March.'

"EMI had just signed up Iron Maiden, and they were fully committed to that band," figures Barry. "And you know, they were going to finance it, in the way that they saw fit. Samson was a much-smaller scale. Our management had money, but they had nothing like the amount of money that EMI were able to put behind Iron Maiden. And yeah, if it'd gone to court and if I'd have lost the case, I could've ended up in any kind of condition."

But clarifications are needed. Thunderstick has also said in interviews that he essentially went to EMI for clearance to do the track. That's crucial, because also in the above telling, he somewhat makes it sound like it was on record already. It wasn't. All copies of *Head On* with the two-tone green GEM label have Steve Harris as part of the credit. Which brings up another point. Thunderstick doesn't claim to have written the substance of "Thunderburst," which is the music and not the drum part, as prominent as it is. In fact, in most band situations, the drummer wouldn't even get credited for adding something like these tuned toms across a musical piece. Ergo, if that's the case, it seems reasonable that the credit for this piece of music could go solely to Steve, but also, maybe fairly or generously, to both Steve and Barry.

So, it doesn't exactly come off as the implied strong-arming of the above telling that Steve would ask to be added to "Thunderburst" and take sole credit in Maidenland. Because let's not forget, on "Thunderburst," he's not even shown as half—it's Steve plus each of the four Samson guys.

Now Thunderstick has also floated the idea that if Steve really thought he wrote this short instrumental, he would have put his foot down and asked for sole credit on both albums. Maybe so, but maybe he was also being overly generous for the Samson situation and guarding his turf for the Maiden situation, essentially ceding more than was reasonable for the Samson record in exchange for sole credit on the Maiden record.

This kind of thing has come up elsewhere as well. Paul Mario Day claims to have written the words and melodies for "Strange World," although sometimes he's made claim to only some of the words. There's the Beckett / "Rainbow's Gold" situation, which we'll hear about in the next chapter, plus the "Running Free" story, to be discussed later. As well, Dennis Wilcock is hellbent for leather staking claim to some lyrics. It's an inevitable turn of events, given how massive Maiden would soon become, as well as given the number of musicians and singers who had circulated through the ranks, not to mention the fact that a good fistful of Iron Maiden semiclassics were pretty much fully formed by 1977.

In any event, back to "The Ides of March," Clive is front and center—but doing his finest Thunderstick!—with finely tuned tom fills across the arrangement. Says Paul, "I'm very proud of that song because Clive Burr came into his own on that. Oh, I can't talk about Clive without getting all teary. I tell you, it's unbelievable. But what an immense drummer."

As for the meaning of the title, although the Ides of March means merely the middle of the month of March, the phrase famously refers to the date on which Julius Caesar is assassinated, said to be in 44 BCE. Therefore, the song, even without lyrics, adheres to the wider record's themes around killing, and hence the title *Killers*.

Then it's Steve's time to shine, with Harris accompanying Burr on an insistent midpaced rhythm before the guitars crash in and Maiden classic "Wrathchild" is presented in all its glory. Originally titled "Rothchild," it's a song worthy of an intro like "The Ides of March," and it just might be the song with the greatest star power

Dave Wright archive

thus far in the Maiden catalog. Says Paul of his leonine, thespian vocal on the track, "I'll tell you what, and I don't want to sound bigheaded, but I don't do more than two or three takes, because if you don't get it right in that time, you shouldn't be doing it at all [laughs]. I think that took about one take, but someone might contradict me on that. The lyrics were all down to Steve on that one. 'I was born into a scene of angriness and greed'—yeah, well, actually, that's not too far removed from what my life was."

As for the next track, "Murders in the Rue Morgue," Di'Anno says, "That one was a nightmare, another three-take job [laughs], three or four. I really didn't like that album much at all, to be honest. I thought we were changing, and not for the better. I suppose in a way we were because it was getting more polished and a little, how should I put it, less aggressive. It was getting a bit too intricate for me. I like it rough and ready [laughs]."

Indeed, the song is fairly fancy, but it's also kind of punk with respect to the verses. Still, there are a number of changeups, with the band turning on a dime one heady rhythmic passage to the next. Edgar Allan Poe's *The Murders in the Rue Morgue* is considered the first detective story, seeing publication back in 1841. Steve is continuing on with his legacy of mining classic dark literature for subject matter, and there will definitely be more to come. In fact, the song contributes to an album that is themed on murder and escape. "Innocent Exile" could be said to be a continuation of this tale, with the innocent bystander witnessing the murder in the Rue Morgue now on the run from the law. The protagonist in "Wrathchild" arguably has violence on his mind, "Another Life" is about suicide (escape), "Genghis Khan" is about both murder and escape, even though there are no words, and on we go even more intensely into the second side.

So yes, rollicking rocker "Another Life" is the brief tale of someone considering suicide, but there's an echo of regret in his furtive fulminations about bad deeds possibly done. It's a song of curiously repeating verses, or a couple of verses mashed together and overlapping. In any event, this sort of repetitive structure, its lack of a chorus, its tempo, its lyric of mental anguish, and the fact that the title is not mentioned in the song accumulates to draw comparisons to Black Sabbath's "Paranoid."

Clive again gets to shine, opening with a tuned tom pattern and then collapsing into one of his signature moves; namely, a beat where he's playing rapidly on the high-hat, two-handed. He switches it up as well, adding lots of fills along the way. There's

Killers eight-track tape. *Dave Wright archive*

even a section that one would have to call punk, in every manner, right down to Clive's manic bashing. It all ends with a massive, "everybody in" windup.

Next, "Genghis Khan" is a rare instrumental for the band, although Steve says that they could have put a vocal on top of it, belying the nature of the song as not excessively unstructured and crammed with musical performance as many instrumentals are. Harris also notes that the title was intentional, that the song was supposed to evoke images of being overwhelmed by an invading horde. There's a bit of an "Ides of March" feel to the track, in terms of its pomp. In truth, it's a little too "notey" for a vocal, although oddly, for an instrumental, Steve decided not to include a guitar solo. Still there are plenty of guitars, with a pile of twin leads placed upon a variety of rhythms, from gallop to frenzied and frantic.

"I absolutely love that one because I didn't have to sing," laughs Paul. "That was the best part of that. I just got rather annoyed. I was listening to that band Papa Roach, and that single of theirs, 'Last Resort'; as soon as I heard it, I thought, 'Oh fuck, they've ripped Maiden off. It's "Genghis Khan."' And then the second one they did, I thought, that's just 'Wrathchild' slowed down. But it's funny, it's just sort of regenerated in a whole big, massive rock band again."

It's Steve who gets to crank up the next one, "Innocent Exile," opening with an angular bass riff accompanied by descending chords before the smart verses begin, Clive once again with two hands on the high-hat. The song delivers on celebrated musical themes around twin leads and tempo changes—this is Maiden's version of progressive metal, much more than tricky time signatures—as well as rhythmic stops and starts blocking off these various sections.

Opening side 2 is the quick-paced title track, Steve again prominent, Clive yet again two-fisted on the high-hat. What ensues is an impossibly fast Iron Maiden gallop, again the end of each verse punctuated by rhythmic exclamation marks. Twin leads of various sorts are assembled throughout on what turns out to be a workout for everybody, but especially Clive. Lyrically, this one is about your standard "Subway Terror," as Starz might say, Paul painting a lurid portrait that matches up pretty well with the Eddie on the front cover. "Killers" is fast and packed with playing, and yet it has a melody that goes down easy. It's proof that Maiden could write in what, again, was a nearly thrash format and yet deliver the hooks.

"To me, melody is the key to the songs," explains Harris. "I've always been attracted to any band or songs that's got melody in their music. There's melody in the guitars and in the vocals. The things with what I've always tried to do with Maiden is basically any guitar melody could be a vocal melody, or vice versa. And I think if you actually go and listen to some of the songs, I think you'll realize that that's true in most cases. In probably 90 percent of the cases, you could put a vocal melody to any of those guitar melodies, or vice versa.

"So, it's always been very central to the part, and essential, if you like. To me, melody is a song. But you try and incorporate that with power and aggression as well, and then you have all those elements—and the progressive thing. This is what we were trying to do. If you have all those elements, it's a pretty potent force. How the melody translates to the live thing I think is pretty obvious. When you see and hear a Maiden crowd that's louder than we are singing along to the melodies—and I was just going back to the last point—they're singing the guitar melodies a lot of the time, as well as the vocal melodies. In a lot of countries, you go to where English is not the first language or they don't even speak the language at all, but they're still singing the melodies. And to me that says it all, really—I rest my case."

Comments Di'Anno on "Killers": "Well, this is the way my sick and twisted mind works. I wanted to get all sorts of different angles on it, like the killer himself and what the public are thinking, you know, trying to get into it. I wasn't that much a writer then. I was sort of just learning. I could do a lot better version of it now. But yeah, it's to mix it up a bit. Three different stories, sort of thing. But yeah, I worked very strangely sometimes. Even I don't like being in my head sometimes."

"Prodigal Son" finds Maiden writing in an interesting progressive rock format, one akin to up-tempo but acoustic Rush. It's rare for Maiden to bring out the acoustics, especially this layered and considered, mixed with all manner of electric texture, very much like Alex Lifeson would do.

The lyric is an ambitious match to the adventurous music. The protagonist has been gripped by a devilish spirit—indeed, one can hear the mental turmoil of the wrathchild, the depressed figure in "Another Life," and the knife-wielding murderer in "Killers" all wrapped up in one. The exhortations for help from Lamia (pronounced "lommia") are curious, given that this being of Greek mythology is a child-eating monster, albeit victimized into that vengeful fate by having her own children killed by Hera. However, the name evolved over time into a general term for a sort of bogeyman for children but also a siren-like sexual temptress. Most intriguing for the story, Lamia was cursed with insomnia, which enhances the story, given that the protagonist is clearly frantic with his current state of possession and likely unable to sleep.

Steve in pants inspired by UFO bassist Pete Way. Fourth Golden Summernight Concert, Stuttgart, Germany, August 15, 1981. © Wolfgang Guerster

"I remember hating doing that in the studio," recalls Paul, "because that little high note thing when it goes up a few steps, I never thought I got that powerful enough, and I thought I sounded like Minnie Mouse. I was a bit pissed off about that. But I'm not a good judge of my own voice. I think I suck 90 percent of the time. I remember I couldn't stop myself from laughing because I didn't know what the hell Lamia was, and I thought, God, that's the saddest name for a demon I've ever heard. Steve wrote it and it says, 'Oh Lamia, please try to help me,' and I said to Steve, 'What the hell is Lamia?' And he says, 'Oh, it's a demon.' And I thought, oh yeah, I'll bet people will be scared of him with that name, won't they? I couldn't keep a straight face. I used to hate doing that song. That was one Maiden song I was really, really ashamed to sing. The music's not bad, but I thought the lyrical content was really awful. But then again, I didn't write it."

Adds Paul on the rare appearance of acoustic guitar on an Iron Maiden song: "Oh, I thought it was great, really good. Steve, I don't know where he was getting his ideas from either. Like I say, to use like the god Lamia, you know, blimey, where did he pick that one up from? But I thought it was brilliant, great—it called for an acoustic guitar; it needed it."

Martin Birch worked Paul hard on that song and indeed the whole album, but ultimately Di'Anno appreciated it. "It was all right, yeah, not so bad. The only problem, as I said, the energy of the first Maiden album is classic, but the production is absolute dog shit. But the songs are fantastic. I wasn't too keen on the songs on the second album, and this is my own personal

A healthy version of Paul catching some rays, Camstatter Wasen, Stuttgart, Germany, August 15, 1981.
© Wolfgang Guerster

opinion. Lots of people think *Killers* is the best-one-since-sliced-bread sort of thing, but to me, we lost a lot of that rawness. Which obviously Martin had smoothed out, after working with Coverdale and all that. But yeah, he got me into that sort of thing of like, go over and over and over it again. Because I'd go in the studio, 'That's it, I'm done,' after the first take. But there's different layers you can put on it, and Martin taught me how to do that, like, 'Try this one and do that and do this.' And I thought that was all right and I still do it today."

Punky speed metal rocker "Purgatory" feels like a continuation of either the "Prodigal Son" narrative, the "Another Life" narrative, or both. Whether the mental meltdown is caused by a demon or overwhelming regret or other internal sadness triggers, the narrator yearns for escape through sleep and dreaming. It's quite an incongruous sentiment set against headbanging metal made for the pit. Still, the music evokes the desperate state at this point, one that perhaps intense insomnia would conjure. Rife throughout are twin leads and quick-picked riffing that one might call proto-thrash—it's no secret that Metallica were huge Maiden fans, and it's songs like this and "Killers" from which the next generation of metal intensifiers would draw inspiration.

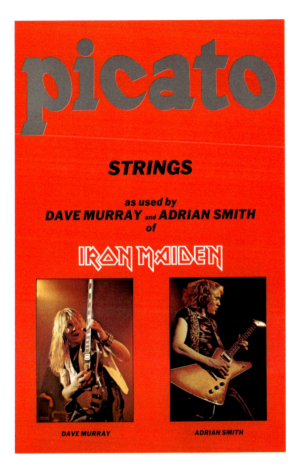

The mark of a band going places: sponsorship.
Dave Wright archive

"'Drifter' was another one [that] Maiden had before I joined them," notes Paul, on the record's closing track. "It was already done and dusted, so I just went along with it and I sang it. I think you can tell the difference between that one and most of the other songs we had done. So that was that. I wasn't too happy with it, but it was massive live. All the kids would just go crazy."

Indeed, this one, outside of the artistic opening gambit, is rock 'n' rollsy and beersy, even punky. Call it a bit of musical levity across what is essentially a collection of songs committed to dark heavy metal at all speeds and then gilded with the formality and timelessness of classical music. Instead, "Drifter" is not far off heavy Sham 69, to conjure a pint-swilling gang mentality band mentioned earlier. Lyrically, if a bunch of nothing, it's still about escape, and at the end of the song, there's another spirited and showstopping windup, allowing the punters to escape into the night, one hopes in time to miss any fisticuffs with the local punk rockers as the pubs close.

Onward and upward, Maiden were now clearly headliners, at least at home. The first leg of dates promoting *Killers* take place February 17 through March 15, 1980, the band playing theaters and city halls up and down the UK. French metal band Trust is the opener on all dates. But Paul seemed to be getting cagey with the situation, expressing of his bandmates, "They all seemed happy enough, and that's when I thought, oh blimey, I don't feel too comfortable with it. But then again, they're probably used to playing all that stuff. I wasn't. I came from punk and hard core. The songs were obviously getting better crafted, if you look at it that way, but for me, I don't know, it was losing its edge. It's a bit difficult. If I can't give 100 percent."

Steve, on the other hand, was drinking it in. "Obviously, at the time, we used to go out and sign stuff after a show for hours. And in the end, it was so bloody cold in some parts of England that we used to get them to come into the venue and we'd sign stuff. We felt that we were no different to the fans. We felt like we were fans, just getting up and playing onstage. So that was a big difference. It wasn't like this whole thing of being completely untouchable, like some other bands were."

Just as Maiden were getting going, wielding what was both a heavier and more world-beating collection of songs, Judas Priest all of a sudden were going in the other

French subway poster. More's lead singer, Paul Mario Day, used to sing for Maiden. *Dave Wright archive*

direction, on February 26 issuing *Point of Entry*, a lighter, less aggressive album than *British Steel*, marking an additional step away from a NWOBHM sound. The band subsequently took some stick for the softer direction, which, in itself, demonstrates that a metal army must have its fill. But in Priest's wake, Iron Maiden were perfectly positioned to capitalize, roaring in and playing the fan's hand.

And so to do so, Rod and the guys keep the pipeline full, on March 2 issuing "Twilight Zone" / "Wrathchild." The single goes to #31 despite lacking the boost of a *Top of the Pops* performance, due to a production strike, the second one to scuttle a Maiden appearance. Recalls Paul, "I remember when we was doing it, actually rehearsing it, bloody 'ell, that's a hard song to sing. But we went into the studio, and it all came together. But it's hard to sing live-wise, which is why I don't do it very often. But no, we pretty much had that all together before we went into the studio anyway, so I knew how I was gonna approach it, just making sure I'm hitting the right notes."

"I went into the twilight zone with this one," says Derek on the garish artwork for the expected and delivered picture sleeve prepared for the single. "It was another weekend job, except they phoned me up Friday. No, he didn't, he phoned me up Saturday and wanted it by Monday; that's right. We've got this single . . . on a fucking Saturday night [laughs]. And the only piece of board I had was called CF10, and it was for line illustration, and it was chalk-coated, and it does not absorb water. And this was the only piece of board I had, and the shops were all shut."

"So, I just started doing it on this CF10, and I thought I could do it in airbrush and painted this and that and it just didn't work. I started painting it, and the paint just

Capital Centre, Landover, Maryland, June 28, 1981.
© Rudy Childs

wouldn't take. The board had got greasy over time, and it was coming out with blotches everywhere and it wasn't working at all. So, I ended up painting it a flat color and then trying to airbrush some shape into it, and it was a bloody mess [laughs]."

"So that figure is really rough, and it's not good. It was a girl looking in a mirror. Of course, a lot of these things have gone into history, and people see the painting now... you just fucking get on with it, discipline. Loads of coffee. Intravenous drip [laughs]. I didn't have time for being stoned or drunk or any of that shit. You can't do it with that stuff; you really can't. Not if you're not allowed to sleep and you just have to work. It's just a matter of getting on with it, and eight hours later you realize you haven't slept yet."

"One time I actually stayed up for a whole week, because I invented a new technique and I was just painting," continues Riggs. "They say you can't go more than three days without sleep, but it's crap, because I went for a whole week. And colors get really vivid, and contrast gets really enhanced and you start to see really strange, but you don't go mad or anything [laughs]. But after a week, I laid down for ten minutes' kip—and I slept for two days."

No sleep till Hammersmith, from March 18 through to May 3, Maiden tour mainland Europe, with the closing Scandinavian leg canceled. Support act is More, featuring past Maiden vocalist Paul Mario Day, with French band Ocean also on the bill for the opening French leg. May 21 through 24, Maiden play five Japanese dates, with the May 23 stop in Nagoya serving as the recordings for a live EP. The opening show in Tokyo represents the band's first concert in Japan.

Explains Loopy, "We did a short British tour towards the end of 1980, with Adrian, just sort of introducing him to the crowd, if you like. It was something like eleven shows. It was all so bang, bang, bang, very fast. Then they recorded the album and then we got ready to go out to do the UK *Killers* tour. Shortly after the British tour, we went out to do Europe. But some of the shows towards the end of the European tour, like Scandinavia, got canceled because the Japanese tour had come up. Back in those days, everything was shipped by sea. So, that's why the Scandinavian dates were canceled, so our equipment could go by sea. So, our gear went out there, and we went and did the Japanese tour."

Eddie threatens Stuttgart. © *Wolfgang Guerster*

In June and July 1980, Maiden support Judas Priest for a second time, this time on the North American leg of Priest's *Point of Entry* tour, a campaign called the World Wide Blitz Tour. Maiden's main competi-tors of the day, Saxon, were support on the first European leg, while Accept got the nod on the second European leg. With Judas Priest promoting the ill-received *Point of Entry*, it becomes a parallel situation to Maiden's support of Kiss on that band's tour for their poppy *Unmasked* album, a commercial flop. The June 3 stop at the Aladdin Hotel in Las Vegas represents Maiden's first show ever on US soil.

Clive Burr donates some sticks to the nation's capital, Landover, Maryland, June 28, 1981. © Rudy Childs

For the second and last time, Iron Maiden would have to sit through a long delay before America got their new album. On June 6, *Killers* was finally out in America. Despite practically no radio play, *Killers* winds up selling about 200,000 copies pretty quickly (en route to its current gold status) and placing #78 on *Billboard*, staying on the charts for a respectable seventeen weeks.

As with the debut, the industry stateside was on board with what Maiden had to offer, being pumped with anticipation by EMI, not to mention word of mouth from the quickly growing metal army of fans across North America.

"Possessing one of the most distasteful album covers in recent memory," proclaimed *Billboard*, "this quintet rocks hard and asks for no apologies. It is an all-stops-out heavy metal quintet. Headliners in its native UK, Iron Maiden plays mostly uptempo material with wailing guitars and frenzied vocals. Best cuts: 'Murders in the Rue Morgue,' 'Prodigal Son,' 'Killers,' 'Drifter.'"

The industry-directed ad for the album in *Billboard*—like the previous year, full page and full color—reads: "The cutting edge of heavy metal is here! The new album already top 20 around the world—United Kingdom, Belgium, France, Sweden, Japan, Denmark, Italy, Germany. Now the axe falls on America! *Killers*—the slaughter continues on Capitol Records and Cassettes." At the bottom in fine print it says, "Marketing memo: Out-of-the-box national consumer advertising, national radio buys, special oversize point-of-purchase poster. See your local Capitol representative."

Punky-looking promo picture. *Dave Wright archive*

EMI weren't exaggerating about the band's success in Europe. *Killers* would wind up gold in France, Sweden, and Germany, with the latter representing a hefty 250,000 records sold. But it's Canada that would prove to be most Maiden-mad, sending the record platinum for sales of over 100,000 copies. Both Canada and Germany would support the debut to the same certification level. Curiously, *Iron Maiden* is triple platinum in the UK, but *Killers* wound up stalled at single platinum.

Also ready for *Killers* was Maiden superfan Brian Slagel, founder of Metal Blade Records, who along with his buddy Lars Ulrich were spreading the Maiden gospel across Los Angeles.

"When I saw the first album cover, I was blown away," recalls Slagel. "At that point it was the best album cover I had ever seen in my entire life. Just the whole vibe of it. To me, being a huge horror movie fan, it was perfect. And of course, the record was phenomenal too. So, the record and the music went hand in hand with the cover. To me, at that point in my life, that was the perfect metal record.

"But favorite Eddie of all time is by far *Killers*. In fact, *Killers* is my favorite album cover of all time. Every element of a metal horror cover I ever want to see is there, with the bloody axe etc. Especially when it came out in 1981, it was such a violently great cover, such a shocking cover, just amazing. I was working in a record store when it came out. And I was able to get as much stuff as I could from Capitol. Because at the time, nobody knew who Iron Maiden was, and someone from the label called up and said, 'Sure, have whatever you want.' So we got these huge posters, displays, a gigantic display in the record store; it was a lot of fun. But to me, that's the quintessential album cover.

"Eddie's brilliant. It's kind of funny how those things worked out. But him being associated with Maiden, once you see him, you know what it is. And it's a whole extra branding of the band, which is a really cool issue too. Some of the greatest concert T-shirts of all time are with Eddie. And it goes hand in hand with the music; it works perfectly. So, I think it helps them get stuff out. Certainly, it's a striking image, and people see that striking image and it leads people into it. When people don't know what the music is like, especially back in the day when we didn't have MTV and the internet, a lot of kids bought albums just based on the cover, and I think their covers helped them a lot as well."

Coincidentally, back home in England on the exact same day as *Killers* hit the shops in America, the first issue of *Kerrang!* debuts as a free insert in *Sounds*. *Sounds* had been the main UK weekly music paper (the others being *NME*, *Melody Maker*, and *Record Mirror*) that tended to cover metal. Response would be so favorable that by October, an additional five-thousand-copy run was deemed necessary.

Crowed Steve at the time, speaking with *Melody Maker*, "What upsets people about heavy metal is the fact that it won't go away. They've tried, but they can't get rid of it. And that really annoys them. The media had to put a tag on it, but there was definitely an upsurge of young heavy metal bands around the same time—Saxon for example—I think because people were just fed up with punk, so they formed bands to play the music they themselves wanted to hear. The thing is the energy. You can express yourself. It's a very aggressive music, and that's a big part of it."

"I was working for *Sounds*, first and whenever *Kerrang!* launched, I did some stuff for them too," adds Garry Bushell. "And I was there when *Sounds* overtook the *NME* [laughs]. We became the biggest-selling music weekly for quite some time in 1981, I think. It was a triumph for what I would call 'street rock' in general, because *Sounds* was very much a down-to-earth cousin, whereas *NME* was for the hip kids; it was for the students, that end of rock. We were more for the guy, the young apprentice, who wanted to go out and have a good time and get his rocks off of a great band, who didn't really want to intellectualize about it. *Kerrang!* was really because of how hugely successful *Sounds* was, and how even the management of *Sounds* realized that there was something different going on, and they were reaching out to an audience that the music paper was now serving. They thought they could take a chance with *Kerrang!* I think it was purely sales driven."

Amid tour dates supporting Priest, in late June, Maiden squeeze in five headline shows in Canada and the US. These are in fact the band's first-ever Canadian dates, June 19 in Toronto and June 21 in Montreal. The *Iron Maiden* debut had already been certified gold in Canada by this point. Same week, the shops in England receive another picture sleeve single from the band, "Purgatory" / "Genghis Khan," both album tracks from *Killers*.

Paul with obi sash? Landover, Maryland, June 28, 1981. © *Rudy Childs*

"Well, I did the album cover, *Number of the Beast*, and the devil figure, the face, was a portrait of Salvador Dalí," explains Derek. "So, I thought I would do that again because I didn't have anything else to do. So, I just had this idea of, where the light hits the devil, in the shadows, that's where Eddie is. So, it's like the light is coming from the same angle as the face is crumbling off. So, in the shadows of the devil, that's where Eddie is. I don't think anybody ever actually picked up on that [laughs]. Eddie is the dark side of the devil. That's pretty heavy, isn't it? [laughs]. The fans always responded to Eddie as a kind of hero. Because as one of the roadies put it, Eddie is much too heavy—if you respond to him as a villain, you just can't handle him. He's just too much. So, you have to handle him as a hero."

Adds Rod Smallwood, "The *Number of the Beast* cover art was going to be the one executed for a single called 'Purgatory,' off the *Killers* album. When the idea was, you know, who is pulling whose strings? You've got the devil with Eddie as a puppet and the devil as a puppet. And Derek did a great job, that whole sort of Bosch-type feel to it, and it looked just way too good for a single, so we scrapped the idea of using that for a single and used the Eddie head rocking to the devil as the single sleeve instead and saved the *Number of the Beast* artwork for the album. And then when Steve actually did the song

Steve in Stuttgart. © Wolfgang Guerster

called 'Number of the Beast,' it all clicked. So sometimes we got lucky like that."

On August 1 and 2, Maiden play two Southern California dates supporting their heroes UFO. Realizing the importance of the event, the band wildly splurges and has their equipment freighted over from its last port of call, Philadelphia. Again, there's an added significance here in that a number of heavy-duty metal influencers were at that show. After the NWOBHM would fizzle in 1983, it would be Los Angeles that would become the hotbed of all things heavy right through the 1980s. Maiden would not be particularly associated with the city or its "hair metal" scene, but along with a pile of 1970s bands behind them, they would all receive a slingshot effect from metal's popularity, helping sustain the band through their slight creative dip past 1984's *Powerslave* firecracker.

Exclamation points upon the genre's robust standing at this time were coming from all facets of media. On August 7, the *Heavy Metal* movie premiers in theaters. The animated film marries fantasy themes with mostly hard rock music. Even though the name refers here to the originating illustrated sword-and-sorcery and sci-fi magazine, nonetheless the popularity of the magazine, the film, and the double-LP hard rock soundtrack help the name recognition of the concept embodied by that term. Attending the debut in the UK were members of Girlschool, Wild Horses, Samson, Stampede, and Iron Maiden.

Also in August, the second issue of *Kerrang!* is launched and a new, regular voice for metal in the UK is born. But it's not enough to float all boats. On September 6, the original Angel Witch play their last show, at the Marquee, before breaking up. Iron Maiden's best competitive doppelganger is now out of the way, although really, once *Killers* had taken hold, it was pretty much understood that Maiden were now competing with the big boys, bands more experienced at the game and yet vulnerable to flash new talent.

August 15 through October 30, 1981, Iron Maiden conduct a headline tour of mainland Europe, support coming once again from somewhat traditional French rockers Trust. In addition to four festival dates, one conventional nonheadline gig is marbled in, with the band supporting Foreigner on August 22 in the Netherlands.

Remarks Rod Smallwood, now forced to raise his game, "It was never a cash business. You've got people like the tax man, the T men. Things had got to be professionally done from the very, very start. Touring a band worldwide is a major operation, and there are various income streams that need to be taken care of, and that's part of my job to do that. And we certainly wouldn't be giving out cash and such. One of the first things I did with the band when I took them on is they all got bank accounts, which at the time, for guys of their background, was something completely foreign. But it was always done that way. In England you used to get bugger all to play anyway. You might get £10 to play a pub gig. You know, that's a round of drinks [laughs].

Japanese tour program. *Dave Wright archive*

"I mean, when Zeppelin were out, that was the beginning of it all. That was like the Wild West. There weren't established promoters, not to the degree there was by the 1980s. I think by the time we came around, we had the benefit of all the bands prior, you know, changing the landscape to make it a more professional business, in terms of the bands getting treated properly and all the deals being properly contracted. Certainly, from when we started. And then we had John Jackson, a proper agent in the UK, and Bill Ellison handling us properly in America, and it was all from big agencies. It was all done by contract, which is obviously the best way around for everybody. Prior to that, in the pubs, like I say, you'd get a round of drinks. But certainly, when I took them on, we were beyond that already. We moved very quickly beyond those £10-a-night shows."

Perhaps as an omen of things to come, Reading Rock '81, conducted on August 28, 29, and 30, was less heavy and more eclectic than the previous year's Reading fest. The NWOBHM was represented by Girlschool, Lightning Raiders, Nightwing, Lionheart, Gillan, and Samson. But the fest would weight heavy of significance upon the Maiden camp, with Rod having a fateful talk with Samson howler Bruce Dickinson.

Says Smallwood, "It wasn't that we said, 'We need to get Bruce into the band.' It was that the problems with Paul were insurmountable, and Paul had to go. We didn't approach anybody or talk to anybody about anything until that was taken care of, just out of respect. And then Steve just said, 'Look, the guy in Samson is fantastic.' So, he and I went down to Reading festival and saw him again, and I had a chat to him after the show and we went from there.

"It just so happened that we thought he was a really great vocalist, who may be available at that time to join us. Paul's a terrific guy [laughs]. He tends to . . . I think people know. I mean, you read the book called *The Beast*. There's obviously a lot of exaggeration there, and Paul does tend to embellish things, and I think he himself believes some of the things he embellishes. He could be quite inconsistent in how he viewed things. But underneath, he's . . . I mean, it's a shame that things didn't work out. Paul sort of wasn't asked to leave the band for any reason other than that he just couldn't consistently perform. He was beating himself up all the time, and he said that himself in his memoirs. It just happened. So, we had to move on or stagnate, and so we chose to move on."

Two sides of Dave Murray. © *Wolfgang Guerster*

September 10 would mark Paul Di'Anno's last concert as lead singer for Iron Maiden, at the Odd Fellows Mansion in Copenhagen, on the *Killers* tour. "Really, it was down to the fact that he just didn't like touring," muses Steve. "We are very much a touring band. When we go on tour, it's like for nine months. So, like, two months into a tour, he'd want to go home. He just wasn't into it. So, there was no way it was going to work on a long-term basis with someone like that."

In the midst of this, almost like a tombstone, on September 14 Iron Maiden issue *Maiden Japan*, a four-tracker showing up both in 7- and 12-inch form, with slight differences in various territories. Total track listing comprises "Running Free" and "Remember Tomorrow" backed with "Killers" and "Innocent Exile." Notes Paul, "I think there were a few overdubs, but it wasn't like Judas Priest *Unleashed in the East* sort of thing. The vocals are live on that all the way through. No, I just think we'd lost a bit of guitar or something. There's very little. I think it was about two bars of a song or something. It just sounded a bit rough, and it got put back in again. Nothing else. Maiden are not that sort of band."

For visuals applied to the EP, much of the world got a menacing shot of Eddie brandishing a Samurai sword, but Venezuela and Brazil got a curious variation, a shot almost in sequence of Eddie in the same setting holding up a severed head, that of Di'Anno—I say almost in sequence, but in the interim, it seems Eddie has put down his sword and taken up an axe for the job.

"Rod saw them and freaked out and had them all burned and had me do another one with just Eddie in it," remarks Riggs on the highly collectible South American variant. "And I discovered afterwards that what happened was, Paul was having a lot of trouble with his voice, and Maiden were looking for another singer, kind of behind his back. And they didn't want him to get wind of this, because he would disappear and leave them without a singer. But he was kind of getting wind that something was going on. So, if he had seen this at that time, this picture of Eddie holding his head up, it just would have freaked him out. He would have blown up. Having Paul in it . . . it wasn't anything I had against anybody; it was just the obvious picture to do at the obvious time for the obvious thing. He was the lead singer, the front man. Instead, we've chopped his head off now, and he's not the front man, actually [laughs]. Everybody knows the front man. There's no sense choosing the drummer. But then because of the circumstances, it turned out to be just too close to the knuckle [laughs].

"They sent one to Rod for proof. Because they send them to the managers, just to make sure everything is kosher the way they wanted it to be, and that they're doing a good job. And Rod hadn't seen it before then. Because there was a bit of a rush on. And he saw this and he was like, 'Oh my God, we can't possibly use this.' And so, we had to do a new one in a hell of a rush [laughs]. I believe some of them survived. You can see them on eBay. But

Killers tour patch. *Dave Wright archive*

A couple more from the Capital Centre, Landover, Maryland, June 28, 1981; Metropolitan Washington, DC, has always been a heavy metal hotbed. © *Rudy Childs*

I didn't even know they were having trouble with Paul. It's always been a bit like that with Maiden. It's a bit weird. You know, we did something and then later on it would happen. It's always a bit beyond coincidence, a bit spooky."

"Somebody showed it to me once," recalls the decapitated lead singer himself, who comes up with a theory at odds with Derek's intention, or lack thereof. "I guess it was kind of a way just to say, 'Well, it's a clean break' sort of thing [laughs]. No, it never bothered me much. I didn't even think about it, to be honest with you."

On September 26, *Sounds* announces that Bruce Dickinson has joined Iron Maiden. But before the deal is sealed, Bruce auditions for the gig, singing "Remember Tomorrow" at a rehearsal studio in Hackney. Symbolically, by shifting from Di'Anno to Dickinson, Maiden shed their last vestiges of being punk in any way. They are now a full-on metal band, set for dominance within the hot music genre of the moment.

"We all got along great, really," reflects Di'Anno, on the changing of the guard. "The only animosity that ever sort of came about . . . let's put it this way: I didn't handle fame very well, to be quite honest with you. Anyone who does know me or has met me, the one thing I like is that they say I'm one of the most normal people they've ever met, if you can define normal [laughs]. It goes right over my head, all this fame stuff. I'm not really interested in it. I want to make music and play it, and that's it. I still do everything else that every other person does.

"But, at that point, it really got to me a bit. I was like, 'Oh, hang on a minute' [laughs]. I've suddenly got all this money in me pocket, and people all of a sudden know who I am walking around the streets and stuff, and I'm like, oh shit. And it really did change my life in the wrong way. I started drinking too much and doing too many drugs, messing around, and you sort of lose sight. It was never really real in the first place, and then it seems less real then. You know what I mean?

"And it all got all out of proportion. I don't know, but there was a reason behind that. It really came to a head after the second album, because I wasn't happy with that album; I didn't like the music so much. I was sort of losing interest in the band. What I should have done is just own up there and then and said, 'Well, this ain't right for me anymore.' But I carried it on, which I suppose anybody would do in their right mind. But I carried on with it only for the fact that I was numbing the pain in different ways. I don't know. I didn't do myself any favors, and I certainly didn't do the band any favors. You have to be 100 percent for yourself and for your band. So, it was time to jump ship."

Above and following two pages: June 19, 1981, Concert Hall, Toronto, Ontario, Canada. © *Martin Popoff.* Three ads, *Martin Popoff archive*

CHAPTER 3
The Number of the Beast

"Sing me a song; you're a singer."

I suppose there are a couple of cases of a newish heavy metal band changing their lead singer just as things were starting to take off. Rainbow and the Michael Schenker Group both had to do the deed, and, curiously, in both cases the new singer was Graham Bonnet. Actually, in the NWOBHM realm, both Quartz and Tygers of Pan Tang were forced to stick-handle this crucial personnel switch-up as well.

But what Iron Maiden was about to do was debated as passionately and vociferously as AC/DC hiring Brian Johnson and Black Sabbath taking on Ronnie James Dio. The noise level around the acquisition of Bruce Dickinson was in fact reflecting Maiden's newfound status as the most exciting new metal band on the planet. And reflecting the youth of the band (or perceived youth anyway), the danger and the bravado associated with the decision almost felt like a positive, in that there was something cool and rock 'n' roll and daredevilish that Maiden would have the audacity to temp self-destruction so early, in some kind of drunken quest to move forward.

Of course, it wouldn't hurt that the band was bringing on board their pirate ship a singer and a front man who would prove to be one of the best that heavy metal would ever serve up. Then again, about London town he was already a bit of a known quantity, having made two albums with Samson. In any event, we've already introduced Bruce Dickinson a couple chapters back, but we'd be remiss not to mention a few additional milestones along the way that got him to his summit with Rod at Reading.

Bruce was already doing his thing by 1976, paying the exact same sorts of dues everybody in Maiden would have to pay; namely, plying his trade at the pubs, first with a band in Sheffield called Styx (original name: Paradox), followed by Speed, which takes him through 1977 and 1978.

Through his side job at university, he got a good look at the hard rock world and how it related to what was going on with punk, which Bruce, like Steve, was fortunately not buying.

"Well, I'll give you an example," says Bruce, always a good explainer. "I mean, I was a history student in college in the East End, and I roadied for two or three years, I was the social secretary at the college, and so, let's look at the bands that I brought as a social set. I booked the Ian Gillan Band, because I was a fan. I booked Hawkwind—I roadied for them. We had two shows, which would be like the *Old Grey Whistle Test*–type stuff, like the Sight and Sound in concert; one was Supertramp, one was Manfred Mann's Earth Band, and then I brought the Pirates and Bethnal, who were a punk band. And I think the Lurkers might've done a show there as well. So, we were booking punk bands. Bethnal were interesting, because they were a punk band with an electric violinist, and they did a great version of 'Baba O'Reilly.' We had the Jam play there. The Jam were kind of local; they were East End.

Dave Wright archive

"And one of the guys was a geography student, called Steve Dagger. And Steve and I used to stand around the jukebox. And he's going, 'Rock 'n' roll is over, mate. It's all going to be punk from now on.' And shove another Deep Purple track on, 'Rubbish,' and then he would put something else on. Anyway, he went off and managed Spandau Ballet, and so yeah, we kept bumping into each other. And I sort of go, 'Well, I've done all right for a washed-up old rocker, haven't I, considering . . .' 'Well, yeah, all right.' But if you look at Spandau Ballet, they were a band that adopted the fashion of punk but actually were a complete pop band. I mean, punk was ambushed very quickly by pop music, because it didn't have the musicianship—or the desire—to be anything else other than a transitory thing.

"You know, when you look at those punk bands who got together, who could barely play their instruments, they jumped around and had a laugh—that's as far as it was ever going to go for those guys. If you look to what McLaren did with the Sex Pistols, he took a bunch of metal guys, who were really good musicians, and said, 'Right, guys, you just go and do what you do. I don't care what it is, don't care about that; we'll dress you up and all this.' But the main thing is we're going to have this sneering guy pissing everybody off, dressed in Vivian Westwood's favorite, you know, pajama trousers and safety pins. You know, annoying grannies up and down the nation. And he was very, very clever, and so to that extent, yes, there was some take-up of things.

"I mean, I could see how punk was entertaining. I could see a band like the Stranglers, for example, who were actually really good at what they did. And they would attract a mixed audience of rock guys and sort of like punk chic-type people. You had Motörhead, who were adopted by punk guys, who just because it was such a blinding wall of noise that nobody would comprehend, oh, it was punk in the first place.

"And you had other strange things, this band the Pirates, which were from Johnny Kidd and the Pirates, which goes right the way back to the 1960s. But they were just an amazing R&B band, R&B in the proper sense of the word. Another band—Dr. Feelgood. Dr. Feelgood came from Canvey Island, and if you look back at the musical genesis of punk, they were a rhythm-and-blues band with harmonica and just really, really harsh, chopping rhythms. And if you look at their style and what they did, they morphed into bands like Madness. So, all those bands, they sort of . . . very quickly, from being punk . . . how long did punk last? Well, let's look at the Boomtown Rats. You know, Boomtown Rats, punk band, they were a pop band! They were produced by Mutt Lange. And Mutt Lange is a pop producer! He doesn't even like heavy metal! I mean, he really doesn't. And so 'I Don't Like Mondays' had all the Mutt Lange devices; very clever guy, great producer, but it was a pure pop record, dressed up as something else."

But Bruce understands why punk had to happen, even if he wasn't going to participate. "I think, to an extent, you had a generation of kids where some of them were into metal and the whole rock thing and the whole prog thing. But if you weren't into that, and you weren't into John Travolta and *Saturday Night Fever* and discotheques and youth clubs and all this, what were you supposed to be into?

"At the end of the 1970s, there was a great feeling that there were a lot of very smart people who didn't have a job that were pretty creative, and they didn't have anywhere to put their creativity. Rock was seen as a fairly traditional medium. It was already its own set of tribal gatherings and beliefs and things like that. If you didn't want to do that, you'd do something else. And so that, I think, is where punk came from, and the genius of the whole punk thing was Malcolm McLaren and Vivian Westwood. I mean, that was it—punk was started as an art school project."

But, says Dickinson, rock wasn't exactly suffering, and he saw promise in sticking with it.

"It was surprisingly quite a healthy scene, to be honest with you. I think, in retrospect, if you look now, the difficulties faced by bands, between not getting paid anymore for doing records and you know, people charging crazy amounts for getting insured just to go out and do the gigs and for noise regulations and 'can't do this, can't do that' health and safety, all the bullshit, affects people just trying to do their gigs now. Back then it was a simpler time. You just turned up to the pubs—and there were quite a few pubs you could do gigs, as a metal band. In actual fact, it was that scene that kept the sort of underbelly of the metal scene going.

"There was no internet," continues Bruce. "There was no way of people getting together to talk to each other, except to go to gigs. People met at gigs. And they didn't meet pretty much anywhere else, unless you went to pubs, which played pop music. So that was sort of the metal scene in the period. You went to a pub and played metal stuff, or you went to a place where there were rock gigs. But at the same time, the punk thing was happening, and it was real; there was a degree of excitement about it, but it kind of coexisted with the whole metal thing. It didn't supplant it or replace it, because you could still go to all the major theaters and venues and see metal acts, and the place would be sold out. Nobody was not going because they were going to see punk. However, where it did supplant it was in the eyes of the media. You had kind of the art school media, which all wanted to be great artistes, and so music really just became an extension of their art school course. In other words, the music had no intrinsic value, as music. It was simply another form of performance art."

Maybe Bruce did appreciate a bit of the punk thing after all, since he's been known to call his band Speed "a cross between Judas Priest and the Stranglers." By late 1978, however, Bruce is in a band called Shots, through to the summer of 1979. Bruce's first recording is a Shots song called "Dracula," recorded as part of a three-song session, with Bruce having just been hired by the band.

As Bruce told *Sounds* in 1985, things were pretty dire at the time. "When I was alone and living on the Isle of Dogs, I never used to have any food. All I owned was a teaspoon and a big china mug. I could cut bread with the handle of the spoon, sort out some cheese on the bread, wipe some Branston on it, and that was my bread 'n' Branston. I was also keen on muesli at the time. I put it all in the mug, stir up, eat it with a teaspoon. The same teaspoon! But that's all stopped now. We've got plates and knives and forks and all manner of modern things."

In August 1979, things are looking up for Dickinson as he joins Samson, after Paul Samson and Thunderstick poach him from Shots, having seen Bruce perform at the

Prince of Wales pub in Gravesend, Kent. Meanwhile, the first wave of indie NWOBHM singles arrives throughout the year. Into April and May 1980, Bruce works on vocal tracks for what will become his first album appearance, *Head On*, the second record by Samson, one of the first bands to the NWOBHM table, with singles or albums. In June the album emerges, with Dickinson credited as Bruce Bruce, inspired by an old Monty Python sketch. The album's first single is "Hammerhead" / "Vice Versa," both tracks from the album, followed shortly thereafter by "Hard Times" in remix form backed with non-LPer "Angel with a Machine Gun."

Samson bassist John McCoy provides a bit of background on the situation, outlining a few extra connections to the Maiden camp.

"That Samson album, I'd just done some sessions with a NWOBHM band called Sledgehammer, with a guitarist called Mike Cook; I did a few tracks with them. And also, in that period just after I'd done the Samson album, I was asked to produce a band called White Spirit, the guitarist being Janick Gers, who subsequently left White Spirit and replaced Bernie in Gillan. And need I say more? He's gone on to great success with Iron Maiden.

"There's also a connection to Iron Maiden as well because the original drummer in Samson—when I was in Samson and we did the first couple of singles—was Clive Burr, who left Samson to go to Iron Maiden. And then by the second album I did with Samson, we brought in a singer called, at that time, Bruce Bruce, who metamorphosed into Bruce Dickinson and, as everyone knows, joined Iron Maiden.

"So, I think without that Samson connection, Iron Maiden would not be the band that it is today. It was a small clique of people that were around. You could go out and see Iron Maiden, Angel Witch, Samson—all these bands were just playing anywhere. I don't want to start swearing, but the feeling behind it was punk is shit; this is what we want to do. It was guys learning to play their instruments properly. Coming up with good ideas, good arrangements, good riffs, great singers, with power and heaviness.

"I had a great time with the punk thing, don't get me wrong. Great fun. But come on, guys, play it properly. Sing a tune. And that's what the NWOBHM thing was about. It harkened back to the early 1970s influences, the Zeppelins and the Purples. That music's going to live forever, and those kids were hit by that, emotionally or however, and the punk thing obviously passed them by. They didn't get it or whatever. And slowly but surely, rock started to take over again. But it was an interesting period. I mean, there are so many guys that came out of that period."

And Bruce was keeping tabs on Maiden from a distance.

"Well, the first time I saw Maiden was kind of like . . . when the Marquis de Sade was locked up in jail, he wrote all these terribly ludicrous sex books on odd pieces of toilet paper, representing all his frustrations and fantasies of being locked in a tower with nothing else but hominines for months on end. Well, for me it was the same thing, but musically. Because I never saw any of the bands that I really got off on, at the start. The Deep Purples or the Jethro Tulls, you know. So, in my mind, I had this kind of insane vision of them that they would be leaping around the stage and doing all these incredible things. I never saw those bands. And I saw those bands—there you go, Freudian slip—I saw Maiden, and I thought, oh my God! This is what I would've really wanted in my dreams; this is sort of the vibe; from what I would've dreamed about some ecstatic Deep Purple concert I never ever saw in my life. And, in a bizarre way, the only thing missing from that dream was me."

In 1980, with Bruce's star on the rise, Speed posthumously issue "Man in the Street" with Dickinson on lead vocals. Up into May of the following year, Samson issue their classic third album, *Shock Tactics*, which would be the last with Bruce Dickinson on vocals. *Shock Tactics* is considered by ardent Dickinson fans as one of Bruce's finest full-album performances as a vocalist. All told, it's a thriller of a record, and perhaps all the more dynamic given Paul Samson's more-rock-than-metal instincts. *Shock Tactics* is absolutely a corker, and possibly this writer's favorite thing with Bruce on it, second being either *Piece of Mind* or *The Chemical Wedding*.

"Paul Samson was a really good friend of mine," begins Neal Kay, addressing why or how Paul didn't quite fit the NWOBHM mold. "Like Steve Harris and his first wife in the early days, my first wife and I, we used to hang with these guys away from work. Steve and his missus would come over for an evening, and we, my wife and I, would go down to South London and visit Paul Samson and his wife.

"Well, Paul was a good guitar player, but Paul was obsessed with the Hendrix, Frank Marino–style culture with blues. That's what he played like; that's what he sounded like. And he used to pull people because he was an old-fashioned guy. People would come to see him do blues. That's what he did: heavy, heavy blues. He played a Gibson SG, which was never the choice weapon of heavy metalers anyway. Whereas in the early stages the Les Paul became accepted as the lead guitarist's dream guitar, especially after the Black Widow came out with gold humbuckers on it and so on. The old-school of guitar went to Fender, the newer school went to Gibson, and that was until the new Japanese guitars and stuff came out much later.

"But Paul played an SG, and an SG was known as a blues guitar, really," clarifies Kay. "It was a solid-body guitar, but it didn't have the real roar, shall I say, of modern young metal bands or hard rock bands. Paul's band was not a hard rock band. He didn't even know there was a NWOBHM. He refused to accept he was a part of it anyway, that rock never went away, and all he was aware of was that he'd play in a pub one week, he'd play a pub the next week, and he'd play a pub the week after. And then suddenly the NWOBHM came along, and he found himself a part of it, but he wasn't really.

"We had what I can only describe as an altercation at my London venue," continues Neal. "I was invited soon after the publicity for the Bandwagon took off to put on a monthly or two-weekly show of my own at the London Music Machine in Camden town. It used to be the BBC TV theater, held about 1,500, which for us was a medium-sized venue. The manager, Nick Parker, contacted me and asked me if I wanted to produce my own three-band live show and DJ the evening, put it all together. Camden town's like half a mile from the center of London, and it was much easier for members of the industry to come up and see a band after work.

"So, I thought, yeah, I've got to do this because it will be good for the bands. So, I took it on, and Paul Samson and some of the others appeared, and by then Paul had got Thunderstick on the drum kit, Clive Burr having gone to Iron Maiden. I don't think Bruce was still with them. I rather fancy Paul as doing the singing. I can't remember, to be honest with you, but basically it was a night that was sponsored by Paul Samson's manager Alastair Primrose.

"Alastair Primrose put together a thing with me called the Heavy Metal Crusade. We had been touring colleges and universities. Not solidly, but maybe do two or three at a time. With Paul Samson always there because Alastair Primrose was his manager, and he put up the money for the Crusade, but it was always either Iron Maiden or Praying Mantis or Toad the Wet Sprocket or Angel Witch or somebody. There were always three bands in the Crusade.

"And this night at the Music Machine was sort of a Crusade appearance night," continues Kay, "and Iron Maiden were in the middle. I can't remember who opened that night. It may have been Toad the Wet Sprocket. Iron Maiden were immediately below Paul Samson, who was going to close the show. The trouble was that as the heavy metal crew gained strength and toured around, it became apparent that the wrong band was headlining. Paul Samson's ideas of explosions and blues and stuff was just not going down with the majority of people who were younger and who were Maiden fans. This is before, obviously, Iron Maiden was signed. It's because Rod came along.

"And masses came to a head at the Music Machine, because the London gig, the Music Machine, most of my fans from the Soundhouse were there—a lot of them. And after Paul Samson played his final chord, instead of rapturous applause, there was dead silence. You could have heard a pin drop. And of course, Paul was fuming, and he came offstage, came over to me, and said, 'Hey you, you made them do this, didn't you? You ordered them not to clap!' And I said, 'No, Paul, no. You ordered them not to clap by giving them stuff they don't want. And they're telling you that. And it's my audience all right, but they are telling you in a Soundhouse way that what you are doing belongs to the old days and it ain't of today. And all you got was the message tonight.'

"And he wouldn't have it. And I'm afraid that acrimonious conversation proved to be a metaphorical divorce in the parting of ways between Paul and I. And Paul had various friends in the music business. One of them was John McCoy, the bass player from the Gillan band, who produced an album for him. He had a lot of friends and a lot of contacts. His manager, Alastair, was someone who should never have been in rock 'n' roll—really and truly just should not have been there. I don't know, he was an estate agent or something and he dabbled in music on the weekend.

"Samson made some good records, but again, there was no continuity," sighs Neal. "And Paul's style of music was not what was going to carry the flag, and that is more the reason why it did not happen for them more than any other. Plus, he went through all these staged histrionics over here back then. Nobody liked flashy, young musicians showing off. Didn't like people wearing stage gears. You could wear biking leather—that's all right—and jeans. That's it. But if you tried to appear as if you were some great, grand touring American band, you'd get the cold shoulder. That was not wanted. To identify yourself as one of the audience was the name of the game. Bear in mind again that phrase 'no radio support.' There was no way of making heroes in this country other than by street word of mouth. Therefore, if you appeared on the street and you were one of the street, you'd do well. But if you stuck your nose in the air and ponced and pratted about, you would not go anywhere."

"Paul went through periods of trying to find the right band, the right players," adds John McCoy. "He was a very, very special guy and a very special player, but you had to understand his way of working, musically that is. In the formative years of any band, I'm sure they've all had gigs where they got booed off. I can remember a few gigs where Neal Kay got booed off, but we won't go there. But Paul, I think there was always a sense, particularly with the Maiden situation, he just got to a level of success with Bruce Dickinson in the band, and it really was a hot band at that time. And then Bruce went off to Iron Maiden, and I think Paul kind of felt, well hey, I gave you a drummer, I gave you a singer, what's going on? But he continued and he had a great singer join the band called Nicky Moore."

CHAPTER 3

And so, in September 1981, Bruce Dickinson and Steve Harris join forces. But first there's something of a formality, as Bruce auditions for the band, singing "Remember Tomorrow." The shift from Di'Anno to Dickinson mirrors Tygers of Pan Tang's shift from Jess Cox to Jon Deverill, both bands acquiring singers who are less street and more operatic and technical. Samson, conversely, will pick up a less photogenic growler to replace the departed Dickinson, even if Nicky Moore can hold his head proud, roaring his way through *Before the Storm* and *Don't Get Mad, Get Even*, two Samson collections that are near equals to *Shock Tactics*.

Men in uniform. *Dave Wright archive*

Says Bruce, "I had to wait three months before they fired Paul, and in the meantime I did some singing and they had to go through a difficult time during which time effectively they'd been unfaithful, and they were waiting for their infidelity . . . waiting so they could have their moment. I mean, it's a terrible thing to say, but it's true. It was an awkward period for them—it must have been. But I mean, I knew that it would work. I knew musically it would work, vocally it would work. I just didn't know if the personalities would work. You know, you can make the personalities work if there's desire. Which is basically what I said to Rod that night."

Maiden had been well on the way with *Killers*, but it was somewhat of a question mark if they would maintain without the beloved Paul Di'Anno putting the crowd in a brotherly headlock. As well, just as Bruce was joining, there were many other exciting goings-on in the lively British scene.

Early October, Budgie issue a second album in a NWOBHM style, *Nightflight*, which, however, is a bit lighter and more melodic than its predecessor, *Power Supply*. Still, the cover art, by Derek Riggs of Iron Maiden fame, is full-on heavy metal fantasy illustration. At the same time, Saxon issue their fourth album, *Denim and Leather*, and announce that they will be touring the UK with a massive 40,000-watt PA and a 30-foot-long eagle-shaped lighting rig buttressed with 150 aircraft-landing lights. The band's October tour dates would be supported by Riot, who found their *Fire Down Under* album issued in the UK due to a petition campaign.

Into November, Tygers of Pan Tang issue their third album, *Crazy Nights*. Even more newsworthy, November 4 finds Black Sabbath unveiling a second album from their Ronnie James Dio era—*Mob Rules* would be produced by Martin Birch. Three days later, Ozzy Osbourne issues his second album, *Diary of a Madman*, which is an instant success, keeping heavy metal exciting for the masses, especially in the US, where the band would tour relentlessly.

The explosion of metal bands that is the NWOBHM, as well as the success of *Kerrang!*, is in part responsible for the founding of a raft of metal magazines around this time, including *Aardschock*, *Acne 'n' Dandruff*, *Hammer*, *Teenage Depression*, *Heavy Music Mag*, *Phoenix*, and *Killing Yourself to Die*. The fourth issue of *Kerrang!*, issued in October, includes in its readers-generated list of Top 100 heavy metal albums of all time Saxon's *Wheels of Steel* at #5, and Motörhead taking the #3 spot with *No Sleep 'til Hammersmith*, and #7 with *Ace of Spades*. Both bands show up again before we get past #25.

But the success of these two bands would not translate across the pond in North America. Iron Maiden would find themselves more so in a pack with a slightly older crowd, elbows raised against Ozzy, Sabbath, Priest, Scorpions, Blue Öyster Cult, and something closer to their age grade, called Mötley Crüe.

On October 26, 1981, Bruce Dickinson performs his first show with Iron Maiden, at the Palasport in Bologna, Italy. Heavy metal has a new and exciting discussion point to replace debate over what Ronnie James Dio was going to do to Black Sabbath. Notes Dickinson on where he got his chops, "A guy called Arthur Brown, who did the song 'Fire' from the late 1960s, was a big influence of mine. Peter Hammill from a band called Van der Graaf Generator, and also Ian Anderson from Jethro Tull, particularly his lyrics. Very different influences. As for Gillan, in the early days it was very much so, but it changed a little bit when I'd been with Maiden; it became much more kind of operatic than the Gillan thing. And Alice Cooper . . . I was pumping gas at a gas station, aged sixteen years old, when 'School's Out' came on the radio. Alice was not so much in the singing stakes, more of just a whole attitude thing at the time when you're fifteen, sixteen years old. Alice is more about focused rebellion; he's a fantastic cartoon character almost, if you like, and therefore he's still successful today—my kid, eleven years old, loves Alice Cooper [laughs]."

"Paul was on his way out before we recorded the first album," reflects Dennis Stratton, he himself now an innocent exile. "They were looking for another singer. If they had got any bigger than what they were at the time, I said to Rod Smallwood, 'You've got to think of going to America and competing with Ronnie James Dio, you've got to compete against Sammy Hagar, you've gotta compete against loads of great singers.' Robert Plant, David Coverdale.

"But Paul never had the range. He didn't have the range. And so, they had to get a guy that had a higher voice. Plus, I think with Paul, he just went a little bit crazy in his head. He couldn't handle the band getting bigger and bigger. He just went very strange. But that has nothing to do with it; the thing was his range—his vocal range wasn't high enough. So, they had to look at competing against your Ronnie James Dio and things like that. To get out there, you only had to listen to the rock stations, and every voice as you know—especially over there; we've only got a few bands over here in our little country—but over there, you've got millions of bands. Every American band you hear has got this great higher voice: Journey, Foreigner. They've all got 'em. So, you have to compete against them. It's a big world, not just England.

"They tried a couple of people out earlier, but I don't think they were good enough, so they stayed with Paul for the first two albums, and then Bruce was there all the time with Samson. Samson was a band that was down at the bottom of the ladder, and when you're at the top of the ladder or nearly at the top of the ladder, you can pick and choose. You take your pick, and they could take their pick of anything; anyone would have joined the band. But I think Bruce was perfect for them. It goes to show how important it is to get the best lineup."

"Well, there were a few things, really," adds Dave Murray, of Di'Anno. "Basically, it got to the stage where we were out touring, in the UK, a few shows in Europe, and it was basically harder and harder to get him to go onstage. There were nights where he would just stand on the side of the stage, and we would have to go on and start, and he would saunter on. And there were times as well where he just refused to go on. And we would say, 'Right, we're going on without you,' and then Steve would sing.

"Basically, he was burning the candle at both ends. But we were there for a reason, to play music, and get out there and have fun onstage and chill out, but he wasn't enjoying it anymore. And I think that the wear and tear of all the traveling and everything was getting to him. It came to the stage where, if we wanted this to be serious enough and continue this, we had to move on.

"He felt the same way as well," continues Murray. "His heart wasn't there anymore. I mean, he complained a lot about his voice, but there's a case where you have to look after yourself. You can go out on tour for months at a time, and you have to look after yourself. I know back then, you're a lot younger, so you think you're strong enough and you can do anything, but perhaps the singer is a bit more sensitive to it, because the voice is their instrument. So, he basically went a bit too far. But he's doing his own thing now, and he's back out. The thing is, he left, and we wish him all the best, but he knew he couldn't sustain the length of the type of touring we were doing. We were getting into it for nine months. And the thing was, he was complaining after a few weeks. You can't live like that. But this band, we're not acting. You're either into it or you're not. It's black or white [laughs]."

Recalled Clive of those days, speaking with *Rock Hard* in 2002, "That was really great. We were driven to the gig venue, then taken back to the hotel before being driven to the next town and so on. We didn't really have time to stop and think about what was happening. Everything was going so fast. It was a crazy schedule: hotel, gig, hotel, gig. When we arrived at a venue, everything was already set. All we had to do was get on stage. You know, I was in a situation where I couldn't say much. I was only a member of the band, and if the band decided to hire a new singer or new guitarist . . . I mean, obviously Bruce and Adrian contributed massively to Maiden. Once again, it was a natural evolution."

On November 15, 1981, Maiden play a one-off at the Rainbow Theatre in London. It is Bruce's first show with the band on home soil. Rod Smallwood throws a party after the successful welcome, and Paul Di'Anno good-naturedly shows up for the festivities.

Wrote journalist Robbi Millar, in a review of the show, "On the evidence of Sunday night, I have more confidence in Iron Maiden's ability to stand their ground. Sounding (and looking) remarkably fresh after their arduous tour

Massey Hall, Toronto, Ontario, June 23, 1982. © *Martin Popoff*

programme, they came over as A Band—and not so much Steve 'Arris'[s] band either!—with a purpose, scoring points for both presentation and marked musical improvement. And while Iron Maiden will never really be the same without Paul Di'Anno, their present state of attack augurs well for the future. Keep your mind open . . ."

Writing sessions for what will become *The Number of the Beast* take place in December 1981 into January 1982, just as EMI reports that Iron Maiden have sold in excess of a million albums in 1981, tallying worldwide totals for *Iron Maiden* and *Killers*. On December 23, the band returns to their old haunt, the Ruskin Arms, for a rare secret pub date, billed as Genghis Khan, to celebrate Dave Murray's birthday.

"Well, there's a contrast to what happened before then, isn't there?" remarks the band's EMI man, Ashley Goodall. "I don't really know all the ins and outs, quite honestly, about Mr. Di'Anno, so I wasn't party to that. What I do find in Bruce is that he's thoroughly professional. I don't know him, actually. But he's thoroughly professional, very focused, good marketing head on him, works hard.

"Now you look at a guy of fifty-something singing the way he's doing today; not many people can do that. He's looked after his instrument. He's kept fit. You've got to be an athlete to be up there, these days. I saw him in Bergen last year and it was amazing. A bit like Mick Jagger. These guys are fit, they're on the case, professional, they love what they're doing, and he's got a great voice still. Now who knows what other people's voices would be like after twenty-five years of heavy rock gigging. Not everyone lasts the course, but he's done pretty well. So, I think he's added that longevity to it, actually. And he's a great front man. He gets up there, he brings the crowd with him, and he's credible.

"You can bring the constituent parts in, and you can add value," muses Goodall. "He's a great singer, operatic kind of big scales stuff, bring it up a notch. That incredible voice soaring over . . . you know what I mean? The Pavarotti of the rock world. And you need that sense of epic delivery as heavy rock became bigger and bigger. Many bands probably suffered a bit, but he carries it off—not many people do."

The presence and vocal prowess of Bruce Dickinson wasn't the only change to the Maiden dynamic this time around. Clive Burr would get a writing credit on the album, as would Adrian Smith, in on three numbers (in fact, "Gangland" is by Adrian and Clive). Also, not only was Steve writing now with his new weapon at the mic in mind, but Bruce is said to have rolled up his sleeves and participated in the penning but had to be left out of the official credits due to contractual obligations still with Samson.

Said Smith on the transition to Bruce, "Well, rock solid, great voice, great range, and he's very musical, he writes great songs, so he made an all-around contribution. He's probably one of the best front men in the business, in terms of performance and still being able to sing; it's pretty amazing. He brought all that. And then later on he contributes to the writing and he's full on.

"Bruce is slightly more operatic and probably has more range than Paul. His voice is a bit more durable; it's more like an instrument. I like Paul's voice; he had a kind of rough, gravely voice. I mean he had technique as well. He could hold notes. That was the difference, really. I'd say Bruce is more operatic. With Bruce's voice we could explore the more proggy side of the band, especially now, as opposed to the more rock 'n' roll side. Although we did some rock 'n' roll stuff when Bruce and I started writing, '2 Minutes to Midnight' and 'Prisoner' and all that stuff, which is more straight ahead."

CHAPTER 3

And he was more than chuffed to join in, says Bruce, "because it was manifestly different to all the other bands; it was just so bloody scary. I mean, it was really a fearsome thing, to go see Maiden. You'd never seen anything quite like it. I mean, most of the bands, most metal bands at the time, were relatively polite, really. And most punk bands were, in their way, quite self-absorbed. You know, they were pogoing or being gobbed on or making sure their safety pins didn't bugger about. But Maiden was just right there, in your face. And musically spot on. You know, musically it was really sharp. And that's what made it completely unique. There was nothing like it."

Reflects Steve, "Going from Paul down into Bruce was a tough transition in a lot of ways, because we had already been successful and it was very tough because we knew there was an element of danger in changing personnel. But we knew we had to do it because we knew we couldn't [in the] long term stay with Paul, because he wasn't really interested in touring and being on the road for long periods of time.

"So that was one of the main elements. And then when Bruce joined, I think he just brought another element to the band because of his enthusiasm, for one thing, but also his vocal style. His voice has a lot more power, so you could actually write more intricate, difficult things, if you like, and throw them at him, and he'd just lap them up. But also, his vocal style was probably more mainstream rock, really, than metal. Though he can sing higher, his vocal style was more akin to someone like Ian Gillan than, say, Paul Rodgers or Robert Plant. So, it gave us a different element yet again.

"And change, it's like anything," muses Harris. "If you have to have a change, make sure it's a good one. You've got to make sure someone's as good or better, and he was better without a doubt. And so right from the start, okay, we'd come out of a really strong album and the pressure was there. The first two albums, bulk of that material, I think there was only three new songs on the second album. It went from the four-or-five-year period before that when those albums were made.

"So, you come to the third album, there's a lot of pressure, we've got a new singer—and we've got no material left. We've run out of material, and we've only got about three weeks to write it. So, there was a lot of pressure, really, to come up with the goods. And that's what set the scene for the way we write to this day. We allow a four-week period to write and just put immense pressure on ourselves. It's kind of a masochistic thing to do, but it works."

Into February 1982, the band got down to work, apparently dealing with poltergeists the whole time. Or maybe call them gremlins, the type that mess with dodgy recording equipment that should have been tossed on the scrap heap.

"That was done at Battery Studios, same as *Killers*," explains Dave, "although really, they both have completely different sounds. So maybe they had moved some of the equipment. But that was 1982, and definitely a sign of the times. The technology back then, and we were kind of on a tight budget as well. To go to any really high-end studio was probably out of the equation. And basically, we were a band where you want to have a little bit of edge to it anyway. But I think if you listen to the album, it's still got the qualities there as a stand-up album.

"There was a DVD put out on the making of that album, and Martin Birch was in the studio going over the album and stuff, and I guess he said that he would have liked to have remixed it. He said he would have mixed it a bit differently. But that's twenty years later. It's easy to say things twenty years down the road. But at the time, it was a case of going in there and putting down these tunes and moving on. And part of the character of the band was the time changes. Even now, with the newer material, there's a lot of tempo changes. But I think it was just that loose aggression and energy. It had that punky feel to it. But you're living on that nervous energy, and that goes into the music. And when you're in the studio, there's an intensity there, and I guess we captured that intensity, as opposed to it being half-assed and lame. It's nice to go in and let it have that edge."

Noted Dave, relating a classic story that had the other vehicle containing a bunch of nuns, "Martin Birch was actually in a car crash when we were recording the album. When he got the bill for the damages, it had actually come to £666. It was just a small dent in his Porsche, really, but it was just the irony behind it."

Remarked Clive Burr, speaking with the *Georgia Straight*'s Steve Newton at the time, "It was the second year we actually used Martin. We had him last year to record *Killers*, so having already made friends with him, we were looking forward to seeing him on this new album. He's more a psychologist, really, than just a producer. He really psyched us up well, without us knowing it. When you go in and record, especially when you're doing high-energy stuff like we do, you're very conscious of the fact that you've got to get that energy going. But it's very difficult without an audience, and you don't want to create a forced energy, because if it doesn't flow freely from you, it sounds false on the recording. You can tell. But Martin really psyched us all up, and it came out really well."

Booze also helps; hence the liner notes indicating that the album was recorded "on Ruddles with a little help from Remy and Carlsberg." Explains Clive, "Ruddles is the beer that we're all into. It's the traditional ale of England. It's brewed in the woods without chemicals and things. And you only need about 2 or 3 pints and then you're gone." Flipping the cover back to the front, Burr remarks that "a lot of people have asked, 'Is this a concept album?' or 'Was this preconceived about all the devil worship?' But we aren't into all that, and it wasn't a preconceived idea, because that cover was in fact a single cover that we brought out a year ago. We had a single called 'Purgatory,' and Derek Riggs, our artist, designed that cover. We thought it was so good that we saved it for a whole year for the new album cover."

On February 12, 1982, the punters get to hear the new guy when Iron Maiden issue "Run to the Hills" backed with "Total Eclipse" as an advance single from the forthcoming *The Number of the Beast*. The single rises to #7 in the charts. By this point, *Killers* had been certified gold on home soil, and the band is in good shape to weather the storm of changing their singer.

Even their pictures sleeves were getting better, and whereas Vince Neil shouts at the devil, Eddie goes for the throat with an axe. Says Derek, "I painted that because I actually wanted to spend some time painting, instead of just rushing things. So, I did that because I just wanted to. And I showed it to Rod, and he liked it and he bought it. If you actually look at the original of that, if you see a print of it, it's actually much better painted than the others. It's much superior. It's just me painting monsters with a good sky."

And also, before the album is out, commencing February 25 through March 20, the band's Beast on the Road tour blankets the UK, with American biker rockers The Rods as support. Rod Smallwood's managing partner Andy Taylor now increases his role, committing to full-time service with an increasingly busy Maiden. On March 16, earlier in the day before the band's show at Newcastle City Hall, the boys shoot some live footage that will be used in their "Run to the Hills" video, an iconic clip that shows what a proper NWOBHM band look like.

Dave Wright archive

Not a week later, on March 22, Iron Maiden issue their third album, *The Number of the Beast*, which opens to the machine gun unison shots of "Invaders," oddly a track that will not rise to prominence as one of the enduring classics from this iconic record. And the boss of the band, Steve Harris, agrees, wishing in retrospect that the guys had more songs from which to choose. Yet, "Invaders" is more than adequate as a trashy fast opener to get the blood flow going. There's some high-quality riffing enclosed, even if, unfortunately, what is remembered is the sing-songy chorus. But the prechorus and the part that one might call the preverse . . . Maiden prove that the high quality expressed across the first two records was no fluke, and that even under duress, they could write at a level indicative of their status as the young metal band to watch.

British rockers love the scary movies of their youth, so it's fitting that "Children of the Damned" is inspired by the 1964 movie of the same name as well as 1960's *Village of the Damned*, both of which were based on John Wyndham's *The Midwich Cuckoos* from 1957.

Bruce points out a more recent influence as well on this semiballad, proggy of surface construction but quite heavy metal in the main. "I love 'Children of the Damned.' I have to say that we were heavily influenced by 'Children of the Sea,' the Black Sabbath song. Take a listen [laughs]. There's a little bit of that about that song in terms of structure. But other than that, it's a beautiful song, almost plaintive at times . . . until it gets going [laughs]."

There's an "olde English" vibe older than Sabbath and older than 1960s sci-fi movies as well, felt especially in the regal chorus chords. Says Steve, "Medieval stuff like Jethro Tull kind of influenced our music, and that British medieval feel came about from the similar schooling that we all had, the subjects we were taught in school, and the whole sort of Britishness, if you like, with the way we were brought up. That had a big influence not only on the melodies—because there's lots of kind of medieval influences in the melodies—but also the lyrics. But if you listen to Wishbone Ash, the *Argus* album, you can hear Maiden all over it. Not because we've nicked bits—because we haven't—but it's just, again, the medieval feel to it. You listen to some of the Jethro Tull stuff, same sort of thing. Even if you listen to thrash now, I think people would be able to hear it."

Dave Wright archive

Which is a good point: Maiden's done this before, but now with even more sharpness. With something like "Children of the Damned," Maiden are laying down the template for all manner of relatively quieter songs from the likes of Anthrax, Testament, Overkill, and especially Metallica, who would score multiple hits with their ballads of blackness—and of course this all started with Judas Priest's "Beyond the Realms of Death." It's of some surprise that it doesn't start with Sabbath or Deep Purple or Uriah Heep, but the line of similarity back to "Beyond the Realms of Death" trumps any other suggested comparative, part for part.

Also of note, Steve has mentioned Be-Bop Deluxe as an influence, and this track as well as "Revelations" from the next record bears similarities to that band's "Sister Seagull," in the regal twin-lead work, in the acoustic-type part played on electric, in the darkness, in the dynamic. There's something dark prog about Be-Bop, similar to Van der Graaf Generator and King Crimson and, yes, somewhat Jethro Tull. But there's also something of a glam sense of swashbuckling style, a combination of David Bowie and Queen. Not sure where Maiden fits in all that, but perhaps through heavy, heavy filters, what they arrived at with these brooding numbers bears some of those hallmarks.

And despite the rickety speed metal of "Invaders," "Children of the Damned" is Bruce's coming-out party with respect to his vocal prowess, both technically and in terms of his stylistic choices and his decisions on notes and phrasing, as well as his tendency to the thespian.

"The Prisoner" is the record's first smart and appreciably novel heavy metal song, hooky and sophisticated of riff, interesting with its shifts in speed. The opening is a snatch of dialogue celebrating yet more British pop culture.

"'The Prisoner' was a favorite of mine, obviously being a huge fan of the TV series," explains Bruce. "I always remember the moment when we got Patrick McGoohan, who was star of *The Prisoner* and who also wrote the series, and we got his permission to use the opening lines of the series. We phoned him up. He's in Malibu; he's a recluse and you can't normally get in touch with him at all. And we got through to him on the phone at home! And we said, 'Hello, we're a rock band from England and we'd like to use your bit.' And he said, 'What did you say you were called?' And we went, 'Um, Iron Maiden,' and he said, 'Do it,' and just put the phone down."

The narration was in fact handled by British DJ Tommy Vance, who had local fame similar to John Peel but more in the metal world. The guitar solo in the track is one that Adrian is particularly proud of, but the rhythm section excels as well, with spirited punctuations and with some novel arrangement in the breaks and exploratory passages.

CHAPTER 3

Capital Centre, Landover, Maryland, October 17, 1982. © Rudy Childs

"A fantastic song, isn't it?" says Bruce of "22 Acacia Avenue," last track on side 1 of *The Number of the Beast*. "I love that one. Steve wrote the lyrics, and I'm sure some Freudian psychoanalyst would have a field day with that one [laughs]. I guess women are big, scary, spooky things, aren't they [laughs]? Much more complicated than beer cans."

The follow-up to "Charlotte the Harlot," this one is distinguished by the tight palm-muted "a capella" riffing at the beginning, another tenet of thrash that Maiden helped develop. The tension is broken as the band collapses into more pleasant and predictable chords for the ersatz chorus. But addressing their celebrated love of complication and surprise, it's almost a different song we are hearing late in the sequence of events as the band locks into one of their many varied forms of gallop.

June 9, 1978, marks the release date for the well-executed hit horror film *Damien: Omen II*. Steve Harris has explained that after watching the movie, he went to sleep and had a nightmare, which was partially the inspiration for the lyrics to the song "The Number of the Beast," title track to the album, second in line in terms of the record's most celebrated songs.

Robert Burns's 1790 poem "Tam o' Shanter" serves as a second historical inspiration for Steve Harris's "The Number of the Beast" lyric, but much earlier than that, 95 CE, John of Patmos puts pen to paper and comes up with the book of Revelation. A few years later, an East End headbanger who plays a mean bass figures he'd lift a few devilish lines from it—specifically from chapter 13, verse 8 (well, partially)—to use as an introduction to this song. The band would also print an excerpt from chapter 21, verse 4, on the back cover of their next record, *Piece of Mind*. Speaking the chilling intro is actor Barry Clayton. Alice Cooper back in 1975 could afford Vincent Price for his *Welcome to My Nightmare* project, but not Iron Maiden in 1982. Price wanted too much money—reportedly £25,000—so the band went with a sound-alike. A year later, Price would build upon the very substantial effect he created with Alice and work with Michael Jackson on "Thriller."

Dave Wright archive

Into the music, the riff to this hall-of-fame metal classic is a little bit sweet and sour, almost too melodic, an assessment that Bruce seems to get.

"Steve writes a lot of the riffs just into a little tape recorder by humming, and then he just transfers it to the bass," explains Dickinson, "which is probably why the riff sounds a bit sing-songy, because that's probably what he was doing at the time. Other than that, I had one of the most frustrating three hours of my life singing the first two lines of that song. Could not get it right. I mean, it's only whispering, really. We were going round and round and round, and I was getting more and more frustrated. I had been singing the song in rehearsals over and over again, and I just wanted to get on with the rest of the song. And the producer, Martin Birch, wouldn't let me get beyond the first two whispered lines. And it was like, if we can't get these first two lines right, we can't work on the rest of the song. Got to get these first two lines right, got to get the right vibe.

"So, I didn't know what he meant, and he sat down and told me a story about Ronnie Dio, the song 'Heaven and Hell.' And the opening line to the song is 'Sing me a song; you're a singer.' So, Ronnie came into the studio and sang the opening lines, and Martin said, 'Stop!' And Ronnie goes, 'What's wrong?' Martin says, 'No, do that again.' And Ronnie goes, 'What's wrong with it?' 'It's not quite right.' 'But I sang it in rehearsal tons of times.' And Martin said, 'No, think about what you're saying. Here you are, heaven and hell, and you're walking out between heaven and hell, and you're saying, "Sing me a song, you're a singer," right? So, you've got to sum up your entire life in those few words. Think you've done it?' And then he went to me, 'And now you have to do those two lines the same way.' That's kind of what it was like working with Martin Birch."

As is expected, Maiden deliver the unexpected as the song progresses, including an elegiac chord structure on which the guitar solo is lovingly placed. Elsewhere, Steve fires off some licks on his own, and Bruce creates the heavy metal version of Roger Daltrey's iconic scream on "Won't Get Fooled Again." Unsurprisingly, this is the song that gets blamed for the lights flicking on and off in the studio and the gear breaking down. More disconcerting, it got Maiden in a heap of trouble during the rise of the PMRC (Parents Music Resource Center) and the attendant satanic panic of the 1980s. Well, not exactly trouble, more like welcome publicity. Not quite glorifying the devil; still, you can't get more direct than Bruce screaming out, with box-cutter enunciation, "Six six six, the one for you and me!" and other violent stabs of hellfire imagery.

"I'm not really anything," muses Steve, on his own religious inclinations. "I mean, I'm not anti- or proreligion, really. I suppose I'm in the middle. I'm not really undecided. I believe in God to a certain degree and religion. But I don't believe religion should rule your life. Too many people have died over thousands of years because of religion. I've just been to Israel, and religion

The storied venue at which Rush recorded *All the World's A Stage*: Massey Hall, Toronto, Ontario, June 23, 1982. © *Martin Popoff*

is so heavy there. It completely rules their lives. Fantastic place, it really is. The feeling of the history there is unbelievable. I love history; I'm really into history. You go to a place like Jerusalem—we just played there—and the history is incredible. You can't really take it all in, to be honest. I'd love to go back there on a holiday."

Next up was our hapless and lighthearted advance single "Run to the Hills," which nonetheless was about a serious topic, the plight of the Indigenous peoples, in North America specifically.

Explains Steve, "Before Bruce joined, I wrote most of the stuff because no one else was writing, so the pressure was on me big time. Once Bruce became embedded in the band and he became more confident and he was able to start writing, then it was great, and we were both heavily into history. So, we both, over the years, have taken a lot of things from historical moments in time, or literary stuff. Sometimes it's fictional, but most of it has a historical essence to it.

"I think he did a degree in history or something like that," Steve says of Bruce. "I didn't get that far with it; I kind of got bored and left. We were both heavily into that kind of stuff, and I think lyrically you're looking for something you can get your teeth into when you're writing. You really need something that's strong that you can visualize when you're writing. You get strong melodies, and then you get a feeling for the melody, and it sparks off some sort of element of what you're going to write about. And then once you've got the basic element of what you're writing about, if you've got something like history, if you don't know about it already, you can go and research it and find out more; it just gives you a lot, lyrically, to use.

"I don't really know why those things worked with the sound of Maiden, really, because we never really analyzed it. We just did it, and that's what felt right to do. So, we never really sat back and thought does this suit it or not, because it just did. And we didn't really question it."

"Run to the Hills" is predicated on a celebrated Maiden gallop, but it's almost comically fast, to the point where it sounds like it's going to break down at any moment. Who will be first? Clive or Steve or one of the guitarists? The best bet is one of the rhythm section.

"I think the gallop thing has worked because it's aggressive," explains Steve, who wanted specifically to evoke the sound of horses for this one. "It's fast, it's aggressive, you can put really good melodies over it. You can interchange and do all kinds of stuff with it. It's sing-along; it kind of does everything, really. That's not to say we sat down and thought it's got all these elements, let's do that. It wasn't like that at all. To be honest, a lot of that really came from Be-Bop Deluxe, believe it or not. There's an album called *Sunburst Finish* and there's a song called 'Sleep That Burns' on it, and it's very much where a lot of that sort of stuff came from."

"'Run to the Hills' was the first track that we recorded together," adds Bruce. "Actually, the whole album was recorded and mixed in five weeks, without a computer. There were no computers in those days. We had to break the board down halfway through because we had to record and mix a single and go right back to square one and record the rest of the album. So that's probably one of the reasons 'Run to the Hills' was a bit rushed."

Amusingly, speaking with *Kerrang!* back in 1982, responding as to why the song was seeing radio play in the US, Bruce scoffed, "It's probably because it's got harmonies on the vocals, something as childish as that. Their taste in music really is very puerile. 'Children of the Damned' has also been played a bit because of the acoustic guitar at the

THE NUMBER OF THE BEAST

The twin-guitar attack of Dave Murray and Adrian Smith, Massey Hall, Toronto, Ontario, June 23, 1982. © Martin Popoff

beginning; they think that it won't put off any potential buyers of Tampax. Radio over there exists more to sell silly, disposable consumer goods than play music. It's a sick situation. People keep coming up to us and asking, 'When are you going to release a radio track?' And we say, 'We're not!' We won't compromise; we'll just have to change the airplay."

"Run to the Hills" scored the band a Top 10 hit in the UK, no doubt helped by the amusing video, which interspersed live footage of this punky offering with sped-up Buster Keaton cowboys-and-Indians footage. Applying a cold and logical eye to the single, it wouldn't be out of line to say that non-LP B-side "Total Eclipse" was the more skillfully crafted track.

Lyrically speaking, Steve crams a lot of information into "Run to the Hills," also providing differing perspectives, that of the invaders to the New World, that of the Native Americans, and then a third-person observation. Bruce delivers all of them with actorly energy and enunciation, rising to some pretty challenging screams for the drawn-out syllables of the chorus refrain.

Moving along, "Gangland" is a simple but speedy rocker considerably derided by band and fan alike as substandard, a spot of filler as it were. The lyrics are a muddle, the performance loose and rushed, and the chord changes are somewhat low rent, down in the neighborhood of any number of NWOBHM hopefuls with a single, a compilation appearance, but no album or proper record deal. The song's fate is entwined with that of "Total Eclipse," with the plan being that whichever song was used as the B-side to "Run to the Hills ("Total Eclipse"), the other one would be stuck on the album ("Gangland"). As mentioned, "Total Eclipse" is a high-quality track, rightly more beloved than "Gangland," and, to boot, would have offered greater hue and dimension and variety to the record's track list.

The Number of the Beast closes in stellar fashion, however, with "Hallowed Be Thy Name," Maiden's most purposeful and forward-amassing prog metal epic yet. And no surprise, there's no reservations from the band about this one, with Harris explaining that "'Hallowed' has been in the set since we first recorded it in 1982. It still feels as fresh as [if] it was written like two years ago or something. And I don't really know why that is; it's just one of those songs. But we've got a few songs like that that we still play—even 'Number of the Beast'—that don't feel old. 'Iron Maiden' itself, from the first album, in fact, still feels energetic and frenetic as ever.

"Again, whatever feels right is right, I think is the answer to that one. That's more where that story ends. It's still feeling right now. We still play it, we still enjoy playing it, it's still a really strong song. If someone had said to me at the time, 'Are you still going to be playing that song thirty years away?,' I probably would have laughed at him. But it's still there and it's still an essential part of Maiden.

"And I suppose if I had to say to someone who's never heard Maiden before, to listen to something that describes Maiden the best, it probably would be that. It's got a good sing-along, it's got melodies, it's got harmonies, it's got a quiet intro, it's got an ominous beginning, it builds up to a crescendo at the end, goes a bit mad at the end, and it's got the return at the end almost, a bit more regimented—it's got everything."

Concurs Dave, "I think 'Hallowed' really sums Maiden up as a band. It has all the qualities, you know, from the quiet intro thing, the melodies, the chord progressions, the complexity. If you want to know what Maiden's about, that song gives a real picture of where we're at."

"What I remember most," adds Bruce, "is that it was blindingly obvious from the moment we started playing it in rehearsal that it was going to be classic. It was one of those songs that was just instant. The biggest Maiden epic before that was 'Phantom of the Opera,' and I remember Steve came in and said, 'That's it, I've got the new "Phantom of the Opera,"' and that was 'Hallowed.'"

Except what is remarkable about "Hallowed" is that it's a song that utilizes many of the tropes and trademarks of the band as we would have them delivered across the balance of the 1980s albums, and yet it's performed by the lineup with Clive. Nicko McBrain is such a signature drummer that his imprint colors any and all Maiden songs moving forward, and so arguably what we get here is a Nicko-era-type Maiden classic, but with this roiling, agitated drum performance so indicative of Clive.

"Hallowed Be Thy Name" came in for a bit of controversy when on March 12, 2018, it was reported that the band had settled a lawsuit concerning "Life's Shadow," from obscure Newcastle band Beckett. Rod Smallwood had been the band's agent at the time, and Steve had seen them live. Maiden's lawyers contended that a portion of the song's lyrics were used as a placeholder until something better could be drummed up, but that in the bluster to get the album done in a rush, they hadn't been changed. "Life's Shadow" appears on Beckett's self-titled album from 1974 on Raft Records. The Maiden guys were fans of the band, with Adrian's old band Evil Ways having covered "Rainclouds," also from the band's lone album. Further, Maiden themselves covered "A Rainbow's Gold" from *Beckett*, retitling it "Rainbow's Gold."

Capital Centre, Landover, Maryland, October 17, 1982. © Rudy Childs

All told, *The Number of the Beast* was a massive success, the record only growing in stature over time, having now sold fourteen million copies worldwide. Back in the day, it peaked at #33 in the US, but on the band's home turf the album entered the charts at #1 and stayed there for two weeks.

"I'm not sure it is still the favorite, but it is certainly the most notorious," muses Bruce, looking back. "What's that word? It's a seminal album [laughs]. In other words, it's the album that really started the whole darn thing, in the eyes of a lot of the people on the planet. And while diehard Maiden fans know the thing was well underway with the first couple of records, the third album of any band is always kind of a make-or-break situation. If the band is doing really well with its first and second albums and doesn't do a great third album, there's a kind of profound sense of disappointment that very often may mean the beginning of the end.

"But a really great third album can kick everything into gear, and in our case it was a great record that really set the scene for the albums that followed. I mean, luckily for us, we followed it up with an album that in my opinion is actually better. But of course, albums are not just about music, they're also a product of their times. And *Number of the Beast*, because it occupied a space and achieved such a legendary status by virtue of its position in the career of the band, it would be very hard to dislodge that. But in my opinion, *Piece of Mind* is a superior record.

"But yes, the third album traditionally is the album that a lot of people pay attention to. And on the third album, they had something extra to throw into the plot, which was me. So, it was a combination of Maiden's style, which was already fairly well established, along with me, and they also had the maturation, if you like, of Adrian and Dave working together. Adrian hadn't been on the first album. They wanted him on, but he turned it down. And so [on] *Killers*, he just came in and played the parts. By the time it got to *Number of the Beast*, we were all jelling together.

"And you know, I think the vocals made a bit of a difference, frankly. Paul had a very guttural voice, and it had a style and a charm which was unique. How far it could go was, you know, questionable. I think Steve was questioning that. He wanted a voice that could do a lot more with a bigger range. And I stepped into the breach, really, and I suppose, as well as the range, I also had a kind of theatrical approach to the presentation, and also to the delivery. You know, I'm not effectively a sort of blues-based American-sounding singer."

Watching on from inside a career that was faltering, Diamond Head's Brian Tatler says, regarding the entirety of the NWOBHM, "I suppose maybe the peak might have been Iron Maiden's releasing *Number of the Beast*, and it becoming like a #1 album, and then being on *Top of the Pops* and things like that. So, it's almost kind of mainstream, isn't it? It was played on Radio One, and most of the other bands could only aspire to that. But it did seem there was a bit of bandwagon jumping. Anybody that was a bit rocky was suddenly 'Oh yeah, we're a New Wave of British Heavy Metal band.' And if you were a true new wave, you kind of looked down your nose at these bands, jumping on the scene in 1982, 1983, 1984, and saying, 'Well, where were you?'"

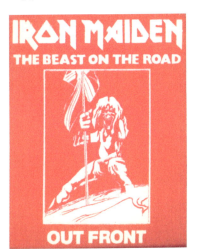

Backstage pass. *Dave Wright archive*

"As HM merchants go, they're pretty fair," wrote Monty Smith in the *NME* at the time, unimpressed with the band's third record. "They're certainly better than the three groups they pay tribute to on the sleeve (Kiss, Judas Priest, and UFO), easily as good as Black Sabbath, and nearly as good as Nazareth. Just why music set so solidly back in 1972 should be so popular in 1982 is, of course, another question. Never mind. With its truly idiotic lyrics, its pristine production, its unvarying dependence on the kind of cascading riffing that can be played only by grimacing guitarists, *The Number of the Beast* is definitely one of the best albums of 1982."

Much more positive was Jon Sutherland from *Record Review*, a boutique magazine with lots of jazz coverage as well that nonetheless found themselves the champions stateside of all things metal for a brief and magical time.

"Now I look at them as the cream of the crop," wrote Jon. "Paul Di'Anno was basically a posing screamer and looks pale in comparison to Bruce Dickinson, who came over from Clive Burr's old band, Samson. When he's really pushing it, he sounds a pinch like Ronnie Dio when he sings fast. Nevertheless, his addition has let the maturing of Adrian Smith and Dave Murray, on twin speedy guitars, hit the sweetest note this side of Marshall stacks. The absolute divine moment in this ode to hellfire is 'Hallowed Be Thy Name,' where the circular guitar riff is reincarnated spectacularly on several occasions."

"I think it was fear, really," laughs Harris, on the key emotion fueling the band's career at this point. "Because the first two albums, apart from three tracks on the second album, were already written in the four-year period before we got signed. So, the second album wasn't that difficult, three other tracks, write those, blah blah blah, whatever. And of course, we come to the third album, no material left. Absolutely nothing. So, you go into the studio for a couple weeks, and you have to come up with an album, material, and it was just complete fear factor, because we were scared out of our wits thinking what are we going to come up with?

A couple of show flyers. *Dave Wright archive*

"But to be honest, whoa! [laughs]. It was exciting as well, because we knew we had to come up with the goods, and that really set the template for every album since, because now it's still a specific period of time and we're under pressure. It worked so well the first time that ever since then, that's the way we do it. And obviously Bruce's vocal range was way different from Paul's, and we were able to throw pretty much anything at him, really, and we did. And he was capable of handling it, so it was just a very different style of singer, really. We were able to push the boundaries, even if we weren't totally aware of that at the time."

Fortunately, it worked. The new singer was accepted, and, really, a large part of that goes to the fact that America hadn't really been pasted with Paul in person by this point. Iron Maiden would be crossing the Atlantic still as a relatively new phenomenon.

"*The Number of the Beast* was a relief in a lot of ways," continues Steve, "because obviously Paul had gone, and even though we felt we made a really strong album, and Bruce is a great singer, we had no way of knowing how people were going to take to that. Whether the fans would take to a new singer or anything. It's all down to that, really. So, it was a bit nerve-racking. But we shouldn't have worried, because the single went straight in the Top 10, and the album went straight to #1, and the tour we did in the UK was actually before the album had come out. The album was towards the end of that tour because we were playing new stuff, which you can't do now because of the internet. But at the time, we were playing new songs off the album, and it wasn't even released yet."

But once the album was out, from March 22 through May 1, 1982, Iron Maiden conducted the European leg of their *Number of the Beast* tour, called The Beast on the Road (a venue-sacking riot ensues at the Metro in Paris). Support comes from southern rock's heaviest band, Blackfoot, for the first third, German AC/DC revivalists Bullet for the second third, and France's punky and concise Trust for the last third. May 1 finds the band playing one show in support of Scorpions. Blackfoot is also on that bill. The tour marks the first appearance of a giant Eddie onstage, at this point about 12 feet tall; previous to this, Eddie was simply played by various roadies wearing masks.

 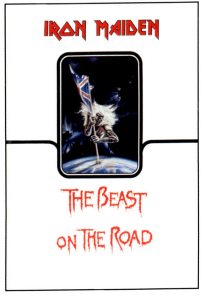

Tour programs. *Dave Wright archive*

On April 2, Maiden play their first-ever show in Spain, and then later in the month, the 26th, EMI issues "The Number of the Beast" as a single, backed with "Remember Tomorrow" (live).

May 11 through the 29, the band transitions to North America, supporting Rainbow, who are out promoting *Straight Between the Eyes*. Ritchie's project is conducting their own experiment with front-man issues, now onto their third lead singer in Joe Lynn Turner, a *very* American American. Maiden goes down a storm, but Rainbow, not so much—*The Number of the Beast* goes on to sell 350,000 stateside in less than a year, while Rainbow would exit this life after seven studio albums without a gold record to its name.

June 1 through 19, Maiden support southern rockers 38 Special for a brief southern US leg of that band's *Special Forces* tour. On June 11 in Memphis, Tennessee, it's Donnie Van Zant's birthday, and who should appear onstage with the band but Eddie? From June 22 to the end of the month, Maiden play five Canadian and two US dates with New York biker metal heroes The Rods. *The Number of the Beast* has by this point gone gold in Canada, on its way to triple platinum. Canada would become the only nation awarding multiplatinum status to Iron Maiden records, sending each of the next three albums to double platinum. Rod recalls the Quebec City show from this leg as the band's first true headlining arena show in North America, with attendance estimated at nine thousand—meanwhile, Paul Di'Anno's first post-Maiden band, Lone Wolf, is out playing the pubs and getting dreadful notices.

Things were going down a storm, explained Clive Burr to the *Georgia Straight*'s Steve Newton. Asked about Yugoslavia, Burr says, "We did a festival out there last year, and we played to—believe it or not—about 30,000 people. It was really weird. I mean the PA was like prewar, and all the bands had to use the same kit. It was very ancient equipment, but the fans were outrageous—they were really into it. Headbangers. I think in Spain and places like that, heavy metal's a sort of new thing, but in places like Germany and France it's always been very popular. And our new stage show is really good. You know, we've got all the effects and things. I can't say too much, but be prepared to be shocked."

Asked by Newton why metal was so big in Britain, Burr figures, "In Britain we've got a different way of making it in the business. We use other media more than we do radio. Whereas in the States it's all done by radio, basically. Once you get the radio play, then people start buying the record. So perhaps we start off with a different attitude. When we're first getting into it, we don't need to make anything, so they'll play it on the radio. We're just given the freedom to style things the way we want. From the very outset, when you're just starting to play your instruments, you're not thinking all the time about hit singles which will get you radio play. You're just thinking about writing songs."

Reflecting the touring methodology of the 1970s and 1980s, Maiden take what they can get, what is negotiated, with Rod capitalizing on opportunities as they arise. July 2 through September 12, the guys and all-gals NWOBHMers Girlschool support Scorpions on the North American leg of that band's campaign for *Blackout*. The band squeezes in three British dates on their own, in late August.

Not about to cede territory without a fight to their doppelganger, albeit on the youthful side, on July 17, 1982, Judas Priest issue *Screaming for Vengeance*, which finds the band heeding the call of their metal army in revolt and reversing the jets on the "pop metal" of *Point of Entry*. Comparatively, the new one is a much-heavier album, even if the sound is still dumbed down and not the cerebral metal that garnered Priest such a reputation in the late 1970s. All told, the record represents the continued Americanization of Priest, which, in the wider context, represents a shift of aggregate metal attention away from the UK toward the US, specifically California. Scorpions do the same thing, as do Rainbow, but Maiden would remain proudly British with their musical mayhem as well as lyrical touchstones, both historical and cultural.

Even a band well out of time and context—namely, Wishbone Ash, Steve's heroes from way back—finds themselves part of the new heavy revolution. September 1982 finds the band issuing *Twin Barrels Burning*, sporting cheap heavy metal illustration for cover art wrapped around the band's heaviest record to date. Demonstrating the UK's increased appetite for hard rock, it reaches #22 on the charts, reviving interest in the band.

Notes guitarist Andy Powell on the whole twin-lead thing suddenly making Maiden distinctive: "Most definitely Thin Lizzy were influenced by our twin-lead sound, because when they first came out from Ireland, one of the first shows that Phil Lynott saw was Wishbone Ash playing the Lyceum Ballroom in London; I know that for a fact. And, of course, Iron Maiden is well documented as a heavy metal band influenced by us as well as more-alternative bands who bring the twin lead into their music. Everybody's influenced by everybody else, and we're certainly influenced by bands that we grew up with.

"We're melodic, and there's an element of English pastorality about our music, so some of our songs are quite mellow and thoughtful," continues Powell. "I mean we can rock—when we need to rock, we certainly rock out—but it's all about dynamics, light and shade. We can be very soft rock, and we can be hard rock. Sometimes people don't have the imagination, and these days everybody is very used to putting music into certain brackets, so they see pictures of us with guitars and they think, 'Oh, this has got to be hard rock,' but it's not necessarily."

Maiden definitely made use of a similar sense of light and shade, occasionally with mellower songs, but mostly through quiet intros. And "pastoral" definitely describes the vibe when they do this, which comes from Wishbone Ash, Be-Bop Deluxe, but also Sabbath and classical music, which is subconsciously ingrained in rockers, more so from Britain and mainland Europe than stateside.

Suddenly glamorous globetrotters, Maiden temporarily jump off their North American tour with Scorpions and play two Reading Rock '82 warm-up dates, in Chippenham and Poole. Then it's time for Reading itself, which is even more full-on metal than 1980's dance card. Friday featured Against the Grain, the Angels, Overkill, Stampede, Tank, Praying Mantis, Baron Rojo, Randy California, Manowar, and Budgie. Saturday features Just Good Friends, Bow Wow, Rock Goddess, Grand Prix, Bernie Torme, Ore, Cheetah, Gary Moore, Blackfoot, Tygers of Pan Tang, and Iron Maiden, in the headlining slot. Sunday features Terraplane, Chinatown, Spider, Marillion, Twisted Sister, Wilko Johnson & Lew Lewis, Bernie Marsden's SOS, Dave Edmunds, Y&T, Jackie Lynton Band, and, finally, Michael Schenker Group. Maiden close their set with a rendition of ZZ Top's "Tush."

Noted Dickinson on the band's Reading stand, in conversation with Dante Bonutto from *Kerrang!*, "We were very nervous for the first half of the set. Up until 'The Prisoner' it was like, 'Oh, my God,' but after that we stopped shaking and really started to fly. In America we played a festival in front of 75,000 people, and nobody was too apprehensive—there was no warblers or anything—but three or four days before the Reading show, we were literally shaking, terrified. You know, the Reading festival is the hardest in the world because—and it's a good thing—the audience is so critical. They've no respect for reputations. The biggest, most sought-after rock star there can die a death here if he does a lousy show."

Massey Hall, Toronto, Ontario, June 23, 1982. © *Martin Popoff*

With a few decades' time to reflect on the band's quick rise to the top, Bruce mused, "I would say if you've ever been on a rollercoaster and you get cranked right the top—click click click click—and then, down the other side, and at some point, you get to the bottom . . . well, we just didn't **get to the bottom. The** rollercoaster . . . we just kept plummeting for about the next four years. So, we were just on an adrenaline rush, for four years, nonstop. I have no idea what that does to you in time [laughs]."

Wrote Bonutto, reviewing Maiden's set, "Not all the audience were committed Maiden freaks, however, and Bruce's joy was dented by a hail of missiles arriving out of the black night sky as iconoclasts got to work. Thus, when he sportingly went across to the other stage to greet lost souls on the 'dead' side of the arena, he was hit with stinging force and swiftly retreated to the arms of Maiden. But the vast majority greeted him with rapturous joy as the boys charged into 'Children of the Damned' and 'The Number of the Beast,' which came complete with horror clip on the video screen. '22 Acacia Avenue' was followed by my favorite drum solo of the weekend, contributed by the lightning-quick Clive Burr, now recognized as one of the nation's best skinsmen. Thence came the duel of the guitarists, and on into 'The Prisoner,' complete with taped introduction and dry ice. Bruce jumped onto the amps with athletic grace and seemed lost in the ecstasy of the band chalking up another milestone in its history. It all seemed a long way from the pubs of the East End."

"That's what I was saying about so much happening in such a short space of time," adds Steve. "So, within two years of making the first album, by the time of the third album two years later, we're a headline act, and we were actually able to headline in, you know, most parts of the world. Because [of] the tour in 1980 in Europe, we toured in 1981 ourselves in Europe, clubs and stuff, and in 1982 we were doing quite big places. So, it was really only in America where we hadn't really . . . I mean, we headlined Massey Hall in Toronto in 1982, but it took to 1983 before we headlined America."

September 14 through October 23, Maiden continue to tour the states, now supporting Judas Priest for the third Maiden and third Priest records in a row. November 7 through December 10, the boys play Australia for the first time, followed by Japan. Last selection on the last date in Japan is the band's raucous cover of Montrose's "I Got the Fire." Support in Australia on all but one date comes from leather rockers Heaven.

But then it's time for another sharp turn for the rollercoaster of which Bruce speaks. It's December 10, 1982, and Clive Burr's last show with Iron Maiden occurs at the end of the band's Beast on the Road tour, the tenth and last show of the closing Japanese leg. His replacement would be Nicko McBrain, fresh from his gig with Trust.

But before Clive would go, he'd managed to get Steve "Loopy" Newhouse fired. As Loopy recalls it, "There were constant arguments. I'm not going to say arguments, but he would give me a ticking off because the kit wasn't set up right. Now, I can defend him to a certain point. But it got to the point where it was somebody else that actually noticed what he was doing. I was setting up the kit the way it should be. It was all marked, so it couldn't be wrong. And he would come in, and he would move something over there and something over there because it wasn't how he wanted it. And he would be sitting there playing, and he'd move this back to where it was, move that back to where it was, and I didn't see him do that. But during the sound check, he would rip my ass. He would really, really . . . like, he would give me a right verbal crap. You know, saying, 'You've done it wrong again. If you don't get it right, we're going to fire you.' And at the end of the Japanese tour in 1981, he got his wish—he fired me. Or he got me fired, by Tony Wigens, the tour manager. But as I say, it wasn't me that noticed what he was doing. It was a couple of the lighting crew."

Dave Wright archive

"I have asked this question," ponders Steve, asked by Jimmy Kay if in this story there is early evidence of Clive's multiple sclerosis. "In fact, I asked his wife, Mimi, because Mimi also suffers from MS. But she controls it. Whereas Clive at the time, we don't know if medically that was a sign. We don't know. But as I said, I can only defend him so far. I met him again at Clive Aid, roundabout 2008 at the Royal Standard. Clive turned up, and that was the first time I had seen him in twenty-two or twenty-five years. And we chatted like we had only seen each other the day before. It was bizarre. But you could tell then that he was in trouble. He'd been in a wheelchair, and it was heartbreaking to see him like that. But I was really surprised when they let him go. When I found out that Nicko would join the band, I was hardly surprised by that, because the amount of times we actually bumped into Nicko on the road was quite amazing."

"Dodgy question," began Clive, speaking with *Rock Hard* in 2002 concerning his ouster. "'The decision was probably made by the band, or to be more accurate, by the man who's always headed Iron Maiden. Of course, I'm talking about Steve Harris. It's always been his band right from the start. And you know, I never came over one day, saying, 'That's it, I've had enough, I quit.' I simply accepted the decision as it was. Doris Day, 'Que sera sera' [laughs]. Then Trust contacted me. As my dad had just passed away, I went to see my mother and visit some relatives in Germany. I stayed there for some time and—I don't know how—I got a phone call from Trust asking me to come over to Paris to rehearse with them. So, I took the car, and I met them there. We played and they asked me to record their new album. I only lent them a hand in the studio."

"Nicko has such amazing chops," reflects Janick Gers, well on the scene but still years away from being part of the Maiden fold. "He has all that jazz stuff happening. A lot of drummers nowadays, they don't have the chops of the old guys. You look at Ian Paice and Keith Moon, these guys come from the big-band era, where there's a lot of emphasis on style and swing. And he has all those chops; he can do all that stuff. A lot of these bands you get around now, the drummers are not really exposed to that kind of playing, the stuff that went on in the early 1960s. I think Nicko loved all that stuff like Buddy Rich, and I think a lot of new drummers tend to not have that swing; it's a more metronomic thing. And to me, it's more about feel rather than being taught to be metronomically in time. Because that movement gives you breath. So, from that point of view, Nicko is very special."

Remarked Nicko at the time, speaking with *Music Express*, "My first reaction was 'What's wrong with the group? Why are they dumping Clive?' I couldn't believe they would want to unload such a good drummer. You have to understand that before I knew Maiden as a band, I knew them as individuals, and they were all mates of mine. When I supported them in Europe, I used to hang out by the mixer and watch them. I used to think they were a great band, and that Clive was an excellent drummer. I felt really strange about being his replacement."

Reflecting on the situation up into 2006, speaking with Ray Van Horn Jr., Nicko explains that "Clive was a great drummer and a good friend too, so it was kind of a double whammy for me, the excitement on one hand of joining one of the top metal bands of that time, but also to actually sit back and go, 'Gee, I've got to fill this guy's shoes! How am I going to do that?' When I joined the band, Steve and I sat and talked about the old material from the first three records, and he said to me, 'Nick, just do it the way you'd do it,' and I said, 'Look, I don't really want to have to copy someone else's playing, because that's not me.' So, I had that freedom. I got to emulate it my way. It was very, very nerve-racking at first; I was biting my fingernails when I first joined the band."

Capital Centre, Landover, Maryland, October 17, 1982. © Rudy Childs

"Well, he had a lot of personal problems back home, personal and emotional things that really got to affecting his playing," explained Bruce concerning Clive, to Steve Newton back in 1983, when this was all fresh. "There was a lot of disagreement, and a lot of stuff went down, particularly in the latter part of the last tour to Japan and Australia. But it was a fairly amicable split. I think both parties realized that things weren't really happening as they should be." As for Nicko, "They're definitely two different sorts of drummers. Nicko's style is more driving than Clive's. Clive used to orient things a lot around his tom-toms, whereas Nicko is real straight and solid. He's amazing. Complete maniac. I mean, a real nutcase."

Above, Martin Popoff archive. Below and next page: a few more shots from Canada. © Martin Popoff

Below
Left: Toronto. © *Martin Popoff*
Right: Maryland. © *Rudy Childs*

CHAPTER 4
Piece of Mind

"Look, it's my song and this is how it should be played."

If it looked to all us Maiden fans that 1983 was the year of Maiden, look again, 'cause here comes Def Leppard, issuing *Pyromania* in January, with those who loved the band's first two records warned about what was to come by advance single "Photograph." The song's poppy bounce foretells the rise of hair metal, which will summarily replace the NWOBHM as the exciting new thing in the vicinity of hard rock.

"We looked more like Duran Duran than, say, Metallica," chuckles then-new Def Leppard guitarist Phil Collen. "So, it had a huge appeal. There were lots of girls going crazy, and a lot of guys liked it as well, so it had a real genuine crossover."

Adds Tygers of Pan Tang producer Chris Tsangarides, "I was working on *Thunder and Lightning*, Thin Lizzy, and my assistant engineer was sharing a flat with Mutt Lange's assistant engineer when he was doing *Pyromania*. So there had been reports going backwards and forwards, because we were actually on the same label, Lizzy and them. And I remember the A&R guy coming in saying, 'Oh my God, they spent however many millions and they're still not finished.' He's pulling his hair out. Well, they all had to eat their words because of the success that they had.

"For me it peaked then, way before then," continues Chris. "The moment they went off to America, they were no longer considered New Wave of British Heavy Metal. Because their music style had changed. They had become kind of Americanized, for want of a better word. That's not a derogatory thing. That's how they evolved, and fantastic. But the old type of New Wave of British Heavy Metal . . . Tygers kept it going until their natural demise. Iron Maiden kept it going until they evolved into the elaborate stuff. But pretty much even their older stuff is similar to the newer stuff. They got their style pretty quickly, I have to say. But yeah, they stopped writing about New Wave of British Heavy Metal. Something else had come up. They had stopped writing about it in those terms. And then of course came the LA business, which was being called heavy metal in the States. And I'm thinking, they're not heavy. What are they talking about? This is rock 'n' roll, rock music, yes, but not heavy metal. It just ain't. Interesting though."

"When you think of it, from that era, there was only two or three bands that actually broke huge in America," says Angel Witch and Tytan bassist Kevin Riddles. "I'm initially thinking of Leppard, who were so big in America because they had what the Americans were looking for, but with a little bit of edge, because of where they came from in the UK. So, they had polished, brilliantly written, brilliantly constructed tunes but still had that little bit of edge. And that's what lifted them up above most American bands.

"The other ones to make it, because they were just damn brilliant, were, of course, Maiden. They just took America apart, because Americans had never really seen a deal like that. But opposite of Def Leppard, there were American bands that seemed more

European, and I'm thinking of Van Halen at the time. I always looked at them and thought they were like a European band wrapped in an American band, because they had that edge, they had that something."

Speaking of Thin Lizzy, that band had arrived at the NWOBHM late for dinner, on March 4, 1983, launching into a flagrant foul of an album called *Thunder and Lightning*. Produced hard on the ears by Chris Tsangarides, this last Thin Lizzy album turned out to be a cynical play for heavy metal status after a bank of highly respected albums that addressed heavy only when Phil Lynott's writing called for it. There was this element of jumping the shark, further proof that the scene was over and about to get replaced.

"I just think that we saw that there were a lot more bands at that point leaning towards the metal side of things," reflects Lizzy guitarist Scott Gorham, "so we thought, well, let's trip the light fantastic on this one, see what happens. It's why John Sykes came into the band, was to have us lean more towards that direction. In fact, I'd gone to Phil a few months beforehand, saying that, you know, I actually wanted out of the band. And I actually didn't really want to do another album. I just thought we should knock it on the head. But he was the one who said, 'No, let's do the one more album, the one more world tour,' kind of thing, and 'I know this kid who is a great guitar player,' and that happened to be John Sykes. And that's how John actually got in. And we started writing the songs and started listening to his guitar tone, and my tone changed a little bit on that one, to kind of match [what] was going on."

Sykes himself would represent the paradigm shift that metal would make in the 1980s, transitioning from ground zero NWOBHMers Tygers of Pan Tang, through his questionable bandwagon album with a 1970s band, and into huge success with Whitesnake, themselves essentially a 1970s concern, then loosely part of the NWOBHM, and then a signature "hair metal" band in America.

And where would Maiden fit in all this? The good news is that they *would* fit and, for that matter, thrive. Along with Def Leppard, they would be a young British band allowed to participate—I say "allowed," but that's due to the forces of nature that are Steve Harris, Rod Smallwood, and their fireplug of a new singer, Bruce Dickinson. A handful of 1970s acts would thrive in this new metal-friendly America as well, but then most of the rest of the success stories would be fresh new American bands, seemingly all from California or at least having migrated there or spent large amounts of time there.

Despite heavy competition, the life of the party. The Spectrum, Philadelphia, Pennsylvania, August 19, 1983. © Rudy Childs

But first Maiden had to get used to another adjustment, that of breaking in their new drummer.

On June 5, 1952, Michael Henry McBrain was born at Hackney Salvation Army Hospital in Hackney, East London, and by adolescence the boy has found his calling, inspired by Joe Morello's drum solo with the Dave Brubeck Quartet. "I must've been about 11½ at the time," explains McBrain, speaking with *Music Express*. "I was so inspired; I got a couple of knives and ran around the house bashing everything in sight. My mother wasn't impressed though. She belted me around the ear hole and told me to shut up. Their attitude was 'Well, that's a five-minute wonder,' but I showed them by playing my first gig almost one year later."

Indeed, into 1969, McBrain is playing with a band called Axe, follow-up group to the likes of the 18th Fairfield Walk, Peyton Bond, and the Wells Street Blues Band. An early mentor was Strawbs and Hudson Ford drummer Richard Hudson, whom Nicko had met at a music store. And speaking of the name Nicko, "I had always hated the name Michael, so my parents called me Nicky when I was a kid, in reference to my favorite book at the time, *Nicholas the Bear*. So, my band were working on some material, and we decided to cut some tracks with two other musicians. When the cuts were finished, we invited all our friends down to the studio for a party to show them what we've been doing. Anyway, Billy Day gets totally sloshed and starts introducing me to everyone as Nicko, the Italian drummer. Everyone thought he was serious, and I thought the name was a gas, so it stuck."

In March 1977, the Pat Travers Band issue their second album, *Makin' Magic*, followed later that year by *Puttin' It Straight*. Drummer in the band is Nicko, in his most significant role before joining Maiden. Into 1978, McBrain is in Blazer Blazer, then playing with Stretch, Jenny Darren, McKitty, Marshall Fury, and Informer, through 1980.

"I don't want to put the knock on Pat," Nicko told Keith Sharp in 1983, "because he is a good mate, but he did have an ego problem and he was difficult to work with. Things just kind of dissolved after we toured in support of *Puttin' It Straight*. The situation wasn't unique to me. Both Tommy Aldridge and Pat Thrall left Pat, and now I hear Cowling's no longer with Travers either."

In October 1981, significant early French metal band Trust issue their *Marche ou crève* LP (*Savage*, in the English-language version issued the following year). "I loved drumming with them because they were absolutely furious," muses McBrain. "They would've done great in Quebec. However, business-wise, things constantly fell apart. There were money problems, exchange problems, and I was in and out of France like a yo-yo. Trust is capable of great music, but they let business and management problems totally screw them up."

Meanwhile in extended Maidenland, January 1982, More and ex-Maiden lead singer Paul Mario Day leave the band, scotching the planned release date of January 4 for the band's second album. Day would land in Wildfire for two albums, this happening while Nicko is leaving Trust. Switching gigs with Nicko, ex-Maiden drummer Clive Burr soon finds himself in Trust, playing on 1983's *IV* and then the French band's *Man's Trap* follow-up from 1984. Also, in 1983 Bruce Dickinson marries for the first time, the marriage lasting four years. On the visual side, in March 1983, UK neo-prog band Marillion issue their debut album, *Script for a Jester's Tear*. The band, recording for Capitol/EMI, the same label as Maiden, instigates what will become extensive and successful use of a mascot. Steve Harris is a professed fan, enjoying the band's overt similarity to Genesis.

But back to business—Iron Maiden have a record to make. As Steve himself pens for a special diary-type feature in *Kerrang!*, "On January 2, we all met at Heathrow once again and headed off to write the album in Jersey for about six weeks. We stayed at this hotel called Le Chalet and immediately hired a table tennis table, pool table, Space Invaders, etc. and a dartboard for Rod 'Rufus the Red' Smallwood. It's a wonder we got the album written at all! Especially as we had our own bar as well. Still, we couldn't go out much as we were right on the coast, miles from anywhere, and didn't want to freeze our nuts off, so we had to have inside entertainment, didn't we?

"The songs came together really well. I tend to write on my own in my room pretty quietly, whereas Bruce and Melvin (sorry, 'H' or Adrian!) write in the rehearsal rooms, amps loud, destroying ceilings, walls, neighbours, etc. (actually, we were lucky as there weren't many neighbours nearby. Well, there weren't when we left anyway!).

"Next was Compass Point Studios, Nassau, Bahamas. The reason for going there wasn't just the sun, honest! Actually, the studio was great, and when you're recording, it doesn't matter whether it's pissing with rain or brilliant sunshine outside; a studio's a studio wherever it is. Still, I must admit that once the backing tracks were done, we were able to get a fair bit of sun in. What we do is record the bass, drums, and two rhythm guitars all together to get as live a sound as possible, once Martin (Birch, that is, our producer) has messed about with sounds, different miking techniques, etc. and is happy with the sound of everything, and we're happy with everything too, of course."

Remarked Bruce on Martin Birch, in conversation with Steve Newton, "His technique is just encouragement, usually. The great thing about Martin is that he's a very subtle producer in the way he works. He doesn't actually suggest anything to do with the music at all. I mean we write and arrange the music, and then he engineers it and gets the performances out of us. He motivates."

"Basically, we don't write songs for airplay or anything like that," continues Dickinson, "so we don't need a producer who produces for that sort of stuff. All we wanted to get was good sounds and a producer who comes along and encourages us. Martin thinks the way we do about the music, so he can be really critical, like, 'You can do a better guitar solo than that.' Or I'll be singing away, and he'll go, 'I think you can sing it a little bit better than that. I think you can go for one more performance and push it a bit more.' And that's how he works. He's always wringing the last drop out of everything you do. I mean, it would be unthinkable to do an Iron Maiden album without Martin."

As to why the band recorded in the Bahamas, Bruce figures, "Because we just got fed up with recording things in England. There are so many distractions, like record companies wanting to do interviews. And also, everybody always gets ill in England; everybody always gets the flu or something like that because we're recording in the wintertime. We've already booked the studio for next year. The sound at Compass Point Studio is incredible. AC/DC did *Back in Black* there and the new album they've just done there too."

Soon it would be time for the punters to hear some new music. On April 11, EMI puts out "Flight of Icarus," backed with a version of Montrose's "I Got the Fire." Also available in 12-inch and 12-inch picture disc formats, the single is the band's first piece of product in nearly a year, and the first featuring Nicko.

"I don't think that worked terribly well," shrugs artist Derek Riggs, on the single's picture sleeve. "But that was done, and it's got Eddie burning Icarus up with a flamethrower thing. Just when they decided to do that as a single, Led Zeppelin decided they weren't making any more records, so that figure, that burning Icarus figure, is a takeoff from Led Zeppelin's Swan Song logo. If you look at that, it's got Robert Plant as an angel with his wings on, so we burned him [laughs]."

"And on the hill beneath him, there are figures writhing in pain, and there's a couple up on the hill who are having sex. So, they took that, and they were making an advert for it in an English magazine, a newspaper. The English music magazines at the time were printed on newsprint, so the printing was a bit rough, and the color didn't always come out. The colors in the sky pretty much disappeared, and the only part that really printed up well were the silhouettes of the figures, which were writhing in pain. And they put a black thing across . . . the falling figure of Icarus, you could see his penis, so they stuck a black thing over that so you couldn't see it. But the most prominent thing in the bottom half of the picture are the silhouettes of the little figures writhing in pain. And right on top of the hill to the left are a couple having sex [laughs]. And they really stand out. So, they did this, but they left that."

Says Nicko of the video, "When they introduced me to the world, we did the 'Flight of Icarus' video in the Bahamas, where we recorded *Piece of Mind*, and Steve was like, 'We need the hooded character that's got his brain and does all of this weird shit!' And I said, sarcastically, 'Ah, the new boy will do it!' They said, 'We're going to paint your face blue and stick this hooding on you; then you're going to go stand on this precipice looking down at the ocean.' I said, 'Listen, I've only just joined the band and you're trying to get rid of me already!' But I look at that guy in 'Flight of Icarus' and I think, 'For crying out loud, who is that drummer?' It's terrible! Just before I joined Maiden, I had my hair cut prior to the Christmas 1982, and then I get the phone call that I'm definitely in the band now, and I'm like, 'You're freaking joking! I just had my hair cut!' I'm joining this classic long-haired rock band!"

A month hence, on May 16, 1983, the new Iron Maiden album hits the shops. Titled *Piece of Mind*, it's a record many Maiden fans consider the band's finest moment. And yet, the band's new singer, Bruce Dickinson, would run a bit hot and cold on it.

"Well, I think we got a huge impetus from Nicko coming into the band. We were just on a roll in terms of the music. There was just so much confidence in the band after the success of *Number of the Beast*. We felt we could do anything. And we really set out to do some interesting stuff on that record, and I think we succeeded. I think it was a great album."

And yet . . . "There are some good songs on it. I always felt that we never did ourselves a favor with the production of it. We never flatter ourselves with production. It's one of my little bug bears. I think it could have sounded a little more . . . I think I would like to do it slightly different. But if the six of us sat down, you'd get six different mixes. That's what a band's all about—it's compromise. As

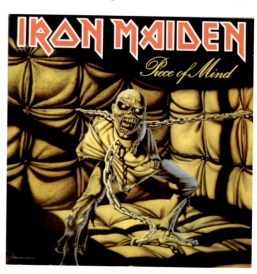

Dave Wright archive

long as it's good and the songs come across, that's all you can hope for. They did a good job on it. Like I say, if you get six guys in the band, Nicko would mix more drums, you know I mean? But with respect to *Piece of Mind*, it's kind of dry. But it's real. It depends on your philosophy of recording. Whether you think the band should sound like they're in a room playing, or whether they're in a huge arena."

"I always find *Piece of Mind* very, very dry," agrees Adrian. "There are some great songs, but it's a bit hard to listen to now. *Powerslave* is a little bit smoother, I think. It was on the way to where we were going with *Somewhere in Time*."

Before the fans themselves could pass judgment, they had to get past the album cover, which featured Eddie chained in a padded cell and lobotomized. As Steve told Jon Sutherland from *Record Review*, "That's right. He was freaking us out. On the album cover he's in a padded cell with all of his hair shaved off. There's a line around his head with a bolt in it. There's a reason for all this, actually. There's a picture on the inner sleeve that shows the band sitting in a banquet hall with the silver trays and all, waiting for dinner to be served. And there's a brain on the table. We thought we couldn't have that. So, we thought we'd put Eddie away for safety. He'll break out soon again, I suppose [laughs]. So many things he can do that we can't do. It's best for us to play the music and let Eddie go on with the crazy things we always dreamed about doing but never found the way."

"The original wasn't aggressive enough," recalls Riggs. "I believe it was only a sketch, not fully finished. But yes, that was the feeling, that it wasn't violent or aggressive enough. He was sitting in the corner, looking a bit mad. When musicians talk about things, they often don't really think about what they're saying. You know, 'Have him sitting in a padded cell, and a bit mad.' When they say sitting, they don't think about it, but I have to work from that. So, I'll paint him sitting."

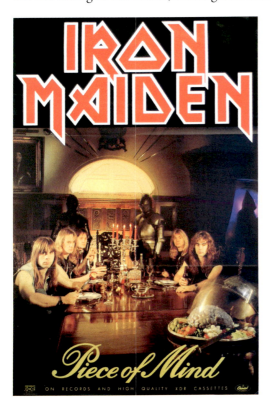

Dave Wright archive

In the end, though, "He had his brain cut out and a few other things," continues Derek. "It was a bit this and that. I don't really know . . . after I stopped doing him, I don't really know what the hell was going on. He didn't seem to have a direction or a clue at all. It was all kind of linked up with football merchandising and crap like that. I mean, really, Eddie is a fucking hang-on for a football team? Yeah, get out of here [laughs]. But as I've said, Eddie just became the things he did—a kind of manic crazy [laughs]. It was like . . . Rod always wanted him to be hyperaggressive. That's what he thought would work. But I don't know. He turned from a monster—he was quite threatening when he turned up—into, I don't know, champion of the poor and oppressed. Eddie, the champion of the people. He became kind of an antihero, I think the word is. As I've said, somebody once said to me, people respond to Eddie as a hero, because he's too heavy to handle as a villain [laughs]. You want him on your side, you know?"

"In the early days, it was pretty straightforward in our briefings to Derek," notes Smallwood. "He would like draw them out; we knew pretty much what we wanted to achieve, and Derek always did a fantastic job executing it. And fortunately, I guess, they always worked. *Piece of Mind* was teamwork. Steve thought about Eddie in a padded cell, which I thought was not quite enough, and it was my idea to lobotomize him. The title was quite hard for that one. I mean, *Food for Thought* was it for a while [laughs], with the brain, but then *Piece of Mind* sort of appeared, and that just seemed to be stronger."

Back at the music, graciously, Steve has the band's newest member open up the wide-angled heavy metal vistas that would distinguish *Piece of Mind*. "Where Eagles Dare" cracks open with a fill, and right way we hear a distinctive drummer who also has a distinctive drum sound, courtesy of himself in collaboration with producer Martin Birch.

"It was a great break for me, but I still had to prove I belonged with them," explained Nicko, speaking with Keith Sharp at the time. "That opportunity presented itself during rehearsals for the material in Jersey. Maiden was giving me plenty of freedom, to add things to their arrangements, and at one point Steve Harris and I started to work out this arrangement feel to 'Where Eagles Dare.' It was a really tricky fill, particularly the middle eight, but some form of eye contact developed between me and Steve, and we worked it out in about ninety minutes. From then on, I felt a part of the band, and the sessions seemed to build momentum from there. By the time we finished *Piece of Mind*, I could honestly listen to the record and feel I had made a distinctive contribution.

"But it was a really awkward six months," continues Nicko, on the initial period where news of his joining had to be kept quiet. "I couldn't say anything to anyone; all my negotiations with the band were done in secret, and meanwhile I'm turning down all these lucrative gigs. My mates thought I was crazy. It was a nerve-racking situation to say the least. Then I had to learn three albums' worth of material as well as rehearse with the band in preparation for the new album. But I once learned twenty songs in four days while playing with Trust, and I heard Maiden's material enough to know pretty well what they wanted."

"I think he's got a lot more control, really," noted Steve, comparing Nicko with Clive Burr for Jon Sutherland in the summer of 1983. "He holds down the beat a lot better. It brings more dynamics to the music. I think that is one of the reasons this album sounds heavier. My style of writing hasn't changed, but the songs seem more solid somehow. It's not that he doesn't do as much technically, because in some ways he does more. Nicko is so experienced. I think his control brings out the climaxes of the songs."

Although Nicko wouldn't feature prominently in the writing of the record, Steve told Jon that he was pleased that the other guys were getting more involved.

"A lot has been made of the fact that I do most of the writing, but that's because no one else is come up with anything. Now Davey, Bruce, and Adrian are getting more and more involved. Davey's a little bit shy as far as the writing goes. He does come up with great riffs, but he doesn't have the confidence to come in and say, 'This is what I want.' So, he needs someone to bring it out of him. I'd like to do this more in the future with

White drums, just like Clive. The Spectrum, Philadelphia, Pennsylvania, August 19, 1983. © Rudy Childs

Davey because he has such good ideas, and all he needs is the confidence to sit down and work on them. He's so modest and so shy, it's great. He could be a guitar hero and really go for it and get the big head, but he never will. He's not like that at all. He's been nice since day one. And nothing's changed him."

As far as soloing goes, Harris says, "Dave just does it off the top of his head. He goes in there and comes out with it. Adrian does it the other way. He tends to work out the parts. So, you have two different styles that are very complementary. Dave plays in his own frantic way, and Adrian is more conceived. Sometimes Adrian's solos tend to stick in your head because they are more worked out."

Lyrically, "Where Eagles Dare" is based on the 1968 spy thriller movie of the same name, screenplay by Alistair MacLean, who wrote the novel version at the same time. "I remember that song quite vividly," says Bruce, "because first of all, I was a huge fan of the movie—we all were. And secondly, there's a drum part on it, which, I mean, I know a bit about drumming. I'm not a great drummer, but I know a great part when I see one. And Nicko wanted to use a double bass drum and we wouldn't let him [laughs]. And he did the whole thing with a single bass drum, and he still does and still refuses to use double bass drums. Because after playing that bit with a single bass drum pedal, he's like, 'No, that's it; I'm going to use a single bass drum pedal. Everybody else is going to have to catch up.'"

Speaking with Steve Newton at the time, Bruce said that "'Where Eagles Dare' is from a movie and 'Quest for Fire' is also a movie. Steve reads a lot of science fiction and watches a lot of movies. We've got a video on the bus, so he just sits in the bus and watches videos all day. These last two he's written about 50 percent. He writes it all on the bass, and then he usually whistles the melody into a little Walkman and writes down the lyrics."

"There was no conscious decision to stay away from the devil debate," said Steve to *Hit Parader*, on the album in general lacking the occult vibe of its predecessor. "We enjoy a good fight every now and then, but we were more concerned with furthering our career than standing up for a cause. We have no particular interest in the devil, so we figured we may as well move on lyrically. I found those charges totally absurd. When I was growing up, I had a lot of interest in horror films, and that interest is carried over to today. Our type of music lends itself very well to that kind of imagery."

"Revelations" slows things down, and even if the song is most remembered for its mellow passages, in fact the verses are of two

Olympiahalle, Munich, Germany, November 30, 1983.
© Wolfgang Guerster

dispositions: stacked power chords, but also with a quiet arrangement—two each, with the heavy verses bookending the mellow ones. Plus, there's a proggy instrumental passage, but then also some quick headbanging. All told, it's one surprise after another. Counter to Steve's assertion, this one is quite dark and mystical. "Well, I was deep into reading all my Aleister Crowley books then," says Dickinson, "and I was major into Egypt and everything else, pyramids, and I just got a big grab bag in of all the imagery I could find, and glued it all together along with the lyrics of an English hymn for the intro and the outro."

Fleshing it out a bit, speaking with Steve Newton, he says, "The first version of it is a hymn I used to sing at school. I was always very fond of the tune and the lyrics." But Bruce wasn't in the choir, per se. "No, I was just part of the congregation. You had to be a bit of a limp wrist to join the choir, obviously. You had to get dressed up in white smocks and all that stuff. It was a bit like wearing a dress or something."

Adds Adrian, "We still play 'Revelations' within the set, and it's one of my favorite songs from *Piece of Mind*. To be honest, I think they're really beautiful lyrics, but I didn't know what Crowley was all about, and sometimes you don't have to be specific. It can just be the way the words hang together and the sound of them. The melody and everything is great. As long as the singer knows what he's singing about and he means it, that's what it's all about. You don't need to know specifically what the song is about for it to still move you."

Next is "Flight of Icarus," a true-blue NWOBHM rocker presented at slow simmer, heavy gallop, as it were, with Nicko helping make this one work with a solid tribal beat with great fills and accents. Anthemic and easily headbangable, the song rose to #8 on the sub-*Billboard* chart called Top Album tracks, as well as #11 in the UK on the main Singles Chart. It's based on the Greek legend of Icarus flying too close to the sun—flirt with danger and you'll get yourself burned—and Bruce twists it universally in lightly suggesting the idea of a headbanging kid skipping off to a show against his father's wishes.

"Me and Steve had a stand-up row in the studio about the tempo of that song," says Bruce. "He, still to this day, hates it and thinks that the studio version was way too slow. I, of course, disagree [laughs]. I basically said, 'Look, it's my song, and this is how it should be played.'"

November 21, 1941, marks the release of the western movie *They Died with Their Boots On*, and *Piece of Mind*'s side 1 closing track is called "Die with Your Boots On." The video from the album's anchor track, "The Trooper," includes footage from the film. This is Bruce's favorite song on the album, "cause it's a basic live track. It's got a great chorus, and I think it sums up our philosophy, really. Which is die with your boots on. Whatever you're gonna do, give it your best shot. Just for the sake of it."

Opening with a classic twin lead, one that stays constant while the melody changes behind it, once the verse starts, we're into straight chords, Steve adding note density along the way. Also included is one of the band's best prechoruses, rising to the chorus, beat constant, before the band collapses into another set of groovy verses. And of course, that groove is provided by Nicko and Steve, great bass sound, Nicko accompanying with a ride cymbal beat and signature bar-ending punctuations. Late in the sequence are more twin leads, lower on the fretboard, underscoring the heft of the track.

Announcing side 2 is "The Trooper," arguably #1 fan favorite of the entire Maiden canon. Guitar and bass perform the opening riff in unison before the rhythm is established, blessed with an iconic twin lead. Shocking the first time one hears it, the music stops dead while Bruce sings the first verse a capella, soon to be aided in battle by a classic Maiden gallop.

Dave Wright archive

"Yes, that was a vocal twister indeed," chuckles Bruce. "The crucial thing about 'The Trooper' is that it starts off at one speed on the record, and as we've played it over the years it's gotten progressively faster and faster, and I've taken more chunks off the end of my tongue as my teeth have collided with it. But we've more or less got it down to a medium-paced gallop now, not the kind of off-the-clock sprint that it was earlier."

Lyrically, we're into a classic Maiden history lesson. October 25, 1854, marks the disastrous Charge of the Light Brigade, which pitted British troops against the Russians during the Crimean War. Miscommunication resulted in a slaughter of the British side. The event, best remembered through Alfred Lord Tennyson's narrative poem "The Charge of the Light Brigade," is the inspiration for the lyric as well as the iconic Eddie portrait used for the single.

Strength to strength, next is "Still Life," another dark and doomy rocker enhanced by band chemistry, beginning up top with a dynamic and actorly vocalist, down through the *Sad Wings of Destiny*–era Priest-proud guitars and into a crack and articulating rhythm section. And speaking of Priest, the solo section feels like a Priest song both in terms of the back track and the dueling soloing—pure Glenn and K. K. to this one. Not knowing the title, one would swear the song was called "Nightmares," given the chorus refrain. It's just another enigmatic characteristic of this mysterious song featuring a tormented narrator drawn into a pool's reflection by evil spirits—inspiration came to Steve from *The Inhabitants of the Lake*, a 1964 short story by Ramsay Campbell. "Still Life" represents Dave Murray's only writing credit on the record, with Adrian getting three music credits, Bruce one ("Revelations"), and Steve the remaining four.

Could do without the intro, especially in light of many, many more of these to come, one indistinguishable from the rest. Before the opening musical passage, however, is a backward message in jest, a jab at the backmasking hysteria drummed up by the religious Right. Played right way around, it's Nicko's impression of brutal African dictator Idi Amin, along with a loud burp. One other trivia note about this one, uttered as part of the lyric, is the phrase "peace of mind."

"I really like 'Still Life,'" reflects" Bruce. "It was never a really successful live song. It's strange that some of my favorite songs on the records sometimes don't seem to make it live. 'Strange World' is another one of my favorite Maiden songs that just didn't really happen live."

Then again, Bruce isn't too sure when asked about these dark-horse songs, because he doesn't play his own records particularly. "No, I just don't see what the point is. I'm always trying to think of something new to do. What's the point of listening to something I did ten years ago? I suppose we should have some big listening party, really, and we should all go get drunk and listen to all our old stuff and get all misty eyed. But it wouldn't do us any good whatsoever in terms of writing a new album [laughs]. I mean, I can remember the songs and most of the stories about how we created them, but I prefer to listen to our stuff by chance. Like somebody playing it on the radio. I was doing a radio show last night live, and it was a phoner, and I was listening to some stuff coming down the phone, because they were playing it in the studio. And as he was playing it, I was thinking, fucking 'ell, that sounds good. I prefer to listen to my stuff like that, than to sit down and indulge myself."

When fans needed to find something to complain about on this superlative record, they all gathered and warmed their hands around "Quest for Fire," Steve taking one step too topical, summarizing one movie too many, this one but two years old. Said Steve to Andy Secher back in December 1983, "The song topics are just a little more expansive this time. When I saw the movie *Quest for Fire*, I was inspired to write a song about it. Originally, I thought it might have to be an instrumental track [laughs]. After all, that movie didn't have any dialogue."

As soon as Bruce hollers "In a time when dinosaurs walked the earth," punters turned tail and ran the other way. It didn't help that the movie bombed (a caveman language was invented for it), or that Maiden's musical strategy for the weak lyric incorporated a sort of timid half-time gallop—one movie too many, one gallop too many.

All is forgiven, however, when "Sun and Steel" cranks up, the band still galloping but more like Vikings on a pillage versus a trot around the stables. Lyrically, this reads like an unforgiving tale of teenage gang violence, even if it was inspired by the life of samurai Miyamoto Musashi, although the title itself is from Japanese author Yukio Mishima's 1968 essay, *Sun and Steel: Art, Action and Ritual Death*, a meditation on Mishima's martial arts and bodybuilding.

The Spectrum, Philadelphia, Pennsylvania, August 19, 1983. © *Rudy Childs*

Piece of Mind closes with "To Tame a Land," "one of Steve's songs based on the book *Dune*," notes Adrian, in reference to the famed sci-fi novel of 1965. "And he wanted to name the song 'Dune,' and he rang up . . . was it Frank Herbert, the author? And he obviously wasn't a fan, because he wouldn't let us use the title, so we had to change it to something else."

A slight variation of the story has Herbert's agents sending through the message "Frank Herbert doesn't like rock bands, particularly heavy rock bands, and especially bands like Iron Maiden." The song is only a shade longer that "Revelations," but it's assembled more like a standard Maiden epic, further made exotic by the Middle Eastern melody to the riff. In 1969, Herbert published *Dune Messiah*, the sequel to *Dune*. More in the series followed (as well as film work), providing ongoing inspiration to practitioners of fantasy metal, with Maiden establishing themselves clearly as pioneers in the realm, preceded in the tradition by the likes of Judas Priest and, really, Uriah Heep before them.

As alluded to, the sum total of Maiden's fourth record is now widely regarded as the band's high watermark, rivaled, really, only by the high regard afforded *The Number of the Beast*. Still, it wasn't like that right out of the gate. Wrote Dante Bonutto in the all-important *Kerrang!* assessment of the record, "With the Birch production rippling muscle and Nicko sliding almost imperceptibly onto a drum stool still warm from the attentions of Clive Burr, this is close to a very good album, a notch above *Number of the Beast* certainly, though Smith and Murray, for my money, don't as yet deliver with enough character or clout to elevate their respective contributions from the level of basic 'playing' to that of 'heroics.' Still, more development in this area and more restraint from Steve Harris (forget the dinosaurs—please!) would result in the next Maiden opus being something special. Men, it can be done! The odd, stuttering step aside, this is plainly a gambol in the right direction."

Examining the record track by track, Bonutto, ardent NWOBHM analyst since the beginning, seems most fond of the following two in particular: "'Flight of Icarus,' the current single, seems to appeal to no-one [sic] I know, but what the hell, vocalist Bruce Dickinson lets rip in a manner not usually pursued by grown men outside the privacy of their own bath/shower, there's some steady bass bringing up the bottom end, and the whole thing doesn't smack, thank God, of any 'Let's write a single and get on *Top of the Pops*' conspiracy. Yes, that's right, I *like* it, though 'Die with Your Boots On,' next under the stylus, is *Piece of Mind*'s standout track. A broadside against superstition and 'end of the world' soapboxing, it takes the form of a restless run-out romp with Bruce submitting his finest vocal performance of the album, supported come chorus time by some off-the-cuff boots 'n' braces backup."

Of note, despite *Kerrang!*'s importance, heavy metal magazines were sprouting all over the place, May 1983 marking the debut of the French-language *Enfer*, which would help Maiden become a strong draw in France, a major market for Maiden to this day.

Piece of Mind promo store display. Dave Wright archive

But the Canadian press performed much the same function in the Great White North, arguably Maiden's top market per capita. Remarked Nicko, speaking with *Music Express*'s Keith Sharp at the time, with the record recently behind him, "I still can't believe I'm with these guys. It gets hard to adjust to being a star (this said with a wink as a couple of groupies hover). It was real tough at first, particularly that initial tour of Britain. I knew I was filling a big seat, and I didn't know how Clive's former fans would take to me, but fortunately, things worked out, and everyone's been great to me. I've got to the point where I've mastered pretty well all the old records, and the new stage act. Now I'm thirsting for new challenges. The chemistry is such that we drive each other to new levels. *Number of the Beast* was a monster record. *Piece of Mind* was a further progression, and now we're gearing for the next stage. I don't know what it's going to sound like, but I do know that I'll be part of it 100 percent."

Being sociable with the growing legion of Maiden fans wasn't proving to be a problem, continued McBrain. "Why not? We're just ordinary people, like our fans. We like to meet them whenever we can, and they're pretty good at dealing with us. There are times when you want to be by yourself, and they start to hassle you a bit. But if you say to them, 'Look, can I catch you later?,' they usually understand. They like us, but I think they also respect us as well."

Now time to deliver the new songs onstage, from May 2 to 28, Iron Maiden conduct the intensive UK leg of their World Piece Tour '83, with poppy NWOBHMers Grand Prix supporting.

"You start off with a concept and you build around that concept," explains Rod, offering a glimpse at how he approaches Maiden's stage sets. "I'm sure there's something we thought that would be a great idea, and then we just thought, well, that is just ridiculously expensive, totally impractical to cart around the world. But you don't really get that far, because you soon get a feel of what works and what doesn't work, and the parameters. Essentially you want to put the best show on but be able to move it internationally. There are some constraints. If you're doing one gig for six months, one venue for six months, or five years, you can do all sorts of extensive staging. If you're moving all over the world, you've got to be practical.

"And so, I can't think of a tour that was impractical," continues the boss behind the scenes. "You've got to reckon we've had the same production guy since 1980, Dick Bell, and at the end of the day, he supervises all that kind of things. He knows what's working, and if something starts getting impractical, he'll say so from the very beginning. It's very much a team. We've got the same sound engineer, same production guy, same bass rig guy, same agents, same merchandising, all sorts of things, since the early 1980s. So that works as a team. We start looking at ideas, and if it's something that's going to be impractical, we're going to sense it immediately, so you never get that far. It would be irresponsible to take something on tour that didn't work all the time; otherwise you get kids in various countries that end up getting very little. Sometimes we had to go with a secondary show. We hope the fans can understand that and appreciate that the band has literally gone out of the way to get up there and play for them, in the best production situation that was feasible at that time."

As Steve Newhouse has alluded to, he was back working with Iron Maiden. "I could see, instantly, what a step up they'd made," remembers Loopy. "They now started to climb the ladder. Obviously, by the time they got to the European tour, they'd already toured America. And when they got back and I joined them for the European tour, they were superb. They were absolutely spot on, so tight, and they just sounded great. And by this time, they owned their own PA. Dave Lights had, to me, the best lighting rig they ever used. I think that just speaks volumes. The way the whole set started with, like there's three triangles, big triangle in the center, two smaller triangles, one on each side, and everything was brought right down just above the drum kit. And all you had were these sort of flickering LEDs. And that's how it started, with the opening music for 'Where Eagles Dare.' And as the music starts, the lights start to lift up. That opening sequence was just absolutely brilliant. It was one of the best I've seen, and luckily I got to see it every night, in Europe."

June 1 through 12, the World Piece Tour '83 moves to the Benelux countries and Scandinavia, with all-female NWOBHMers Rock Goddess as support. Final day of this leg, EMI issues "The Trooper" as the band's ninth single, backed with a cover of Jethro Tull's "Cross-Eyed Mary." The song reaches #28 on the US Mainstream Rock charts. In 2011, "The Trooper" was picked as the opening theme in VH1's eleven-episode *Metal Evolution* series, produced by Banger Films, with the author on board as part of the team. Codirector (with Scot McFadyen) Sam Dunn, not coincidentally a bassist, has repeatedly called Iron Maiden his favorite band of all time. But back to 1983, the following month Maiden were making their own metal movies, issuing a four-track compilation called *Video Pieces*; it is their second video ever.

Smallwood recalls an incident caused by "Cross-Eyed Mary." "We had the B-side in England, because Steve was a big Jethro Tull fan, as people know, and for some reason it got picked up by an American radio station and it spread from there and got quite substantial airplay. And the label wanted to add it to the album, which we flat refused to do. It just wasn't the way we wanted to work. A lot of fans had already bought the album, and it was completely unfair to them to put the track on, after they bought the album, with the expectation of buying it again. We just didn't work that way. The first thing has always been the fans for Maiden, which is probably why they are still here."

Dave Wright archive

Remarked Derek Riggs, on the iconic artwork for the single (of which a flag-waving Bruce in uniform would essentially bring to life onstage), "People keep asking me, 'Why is he wearing that uniform?' Look, the song is about the Charge of the Light Brigade. He's wearing the uniform that the Light Brigade wore when they charged. Get over it [laughs]. It's not World War II. But yes, this is always a really popular one with the fans. That one is gouache and a bit of airbrush, on illustration board. This Light Brigade, it was an ill-fated attack by the British on the Russians. I'm not sure of the details, as I didn't pay attention in school. They went into a valley, a general and a small brigade of soldiers, and he decided to charge the Russians, and the Russians had barricades of cannons and things like that, and he was a rotten general and he made a really bad choice and they got murdered. There were stories of guys having their horses blown out from under them and things. It was a complete massacre."

An unchained Eddie escapes the asylum. The Spectrum, Philadelphia, Pennsylvania, August 19, 1983. © Rudy Childs

June 21 through October 25, Maiden take their World Piece Tour '83 to North America for an intensive blanketing of the US and Canada. Support through August 2 is Fastway and Saxon (the author's first Maiden show ever is the early Spokane, Washington, stop, on June 24). Support then shifts to Fastway and Canadian hard rockers Coney Hatch. September and October find Quiet Riot supporting, with the last three dates, rescheduled ones, featuring Coney Hatch and Axe filling out the bill.

Asked by *Hit Parader*'s Andy Secher in 1983 what he did for fun on the American leg, Harris remarked, "Well, I'm very happily married, so that eliminates a lot of possibilities right there! What I like to do is go to clubs and see local bands, especially if they're good rock 'n' roll groups. I'm not into disco, so I go to rock clubs. One of the problems I've been having lately is that I've been recognized. I like it when people come up to me and say hello and ask for an autograph, but sometimes I just want to hear the music. There are a lot of good American club bands, but regrettably, they seem to feel the need to play cover tunes instead of original music. I realize that it's probably the owner of the club who's telling them to play the covers, but I'd like to see them get a chance to play their own songs as well. That's the way a lot of British bands have gotten their start."

As for what he was listening to at that juncture, "One of my favorites are the Tygers of Pan Tang. They're very interesting. I also like Raven; they remind me of Maiden a little bit. On a more progressive side, I enjoy Marillion very much. I was a big fan of early Genesis, and Marillion can be amazingly similar to Genesis in their sound and style."

"It looked like we were all going to break, actually," explains a rueful Biff Byford, legendary longtime NWOBHM soldier and singer for Saxon on the band's historic campaign with Maiden. "It was a massive tour. I think we were all in the *Billboard* charts, weren't we? And Maiden did break off that tour. It would've been nice to finish the tour,

Steve and Nicko in full Maiden gallop. The Spectrum, Philadelphia, Pennsylvania, August 19, 1983.
© Rudy Childs

but we only did half the tour for some strange reason. But it was a great tour. We really should've broke off that. We didn't get kicked off. Our manager . . . yeah, it would be nice to say that, but the truth is the manager just had a contract for half of it; he was a greedy bastard. I mean, we went out headlining after that, which was probably because it made more money for him. But Maiden, yeah, we were all supercompetitive with bands. English people are like that [laughs]. We're very competitive. But no, we really didn't have any problems with Maiden. I talk to Maiden's manager once a month; we're good mates, from the same town as me. I think they've always been very competitive, Maiden, and always been very secretive. You don't really know anything about the inner workings of Maiden. And I think that's the same with a lot of bands—AC/DC are the same."

A couple of satin backstage passes.
Dave Wright archive

Adds Saxon guitarist Paul Quinn, "Fast Eddie (Fastway leader; ex-Motörhead; now, sadly, deceased), he's got a sardonic sense of humor, so we could relate to that, being British. We were fans as musicians anyway. They'd been through some famous bands themselves. Maiden, we'd known quite a few years. I saw recently on a Facebook page . . . I forgot who posted it, whether was it Bruce, but it was this ticket from Manchester University, which is kind of the University College, of us, Maiden and Nutz playing together, which is when we first met them; I would imagine it was 1978 or 1979."

"Yeah, it was a management thing," agrees Saxon drummer Nigel Glockler, on why the band didn't stay with Maiden, "which I was pissed off about actually. We were on an equal footing with Maiden, audience reaction-wise, definitely. I think if we had stayed on that, we would've broken America big time. It's very frustrating that they didn't commit us to do that, but you know, I'm not one of these people that feels bitter. It's like, well, what's the point in bloody worrying about it, quite frankly. We're still here now, and we're on the up again, and I figure, you know, that's great. I mean, a lot of bands of that era are gone. We're still here and we're still relevant to the fans because they're still buying our albums and coming to shows. So, you know, great."

"Fantastic, great," chuckles Saxon bassist Steve Dawson, providing the final word on this landmark tour. "Yeah, we all got on very well. Nobody got a big ego, so nobody was wanting to put one over on the other, as in not enough room on the stage or the sound or anything. We worked with Fast Eddie before, when we toured with Motörhead on the *Bomber* tour, so we were old mates. But Fast Eddie is a really funny guy. He's just got like a really dry sense of humor. And Dave King, the singer at that time, he had just been in local bands in Ireland. It was all new to him, and so he was just having a fantastic time."

"And everybody in Iron Maiden—Bruce, Steve Harris—we were all just sort of . . . you see, we all worked together before. Iron Maiden and ourselves were on the tour circuit in England for a long time before we got a recording contract. So, we knew them, you see; we'd come across each other lots and lots of times. And in fact, on one bill, we played in London when Paul Di'Anno was singing for Iron Maiden—it was Iron Maiden, Saxon, and Samson, and Bruce Dickinson was singing for Samson at the time. All three of us on the same bill, and we did that lineup for about four or five shows. I mean, at that time we were all skint and got no money, and we shared a common goal."

Arguably, Saxon didn't stand a chance, because July 25, 1983, marks the release of something called *Kill 'Em All*, by an obscure pop combo called Metallica. This groundbreaking record reads like a harsh and unkind summary of all the bits of shrapnel from the NWOBHM that strike the listener straight between the eyes. Adding insult to injury, many of the most eager headbangers who bought the album wound up with an English copy, on feisty upstart Music for Nations, a phenomenon that would be repeated with regard to the band's second album. The Americans were about to take over, slaking off all the heaviness the British just brought, and spitting out any other nonsense.

Olympiahalle, Munich, Germany, November 30, 1983. © *Wolfgang Guerster*

And then on September 26, Mötley Crüe issue their second album, *Shout at the Devil*, and suddenly the metal axis shifts to Los Angeles with a resounding round of "Shout, shout, shout at the devil!" There's thrash, to be sure, but it is hair metal, through the likes of Dokken, Ratt, Quiet Riot, and, across the country, Twisted Sister and Bon Jovi, which would soon be all the rage.

The Spectrum, Philadelphia, Pennsylvania, August 19, 1983. © *Rudy Childs*

Remarks Diamond Head guitarist Brian Tatler, "Well, I suppose I thought it was strange, all the makeup and the big hair and hairspray and all that. It just wasn't for me. And I look back to the older bands, like Deep Purple, and they wouldn't do all that. It was a band that would go onstage as they were. They might have a nice shirt on, I don't know [laughs], but I thought, I don't want to be wearing makeup and having me hair done and all that. And so, it didn't really appeal, to go down the image route. It just seemed wrong somehow. We didn't want to have to do that to get noticed."

Nor did any band from Britain. Saxon shamelessly played ball for a bit (and there were Shy and Wrathchild), but in the main, records from the UK just stopped getting released in the US. Hell, they stopped getting made. Bounding up the middle was Iron Maiden, already invigorated by all those hard-won nights playing the pubs and the various lineups, arriving as a band of distinct personalities all about the music and not the image, which, more so through smarts than by accident, they relegated to their green and leathery mascot Eddie so that the guys could concentrate on what they did best.

"Eddie's a bit of a character, but we don't overuse him," cautioned Bruce, speaking with *Music Express*. "He may be symbolic of the band's image, but we only use him on stage for one number. I mean it would be really easy for us to hire people with banners to picket our concerts and create a lot of bad press, but why bother? We can sell tickets without the controversy."

Three days after the release of *Kill 'Em All*, *Piece of Mind* goes gold in the US for sales of over 500,000 albums. This marks the band's first RIAA certification, which comes two and a half months after the album's issue, and in the midst of the North American tour. By October 4, as the guys wind up their North American campaign, they receive a second RIAA gold certification, for *The Number of the Beast*. November 5 through December 18, the World Piece Tour '83 winds its way through mainland Europe, with the Michael Schenker Group as support on most dates.

The Spectrum, Philadelphia, Pennsylvania, August 19, 1983. © Rudy Childs

Meanwhile, Paul Di'Anno's much-publicized band Lonewolf is put to rest, with Paul citing lack of gigs, poor management, and fan reaction to the band's metal-lite direction as deciding factors.

Bruce Dickinson, the thespian, again from the Spectrum in Philadelphia. © *Rudy Childs*

This page and following three pages: more action-packed shots from the Spectrum in Philadelphia, Pennsylvania, August 19, 1983. © *Rudy Childs,* and *Martin Popoff archive*

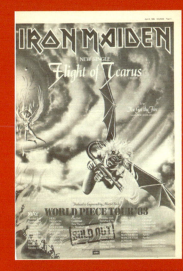

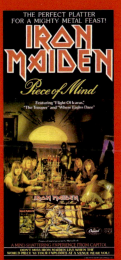

CHAPTER 5
Powerslave

"We used to call it pyramid power."

"Oh God, I was hoping you wouldn't ask that one!" laughs Paul Di'Anno, who in 1984 isn't quite killing it like his old bandmates, issuing an album called *Two Swimmers & a Bag of Jockies*, even if that was the title only in Japan. "Right, well we had a band called Lone Wolf, yeah? And then the record company decided to change the name. And what it was, you know over in London, there's the Cockney rhyming slang, yeah? It's from East London, where I come from. But we tried to put a new slant on it. And it was two swimmers and a bag of jockeys. Well, jockeys are chips, not potato chips but French fries as you call them, and the swimmers were fish, so you have fish and chips. Basically, that's it [laughs]. We must have been on drugs!"

Indeed, Paul's new band was now called Di'Anno, and the album in the West would be a self-titled. Recorded at the venerable Rockfield Studios, the surprisingly radio-friendly *Di'Anno* would be issued on scrappy small imprint Heavy Metal Records, a.k.a. FM, with the hopeful "Heartuser" being pushed as the first single.

"The closest we got to Iron Maiden was we did an album with Paul Di'Anno, and then later of course Bruce Dickinson produced the Wrathchild videos for us," notes Heavy Metal Records boss Paul Birch. "They're on Nuclear Rockout. He was an interesting man, very clever. Paul Di'Anno didn't enjoy great health, to be fair. He was managed by a husband and wife, the husband being Olav Wyper, interesting chap, who founded Vertigo. And I'm not sure just how many people acknowledge that, because I was a big fan of Vertigo. I mean bloody 'ell, anybody interested in rock music should be, because we've got a lot to thank Vertigo for, frankly. Certainly, the album that Paul came up with for us was a lot lighter, AOR kind of lighter. And I'm not sure that was exactly the right direction for Paul. I went to a lot of Paul's gigs, and we never saw audiences of more than three hundred people. This would be 1984, but then it was something new."

"It was funny," recalls Loopy, "being at home and not expecting a knock on the door. Paul Di'Anno is standing there, and I go, 'Aren't you supposed to be somewhere?' 'No, I've quit,' which is actually his version. I don't know whether he jumped or whether he was pushed, but we ended up sort of hanging out together again, and that's when we started putting together Lonewolf. That's when we started putting all that together. I don't think *The Number of the Beast* with Paul would've worked. And the *Di'Anno* album, the very first one, that was originally Lonewolf. He used most of the members from Lonewolf, except he used a different drummer. But no, they went off to do that at the studio in Wales, Rockfield. There were keyboards, there were backing vocals, the songs are very American oriented. I've heard better, but I've heard worse. Middle ground, if you like. By that time, I think I was back with Maiden."

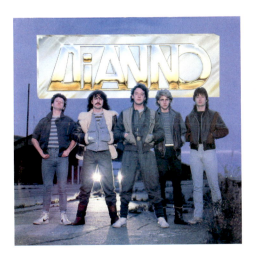

Front cover of the *Di'Anno* album.
Dave Wright archive

Not anything new, thank you very much, would be the next very dependable and sturdy raft of songs from Paul's old band. Iron Maiden would deliver on the promise both of *Piece of Mind*'s stack of songs and the five guys who played them. What I mean by that is, first, stylistically, there'd be no wavering, and second, the chemistry of the band, now with Bruce and Nicko, would be further underscored—if anything, the guys found themselves loosening up across the performances on what would come to be Iron Maiden's fifth album.

Some of this surely comes out of the band's proven and winning formula. Rigidly sticking to their tidy year-by-year compartmentalization, the guys took three weeks off over Christmas and early January, before returning for writing and inspiration to the Channel Island of Jersey off the coast of France. February through June 1984, the operation transitioned (again like last time) to Compass Point Studios in Bahamas for drinks and takes.

"We were pretty well behaved, actually," remembers Adrian. "It was a fantastic environment, in some ways, to work. It was beautiful. We had apartments right on the sea. The studio was right there. It was very isolated. Every now and again we would get what we would call island fever, and we all had to go into Nassau and party for a couple of days. But we did manage to get quite a bit of work done amongst all the fun. Not much arguing about anything. I think that might have come a little bit later [laughs]. At the time, we were kind of riding a wave and having a great time and flying high.

"Sort of the same," figures Smith, on whether *Powerslave* would constitute more work than *Piece of Mind*. "We had a process set up. We would go to Jersey and rehearse for a month or six weeks and then go to the Bahamas for a couple of months and then go mix it. It was about the same, three months."

"Yeah, we saw Robert Palmer a few times, and Talking Heads," points out Dave, twisting the tale toward somewhat surreal (Talking Heads' *Speaking in Tongues* would be partially recorded at Compass Point). "The drummer from Talking Heads lived down there. And obviously there were a lot of reggae bands coming down and recording there. We saw Eric Clapton down there. It was just a great working environment. Obviously, we focused on doing the album, but you could also chill out at the same time. There were three, four studios there, and there would be a poolroom at the end of them, so between takes we would go in there and hang out, play pool, and you've got these guys in dreads, all these Rasta guys, and they were just really cool guys. You would walk past and listen to this stuff coming out of the studio, and it was that real heavy reggae, great sounding stuff. So that just gave you a little twist, a complete opposite. Opposites attract, you know? [laughs]. You've got the one studio with the heavy rock thing going on, and then next door you've got this reggae thing happening. It was a nice contrast, and they were really interesting. We would just sit there and chat with them and stuff, hang out; really cool dudes."

While Maiden were ensconced in their sunny self-imposed exile, metal life went on around them. In March, Samson issue *Don't Get Mad, Get Even*, that band's second album featuring Bruce's replacement Nicky Moore on vocals. Two singles are floated from the record—namely, "Are You Ready" and "The Fight Goes On," but two months later the band calls it quits. Up into September, a slapdash Samson compilation would emerge, on Thunderbolt, called *Last Rites*. Paul Samson quickly disavows the release, cognizant that it hails from a different time and space, the songs amateurish, albeit featuring a certain very famous lead singer.

On April 16, Saxon issue their *Crusader* album, which is seen as a bit of a sellout after the ferocious *Power & the Glory*. Recorded in LA and produced by Kevin Beamish, the band's sixth record represents a bellwether that the NWOBHM is on the decline. If a leading band like Saxon is losing steam, maybe the whole scene is fit to be buried. Further confirmation of that nagging thought comes on July 24, when Metallica issue their second album, *Ride the Lightning*, a heavy metal masterpiece that makes the most-powerful and most-professional NWOBHM statements of all time look twee and thoughtless by comparison—even if Maiden are still in the ascendance commercially, creatively they suddenly now look old-school.

In any event, the first spot of new music we get from Maiden is a tidy bit of truly lovable songwriting in the form of "2 Minutes to Midnight," issued in picture sleeve on August 6, backed with a cover of "Rainbow's Gold" from aforementioned one-record Newcastle band Beckett. Also included is a gut-busting backstage Nicko rant that is given the name "Mission from 'Arry." The loud 'n' proud A-side presents Maiden as keepers of the NWOBHM flame, admirably, against the pressures there must have been to suppress the band's Britishness. As to why the band had now emerged as the only keeper of the NWOBHM flame with a career, Steve figures, "It's difficult to say, but I think it really all boils down to songwriting and strength of material. Because I think that's the key. You can be the best singer in the world, and if you're not singing or playing great songs, people aren't going to want to listen to 'em. But I think the songs are really, really strong. The standards that we set for ourselves are really high, and to me it's that, mainly, I suppose."

Even before the record's out, Maiden get themselves together and begin touring. August 9 through September 8, the band conducts the mainland European leg of their nearly two-year World Slavery tour, in support of the upcoming *Powerslave* opus.

No longer with the band, guitarist Dennis Stratton has to admit that Maiden had won by this point. "Out of the New Wave of British Heavy Metal . . . see the thing is, when I was growing up, I was listening to Uriah Heep and Deep Purple. David Coverdale has always been my favorite

Martin Popoff archive

Maple Leaf Gardens, Toronto, Ontario, Canada, November 30, 1984. © *Martin Popoff*

vocalist, with Paul Rodgers. Next generation, the bands that you had coming from England at the time were Tygers of Pan Tang, Def Leppard, Saxon, Maiden, Samson. There were bands that were all trying at the same time, which was the NWOBHM, but Maiden had the biggest record company in EMI. We were all doing the same-sized shows, but it was only a matter of time, when it got to the 1980s, that you saw that Maiden were gonna keep going up and up and up and up and other ones were falling behind. I think that goes to show now.

"The biggest surprise was Def Leppard, who couldn't play a gig in England," continues Stratton, in 1984 trying his hand with his own glossy AOR band, Lionheart, and a debut record called *Hot Tonight*. "They couldn't sell a record and yet they went to America, and they became huge. That just goes to show, just 'cause you're not big in your own country, it doesn't say you can't do it somewhere else. When Def Leppard came back to England, I did a tour with them with Lionheart after Maiden, because we actually had people coming to our shows. They had to have three or four bands on the list because they couldn't sell tickets. Then they get a multimillion seller in America. It was just strange. But that list of bands on the heavy metal side of it were also-runners. They just didn't have what Maiden had."

But proving the axis had shifted, making Maiden an outlier, the fifth Monsters of Rock, or Donington (conducted mid-August, just as Maiden's record was about to emerge), features Mötley Crüe, Accept, Y&T, Gary Moore, Ozzy Osbourne, Van Halen, and headliners AC/DC. There's a complete absence of NWOBHM acts, and in fact very little British content at all. Again, the presence of Mötley Crüe on the bill represents a paradigm shift toward hair metal and the dominance of California, regionally speaking, that would persist for the rest of the decade.

But then it's Maiden's day in the sun, with September 3, 1984, marking the release date of *Powerslave*, the band's fifth album in five years. Widely viewed as "son of" *Piece of Mind*, the album nonetheless was well received, vaulting Maiden onto exalted metal par with Ozzy Osbourne, Scorpions, Van Halen, and Judas Priest (i.e., playing the same type of US hockey barn circuit, while representing—and championing—a new heavy metal generation), even if their sound looked somewhat conventional against the likes of Metallica, Slayer, and Anthrax, not to mention the new meta-Maiden as it were, Queensryche.

"It was a nightmare," laughs Derek, on the *Powerslave* album art, fresh and nonmetal of color, globetrotting of theme. "It started out . . . Steve had this picture of these five guys dragging this pharaoh's head along, some engraving he'd found. I started drawing it and it just grew and grew. I started on a little piece of A4 layout pad; it's like tracing paper. So, I started drawing it on that, and then I ended up with a piece of paper . . . it's like patching pieces of paper together, because it kept getting bigger. And in the end, I went to Rod, and it was about sixteen pieces of A4 paper that were all patched together. 'Look, I've done this. Should I paint it?' And he said, 'Yeah, all right then' [laughs].

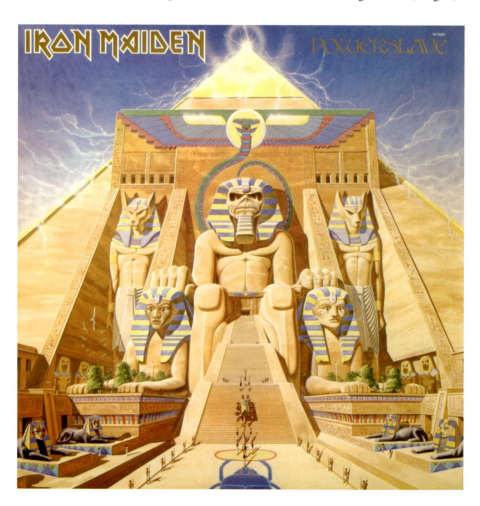

Dave Wright archive

"And I was in the Bahamas at the time. They had flown me over to the Bahamas for some reason. And it's a nightmare over there if you want to do a painting. You couldn't get the paint. I had flown the paint over. I had to fly an easel over. Couldn't get an airbrush. Had to fly an airbrush over. Had to fly my brushes over. Then I started work, and I got some sheets of drawing board flown over. Because the island sold nothing. It was like they've got four tubes of water painter something, and that was it, on the whole island, some of these kiddies' palettes [laughs].

"So, the airbrush and the compressor and all that were flown in, and then I get a sketch and started working, and, well, it was very humid there. It was coming into summer. And when you compress humid air, it compresses the water out. The water condenses out. And so, it started spitting big gobs of water at my painting. And I was working in watercolor, so this wasn't really appreciated [laughs]. So, for the next five hours, I was trying to remove this blodge from Eddie's nose. So that had to stop. So, we got a water filter, and that didn't really get it. And what we ended up with, I was in this little room somewhere. So, we had a dehumidifier working at one end, and had about four of these air filters that were supposed to remove water from the air, in a row, and it was still spitting sometimes. And it took ages, because every time I felt like it was going to spit—because you could kind of tell after a while—I had to squirt it on a piece of rag or something. It took ages, and it was a nightmare. You think going down to the Bahamas, it's lovely, but there's nothing much to do. And then when your equipment doesn't work, it gets a bit painful."

Dropping the needle onto *Powerslave* back in 1984, I remember thinking, well, here's the new "Invaders" and not being particularly thrilled of that comparative. But "Aces High" is better, and it's grown in stature over time. Lyrically, this is one of Steve's World War II tales, identified that way mainly through the reference to the Me 109, which is what the Allied forces called the Messerschmitt Bf 109. Amusingly, the nuts-and-bolts telling evokes images of Maiden gearing up to hit the stage, no doubt armed and ready with a fast opener like this one.

Reinforcing the narrative moving forward, the band would intro the song with an iconic bit of spoken word Britishness. On June 4, 1940, Winston Churchill makes his classic wartime speech of defiance. This the band would use as the intro to "Aces High" in the live setting, again, Maiden tacitly drawing parallels to themselves as battle-worn Englishmen with stiff upper lip defiantly delivering old-school metal despite being dismissed as iconoclasts. Unsurprisingly, the song is also partially inspired by the 1976 movie of the same name.

In any event, the gaffer-taped construction of "Aces High" reveals a barnstormer perhaps only one brick short of a full load, evidenced by a nice enough musical intro that pointlessly dissolves into an unrelated verse, perhaps the first clue that this record will be less brilliantly and logically conceived versus *Piece of Mind*, yet somehow more in the lively metal spirit of things. Indeed, after the rootedness of its predecessor, "Aces High" and what was to follow felt like the last-minute homework turned in by a Maiden on a merry metal roll, drunk, punked, and randy, a somewhat ragged, wayward affair that was a kitchen sink catchall, but fortunately the work of a band in their element—for a magic moment, a band that could do no wrong.

Adrian figures that "Aces High" set the tone for a bracing level of productivity for the songs to come. "The first time we played that was in Jersey, where we used to rehearse, in the Channel Islands. It's a typical Iron Maiden song, one of Steve's better songs, I think. It's really exciting and up tempo. It was like, yeah, if this is how this album is going, this is going to be a great album."

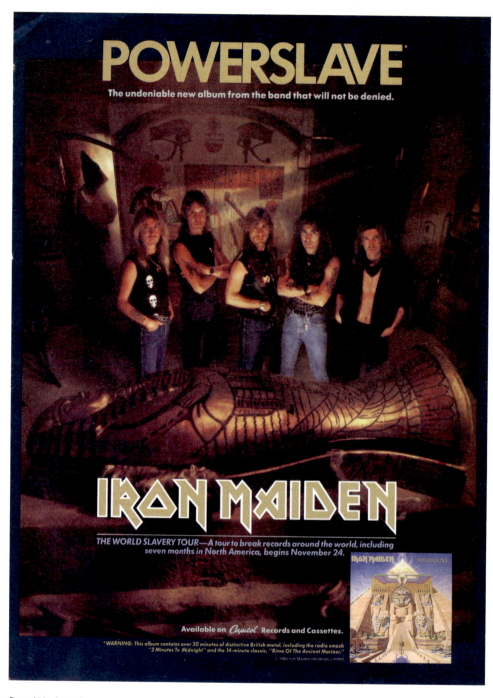

Dave Wright archive

"Aces High" was issued as a single on October 22, backed with "King of Twilight," yet another obscure cover, this time the band celebrating proggers Nektar and their 1972 album, *A Tab in the Ocean*. Maiden's take is actually a melding of the last song on that album, "King of Twilight," and the one just before it, "Crying in the Dark." This was also released in 12-inch and 12-inch picture disc formats, with the additional B-side being a live version of "The Number of the Beast."

In 1953, both the US and the Soviet Union conduct tests of thermonuclear devices. It is the only time in history that the "doomsday clock," initiated by scientists at the University of Chicago in 1947, reads, as Bruce Dickinson phrases it on the *Powerslave* album, "2 Minutes to Midnight."

"Well, that's basically a hard rock tune," chuckles Adrian, "People know me, and that's what my thing is in the band, and it runs through to what I did with Psycho Motel. I'm guitar oriented. That's where my writing goes. I was one of the first of us to get a little four-track, a multitrack sort of recorder, and I was sitting in my hotel room in Jersey working on this riff. And there was a banging on the door, and it was Bruce, because we had taken over the whole hotel to rehearse, and he's banging on my door and saying, 'Wow, what's that riff?' So, I played him the music to it, and he had a bunch of lyrics and he started singing and we had '2 Minutes to Midnight.' We wrote it in about twenty minutes [laughs]."

Whatever its germination, it wins the day for Maiden by being a rare title we might call "rock 'n' rollsy," fresh, riffy, something that is inherent in Adrian's playing more so than Dave's. Essentially the song steps outside the half-dozen rules to which Maiden is by this point becoming increasingly tethered. It is mature, dangerous, groovy, and lyrically intelligent, and yes, effortlessly groovy, something you might hear from more of a lunch bucket NWOBHM band.

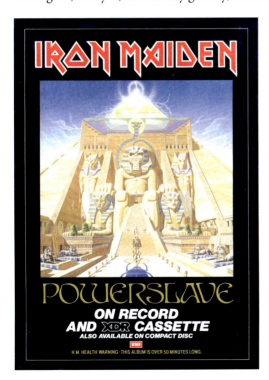

Dave Wright archive

"Bruce wrote the lyrics to that," Dave told Steve Newton back in the day, "and apparently, it's about the doomsday clock—when it strikes midnight it's like the end of the world. It's probably something that he feels strongly about, and it's good that he can express it through writing the lyrics."

Indeed, the lyric was timely. Moved up to two minutes back in September '53, with Reagan conducting a chilly cold war with the Russians, here in 1984 the clock had moved from twelve minutes to midnight in 1972 back up to 11:57. Steve later intimated that the message is less about the Cold War and more about the romance of war, people's fascination with the topic. In 2018, the clock was back at two minutes to midnight, due to the threat again of nuclear war (traditional but also from rogue nations) but also to the threat of catastrophic abrupt climate change.

One B-side to the single release of the song is the aforementioned Beckett cover, "Rainbow's Gold," but there's comedy gold too. "Mission from 'Arry" is nothing more than a type of surveillance recording, captured back on August 18, 1983, in Allentown, Pennsylvania, of Nicko throwing a tantrum about being interrupted during his drum solo. And he's friggin' got a point—the request was reasonable, albeit badly delivered. Steve's bass rig was acting up, so the "mission" was to get a roadie to tell McBrain to extend his solo. Frustratingly, repeatedly, Nicko couldn't hear what he was on about, and it threw him off his game.

Next up is "Losfer Words (Big 'Orra)," which is a pretty standard galloping instrumental, not particularly action packed (i.e., pretty much able to support a vocal without sounding weird). Still, there are interesting shifts passage to passage. But again, the song betrays a scrappiness of sound and devil-may-care execution not evident across the previous record's more-sober performances. For example, Steve's bass has gotten more articulated toward the likes of John Entwistle, Geddy Lee, Chris Squire, and Lemmy, not in the realm of buzzy, more so, as Paul is wont to say, "clacky."

Next is "Flash of the Blade," a combative if workmanlike quick-paced rocker albeit blessed with a killer intro riff. Lyrically, it's essentially three vignettes, concerning a kid playing with a wooden sword, a roustabout, and then a fencer. It's not much, but one can ponder which one of the latter two used to be the "young boy chasing dragons."

"Yeah, that was a good little song," recalls Adrian, "one of Bruce's; a good, tight little song. We never played it live, but I enjoyed playing it in the studio. I actually added quite a few more guitar lines to it. A lot of the harmony stuff you hear, I actually overdubbed. Good little song. And everybody knows Bruce is a fencing nut."

Further on the subject of twin leads, Adrian explains that "We actually used to work separately. Dave would go in for a couple of days and do some solos, do some guitar lines, and then I would go in and do my solos and put the harmony to what he'd done. And if it was Steve's song, Steve would be there, but both of us were in there, just making sure it's what he wanted. He's very meticulous about his stuff, you know. But on 'Flash of the Blade,' for example, there were certain parts I didn't feel were strong enough, so I overdubbed harmonies myself on top of what was already there. So occasionally we would do separate harmonies, but mostly we would do them together."

Steve's galloping and somewhat shuffling "The Duellists" closes side 1 of the original vinyl. It's a bit of a *Piece of Mind* rehash—"Where Eagles Dare," to be specific, or, for that matter, this record's "Losfer Words (Big 'Orra)", further evidence that quite possibly the guys' well of creativity is becoming a bit parched, with the band now having made a full first pass through the traditional manor house home library, brandy snifters in hand (even if for a spot of positivity, Adrian is quite pleased with his guitar solo in that one).

Side 2 of *Powerslave* has its own problems, but the guys put on a brave face, starting the proceedings with "Back in the Village," a boisterous knees-up romp propelled by a complex and fluid Allan Holdsworth–like riff, along with piquant and sophisticated vocal phrasings from Bruce.

Notes Adrian, "That was a riff I had been playing all through the previous tour at sound checks, and people kept saying you've got to do something with that riff. So again, Bruce and I got together, and we came up with the idea, 'Back in the Village.' He's a real fan of that old British TV show *The Prisoner*, and I think the lyrics are all involved with that. It's a song we also did in the Untouchables [one of Adrian's fun bands during his '90s hiatus], and I actually sang it, believe it or not [laughs]."

Indeed, September 29, 1967, marks the first broadcast date of hit British crime drama *The Prisoner*, inspiration for the Maiden track of the same name on *The Number of the Beast*, as well as this *Powerslave* pacemaker. Bruce's lyric is stuffed with imagery, and yet it's kept quite abstract. The fighter pilot vibe to some of the lines brings consistency with "Aces High" and indeed the violence strung across every other song thus far in terms of lyrics.

Powerslave's title track is arguably the album's second-most-convincing composition after "2 Minutes to Midnight." It triggers the Egyptian musical theme carried over to the cover art, with fully two-thirds of side 2 containing these Jimmy Page / Ritchie Blackmore Middle Eastern tonalities if one takes into account much of closing track, "Rime of the Ancient Mariner." Our dateline takes us back to 2500 BCE, where Horus and Osiris are referenced in the Egyptian pyramid texts. Both music and lyrics are credited to Bruce, who tells the story of a dying pharaoh, rueful of his brutish life and incensed that he must die, having lived his life as a god, or so he thought.

"In fact, the theme of the album is contained in the song 'Powerslave,'" explained Dickinson, to *Enfer*'s Philippe Touchard. "The other songs deal with completely different things. 'Powerslave' tells us about a dying pharaoh. He's about to die, and he finds himself a slave to the power of death, as well as the slave to his own power. When a pharaoh dies, all the slaves that built his grave and prepared his funeral have to die too. Even if he didn't want it, his power implies without questions that these people must die, far beyond his own will. Basically, he's a prisoner of his power. The power has got its own logic in order to last, and that means that those who want it have to be sacrificed. It's horrible! In Egypt, the pharaoh incarnates life, he's a living god, and controls the essential substance of the earth. When life departs his body, it must also quit the bodies of those who served him, as the rule dictates. The paradox is that even if he's a living god and decides on his deathbed to carry on living, well, he can't. His power is enslaved to the power of death."

Dave Wright archive

Speaking about Derek's artwork for the cover, Bruce says, "The concept that you find on the cover deals with the typical Egyptian philosophy. After we trepanated Eddie, we made him reborn in another world, and his power has been amplified, as you can see from the illustration itself." Bruce adds, somewhat tongue in cheek, "You must look for the answers in the illustration. In fact, there are many clues all over that cover, and if you find them all, you'll get the answers to your questions."

Olympiahalle, Munich, Germany, October 24, 1984. © *Wolfgang Guerster*

Continuing with his analysis, Bruce explains that "at the beginning of the song, the pharaoh dies. At the end of the song, he's still alive, but a change has occurred. His spirit is still alive and tries to break free from his dead body."

Dickinson divulges that he came up with the idea for "Powerslave" "while having breakfast. I was thinking about 'Revelations,' on the previous album, and I was looking for something missing. And I indeed found a 'missing link.' In 'Revelations,' there are all sorts of signs related to the Hindu and Egyptian mythology about life and death. But there was something missing: the power of death over life, which is a theme you find very often in Egyptian mythology. So, I basically wrote 'Powerslave' while listening to 'Revelations,' a cup of tea in one hand and bacon in the other."

Asked by Touchard if there are lessons here for Western civilization, Bruce figures, "Yes, in the way that power is always in the hands of a few privileged people who won't let go of it. The power gives them a certain status, and this status makes them slaves to their power. In Egypt, power was spiritual before it was material. In our society, it's the opposite. There's been a great awareness of this phenomenon when people in the US started imagining that Nixon could start World War III. I hope people who listen to this song will draw the same conclusions. If not, well, never mind; it would have just been another good story to tell."

At the musical end of "Powerslave," if the verse is sturdy, the chorus is panoramic, even more successful, assembled almost like a song in itself, building to an apex before nomads on camels invade for another verse.

"I'll tell you a great story about 'Powerslave,'" says Adrian. "We were in the Bahamas, and, like I say, we used to party a lot. I had been in the studio with Martin Birch and the engineer, and we had finished the night before and we'd been working quite hard, so we decided to have a little bit of relaxation, if you know what I mean. Anyway, about five o'clock in the morning we were all kind of staggering around, and I said, 'Look, man, I've got to go to bed.' So, I left, fully expecting to have the day off the next day.

"And then the phone rang at about two o'clock in the afternoon, and it was Martin. He was the last person who I expected to hear from. And he was slurring, 'Come down to the studio and let's do some work.' And I thought, oh my God, no. So, I went down to the studio, and apparently he had been up drinking with Robert Palmer all night, because he lived next door to the studio. So, Robert Palmer is sitting there in his dressing down, and they were both drinking tequila and they wanted me to work. And I was completely hung over, and I felt like death, and I was totally intimidated because Robert Palmer was there, big-name guy. And I plugged my guitar in, and I think I did the solo in 'Powerslave,' my first take. I don't know how I did it, because I felt at death's door. And Robert Palmer was jumping up and down and really getting off on the track. It was bizarre. And then after that we went home and slept for a couple of days."

In 1797 and 1798, Samuel Taylor Coleridge writes "The Rime of the Ancient Mariner," published in his book *Lyrical Ballads*. A few years later, excerpts of the long poem are nicked for *Powerslave*'s epic 13:45 closing track of the same name. The song is a live favorite of both Bruce and Steve, with Harris taking sole credit for the song, meaning music and lyrics. A suite of many movements; central, however is a time-honored Maiden gallop, punctuated by an extended rhythmic windup.

"It was definitely a lot of work," recalls Adrian. "Steve walked into the studio and said, 'I've got this song,' and he held the lyrics up and sort of let the paper go, and it came down to the floor, you know what I mean? And so, Bruce was doing the guide vocal when we were rehearsing it, and we had to get something to pin the lyrics to so we could read them. And we found this huge stepladder and pinned the lyrics to the top of the ladder so they could hang down and you could see all the verses. We used to call it pyramid power."

"Yes, there was a ladder," adds Dave. "This ladder had been sitting in the studio, and it was kind of like the pyramid thing. Someone took it away, and that's when everything started going wrong. It was one of those jinx things, so we had to drag the ladder back in again, and everything got moved up again. But basically, those songs were great for playing, and they stood the test of time; plus, they were great for touring."

Because this idea of tapping classic literature more or less point blank for adaptation into song is still a somewhat fresh idea within the Maiden camp—Rush is a good predecessor with "Xanadu"—"Rime of the Ancient Mariner" was enthusiastically accepted by fans of the band, and it lives on as a classic. The song is perhaps in need of a bit of an edit, but only

Maple Leaf Gardens, Toronto, Ontario, Canada, November 30, 1984. © *Martin Popoff*

a bit. Somehow the energy of a good Maiden gallop is maintained, most likely due to the song's circuitous yet catchy riff. It is also inspiring how the song does not begin with one of Steve's dreary intros—we are into the thick of the action immediately. But Steve gets us back later, dredging the melancholy feel of those sailors parched and dying without a drop to drink. I would think that the last thing they want to hear is a bass solo from Steve.

Amusingly, Dave cites a tale similar to Adrian's with respect to "Powerslave" (and in fact, he might be referring to the same couple of days). "Martin was part of the band, really. In fact, there was one song I remember, 'Rime of the Ancient Mariner,' and we were recording that in the Bahamas, and Steve was working on the song, and we're thinking, okay, this is kind of like a free day. So, everyone was out, and we were drinking a few margaritas and basically just chilling out. And suddenly early afternoon we got a knock on the door from Martin, and he was standing there, sort of like the headmaster; 'We're going to go in and start working on this song' [laughs]. So, we all went in a little bit worse for wear, but we got through it. So he would be there like any producer, keeping you on your toes. But that was a pure innocent mistake. We thought it was a nonworking day there, but we went in there and we still got it. And that was kind of like a fifteen-minute song or something, so we kind of had time to get our heads around that. But he was great, the captain of the ship, and he was basically gluing everything together, holding the thing in place, although we kind of knew as a band anyway what we wanted to put down."

Speaking with Steve Newton back in the day, Dave explained that "Steve has always been interested in English literature and all that. It's a Coleridge poem, and it's long, so Steve sat down and read it and interpreted it in his own way. He actually wrote the song when we were recording the album in the Bahamas. I remember when he first came out with the lyrics—there were pages and pages of them. And it's good because we don't really stick by the mainstream and just write three-minute songs. From each album we've had a song which is maybe eight or nine minutes—like on *Piece of Mind* it was 'To Tame a Land.' We like to make big songs, like a short story really, and try to make them as interesting as possible. But probably the hardest song to record on the album was 'The Mariner,' because it was the only one actually written in the studio. Steve and Nicko put the bass and drums down, then me and Adrian would come in with the guitars—we were actually in there learning it as it was coming along. But it was great fun because it kept us on our toes."

In the harsh light of history, Maiden have found themselves in the fortunate situation where camps are divided with respect to what their favorite Maiden albums are, with interesting arguments to be made for any number of them. *Powerslave* and the two before it are often mentioned, as is, oddly enough, *Seventh Son of a Seven Son*. Whatever the preference, *Powerslave* is somewhat of a lightning rod, inextricably linked with *Piece of Mind* and then debated against it endlessly. Comparatively, it is the work of a Maiden unleashed, maybe even off the cuff, more energetic but almost hyperactively so, running on fumes. It also marks a point where the sands of time shift between the old, succinct Maiden and a band with many more-progressive elements. It is an unhinged record of many motivations, and for that reason always an interesting scrapyard to revisit, the listener always energized, both physically and mentally challenged, upon exit through its front rusted gate.

Victory, 1984. © Martin Popoff

With the band's wild new songs barely caged, now it was time to tour—and what a heroic odyssey it would be. September 11 through October 12, 1984, the World Slavery tour blankets the UK, with support coming from Waysted, featuring Pete Way and Paul Chapman from UFO. Big UFO fans, Maiden also took out MSG previously, featuring another UFO member, Michael Schenker. October 15 through November 14, the tour transitions back to mainland Europe, this time with Mötley Crüe in tow, a trip behind the Iron Curtain a highlight for the boys.

"Well, that was a great experience," remarked Dave, speaking with Steve Newton. "We did ten shows there altogether, and the reaction from the kids was superb. It's so rare that you get bands going over there. For one thing, you can't buy records over there much, which is a drag. You have to get people to send you albums. They're pretty much suppressed when it comes to music, so when they do get a concert it's incredible. They were saying that it's probably the first—and maybe the last—rock concert they'll ever see. So, it was really emotional in a way.

"There was a riot squad, they had strict security, and by the end of the show the guards were jumping up and down. We've got quite a collection of police hats at the moment, you know, which we're gonna auction off at the next gig. I'm not sure exactly how we got over there really—it was done through our agency. We just got our visas and everything. Actually, they gave us a great welcome when we got there. There were all these soldiers at the airport, because quite a few fans turned up. And a TV station turned up. It was great.

"We might go back in 1986," continued Murray. "But we filmed everything for a documentary when we were over there. It went out on MTV about a month ago. So hopefully we might have opened the doors now for more bands. We've also been to Japan twice and Australia once, and in Japan the audience is like 95 percent female. And they're very polite. They come to the concert, and they're not allowed to get up in their seats, so they all sit down. I mean it's all girls, right, and they just . . . you know, it's great! And in Australia there's the hard-core heavy metal fans, who are pretty much the same all over the world. They've got their own fashion—they all dress the same with denim jackets and patches."

On October 23, 1984, Maiden issue their third video package, a live set called *Behind the Iron Curtain*. It consists of two live tracks and two studio tracks plus interview footage, totaling thirty minutes. Meanwhile, also this month, Stratus, featuring a couple of Praying Mantis guys plus ex-Maiden drummer Clive Burr, complete tracking in Frankfurt for their *Throwing Shapes* album, which will emerge in early 1985.

On November 7 the band receives their third US certification, when *Powerslave* goes gold two months after the record's release, just in time for an eleven-date cross-Canada tour leg November 24 through December 3, support coming from Twisted Sister. "Losfer Words (Big 'Orra)" and "22 Acacia Avenue" would be dropped from the set list at this point as the band transitioned to the Canadian dates of the tour.

Recalls Twisted Sister's Dee Snider, "We did the *Powerslave* tour, and I don't know if it was the biggest Eddie, but it was one of the biggest Eddies. They called it Eddie on a stick. He used to burst out of the *Powerslave* logo at the end, and it was just an upper torso, and he was matchsticks [laughs] and he was on a cherry picker. It was hysterical how big Eddie got. He's one of the biggest-selling merchandising things. I know at some point they were frustrated by Eddie being more prominent than the band was, visually. They went through a period with that, where they sort of were frustrated to be overshadowed by their own mascot. But I think they eventually realized, hey, fuck it, we're making a lot of money off of this damned mascot. He was entertaining. But yeah, he got bigger and bigger with each tour."

A month into the North American campaign, *Powerslave* would go gold back home in the UK, for sales of over 100,000 units, just as an expensive version of Frank Herbert's sci-fi saga *Dune* written and directed by David Lynch hits theaters, reminding fans of a fine song from Maiden's previous record.

From December 10, 1984, through March 31 of the following year, the band executes the first of two American legs on their exhaustive World Slavery tour, with Twisted Sister continuing to support, along with sporadic shows from Queensryche, W.A.S.P., and Quiet Riot, with Bruce telling

Bruce takes us back to ancient Egypt. Maple Leaf Gardens, Toronto, Ontario, Canada, November 30, 1984. © *Martin Popoff*

Hit Parader at the time, "The stage set we're using this time was specially designed for us. We wanted something that would tie in with the theme of *Powerslave*, which is Egyptian mythology, so we put together the idea of constructing an Egyptian temple complete with hieroglyphics and tombs. It's quite spectacular to look at, and even more fun to play on. That's an important factor for us—when you're working in the same environment every night, you might as well enjoy where you're working."

"We love the road," added Steve, in the same chat with Rob Andrews. "That's something that will never change. When we write songs, we're always picturing how they will sound when we play them in front of an audience. This tour is unquestionably our most complicated ever. Before, when we would be special guests on someone else's tour, we'd just throw our gear aboard and have a great time. As headliners, you're responsible for everything. You obviously stand to gain a great deal more financially as the headline band, but there's a great deal more work involved as well. We all get very excited before we go on stage, and each of us have [sic] different ways of showing it. Some of us tune our instruments; others take a drink and sit quietly. Bruce just gets himself mentally prepared. He channels all his energies into the performance. He has to expel more energy than the rest of us, and he feels the need to prepare himself for the effort.

"People sometimes ask me if I get bored by the music Maiden plays," continued Harris. "They seem to feel that all our songs follow a similar pattern. Obviously, those people aren't familiar with our music, because our real fans often criticize us for changing our sound too much from album to album. There's no way the material on *Powerslave* sounds similar to the things that appeared on *Piece of Mind*. Sure, there's an Iron Maiden style, but the songs have little in common. We've covered different lyrical topics this time, and we presented them in a more refreshing way."

Amid Maiden creating their magic moment, with this live and lively band operating at the peak of world excitement for what they were selling, a small gig signifying a further changing of the guard is taking place back on the band's home soil. On December 20, Metallica play a one-off at the Lyceum. Support on the night is Tank and Bernie Tormé's new band Tormé, both of whom sound dated, arguably to the point of irrelevant, next to the American bounders. It is an ultimate irony that Metallica's drummer, Lars Ulrich, turned out to be so much of a Maiden fan that he was one of the few American musicians to go through the trouble to travel to the UK to witness the NWOBHM movement close up. The lessons he—along with his buddy Brian Slagel—took away from the experience would change rock history forever.

"It was the energy," reflected Lars, on the scene Maiden had led proudly, chin up. "First and foremost, there was a different energy. If you do a quick lineage thing here, the NWOBHM was basically hard rock metal's answer to the punk movement, which got off the ground in England 1976/1977 type of thing. And the punk movement was basically a direct contradictory element to the kind of bloated dinosaur rock of the 1970s. There was just a whole group of people in England who felt disenfranchised and could not relate to the Zeppelins and the Genesises and the Deep Purples and the Pink Floyds, and the Emerson, Lake & Palmers and the twenty-minute keyboard solos and that bloated, let's all take a big pile of drugs and just watch these people do their thing.

"So punk, three-minute songs, it became all about the idea that the audience could do what the people onstage were doing, and it became kind of a bond and all of us as one and that type of stuff. But with punk, it was mostly about energy and about kind of doing it yourself. And there were a bunch of the metal dudes that then took the energy and the spirit of punk but made the riffs heavier, made the riffs a little more blues based, made the riffs a little more intricate, and there was just a slightly different level of musical weight to it. The NWOBHM, spearheaded by Iron Maiden, Saxon, Diamond Head, and some of these bands, was just metal played with the energy and the spirit of punk and the accessibility of punk and how the musicians were sort of on the same level as the audience and everybody felt they could relate to each other. There was a big kind of lovefest between the audience and the musicians, you know?"

"I think it was a big change," agrees Steve, "because a lot of bands had a different attitude and wanted to prove themselves and wanted to do something a little different to what had gone on before. I think it was still a lot of influence. You could still hear all your influences coming from the early stuff, but it was just a different edge to it, that's all. And the new young fans out there, it was their music as well. It became a thing that they got behind because they felt that it was theirs."

But by this date, certainly, as 1984 comes to a close, it was all over. A tight fistful of UK bands crossed the ocean, experiencing varying degrees of success, but most just hung it up. Everything that was magic about the NWOBHM was now being demonstrated and experienced twice as hard and twice as fast by the likes of Lars and Slayer and Exodus and Anthrax.

"Obviously you can't just keep going, can you?" shrugs Brian Tatler, of Diamond Head fame. "And the press always wanted something that was new. And at that point, a couple of bands had shown themselves as the forerunners, and they just focused on those bands, and everyone else would just drift away. And that's just the nature of the beast,

Eddie invades the Olympiahalle, Munich, Germany, October 24, 1984. © *Wolfgang Guerster*

isn't it? How many punk rock bands survived the punk explosion? There were hundreds of punk rock bands, and there's only a couple survived, didn't they? You know, the Clash and the Damned went on; the Sex Pistols didn't last for long, but everybody remembers them. But the same thing happened with New Wave of British Heavy Metal. There were apparently about four hundred bands that claim to be New Wave of British Heavy Metal, and there were only a couple of handfuls that made a good living at it and are around to this day making records.

"At the time, generally, a lot of fans continued to follow Iron Maiden, and then you had Saxon, Van Halen, Scorpions, AC/DC, Judas Priest, all those bands who pretty consistently were releasing albums. Dio came along. They probably just swallowed up anybody they could get their hands on. I can remember when our *Canterbury* album came out; it was a faulty pressing. The first 20,000 copies jumped, and people would take it back to the shop and get another copy. And then that jumped, and I remember this chap said, 'I took your album back,' you know, ten times or whatever, and then he eventually bought *Holy Diver* [laughs]."

Adds Tygers of Pan Tang's Jess Cox, "In every genre there's two or three bands, and that was Iron Maiden and, to a point, Saxon, but really it was Def Leppard and Iron Maiden. I just think England is very fashion led and they were ready for the next thing. They went on to a thing called "new romantics," which was kind of Spandau Ballet and whatever else; they just went that way. On the metal side, I think it was kind of the Mötley Crües of the world and whatever else started to take up the flame."

'Arry puts in another day at the office, playing Toronto's largest hockey barn. © *Martin Popoff*

"It was probably because it was such a pigeonhole to put bands into," figures Kevin Riddles, former Angel Witch and still struggling late with Tytan. "To call us the New Wave of British Heavy Metal suited at the time, but you couldn't be sort of post–New Wave of British Heavy Metal. You can't be one of those bands . . . if you weren't there at the time, you were not New Wave of British Heavy Metal. And a couple years down the line, of course, it wasn't new anymore. It was sort of the old New Wave of British Heavy Metal, if that makes the slightest bit of sense.

"And of course, the whole sort of anti-epic rock 'n' roll movement was in full swing. You were starting to get the new romantics and those sorts of people, postpunk, the sort of punks all grown up, wearing face paint and stuff. You saw Adam Ant and Siouxsie and the Banshees, fantastic people and brilliant material, but obviously they were filling the space that punk and rock had been occupying.

"And also, this was combined with, especially in the UK, a lot of clubs closing down that were putting on live gigs. Because disco was king. You could literally open up a club for like twenty bucks, because all you needed was a sound system. You didn't need to put in stage lights and PA and God knows what else. You just needed to have someone come and spin the records, and you would pack the place every night. That's where, in inverted commas, 'music' went, in the mid- to late 1980s. So, the Soundhouse was one that shut down, for a start, that Neal Kay had in Kingsway. Places like the Music Machine suddenly became . . . what the hell was it? It was bought by Steve Strange from Visage; he bought the club and turned it into a nightclub. And you had to be the right sort of person to get in there, that sort of thing. Places like the Bouncing Ball in Peckham was great, the Cats Whiskers in Wardour Street, and even the Marquee club, also in Wardour Street, closed down."

"All they wanted was to be given a chance," sighs Neal Kay, spark-lighter of the NWOBHM flame for Maiden and so many other bands, really, only a short five years ago. "A lot of them probably knew that they weren't going to go far for a million different reasons. But the thing is, all they wanted was that chance to be a hero for fifteen minutes, to be somebody for fifteen minutes, to have somebody listen to their music, and until all this happened, no one was. And I personally thought that was utter shit, you know?

"And it awakened a kind of a passion in me, something, I don't know. It was like a war thing—I just had to go. I had to do it. Something made me do it. It may have been God-directed or spiritually pointed or something, but I had to do it. I couldn't not do it.

"I've always felt that I've been proud to have anything to do with it, actually. I mean, basically I was a furniture trucker at the time, and I got given the opportunity, the chance, the one in a million to make a difference.

"I didn't realize it at the time—and I am utterly convinced that no matter who you interview—at the time that it happened, none of us did. We just followed our heart and our soul and our spirit and our drive. We didn't do it to be remembered, we didn't do it for the media; we did it for rock 'n' roll. And if you're a real rock 'n' roller, that's all you can ask of anybody. I mean how they speak of you afterwards, how they label you, what they say about you is all in retrospect, because most of them weren't bloody well there anyway.

Munich, Germany, October 24, 1984. © *Wolfgang Guerster*

"It's the same as any great band of brothers that find themselves together in a moment in time with a huge objective that they must win," concludes Kay. "The guys that spend time fighting the war, the Second World War, the real band of brothers, if you want; their lives were changed forever by the experiences that they underwent. There always is going to be a band of brothers, where the winning requires extreme action of one kind or another. And when you're together there's an incredible sense of being together. That is the brotherhood. And if the Soundhouse started that, then I'm more proud than ever because it's nice to know that as we all get older, that spirit, that thing, that indefinable thing, it matters to people so much that they still have that spirit in them today—it's the only way to live."

"It was a journalistic conceit—there you go" is how Bruce remembers the NWOBHM. "That's what it was. Quite a bad one, as well, because who else would have thought up such an unwieldy and absurd title? They must've been rumbling around in their beer when they drafted it up. And they did dream it up. It was dreamt up at a drinking session at, you know, *Sounds* magazine, I believe. And so now having served up this movement, they now went out in search of it."

"But I think to an extent, they were just looking at the success that punk had had, and they sort of go, 'Well, we are kind of caught with our trousers down here.' You know, 'Why didn't we get a bullshit movement? Why don't we invent our own bullshit movement and call it the New Wave of British Heavy Metal?' Because punk was a bullshit movement. Nobody knew they were supposed to be punk, and all of a sudden everybody was putting their safety pins through their nose or trousers or whatever; it was a fashion thing. And so I think it was their revenge on being caught unawares.

"There was no explosion of bands. These bands didn't explode. They'd been around for years. I hate to say it, because it's not very romantic or anything like that, but if you look back on it, it's a question of some clever guys doing some great marketing, and some guys who wanted to sell newspapers. And it worked. It could sell newspapers. People went, 'Hmm, well, a new movement; yes, I can get into that.'

"And all of a sudden they went to see all these bands," continues Dickinson, part of four of them. "Some of them were terrible, some of them were quite good, some of them should have done better than they did, and some of them were thoroughly excellent. You know, some of them didn't deserve the success that they subsequently attained. By hook or by crook, they were manufactured, they were molded, they were picked up, other people sang their parts. Session musicians came in and played on their stuff, and in that respect the music industry has not changed in two hundred years. Because Tin Pan Alley and all that stuff, in which songwriters came in and a guy sang a song that he was paid to sing and dressed up in a silly suit and had a hit, that was all going on at the turn of the century. So, nothing really has changed.

The two originals, Dave and Steve, in Toronto. © *Martin Popoff*

"But in the end, the bands that have the longest longevity have got something about them that is special. And actually, most of them are special, way outside whatever genre gave them the little catalyst, whatever gave them the little nudge onto the first step, so that people noticed them. What people noticed about them was that they were different. And when they went to see them live, they were extraordinary. And that's why those bands happened and are still around."

Opposite
Top: two more shots from Toronto. © *Martin Popoff*
Bottom: across the pond in Germany. © *Wolfgang Guerster*

Above: FM Records does their part in trying to make Paul an AOR star, issuing this ad to the UK music newspapers.
Martin Popoff archive
Top and right: Olympiahalle, Munich, Germany, October 24, 1984. © *Wolfgang Guerster*

This page and next three: Ohio Center, Columbus, Ohio, January 5, 1985. © Rod Dysinger

Chapter 6
Live After Death

"Five young guys steaming around the world on tour buses."

For five years running, like clockwork, Maiden dropped upon its fans a studio album, reflecting the visions and ambitions of the guys' favorite rock 'n' roll heroes from the 1970s and the crazy schedules they kept until they burnt themselves out. But for 1985, Rod and the band had another ace up their sleeve, one that also reflected 1970s traditions; namely, a double live album gate-folded and stuffed with pictures.

Live After Death would document the red-hot World Slavery tour, which was still ongoing as 1984 ticked over into 1985, kicked off with a career highlight when, on January 11, the boys invade Brazil. "I suppose when we played in Rio in 1985 was amazing," recalls Steve, asked for milestone moments. "We weren't headlining, but we were special guests of Queen and Whitesnake and a few other bands on the bill. It was the first time we played a major festival, with like 300,000 people showing up. So that always sticks in my memory. Also, the first time we headlined Donington, or both times really. But the first time really, because we had over 100,000 people there, in our own country headlining."

On March 15, Maiden's Long Beach concert is captured in audio and video for use on the upcoming live package, with Bruce specifying that "*Live After Death* was not just one concert. It was assembled out of different songs from different nights. We recorded at least three nights, and then we assembled the best out of those three nights."

With Long Beach safely put to tape, from April 14 through 25 Japan gets to experience Maiden's World Slavery tour, with the band playing eight dates before moving on to Australia for seven dates in May, supported by Aussie biker rockers Boss. Back in North America, on May 20 and 21, Dave and Adrian guest as primary rhythm guitarists on the song "Stars," in Hollywood, for Ronnie James Dio's *Hear 'n Aid* charity project in support of famine aid for Africa.

In peripheral Maiden news, also this year, supergroup project band Gogmagog record a three-track EP consisting of "I Will Be There," "Living in a Fucking Time Warp," and "It's Illegal, It's Immoral, It's Unhealthy, but It's Fun." The band lineup is Paul Di'Anno (vocals), Janick Gers (guitars), Pete Willis (guitars), Neil Murray

Dave Wright archive

Dave Wright archive

(bass), and Clive Burr (drums). Also, in 1985, Clive, along with members of Praying Mantis, is featured on *Throwing Shapes* by Stratus, formerly Clive Burr's Escape.

"For the Gogmagog project," explained Burr, "I have to say that it was a bit like, 'This is *the* next band, something that'll become big, huge' and so on. We were conditioned to reach this goal. We'd just recorded our first EP, *I Will Be There*, but our management didn't support us tooth and claw. It was the same with the record company. They didn't put out a promotional campaign worthy of this name in any country. It's a shame because it was basically a good band. None of us wrote anything except Jonathan King [producer], who wrote all the tracks. Once again, this project was his idea; it was his band. We simply were playing the songs he'd submit to us in the studio."

Having helped Ronnie, two days later Dave and Adrian are back in the fold for a second extensive North American leg of the World Slavery tour, this time with Accept supporting on most dates.

On August 3, *Billboard* magazine celebrated Iron Maiden with one of their famed "dedication" issues, in which multiple ads are run featuring various segments of the music business congratulating the band on their success. Into September, the US Senate begins hearings on obscenity in rock, prompted by the activism of the Parents Music Resource Center, or PMRC. Dee Snider and Frank Zappa famously speak against censorship, and

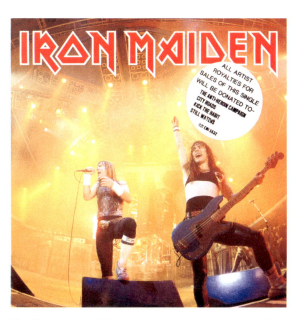

The "Running Free" live single, along with an ad for it. *Dave Wright archive*

although Iron Maiden doesn't make the list of the "Filthy Fifteen" most-objectionable songs, the band is regularly pilloried, along with Ozzy Osbourne, Led Zeppelin, Mötley Crüe, Kiss, and AC/DC, as being among the worst of the devil-worshipping heavy metal rock acts messing with the heads of America's teenagers. Predictably, it's really down to the band calling one of their records *The Number of the Beast* and then putting a monster and the devil on the album cover. But a picture is worth a thousand words—Eddie is everywhere in 1985, and, barring any study of the situation, he's viewed upon as evil.

Four days after the hearings begin, September 23, Maiden issue the "Running Free" single, backed with "Sanctuary" and "Murders in the Rue Morgue," all songs performed live. It's billed as a double A-side, given that "Running Free" and "Sanctuary" had been the band's first two singles. Adding value to the item, "Sanctuary" and "Murders in the Rue Morgue" would not be songs featured on the band's forthcoming first live album. Additionally, all royalties from the single are earmarked for charity, the recipients being the Anti-Heroin Campaign, City Roads, Kick the Habit, and Still Waters. Said Bruce Dickinson, in a statement, "We certainly hope that all metal fans have the sense to say 'No'—remember, sport and music is a far better high than any drug, so take care."

Then it was time. On October 14, 1985, Iron Maiden issue their first double live album, *Live After Death*, with the multiformat video release following on October 23. Remarked Steve, speaking with Winston Cummings from *Hit Parader*, "The idea of releasing a live LP has always been very exciting for us. It's perhaps the ultimate Iron Maiden album. We've always considered ourselves a live band, and the chance to do a live recording that captures the energy and excitement of one of our shows is one of the big thrills I've had. If it was possible, I'd love to try recording an album of new material live, sometime in the future. You know, write new songs, rehearse them, play them in front of a crowd, then release the new tracks in album form."

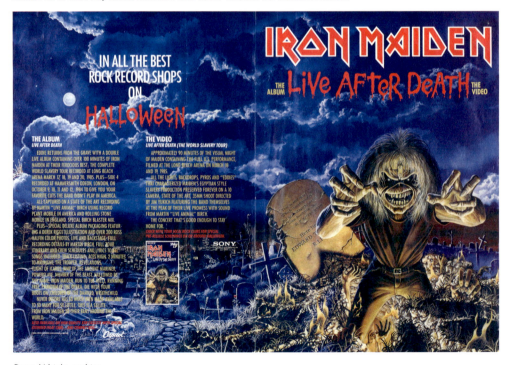

Dave Wright archive

Derek Riggs outdid himself on this one's cover art, going with a relatively monochromatic blue-and-yellow theme. Then there were the usual in-jokes. "The tombstone on the front with the Lovecraft quote, I just put it in. They didn't have any say in it. My suggestion for the title of the album was *Let It R.I.P.*, as in Rest in Peace. But they didn't like that because it had wit and intelligence. I thought it was quite good because it's something they never do, 'rest in peace.' Iron Maiden . . . get a life [laughs]. It's not going to happen, you know? On the back, you've got Live with Pride on one of the tombstones; that was a slogan that was going around for live music or something. They asked me to put that on there. There were a lot of things against disco and lip-synching in those days.

"The cat is from way back," continues Derek of the halo-topped kitty, also on the back cover, lower right. "That goes right back to *Killers*. Because it was an alleyway, it was an alley cat. So, the cat was floating around for years, and I just stuck the halo on him and made him look sinister because 'What's that all about?' Well, it's not about anything really—it's just a cat with a halo [laughs]. I'm good at making things look unusual and sinister. There's this idea I came up with to get people's attention; you've got to get people to look at something and wonder what it's about. And the best way to make people wonder about something is to do something a little bit weird. It's not there because it's great, deep, and meaningful. Its total reason for being there is to make you go, 'What's that there for?' That's all it's there for. That's its total reason for existence. To make you stop and go, 'What's that all about then?' The rose on the grave, Here Lies Derek Riggs, R.I.P., I killed myself. This thank-you on the gravestone . . . do you know what that's about? 'Thank you' on a gravestone: it's the Grateful Dead! [laughs]. Here lies Faust in body, only because Faust sold his soul to the devil. Part of him is missing."

Live After Death is one of the rare covers that has a full-blown alternate piece of art lurking in its nether zones. "Well, you see, it was wrong, in my opinion," explains Riggs. "They wanted Eddie coming out of the grave going, 'Grrrr.' A figure coming straight towards you has no dynamics. It just looks static; you can't get movement side to side when it's coming straight at you. It doesn't really do much. So, I was never really happy with that figure. It just wasn't really happening. But the background was more fun. You went across the graveyard, and it had a little tiny Michael Jackson and dead people coming out of the grave, and in the background was, I think, the house from *Psycho*, on the hill. But then it was an oil painting, and it was pretty large."

A trio of backstage passes. *Dave Wright archive*

The label centerpieces featured a blank tombstone, with Eddie's hand emerging from the grave. "That was designed so they could put the song titles on, obviously. I did that one bigger because I thought they might want to use it for other things. You get the image and then you work it. So, the image sticks in people's minds. And you know, it works. As I've said, you get the image, and you work it around. So, it's done basically for the label, but it was also used for adverts and probably on T-shirts somewhere. It's *Carrie*, the horror film. You know what happens at the end with the hand coming out and it grabs the girl or whatever? I'll steal everything. I'm not proud [laughs]. If you've got a good idea, I'm going to get it off you."

Into the record, and the band opens with the excerpt of Winston Churchill's famous June 4, 1940, House of Commons speech before the band tears into "Aces High." The sonics of the album are visceral and the performances tight and brisk. Side 1 of the original vinyl progresses to "2 Minutes to Midnight" and then a three-pack from *Piece of Mind*; namely, "The Trooper," "Revelations," and "Flight of Icarus." Bruce periodically ducks notes, and he's a little flat on "Revelations," but this is a man working through demanding songs, running all over the stage, and doing it in the midst of an epic tour.

Side 2 features "Rime of the Ancient Mariner," which is somewhat undermined by the musical passage evocative of the ship stuck with no wind. Wind temporarily out of the show's sails, we're soon into "Powerslave" and "The Number of the Beast" to close out the side.

Pull the second vinyl out of its own glossy sleeve plastered in live photography and we get "Hallowed Be Thy Name," "Iron Maiden," "Run to the Hills," and "Running Free" for a nice trip down memory lane. All of this thus far is from Long Beach, but the five performances on side 4—"Wrathchild," "22 Acacia Avenue," "Children of the Damned," "Die with Your Boots On," and "Phantom of the Opera"—are from the Hammersmith Odeon in London, October 8, 9, 10, and 12. Steve kind of wished the whole album could have been done at the Hammersmith Odeon, but he found himself pleasantly surprised by the band's performances in California—and why wouldn't you want the milieu in the mind of the listener to be of a certain type of elevated victory, specifically that of East End Londoners conquering the hockey barns of America? As well, this way the video would match up to the audio better. The band had director Jim Yukich on the case, shooting two of the band's four shows from that stand, March 14–17, 1985.

All told, the track list of the album had the catalog evenly represented except for *Killers*, which contributes only one track; a 1995 reissue of the album would add "Losfer Words (Big 'Orra)," "Sanctuary," and "Murders in the Rue Morgue".

Is *Live After Death* the first and last great heavy metal live album of the 1980s? Possibly so. First off, none of the big new 1980s bands, Maiden's contemporaries such as, say, Def Leppard, Mötley Crüe, Bon Jovi, or Guns N' Roses, or, downwind, Saxon, Krokus, Y&T, or Accept, struck when the iron was hot with a standard-issue deluxe double record like Maiden's. Second, with all of the 1970s bands who put together fan-lauded double live packages in the 1970s, even if many of them did a double live in the 1980s—Rush, Blue Öyster Cult, Thin Lizzy, Scorpions, Deep Purple—it was unanimously seen as inferior to the first one. Priest followed a classic single with a droopy double, while UFO followed an even more revered double with nothing at all. Kiss did two in the 1970s and none in the 1980s. Sabbath finally put out an official live album, but it was with Ronnie, and then Ozzy did two double-lives, but both of them were special cases.

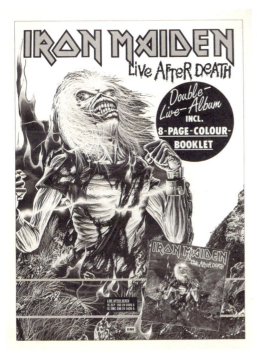 

Two full-page ads from the British music newspapers. *Dave Wright archive*

And then there was *Live After Death*, essentially Kiss *Alive!* for and from the NWOBHM, flung to the seething Maiden masses from the vantage point of the band's white-hot peak, the guys tearing it up around the world and barely containing their youthful superlatives on vinyl.

"It's hard for me to say what *Live After Death* means to other people," reflected Adrian, speaking with *BW&BK*'s Dom Lawson in 2008, on the occasion of the release of the video version of the album on DVD. "I can only say what it means to us, and I suppose it represents the high point of our success, particularly in America, during the 1980s. Doing the four nights at Long Beach Arena was a pretty big deal for us. I suppose to real Maiden fans it would represent something special—I can see that. Some of my all-time favorite albums have been live albums. Like Free's *Live!*, if anyone can remember that! It's not about technical perfection—far from it. In the first song on the Free album, something goes wrong with the guitar, and then it drops out and there's all this spontaneous stuff going on. To me, I found that very exciting when I was a kid, so I can relate to the way people feel about *Live After Death*. It's got energy. I watched the video a couple of years ago. We were about to go out on tour, and I wanted to get back into the vibe of it, and I thought, 'That ain't bad!,' you know? If you see us playing live, it all makes more sense. If you were an outsider, you probably wouldn't get it, but if you can see the energy of us playing as a band, it makes all the difference.

"It was just a very creative time," continues Adrian. "There was lots of touring, lots of energy crackling around. We knew we had to write an album each time, so we always used to go away to prepare. We had a routine. We'd go to Jersey after Christmas to write the album, and then we'd go to the Bahamas to record it. It sounds amazing, doesn't it? And it was [laughs]. I remember that we used to go to Jersey and not do anything and cram ideas in the last couple of weeks. It's like anything else though. We needed a bit of pressure to get the creative juices flowing and to get you working. I think we're still coming up with good stuff, but back then it was the coming together of the creative side and all that energy from all the touring we were doing. We played to so many people, it had to be inspiring for us."

Wrote Lawson, reflecting on the significance of the record from his 2008 vantage point, "It's hard not to be envious of the thousands of folks who actually saw Iron Maiden at Long Beach Arena back in March 1985. But then those of us who have worshipped at the altar of Iron Maiden for the last three decades have spent so much time immersed in *Live After Death* that it's almost as if we were there, in spirit if not in body. Aside from being able to cite verbatim Bruce Dickinson's onstage banter, there will be plenty of people reading this who can quote facts from the album booklet—152,000 watts of power coming from those front-of-house speakers, right? Four miles of cable? 6,000 pints of milk?—like sacraments from some divine nostalgic ritual. But for Maiden themselves, the relentless trek around the globe that was the World Slavery tour has now been reduced to a warmly remembered blur; a pivotal moment in their career, of course, but one that they were far too busy to truly appreciate at the time. 322 days on the road, anyone?"

"I've never really gotten to grips with this live album business," opined Robbi Millar, reviewing the record for *Sounds* back in 1985. "But this *Live After Death*, this four-sided, glossily packaged, warts 'n' all monster monolith, this just might make me change my mind. Because it is quite possibly the best record Iron Maiden have ever made. No bullshit! All it really takes to make a great live album is a great live band—and Maiden are surely amongst the guardians of the genre, one of the few bands who truly understand it, swallowing the heat 'n' dust and spitting out an atmosphere fraught with tension, communication, straight down the line. Recorded at Hammersmith and Long Beach, California, on the '84/'85 tour, Martin Birch at the controls—and all wrapped up in a photo-line gatefold, Eddie reincarnated on the graveyard sleeve, fact-pack tour mag within—this album is more than a live collection. It's a document, a synthesis of the workings of a rock band who have deservedly taken this decade by storm. History. Make it part of yours."

Dave Wright archive

As a postrelease birthday present for the band, on November 1, 1985, *Killers* received its gold certification back home in the UK. As the years rolled on, *Killers* would represent a kind of odd and somewhat forgotten period in the band's history. Even if the self-titled debut is the comparatively wobblier record of the two, the pushing forward and perennial celebration of "Phantom of the Opera" and "Iron Maiden," and to a lesser extent "Running Free," would keep *Iron Maiden* firmly in the hearts and minds of Maiden fans as the decades mounted.

Before the year is out, German "power metal" band Helloween would arrive on the scene with their full-length debut album, *Walls of Jericho*. The band was quickly framed by journalists and fans as a younger, flashier, more frantic and speedy version of Iron Maiden, proving the dictum that a band always has to keep progressing and looking over its collective shoulder for the next wave looking to make a play for first place—just like Maiden did in 1980. So now there were bands proposing to beat Maiden at their own game—Helloween, yes, but also Queensryche, Dio, Fates Warning, and soon Blind Guardian and Gamma Ray. And then there was the whole other newer thing, the bands of the thrash "Big Four," who were going to make Priest and Maiden and any of their imitators sound like anachronisms, antiques to be handled with care and put in the corner.

But that's no reason to stop. Especially if you've found a sound all your own and you believe in that sound. On December 2, 1985, EMI issues on behalf of the boys the "Run to the Hills" single, backed with "Phantom of the Opera" and "Losfer Words (Big 'Orra)," again, all tracks performed live. Two weeks later, Maiden receive their fourth RIAA gold certification, this time for the new one, *Live After Death*. The next day, December 19, for a spot of fun, Adrian Smith re-forms Urchin for a live gig at the Marquee Club (also including in the lineup Nicko McBrain), the results of which are issued as the low-key *The Entire Population of Hackney*. Members of Maiden cameo at the relaxed show, and fully three compositions performed at the show would be covered by Maiden and used as B-sides on the band's forthcoming singles, continuing the tradition of value for money that Rod so admirably pushed in all facets of the band's business.

Dave Wright archive

"It's difficult to remember those times," says Smith, in closing, on the World Slavery tour (slavery, yes, but for whom?). "It's one of those things where you're on the road for six or seven months and then you realize that you're only halfway through. Mind you, we did it, we reached the end, and that's what matters. That's what bands do at that stage in their careers. You go out for a long stretch or a couple of long stretches. I'm sure we're not the only band to tour that much, but maybe we're the most high-profile band to do it. We just wanted to play anywhere and everywhere.

CHAPTER 6

Live After Death–era publicity shot. Dave Wright archive

"It was five young guys steaming around the world on tour buses, so of course there was a fair bit of partying," continues Smith, allowing himself a wry smile. "I think it was worse before that tour, to be honest, when we were the support act. Then things were a bit more out of control. But when we started headlining, I think we started to get a bit more professional. You had to be onstage for two hours every night, so you couldn't afford to be too tired or hung over. Inevitably we were, sometimes, because of the nature of the schedule, and if you weren't careful, you'd get into a cycle of always being tired. But youth is a wonderful thing, isn't it? You can just do it. Your days are mapped out for you. That's the wonderful thing about being on tour. All you have to worry about are those two hours onstage. The rest of the time you're just being carted around like pieces of equipment. That's the game.

"I suppose it's surprising, but we did all get on pretty well," he shrugs. "We had our moments, but I won't go into that! [laughs]. It would be naive to think that we all traveled together and lived together for thirteen months without someone getting on someone else's nerves. If you put a group of people together for that length of time, under that sort of pressure, that it's always going to be fun . . . I don't think we had major bust-ups, but there were certainly times when you'd think, 'Oh for Christ's sake, I wish he would shut up!' or 'I don't want to be around that person today,' but you just deal with it. It was probably good that we took a break after the World Slavery tour. We had the good sense to realize that we needed a break from each other, and I think a lot of bands don't do that, and that's why it all goes wrong. They keep doing it, and it's the death knell for a lot of bands. It starts with something petty and then it festers, and if you don't have a break, it can easily get blown up. But I think we did the right thing, and we've done all right, haven't we?

"The fans come to the show, and they want to be part of it, and they are," figures Smith, on the support they get from their singing-along throngs. "It's like that cliché about a football crowd. A good crowd is like having a goal head start. You walk out, the crowd erupts, and it makes you feel at home straightaway, like you don't have to prove anything. You still do try to prove yourselves anyway. We've got our standards! But the Maiden fans are very passionate and warm and responsive, and it's a privilege to walk out and play for those people. We've all spent a large part of our lives on the road and making records and building a following, so it's a nice payback to walk out there and get that kind of response. It makes me feel 10 feet tall sometimes; it really does."

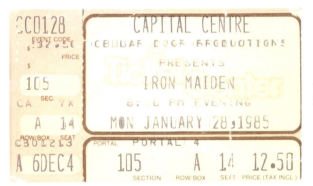

Were you there to witness the World Slavery tour? *Martin Popoff archive*

CHAPTER 7
Somewhere in Time

"I was absolutely shattered mentally."

After a much-needed five months off, in January 1986 Maiden commence work on what will become *Somewhere in Time*, recording rhythm tracks at Compass Point in the Bahamas before moving to Wisseloord Studios in Hilversum, Holland, to record guitars, vocals, and the band's new controversial guitar synthesizers. Mixing then takes place at Electric Lady Studio, in New York City.

Remembers Dave, "Half of that, bass and drums, was recorded back in the Bahamas; then we decided to leave there and record the other half of it, guitars and vocals, in Holland. That was another album where the actual tour got, as far as production goes, huge. We had inflatable space cars, flying saucers, icebergs. Everything was big. It was just a sign of the times as well."

Explained Steve of the break, speaking with *Enfer*'s Pierre Thiollay, "Bruce was practicing his favorite sport, fencing, Nicko was perfecting his flying, Adrian went fishing in the cold streams of the Canadian Rockies, Dave, who just married a lovely Hawaiian girl, was enjoying his new house next to a gorgeous beach, and I played football. We all needed some rest, and it was very important that we could let off steam, independently of each other. We'd been leading a very 'metal' kind of life, as you say, for the past six years, and this was a necessary break. Necessary for ourselves and our health, therefore our lives, which was at stake, and also for the band, because such a 'metal' lifestyle could've threatened its cohesion and unity. Life on the road causes inevitably some tensions, and now we're almost all married and have children. We have to consider the needs of our wives and kids, so we have to come home from time to time. I'd be extremely pissed off to have a successful 'public life' while my private life suffers from it. I can't even imagine that."

And Bruce was most definitely serious about the fencing, explaining to *Hard Force* magazine in April 1987: "I just passed the exam I had been preparing for for a while. It's only a start in the apprenticeship of the field: teaching fencing. Summer, after the tour, I'll take more exams for a week or two in order to perfect this. You get better every time. In January 1986, for instance, I changed my stance. Knowing that my father is ambidextrous—left-handed, in reality—and that I have some slight coordination problems with my movements, I switched to my right arm—I've really progressed since! Much more evolution than in the previous seven years of practice and using my left hand in competition. Who would've thought that I was ambidextrous too?

"But I can't do it as often as I'd like," continues Dickinson, at this point becoming a Renaissance man of sorts, and progressively over the years adding more dimension to his persona. "At times I can practice two days a week, at most. But I'm on the road the rest of the time. I keep fit through my performances onstage. That's real sport! In the changing rooms, I always have my equipment with me. So, when we tour, I always try to find a fencing club on the way, more precisely in France and Germany. Before the Somewhere on Tour, 1986, 1987, I trained in Offenbach, five days a week in a very tough club, including a 5-kilometer run every morning. Sport physically develops me, and the tour keeps me fit."

Back home, Bruce was practically a country squire. "I've got a large house with a massive garden. I have two dogs. In the house, I love this little room, a kind of library where I have six hundred or seven hundred books. I write some songs there, finding the inspiration in front of my window. I love reading. My sources of inspiration are quite diverse, and I use old books, like the one I recently acquired, published in 1890, which deals with fantasy and imaginary subjects. I like magic treatises, occult stuff. I'm less interested these days, though, as I found out that a large number of those books are pure bullshit."

Leading up to the release of the record, Bruce told Nelly Saupiquet from *Hard Rock* that "unlike what we usually do, we didn't write anything while on the road, and we've had a six-month break. For the previous albums, at least one of us was writing stuff while on tour. But as we never took any holiday, we arrive in the studio in a state of excitement, with the right number of songs for the release of a record. This time, however, there's been some innovation! We got together in Jersey at the beginning of January, and we were all slumped! Absolutely everyone had written songs, and I don't mean only the music, but the lyrics too. Let's see . . . I had at least nine songs, so had Adrian, but Steve was the worst: he had written so many songs that he could've filled up the album by himself! After much choosing and clearing up, we have now only nine left, but they're absolutely superb.

"I personally use an acoustic guitar, which isn't always the best," continued Bruce, on how he writes. "All the songs I'd written sounded very much like Spanish folk music, and I didn't even realize. I remember, in Jersey, playing my serenades to Steve. Everybody was in stitches! So, there's only one song from me, four from Steve, three from Adrian, and one from Dave."

Of note, however, is that in the end, there would be none from Bruce. It's a strange episode, this acoustic song thing. Somewhat smoothed over, essentially this is Bruce addressing his strong instincts that the band was stagnating. As he put it, it was time for Maiden to come up with their *Physical Graffiti*, and of course *Somewhere in Time* would be far from that. The way would be paved for Bruce to eventually depart after too much more of the same. Ultimately, the conclusion a sensible student of Maiden would have to arrive at is this: a hard look at the catalogs of both Maiden and Bruce Dickinson as a solo artist would reveal *The Chemical Wedding* as the best album-length artistic statement Bruce would ever craft. Shocking, but, again, a conclusion that is sensible. With a few of his other solo records in the running as well.

"The album is very different from the others," framed Dickinson, feeding the press machine. "It's the best one since *The Number of the Beast*, but I don't mean that we used drum machines or synthesizers—not at all—and we're not going to do it. There's a lot of feeling, a lot of space, on this album. It's not going flat out either; we really worked a lot on this album. There are a lot of melodies, guitars, vocals, and choruses. The vocals are sometimes very bluesy, and I'm proud of that. Wasn't I a blues singer in the past? There is also some singing in a very open 'operatic' style. It's the diversity that I like so much in this album. You'll see—no one will be disappointed."

Adrian has a fond memory from the mixing trip. "Yes, I remember *Somewhere in Time*, in New York, Electric Lady Studios, it was me and Martin Birch and the engineer, and we were listening to a mix. Steve was there but he had gone off to get a couple of drinks, and we said let's go back to our hotel and listen to it on the little system in the room; so, we went back there. We've all had a few drinks by this time, and I had seen Tom Jones in the bar earlier. And they didn't believe me. This is quite a nice hotel in New York, Parker Meridian. I swear I saw him; they say, no, no. Anyway, we're sitting there listening to music, and there's a knock on the door, open the door up, and there's Tom Jones. He's got a bottle of champagne in one hand, cigar in the other hand, and he's got this really rough voice. He said, 'I heard the music; do you mind if I come and have a listen?' I said no. So, he came into my room with his bodyguard—it was actually his son—and we sat there all night, talking, drinking, listening to music; it was great. It was like being in the room with a living legend. And he had these contact lenses, and his eyes were like shining [laughs], so it was a bit weird."

Dave Wright archive

Meanwhile, as the video version of *Live After Death* goes gold in the US, over in a parallel universe Paul Di'Anno's Battlezone issue their debut album, *Fighting Back*, in July 1986, on Raw Power Records in the UK and Shatter Records in the US. But our intrepid exile as usual is finding it hard to come up with lyrics. "Oh, that's the one," laughs Paul. "I hate doing that. I have a little tape recorder under my bed, and it's not very nice when you're with your girlfriend. It's like, 'Wait a second, hang on, I've got an idea.' But when I'm at home, I watch TV, and something will catch me, and I will elaborate on that or something I see or read. Most of the stuff is what happens in real life. I'm unhappy with myself sometimes. I read about three or four books a week. I'm an avid reader and I collect books as well. Unfortunately, they are very limited. I like thrillers, espionage thrillers, because I think they're the most devious people in the world, aside from politicians. The person who can write a great espionage novel is absolutely brilliant, the devious tricks they get up to. I don't know, it just makes me happy to think that there is some fucker who is worse-minded than I ever could be."

Turns out to be a pretty good album, *Fighting Back*, but then it's time for Maiden to answer, with the first spot of new music from the band since two years earlier, pretty much to the day. On September 6, 1986, Maiden issue "Wasted Years" (working title "Golden Years") as a single, backed with an old Adrian Smith project song, "Reach Out," and "Sheriff of Huddersfield," a joke track needling manager Rod Smallwood for moving from the UK to LA, specifically the Hollywood Hills.

Quick to follow is the full record, on September 29, with Iron Maiden presenting their sixth studio album, *Somewhere in Time*, which, again, will feature no Bruce Dickinson songwriting credits across the entire record.

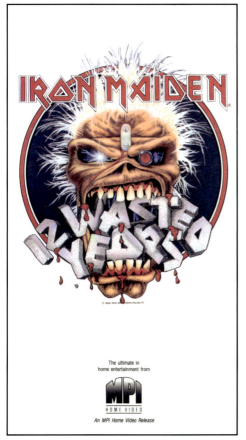

Dave Wright archive

"Well, I haven't listened to that album for ages and ages and ages," explained Bruce, years down the line. "My thoughts on the record are so colored by the state of mind I was in when I recorded it. And I was not in a great frame of mind when I did it, really. We came off the *Powerslave* tour and I was absolutely shattered mentally. I wanted to take a big, long break, and I actually was going to take such a long break, but I wasn't even sure I was ever going to come back. To music at all. Because it was doing my head in. And we took a break, and not really for long enough, certainly for me, and we came back and started writing. And I had a combination of, I didn't know whether I was enthusiastic about writing or not or whatever, and I had this vague sense that I wanted something to be different, but I didn't know what it was. And anyway, I ended up not writing anything for the record. And I thought maybe I should just be the singer. You know, just chill out, take a back seat, just be a singer, and have a rest while you're singing [laughs]. And I kind of chilled out after that, and it put me in a good frame of mind for *Seventh Son*."

Interesting comment, and prophetically the album would mark a slide in enthusiasm for Maiden from the outside as well. Complaints would come about the record's so-called guitar synths, which you'd think the guys would have avoided, given the drubbing that Judas Priest had just taken for the idea on their *Turbo* album, released earlier in the year.

Subtly, perhaps the band was becoming more about catalog at this point. After all, simultaneous with the release of the new record on October 2, *The Number of the Beast* becomes Iron Maiden's first RIAA platinum album, the band celebrating sales of over a million copies, although, interestingly, despite the record's positive fame and notoriety, it has yet to be certified any higher than platinum.

"Maiden never exploded," reflects Rod, stating a reality about Maiden that bugged the guys in Priest about their own band. "The first album did 350,000 worldwide, the second one did about 750,000, *Beast* did about 1.2 million, something like that. But you've got to reckon, in France alone, *Killers* did 300,000, so *Number of the Beast* was actually a letdown in France when it did about 150,000. There were markets around the world where Maiden were already very strong when America picked up on it, which was with *Beast*. But you've got to reckon, we were headlining on *Piece of Mind* in arenas at a time when *Number of the Beast* hadn't even sold 400,000 units. Do you know any band who can do fuckin' arenas without selling over 400,000 units, not even a gold record? But there was a madness about it; we had a very smart agent with us at the time, and we reckon we didn't want to support anymore, we should headline, and we just had the energy to work. The first show in North America was Seattle Arena, 11,000, sold out, and we thought we'd got it right for a change. It was a fantastic tour and word of mouth . . . jungle drums are what metal's all about, jungle drums and the web, and gossip [laughs]."

Even *Somewhere in Time*'s album cover was vaguely unsatisfying, in fact, even to its creator. "*Somewhere in Time* was a complicated picture, but it was so complicated, it all gets lost," says Derek. "It falls down a bit there. All the jokes are my idea, like the reflection in the window that says, 'This is a very boring painting.' Occasionally someone would come up with an idea for an actual picture, but the brief for this one was, we want a city more like the *Blade Runner* city rather than something like *Star Wars*. They wanted a science fiction city. So, I worked with that brief and created a picture. I had put in a bunch of well-known starships like the USS *Enterprise*, but they didn't want to get sued, so I had to take them out. But I did manage to squeeze in Batman—this is three years before the movie came out. He's on the back, standing on a ledge, which is just above the *Powerslave* cartouche.

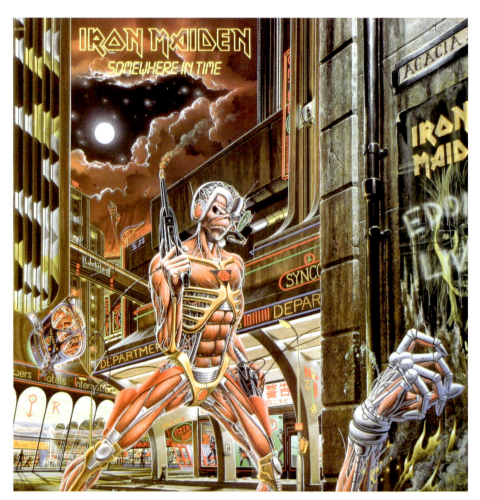

Dave Wright archive

"Webster's—that's for Charlie Webster; I'd forgotten all about him. He was the art director at EMI when we were doing this cover. This Cyrillic above the words 'Pizza Hut,' I think it says sour milk in Russian, if I recall correctly. [This might also refer to yogurt, or something short and to the point to designate a store that sold milk and other dairy products, in Russia.] The Chinese there . . . I copied it from a Chinese or Japanese magazine, and it was an advert for zit cream. I copied it, I wrote it down, and a friend of mine, who is Chinese, says, 'Why did you write that in there?' I said, 'I got it out of a magazine.' And he says, 'Do you know what it says?' And I said no. And he translated it for me and said—because a lot of Chinese is based on context—'As far as I can tell, that says: Danger, yellow bikini' [laughs].

"And Eddie's got a nuclear-powered willie," continues Derek, pointing out the biohazard sign on Ed's crotch plate. And the cramped hand rising from the lower right? "That's a joke! It goes way back to *Creature from the Black Lagoon*. Now, *Creature from the Black Lagoon*, the original black-and-white thing, was done in 3-D. He comes out from the lagoon and he kind of rips up somebody's tent and kills them. That shot, from the *Black Lagoon*, all these victims, they've all got one hand like that. They're lying on the ground, and they've all got one hand sticking up like this. And it's a joke amongst horror fans—always that hand. So that's what that is. And Eddie's actually in the pose that toy soldiers take up. That pose was always used by soldiers or cowboys. I never really knew why they were standing like that, because they weren't actually doing anything. 'Why is he pointing his gun at the ceiling, Dad?' 'I don't know, son.'"

And that space-age toaster trailing Eddie? "That's his spaceship; it's what he rides around in. It looks just a bit peculiar—I just wanted a little buggy." Adds Derek on the busy text seemingly everywhere, "I just wanted lots of logos. If you go around town, it's all company logos. So, I had to invent company logos, in order to make it look like a town. Bradbury Towers, that's a statement, not the name of the building—Ray Bradbury Towers. See, in *Blade Runner*, the building that he's in, I think it's called Bradbury Villa or something like that. It's referring to that; it's a science fiction joke."

The name "Acacia" refers of course to "22 Acacia Avenue," and below that, "That's the very first Iron Maiden poster there. And right in the middle on the front, that's the lamppost from the very first cover, complete with sign and garbage can. It all feeds back on itself. Icarus is falling off the top of that building on the back. There's some Jewish— it's God written in the shape of a man, deep mystical stuff; Jews pick up on it. That would be Caballic [kabbalistic] stuff.

"And they've got the football scores there, and *Live After Death* and *Blade Runner* showing at the cinema; Phantom Opera House, as in 'Phantom of the Opera.' Ruskin Arms, that's the pub they used to go to, and Rainbow, that's the Rainbow pub in LA. L'Amours is in New York. Hammerjacks is a nightclub in Baltimore they used to go to. There's the TARDIS from Doctor Who. Doctor Who flies around in a time machine called a TARDIS (time and relative dimensions in space). The time machine had a chameleon circuit to make it blend in with the background, but he landed in 1960s London, and it disguised itself as a police phone box, which were around in 1961 or something. But the chameleon circuit broke, and it got stuck as a phone box. So, he's flying around in a time machine that looks like a 1961 phone box.

"There's Fireball XL5, which most people don't remember—this had all the spaceships in it, didn't it? Jerry Anderson had Thunderbirds and Stingrays, and one of his early ones was called Fireball XL5, and it was a rocket ship. The one before that was called Supercar. You have to get one of the DVDs; they were brilliant, better than *Star Wars* [laughs]. And that big thing there, that's a pyramid, and we've got death floating around, and there's the Tyrell Corporation in the background. That's the name of the corporation in *Blade Runner*. They're the company that makes the clones that Harrison Ford is trying to shoot. 'The Mekong Lives in L.A.' is written just to the right of that. The Mekong is in Dan Dare, a science fiction comic book from the 1920s, 'Dan Dare, pilot of the future.'"

Continuing the tour, Derek points out that "this is whiskey in Yiddish and that's Bruce with a brain. They told me to paint portraits, and they complained because they didn't look exactly like them. Hello? They're inches tall. They're the size of postage stamps [laughs]. The whole painting would have been about 15 inches high by about 32 inches long. *Powerslave* is 23 inches, I think, because that's as big as a sheet of board as I could get, so that would have been probably 23 × 26, and we would have had to trim it down to make it square, or just paint blue at the top or something. But yes, there's Sanctuary Music Shop. There's an HMV store, because they were signed to HMV. There's Gypsy's Kiss, which was Steve's first band. There's the Spitfire from 'Aces High,' so there's the Aces High bar over there. That's a flying saucer, a UFO . . .

"And with Eddie," says Derek, getting back to the core of the busy shot, "the whole concept was that it carried on from one album to the next, which is why he kept the artificial eye and all the things that happened to him. I just like rolling him on like that, seeing what you could do with him next, which parts you could keep."

Other interesting tidbits include the clock set at two minutes to midnight, the football score with West Ham naturally ahead, a name-drop for Philip K. Dick, who wrote the book that *Blade Runner* was based on, Nicko's "Iron What?" T-shirt, the Eye of Horus, the cat with halo (see *Live After Death*), the Asimov Foundation building, and Tehe's Bar, the place where the band copped some backup vocalists for use on "Heaven Can Wait."

Dave Wright archive

Somewhere in Time opens with its erstwhile title track, "Caught Somewhere in Time," being a spirited though standard Iron Maiden gallop, an anthem built for the stage. This one's credited solely to Steve, who can be heard quite distinctly and dirty instantly behind Dave's and Adrian's dreamy intro twin leads. Before the lyrics arrive, the song switches gears and speeds up somewhat pointlessly. But soon the listener is wrapped in Steve's enigmatic lyric, with Harris inspired by the 1979 Jack the Ripper–themed movie *Time After Time*.

"The whole album deals with the notion of time," explained Steve, speaking with *Hard Rock* in October 1986. "The basic idea is the following: someone sits next to you, he tells you he's invented a time machine, and he asks you to join him in his travels. Would you go? Would you have the guts to follow him just like that, without telling anyone? And without any luggage? Would you really go? Now that I think of it, there's only one song, 'Sea of Madness,' that has nothing to do with time. All the other songs are somehow related to the idea of time. And that's only a coincidence!"

Turns out "the notion of time" weighed heavily on the recording of the album as well. "We only had a broader vision of the composition of the album and of the way it was going to sound," continues Steve. "We recorded the bass and drum tracks in Nassau, and then we went to Holland to do the rest. When everything was done, it wasn't quite what we expected. The songs were longer than we thought, and there weren't as many of them. *Somewhere in Time* is a very long album, with almost fifty minutes of music. At least the kids will get their money's worth! At first, we had many ideas and different musical themes, but as we progressed, we didn't finish some songs, or we used some parts for other songs to reinforce them. When we got enough songs, we didn't look any further."

The "Wasted Years" 7-inch. *Dave Wright archive*

Remarked Steve on his writing style, "I usually work alone. It's a habit. In the beginning I had to do everything myself. It was some sort of routine. But I did write some songs with Dave and Adrian. For this album, Adrian worked on his side. This is why Bruce didn't write anything. He used to work with Adrian, but this time he found himself writing alone. Adrian even wrote all the lyrics by himself. What Bruce had written didn't quite suit what we'd done. So, we kept his songs for the next album. As for Dave, he only writes half a song once in a blue moon [laughs]."

At the music end of "Somewhere in Time," the best twin lead comes as a preamble to the chorus, which doesn't arrive until fully two and a half minutes in. With Bruce simply singing the title stretched and crooning, the song suddenly becomes anthemic, winning the listener over. Despite the talk of guitar synths, really, the sound and composition and everything is business as usual. That kind of talk usually doesn't impress, but amid a few ideas that are a little worse than business as usual, "Caught Somewhere in Time" will prove to be a high point on the album.

Next is "Wasted Years," a kind of new, fresh thing for Maiden, a real sort of thumping, four-on-the-floor, rootsy song that instantly connected with the fans, to the point where it would rise to #18 on the UK singles chart. It's distinguished as the only track on the album with no guitar synths, although as hinted at earlier, the use of these new testy machines is not that prominent across the record. "Wasted Years" is further made true and strong by a memorable and passionate chorus, one that takes the song in a bit more of a traditional Maiden direction.

Comments Bruce, "'Wasted Years' was written very much in the middle of the time when we were on the road so much that there was a certain sense of irony about that song. Because when Adrian wrote that lyric, I think he was, along with all of us, sitting there on the road going, well, this is great. And there are some people that would cut their limb off to do this full time. But boy, there are some days when we really feel we could do with a break [laughs]."

Framing it slightly differently, speaking with *Hard Rock* magazine at the time, Bruce explained that "Adrian writes songs in a much more medium tempo. His lyrics are pretty much, say, traditional, mixed with a Bad Company kind of style, very open, but also based on personal experiences and feelings. There's a song that deals with the way you feel when you reach the top with your band. It's the best time of your life; you have to enjoy it, to live intensely every moment of it."

And as Steve told Nelly, "It's a song written by Adrian. The basic idea is something like, 'Could I have done it better?' Adrian must've spent the night in a pub to write such a song! It's also certain that Dave must've cheered him up with some lager [laughs]. You know, when you do what you think is right at the time, you shouldn't regret it afterwards [laughs]. No, we are busy with the present and preparing the future but were proud of our past. Anyway, even if we had regrets, we couldn't change anything, so . . .'"

"A bit of a compromise was 'Wasted Years,'" laughs Derek Riggs on the picture sleeve for the single release. "If you look at Eddie, that's such a departure from the last time," notes Derek. "For *Somewhere in Time*, Eddie is stripped down as a robot. Now this was a bitch of a single, this 'Wasted Years.' We had to have something that had Eddie in it somehow, but we didn't want to preempt the album look of Eddie. Because it would take the shock away from what we did to Eddie, right? [Derek is referring to the fact that the single came out slightly ahead of the album.] We didn't want to give away the game before we started. So, we were stuck for what we could do. You try illustrating 'Wasted Years.' What do you do? If you put four guys on there playing guitar, and you put the title, 'Wasted Years,' it looks like they've been wasting their time playing guitar. If you have a picture of Eddie chopping people up, it's like, he's been wasting all these years chopping people up—what can you do? Whatever you do, it turns it into a negative.

"So, we said, we couldn't use Eddie too much, because it was such a radical change to Eddie that even giving a bit of Eddie away, we'd kind of blow it. So, I think Rod said, 'What about using him as a reflection in something, so you could only see part of his head? So, you can't really see what's going on, but it's still got Eddie on it.' So, we played with that for a bit, and we said, What about a time machine? You know, wasted years / time machine. And that was the only idea we could find that could work properly and fulfill all the specifications of what we needed to do with it. It's got a TARDIS in it again, that spaceship that looks like the police phone box. So, it's a duffer. It's a technical illustration of a keyboard of a time machine [laughs], with Eddie reflected in the window, because it was the only thing we could think of, that wouldn't give Eddie away, which fit 'Wasted Years,' without becoming a kind of self-defeating illustration."

"Wasted Years" is a clear demonstration that Adrian is a secret weapon in Maiden, allowing a different dimension, especially that all the other writers—in fact, both lyrically and musically—tend to be indistinguishable from each other. But Adrian, having cooked up the song on his four-track, was in fact reluctant to bring it to Steve, thinking it was too commercial.

"Sea of Madness" is a third strong opener on the record, and it's surprising that it's been essentially passed over for live play. Bolstered by a strong verse riff and rhythm, the song gets even better come chorus time; or, more accurately, there barely is a chorus, but what feels more like a prechorus is a sublime highlight, evocative of the best bits of "2 Minutes to Midnight." It makes sense that the song is credited solely to Adrian, because again, it's well out of the box for Maiden, adding welcome dimension to the record.

"Heaven Can Wait" is an interesting one, turning almost pop punk after a gratuitous intro. Come chorus time, things get even more melodic.

"Ah, the bastard!" says Steve, after being told that Bruce had been calling the song "mainstream" in interviews. "Here's the truth: when I started writing, I found a chorus, the one on 'Heaven Can Wait.' It's true that I thought it could sound 'mainstream.' Bruce listened to it, and I told him about my worries. But I knew that as soon as the others would start working on it, it'd be arranged in a very different way. And Bruce made a story of this! Then again, I'm not completely against mainstream stuff. It's just not my thing. We continuously progress, and this album has many choruses. But it's hard to explain. It is very different to our first albums. At the time, we had songs we'd been playing for a while. In a way, any band's first albums are really 'best of.' They contain the best ideas, those that have been worked on for months before the first deal. In a first album, you really have to give your best. But it doesn't prevent our other albums from being excellent."

Lyrically, this one's the tale of dying, perhaps on the operating table, although it's not clear, the narrator then struggling with hell (his "only foe"), a "lust" for the earth (i.e., returning to his body), and heaven, which can wait till another day. The ultimate battle is a purely musical one, culminating in gang chorus chants over a gallop, then guitar solos, then a fast and somewhat proggy passage before the song collapses back into the resolving verse, where our struggling NDE sufferer returns to Earth.

Said Steve of "The Loneliness of the Long Distance Runner" (chase with Rush's "Marathon"), speaking with *Enfer*, "As usual, it was impossible for me to write cheesy love songs like 'I love you, you love me, what a wonderful life.' Anyway, I've never been interested in this kind of thing. 'The Loneliness' was inspired by an old British film with the same title. The theme is dead simple: in life, you have to run, move forward, even if it means that you have to run alone. Just move on without a care about what people might say about you."

Indeed, in 1962 the 1958 Allan Sillitoe short story, *The Loneliness of the Long Distance Runner*, was turned into a movie, directed by Tony Richardson, adding to the long list of films that inspired Steve to put pen to paper.

Musically, this one's framed upon a brisk metal gallop, Bruce spitting out the lyrics in unison with the riff, which serves to make the topicality of them all the more jarring. There's much Maiden melody everywhere, including across twin leads and a single lead that sounds like Queen. Back at the vocal end, it's a strange key for Bruce, with some of the notes he has to hit necessarily because of the unison rule, with the riff coming off a tad flat.

Japanese 12-inch for "Stranger in a Strange Land." *Dave Wright archive*

On June 1, 1961, Robert Heinlein's science fiction classic *Stranger in a Strange Land* was published by Putnam, with Steve explaining to *Enfer* that "'Stranger in a Strange Land,' although inspired by the title of the Robert Heinlein book, has a strange origin. Adrian remembered a story that was published in the press a few years ago about this old sailor who was found dead, perfectly preserved in the ice of the North Pole. In fact, he was a member of an expedition that had disappeared after an iceberg had struck their ship. When he found his body, they awarded him a posthumous medal."

Indeed, this is another Adrian Smith composition from top to bottom, and it's a midcatalog classic, by no means a famed Maiden anthem, but classy, interesting, looming doomy, with a gravitas somewhere along the lines of "Flight of Icarus." Secret weapon is Nicko, who finds various ways to make a slow song interesting and groovy.

Adds Bruce, who further improves the song through a novel vocal melody, "They had just brought out the first Roland guitar synthesizers, and you could play kind of Hammond organ and guitar at the same time. Well, all the new toys came out, so all of a sudden we sounded like Deep Purple on that one. It's strange that some of my favorite songs on the records sometimes don't seem to make it live. 'Strange World' is another one of my favorite Maiden songs that just didn't really happen live. But 'Stranger in a Strange Land,' again, everybody in the band thought it should be a great live song, but it just never seemed to work."

Dickinson is correct that on this one, the "guitar synthesizers" can be heard clearly. But again, this isn't the obtrusive buzzy sound that Judas Priest got on *Turbo*. Instead, there's just a periodic background texture that sounds like regular keyboards, clear, of single note, not dated, because it's barely noticeable. The bluesy, reverb-drenched solo is by Adrian (after all, it's his song), and again, Smith's decisions make Maiden more universal, less classical, and proto-power metal.

Noted Dave Murray on the concept of keys in Maiden, "The thing is, we used these guitar synths because you're trying to create keyboard sounds. It was that time; bringing in keyboards was an area we were looking at strongly. So basically, the guitar synths were great, because you were strumming the chords and you were creating a synth-type effect. The thing is, they can be a bit of a pain because there was always a slight delay with the technology there. But basically, it was kind of to fill out the sound, give it a bit more ambience and color and background, more like washes to the songs. Obviously, now we've just been using keyboards, hands-on keyboards [laughs]. Basically, it just developed the sound, made it sound a bit more mature. It just broadens the scope. As opposed to, you can have a three-piece band, a four-piece band. And some of the songs, some of the riffs sounded like they needed to be orchestrated. We would say, let's make this sound like cellos, you know? [laughs]. Or a nice keyboard sound."

The two B-sides covered for the single—namely, "Juanita" and "That Girl" (plus "Reach Out" on the back of "Wasted Years")—came to Maiden from the two Entire Population of Hackney gigs thrown together to blow off steam during the long time off from Maiden business. The haphazard band was centered on Adrian and Nicko, plus some buddies from Urchin and FM, and then everybody else from Maiden as guest cameos. The experience formed the basis for Adrian to eventually leave Maiden and form the short-lived A.S.a.P. in 1989, with Dave Colwell and Andy Barnett, who had been on for these two impromptu shows.

Commented Adrian back in 1987, "It's difficult to say what might happen in the future. But I've been in this band so long I can't really imagine doing anything else. But yes, I admit it, I'm a frustrated singer. I'm singing on the B-side of 'Wasted Years,' on the song 'Reach Out.' Because we were on vacation last year, me and Nicko had a little band that we played in purely because we were bored. I was the singer in it, and I loved it. Because I was the lead vocalist for Urchin, five years before my Iron Maiden days, I still have a yen to do that. So maybe someday I'll get back into singing; I dunno."

Dave Wright archive

"They wanted Eddie in that bar in *Star Wars*," notes Derek, on the picture sleeve done for the single. "So, I knew I needed the bar in *Star Wars*, but I did him as Clint Eastwood. And it's the scene... you know, Clint Eastwood walks into the bar, and there's two guys playing cards, and one of them pretends to reach for the cards, but you know he's really going to reach for the gun, because this is the bit where Clint Eastwood shoots them all and doesn't incur any bullet holes himself, somehow. You know, he's the stranger with no name, the stranger in a strange land. It's even got Clint Eastwood's physique, if you look at it, plus the little cigarette thing and everything. *A Fistful of Dollars* might be the actual movie, and I mixed the two up and made them work together."

After "Stranger in a Strange Land" fades out (very rare for a Maiden song), here comes another pointless intro, this one duct-taped to the beginning of "Deja-Vu," in which Steve very plainly lays down the definition of déjà vu. "In the band, we used to say that Dave was 'giving birth' to a song every three years," noted Steve back

Bruce, Somewhere on Tour, Assembly Civic Center, Tulsa, Oklahoma, January 28, 1987. © Rich Galbraith

in 1986, speaking with *Enfer*. "The last time he did was on the *Piece of Mind* album. Well, we can say that Dave has for an excuse being a newlywed. What I'd like to say about Dave's songwriting is that he always comes up with great riffs and very flashy solos. But he often has problems writing lyrics that match the melody. This is where I help him out."

Unsurprisingly, we've not ever seen a solo album from Dave. "I'm not really into these self-indulgent things," demurs Murray. "If I did, it would be way after Maiden hung up their boots. To me, I'm happy doing this. It would be more for fun, really. The thought of going out and starting over in the clubs doesn't really appeal to me. I'm happy being part of a team."

As Dave told *Metal*, "I used to like the spontaneous thing of doing a different guitar solo every night on stage. But I've changed a little. I like the actual thing of spending three months in the studio, concentrating on getting one thing right. You have to sit down and really work at it, whereas on stage you can get away with a few things because of all the excitement. I think there's actually more pressure now in the studio, but I love it. It's a challenge. Writing is also an inspiration for me—it's especially rewarding to see your own song take form."

Bruce sings "Deja-Vu" mixing his usual operatic style with an uncommon bit of vocal fry. It's another high-speed rocker, loose and heavy, somewhat of a gallop, two sets of very melodic twin leads included—arguably the album's most obscure track.

As we progress toward the album's last and longest track, here comes another bluesy mellow intro indistinguishable from what came before and more to come. This one's to build anticipation for Steve's triumphant and galloping "Alexander the Great," which feels a little too close to comfort next to "Rime of the Ancient Mariner," last and longest track on the last album.

For this one, Steve goes all the way back to 336 through 323 BCE, when Alexander the Great reigns Macedon, currently northern Greece. The Egyptian city of Alexandria was named for this fierce warlord of yore—Alexander died young and mysteriously, in Babylon at the age of thirty-two. Steve cites "a fever" as cause of death, but other theories include poisoned wine as a possible cause of death—Alexander had many enemies and was constantly surrounded by assassination plots.

As Harris told *Enfer* at the time, "My most ambitious composition is certainly 'Alexander the Great,' a story based on true facts. When we started working on the LP, I was immersed in the story of Alexander the Great, a man who had a fantastic and incredible life. I fell in love with him, and quite naturally, I wrote the song and the lyrics, all this within two weeks. I must say that I'm very proud of this track."

Album complete, Maiden work toward shaking off the rust of months away from playing live, from September 10 through 25 conducting an eastern European leg of their so-called Somewhere on Tour campaign, supported by Waysted, whose leader, Pete Way, was somewhat of an inspiration for Steve both musically and visually. Somewhere on Tour featured a futuristic sort of cyberworld stage set and is distinguished as the first campaign on which Steve's tech Michael Kenney played keyboards, despite the band also bringing the

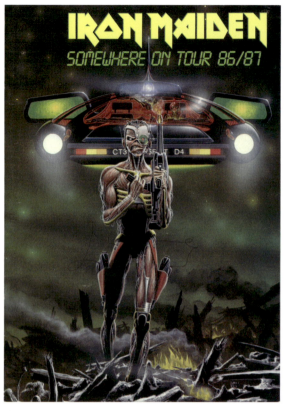

There were many custom Eddie artworks outside of the LPs and singles. Here's our hero looking futuristic on the tour program. *Dave Wright archive*

guitar synthesizers into the live arena. Tracks from the new record regularly played are "Sea of Madness," "Stranger in a Strange Land," "Wasted Years," "Heaven Can Wait," and "Caught Somewhere in Time," which opened the show after the intro music, which was the theme from *Blade Runner*.

"We always liked keyboards, but we never used them," recalls Dave of this period. "I remember we were in Japan, and we had these Roland guitar synths lying around, so Adrian and I tried them out. After that, we brought in keyboards. In fact, Mike Kenney, the guy that does Steve's bass rig, is the person who's been playing keyboards since then. He actually plays them onstage now. I think keyboards can really add a lot of color, and it can open up the sound. We'd come from twin guitars, bass, drums, vocals, and put in a wash of keyboards. You can keep the melody there but have a solid rock foundation underneath. It just makes it more musical. We've always been a very heavy band, but with melodies on top. With the keyboards, it added a bit more to it."

But with respect to his own domain, Dave kept it simple. "I started collecting guitars in the early 1980s," explained Dave in 1996. "In fact, I've gotten a lot in America. I've got about fifty-five. A lot of them are old Strats and Gibson 335s and that sort of thing, so I've got an abundance. During that period, I was using a Strat, and an SG. The Strat used to belong to Paul Kossoff from Free. I got that in 1976, and I'd been using that for the first couple of albums."

Steve puts his feet up at the Assembly Civic Center, Tulsa, Oklahoma, January 28, 1987. © *Rich Galbraith*

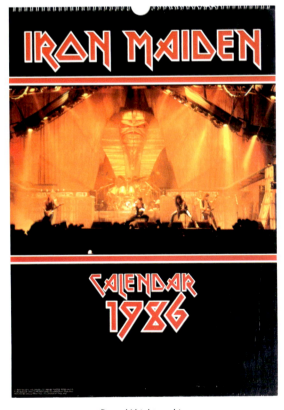

Dave Wright archive

Although this guitar was originally white, Dave had it painted blue. Murray had bought it off an ad in *Melody Maker*, and to verify the claims of it being Kossoff's, he ran a check on the serial numbers past the musician's union.

Continues Dave, "I also put some humbuckers on there to fatten up the sound. Really, it was the Stratocaster and the Marshall amps in that period. Pretty much that was it, apart from using choruses and echoes and the wah metal. I just try to get that rock sound you can get from a Marshall amp. Right up until today, we still use Fenders and Stratocasters. We still use Marshall amps, but there is the 9100 series, which are the new amps they have now. Throughout time, it's been Fender Strats and the Marshall amps. It's the traditional thing that Hendrix was using in the '60s. I found you can get a good combination of really heavy sound, but a nice clean sound as well. As far as an all-around instrument, the Fender seems to be the one. It's also the shape of them—they sit on your body really well. You can throw them around, and if they fall apart, they're easy to put back together!"

October 3 through November 9, the tour crisscrosses the UK extensively, with Bruce's old bandmate Paul Samson supporting, under the moniker Paul Samson's Empire.

Noted Bruce at the time, speaking with *Metal* magazine, "I don't mind them supporting us. I was more concerned how they felt about it. But our parting was very amicable. Musically, we were drifting apart. When Rod Smallwood came to me about joining Iron Maiden, I went for it, all guns blazing. I'm like a real step-on-your-toes kind of sod, and if you don't like it, throw me out. There had been several lead singers in Iron Maiden before me. So, I just told Rod, 'I have my own ideas about music and songs, and I don't want to have anything to do with what went before. If you don't want to go along with me, you will have to fire me because I'll be a real pain in the ass!' Actually, I can't believe I said that, but I really did!"

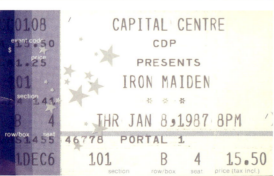

Cause and effect: show flyer, ticket stub, T-shirt. *Dave Wright archive*

Added Bruce, on how we got into this game in the first place, "We used to have rock concerts in school twice a term. We used to sit around with cans of Mars bars and sweets, because alcohol was out, of course. The first band I ever saw was a band called Wild Turkey, with Jethro Tull's future bass player, and I went crazy. I saw a lot of art rock bands at school: Queen, Genesis, Arthur Brown. At first, I didn't think about singing. But I did get into acting. I was always dithering between joining the army and acting. I guess I've been in training for all this ever since I was knee high to a grasshopper. When I was ten years old, I played Mole in *Wind in the Willows*. And I've always had a loud voice! I got my first gig by just singing notes into a tape recorder. I didn't know any songs to audition, so I just sang notes."

On November 5, *Piece of Mind* becomes Iron Maiden's second RIAA-designated platinum album, just as the band transitions to mainland Europe supported by W.A.S.P. Two weeks later, the current record goes gold, two months after release, rising to #11 in the charts. The record currently sits at platinum, which also aligns it somewhat inauspiciously with Judas Priest's *Turbo*, both 1986 offerings selling well despite not being particularly beloved by the fan base. Incidentally, Canada continued to love their Maiden, sending the album double platinum for the third record in a row, with *The Number of the Beast* currently sitting at triple platinum, for sales of 300,000 copies in a country with a population of twenty-six million in 1986 (the album also went gold in Germany, Japan, and the UK).

Taking a break for Christmas, from January 7 through May 2, 1987, Maiden execute the North American dates promoting *Somewhere in Time*. Support for the first batch of dates is Yngwie Malmsteen. The middle dates feature Vinnie Vincent's Invasion. Waysted return yet again to support for much of the back half of the tour (a special Day on the Green stop in San Jose included Y&T and Tesla, both Bay Area bands). On January 20, *Killers* finally goes gold in the US, almost seven years after its release date. May 11 through 21, Maiden close out their Somewhere on Tour with a half-dozen dates in Japan, capping a substantial campaign, albeit not the stress test that was the World Slavery tour.

Eddie conducts an examination of the Assembly Civic Center in Tulsa, Oklahoma. © *Rich Galbraith*

The balance of 1987 would be quiet for the band. On August 14 the video version of *Live After Death* reaches platinum, and then up into October there's another video compilation put together called *12 Wasted Years*.

"I did like *Fighting Back*; I thought it was really good, very punky in a way," says old Maiden howler Paul Di'Anno, who finds himself proud father of a second Battlezone album, called *Children of Madness*, birthed in June 1987. "That was the thing I wanted to do. You see, it's the same mistake again. It seems to sort of come about. I thought the first Iron Maiden album was great, but I thought *Killers* was a bit too polished, and it didn't feel right for me. That's why I wanted to get out of it. And then it happened again. The *Fighting Back* album I thought was great and raw and it felt good, and then we did the *Children of Madness* album. We gave them a load of material before and they said, 'Well, we can't change the recording sessions and the times and that, and these songs aren't suitable.' So, we had to change it. We had to write, oh, seven songs in about two days, which me and Joe Wiggins went ahead and did, and I think it suffered for it. It ended up sounding like a third-rate Queensryche, and I wasn't into that. I mean, they're a great band, but it wasn't the kind of stuff that I do, so I got a little upset with that."

If Paul seemed bereft of ideas in June 1987, his old boss Steve would conversely find inspiration when American novelist Orson Scott Card, also this month, sees the publication of his first book in a series known as *The Tales of Alvin Maker*, concerning American frontiersman Alvin Miller, who is, in fact, the seventh son of a seventh son.

Martin Popoff archive

CHAPTER 8
Seventh Son of a Seventh Son

"God damn it, artistically we were in second place."

As if the guitar synths weren't a meaningful enough presence across *Somewhere in Time*, Maiden would bring actual keyboards to their seventh album, although yet again, no one would accuse Steve and the boys of being anything other than a nuts-and-bolts—and even artisanal, organic, and grass-fed—heavy metal band.

As alluded to last chapter, Steve had been inspired by Orson Card's novel *Seventh Son*. After conferring with Bruce, Harris had Dickinson's mind racing, and Bruce was back in the fold as a writer. Recording of the record took place at Musicland in Munich, February through March 1988; however, rather than mainstay at that studio Reinhold Mack producing, the band convened once again with their exclusive charge, Martin Birch.

March 20 would bring us the first new music from what would be Iron Maiden's first concept album. "Can I Play with Madness" is issued as an advance single from the forthcoming *Seventh Son of a Seventh Son*, finding much success in the UK, where it reaches #3. Its B-sides are non-LP original "Black Bart Blues" and a cover of Thin Lizzy's "Massacre."

"The studio back then was in a hotel," recalls Dave on putting together the album. "We spent like three months living in this hotel. So, we got to know the area real well. Unfortunately, when we went down to the studio recently, Musicland in Munich, it was gone. Because they built a metro near it, and the train kept interfering with the studio. The studio had a lot of magic. Deep Purple recorded some stuff there; Queen recorded there. The walls just oozed with magic. The vibe was also in the concept as well, you know, with the prophets and that sort of thing. We were moving on musically and lyrically."

Nicko celebrated the finish of the sessions by appearing on the popular UK series for toddlers, *The Sooty Show*, on March 10. McBrain recalls speaking with *Hard Roxx*: "Rod phoned me and said, 'Are you sitting down?' He said, 'You've been asked to do *The Sooty Show*,' and I laughed me fucking head off. I said, you've got to be fucking joking, haven't you? He says, 'No, I'm not. Why did you think I'd be joking?' I said, it's not the sort of thing a heavy metal drummer's going to go on, is it? He said, 'Well, think about your boy.' Because my Nick was only four and a half years old, so I thought, that's not a bad idea. He can tell his friends that his dad's on *Sooty*."

A month later, April 11, 1988, the record hit the shops, not that the world was waiting with bated breath, given that the likes of Poison, Whitesnake, and Guns N' Roses were all the rage at this juncture, not to mention a surging Aerosmith, Kiss, and Alice Cooper, due to adaptation to then-current hair metal realities.

"*Seventh Son* really revitalized my enthusiasm," notes Bruce. "The idea of doing a concept album, I loved. It was a great idea. I was probably responsible in a large part for the cover, with Derek. The idea was to do something surreal. We wanted a surrealist Eddie. And Derek came up with that, which I was really pleased with."

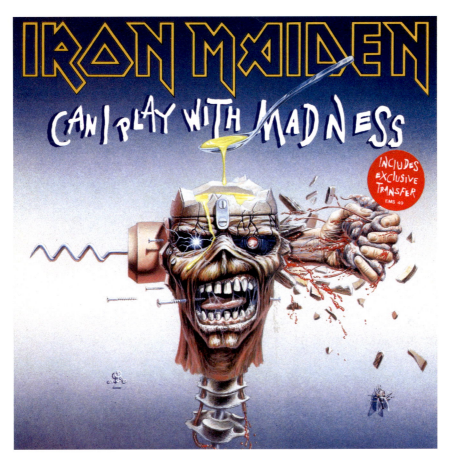

"Can I Play with Madness" 7-inch sleeve. *Dave Wright archive*

Indeed, the *Seventh Son* artwork would be stark and definitely surreal. What's more, it presented to fans a fresh color palette, like *Powerslave* three records earlier.

"They said they wanted one of my surreal things," confirms Riggs. "'It's about prophecy and seeing into the future and we want one of your surreal things.' That was the brief. The first two albums, they had no idea at all, because I painted them off my own plan. The singles are pretty much what the single is about, if you can work out what the single is about [laughs]. But it's always like, we want a guy and a television set and go and do it. The jokes and all that . . . you know, half the time they didn't know what was going to be on the cover because I didn't know what we were going to end up with because I was making it up as we went along; I was just winging it. And half the time I would [make] changes halfway through because I knew it wasn't going to work.

"But yes, for *Seventh Son*, I had a limited time to do the picture, and I thought it was pretty weird, their concept, so I just went with that. I don't know where the ideas come from. I read a lot and I stick a lot of pictures in my head. I've got a lot of wildlife books, and sooner or later something goes in but mixed up. The idea was that they were doing an album that was a bit more thoughtful than some of the others. It had a concept behind it; in other words, it was telling a story. It was about something weird. The seventh son of the seventh son is supposed to be psychic. That's the departure point. So, the thing is actually a concept album about stuff that this guy goes through.

Dave Wright archive

"And I thought, you know, I don't feel like painting all of Eddie, so I'll get rid of him [laughs]. I'll chop him off and make it look kind of nonpleasant. And it's got the apple, which is Garden of Eden stuff, and the baby, and it's got some of his machine parts plus a burning head, which was actually a symbol for inspiration, which I stole from Arthur Brown, as in the Crazy World of Arthur Brown, who used to dance around onstage and set his head on fire and sing about fire. But I actually had the album way back when. And on the album, the stuff about fire is not about the devil; it's actually about inspiration. It's kind of about the devil and suffering, but it's about inspiration, so I kind of stole that. And the apple has got yin yang on it. Red and green is yin and yang. They're opposites; plus, red and green are opposites in the color spectrum."

On April 14, 1920, the Great Beast himself, Aleister Crowley, founds the abbey of Thelema, the Cefalu, Sicily, location of his most-satanic deeds. Bruce's "Revelations" lyrics from *Piece of Mind* would be inspired by Crowley's life story. As well, Crowley would pen a novel called *Moonchild*, which is also the name of the opening track on the *Seventh Son of a Seventh Son* album. Indicative of the slight wobble the record exhibits conceptually, the lyric of this one is most definitely part Crowley's *Moonchild* and only part Iron Maiden's *Seventh Son of a Seventh Son*, essentially a befuddling of the two, although its unlikely that Bruce did it by accident; rather, Dickinson going more for the idea of a bank of lyrics being able to be read on multiple levels.

At the music end of things, "Moonchild" represents one of Adrian's three credits on the album. Now, Smith would be gone come the next Maiden record, and one can almost hear him giving up the ghost right here, turning in a musical track that is more like a typical meat-and-potatoes Steve song. It's almost as if the band was so enthused about writing a concept album, and how Steve and his prog-loving past and indeed the working parts of Maiden stylistically added up to this destiny, that the music itself took a back seat to the fancy-pants literary narrative. Indeed "Moonchild" sounds like a Steve Harris deep album cut politely that deserved to be politely put to the side when it would come time to draw up the set list.

"Infinite Dreams" is an interesting one, surprisingly solely credited to Steve, although it's the most Adrian-sounding tune on the record, perhaps tied with "Can I Play with Madness." There's an obligatory intro, but not the expected explosion. First verse is sung to the tune of an up-tempo ballad, bluesy pop as it were, but then rootsy power chords arrive to fill it out. Still, it's music that is appropriate to a concept album. It's music that gets out of the way for story, further underscored by Dickinson's contemplative, ruminating, low-key vocal. At the lyric end, this one's in the growing tradition of Maiden songs about the visitation of nightmares upon a restless sleeve, or more so, as in most cases, not just conjurings of the mind but actual psychic events.

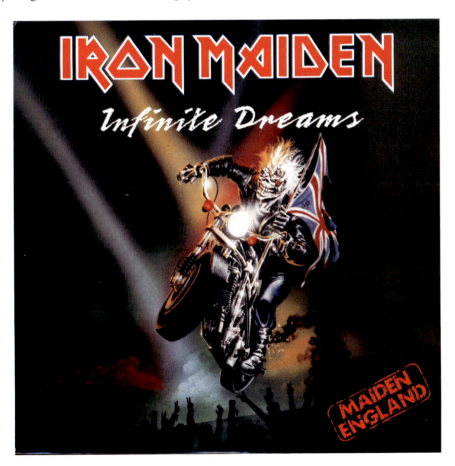

The "Infinite Dreams" live 7-inch from 1989. *Dave Wright archive*

Speaking with Sylvie Simmons back in 1988, Bruce explained that "Infinite Dreams" "starts out really dreamy and Hendrix-y and has all kinds of strange things all over it, and the whole thing just builds up. We really had difficulties with Nicko on this one. He started hammering away like crazy. We told him, 'No! Play it more soft, more soberly!,' and the track built itself up. All the notes are the same for 24 measures, and the only thing that changes in is the intensity of the interpretation. It's really nice to listen to because you have this impression of several repeated themes. Every time you listen to it, you hear something different.

"We took a more laid-back approach for this LP," continued Dickinson. "We gave ourselves a starting point. We all guaranteed that we would not bother each other until this point, and then after that it was really a free-for-all. We wrote the album 'round Steve's house in Essex in his old barn, which sounds great, a good atmosphere to work in. We played our respective material and recorded the lot on tape, with an acoustic guitar and bass. Just ideas we had in mind. And Adrian came around my house a couple times, and it's at that time that we wrote those three tracks on the album. Then we all went into the studio."

"Infinite Dreams" plays seamlessly into "Can I Play with Madness," the record's first single and the song destined to dominate and outlast all others from this record. A combination of "Wasted Years" and Ozzy's "Crazy Train," this one's a thumping, upbeat, commercial rocker that the fans accepted into their hearts. The verse is a bit hapless, frankly, exposing Martin Birch's declining success at getting both a good sound and performance out of Maiden—at this point they are becoming the Rolling Stones of metal—but then an abrupt shift of gears takes us to a melodic and "commercial" yet comfortably Maiden-like chorus, one for the ages, blessed with a thespian performance from Bruce and that valuable voice of his.

Notes Dickinson, "We had a big row in the writing of that one. There's that whole bit in the middle where it goes into a sort of guitar solo bit and then just stops abruptly and goes 'Can I play with madness?' And you get the a cappella bit and then it goes back into the chorus. That whole bit in the middle was just completely inserted, like plunk, stuck in the middle. And it was Steve's bit. And he said, 'Oh, this will work,' and he put it in there, and Adrian absolutely hated it. I was unfortunately the one who sat in the corner thinking, 'Well, Adrian hates it and Steve thinks it really works,' and then I was thinking, actually, 'It does kind of work,' so I chimed in and said, 'Actually, it does seem to work, guys,' and it was like, 'Oh dear' . . ."

At the time, back in 1988 speaking with Simmons, Dickinson framed the song this way, filling in a few blanks. "The single's a real collaborative effort. The beginning bit, the riff—with apologies to Pete Townshend!—was me on acoustic guitar at home. Then Adrian came along with some chords, and I went, 'Hang on a minute, I've got some words here that fit.' So, we sat around and worked on it. And I said, 'Can I write an instrumental bit in the middle?' Because I normally don't write bits like that since I don't have to play them. And Steve came in with the time change bit, the Zeppelin-y bit, and we had a tremendous argument with Nicko saying, 'Oh, it won't work; it's too radical.' And I thought, no, it will work, so long as everyone takes the plunge and does it. Many ideas were thrown into this album, a lot of rhythms. Instead of looking at it like Lego bricks—this bit goes here, and that bit goes there—it was just getting the feeling right that made it work. Whereas before I think we tended to plan everything out a lot; on the new album we sort of loosened up a bit, and that made all the difference.

"I'd really like to have a hit single," mused Bruce. "We haven't had a genuine hit single since 'Run to the Hills.' I think this one stands a chance because of the kind of song it is—the chorus is quite catchy. And it would be nice to go out and do an absolutely rip-roaring tour. We'd like to give everybody something to think about before the 1990s. Like, there's life in them there hills, and nobody's going down without a serious fight!"

"Can I Play with Madness" is in fact credited to Adrian, Steve, and Bruce and arises from something of Adrian's called "On the Wings of Eagles." As the band's sixteenth single, the song soared to a #3 placement on the English charts. Sadly, the video for the song would represent the last appearance of Graham Chapman of Monty Python fame on film before his death from cancer on October 4, 1989.

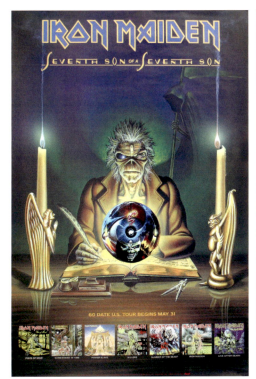 

A couple of *Seventh Son of a Seventh Son* promotional posters. *Dave Wright archive*

Just as "Moonchild" serves two purposes, "Can I Play with Madness" can be seen as an integral part of the story, featuring the central character, an old seer, and a crystal ball. But just headbang to it live, and the song can be seen as an anthem to youthful rebellion. It's the same way that "Flight of Icarus" can be about a formal and scholarly Greek parable at the same time that it's about escaping out the window and going to see Angel Witch, Spider, and Lightning Raiders warm up the crowd for Saxon and Motörhead. The video, although complex and representative of a third story line, essentially supports this idea, featuring both mysticism and a rocker who loves his Maiden, reading about the band, drawing Eddies.

The year is 1599, and William Shakespeare writes *The Tragedy of Julius Caesar*, which inspires the title of "The Evil That Men Do," a bracing arch-Maiden anthem, galloping, grinding, built for the stage. Comments Bruce, "'The Evil That Men Do' was conceived . . . I got about halfway through writing a story to go with the album. And a couple of my songs that I did lyrics for fitted in with this general concept of the story. And 'Evil That Men Do' was one of those, and the idea was the corruption of innocence. And in it, the seventh son of the seventh son is tempted to sleep with the devil. And he comes down as this gorgeous woman who basically takes his virginity and disappears, basically leaving him lonely and pissed off and empty."

It must be noted that the concept of the seventh son doesn't originate with Orson Card, but that there's a long literary and mystical record of stories about the magical and visionary powers that both bless and curse the child who happens to be born the seventh son of a seventh son. There's even a Christian name for one of these—Septamus. Also, seven is the number of perfection in Hebrew tradition, as well as, over the eons, becoming the number most associated with God, just as 666 is the number of the beast.

"The Evil That Men Do" is credited to Adrian, Steve, and Bruce, reflective of this idea that the band was collaborating a bit more, necessarily, because all the lyrics had to fit a story line. Therefore, as Steve says, there was more monitoring going on versus quiet communion with four-tracks at home. Helping turn the song into a typical Maiden call to arms is a sophisticated if brief prechorus gesture—the song could have just as

"The Evil That Men Do" 7-inch sleeve. *Dave Wright archive*

easily been called "Living on a Razor's Edge"—followed by a chorus that simply repeats the title in long, soaring notes from a man who is arguably heavy metal's best or most beloved (or both) and storied singer, certainly in lockstep with Rob Halford and Ronnie James Dio.

Opening side 2 is the record's title track, which, at ten minutes long, does most of the heavy lifting conceptually. But even if the lyrics plainly lay out and reemphasize the concept, they are surprisingly sparse. And then, at the musical end, "Seventh Son of a Seventh Son" finds Steve (sole writer on the track) lapsing into form, structuring the song around a slow gallop and Middle Eastern tones. Suddenly we're at "To Tame a Land," "Rime of the Ancient Mariner," and "Alexander the Great" all over again, and the optimistic fan has to tell himself, well, another year and more of the same means another Iron Maiden epic, so I'm happy.

Oddly, we are halfway through the album, and the seventh son is just being born. But then again, "Moonchild" can be interpreted as a cautionary tale about preventing him from being born, and then much of side 1 reflects visions and dream states. As well, it's a common rock 'n' roll trope to throw up a smokescreen and reorder the tracks of a narrative to make the listener work harder to discern what's going on. Additionally, when you do this, new meanings perhaps personal only to the reader fall out of the now more abstract telling. It's a bit like David Bowie and the cutup technique, where he'd physically have words and phrases in bits of paper in a jumble and then assemble them to the point where a new idea lives between two independent thoughts.

If you can stick around through another hit dog break of a dreary intro, Steve and the guys will eventually turn on the electricity, bringing "The Prophecy," built of a proggy and very much Celtic-flavored slow gallop, replete with a Thin Lizzy twin lead. This one features another rare Dave Murray credit, and given the "olde English" feel to the song, once again it's proven that Dave, Steve, and Bruce tend to write very much the same kinds of songs. All told, it's an airy enough, slow-burning frame on which to get conceptual. And Steve most surely does, having our tormented narrator foretelling of doom for the village at the hands of a smiling Lucifer but getting blamed for it instead.

"The Clairvoyant" has our erstwhile Septamus or Alvin Miller character coming to terms with his powers, focusing through the psychic turmoil to distinguish reality from mere nightmares. But again, headbang to the song live, and a new meaning struggles to the top of the pile through the repeated chorus, that of coming to

Seventh Son of a Seventh Son press kit. Dave Wright archive

terms with death. In this respect there's a bit of "Powerslave" to the song. Drawing attention to this and away from the conceptual story line is the fact that musically, these chorus parts are placed on an infectious and comfortable—to the point of predictable—slow Maiden gallop, sort of like "Fear of the Dark."

But much more than this goes on musically. "The Clairvoyant" represents a strange and disconcerting mix of the above, with sweet and sour, sing-songy passages that are almost pop punk, but then a verse structure that is one of the strongest on the album, featuring dark, urgent chords, sophisticated textures, and a novel rhythm from Nicko. In totality there's the Maiden you love and the Maiden you love to hate, all wrapped up in one fragmented song.

Steve says that the song was the first written for the album, and that it was inspired by the death of psychic Doris Stokes.

"The Clairvoyant" 7-inch sleeve along with the picture disc version. *Dave Wright archive*

And then, almost as if the band realized that the part from "The Clairvoyant" that goes over best with the 'Edbangers is the gallop, they close the album with "Only the Good Die Young," which gallops right the way through, no meandering intro necessary. The lyrics across the verses are quite shocking, evil, and violent, but again, all that is remembered is the title sung over and over again, perhaps a pithy sentiment, but at least it ties in with the rumination-of-death theme of the last song and indeed so many tunes across the catalog.

"If you asked Steve Harris what his favorite record is, he'd say *Seventh Son*," says Dave, summing up. "We actually tried to hit on a concept where the seventh son is a magician telling the story throughout the album. In fact, it's one of my favorite albums as well. I don't think it fell short of anything. As for the themes, and the story line running through it, I think it's a strong album—every track is really strong on it."

Two weeks after Maiden had served up *Seventh Son of a Seventh Son* for debate, on May 3 Queensryche issue their third album, *Operation: Mindcrime*. Already, with the band's debut EP, the Seattle upstarts were seen as a new and improved version of Iron

Maiden. Now, five years later, they somewhat steal Maiden's thunder with a heavy metal concept record that made *Seventh Son of a Seventh Son*, as Bruce explains, look ragged and amateurish by comparison.

"I guess what I found strange is that we took the album to a certain point, and then it never got developed any further. And in the same year, while we were in the midst of mixing or something, I heard some advance tracks from Queensryche, *Operation: Mindcrime*, and was blown away. And I remember thinking, [as] I was driving down a street through a park in Germany, and heard these four tracks from *Mindcrime*, and then stopped the car and sat there with my head in my hands, and thought that they had made the album that we should have made. *Seventh Son* should be this. And could be this. If we'd only forced it, if we'd only thought it through and sat down and planned it and discussed it. You just don't make a concept album like that in five minutes. You don't just loosely glue a few things together and say, okay, that's a concept album. So that was my feeling. I was proud of it, but there was always this thought [that], God damn it, artistically we were in second place. Review-wise we were as well. In terms of the way the world perceives everything, *Mindcrime* was a groundbreaking album. And *Seventh Son* was not quite. For Maiden fans it was, but there was this feeling I had then that there was this world of Maiden, and there was the rest of the world.

Seventh Son of a Seventh Son—era press photo. *Dave Wright archive*

"So yeah, *Seventh Son* was funny, because the album of the year for me was *Operation: Mindcrime*. They made the record that *Seventh Son* should've been. We could've made a record as good as that, but we didn't. We made a record that was halfway. There wasn't a desire to follow the creative process all the way through, in terms of a concept album with a story line that fully develops. We made a pretty good stab at it, and it is one of the better post–*Live After Death* albums. You can pretty much split the band down the middle with pre–*Live After Death* and post–*Live After Death*. All my favorite stuff is up until *Live After Death*. After that, it's the band trying to regain the momentum it had."

Bruce makes a good point; in the insular world of Maiden, the band could do no wrong (within reason). But even outside, during this era, the band was getting a pass from critics, with writers politely abstaining from scathing reviews but not exactly exalting the band's accomplishments either. Even among the faithful, outside of the concept extra, *Seventh Son* was essentially more of the same, Maiden checking off all the boxes they'd squared up for themselves since *Piece of Mind*.

Thrash was the exciting new music, with the big four, conspicuously, all American bands entering their gold-record period. The trash rockers up strutting up and down the Sunset Strip and being seen at the Rainbow along the way; well, no one was calling that high art. But then again, that's where the easy platinum was coming from, with the occasional breakout to multiplatinum, such beginning with Ratt, Quiet Riot, and Twisted Sister and, toward the exposed midrift and the tail feathers, Whitesnake, Warrant, Cinderella, Bon Jovi, and Guns N' Roses. Meanwhile Maiden was struggling at gold, and they weren't making it easy on themselves by playing what was essentially castle rock recorded roughly.

Hitting the road, the band celebrates the author's twenty-fifth birthday, April 28 and 29, with two secret tour warm-up gigs at the Empire Club in Cologne, Germany, as Charlotte and the Harlots. On May 8, the band plays one more warm-up club gig before beginning Seventh Tour of a Seventh Tour five days later in Canada. It is at famed New York metal local L'Amour. May 13 through 30, Iron Maiden embark upon the huge North American leg of the campaign, beginning with ten dates across Canada, supported by Guns N' Roses.

Noted Steve in 1990, speaking with *M.E.A.T.* magazine, "It may have seemed that we were drawing poorly, but really, we weren't. A lot of people didn't realize we've never sold out in the secondary markets. We do well in the big places like Toronto, New York, Chicago, and LA, but never in the smaller ones, even when the touring market was on the upside. And instead of selling 7,000–8,000 tickets, it was down to 6,000, so that wasn't too bad. And they were fans who were totally into Maiden, whereas the 1,000–2,000 who didn't show were mostly always just tagalongs—the periphery audience who just came along 'cause it was a rock show. Our fans' reactions were actually better. People say we are on a downslide, but we took along bands like Guns N' Roses and Zodiac Mindwarp who didn't really appeal to our audience. And it was the first time we'd ever done a summer tour, and there was Monsters of Rock, Def Leppard, and AC/DC, all competing for the fans' dollars. Some of our timing may have been off, but we did good business."

May 31 through August 10, Seventh Tour of a Seventh Tour assaults America, with Frehley's Comet supporting for the most dates (perpetuating a trend whereby Maiden take on solo or side acts from root bands they supported in the past). Also supporting for multiple dates are Megadeth and major-label Canadian signing Killer Dwarfs. Just as the tour kicks off, the guys get some good news when the new record receives its RIAA gold designation. Back home, on August 1, EMI issues "The Evil That Men Do" as a single in the UK, where it peaks at #5. B-sides are the studio rerecordings, "Prowler '88" and "Charlotte the Harlot '88," the 7-inch getting just the first one, the 12-inch including both. Also issued was a shaped picture disc with the two songs, as well as a CD single, as the industry now slowly proceeds along its conversion to the compact disc format.

Dave Wright archive

August 20 through October 5, the mainland European leg of the Seventh Tour of a Seventh Tour encompasses twenty shows in fifteen countries, beginning with a nonmainland date—namely, Monsters of Rock at Donington, with other "Monsters of Rock" bills marbled throughout Europe. The "baby" Iron Maiden, Helloween, support on a few dates toward the tail end of the tour. On November 7, EMI issues a live version of "The Clairvoyant" as a single, backed with "The Prisoner" and "Heaven Can Wait," also live. The loosening up into the live realm and the recent rerecorded versions represent a slackening of standards—to come will be all manner of live album, none of which will possess the fire, the mystique, and the "reason to be" as the peerless original, *Live After Death*. In time for the single, November 18 through December 12 finds the band executing the UK leg of the Seventh Tour of a Seventh Tour. The final show, an intimate affair at the Hammersmith Odeon in London, would be Adrian Smith's last with the band for eleven years. Support throughout the UK comes from Killer Dwarfs.

Iron Maiden close off the 1980s again, showing their fatigue, their creeping lack of enthusiasm for the project. On January 5 the *12 Wasted Years* video goes gold, on February 28 the *Behind the Iron Curtain* video goes gold, and on November 6, EMI issues a live take of "Infinite Dreams" as a single, backed with live versions of "Killers" and "Still Life." The message is that the old songs were better, and that the studio versions of the new songs didn't have as much pizzazz as what the band could do to them live. Or it was just value for the money, but where was the modern-day equivalent of "Women in Uniform" or "I've Got the Fire"? A couple of days after this nonstarter, EMI issues a fifteen-track live video called *Maiden England*, culled from two Birmingham NEC live sets, November 27 and 28 from the previous year, to be reissued as a limited-edition video/CD set five years later.

Maiden England store display and patch.
Dave Wright archive

Meanwhile Clive Burr resurfaces. Twisted Sister vocalist Dee Snider, bassist Marc Russell, Bernie Tormé (Janick Gers's predecessor in Gillan), and, on the drums, Clive record what would become a shelved album under the band name Desperado. The album would see authorized issue in 1996 on Destroyer Records and then be reissued in 2006 through Cleopatra/Deadline.

"There again, that was a good band," recalled Clive. "Bernie Tormé was in it. But I ended up in the situation where not enough money was invested into the band. Moreover, the record company executives decided all of a sudden that they weren't going to produce albums from rock bands anymore. So obviously it all went pear shaped once again."

Says Dee on Clive, sadly to succumb to multiple sclerosis in 2013 at the age of fifty-six, "The funny thing about Clive was, Bernie and I were trying to figure out, okay, the people I originally thought I would play with aren't going to be right for this project. And I said, 'You know a drummer I've always liked? I've always liked Clive Burr's playing. He's a very creative, different kind of drummer. If we could get someone like Clive, that would be great.' And Bernie says, in his . . . he has a bad stutter, goes, 'Well, why don't we get Clive?' [laughs]

"And I never thought, pick up the phone and get Clive to play. I said get somebody like Clive. 'You know how to get ahold of him?!' He says yeah. So, he calls Clive, and they jam together, and Clive was different from any drummer I've ever experienced—on so many levels. One thing about Clive, which I found intriguing: he was the only one I ever worked with who would never finish his drum parts until he knew the words. He worked off of the vocal, not off of the guitar or the bass. I've never . . . he was a melody-driven drummer, which might have explained some of the very creative drum parts you see, especially in Maiden, where there are almost no rules there. For what is accepted. So, it was intriguing that way. And one of the most joyous drummers. When he had the sticks in his hands, he was just in heaven. He would love fucking playing."

Famously, Bruce would eventually leave the Maiden fold, realizing that there were more-creative peaks of purpose to climb. But first it would be Adrian, who tested the waters in October 1989 with his solo band (with roots in his pre-Maiden act Urchin) called A.S.a.P., which stands for Adrian Smith and Project. A formal-attire-only record called *Silver and Gold* would emerge, with Adrian handling lead vocals as well as guitar.

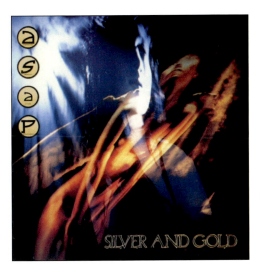

Silver and Gold album cover. Dave Wright archive

Explained Adrian on his ramp-up toward leaving Maiden: "The very fact that I went off and did a solo album, and it was the first one . . . well, there was Bruce as well. And I think that kind of unsettled people. Especially Steve, who was just kind of wondering what I was doing. So that was sowing the seeds. I really liked where we were going with *Somewhere in Time* and *Seventh Son*. I thought they were a little bit more mature and a bit more polished. That's where I was coming from and felt like going. I wanted to do something that was really polished."

"A.S.a.P. was kind of a shining, gleaming, produced record, which is what I wanted to do. I was quite pleased with that, although obviously it was a radical musical departure, which threw a bit of a curveball. But that just shows where I'm at. I have a wide range of tastes. Also, with A.S.a.P., I was heavily involved with a couple of other guys. It wasn't strictly speaking a solo album. I mean, the two friends that I had for a long while, I grew up playing with. They were always encouraging me to do a solo album. But they also had a lot of encouragement in the way that they helped me find a producer and did all the songwriting with me. To be quite honest with you, I almost got thrown into that situation because I made some demos a couple of years earlier which Sanctuary Management really liked. And they were as encouraging to me as anybody to do a solo album. But I wasn't really sure what I wanted to do, and I kind of just went along with everything and ended up in the studio doing this project. And I spent a shitload of money."

So how would Iron Maiden face the 1990s?

Fact is, almost ironically, they would ride out the grunge sensation, the rise of Soundgarden, Nirvana, and then Alice in Chains and Pearl Jam, slightly better than their heavy metal compatriots. Why? Because Steve and his charges were already considered dated and old news—how much further from the latest pop headlines could they fall?

Not that the first two records of the new decade—*No Prayer for the Dying* and *Fear of the Dark*—would be great shakes, but the band would nonetheless cash in on the enormous goodwill built up through their endearing "people's band" work ethic. It was their saving grace then, in what was a notoriously tough time for heavy metal, and it became their saving grace through their inspiring rise back to the top of the heap, beginning palpably around 2005.

And to be sure, the sag in excitement vis-à-vis American crowds would be noticeable, but Maiden would also ride the typical to rock 'n' roll delayed effect of Western decline not spreading for eighteen months or two years into the rest of the world. In other words, when the love was gone stateside—gone first to the Sunset Strip and then gone to Seattle—it remained in markets around the world, markets that Maiden would come to embrace in the 2000s, again, Rod's timing proving to be impeccable.

As well, back to the songs. However anachronistic the records would be through the late 1980s and into the 1990s, it has to be said once more that the band found their identity right 'round *Piece of Mind* and felt so comfortable within it that they defiantly bucked all trends along the way, believing steadfastly in the siege mentality that made the New Wave of British Heavy Metal so magical and heroic of purpose. For this, Iron Maiden were eventually awarded with their current status as really—arguably but still sensibly—the greatest heavy metal band of all time. Unfortunate for the millions of fans around the world wrapped head to toe in their Eddie gear, there's been talk of retirement. But if any sort of heritage act from the low 1980s has gas in the tank for a few more records and Bruce-piloted world tours, it has to be Maiden. Long may they reign.

But to be sure, Iron Maiden had already been a mature and rather large rock 'n' roll franchise for a long time now, as the 1980s came to a close. And they'd managed to keep an even keel due to the strict divide between sturdy management and band, and then once the line is crossed into band, the undisputed leadership position of Steve Harris within that realm.

Closing words of this chapter go to Rod Smallwood, who explains essentially why we still have a vibrant and vital Iron Maiden to this day now, thirty more years down the line.

"Steve founded the band," begins Rod. "He's the main songwriter, and if he needs to make a decision, he'll make one on behalf of the band in a very democratic way. With Maiden, a lot of it's been me and Steve and our standup fights basically—that's what we do. But Steve's always had complete control of the music and the studio and the producers and what we play onstage and all that. I'll have my viewpoint, and we'll argue the toss about it.

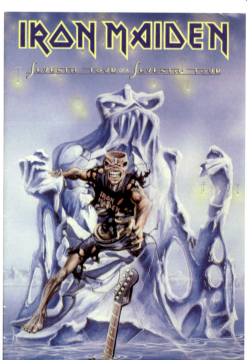

Seventh Son of a Seventh Son tour program. Dave Wright archive

"My side's the marketing and the gigs and all that side, which we'll discuss. Historically we've pretty well all gotten along. Sometimes there'll be 'Well, we don't really want to do that gig there' or 'We want to make that a bit shorter,' but generally speaking, we know each other so well we sort of know where we're going. Business-wise we've always taken care of it. It's good they've never felt a need to. They've got their own accountants and lawyers and everything else, but it's something we've always taken care of. And I think because we've done it well, then everyone's always been very happy. And Andy's very smart on how to operate the company's international tax side. These things are important for a band. Certain bands, like Maiden, aren't driven by money, but at the end of the day, if you're working as hard as they work, you want to get your just rewards for it. We make absolutely sure they get their just rewards.

Backstage pass. *Dave Wright archive*

"Nothing's ever blown up," continues Smallwood. "Believe it or not, it might sound totally impossible, but nothing's ever blown up. We've always been very sure about what we do, and we've always planned it ahead. Particularly in the 1980s, I mean you've got to reckon, I was on the road with the guys right through when I got married in 1989. I was there all the time. We lived, ate, breathed, slept everything Maiden. We'd tour, then we'd come back and write an album. We'd go to Jersey somewhere, lock ourselves in a hotel, write an album. We'd go to the Bahamas, lock ourselves up there, and make the album. Then we'd lock ourselves up and rehearse, and then we'd go on tour and go mad."

"It's a very, very close-knit family. Half of our crew, or three of our key crew, have been with us since 1979 and 1980. You know each other really well. Actually, the way we look at it, we're all working for Iron Maiden. We're all working for something we've got great respect for. We've also got different jobs to do for this employer called Iron Maiden. Steve plays bass and writes songs, Bruce sings, Nicko's on the drums, I'm the manager, and Andy's looking after the business side. We've all got our jobs as part of it, and when we go on tour it's like going on a rugby tour. Everyone does their job, and then we go down the bar afterwards and have a good time. We're too close to miss a point by a mile, to have a major blowup.

"At the end of the day, Steve's got his side that he makes decisions on, and I've sort of got mine in terms of certain aspects in my territory. If we disagree, then if the one who wants it is still saying after hours of shouting that this is the right thing to do, we decide that if you feel so strongly about it, you must be right, and get on with it. I think any partnership's like that, isn't it? So, I can't recall ever having anything even close to unpleasant. Really, we've argued things out of passion for what we believe is right for Maiden, with different takes on it. But you can't fall out over stuff like that.

"But yes, we have total control—we always have had. Total. I mean nothing passes in Iron Maiden without me seeing it. Most of it goes past Steve as well. The only thing that doesn't go past him are more day to day. I see everything that goes on. We've always been completely in the creative process. You look at the old artwork, and that was all from ideas from myself and some from the band which Derek executed. But the actual ideas and designs and things, a large proportion were ours. It continues on like that. We've always had a complete grip on what we're doing. We've always had a lot of control, but we've always ensured we're in a situation to have the control. If we don't know how to do it, who the hell does?"

CHAPTER 8

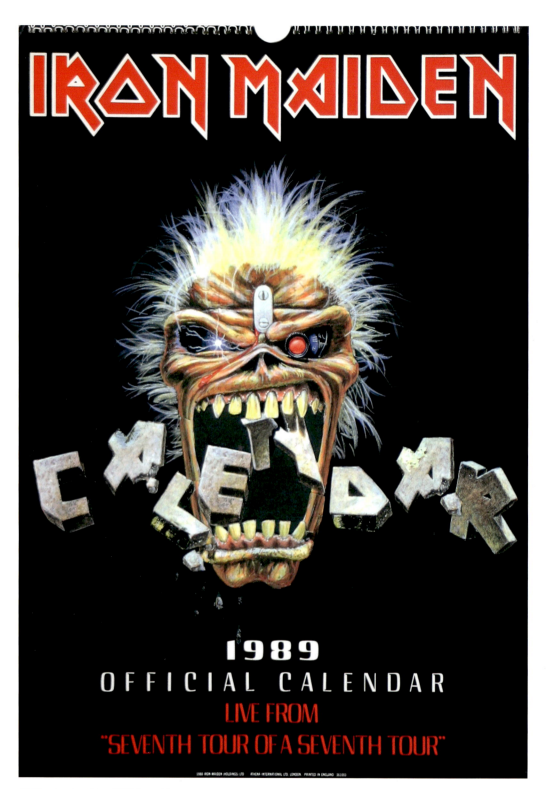

1989 calendar. *Dave Wright archive*

CHAPTER 9
Tattooed Millionaire and No Prayer for the Dying

"We went into a sort of collective madness."

Having conquered the world in the 1980s, their glory years culminating in the *Live After Death* album of 1985 and the Herculean tour that produced this "New Wave of British Heavy Metal" exclamation mark, Iron Maiden entered the 1990s filled with self-doubt and fears of obsolescence.

The band's John Paul Jones, thoughtful guitarist Adrian Smith, had left the band, and meteoric lead singer Bruce Dickinson wasn't exactly solid within the ranks. Dissatisfaction had lingered all the way since *Somewhere in Time*, and now Dickinson was striking out with a solo album, the ultimate expression of creative restlessness in rock 'n' roll bands, the roiling spoiler inevitably holding up a mirror to the mess that is the main franchise.

To kick off the year, Iron Maiden would conduct writing sessions in a campaign to bolster their relevance by way of their first album of the decade, after two records—*Somewhere in Time* and *Seventh Son of a Seventh Son*—that were a letdown from their peak performances; namely, *The Number of the Beast*, *Piece of Mind*, and *Powerslave*. But Adrian Smith would not be part of the creative dynamic, leaving Bruce and chief executive officer Steve Harris to come up with the goods.

"At the time, I just felt I had been in the band for ten years and done a lot of touring and recording, and I just felt the urge to do something different," says Smith. "And to be honest, at the time I felt a bit stifled in the band. Obviously, these things are never black and white, they're very complex, but I guess I basically wasn't pulling in the same direction as the other chaps. You know, Steve's very prolific, and he's always going to come up with a lot of stuff. His material is kind of the backbone of what we do. Also, at the time there was some movement in the band to go back to a really raw sound, almost garagey, and I really wasn't into that either.

"And we started to do the record, *No Prayer for the Dying*, and I just lost my enthusiasm and things came to a head, and I think I was just burned out as well about the last ten years. I'd started working on a few things, and it just wasn't sparking. And we sat down and had a chat and that was it, really [laughs]. To be quite honest, I didn't know what to do with myself when I split with Iron Maiden. I was so used to being involved with Maiden on a day-to-day basis for ten years, I just kind of sat at home and chilled out and had a regular life for a little while."

Asked by the author whether he went and got a regular job, Smith chuckled and said, "No, no, I wasn't that shaken up, no."

"Overall, Adrian wasn't really into the band all along for the past little while," said drummer Nicko McBrain at the time. "He was really unhappy, and he had to do a solo record. Whereas Bruce is a totally different story. He did it 'cause basically he's so hyper, he had to do something. He had a totally different attitude to it—he did a one-off single, then followed it up with the solo record. It wasn't preconceived like Adrian's. We didn't expect him to leave, and we didn't want it to happen. But we've now got Janick, and he's great."

Speaking with Jon Hotten, Bruce said that "when Adrian left, there was no personal crap anymore. It's not like there are any shitheads in the band. Everyone has an ego, of course, but everyone knows how to handle each other. He was obviously so unhappy with the band thing. It really was a question that he wanted to be somewhere else, somewhere totally different. I mean, his record is so totally different. We noticed it more onstage than anywhere else, little things like eye contact, body language. There was always something wrong. He didn't seem to be happy on stage."

Meanwhile, life went on, Adrian gone, uneasy truce with Bruce. *The Earthquake Album* by Rock Aid Armenia is issued, including in the track list Maiden's "Run to the Hills." Dickinson guests on the anchor track, an all-star version of Deep Purple's "Smoke on the Water." As well, Bruce's wife, Paddy, gives birth to the couple's (and Bruce's) first child, Austin. Griffin would follow in 1992, and Kia in 1994. Paddy represented a second marriage for Bruce, after having been married to Jane from 1983 through 1987, that marriage producing no children.

February through September 1990, Iron Maiden work on what will become *No Prayer for the Dying*, using the Rolling Stones Mobile Studio and a barn (a.k.a. Barnyard Studios) on Steve Harris's property in Essex. The Stones Mobile was proposed because Battery Studios proved to be unavailable until mid-April, and the band was enthusiastic to start directly following their writing sessions.

So yes, a notable lineup change finds Adrian Smith replaced with Janick Gers.

As Steve explains to *M.E.A.T.* magazine's the Sledge at the time, "When Janick came in, all the material had already been written and arranged, so yeah, he just had to learn the parts, which he did quickly and plays them excellently. When we recorded it, we did everything in one or two takes to get a live feel to it—I commented to the guys that if we were to stick some audience parts in, you'd swear it was recorded at a show. It sounds that live, which is exactly what we've been trying to get all these years. And Martin [Birch, producer] had worked before with this mobile, so that went smooth too. It was a real fun and relaxed album to do because we did it in a familiar atmosphere where we could have a few beers at the local pub afterwards. I think that from now on we'll always record there. The main thing at the end of the day is the sound and feeling, which we really like on this record."

But long before the release of *No Prayer for the Dying*, Bruce would emerge on May 8, 1990, with *Tattooed Millionaire*, prefaced by a taster in the UK via the title track, on April 17 (also considered for the album title: *First Offence*).

Wrote Phil Wilding of Bruce's introductory volley (namely, the single), "Someone told me this was about Steve Harris. It isn't. Actually—and I know this is going to surprise you—but this is what's known in the trade as Really Rather Good. No pomp, no inflated yelping, no overdone histrionics, and Dickinson really singing. Where this newfound vocal grit has risen from, God only knows. Could I possibly get an album? Now what are you going to write about? There's always your medical problems, I suppose."

If seeing Bruce on a party rock record wasn't surreal enough, at the same time, book company Sidgwick & Jackson publish Bruce's satirical novel *The Adventures of Lord Iffy Boatrace*, which upon release promptly sells 40,000 copies. Two years later, Bruce pens a sequel called *The Missionary Position*.

CHAPTER 9

"I've actually put this album out at the wrong time in accordance with my career with Maiden, as I really had no time," mused Bruce with a smile back in the spring of 1990. "But I'm a great believer in being an opportunist, so when the opportunity arose to cut a song with some friends of mine, I immediately took advantage of it, and it turned out to be such a fantastic feeling—so much so that I saw a direction building and knew it was time to do the solo album, so I just went and did it. The whole record was written in a week. They just kept coming out.

"It's not that much different from when I write songs for Maiden with Steve," continues Bruce, "as we can come up with four songs in a day. For this record I wrote the songs in collaboration with Janick Gers—it works out to a 70/30 split between me and him, with me controlling the direction of the whole thing. It's a great rock 'n' roll record. It should never be compared to a Maiden record, because it's a different beast. I would never dream of writing this material for Maiden, 'cause it wouldn't fit them. I wrote this material with the guys who are going to play it. I must admit, though, that I did have some extra freedom—it was enjoyable doing some different lyrics and plays on words, and I feel that people will be surprised by the quality of the songs."

Indeed, *Tattooed Millionaire* would serve as a launching pad for Janick Gers—formerly with White Spirit and Gillan—into Iron Maiden, via the solo record. Everybody knew Janick quite well. White Spirit was a Deep Purple–influenced NWOBHM band with a lone record from way back in 1980, when Bruce was in Samson. Gers replaced Bernie Tormé in Gillan, playing on the band's last two records, *Double Trouble* and *Magic*. Then there's virtually nothing (other than, commendably, a humanities degree), right up until *Tattooed Millionaire*.

The initial song Bruce refers to is his writing and recording of "Bring Your Daughter . . . to the Slaughter" for *A Nightmare on Elm Street 5: The Dream Child*. Admirably, Bruce's label, EMI, left this off the record, and it would enjoy renewed life through Maiden. In its stead, the title track would be launched, reaching #18 in the UK charts, with the band's cover of "All the Young Dudes" reaching #23.

Dave Wright archive

As Bruce explained to *Kerrang!*, "I wandered into the studio with no intention of doing a solo album, to do this, 'Bring Your Daughter . . . to the Slaughter' track, which I really did because I thought it's only gonna take a week and I've always wanted to do something with Janick. The vibe was so good that I thought, 'There's an album here.' It's just one of those things where the whole thing meshes, and you see what shape it's going to be.

"One of the things I found majorly unattractive and had a bee in my bonnet about," continued Bruce, "is that for a country that

Dave Wright archive

basically single-handedly created the entire music form that is heavy metal, England has this thing about trying to dress up like male bimbos from LA. If you look in the back of *Melody Maker*, all the bands are influenced by American bands, and half these bands are shit! There's no feel, there's no soul, there's no nothing. There's a brain scan of zero going through these people. If the whole world started sounding like the Carpenters, they'd get dressed up like the Carpenters and play that instead. They don't owe allegiance or loyalty to anything like that. There's no point to what they do.

"What I'm really against is lack of honesty. It's all the wannabes. They just wanna be the attitude and not the content. All music, art, anything that purports to be in the creative arena, has always got a conflict between style and substance, right? There's always a line. What I'm saying is that for me, a lot of metal music has gone too far towards style. Style, when it becomes utterly insular, utterly introspective, just becomes boring and meaningless. If you have a linear style, it's boring. But if you have a lateral style—same ideas in a different context—that makes people see the same idea in a different way."

Produced by storied British stalwart Chris Tsangarides (Y&T, Tygers of Pan Tang, Thin Lizzy, Judas Priest), working at Battery Studios, for all the high ideals, *Tattooed Millionaire* would sound like a tight, efficient, and glossy cross between Maiden, lunch bucket metal, and hair metal. In other words, it's a bit anchored to the times but not an embarrassment. More graphically, next to the Iron Maiden of *No Prayer for the Dying* and even *Fear of the Dark*, it sounded vital, relevant, even confident. But still there was really no band vibe to the thing. Janick was the record's only guitarist, and bassist Andy Carr and drummer Fabio Del Rio were unknowns, remaining that way moving forward.

And despite his enthusiasm for the solo record, in interviews to promote it, Dickinson was only too happy to talk about what the next record with Maiden will sound like.

"Heavy as fuck! There's no title yet, and definitely no concept," enthused Bruce in 1990. "It's just a bunch of songs put together for a great record, like on the *Number of the Beast* and *Piece of Mind* albums. We were doing album after album after album, and I feel that it was starting to show after a while that we were doing too much too soon. We got into a bit of a rut, especially me personally. But now we've got a clear mind for this record, and we been cleaning up our own house. We've been shortening up the songs. We're bored with the thirty-eight-bar guitar solos. We want to make things a bit more concise. We got a bit guilty of overblowing things.

"Getting away from it for a couple of years and then coming back is like getting back to the roots and rediscovering what it's all about. And for me it's doubly good that I am doing the solo thing now, so that I really get back to the roots. I feel that the break was good for all in Maiden, and that the new album will blow people away. So, by doing this solo record, I've got some inspirational juices going again. It's only going to make my performance on the Maiden record better for it. I'm confident though that both albums will do extremely well because they're both killer."

Back to *Tattooed Millionaire*, the album opens with "Son of a Gun," a slow, heavy number that sets the mood right with loads of tradition. Next comes the title track, which is essentially solid hair metal, played airtight and efficient. The song's melodic chorus is a bit of a shock, but it's well written, so Bruce fans were won over. The song was given the full video treatment, with the clip produced by Storm Thorgerson of Hipgnosis fame. Nikki Sixx seems to think that the song was written about him and a love triangle that might have taken place between the two and Bruce's wife. Indeed, Bruce has intimated that the lyric was inspired by watching what was going on from visits to the Rainbow on the Sunset Strip in Hollywood, watching how all the hair metal bands conducted themselves.

"Born in '58" is even more melodic, a sort of pop song and thus sensible as a single, which it was, getting issued as the album's last kick of the can on March 25, 1991, backed with live versions of "Tattooed Millionaire" and "Son of a Gun." The autobiographical lyric has Bruce reminiscing about being raised by his grandparents.

"Hell on Wheels" is also indicative of the straight commercial metal of the day, but a little more slanted to the 1970s. Again, a strong chorus shores it up. Like the album opener, Bruce sings this one with a lot of vocal fry, lending contrast and reminding us of his robust work back with Samson.

Next up is "Gypsy Road," which is your basic hair metal take on the southern rock ballad, something you might hear from Bon

BRUCE DICKINSON

Dave Wright archive

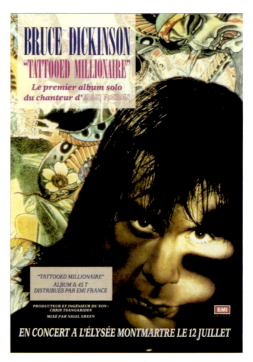

Martin Popoff archive

Jovi, Mötley Crüe, Guns N' Roses, or Cinderella, who also wrote a song with the same title. Despite the massaging in of acoustic guitar, the song can't be saved. One, it sounds odd coming from Bruce; two, it's too LA; and three, the stiff playing and production leaches all the potential southern soul out of it.

"Dive! Dive! Dive" comes next, with Bruce turning in a lascivious party rocker, all sexual double entendre and choral gang vocals. Concerning the narrative, Bruce was inspired by a British comic strip and TV cartoon character called Captain Horatio Pugwash. Not much to Janick's riff, which is the problem with these songs—they are likable but not lovable—even if his solo is highly inventive. Dickinson then switches things up for his cover of Mott-circa-Bowie's "All the Young Dudes," again, not given much of a chance with the rigid, corporate drums and the bass snapped to grid by producer Chris Tsangarides—this is arguably the stuffiest-sounding and arguably least inspired record of the man's long and varied résumé. Still, Bruce gives the vocal the ol' college try, pushing lots of air, effecting a slight English accent.

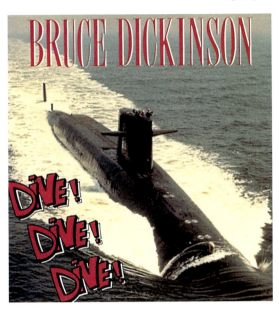

Martin Popoff archive

"Lickin' the Gun" and "Zulu Lulu" contribute further to this unstated mandate of party metal with one foot in the 1970s, one foot on the Sunset Strip, the first funky, the second a bit glam of both sorts; namely, UK glam from the early '70s and the hair metal of the late 1980s. The record's most serious song—and most seriously rocking—is left to last, "No Lies" being an ambitious song of novel chorus-first construct and later a sort of bluesy jam. It's a thoughtful way to end the record, with a song that demonstrates creative potential that would emphatically be fulfilled as Bruce's solo career develops.

Time to promote, and from June 18 through 28, 1990, Bruce conducts a solo tour of the UK, supported by Jagged Edge. Then it's over to the States, where on August 14, 1990, Bruce and his band perform a concert in LA that is later released as the *Dive! Dive! Dive!* VHS video. "One bus for the band and crew to live on," chuckled Bruce of the US campaign, "with the equipment underneath. Just like the old days. We've only got five weeks to do a whole bloody country."

As he told Jon Hotten, "Steve thinks my solo album has a good chance of outselling Maiden, especially in the States. If it sells one million in the States, it'll sell three. If one song gets away, there will be five songs to get away, and it'll be huge. Steve knows that because it's one of his favorite albums. We sat around talking about it, and I said, 'Look, I'm doing a short tour of the States, clubs, one tour bus, all the gear slung underneath, in the same spirit in which the album was made.' I've scheduled my solo album around the Maiden tour."

CHAPTER 9

You know, both of these industry veterans were making some sense here. This record—pertly played and packaged, with Bruce's beloved, snappy title . . . *Tattooed Millionaire* could have been a smash hit. It's not out of the question calling the thing three, four singles deep, and really, all the right choices were made in that respect. Arguably, it's arriving a few years too late, with respect to metal's arc as well as Maiden's. If it had been issued when Maiden was meteoric, the sky for the band's fireplug of a singer would have been the limit. The fact that the album wasn't particularly exciting was neither here nor there. It still could have sold buckets, in an era when safe music hammered into submission by superstar producers was the order of the day.

As Steve confided with Mick Wall, "The only thing I was a little bit concerned about was that it would be a bloody great album, and it would do so well he'd want to leave. The grass is always greener on the other side. I actually said to Rod, 'I hope he doesn't do a Fish and fuck off and leave us in the shit, because at this stage, to find another singer would be really bad news!' But Bruce made it quite plain that he really doesn't want to leave Maiden. It's not that he has a burning desire to do a solo album in the first place. That was the thing with Adrian: he always had a burning desire to do a solo album, and when he did it, I think it showed that maybe he wasn't as content being in Maiden as he thought he was.

"Bruce's thing was much more spontaneous; that's the difference. I think now that he's done a solo album, though, in the future he'll maybe want to do . . . he's seen another side of himself that might not necessarily fit in with the Iron Maiden mold, which he'd still like to pursue. I don't see why he can't do both. He said the same thing himself. Sure, why not? He's still into being our singer too, so why shouldn't he? As long as he's still enjoying himself in Maiden, then why leave? And as far as I know, Bruce is still enjoying himself in Maiden, so there's no problem. If any of us stopped enjoying it, we'd leave."

More on *Tattooed Millionaire*, specifically its fate in the States, Harris says, "It's doing all right. It's not gone mental. Personally, I thought it would've done better than that. But he's only released one single so far over there, with one underway now that may or may not take off. But then he's also got another two or three other songs that could go mega."

Indeed Dickinson, feet on the ground, was letting the world know that his place fronting Maiden was not in jeopardy. Still, he was reflective, telling Hotten, "Look, I think to some extent this thing exists more in Rod's [Smallwood, manager] mind than it does in ours [meaning Maiden]. I mean, you won't see the five members of Iron Maiden joined at the hip walking in and out of the Hippodrome in step like some kind of millipede. But I wouldn't expect five people, with an average age of thirty-two or thirty-three, most of whom are married and all of whom have got children or have children on the way, to be out pubbing it out on the town every night. That's unrealistic and stupid. The relationships that are forged in ten years on the road, six of them pretty much constant, are relationships that last a long time. I may not see Steve for six months, but when I see him, he's exactly the same Steve I ever knew.

"I'd be foolish to turn around and say Iron Maiden are still going to be happening in 2010," continues Bruce. "I don't know; maybe we will. It depends how foolish we feel. My personal feeling is that, again, when it feels right for us to bow out, we will. I think we'll do it fairly graciously. There are gonna be no acrimonious bust-ups in the band. We've been together too long."

On September 3, longtime Maiden rivals Judas Priest issue their high-quality and nearly thrashy *Painkiller* album, posing a serious challenge to Maiden's dominance as the UK's premiere heavy metal band, a title Maiden arguably wrestled from Priest upon the issuance of that band's "glam metal" *Turbo* record in 1986. Interestingly, the producer turning Priest into a throaty, gleaming machine is Chris Tsangarides, who emphatically had not made the same manly impact with Bruce on his solo debut.

And how would Maiden respond to the heavying up of heavy metal as the new decade dawned? "The way we've always felt is that people can think what they want to think," said a dismissive Nicko McBrain at the time. "We do things the way we feel is right—we've always just gone by the way we feel at the time. It's no good sitting down and looking at what's happening now and try to analyze it, because otherwise we wouldn't be able to be Maiden. We'd have tried to make a thrash album or something, which would be like totally false for us to do that. We are from a different era. We are more influenced by '70s stuff, and it'd be wrong for us to go out and try to be in vogue or to stay young, if you know what I mean. I like some of that stuff—it's just that it wouldn't be natural for us to do it."

We'd hear soon enough that Maiden weren't about to change their age spots. On September 10, "Holy Smoke" is issued as an advance single from the forthcoming *No Prayer for the Dying*, backed with covers of Stray's "All in Your Mind" and Golden Earring's "Kill Me ce Soir," both impossibly and amusingly obscure. Sniffed longtime cover illustrator Derek Riggs on the sleeve for the thing, "At this point they thought they were coming up with all the ideas, so I let them, and I stopped contributing, because they were getting a bit snotty. And 'Holy Smoke' was somebody's idea about all these preachers on television. Basically, it was Eddie smashing things or Eddie sitting in a chair, and they are still kind of doing that."

A week later, on September 19, Bruce's solo guitarist Janick Gers plays his first show with Iron Maiden, at the Woughton Centre in Milton Keynes, England. It is a "secret" warm-up gig, with the band billed as the Holy Smokers. Framed Bruce on his mate at the time, "Rhythmically more like a machine gun—choppy and wicked. What's great is that he's come from the same time period as us. We've all known him for ages, so he's not new to us in that respect. For about the last two or three years, or over the last two tours, Adrian was noticeably not very happy onstage. We weren't getting any enthusiasm or reaction from him, and when it became clear on this new record that we weren't going for anything commercial at all, he just came to us and said he felt he didn't fit anymore. We respect him for it 'cause he was honest about it. We wish him the best of luck."

Through October 18, Maiden conduct their Intercity Express tour of the UK, playing theaters and other venues smaller than they had become accustomed to, in tandem using a stripped-down stage show. Support comes from Wolfsbane, whose front man Blaze Bayley would soon become Iron Maiden's new lead singer.

"There's no jealousy going on with the band and me over the solo record," said Bruce, juggling. "Nor am I dissatisfied with Maiden's music. It's just like Phil Collins and Genesis—I've got the best of both worlds. I feel I'm smart enough to deal with both things without developing a crazed ego-inflated attitude. The band loves my solo record, and Steve has already said to me that he thinks it'll outsell Maiden, because it's got the kind of stuff on it that radio will like—they've never played Maiden."

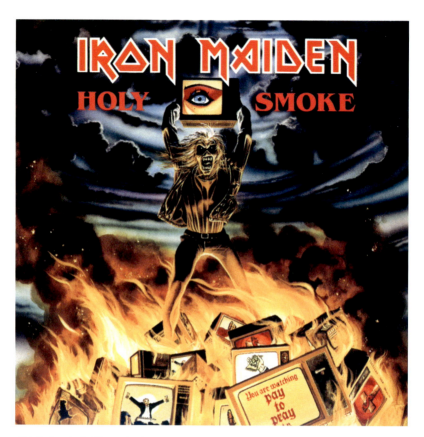

"Holy Smoke" CD single. *Dave Wright archive*

On September 23, 1990, surprisingly, Maiden perform their first ever show in Ireland, with the first in Northern Ireland taking place the following night. This is followed by an even greater cause for celebration, when on October 1 the band issues *No Prayer for the Dying*, their eighth studio album, which instantly goes gold in the UK.

"We were halfway through, and Adrian left and Janick came in," remembers Dave Murray, setting the scene. "We recorded that on the Mobile, and it was parked outside Steve's house. And basically, the Mobile itself was from the 1970s, so it kind of had that sound and feel to it. But we obviously had Martin Birch there at the helm, and basically each album, once you've done it, you let it go. It's that period of your life, history [laughs]."

"But I've enjoyed every album we've done. *No Prayer* is a really stand-up album. I think it's one where the band went off on a little tangent. There's some really good material on there, but it's such an individualistic thing, 'Oh, I like this album better or this one.' I kind of just take them and you're done with it, and you're so proud of it and you move on.

"*No Prayer* wasn't recorded under any pressure," continues the blond axman, suddenly the last link besides Steve to the early days. "No album's been recorded, really, under any pressure. It's just [that] at the time there were a few changes going on, and so basically, you've got this period of time, and you put that recording hat on and do what you're supposed to be doing. You go in there and the rhythm tracks are going

Intercity Express tour booklet. *Dave Wright archive*

down and you're playing as a band. And then you'd start layering things. You would go in there for a couple of days or Janick would go in for a couple of days. So, we weren't going in there and beating our head against the wall every day, twenty hours in the studio. We'd go in there for half a day, a couple of days a week, so it was never thrashing around.

"But *No Prayer*, for sound, because of the environment it was recorded in and the stuff we were using . . . but then maybe, hey, it was time for a little change; let's throw a spanner into the works [laughs]. At the end of the day, we've played a lot of those songs live, and they probably sound better live than they did on the album. The playing was still there, but at the time, I think it did sound a bit dated. But then, it was just, hey, let's do it, another feather in the cap."

As Steve told *Hard Force*'s Henry Dumatray, the album "was recorded from January to April 1990 at my place, in my private recording studio. Originally, the recording was planned to start in April, at the Battery Studios of London. But as the new songs were written quickly, we started earlier and started working at my place so we could put everything on tape as fast as possible. As we'd recorded the stuff in the barn we use as a rehearsing studio, we were all very relaxed, without any external pressure, which accounts for the very 'live' sound of the album. It's mainly more aggressive than the previous albums. I think that some of our fans were disappointed in the musical orientation we had taken lately. So, I think they'll be happy to see that we're going back to a more aggressive and powerful style. The band still has the fire anyway."

Concerning Maiden's new guitarist, Steve remarked that "we've known him for a while now, and I think he's a really nice bloke, which is also one of the reasons we took him on board. We'd seen him play with Ian Gillan while he was in his band, and we therefore knew that he was a good guitar player. We just needed to know whether his style would suit that of Iron Maiden. We asked him to learn four songs of ours, and the audition went really well. Janick moves much more than Adrian, but I don't know if he'll be able to move that much onstage with Maiden, as our songs are fairly technical. And as I like to move too, we'll have to be careful not to run into each other! [laughs]. He may well be a bit nervous at first, but I think he'll get over it."

Noted Murray on Gers, "I didn't really want anybody else after Adrian left, because we were all such close friends. But I saw Janick play with Gillan, and I thought he was amazing—his stage presence and everything was so exciting. I think his playing really shows on the album. Actually, the first day Janick played with the band, it was just immediate. We played 'The Trooper' and we thought this was it. We felt the intensity in the studio. It was electric.

"About halfway through the first song, I knew he'd fit in," Dave told Chris Welch from *Metal Hammer*. "The band felt the same way too. Then we played 'Iron Maiden,' 'The Prisoner,' and 'Children of the Damned,' and that was great, mostly that Janick only had twenty-four hours to learn them. Afterwards we were all silent for a moment, motionless, looking at each other. All you could hear was the buzzing of the amps. That's a moment that meant a lot to us."

Getting down to work with Janick, Dave said that "at first, we recorded separately. Then we decided to work together on the solos, so we wouldn't play in the same tones. Then we worked on the harmonies together. It was the first time that Janick was playing with another guitarist. Before that he'd only collaborated with keyboard players.

"Many songs were recorded in one take per instrument," continues Dave. "In a lot of cases, we just placed microphones in the room to capture the live aspect of our sound. I wonder what the carpenters who built Steve's house some three hundred years ago would have thought if they'd known that a rock band was going to record an album there. This place has a past, just like the mobile studio we used, that was also used for the recording of Led Zeppelin's *Physical Graffiti*. In fact, we'd use this mobile studio several times in the past, during the airing of the Donington gig on the BBC, or for the *Maiden England* video.

Publicity photo featuring the new guy, Janick Gers, *second from left*. Dave Wright archive

"I've always been very pleased with all our albums, even those where we experimented a little bit, but this particular album sounds like dynamite. It's been like going back to our roots. What happened is that we found ourselves in the same state of mind as at the beginning, with the same thirst for success, the same rages we had ten years ago, but this time with the experience that you get from ten years of a successful career."

Derek Riggs's art for *No Prayer* was as dark, rough, and disorienting as the enclosed music. It was hard to cotton on to what was going on, but if you squinted and lingered, you'd realize that it had something to do with the awkward mouthful of syllables that composed the titling.

"I did that as a painting," explains Riggs. "The first version with the man standing next to the gravestone is all painting—gouache, watercolor. Later on, they did a reissue of it, and Rod said he would quite like to change it. Because he never really liked the guy; he didn't think the man worked very well. So, at that time I was working digitally. You couldn't have done this any other way. I took it off. I patched up the gaps where the man was, and patched up all the faulty bits which were left from taking the guy off. And then from that, I constructed a new background, which was skeletons lying on a stone floor, and they're all lying in piles of dust—they're turned to dust. That was the background. I replaced the whole thing. I basically had to redraw 70, 80, 90 percent of it. It took a lot of removing. Because there was more of it than you see in the final new cover. I had to basically slice it apart and put it back together again. It's the original painted Eddie. I've taken him digitally out of the artwork, the standing artwork, and patched it together with the bits I had, and re-created the background."

Dave Wright archive

I remember thinking when the album came out that the man looked a bit like Rod Smallwood, seriously thinking that Derek and even Rod and the guys were giving boss #2 a bit of a send-up, in the same way that Paul got beheaded on an earlier single. Maybe that's why Rod didn't like it—he thought he was the gravedigger about to get beat to hell by Eddie. This redoing of the covers for reissue is a contentious idea, reaching its zenith with the digital rerender of the debut cover, an iconic image that should never be compromised. Of note, all of this might not have come to be—the working title for the record was *008*, complete with a James Bond theme for Eddie!

No Prayer for the Dying opens with a welcome rumble and a roar, "Tailgunner" sweeping into view as a sturdy, quick-paced rocker in the spirit of "Aces High." However, a smart, creative verse riff gives way to a bit of a weak chorus, although all is forgiven by the happy race to the end. Noted Bruce at the time, in an uncredited chat, "The title came from a porno movie, about anal sex, and then I thought, well, I can't write the lyrics about that! So, I wrote it about real tail gunners. I had some words which began 'Trace your way back 50 years, to the glory of Dresden, blood and tears.' I know we shouldn't mention the war, but it's about the attitude of bombing people. It was real death in the skies back then. But there aren't any tail gunners on planes anymore. It's all done by computers using missiles. At least it used to be man on man, but now it's machine on machine. Who uses bullets anymore?"

A single that never stuck, "Holy Smoke" is next, this one fully in the spirit of the record's mandate, this idea of quick, casual, a bit loose and rock 'n' rollsy, with Bruce's raspy voice recalling the style of his predecessor Paul Di'Anno, befitting of the barn-crafted music behind Bruce's verbal attack. The song's open hanging chords remind this writer of "Never Say Die," even

"Tailgunner" promo sticker. *Dave Wright archive*

more so when one recalls that Sabbath were similarly looking for a gritty vibe with the album of the same name and then proposed a fast simple song as a single. "Never Say Die" was even more of a surprise style change for Sabbath than "Holy Smoke" was for Maiden, but both indeed were propelled by what one might called stacked pancakes of power chords rather than note-dense riffing. Says Bruce, "This is about TV preachers and all the various lies they tell. I just had this big image of all those ovens in the death camps with the preachers' feet sticking out and holy smoke going up."

Maiden had a long tradition of poking priests, but after all the TV evangelist scandals of the 1980s, the idea was ripe for a return visit—just ask Ozzy, who scored a midcareer highlight hit with "Miracle Man."

Conversely, next, "No Prayer for the Dying" is a sincere address to God in times of depression and turmoil. For music, the band goes with a sort of full-band Renaissance music ballad, although quickly that goes up in holy smoke as the boys double up on the speed and hit a jam, and then Bruce delivers the direct plea to God.

"This song has Steve's lyrics," explains Dickinson. "And for me it has the best vocal on the album, the one I like best, even though it's like just two lines. It's one of the best 'quiet beginning' type [of] songs I've ever done with Maiden, and I really like the melody line."

With respect to the odd turn of phrase "no prayer for the dying," Steve told Mick Wall that "we were just going through the songs, searching for something that might make a good title, and Eddie certainly wouldn't give anyone a prayer! [laughs]. It just felt like a good title, something that conjures up some sort of imagery. You need something like that for Eddie. It's like, he's done it all so far. He's been mummified, killed himself off, and gone into the future. Where can he go from here?"

"Public Enema Number One" is a raging rocker, underrated, maybe the fiery heart of the album, Bruce alternately sneering and howling, Janick and Dave slashing out a demonic chord sequence, Steve and Nicko grooving trashy. Hidden jewel within a jewel is the half-time chorus, with an ominous melody that is the perfect foil to the nearly off-the-rails verse. Dave Murray gets a rare writing credit on this one, and as Steve champions, the guys rarely get a song out of Dave, but it's usually a good one when it happens.

"It's actually about green hypocrites," says Bruce, who takes the lyric credit. "It's about a big guy with his fast car, and he's leaving the city in a cloud of smoke, leaving the children crying in fear. He's got a one-way ticket out of here. Fine, see ya. Because he can afford it, he's left everyone else behind. And in the cities, there is overcrowding, guns, and riots, and it seems like everything is gonna snap. The politicians just lie to save their own skins, gamble that they are gonna do the right thing, and they give the press scapegoats all the time. The whole thing is based on a cross between New York and LA, and I just hope the kids of today have more brains than the frazzled remains of the 1960s and the 1970s generations. California dreaming and the earth dies screaming! That's what it's about: people talking about the environment and not doing anything."

"Fates Warning" is another somewhat forgotten song that shouldn't be. Past the mellow intro, the song heats up with a nice gallop topped with a guitar sculpture that is part simple chords, part simple high lead riff, a novel construct but an effective one. The chord sequences are malevolent, passionate, and blustery, with a vibe like "Flight of Icarus."

What's cool about the record thus far is that there's barely a song much over four minutes, and in fact once it's done, there's only one that eclipses five. Ergo, the track lengths further feed this idea that the band wanted an album with more immediate bite—and boy does *No Prayer* snap like a rabid dog.

"Steve's words again," says Bruce, of "Fates Warning." "This is about feeling secure when everyone's life can hang by a thread. You can go any time. And who knows why or how?" The title of the song also pays winking tribute to New England rockers Fates Warning, who, along with Queensryche and Iron Maiden (slightly more loosely), form a triumvirate of bands building upon what Rush invented—progressive metal. In fact, Steve Harris arrived at what he would do from very much the same set of influences that Rush appreciated, which was a significant library of straight-up progressive rock.

Next is "The Assassin," another Maiden track rendered wholly obscure. This one makes use of a Nicko rhythm that reverses upon itself from verse to chorus, and a melodic structure that modulates. Also, during the verses, there's prominent bass and high guitar rather than much power chord riffing. Can't say that any of the parts work particularly well, with the chorus hampered by a sing-songy vocal melody.

"Here we are trying to get into the head of a hired killer," says Bruce. "He doesn't do it for money, but because he likes it and he's cool, calculating, cold, and sadistic. These are Steve's lyrics again."

Tortuous intro notwithstanding, "Run Silent Run Deep" is another salt-of-the-earth Maiden romp that deserves to be heard more. Built on a typical gallop (albeit with discombobulating time signature), it's quite sophisticated melodically, and the anthemic chorus fits well. The song's aggression is underscored by Bruce's roughshod vocal, with Dickinson doing a good job of maintaining the mandated sonic scowl as we run deep into the track list.

"These are some words I wrote for the *Somewhere in Time* album," explains Dickinson. "That particular song never made it, but I kept the words, and when Steve came up with something, I said, 'You know what will fit brilliantly there? These words.' It's a song about submarines, actually, the first song about submarines. 'Dive! Dive! Dive!' came later. This is a slightly more serious version. The title comes from one of my favorite war movies. We do use a lot of films and book titles, because they always inspired good material for us. But then books crop up a lot in films! This is about the dog-eat-dog, no-mercy world of life and death at sea during the Second World War, and it was as rough for the guys below as it was for the guys up top, both engaged in this evil struggle without any mercy. And the sea didn't have any mercy."

"Hooks in You" is the lone track on *No Prayer for the Dying* that features an Adrian Smith credit, which makes sense given the song's utilitarian rock 'n' roll vibe, with a riff akin to the Michael Schenker Group's "Armed and Ready." Adrian downplays this type of generalization, and indeed later in life his music writing was more along the lines of the other guys. But back during his first run with the band, we could count on him for a certain pint-clinking crossover charm. Of course, he's out of the band by this point, but he had been around in the early stages, contributing a bit of writing.

Dave Wright archive

"It's a slightly tongue-in-cheek thing," remarked Bruce. "Me and Paddy went to look at a house to buy, and it was lived in by three gay guys. We looked around and it had all these beams, and one of the guys was obviously into S&M and leather and stuff, and in one room there were these enormous industrial hooks screwed into the beams. My mind boggled at what they could be used for. I went home and wrote 'Hooks in You,' with the line 'hooks in the ceiling for that well-hung feeling.' I couldn't write it about gay guys, but what if you went around to the house of Mr. and Mrs. Average and you found all these hooks in the ceiling? What do they get up to? At the end of the song, the guy thinks his wife has been unfaithful, and sets her in concrete in the foundations."

Next is the aforementioned "Bring Your Daughter . . . to the Slaughter," which, indeed, in a validation of the band's better instincts and became a semifamed selection from this generally overlooked record. As discussed, this sprung from Bruce's first stab at a solo career. As Steve told Mick Wall, "What happened was, Bruce played me the song, and I said, 'You bastard, it's a fucking great song! We could do a fucking great version of that!' Mainly, I was thinking of live. It's a totally Maiden sort of song. It would go down great with the punters; I know it. But if he really wanted to do it on his solo album, then I'm sure he would have. But the way it worked out was, they asked him if he'd rather do an album, and Bruce said fine, so we ended up getting the song."

And so, in Bruce world, it remained a song generated for a movie. "Here I tried to sum up what I thought *Nightmare on Elm Street* movies are really about, and it's all about adolescent fear of periods. That's what I think it is, deep down. When a young girl first gets her period, she bleeds. And it happens at night, and so she is afraid to go to sleep. And it's a very terrifying time for her, sexually as well, and *Nightmare on Elm Street* targets that fear. The real slaughter in the Freddie movies is when she loses her virginity. That is the rather nasty thought behind it all, but that's what makes those kinds of movies frightening."

No Prayer for the Dying ends with a track that fits in that category of "forced" Maiden songs along the lines of "Quest for Fire," sort of too topical, grasping at straws, vaguely unsatisfying for a number of reasons. "Wind of Change" was a massive song for Scorpions, but that doesn't mean it's a creative triumph. And when Accept or U.D.O. pandered to the Russians, after a couple runs at it, it started to sound cliché. "Mother Russia" finds Maiden imagining a heavy metal version of Russian military music, and it falls flat, especially when Bruce has to sing like a Russian soldier over top of it.

As Steve told Mick Wall, "It's an epic-sounding song, even though it's not epic in length. Before the Berlin Wall went down, I had this Russian-sounding idea. I wrote the lyrics before the music, which is unusual for me. Musically, I wanted to try and capture the sort of Cossack-sounding thing. I don't know . . . Bruce made me burst out laughing because when he heard it, he immediately started doing this Cossack dance. But it sort of broke the ice. I was self-conscious about playing it to the lads for the first time because it is so Russian sounding, and it's one of those things that if it's not done properly could end up sounding really corny, really bad.

"We were the first major rock band to play in the Eastern Bloc," continued Harris. "We played in Poland in 1984. I think UFO and Budgie played there before we did, but they just hired local gear. We took the whole Iron Maiden show. We went there because we wanted to see what the place was all about, and we really enjoyed it and went back again on the next tour. We played in Warsaw, and half the Russian embassy came to the show!

"But 'Mother Russia' itself isn't particularly about perestroika. I didn't really want to get into that, because it seemed to me [that] everybody else was doing that already. I wanted to deal with Russia's past more and compare what's happening now with then. The key line in the song is probably 'Mother Russia, can you be happy now that your people are free?' That's the question nobody has the answer to yet. Obviously, in a country that size, it's going to take a long, long time before they catch up with the rest of the world now that the doors have finally been opened by Gorbachev. But I think they'll make it. I hope so."

Summarizes Bruce on the lyric, "It's about the tragedy of a great land which has an incredible history of being overrun and people being massacred for centuries. And this song says, wouldn't it be great if Russia could finally get itself together now and live in peace?"

All through the making of *No Prayer for the Dying*, Dickinson was finding the making of Iron Maiden's eighth record unsatisfying, further sowing the seeds of his discontent. After it was out and he got some distance from it, those ill feelings hadn't changed.

"*No Prayer for the Dying* was an album that I have to share collective responsibility and also blame for possibly being the worst-sounding Maiden album ever, with the exception of the first Maiden album," pronounced the Air Raid Siren. "We went into a sort of collective madness and recorded with this antiquated Rolling Stone Mobile, in a barn in the middle of winter. In a fit of enthusiasm, gosh, we'll be terribly hip because we'll be agricultural, and we were running around with straw in our hair doing guitar solos and things. And it just sounds like a dreadful album. Just the sonic quality of it. It's awful."

Derek Riggs–signed promo print. *Dave Wright archive*

Adds Dave, "The Mobile is quite an archaic piece of machinery. We felt like, let's try it, but I think the sound that came out actually sounds a little dated. As far as singles go in the UK, we had a couple of major hits from that album: 'Holy Smoke' and 'Bring Your Daughter . . . to the Slaughter.' When the first single was released, it was the first of the new year and it went straight to #1. In fact, it knocked off a Christmas song, a Cliff Richard track or something like that."

Speaking with Mattias Reinholdsson from *The Bruce Dickinson Wellbeing Network*, Bruce framed the situation this way:

"By the time we got to *No Prayer for the Dying*, Martin wasn't making any records at all, apart from an Iron Maiden record every year and a half. He'd basically gone into semiretirement. He earned his cash doing the Iron Maiden records, and he gets lots of royalties from back records from all the other bands he's done as well. And Martin was a character who would push himself to the point of destruction making a record. Far more so than anyone else in the band. Martin, as a producer, threw himself into albums to the point where he would almost have a breakdown. In fact, at one point he almost had a complete breakdown. He went through a very rough time when he was working really hard, and he was under a lot of pressure. He's not the kind of person that compromises easily, in terms of creativity. But after *Live After Death*, basically I think that Maiden had become quite civilized.

"I'm not sure if it was necessarily conscious," continued Bruce. "I think it was just something that everybody had slipped into. And I saw my position in the band as being the one to try and take Steve's ideas, reinvent them, and fuck around with it as much as I could, or as much as he allowed. For example, Rod, the manager, would ask me, 'Is there any chance you could get Steve to try and do this?' And I just said, 'Fuck, why don't you ask him yourself? Why come to me?'

"So, we'd go through these things, and I must say, when we got to *Seventh Son*, I was quite optimistic about that album. I think it was the last really good record the band made, and it was a record where everybody was really trying hard to come up with directions. But it was so slow developing that record, and it took such a long time to record it and it was so terribly expensive. But it was a pretty good record, and there were several ways the band could have gone at that point. But as it turned out, the next one, *No Prayer for the Dying*, was a huge backward step, I thought. I don't think that the production of that record was in any way correct."

Reminded by Mattias that the mandate was to record simply and directly, to make a record that sounded back to the roots, Dickinson counters, "Yes, but not one that sounded shit. The idea was to do something low key and not particularly complex. The idea was to do something that was the opposite to *Seventh Son*, and the idea was to do something that was very street, very happening, and something that was gonna sound good. The fact is that it sounded terrible, and everybody kind of acknowledges it now.

"We all collaborated with it, and we all had a great time making it because we were out in the middle of a field making a record in a barn on a twenty-year-old mobile truck. But basically, the Rolling Stones Mobile is a piece of crap! It's exactly the same as when Deep Purple recorded *Machine Head* on it. And the only reason they recorded *Machine Head* on it was that their real studio had burnt down. It wasn't because it was such great-sounding equipment, and it certainly sounded much better twenty years ago. They didn't even have a pair of monitors in it that were suitable for mixing on, so they got in a pair of small monitors, and I believe they mixed the album on the Rolling Stones Mobile as well, which, I think, is completely crazy.

"Martin Birch suggested that we do the album in a proper studio at the very beginning, but everybody was like, 'No, no, no, this'll be really cool.' And Martin did the best he could. Steve at that point started getting very interested in the idea of himself being a producer, and he was already editing Iron Maiden's concert videos. Something which I argued with him against as well. I said that I didn't think much of his editing, basically."

Truth be told, *No Prayer for the Dying* is not far off the others in terms of the sound picture, but one could imagine that Bruce, being the singer, is significantly taking into account, more so than anyone else would, the vocals, which, again, are aggressive and combative, negatively speaking, a bit worn and shot. When he listens back, he hears the ongoing exhaustion from the World Slavery tour through all the ensuing years, an exhaustion that wouldn't let up until his break from the band to come.

Wrote Neil Jeffries in his (overly generous) four out of five K review of the record for *Kerrang!*, "The only nagging doubt I have is that in going back to the roots, they've forgotten to move forward from the 1980s. For that reason, *No Prayer for the Dying* is littered with the echoes of Maiden Classics We Have Known. That might be what the most-diehard fanatics or the next generation of Irons supporters will want, but to me it tarnishes an otherwise crackin' good comeback, so I've docked the fifth K. It may seem churlish to attack a band for delivering what the fans will want, but I still think that maybe if Gers had arrived in time to add his ten-pence worth to the arrangements, this could've been the LP to really take Maiden into the 1990s. Who knows? What is beyond question is that their approach to the material here and the way the guitar solos slash out of the speakers like barbed-wire bullwhips make this a record Maiden can be proud of. It's just the album they needed and pretty much the answer to all our prayers."

October 21 through December 22, 1990, the band begins their tour dates for the album, a mainland European leg with a few British dates included. Main support comes from Anthrax, with King's X chiming in on a few German dates, inspiring that band's popular song "Lost in Germany." On October 29, Maiden issue a video compilation called *The First Ten Years*. The set was to be reissued as *From Here to Eternity* two years later. *The First Ten Years* was also issued in CD / double 12-inch vinyl single form. On November 19, the *Maiden England* video goes gold in the States, followed eight days later by *No Prayer* getting its RIAA gold certification, two months after issue. It would be Maiden's last album to achieve certification levels in the US market.

On December 24, "Bring Your Daughter . . . to the Slaughter" is issued as a single, becoming the band's only #1 on the UK charts. Its B-sides are covers of "I'm a Mover" by Free and "Communication Breakdown" by Led Zeppelin. Comments Derek Riggs on the single's picture sleeve, "There's Eddie standing there, waving his axe around, and there are all these monsters coming out of the pavement and he's got this girl on his arm. Well, the girl is that cartoon from *Roger Rabbit*, that long thing, the redhead, what's

The First Ten Years box. Dave Wright archive

her name, Jessica or something, the lead singer, the one that was based on Diana Dors, in the red dress and everything. And in the dustbin on the right-hand side, there's Oscar the Grouch, the Muppet, the one that lives in the dustbin, silly shit like that."

Into the new year, January 13 through March 19, 1991, the No Prayer on the Road tour crosses the Atlantic for an extensive North American leg, beginning in eastern Canada, then blanketing the States and hitting western Canada, before winding down in Salt Lake City, Utah. Anthrax continues on as support. "We're not going out with a big, massive stage production like we've done before," said Steve at the time. "We're going to concentrate on lights and backdrops. We've done four mega-show productions, and we can't see us doing anything better now—I mean, how much further could we go? Eddie will still be around, but different from the last two times. We want to play a lot of new material, but we're also going to play a lot of older material, 'cause if we didn't, the punters would kill us."

March 28 through April 5, Maiden play five dates in Japan. Dave Murray finds himself having to step up his game live now that Janick is in the band, telling *Kerrang!*, "Janick's got so much energy, it rubs off. Before this tour, I got into the habit of training and going swimming. Previously my idea of a workout was a jog down the pub! I just felt that I needed to move around more now that there is more interaction between the four of us out front. It's actually more fun. Exhausting, but fun! It's important that we create as much energy now that we're stripped to the bare essentials. There's no polar ice caps and inflatable hands this time. We're not bad for a bunch of old gits, are we?!"

On June 17, both *Live After Death* and *Powerslave* are certified platinum in the US, proving a subtle thing about Maiden that persists to this day: despite lack of excitement at any given point as pertains to the band's current state, the critical mass of the past is so appealing that the business can't help but tick along efficiently.

June 29 through September 21, 1991, Maiden play select European dates to close out their tour in support of *No Prayer for the Dying*, this final leg called *No Prayer for the Summer*. Meanwhile, the following month, Nicko McBrain issues a single in regular 45 rpm format plus picture disc pairing "Rhythm of the Beast" with "Beehive Boogie," and Picture Music International issues a Bruce Dickinson live video called *Dive! Dive! Dive!* In extended alumni news, also this year, Praying Mantis, with Paul Di'Anno and Dennis Stratton, issue *Live at Last*.

Another fresh Eddie dedicated to one of Maiden's regular calendar issues. *Dave Wright archive*

CHAPTER 9

Alas, as the year winds out, the sense of Maiden being swept aside in terms of any sort of dominance or even significance in the hard rock narrative of the day would be represented by the confluence of a number of major album releases creating a tsunami of attention for the artists behind them.

On August 12, 1991, Metallica issue their smash hit self-titled record, widely known as *The Black Album*. Metallica now become the world's biggest heavy metal band, leaving the likes of Maiden sounding dated and redundant in the process. Meanwhile, Ozzy Osbourne's career shows no sign of decline, with the ex-Sabbath singer about to issue the hit *No More Tears* album the following month.

On September 24, Seattle grungesters Nirvana issue their second album, *Nevermind*. Currently sitting at worldwide sales of over thirty million copies, the record's instant smash success signaled the end of the party for traditional heavy metal, outside of a handful of monoliths such as the aforementioned Metallica and Ozzy Osbourne, as well as surprise comeback kings Aerosmith, with *Pump*, and AC/DC, with *The Razors Edge*. However, the last gasp for metal from the Sunset Strip would be a loud and gassy one: the week previous to the Nirvana drop would find Guns N' Roses issuing two long and long-awaited albums on the same day, *Use Your Illusion I* and *Use Your Illusion II*, but that would be the last big news to come out of Hollyrock for a long time.

Aggregate all this effortless "multiplatinumness" happening at once, and there was no room left for a Maiden record made in a barn, much less Wolfsbane's second album, *Down Fall the Good Guys*, issued in October, featuring a lead singer called Blaze Bayley.

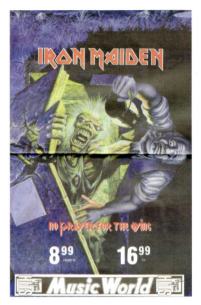

Martin Popoff archive

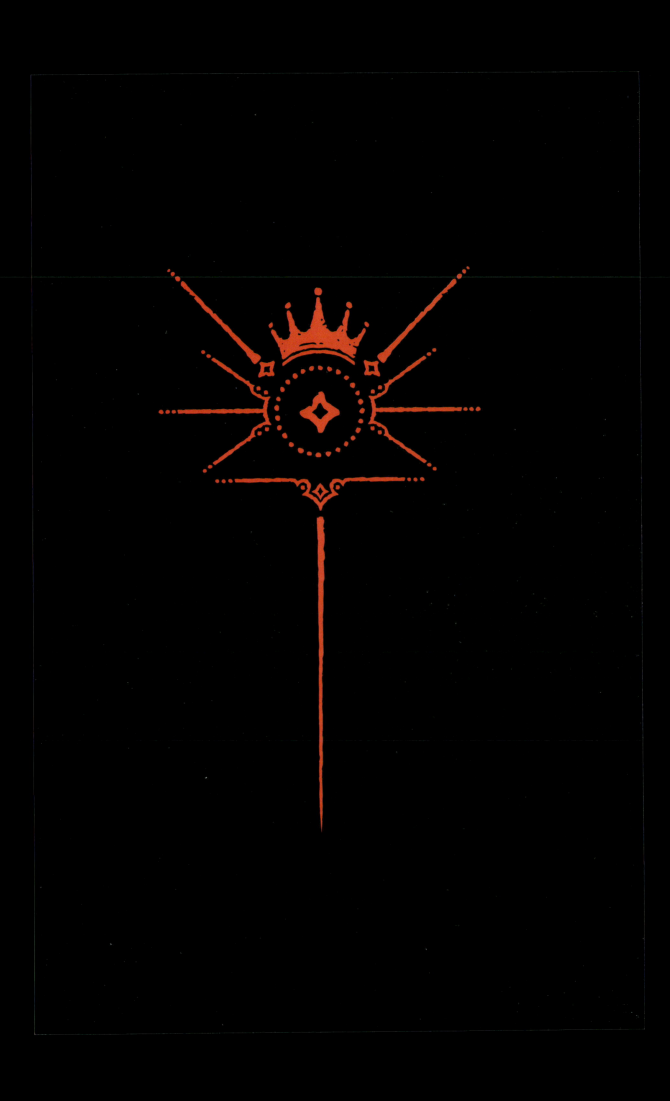

CHAPTER 10
Fear of the Dark

"Get back to some basic rock 'n' roll."

Arguably, Iron Maiden albums to date had fallen into a sort of pairing pattern. There were the two albums with Paul that are of a piece because of that, but then *The Number of the Beast* stands alone. *Powerslave* is son of *Piece of Mind*, and then a momentous live album puts an exclamation mark on that idea. *Somewhere in Time* and *Seventh Son of a Seventh Son* stick together as the so-called keyboardy albums, although I say "so-called" because that narrative is overplayed. Soon enough there would be two quite similar albums in *The X Factor* and *Virtual XI*, similar in sound and in titling, and similar even more so because they are the only ones with Blaze Bayley as vocalist. And then at the current juncture, I'd argue that *Fear of the Dark* is of a set with *No Prayer for the Dying*, both ragged and casual, marking a gritty, almost bitter entrenchment of Steve barricaded with his sound, refusing to come out.

This record's version of "Tailgunner" arrived in the shops on April 13, 1992, when "Be Quick or Be Dead" is issued as an advance single from the forthcoming *Fear of the Dark*. Its B-sides are comedic original "Nodding Donkey Blues" and a cover of Montrose's "Space Station No. 5," on which Dickinson quips, "Here comes Metallica in the rearview mirror." And there they go zooming past. Which Bruce would see as rueful validation of his assessment of Maiden's drift, completely warranted. Embedded and unlisted is a second comedic offering called "Bayswater Ain't a Bad Place to Be," which is a send-up of manager Rod Smallwood, a sort of follow-up to "The Sherriff of Huddersfield."

The band would work once again with Martin Birch, although you wouldn't know it, the sound picture bearing more the imprint of Steve Harris as producer in his own Barnyard Studios than of Birch using his own toolings. Still, the parties were of like mind, Dave explaining of Martin that "he's into the traditional type of recording, using mics close-up and room stuff, room mics. It was a pleasure to work with him, and he was inspiring because of his track record as well, the bands he had recorded. So, we were huge fans of him. He would go in and it would be traditional. And also, stuff like doing solos, which I'd never done before, where you would actually go into the studio, sit next to him at the desk, and

Dave Wright archive

work on stuff there, as opposed to sitting out in the studio with your headphones on, in kind of no man's land. So, you're in that environment and you're getting a truer sound. So that was a great thing, sitting side by side, and he'd be messing around and getting sounds. It's kind of inspiring that way.

"There's a lot of aggression on the record," adds Murray, framing *Fear of the Dark*, "but it has those progressive qualities also. This album's been three or four years in the back of our minds. The whole musical direction of the band has leapt forward. The material on *Seventh Son* was really experimental. We were going off on a tangent, really. It was something we wanted to do. We kind of went around full circle with the last album. It's important for bands to travel those experimental avenues. Maiden's always been experimental with everything they do, with the lyrics and the music. This album was recorded in digital, so the sound should be brilliant. This is the first time we've recorded straight to digital. Everything is so precise, and it really comes through."

This would be the last record for Martin, and the last since he came up with the novel idea about ten years previous of going exclusive with Iron Maiden to close out his career.

"That was Martin's choice," explains manager Rod Smallwood. "Martin had spent a lot of time in the darkened studio with all sorts of bands making all sorts of great records. And really, a couple of albums with us, I think he felt he didn't want to do that anymore, so he just worked with us. It was completely his choice. It wasn't like, 'Martin, if you want to work with us, you can't work with anybody else.' Not at all. We would have been quite happy for him to work with other people. But I just think it was a time in Martin's life, and obviously, we were selling a lot of records, so financially he was in a good position on it, and I think he felt he wanted to spend more time with family, start playing golf, do a bit of fishing, and work for a couple of months a year with us, which is a pretty smart move. Martin knew completely what we were about and what he needed to do, and he was very funny."

Dave Wright archive

Remarked Bruce on working with Martin on the record, "He's an old-school producer. The new-school guys, they start rearranging the songs, then they bring in other musicians; they want to do the backing vocals themselves. These new hotshots turn up with a CD of drum sounds and samplers, plus a shitload of computers. The point is, do you really want to sell fifteen million records, or do you want to make the record that you want to make and have fun? We sell two, two and a half million records around the world every album. That's enough; I'm happy with that."

It's an interesting comment from Bruce there, since ten, twenty years later, a "new school" guy would have other ways of making a record "perfect." But in the early 1990s, for sure, the top records were the domain of marquee name producers getting paid a lot of money, and indeed using session musicians, really synthesizing drum sounds and coming up with gang backup vocals that don't particularly sound like the four guys in the band. At least one nod to getting serious over and above the last record took place, and that was ditching the Rolling Stone Mobile and heavily upgrading Steve's pile so that it was a proper studio. Martin took on more of a role as well, but the experience in Barnyard's cramped and still somewhat technologically limited locale wouldn't be enough to keep Bruce enthused about Maiden's ability to compete.

"I think a lot of the sound is due to Steve's involvement with it," noted Janick at the time. "On the albums I've done, his mark is on every track as a producer. Martin is very much an idea man and an engineer that will get the sounds right. Steve's always there with his input. Also, it's good to have someone from the band that is close to the material in with the producer, because if you've been in there for eight hours or more, you can't tell anymore. But it's got the rawness and the energy of Maiden. You'll never hear Martin giving suggestions to sweeten things up, like a lot of producers who think of record sales, or record companies. I think it's the way it had to go. You couldn't really go much further forward in a particular direction. Maiden push the boundaries. When I came in, the whole feeling from my point of view was to get back to basics and keep it hard hitting. Get back to some basic rock 'n' roll. I think everybody felt like that."

"Every album we do we try to write the best album we can," adds Steve. "Our standards have been pretty high as far as that goes anyway. On this album, it's more varied, because there are four different writers. There's quite a few different directional styles happening, really. It's really refreshing as well. There's some heavy stuff, some fast stuff, and some progressive stuff. We really felt we didn't have to change producers to change the sound. All we had to do was sit down and talk about what we wanted to do and do it. Martin is such an excellent engineer that whatever sound we want to get, we'll get it with him. If you listen to some producers who work with different bands, all the guitar sounds are the same. I think these bands lose their identity. Whereas with us, we do exactly what we want to do. We don't need someone to try and change it. If we want to change, we'll change it ourselves, which we have done this album. Sound-wise, I think it's a bigger sound; it's a change for the better, but it still sounds like Maiden."

The record would hit store shelves on May 11, 1992. Demonstrating that there was still life in the old dogs, it would reach #12 on the US charts, but, even more surprisingly, #1 back in the UK, sending it to gold certification at home immediately—the record would be the first Maiden album of the Bruce era not to reach gold in the US. *Fear of the Dark* would also be the band's first album fully immersed in the CD age, which arguably began in 1990 with the last record, but not really, especially in Europe. At this point, compact disc is overwhelmingly the format of choice, and in recognition of that fact, the band packed onto their new record fifty-eight minutes of music, after the previous time out offering only forty-four.

Curiously, also this month, Paul Di'Anno's Killers issue *Murder One*. Di'Anno, unlike his old mates in Maiden, is trying hard to update his sound, going for a Panteraesque thrash vibe. Among the myriad parallels between Maiden and Judas Priest, here's another one: both had ex-singers impressed with the world-beating Cowboys from Hell, Rob Halford saying as much with his *War of Words* album issued under the band name Fight in September of the following year.

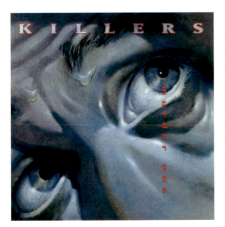

Dave Wright archive

Fans picking up their new tiny Iron Maiden album (albeit perhaps in long-box packaging, to thwart theft), would be surprised to find out that the front cover was not painted by Derek Riggs, but rather by Melvyn Grant. Rod had decided to open up the competition for new Eddies, having always butted head with Derek. But like an old marriage, the two would continue to work together through their bickering, despite Grant doing more work for the band moving forward as well. On *Fear of the Dark*, Grant goes for a muted color palette of the band's trademark cartoony blue and yellow, but he's come up with quite the remarkable Eddie, portrayed essentially as some sort of a living tree (in popular folklore, a driad or dryad), with "limbs" that might grasp and eat anyone (or any squirrel) that might venture too close.

It may be a bridge too far to say that it's a progressive idea that ties the record to the progressiveness of *Seventh Son of a Seventh Son* (i.e., a record with a similarly extra-thoughtful Eddie), but if we're to believe Steve, *Fear of the Dark* is an all-around smarter album than its predecessor, and to be sure, this is quite the surreal depiction of Eddie.

Comments Dave, "Derek didn't do *Fear of the Dark*. He came in with some artwork, but it just wasn't jelling. The vibe wasn't there. He got more into the music side of the album, so he was drawing along those lines, and I think his interest waned a little bit in terms of coming up with something that's really stunning. So someone else came in that we chose from all the artwork submitted. We chose the artwork of Eddie in a tree—*Fear of the Bark*."

As Steve told *Hard Rock* magazine, "Derek had drawn Eddie intruding into a kid's dream to transform it into a nightmare. But we wanted something totally different. So, we tried out other artists who sent us some drafts. One of them had imagined Eddie as Nosferatu, but we eventually chose the one you already know, Eddie as a tree monster."

The album opens with its advance single, "Be Quick or Be Dead," which, commendably, is about political corruption. There's not a lot of words, but they paint stark and violent images, especially the way they are spit out by Bruce, while also echoing biblical verse. The picture sleeve picked for the release references various banking and stock market scandals (including the BCCI debacle), underscored by a casually dressed Eddie about to twist off publishing magnate Robert Maxwell's head. The song is uncommonly "quick" for Maiden, and it marks the first single-release writing credit for the new guy, Janick Gers.

Explained Steve, speaking with Jason Arnopp, on issuing the song as the record's first single, "We thought it'd be a good one, 'cause it's got a good hook line to it and it's a fast, up-tempo song. Right in your face, like get some of this! 'The boys are back' type of thing. It sets up the album nicely. Although it might be a bit deceiving, I suppose. It is the heaviest track, but a lot of the other songs are heavy in different ways. It really doesn't make any difference. We could release any song off the album. We could put the album's longest track out, but it doesn't seem to matter. The single comes out, the fans hopefully buy it, it goes straight in the charts high, and it goes straight back out again in a couple of weeks! It's like when 'Bring Your Daughter' went to #1. That's a great song, but I reckon we could've released any song off *No Prayer for the Dying* at that stage and it would've done the same thing. We seem to be kind of unofficially banned from radio anyway.

"Bruce wrote the lyrics and Janick wrote the music," continued Steve. "He basically wrote that all about the scandals going on. Big, bad business stuff. It's the sort of lyric he likes, 'cause he can spit it out with a bit of venom. And he does! I mean, we've done fast stuff before. 'Aces High' was pretty up tempo, and in retrospect I think we should've released 'Tailgunner' as the last album's first single. 'Holy Smoke' seemed right at the time because we had the video and all that. It went in at #3, so can't complain, but in some ways 'Tailgunner' might've been a better choice."

Dave Wright archive

With "From Here to Eternity" we're really not that far away from *No Prayer for the Dying* at all, this song being a scrappy meat-and-potatoes rocker along the lines of "Bring Your Daughter." It is in fact the fourth and last in line of the very loose Charlotte the Harlot saga, beginning with the song of that name, through "22 Acacia Avenue," through the last record's "Hooks in You," which also bears earthy rock 'n' rollsy similarities to the current track. Whether "Hooks in You" is part of the sordid tale is cause for debate, the link being the reference to street number 22, rather than Charlotte by name. Come chorus time, the band weakly attempts to participate in the world of hooky American choruses, and it worked just a little bit, the song getting issued as a single and then reaching #21 on the UK charts. The picture sleeve for the single release, issued July 14, skipped over Eddie for a live shot, a still from the song's video.

For B-sides, the band went with "Roll Over Vic Vella," a comedic tribute to an early Maiden roadie, plus a cover of Budgie's "I Can't See My Feelings" and live versions of "Public Enema Number One" and "No Prayer for the Dying." Further giving the song recognition, on the same day as the single issue, Maiden put to market a promo video collection called *From There to Eternity*.

Steve was not kind to Charlotte with his lyric (incidentally, Harris is credited with the music as well, as if the bass chords didn't tip you off). Quoting with a wink AC/DC, Harris forewarns for Charlotte that "hell ain't a bad place to be." What ensues is that the devil roars by with his motorcycle, and Charlotte gets on. Satan then essentially deliberately crashes the bike, taking Charlotte back to hell with him for all of eternity.

"Afraid to Shoot Strangers" is a ballad in 3/4 waltz time for the first half of its nearly seven-minute length, after which the band cranks up for what is mostly an instrumental break. Then we're back to the waltz bit, Nicko sounding clunky and Janick and Dave executing the Renaissance music twin lead that acted as the song's second movement before the metal bit. It's an interesting construction, with all the verses front-ended.

The "From Here to Eternity" 7-inch. *Dave Wright archive*

Steve pens an antiwar lyric for this one, reflecting on a soldier's conflicted feelings during war, although, as he indicated at the time, he wasn't specifically writing about the Gulf War, which was raging at the time. Further, at the time, Harris said of the track, "This song, I think, is going to be . . . I don't want to say 'classic,' 'cause that sounds bigheaded. But it could become a really big song of ours. 'Afraid' is definitely one of the best songs we've written in a long time. It's got a great feel and a good emotional kick. It's about what is going through someone's mind before they go to war. I tried to put myself in that position, although I don't know how I'd feel when it came to the crunch."

"It's about a soldier who starts shooting during the Gulf War," countered Bruce, speaking with *Hard Force* magazine. "He doesn't want to kill anybody, but he knows that his duty will force him to do it. But if he doesn't shoot, maybe another one will shoot him. So, he hasn't got much choice. It's a cruel dilemma, but there's no other way to get out of it."

Commenting on the real-life drama unfolding, Bruce says that "I think that what the politicians really wanted to achieve was to suppress Iraq's military potential, all those chemical weapons and those plans to make a nuclear bomb, in order to render that country harmless. I think that no war is good. I really have a lot of mixed feelings regarding this offensive in the Gulf. I'm not really able to decide whether it was justified or not. I must admit that I'm not a great pacifist either—some things have to be done. You have to be able to fight for the right cause, and I'm convinced that what Saddam Hussein did was entirely reprehensible. What's not so clear are the real reasons why the countries took part in this war. Anyway, we've been told too many lies to have a clear idea about this."

CHAPTER 10

Promo *Fear of the Dark* flashlight along with a patch from that period. *Dave Wright archive*

"Afraid to Shoot Strangers" was usurped only by "Fear of the Dark" in terms of its appearance in Maiden's set lists over the ensuing years, also enjoying repeated plays during the Blaze Bayley era later in the decade.

Next up is "Fear Is the Key," music from Janick, lyrics from Bruce. As Dickinson told Henry Dumatray, "'Fear Is the Key' is about the fear that exists nowadays in sexual relationships because of AIDS, of course. 'Sex' has become a synonym for 'fear.' When we were writing the songs, we heard about Freddie Mercury's death. There's a line in 'Fear Is the Key' that goes, 'Nobody cares till somebody famous dies.' And that's quite sadly true. In the States, mostly nobody really cared about AIDS until Magic Johnson, the basketball player, announced publicly that he was HIV positive. As long as the virus was confined to homosexuals or drug addicts, nobody gave a shit. It's only when celebrities started to die that the masses began to feel concerned."

At the musical end, Janick first creates a slow gallop with an Egypto melody evocative of Rainbow. This gives way to a novel riff come verse time. There's also an inventive prog rock break that truly feels like a break from the hot desert slog of the rest of the song. Steve puts aside overt articulation on the bass, creating with Nicko a huge backbeat.

"Childhood's End" perpetuates the aforementioned established prog vibe of the record, given its long intro and interesting and quite tribal one-and-three beat. As well, there are overtly melodic breaks in the action. On bass, Steve's articulation is back, Harris accenting hard with McBrain—it's funny, but one of Steve's assessments with respect to Nicko is that he is often in charge, running the rhythm section, spurring Harris on to keep up both tempo-wise and creatively.

Deep album track, this one, often forgotten in discussions about the album. Notes Bruce, "This one mentions the fact that there isn't a single place in the world where humans can remain kids. In ten years, we've made the water, the air, and the sun almost completely disappear, and now you have to be out of your mind to be willing to give birth to children when you see the current state of the world. So, we wonder where this will all end." That's a crazy, prescient comment in light of the intensity of concern over climate change right now, nearly thirty years later. It's also a sad commentary on how long the narrative has been around, with little being done to change things.

"Wasting Love" finds Maiden reviving a composition from Bruce's *Tattooed Millionaire* sessions. It's a dark Sabbathesque power ballad that is disciplined of construction, as well as featuring a mournful twin lead, a solo by its writer Janick, and, most notably, rare and pervasive use of acoustic guitars.

"Wasting Love" CD single along with a promo flat touting the track. *Dave Wright archive*

Reflects Bruce, "It's about those who jump from one bed into another, those who sleep with whoever come their way, without giving or receiving whatever they're looking for, because they are very lonely. They are lonely within themselves, but they are continuously in action, collecting short-term relationships in order to fill the void they feel. I've often seen people like that. Life on the road is tough, and I know that many musicians find it hard to emotionally 'open up,' because they have those worries and those feelings that they cannot share with anyone, and that they keep buried within themselves. They believe that in their position it's impossible to have 'true' relationships with people, so they end up in bed with those of the opposite sex without thinking any further."

"Wasting Love" was issued as a single, but in the Netherlands only, backed with live (at Wembley) versions of "Tailgunner," "Holy Smoke," and "The Assassin." The plush production video cooked up for the song was directed by Samuel Bayer, who cranked out dozens of videos beginning in 1991, including Nirvana's "Smells like Teen Spirit."

Deep into the wilderness portion of the record and the deep album tracks, the uncelebrated songs of the canon keep coming, pretty much relegating *Fear of the Dark* to status as an album generating one lasting song. "The Fugitive" is another one of these ponderous prog songs that had the fans scratching their heads. There's keyboards, prominent bass, ill-fitting parts, and overt melody. "That's one of Steve's," notes Bruce. "The story is pretty straightforward, a bit like an adventure. It's about someone who's on the run. He escaped from prison and everyone's after him. The lyrics are therefore quite paranoid, to tell the truth! He eventually makes it, he gets out, and he's still running at the end of the song."

There's an uptick in quality come "Chains of Misery," with Maiden writing what sounds a bit like a hair metal song, complete with gang vocals for the chorus. This one groups with "Wasting Love," "Judas Be My Guide," and "Weekend Warriors" in terms of the band trying a few things that one might call American.

As Dickinson told Dumatray, "'Chains of Misery' is about the little devil that sits permanently on our shoulder, this little devil who can ruin your life. For instance, you meet a girl, you have a great relationship, and all of a sudden you do something stupid, with no apparent reason. And you wonder, 'Why am I doing this?' You don't really know why you act the way you do, but you feel that you have to do it. Maybe it's a feeling of guilt that drives you. Maybe you feel that you're not 'good enough' to deserve all this. In any case, you act against your own interest without really knowing why."

With "The Apparition," we are back to a bit of a Middle Eastern feel, albeit faint, upon a halting, heavy 4/4 beat. "These are Steve's views on the world," says Bruce. "He exposes all his feelings, his anguish, his fears, his preoccupations." Late in the proceedings, there are some typical extra and extraneous parts (i.e., some of them working, some of them not). Part of the problem with this one is the strange harmonizing of Steve's bass with the verse chords, especially given that the guitars are somewhat buried in the mix, indeed behind the bass. Bruce tries in vain to support the melodic mass of the thing by singing a vocal melody that is in unison with the riff, but ultimately, this one sounds sour.

Irving Meadows Amphitheater, Laguna Hills, California, July 2, 1992. © *Tom Wallace*

"This is a pretty ironic song, actually," says Bruce, addressing the aforementioned "Judas Be My Guide," lyrics by Bruce, music by Dave. "I don't know if it will be well received, because it's somehow perilous to be ironic in the world of rock music. It's about the dark side in all of us, and I decided to call this dark side Judas. It's this trend that would make anyone sell anything, that would make them care about nothing. That's this little Judas who's inside all of us, and if he becomes powerful enough to rule the world, then . . . bye-bye! [laughs]." As alluded to, this one has a hint of the American to it, especially the chorus, which sounds full-on hair metal despite the biblical lyric.

"Weekend Warrior" is a stomping roots rocker with a bit of AC/DC to it, and even a bit of southern rock come the mellow bit. The chorus is interesting, for the massaging in of an acoustic guitar track with the electrics.

"That's a very good song," figures Bruce. "Steve wrote it. It's about football and all the violence that surrounds the sport. Hooliganism is a terrible thing. You have those people who don't have any other interest in life but the football game on the weekend. Those people indulge in whatever violence they're capable of during the game, having fights with supporters of the other team, screaming insults, and then they go back to their little jobs on Monday morning, and that's when you realize that they're nothing."

No surprise that Harris, a huge football fan, would be writing a lyric like this, and what he's done is a good fit to Janick's music, which is party rock but with a few interesting twists, including a shredding guitar solo.

The album's title track, lyrics and music by Steve, takes us out, Eddie lurking in the shadows. "Fear of the Dark" would become a massive Maiden anthem, arguably the most famed song from any record past *Powerslave*, albeit perhaps part of a photo finish with "Wasted Years" and "Can I Play with Madness." Eminently catchy, the song wedges into the memory banks aided by its mix of tempos (i.e., up tempo, full throttle, and half time), with the half time also being a signature Maiden gallop. As well, as the record's longest song, it's not packed with parts that don't fit. Rather, the band hammers away at the same half-dozen themes throughout, making sure each sinks in.

Comments Bruce, "'Fear of the Dark' was one of the standout tracks on the album, very atmospheric, a great live track to do, and one that is very satisfying to sing vocally, because it's a really full-bodied kind of vocal." Adds Janick, "Steve came in one day and played that riff on the bass and sang the tune to us. It was the two of us, me and Dave, and Bruce, and we just sort of sat there as Steve dabbled on the bass. I just knew straightaway this was a classic Maiden song, you know, when the hair stands on your back. It just had that particular something."

The song was in fact nominated for a Grammy in the Best Metal Performance category, losing out to "I Don't Want to Change the World" from future nemesis Ozzy Osbourne. In 1993, a live version would be launched as a single, featuring the celebrated crowd participation element of the track, merely one of many points in a Maiden show where the throngs help Bruce out with the type of gang vocal we might get from the lads celebrated on "Weekend Warrior."

When asked by Jason Arnopp at the time whether what we have here is in fact a concept album, Steve says, "It's really funny you should say that, because I've been listening through the mixes. I only really noticed it by hearing the songs back to back. But yeah, you're half right. That's totally coincidence, believe it or not. We've got 'Fear Is the Key,' 'Fear of the Dark,' 'Afraid to Shoot Strangers,' and a number of the others mention it, but this is definitely not a concept album! Rod actually wanted to call it *Fear*, but we told him it was bloody crap! To me, the album title conjures up so many things, like reaching nervously into a dark room for the light switch. People do things like that all the time, even if they don't admit it, and darkness does tend to freak people out a bit. I remember being horrible to my sister when we were young, by telling her dark tales and frightening the bloody life out of her. She usually brings it up in conversations these days to embarrass me."

All told, once the initial excitement wore off, fans found themselves unimpressed with *Fear of the Dark*—and *No Prayer for the Dying* was not aging well either. As Bruce explained to me years later, "*Fear of the Dark* sounds considerably better, much more like a Maiden album. But at that point, I guess I was starting to get a little disenchanted with the complacency—I suppose complacency would be the right word; at least that's the way I saw it. We weren't doing anything on *Fear of the Dark* that we didn't do on every other damn Maiden album. And I was like, 'Ah, shouldn't we be trying a bit harder? Like, shouldn't we be worried?'"

Speaking with Mattias Reinholdsson, Bruce related that "we did *Fear of the Dark*, and I took Nicko aside and said, "Have you heard this band called Dream Theater?' I had some demos of theirs and I played them for him, and I said, 'Listen to these; these are twenty-four-track demos, no samples, no nothing, no machines—listen to this band.' And then I said, 'Now listen to *No Prayer for the Dying*. This is our album, and these are their demos. It blows Iron Maiden's sound into next week, and it shouldn't.' I said, 'We've got to get our shit together and make a good-sounding record.'

"*Fear of the Dark*, then, was recorded in Steve's studio because he wanted it to be. He'd bought it and he'd paid for it, and the band were gonna pay him back for using his studio, so it was a foregone conclusion that *Fear of the Dark* would be recorded in his studio. I think it was the first album where we were attempting to recapture something in the past. In many ways I think that we were looking backwards to other albums that we've done in the past, while other bands are looking forward to something new. And that was the last studio album I made. Shortly afterwards I just woke up to the end part of the twentieth century and went, 'Shit, I'd better try and do something different.'"

Something would eventually have to give, but for now there was a tour to be conducted. On June 3, 1992, Maiden play a warm-up gig for the forthcoming *Fear of the Dark* tour in Norwich, England, as the Nodding Donkeys, with the first date proper taking place in Iceland, on June 5, before hitting New York's the Ritz for a club date supported by Dream Theater, originators of a next wave of progressive metal. The North American campaign begins proper in Maiden-mad Quebec City, with Corrosion of Conformity and Testament supporting on all dates.

Opined Janick Gers on the band's musicianship, "I've always known that Maiden were really good musicians, yet there seems to be a general feeling that people have refused to admit it. Other musicians tend to put us down. Now, I don't know why, but I've seen it happen, and it's apparent as soon as you join a band like this how good the musicianship is. Nicko is one of the best drummers around. Davey, to me, is one of the best guitarists around, and I'll tell you why. People don't realize how difficult it is to have an identity. Davey plays one note, and you know it's him. Everyone knows it's Dave Murray. To me, when you start playing guitar, you create for yourself an identity so that everyone knows who you are; that's the most important thing. There are lots of guitarists who are clever, but not that many that have the identity like Dave does. He plays his own way; he's very individual and he wouldn't fit into a lot of other bands. A lot of other bands wouldn't be able to play around what he plays. I just feel the band's full of professional people."

Irving Meadows Amphitheater, Laguna Hills, California, July 2, 1992. © Tom Wallace

On July 20, *Somewhere in Time* receives its platinum designation in the US, extending the run of good sales for the band's initial run of records into 1986. Also in 1992, further compromising his focus on all things Maiden, Bruce spots an ad for flying lessons while on vacation with his family in Florida. The next year, back in Britain, he would begin his exams to become a pilot, soon to become the second flier in the band after Nicko McBrain, who received his pilot's license in the mid-1980s.

M.E.A.T. was a Toronto heavy metal magazine run by Drew Masters, a good buddy of the author. Martin Popoff archive

Martin Popoff archive

Dave Wright archive

CHAPTER 11
A Real Live One, *A Real Dead One*, and *Live at Donington*

"We haven't been deemed as being a 'cool' band for some time now."

Like Rob Halford across the divide, Bruce Dickinson sensed he was beating a dead horse. But he rolled up his sleeves and continued to show up for work, even if at times that's kind of all he did. July 23 through August 4, 1992, the *Fear of the Dark* tour hits South America. The proposed date in Chile is canceled after protests by the Catholic Church. Support comes from bluesy UK hair metal band, Thunder, like Maiden—and Wolfsbane!—*Kerrang!* favorites. August 15 through September 19, the band embarks on a mainland European leg, with main support coming from Warrant, although Testament step up for the Scandinavian dates. Much of the circuit is billed as Monsters of Rock dates.

On August 22, Iron Maiden play Donington, with Adrian Smith guesting for the band's rendition of "Running Free," marking Adrian's tentative return to rock after having left the band two years previous. The cameo is captured on Maiden's *Live at Donington* album, an official release of this concert.

"That was great," Steve told Vincent Martin. "We only worried about how we could make it even better than the first one. Finally, everyone told us afterwards that the gig was, without any doubt, better than the one in 1988, and that's also what I think. But I still hold a grudge against the British press who speculated about the fact that we only sold 72,000 tickets. What you need to know is that back in 1988, we only sold 66,000 tickets before the festival, then another 40,000 on the day of the gig. But at that time there was no limit to the number of people coming in. In 1992, the capacity of the festival was limited to 72,000—we couldn't sell any tickets on the day. But anyway, everybody started making those stupid comparisons and said we were about to go under. I don't think anyone has sold that many tickets at Donington ever since."

Noted Dave, speaking with Alex Ristic, "To headline on your home turf to that amount of people with such a great bill, it was like a great achievement. It doesn't get much better than this. The atmosphere there was just fantastic. It shows the band in a festival situation. And I think it sounds completely different from the other live albums that we've put out. There's some magic there from that day, and it's one of the highlights of the band's career, I think."

Explained Adrian about this time in his life, "I did a lot of writing and I got married and stuff and got a house and lived a regular life for a couple of years. Then my brother-in-law, Carl, came to stay with us; my wife is from Montreal. He came over, and he is also a musician, and he said, 'What are you doing, man? Why don't you get out and play instead of sitting around feeling sorry for yourself?' And we formed a little covers band, Carl and I and Jaimie Stewart, who used to be in the Cult, and we were called the Untouchables and we played down the local pub. And then we started doing a few originals, and things grew from there and then it was all originals, and we became this bluesy kind of rock band.

Irving Meadows Amphitheater, Laguna Hills, California, July 2, 1992. © *Tom Wallace*

"But around 1990 the musical climate changed absolutely dramatically, so us going out doing this ZZ Top–meets–Bryan Adams stuff was a waste of time. But I had a great time. There were a couple of versions of the Untouchables, and then I had a band called Skeleton Crew, which was a three-piece power trio thing. And then I got a singer, and then that was the first Psycho Motel with Soli, a Norwegian guy, and that's when we did *State of Mind*."

On September 1, as mentioned, "Wasting Love" is issued as the third single from *Fear of the Dark*, backed with live versions of "Tailgunner," "Holy Smoke," and "The Assassin." September 26 through October 10, Maiden play six dates in Puerto Rico, Venezuela, and Mexico. These are the band's first shows in any of those countries, a significant step in transforming Maiden into the panworld favorite they are today. October 20 through 23, the band plays three dates in New Zealand—also for the first time—plus Australia. Then it's seven dates in Japan, ending November 4, these shows representing the close of the band's *Fear of the Dark* tour and all activity for the year.

Low point of the year to follow, besides the exit of Bruce from the band, is Steve's divorce from Lorraine, his wife of sixteen years. The tough personal struggle, intertwined with his views on faith, are to be reflected in the dark nature of Steve's writing for what will eventually become *The X Factor*. "Yeah, I suppose these last few years have been pretty rocky," noted Steve at the time. "I suppose you can't help but be influenced by what's going on around you in the world anyway, and I suppose personally as well. So, it's bound to reflect. You're right, really. It's bound to affect the way you write."

But as alluded to, Bruce makes it known he is leaving the band; oddly, with many more shows still to be performed. "I suppose it was about three weeks before the tour started, at the end of February," explained Harris just after the rift. "He spoke to our manager, Rod Smallwood, about it, and he asked him not to phone me because I was mixing *Live* in Miami, and he didn't want to disturb me. So, I got the news when I got back to Europe. We were rehearsing for this thing in Portugal, and that's when he told me.

"Surprise, annoyance, sadness, all rolled into one. It was very weird. There's no animosity or anything like that—we're just getting on with it. It's strange going out on tour with somebody who you know isn't going to be there at the end of it, but we're big enough to be able to deal with it. It's been pretty positive, pretty much throughout. Most of the people are more concerned that we're not going to split up than we are changing singers, which is really encouraging. Obviously, there's been a couple of people saying, 'Oh?! Maybe you should split up.' The way we look at it is why the hell should we give up just because he's gonna leave? We feel we have a lot to offer, and that we're enjoying ourselves far too much to give up. I suppose, to be honest, we were pissed off when we first found out. It was a surprise timing-wise, because it was in the middle of these tours, but it wasn't a total surprise, because I always thought that he probably would go at some point because he was doing so many different things."

Speaking with *Kerrang!*'s Jason Arnopp in the spring of 1993, Nicko was pretty forthright about Bruce leaving. "He's said, 'Fuck you, I'm off.' If that ain't shitting on you, then what the fuck is?! It seems to have been a combination of things for Bruce. He's been writing screenplays, books, he's got his fencing and his family. It could have been pressure from his wife for all I know. He hasn't said anything, but it's a possibility. Plus, he went to LA, and you know what the fucking wankers are like out there! 'Oh, fuckin' Bruce Dickinson, you awesome motherfucker, dude! Yeah, you'll make a great fuckin' career in your own! Leave that bunch of fuckin' has-beens behind!'

"Some nights I see Bruce sing like he hasn't sung before," continued Nicko, addressing the strange situation the guys were currently in with respect to touring but knowing that Bruce was leaving. "Tonight wasn't one of them. Sometimes I can hear him and wonder whether me monitors are fucked! He's skylarking about . . . that's okay; that's the way he deals with it. But I eat, live, breathe, and shit this band. And I do feel that he don't really wanna be here. Everyone's felt a little bit of the same about Bruce's effort, and how he's been performing.

"But we mustn't let it get to us. We've got so much strength from each other, and from the whole fuckin' deal, that has bonded us together. To me, this is still a *Fear of the Dark* tour. It's not a Farewell to Bruce tour.

Acoustic Janick Gers. Irving Meadows Amphitheater, Laguna Hills, California, July 2, 1992. © *Tom Wallace*

It's got fuck-all to do with that. What I feel, although in a positive way rather than a hateful one, is good fucking riddance! I can't wait to get to the end of this tour and find a new singer. He and I have done interviews together, where I've said stuff like, 'I'm gonna take him outside and fuckin' do him!' It's a laugh, but there's also an element of truth in that! In my heart of hearts, I don't want to be doing this. I want us to find a new singer and do a new album. There's still a good fuckin' bit of mileage left in this band. We ain't dead yet. Where there's a will, there's a fuckin' way. It's gonna work for us; I know it will. Everyone's so positive. It's like the Phoenix rising. We will rise again, as a stronger and more positive bird."

Years later, as Bruce explained to Mick Wall after a pile of distance, "I always thought of myself as more than just the singer in Iron Maiden. I wrote a couple of novels, I did some work as a presenter on MTV and some other TV and radio work, I continued my fencing, and I qualified as a pilot. I didn't want to pin myself in trying to conform to the established Maiden routine. Meanwhile, Sony were making noises saying they wanted another solo album, and there was gonna be this big gap in the middle of the Maiden tour, where the live album was being mixed, so I was writing a lot of stuff and I borrowed Skin to be sort of a backing band. We got as far as doing all the backing tracks, and then Rod pulled me to one side and said, 'Look, if you're gonna do a solo record, don't just glibly do a solo record; do a really fucking good one.' And that's when I realized I was just going along with the flow, making my solo album in the same way we were motoring on with Maiden. So I went, right, full stop, and pulled the whole thing.

"I wanted to do something quite unusual and quite mad," continued Bruce. "I realized that I had reached a creative fork in the road. I thought if you want to, you can stay with Maiden, but things are sure not gonna change. Or I could take a chance and go somewhere else. Potentially, I knew I could be facing the prospect of commercial oblivion, which didn't scare me at all. Because, for one, I've had a great living and career out of Maiden, which is more than anybody could possibly ask. And also, I just thought, if that's as far as I'm supposed to go in this lifetime, if that's all I'm destined to do, then that's fine with me. But I wanted to find out. I realized there are so many other things I could be getting on with in my life. And that was when I decided I have to leave now. I have to tell people now, and then I'll try and decide what on earth I want to do later on if anybody understands."

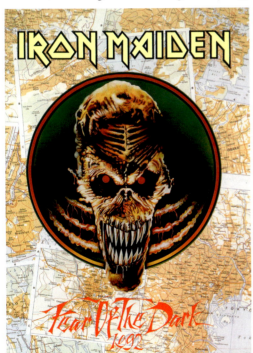
Fear of the Dark tour program. *Dave Wright archive*

As for playing more shows after the announcement, Bruce told Mick, "I thought it wouldn't be a problem to go out and do the shows at all. It could be great, be a good vibe and everything else. But it wasn't a good vibe at all. And this is not necessarily from the band. This was when we walked on stage, and it was like a morgue. The Maiden fans knew I'd quit. They knew these were the last gigs, and I suddenly realized that as a front man, you're in an almost impossible situation. If you're like, 'Wow, this is really fucking cool tonight, man!,' they're all gonna sit there going, 'What a wanker. He's leaving—how can it be cool?' Or do you go on and say, 'Look, I'm really sorry I'm leaving. Not to put a damper on the evening, but I am quitting.' I mean, what do you do?"

On March 22, 1993, Iron Maiden issue the *A Real Live One* live album, consisting entirely of songs written and recorded after the previous (and first full-length) concert album, *Live After Death*. All performances are taken from the August and September European leg of the *Fear of the Dark* tour. In advance, on March 1 the band issues "Fear of the Dark (live)" as a single, backed with additional live tracks.

Recalls Dave, "*Fear of the Dark* was Bruce's last studio album with the band, and in fact, that was his last tour. Halfway through the tour, he announced he was leaving. The CDs were done pretty much before Bruce had announced that he was leaving, recorded on the first part of the *Fear of the Dark* tour. Really, we hadn't released a live album since *Live After Death*, so we thought we could sort of justify it because we had four studio albums in the can since. We felt we could draw from those resources, and it was about time. Plus, Bruce was leaving, so it was the end of an era. It was like bringing everything up to date."

Dave Wright archive

"We decided long ago not to do it as a double album simply because of the cost, especially to the fans," remarked Harris. "Originally, we were going to release one at the start of this European tour, and one at the end of it, and then of course Bruce decided to leave and that sort of changed the game plan. So, we recorded a few more gigs, and now the second one will come out in September. There will be a few different tracks than we originally planned—four to five songs that we haven't done for a long time, stuff like 'Prowler' and 'Transylvania.' I was originally going to coproduce it with Martin Birch, but he, for his own reasons, pulled out quite late on. But I thought I might as well do it myself, as I thought I was ready for that anyway. I felt a bit nervous about doing it on my own, but at the same time, once I got stuck into it, I felt pretty confident and really enjoyed it. We are still friends, but I just think that after this—us having to change anyway—we feel that maybe it was the right thing to do now."

"From the moment that I said I was leaving, that wasn't my business anymore," dismissed Bruce, speaking with Ravin' Pestos. "It's a live album, not my album, only the recording of my voice. Steve wanted to produce it—fine. If you leave me in a room with Steve Harris, nothing works anymore. Our views on music are radically different. This is why our first three albums together worked so well. We were working together, and we never were on the same wavelength. We were dragging each other in the mud so one would give in. All the energy of these records, this rebellious aspect, comes from there! I got fed up with shouting at him all the time. Even if I'm not naturally a quitter, Steve is honest and straight all the way. He is Iron Maiden. It's his thing, his creature; nobody else but him can claim the tiniest part of the band. Why should he allow it? He's got his own recording studio, makes us rehearse and record the albums at his place. The other members of the band are delighted to work in such conditions—good for them. As far as I'm concerned, I thought that a band was a collective thing."

Playing these final gigs was getting to Bruce. "I like shows when they are creative. There's nothing more boring than to repeat fifty times the same gig. You play the same songs, you move the same way, you do the same things. I resigned myself to it out of respect for the audience, but that was a meticulously prepared performance. It didn't go straight to the heart of people; it was just a performance. In this way, to me, it'd simply become a job. Leaving actually scared me at first, because it was a fucking good job."

A couple of *A Real Live One* publicity photos. *Dave Wright archive*

"Writing Maiden stuff was never a problem," continued Bruce, turning to his solo future. "I could've written several more albums. But what the hell? In ten studio albums, we seem to have done whatever can be done in the genre, and probably repeated it at least once. I think it was time to do it. When I was working on the record [what would become *Balls to Picasso*], an idea came to me as evidence. The notion that art, music in my case, allows you to concretize the images that are in your mind. You put those images with sounds. So, you make films with sounds. I couldn't do that anymore. With Iron Maiden it was all right at the time of *Number of the Beast* or *Piece of Mind*. I was young, and those were the images I wanted to see take shape with the riffs, rhythms, and chords. Today I aspire to more feelings and harmonies. My new record is full of colors and drama. It's an abstract painting. I've already recorded about twenty songs. I've spent eleven years of my life writing in the same way, and all of a sudden I'm now completely free to do whatever I want. I want this album to be a reflection of me, a real record that comes from the depths of my soul."

Derek Riggs was back in Rod Smallwood's good graces, providing the cover art for the new live album.

"Sometimes it doesn't improve the picture, you know, sticking all this stuff in. Sometimes you're better off with a very simple thing. I think *A Real Live One*, where he's holding the electric cables, that was my reaction against doing those things with tons of detail in them. Because they just stopped making albums, and they were making CDs now. And the albums were like 5 percent of the total market now with CDs taking over. And I was reduced from doing 12 inches square down to 5 inches square, which is less than half the size. And you just can't do that detail on a size like that. It works like camouflage.

"So, I felt the need to do something strong and punchy, without all the detail in it. I still painted them 12 inches, because painting on 5 inches square, you couldn't get anything in it. It would just be a nightmare, really. But I would never do them much bigger, because otherwise you just spend the time filling space. You might as well be using a 2-inch house brush. Smaller than that, you go blind [laughs]. So, there's kind of an optimum which is around 12 inches. But *A Real Live One* has a lasting appeal, I think. It's strong, very straightforward. That was my idea for the cover. I said, 'This is a very simple picture; it doesn't sound like anything if I tell it to you, but it's going to work. It'll look good. It's just Eddie ripping a cable apart, getting electrocuted.' Rod said, 'Well, all right, go on, paint it.' So, I did, and they liked it. It's just the dynamics of the figure and the lightning, and it works. You needed the live background for it.

"I never even had a personality planned out for Eddie," muses Derek, on his creation and considerable claim to fame. "Eddie just did stuff. That's all it was. And after I left, it degenerated into Eddie breaking things, or Eddie sitting in chairs quite often [laughs]. There's a lot of sitting in chairs, after I left. So, it's not so much a characterization, it's more about what you've got and what you can do with him. He wasn't anybody.

"Eddie was just something I thought up one day when I was trying to make a symbol for wasted youth, all that punk thing that was going on. So I just did this corpse, and this corpse had to run around and this corpse had to do that, and the single was called this, so what can we do with that, what fits with that? And that carried on from the last thing, so it started making a kind of narrative. You know, you get twenty pictures of the same character, somebody, somewhere is going to invent a narrative. So, there was never any thought about what was Eddie like or what did Eddie think?

The *A Real Live One* tour program. *Dave Wright archive*

It was just what could we do with Eddie that fits in with this song? It's basically what you do with him, or what could you do *to* him? [laughs]. There's no thought of actual characterization—what's he like, what is his personal philosophy and all that crap. It's 'Who can we kill?' [laughs]."

A Real Live One comprised eleven tracks, with the record clocking in at fifty-nine minutes. *Somewhere in Time* was represented by a single track, "Heaven Can Wait." There were three songs from *Seventh Son of a Seventh Son*, two from *No Prayer for the Dying*, and five from *Fear of the Dark*. The live "Fear of the Dark" single managed a #8 placement in the UK, where the album hit #3 and went silver, for sales of over 60,000 copies. Maiden stronghold France responded with a gold certification for sales of over 100,000 copies.

March 25 through June 4, 1993, Maiden conduct the Real Live tour, in support of the new concert album. Support on most dates came from Sanctuary stable act the Almighty. Says Steve, "It was pretty depressing when Bruce left. Not the fact that he was leaving as such, but the timing of it. It was like for a while we were four people in the band instead of five. Before, any time when we had changes, there always seemed to be someone there to step in. So, it was never very long until we were a unit again. So that was a bit strange. But to be really honest with you, there haven't been too many low points, really. I've been very lucky in that respect. We've had a lot of success, and it's always been success on our own terms. It's been very enjoyable."

On August 27 and 28, 1993, Bruce plays his last shows with the band before the 1999 reunion. The occasion is a two-date session at Pinewood Studios for the purpose of the *Raising Hell* video, which pairs Maiden live in concert with horror magician Simon Drake. "I think he just lost the passion for the band," reflects Steve. "He's always been into doing a lot of other things, writing books and screenplays; this, that, and the other. And he went off and did a solo thing. I think he just . . . I don't know. Maybe he just thought he didn't have time to do everything. Something had to give, I suppose."

As Bruce reasoned the following year, "It wouldn't be fair to myself if I stayed with them. I'd just be shutting down 50 percent of myself to continue playing. The live thing was never a question. We were always a good live band. It was the long periods in between. 'Wouldn't it be great to do this,' and you realize you can't do these things, because they don't fit with the Maiden image. If there's one thing that that band has, it's a rock solid identity. I think in some ways this identity is just as important as the music. If you're going to try and make important music outside of Maiden, you really have to leave the band. Because the identity is so strong, it will swamp anything you try to do on your own.

"You can pretty much split the band down the middle with pre–*Live After Death* and post–*Live After Death*," continued Bruce, revealing but one source of his dissatisfaction. "All my favorite stuff is up until *Live After Death*. After that, it's the band trying to regain the momentum it had. *Seventh Son* was funny, because the album of the year for me was Queensryche's *Operation: Mindcrime*. They made the record that *Seventh Son* should have been. We could've made a record as good as that, but we didn't. We made a record that was halfway. There wasn't a desire to follow the creative process all the way through, in terms of a concept album with a story line that fully develops. We made a pretty good stab at it, and it is one of the better post–*Live After Death* albums."

As Dickinson told Jason Arnopp, "Experienced Maiden watchers were probably geared up to have me disappear two or three years ago, around the time of *Tattooed Millionaire*. At the end of this tour's first chunk, I was due to make another solo record, and looking back at the whole *Fear of the Dark* thing, it hadn't quite worked out as I thought it might. I still think it's the best album we did since *Powerslave*, but I also think I've been creatively sleepwalking for the last five years. The rest of the band and all the fans love being locked in the straight, narrow direction that is Maiden, and there's nothing wrong with that. But I kept trying to deviate from the rut, saying, 'Look, what's up here, guys?' I just ended up drained. I realized that I was trying to drag this huge thing somewhere it didn't wanna go!

"It will probably become very much more Steve's baby now, and I certainly don't think it'll plummet just because I've gone. Iron Maiden is like an old warhorse. The Trooper, the charging, Roy of the Rovers, the straight arrow, the ball at the back of the net—that's what Steve is. From a personal point of view, I wouldn't like to see Maiden play Guildford Hall. I think that would be very sad. But then again, if people are happy doing that, it's okay!

"We haven't really had that many conversations over the last ten years," says Bruce, asked about any heart-to-hearts over all this. "He's not really the kind of bloke you could sit down with in a pub and pour your heart out to! He's more of a 'Pass the salt' sort of chap. We have different approaches to feelings. He keeps all his locked up, and I'm in the process of trying to splatter mine all over my music. I would have liked to splatter more emotion over Iron Maiden's music. But it doesn't work! It's not the kind of music you can do that with. At first it was quite intriguing because no one was doing it. But after a while, all the allegorical stuff I tried to slip in became so tenuous. I started to think, 'Why don't you just say what you mean?!' If I'd had my way, Maiden would've expressed more feelings and opinions from the very beginning. Steve has always felt that it's dangerous to overanalyze things, and most of the songs are about fear."

On October 4, Maiden issue a live version of "Hallowed Be Thy Name" as a single, backed with live versions of "The Trooper," "Wasted Years," and "Wrathchild." This is to commemorate a soon-to-arrive companion piece to *A Real Live One*.

Notes Derek Riggs on the artwork for the single, "That was on purpose. Yeah, do a picture of Bruce getting fried over some flames because he's leaving. So, that's what I did. We toasted him [laughs]. Bruce decided to leave, so the manager said, 'Well, the last time we had a lead singer, that single happened, which we shied away from using. So, let's do it to Bruce. Let's toast him.' So, we stuck him on a pitchfork and toasted him." Derek is referring to a previous instance where he had drawn up a decapitated Paul Di'Anno!

On October 18, the band issues a paired follow-up live album to *A Real Live One* called *A Real Dead One*, the set list of which featured only songs from *Powerslave* and earlier. Revealed Bruce, "*A Real Live One* and *A Real Dead One*, those are like Frankenstein's monster. There are bits of vocals on there that weren't even on the same night; the same with guitar lines and everything. Because Steve had just discovered ProTools, so he decided that in order to make the best job, he would just cut and paste from all kinds of different performances, even on different nights."

Interesting that Bruce would say that, because the cover art even goes a step further. Even though this is a live record, on the front is Eddie screaming out a vocal . . . in a studio! The hour-long album features fully six selections from the band's self-titled debut

The "Hallowed Be Thy Name" live 7-inch. *Dave Wright archive*

from 1980 and zero from 1981's *Killers*. *The Number of the Beast* is represented with three songs, *Piece of Mind* with two, and *Powerslave* with one—namely, the greatest Maiden song of all time (!), "2 Minutes to Midnight." The album would reach #12 in the UK charts, propelled by the "Hallowed Be Thy Name" single, which got to #9. In the US, back on *Billboard*, the album would stall at #140, a drop from the performance of *A Real Live One*, which got to #106.

Not three weeks later, on November 8, Maiden issue yet another live album, a twenty-tracker called *Live at Donington*, available in two-CD format and on video. Granted, the album would be issued in the UK only, and then in the States five years later, with an upgrade over the original's black-and-white cover art.

"It was meant to look like a bootleg," explained Steve. "Basically, we'd just released two live albums, *A Real Live One* and *A Real Dead One*, and we didn't intend to release any others so soon afterwards. As I was mixing the sound of the Donington video, I realized that the quality was really excellent. So, we thought that it might be appropriate to release it as a limited edition. We didn't want this record to be considered Maiden's new album, so we didn't order any artwork for it. We only tried to reproduce the cover that a bootleg would have had. This is quite ironic, in fact, because nowadays some bootlegs have splendid covers that are probably just as good as ours."

Despite all this discographical activity, at the time Steve was beginning to lament the band's waning fortunes in North America. "We're still really popular everywhere, except for North America, and, to a different degree, Canada. In Canada we're still doing well, but we have sort of lost the ground in North America with the last couple of albums.

It's very difficult to say why we've dropped off. I think partly it's because of the vogue thing that's happening with all these Seattle bands—we haven't been deemed as being a 'cool' band for some time now."

"And partly, with the US, we did two albums with Epic, which was probably a bad move. We're on EMI in the rest of the world and have gone back to Capitol/EMI in North America, so it will be interesting to see if we can get that ground back. I'm not blaming it completely on them—there's been a lot of factors—but the thing is we've still got a hard-core following everywhere, and it's just not as big as it used to be there. Perhaps people have grown out of it? In North America, we haven't really gained too many new young fans, whereas in the rest of the world we have. The *Fear of the Dark* album, for example, was the biggest-selling album we've ever had with fans in Italy and places like that. And last year we headlined the Monsters of Rock festival in Europe. It just would be nice to have North America back. But it's not the be-all and end-all."

Irving Meadows Amphitheater, Laguna Hills, California, July 2, 1992.
© Tom Wallace

CHAPTER 12
Balls to Picasso and Alive in Studio A

"It's emotional catch-up time; it's 100 percent me."

As Iron Maiden went into a combination of hibernation and apoplectic fits, marked by all manner of rumor around who was going to be their new singer, Dickinson followed the path of Rob Halford and courted relevance. Halford had executed his return with Fight, his combative, compact, and youthful new band marching into the metal culture fray in September 1993 with a debut record called *War of Words*.

Dickinson would take a different tack, going a bit Robert Plant, conjuring some new music that was somewhat different for difference's sake, as it were. *Balls to Picasso* would draw measured inspiration from the Seattle grunge movement but would emerge a strange hybrid of styles, courting both the expected metallic and a somewhat more surprising murky and rhythmic dimension.

However, our first taste from the ensuing record wouldn't be any of that. On May 28, 1994, Bruce issues "Tears of the Dragon" as the first single from the forthcoming album, and stylistically what we get is an accomplished and substantial power ballad, an improved version of "Wasting Love," as it were.

"'Tears of the Dragon' started off as being called 'Pendragon's Day,'" explains Dickinson, "and was very much King Arthur, Knights of the Round Table, misty English hillsides, an atmospheric-type tune. And the producer I was working with at the time was like, 'Who is this Uther Pendragon?! Nobody knows who this guy is!' I said, 'Well, who cares? And besides, they'll know after they listen to the song.' And he said that's not the point.

"So, I went away and scratched my head and said, well, there have been a lot of people singing about King Arthur and stuff like that. I can see how it can be seen as kind of a cliché. And out of that I just started thinking, 'What do I feel and think of when I think about those kind of images?' And I think it was something about water, you know, the Lady of the Lake, Excalibur, and reincarnation. And that's how we got to all the water imagery in the song. And for me, it's still very much an Arthurian, romantic kind of song. It's the romance of throwing yourself into a raging torrent and just letting the water take you wherever. It's a very romantic sort of ideal. And of course, 'Pendragon's Day' to 'Tears of the Dragon' isn't really that much of a leap of faith."

The producer of which Bruce speaks was Roy Z, who would become a collaborator for Dickinson for years to come. "Obviously 'Tears of the Dragon' is a monster," says Roy. "I just felt that the mix was never right for that song. I think all the parts are there, just not the mix. I would have done it differently. Because that song is mission accomplished. Bruce has other versions of it and they're really good, but they didn't quite have the elements and the vibe that he wanted, and we got it right off the bat."

Bruce had met Roy through a process that had Dickinson first working with the band Skin, then producer Keith Olsen, with both those situations flaming out. In

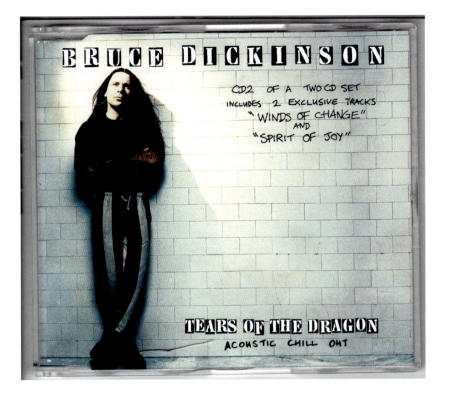

Martin Popoff archive

conjunction with LA-based guitarist Roy, Bruce also got his latest band, the Latin-rock-leaning Tribe of Gypsies.

Further on "Tears of the Dragon," Bruce told *The Bruce Dickinson Wellbeing Network* a few years after the fact, "Actually the song's more about . . . if you look at the video, the video is about this big fucking thing that I beat with a stick. And there's this general feeling of being held back by some kind of strange night of the soul in which you're seeing things, but you can't break through. It's just this thing, and when it comes, you're gonna smash through before you can just go with the flow. 'Tears of the dragon' sounds great. Dragons don't cry. For a dragon to cry, something's gotta be really sad. A dragon breathes fire and it's supposed to be evil, but for a dragon to cry, something's gonna be really wrong it should not be happening."

Bruce wanted to call his new record *Laughing in the Hiding Bush*, on the basis of a remark from his son Austin, who is credited on the song of the same name. He had also considered *A Thousand Points of Light* for the album title. Along with this, there was to be Storm Thorgerson artwork, which Bruce couldn't afford, that image going to Anthrax instead, who used it on their *Stomp 442* record. What Bruce used in its place was a scrawl he did on a bathroom wall, which went just fine with the earthy, provocative album title and the record's street-level sound.

Back to the timeline, on June 17 a plush production music video for "Tears of the Dragon," emphasizing the above-stated water imagery, is released to MTV. Inspired by the closing scene of 1968's *Planet of the Apes*, in which we see the Statue of Liberty half buried, Bruce and director Howard Greenhalgh wanted a similar sort of terrain, which they found at the site of the Durdle Door in Dorset, England. Ten days later, the band's US label, Mercury, releases "Cyclops" to metal radio, in conjunction with the launch of the album, which would surprisingly wind up as Dickinson's biggest solo seller in the US, by early 2005, sitting at 65,317 copies.

Remarks Bruce, "When I started off doing solo stuff, the first album I did, I suppose, is the odd one out because I didn't intend it to be part of a series of albums or an alternate career, *Tattooed Millionaire*. Then when I left the band, I started off on an experimental road, I guess you could say, spreading my wings a bit in terms of hard rock music or metal. So, *Balls to Picasso* was one of those albums with a lot of Latino percussive things going on, but in a metal sort of context. We were trying to use lots of interesting rhythms in ways you didn't necessarily hear them used on traditional metal records, particularly stuff out of the 1980s."

Dave Wright archive

"It was a situation where I hired a guy to mix my Tribe record," explains Roy, on how the fruitful collaboration came to be. "I didn't know at that time, but he was working with Bruce. He was Keith Olsen's engineer, and this guy saw us in a club, and I had an indie German deal. And he said, 'I like you guys; I'm working with this guy and that guy, and the Scorpions and we're almost done tracking, and we're going to get ready to mix,' and he said, 'Let me mix your record.' So, I went ahead and struck a deal with him and let him mix a song, and he did a great job.

"So, we went into the studio, and we were moonlighting. Basically, we would come in late at night and we'd be mixing. And during the day he was working with Bruce. We knew that Bruce was there. So, one day he said we're going to have a few days off, so come in early and we'll get your thing done. So, I walk into the studio one day, and I see this dude in the studio, and he's in the control room headbanging to one of my songs, and I'm like, 'Who is this guy?' This isn't even headbanging kind of music [laughs], and it turned out to be Bruce. He's saying, 'I love your band; I want to help you' blah blah blah.

"He wanted just to give us the world basically. And I was just blown away because I had always been a Maiden fan. One of my first concerts ever was Maiden. And he was helping us out, hooked us up with some management people and whatnot, and then, you know, he's listening to his record and then he would listen to ours, and he just bailed on his. He just bailed on it. And he said, 'Hey, I need some of your kind of stuff on my record.' And I'm like, 'Dude, my kind of stuff doesn't fit.' And he says, 'Well, just give me some of the vibe.'

"So, I went over there, and we wrote together, and it was great, and we did like three songs. And he said I'm going to have you over and record three or five songs. And we went over there and recorded with him, and he's like, 'Well, now it doesn't match with the rest of my record, so we're going to have to do a whole record' [laughs]. And it was

Dave Wright archive

a fun experience, it was a great time, but it was difficult, because I was clashing a lot with the producer. He and I just didn't see eye to eye on how this record should sound. I was trying to make it sound more like Maiden, heavier, and he was trying to go for some sort of commercial sound."

Balls to Picasso opens with the Latin texture referred to but cross-stitched onto a sort of disconcertingly casual doom song, with "Cyclops" being too long, too jammy, but a promising start in terms of creativity and ear-to-the-ground relevance— this was not the mainstream Bruce of *Tattooed Millionaire*. The second track, "Hell No," is of a similar casual quality, textured, percussive, a bit of Soundgarden to it, as well as the general alt-rock idea of whisper to roar, from verse to prechorus to chorus. Curiously, both songs address a person's inner dialogue, secret life, subconscious motivations.

Even more curiously, the record's third track, "Gods of War," perpetuates the record's theme of stinginess with hook or action, most notably during verses. It's also the third somewhat slow song, this one a languid 3/4 time, with signature percussion by Doug van Booven augmenting the drum track of David Ingraham.

"1000 Points of Light" retains the trashy, open-architecture drum vibe we've heard so far, but all told, it's more of a metal song with critical mass, cool origami funk riffing for the verse, and doomy prechorus giving way to an unexpectedly melodic chorus. This track and the previous one pair up like the first two, Bruce addressing the pointlessness of war and then the pain of gun violence, both artfully, his lyric skills ever advancing, perhaps blooming by being freed from the primary-colored but somewhat self-imposed constraints of Maiden.

"Laughing in the Hiding Bush" is a fit to previous themes, helping grow a clear identity to this record—namely, doomy, reflective, quiet bits underscoring the power of the loud bits, but then the sort of spare production and arrangement holding back potential explosions. "Change of Heart" sees Bruce's band applying Latin percussive grace to the record's first ballad, one distinguished by pervasive clean and bluesy guitar licks. This song features new Dickinson lyrics on top of a track originally written by Roy Z and Rob Rock for their band Driver; Roy and Rob would eventually present their original idea on 2008's *Sons of Thunder*, the first of the band's two records thus far.

  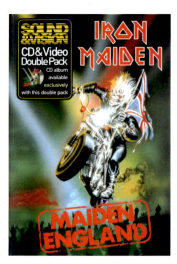

While Bruce takes the spotlight, Iron Maiden Inc. remains in business. The 1995 calendar along with a couple of videos from 1994. *Dave Wright archive*

Next comes the album's most stadium rock song, "Shoot All the Clowns," unsurprisingly seeing launch as a single complete with fancy production video, with Bruce emoting up a storm against a sort of secret-society narrative that gets surreal but fast. Late in the almost Guns N' Roses hair-metal-styled song, Bruce goes into what can only be described as a rap, placed over funk guitar that reminds us of the record's slight panworld mandate. What's interesting is that the incongruously commercial track was put together at the end of the process, at the label's insistence, because of concerns that the record sounded too obscure. As the story goes, Bruce and the guys were told to deliver a song that sounds like Aerosmith, who at this point were grossly multiplatinum three records in a row.

The wacky six-track single issue of the song includes "Tibet," which sounded squarely like Peter Gabriel or at least Dan Reed Network. There's also a radically different version of "Tears of the Dragon," which percolates with poppy, percussive world music snap, not to mention piano. It's a percussion tour de force, and arguably better than the stripped-down and dour version put on the record and released as a single and video. Moving on, there's an extended version of "Shoot All the Clowns," followed by "Cadillac Gas Mask," another huge production piece, but this time applied to what might be described as poppy hair metal. Stripped to a power trio performance (albeit with requisite hard rock Hollyrock overdubs), this would have fit fine on *Tattooed Millionaire*. Finally, there's "No Way Out . . . Continued," a massive, ambitious, and progressive pure metal track that points to the smarts of Bruce's later beloved solo excursions.

"Tears of the Dragon (First Bit, Long Bit, Last Bit)," "Cadillac Gas Mask," and "No Way Out . . . Continued," along with another non-LP track to surface later called "Over and Out" (cowritten with Saga's Jim Crichton!), hail from Bruce's sessions with superstar producer Keith Olsen, who throws everything 1980s at the songs, creating a dated sound wisely left at the curb.

Back to *Balls to Picasso*, next is "Fire," on which Bruce and Roy share songwriting credit with band bassist Eddie Casillas. This one's slow but squarely metal, like *Dehumanizer*-era Sabbath, but disciplined like hair metal and yet still somewhat disconcertingly marred by loose drumming, tight high snare, and needless piddling percussion. "Fire" is followed by "Sacred Cowboys," which is another type of departure, a sort of alt-metal with a rapid-fire monotone verse vocal, essentially a rap. This radical section is tempered by a typical soaring Bruce chorus, "Sacred Cowboys," adding to the roiling, disorienting creativity of this searching album of oddity.

Closing the album is "Tears of the Dragon," which, now after the brambled terrain of the previous nine tracks, sounds downright Maidenesque, even if it is a ballad. Turns out that the advance single would be nothing like the rest of the record, with Bruce and Maiden fans leaving perplexed but intrigued by the man's *Balls to Picasso* period, respectful of the fecund creativity applied to the project, but predictably put off by the overall lack of hooks.

If the album wasn't wacky enough, up into 2005 there would be a reissue of it that adds a second CD of fully sixteen tracks of non-LP songs, live tracks, and alternate versions, just to drive home the point about how untethered, upbeat, and up for anything Bruce was during this period of total freedom.

"I don't think I'm any more special than the next guy," said Bruce at the time, summing up his record and his place in rock 'n' roll. "But I think my record is special. That's really how I'd like to slant things. The personality thing is just a conduit to the music. It's a way to lead people towards the record. There can always be another talking head.

"It's emotional catch-up time; it's 100 percent me. There was a lot of me that wouldn't fit on Iron Maiden records. A lot of things happened in my life. I got married again, and I've got three children now, so there's all kinds of emotions that spring from that. I started to realize that maybe I could write songs about these things. I couldn't write songs about these things in Maiden, because it just wouldn't have fit the style of music that the band wanted to play. These songs were so important and personal to me, and I wanted them to be taken seriously. I just wanted it to be a good, honest record, and I figured the only way people would listen was to leave the band.

"That's why I got into music in the first place," continued Bruce, on remaining creative. "Over the years, I've gotten close to it, but most times I've drifted away from it. Certainly, with Maiden, I drifted away from it. If you're going to continue as an artist and have anyone listen to you, you better have a good reason why. At thirty-five years old, having been with a band like Maiden, who had such a strong identity, it's quite tough to step outside of it. I think people need to be aware that this is quite a unique record. It's not the beginning of another band project; it's something special. I will try to do something special for the next one.

"I can't justify anyone buying this record because I'm Bruce Dickinson, former lead singer of Iron Maiden. You'd better come up with a better reason than that, because there are plenty of ex-singers, plenty of new bands that are playing some really heavy shit. The world doesn't need another one from me. This is the best that I've sung on a record since *Number of the Beast* and *Piece of Mind*. You don't have to have a degree to see that a lot of people have stopped buying Iron Maiden records in North America. I can't believe that all those people stopped buying music.

"Some things are universal: passion, emotion, and truth," figures Bruce. "If those exist in a record, then people will be drawn, because there are so many records that fall short of that mark. There are more people in the world who want to live their lives through love and passion than those who want to live through manic depression and death. This record is all about love and passion. If people can't see that, then that's okay; they're not ready for the record yet. But for every person who doesn't understand it, there's another ten people who will see it immediately. It's all about bringing people in without making them feel that they have to be part of the gang. Heavy metal records traditionally made you part of a big gang. I really don't want people to feel like they're part of the gang. I want it to be a personal experience—one on one, you and your headphones."

Commenting on the making of *Balls to Picasso* with a few years of hindsight, Roy Z told *The Bruce Dickinson Wellbeing Network*, "*Balls to Picasso* is a different album because Bruce didn't want to sound like Maiden. He didn't want to have anything to do with that. I tried to sneak things in [laughs]. But I think it's a great album. The standout tracks are 'Cyclops' and 'Tears of the Dragon.' There are other parts that are really cool. I think no one really knew what we were doing on that except for those songs. So, *Balls to Picasso* was a lot of guessing. From all our parts, we were like, 'What are we gonna do?' We didn't know what we were doing then, to be honest with you. We just had no idea.

"My thing is that I never liked the sound of the album," continued Roy. "I think the producer was kind of whacked out [laughs]. We were all having too much fun. We were all in England working. My whole band was there. Everybody was crazy. We were all working hard, but you had the occasional joint or too many beers or whatever it was it was you were doing. I think we all were there just going for it, not knowing what was happening. I don't like the sound of the guitar. The drums are okay, but even those are real thin. I'm always telling Bruce, 'Man, please let me remix "Tears of the Dragon," please!' Because I want to hear the lead solo. It's hard to hear the lead solo for me. The drums are real thin and the picking guitar in the beginning is too squeaky. I mean, the sound could have been more direct on the drums. It has like a garage/room sound. I prefer either no room sound or [to] control that a bit. I wouldn't have thick reverbs or things like that. I would just make it a bit more focused."

And then just like that, Bruce would perform a rethink and get a new band to help hone his evolving vision, touring the record with them and presenting on *Alive in Studio A*, issued in March 1995, with Alex Dickson on guitar, Chris Dale on bass, and Alessandro Elena on drums.

This page and next: A couple of *Alive in Studio A* press kit photos. *Martin Popoff archive*

Recalling the germination of the experience, Dale told *The Bruce Dickinson Wellbeing Network*, "I'd been playing bass in a band called Atom Seed, who I did a bunch of touring with and a couple of albums. Then I met Alex Elena in a short-lived band called Machine. We weren't really enjoying the band, so we teamed up to audition for Bruce. I'd read an interview in *Kerrang!* where Bruce said he was looking for a rhythm section. So, me and Alex Elena sent a tape to Sanctuary Management with all the usual CV and photo stuff as well as recommendations from Myke Gray and Janick Gers, both of whom I'd known for a while.

"That was enough to get him to audition only us. It turned out he'd only received half a dozen tapes from people, mostly either just bassists or drummers, not pairs and not very well done. So, the lesson for

all aspiring musicians is that when you hear someone's left a band, it's no use thinking, 'Oh, I bet thousands of brilliant people are going for that.' It's always worth finding their management's or record company's phone number from directory inquiries and sending a well-presented tape/CD, photo, and CV; there's probably less than ten people running for it. I first met him at the studio where we auditioned. I was quite impressed when he helped me carry my heavy bass cabinets into the studio. I thought he'd leave that kind of thing to his roadies. Not many millionaires put their back into lifting things."

An interesting release originally slated for promo radio play that never happened, *Alive in Studio A* has on its first disc live-in-the-studio versions of songs from *Tattooed Millionaire* and *Balls to Picasso* recorded on August 19, 1994, at Metropolis Studio A. The second disc finds the band playing much the same set, but now at the Marquee club in London on October 18. The new record was the first spot of product after Dickinson's departure from EMI (he was on Mercury in the US), which took place in January 1995. *Alive in Studio A* would emerge on Raw Power (with Castle distribution) in the UK and on CMC International in the US. Bruce insisted at the time that leaving EMI was his decision, intimating that they didn't appreciate his new direction and that therefore the enthusiasm wasn't there from the team in terms of promotion.

In any event, Bruce—taking his time, really—had now waded into solo-artist waters with mixed creative results and attendant commercial indifference. His nemesis Steve Harris, looking on—also taking his time—was about to respond. He would soon realize, like Bruce must have been starting to wonder, that life was much bigger and bolder when the team was intact.

CHAPTER 13
The X Factor

"Get this—you put a card on the doorknob and someone comes around and cleans your room for you!"

In January 1994, after ostensibly combing through a thousand audition tapes, Iron Maiden choose Blaze Bayley to be their new lead vocalist. Speculation (mostly on the part of the press) of who is up for the gig includes Joey Belladonna from Anthrax, Michael Kiske from Helloween, and even Paul Di'Anno. This is all going down as Blaze's Dennis the Menace of a band Wolfsbane issue their third studio album (amid EPs and a live album), a self-titled. At this point the band has been demoted from Def American to Bronze/Castle. Shortly thereafter, Blaze Bayley would depart, not without regrets.

Recalled Blaze, "I looked under the sink, because I thought I might have an old bottle of champagne there left from years ago on an old Wolfsbane tour, where the support band gave us a bottle. And there it was! So, I popped that, and I thought, well, I'll probably be able to afford another one of these now. But that was it, really. I was just relieved for two reasons: one, that the waiting was over, and two, that I'd be able to carry on making music and singing."

"By the time I auditioned for Iron Maiden, Wolfsbane were over," Bayley told Jimmy Kay of the *Metal Voice*. "I had the audition, and a lot of different people auditioned, then you had to have a second audition, which was going into the studio, and you had to sing along with some different things, recorded as well. And then it was a few weeks after that that I had a meeting with Rod and Steve and they said, yep, we'd like to offer you to be in Iron Maiden. And of course, I was absolutely over the moon but tinged with sadness that I hadn't made it with Wolfsbane, where we thought we would make it.

"But Iron Maiden was just the dream job, doing tours that lasted nine months of the year, doing albums, no compromise musically, doing the music and lyrics we wanted. The record company couldn't be involved. Nobody could tell you what to do. It was all about what the band was doing themselves, and their own ideas. So, it's fantastic, really, just a brilliant opportunity. There was no music written before I joined Iron Maiden, so *The X Factor* album, my first album, was written with Steve Harris, with Janick Gers and Dave Murray and Nicko, and we worked on all the music together. And it was a real collaboration; I think there's five or six of my ideas that are a part of that first album. And it just worked absolutely great."

"Blaze has to be happy as a pig in shit," commented Bruce at the time. "He's got himself a great job and I think he'll do really well. It should be interesting to hear what he sounds like. I don't have any beef with the guys in Maiden, and I'm not setting up shop in competition with them. People can buy both records if they want. I'm happy with everybody free to do whatever they like. I really don't have anything but good feelings and good memories. People keep asking, 'Is there any chance of reunion?'

Absolutely not. It's not fair to anybody: me, the band, the fans, or Blaze. This is not going to turn into a Deep Purple thing. I'm a huge fan of Purple. They were the band that really got me started, but I'd rather not talk about their current state!"

Bayley Alexander Cooke, born May 29, 1963, came into the world destined to be part of this music, having been born in Birmingham, the home of metal, as it's known. "I've lots of memories," says Blaze, asked about being exactly the right age to have experienced the New Wave of British Heavy Metal firsthand, just a few years behind the Maiden guys themselves. "But in one way I kind of missed it—because I was in it. I'd never even thought of it. 1976 was the absolutely pivotal year where you had the Sex Pistols, but alongside that, for me anyway, as a music fan, you had Motörhead and then Iron Maiden and Saxon and all those other guys. So, there was this real music in the charts, and the charts were important. You still bought 7-inch vinyl. You saved up your pocket money for the week so you could buy one of these. That was it for me. We were all, you know, at school, going to friends' houses, 'Oh, I got this record.' It was just a wonderful time."

But Blaze's exposure to music was limited. "Yes, because my family circumstances were prohibitive. I wasn't allowed to go to concerts or anything like that. I took great joy in listening to the music. And, you know, the chart was just on BBC Radio One on Sunday; that was it. There was hardly any commercial radio, and you listened to that, and I bought the odd piece of vinyl. It was great when Iron Maiden got into the charts. It was just a great time for music. And growing up, you becoming aware of music at that time and you start finding out about Deep Purple and Led Zeppelin—just fantastic."

Asked if his parents were strict, Blaze told me, "Well, yeah, it was very unusual. Not unusual—that's not the right word at all, but yeah, I wasn't really allowed to listen to music at home when my parents were in. So, I'd have to wait for them to go out, and then

The Palace, Los Angeles, California, April 4, 1996. © Tom Wallace

I could put the record player on. The only time I got to listen to it, really, up until I was seventeen, was on the radio, or when my parents were out, or at my friends' houses. I moved to my grandmother's house when I was eighteen and got my own place when I was nineteen. I worked in a hotel, and I had my own room, and that was it, really. I could listen to the music I liked all day long, and I just fell in love with heavy metal."

As to the significance of Birmingham to metal, Blaze says, "I had friends who saw Earth, and friends who saw AC/DC with Bon Scott. But . . . it's not really a shadow, but it's as if a Sabbath shadow was over Birmingham. There was the thing of Sabbath being out of Birmingham. There was also Trapeze and Magnum. And of course, you had ELO, which is not heavy metal, but just this fantastic innovative, musical band. And the guys that worked at the hotel, we all loved all those guys and we all loved metal. We all loved heavy rock and [would say,], 'Have you heard this band? Have you heard that band?'

"But the Birmingham thing, I didn't understand it at the time. After Wolfsbane, really, when I really started traveling to different countries, that's when you think, oh, Birmingham, the cradle of heavy metal, because of Judas Priest and Black Sabbath and a lot of other bands. The scary thing about Priest is that the guys at school that were into Priest were just a little bit weirder than other guys. That's about the best recollection I've got of it. Black Sabbath and Judas Priest were just there in the fabric of everything that was happening."

As it turns out, Blaze's hotel job turned out to be salient training for his job fronting Maiden. "*Number of the Beast* is a very important album, because when I was working in the hotel, I had that and *Piece of Mind*, back to back on an old C90 cassette, when I was cleaning the hotel. So that was something that I was very connected to. I think my introduction to Maiden was 'Run to the Hills' going into the charts. I was aware of Iron Maiden before that, but that was the single that I bought, when Bruce joined, and that was the thing that I played the most over and over. And then, like I say, I listened to those first two albums with Bruce back to back just incessantly—I lived them. Those were the two albums that really inspired me and got me into them.

"But the album that's the one I never skip a track on is *Seventh Son of a Seventh Son*. We played many songs from that live when I was in the band, and whenever I had to learn a song from that, I would always end up listening to the end of the album. There's

Dave Wright archive

just something about it, the style of the songs on there, the way the music goes . . . something really got me about that. So, I would say that overall that that is the pre–*X Factor* album that is my favorite now, *Seventh Son*."

In terms of game changers for Blaze pushing him down the path toward singing, he cites *Holy Diver*. "When I first heard Ronnie James Dio at Birmingham Odeon, on that tour, that was a beautiful moment in my life. When I heard him sing 'Children of the Sea,' I didn't even think it was possible to sing that way. I'd never experienced it before. And so *Holy Diver* is something magical in my life. Next, it's got to be *Highway to Hell*. One of the influences I have is Bon Scott. His approach to vocals, not the greatest technical singer, but there's a story in his voice. He's like he is in his voice. It's a man talking to me, telling me what's happened, and it's pretty cool. And I wanted in my voice not to sound like Bon Scott, but to have that feeling that when you listen to him, it's not just singing; it's a story. And a connection that you're getting with the person."

In later years, on the path toward Maiden, Blaze found himself inspired by *Operation: Mindcrime*—in effect, this record is one of the reasons that Bruce Dickinson realized being in Maiden wasn't so hot anymore. "It's classic Queensryche and it's a classic album, and I'm always in search of classic in my own life. I want to make something classic that will live beyond, and that for me is a primary example of that. I got that album when I was in LA, and I had it on my Walkman and I skateboarded through the underground car park for hours at a time, listening to that album."

And what was Blaze doing in LA? "I was recording my first album, at Sound City Studios, the famous studio. Yeah, I don't think I really mention much the time that I kicked down the front door of the studio when I was trying to pick a fight with Rick Rubin. I seem to gloss over that."

Blaze also has intensely fond memories of *A Day at the Races*, *The Song Remains the Same*, and *1984*, but then, more adjacent to when he was actually playing rock star himself

The Palace, Los Angeles, California, April 4, 1996. © *Tom Wallace*

... "Guns N' Roses, at their first concert at the old Marquee, in Wardour Street. They were just young, played two or three nights there, and I can remember the songs. The album wasn't out or anything. Just the single 'It's So Easy' was out. And that marked a time in my life when I was trying to get on with the band, with Wolfsbane, and we had something about being real and urgent, having that sense of urgency.

"So, to be around at that time . . . I saw them there at the Marquee in London, and then later supporting the Rolling Stones in the LA Coliseum. So, I saw them on that journey. And I gave Slash my Wolfsbane demo tape, at the Marquee. Just like guys do to me. They give me their stuff, and I gave that to him. And, you know, a while later, I met him backstage at an AC/DC gig, and I said, 'I don't know if you remember, Slash, from the Marquee in London, when [we] were there.' He goes, 'Yeah, Wolfsbane, yeah.' And he goes [sings a riff], and he sings 'Loco,' the intro to it. Man, just the coolest thing ever. Absolutely the coolest thing ever. That was amazing.

"*Live Fast, Die Fast* was a living hell," continues Blaze, summarizing the tale of Wolfsbane for us. "It nearly broke the band, and it took us a long time to recover from that. We didn't expect Rick Rubin to be such a radical producer. He wanted to pull the band to pieces and restructure it. Everything he signed us up for and liked about us he kept trying to change. So that nearly ripped the guts out of the band. It nearly split us up doing that record. We were from a small town in England, and we had done everything on our own. We had loads and loads of fans around the UK, because we'd played in all the pubs and bars, and always kept playing.

"Def American were the only label willing to do metal at that time. They signed us up, and we ended up hardly doing anything for about the six months it took us to do the first record. And we were a band that could do an album in eight days. It was ridiculous. But it was the same for that other band they had, Trouble. I mean, they should have been incredibly huge. It's just a crime what happened to them. They were there before Metallica playing Metallica stuff. They were there before Alice in Chains. They should have been just living on a bus. But no, no, no, just take ages to make the record, not sure about this, that, or the other. They were a fucking brilliant band, they were. It's a complete tragedy what happened to them. But that's just labels; labels from all over do that. And it took us awhile to get over that. But we really enjoyed our experiences in Los Angeles."

Then there was a live EP, followed by another record for Def American, *Down Fall the Good Guys*. "Yes, that was great, recording that one. Because that was Brendan O'Brien, who came over to the UK. We recorded the whole thing in a few days. We had two days of rehearsal with Brendan, and then we went into the Roundhouse studio, where AC/DC and Queen had worked before. And we just blasted through it the same way that we played them live, and that was it. We were on tour with Iron Maiden after that.

"That turned out to be the prophetic album, didn't it? *Down Fall the Good Guys*. Because we were the good guys, and down we fell after that. So, we did this brilliant tour supporting Iron Maiden, twenty-one dates sold out in the UK. Then at Christmas time we got to open up for Ozzy Osbourne at Wembley in front of 12,000 people, live on Radio One, national radio, and it was all buzzing for us. We were getting great reviews; we got the best reviews of any band on the day in a couple of papers.

"And we said to the record company and our management, 'Let's go on tour now; let's go and do our own tour.' And they said, 'No. Go and make your new album.' And they wouldn't give us a date that we were to go into the studio. As much as we had written, it took us over a year before the album came out. And by the time it happened, we were starting from scratch again. Our audience had practically disappeared, and that was really the clincher for us. We managed to get back a bit of ground, but by that time, of course, the label were blaming us for the album not selling and all that." The band closed shop (until reunion) with a self-titled.

"We were finished with Def American then," explains Bayley. "The contract had actually expired. We had kept quiet, and we had let the option finish. Because the way it was with Def American, we couldn't actually make an album, right? They wouldn't give us any money to make an album. They wouldn't give us any money so we could live, so we had to go on welfare, right? We were in a horrible situation. So, what we thought was stay quiet and let the option go. And we just wrote to them and said, 'Look, we're out of this deal because you didn't pick up the option.'

"And then we just went to a small label in the UK called Bronze, with a man called Pete Winkleman. He didn't have any money, but he said, 'Yeah, let's do two albums together.' So, we did a live album, *Massive Noise Injection*, which we recorded one night at the Marquee. We just wrote to all our fans and said, 'Right, you can be on a live album; it's going to be you, just come down to the Marquee on this night.' And they did and it was fucking brilliant. We took that one night to record the album, and then we took two weeks to mix it. And then we just did an album called *Wolfsbane*, but by that point it was just too late—we were massively in debt. We couldn't get any money to tour. No English label would pick us up. That was it. It was all over.

"We never recouped and we never had a royalty check. We never had any money. We were all living at home with our parents! We just lived for rock 'n' roll! We just lived for music! That's why we were such a crazy band and people thought we were wild. That's because it was our only chance to get away from home. We thought, fuck it. We just lived to go on tour or go into the studio. Every second that we were on tour, we were just crazy all of the time. Because we never wanted to go home. Because we had such shitty, boring lives at home, no money, completely broke. At least when you're on tour, you have the dressing room full of booze, you've got sandwiches, or maybe one hot meal a day. That was enough for us—and you got to go to a gig every night. Fucking brilliant.

"If it was a crest of a wave, we were right behind it," sighs Blaze. "If we were in a surfing competition, we were still out there on the ocean, probably. We had what I considered to be great music, with our own edge, very serious about what we did, and we just did not get the opportunity that we wanted to just live in a van and be on tour. We'd done that in the UK, and we'd been reasonably successful. But after coming back after that first album, things weren't good.

"And we never went to Europe. And I think that's what really changes you as a band, when you have to go and communicate with people with just your music, where English isn't their first language. That really shapes you; that really makes a difference in your music. And when I look back, that was what didn't happen that we wanted to happen. And since I've been independent, all I've ever tried to do is do what we didn't do in Wolfsbane. And fortunately, I've done that with a certain degree of success."

But with Maiden, right from the beginning, little seemed to be going right. As soon as Blaze joins, a short eastern European tour that was supposed to begin on February 2, 1994, is canceled due to Bayley having been in a motorcycle accident. This would contribute to Rod answering, when asked about the most difficult record the band ever made, "I think the only one that would come close to that would be *The X Factor*, because with the changes, and then Blaze had a motorcycle crash, which put it all back. We did it in Steve's studio, and it took a long time to make that record—it was a difficult record to make and a very complicated record to make. There's a lot of serious playing on that album."

On May 10, Maiden issue the seventeen-track *Raising Hell* video, an in-studio concert affair featuring Bruce's last performance with the band until the reunion five years later. As the year grinds on, on August 8 there's limited-release thirteen-track CD and video package called *Maiden England*. Over in the alumni class, on October 4, for the high-profile Black Sabbath tribute album *Nativity in Black*, Bruce collaborates with Godspeed on a rendition of "Sabbath Bloody Sabbath," and the following month Paul Di'Anno's Killers issue *Menace to Society*, their second, with Paul pursuing an ill-advised Panteraesque direction. In July 1995, Di'Anno and Dennis Stratton, coguitarist on the debut Maiden record, issue an album called *The Original Iron Men*, following up with a second volume in 1996, plus *As Hard as Iron*, also in 1996.

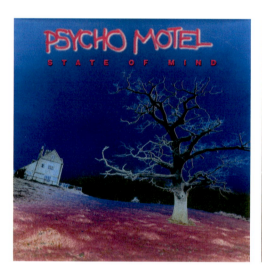 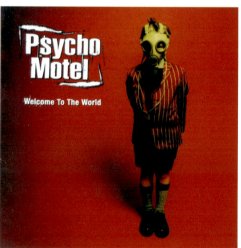

The two Psycho Motel albums. *Dave Wright archive*

Into the new year, in February 1995, Adrian Smith's heavy-alternative-metal act Psycho Motel issue their debut album, *State of Mind*, but only in Japan. It emerges in the rest of the world the following year.

"I wanted it to have classic influences like Zeppelin and old Sabbath," explained Adrian, on the mandate for the band, "and Soli was more into the modern side of it. I also like bands like Soundgarden and Alice in Chains. As far as I'm concerned, they were just damn good rock bands. So, there's a bit of that in it as well. And there's a lot of tradition in this sound simply because of my guitar style, my lead style. And the title track has almost a Hendrix influence. Old rock meets new rock, basically.

"There's a band I've only heard a little bit about, Candlebox, and I heard a couple of their tracks and thought, well, that's cool. I pulled a few favors and put some of my own money into it. We did half the album in sort of a run-down studio with very good equipment. I remember it was the summer of 1997, the hottest summer we've had in Britain for several years, and there was no air-conditioning in the studio, so you can imagine what it was like. But I had a great time. I actually sort of produced that album as well; I had a great engineer. But as far as doing vocals, I was right there with Soli. I really enjoyed doing that; I thoroughly enjoyed the whole experience.

"It came out in Japan, and it came out in Europe," continues Smith. "Again, it's different than Iron Maiden. Getting a new band off the ground, I mean, I don't think I even realized the work it took. And the management insisted I make it a band project. I think in retrospect it would have been easier just to have stuck my name on it and marketed it like that. You know, Psycho Motel, *State of Mind*; people don't know it. And now with the reissues, there are stickers on them, but at the time there weren't. There's so much . . . I don't know, there's been problems with the marketing. I think if I was to do another album now, I'd just put Adrian Smith on it, so people know where they stand."

Bruce was to soon regret going solo as well, although sticking his name on it made the situation different from Adrian's, so that didn't turn out to be the solution to his lack of commercial success. Suffice to say he had the same problems, and most of that was related to "getting a new band off the ground," but also metal's decline of fortune in the 1990s. As well, any big-band guy who goes solo is usually overwhelmed by the responsibility and the focus placed on his shoulders. Some grow from it and some are just traumatized.

On May 29, 1995, German power metal band Gamma Ray have themselves a new record. Somewhat the offspring of bands such as Maiden and Priest, Gamma Ray also sound very much like Helloween, associated by personnel. With metal out of favor, this nascent power metal movement was busy, mostly in Germany, slowly bringing pure metal back. Gamma Ray, with this album, start using an Eddie-like mascot, on the cover of their *Land of the Free* album, issued on this day through Noise Records. Derek Riggs, creator of all the early Eddies, would subsequently be commissioned to create artwork for the band, as would Hervé Monjeaud, painter of later Eddies.

Finally, in August 1995, Maiden complete work on what will become *The X Factor*. "We just wanted it to be natural," remembers Blaze, concerning the sessions. "We thought, well, let's get together and see what comes out, and whatever is the best stuff, then that was what will make the album. But we were all asked for ideas. We wrote it all from scratch. When I joined the band, there was nothing written for the album. We just started writing the album more or less the next month. And we recorded at Steve's studio, which is a separate place. He lives in an older house, and it's an old barn that he had converted into a studio, so it's all like state-of-the-art recording inside. He converted his whole barn. It was just a derelict building on the back of his house, because it was an old farmhouse. So, he decided to convert it into a studio. We had some good vibes in there. And then there's the pub, which was just another part of this house."

Noted Steve on the wait at the time, "We've taken some stick—especially from our manager—about taking so long over the recording. But this is obviously a very important time for us with the new lineup. It takes time to fully integrate a new singer. When Bruce Dickinson replaced Paul Di'Anno, we were able to quietly go off to Italy to tour before going into the studio to record *The Beast*. Now it's impossible to do anything 'quietly.' So, we spent a lot of time in rehearsal just playing, relaxing, getting the right feeling before getting down to the actual recording. This way we felt we were a band once recording started.

"Everything went really well with Blaze from the word 'go.' We knew him before from touring together. I always loved his vocals. He was just very Maiden. We still checked out thousands of tapes and auditioned a number of singers, but when we'd been through it all, Blaze was definitely the man for the job. So it was no great surprise that things jelled so well. It was very satisfying. Anyway, we all feel that this album would be something very special. This will be reflected in the title, which is a well-kept secret just now. We're very proud of the songs, and the playing is as good as ever. We're spending more time on the actual sound. All in all, we're delighted with the way things have gone, and can't wait for the fans to hear Blaze and the new material. Also dying to get on tour again. It's the longest we've ever been between gigs."

Asked by Vincent Martin about not working with Martin Birch, Steve said that "Martin ceased all activity after *Fear of the Dark*, and he was only working with us because he didn't want to do anything else anymore. As I coproduced *Fear*, with him, I'm quite familiar with his techniques and I know what to do. It wasn't a problem. I chose Nigel Green (coproducer) because of his background and because he can adapt really well. He can work with AC/DC or Def Leppard as well as with Billy Ocean or Iron Maiden. My greatest fear is a producer like Mutt Lange, who has his very own sound and who doesn't grant much importance to the artists he produces. *The X Factor* is not perfect, but we did well."

Added Bayley, "I can't wait to get out touring with Maiden. I supported them on tour a few years ago, and it was awesome. I wanted to get out and play the UK straightaway, but the rest reckoned we should get some gigs under our belt first, get things really revved up. We're doing the UK in two parts, some before we do western Europe and some more a bit later. All the gigs are standing, so they can really get rowdy. It's gonna be fuckin' great."

On September 25, "Man on the Edge," written by Blaze Bayley and Janick Gers, is issued as an advance single from the forthcoming *The X Factor*. It is issued in two parts, and in picture disc form. Two non-LP tracks are featured, "Justice of the Peace" and "I Live My Way." Bayley appreciated having one of his songs out front like this, not only as the first single but as an advance single.

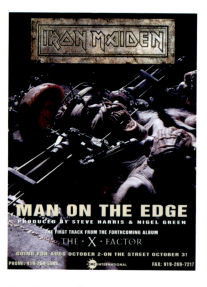 

Dave Wright archive

Indeed, the gesture from Steve was not lost on Blaze.

"Absolutely, the biggest influence working with the guys in Maiden is the level of confidence, working with Steve and him mentoring me in my songwriting," explains Bayley. "I'd written many songs before Iron Maiden. I was very pleased with a lot of them. The thing I learned from Steve Harris was to take the sound in your head and get that to be the idea that is on the album. That's another way to look at things; working with him really taught me that. But the level of confidence when you write a song and it becomes the single, and it's worldwide, and in the Top 10 of the rock charts, and in some countries is #1 in the charts . . . when that happened to 'Man on the Edge,' which I wrote the melody and the lyrics for that song, that's a huge amount of confidence. That my idea is good enough and my song is good enough. But like I say, you have to get them over to people. Learning that was the greatest gift that I got from those fantastic years with Iron Maiden.

"'Man on the Edge' was one that I wrote with Janick," continues Blaze, "and Steve came in on that one as well towards the end. We did the song on the *Top of the Pops* show in the UK, and yeah, it was good. That was the first big chart hit that I'd ever had, really, so it was really great fun. That was one of the very first ideas I had. I went to Janick Gers's house, and he's got the little home studio there, and we sat down, and we were going through things.

"That song is based on the movie *Falling Down* [in theaters on February 26, 1993] with Michael Douglas, which really touched me. It may sound really cheesy, but that guy is pretending to go to work every day because he's ashamed that he's been fired from his job. He's been let go from his job. When I was a very young man and I had a paper round, I did exactly the same thing. I went to do the paper round every day, because I was scared of my stepfather and what he would say if he found out that I didn't have my paper round. I'd been fired by the shop. He said we don't want you anymore to deliver papers.

"And I was so scared of my stepfather that I went every day, out of the house at 7:00 a.m., just to give the appearance that I still had that paper round. And so when I saw the movie *Falling Down*, it really resonated with me. It came together so quickly. I said, 'Oh, well, try this,' and Janick said, 'Yeah, a bit of this,' and we took it to the rest of the band, 'What do you think about this?' And they just went crazy, and it was the first single chosen from the album. The video was great too.

"So for me, as the first hit song, really, Top 10 all over the world in the rock charts, it was incredible that I'd been a part of it. I'd written a lot of songs before that, but it was so meaningful to me that it was something that resonated with me personally, and it was also this big song that went everywhere—and my idea was good enough. That was something very special. And that confidence that I got from working with the band, that transferred to my solo work. If you listen to the *Infinite Entanglement* trilogy, you can see the direct influence—more, perhaps, than on my other albums—of working with the guys in Maiden and learning all of those things, melody parts and making sure the instrumental really says something. Steve Harris had said, 'The instrumental is as important as the vocals. It has to do something. It has to go somewhere and tell its own story.' And I get that.

"It was a lot different for me," reflected Blaze, speaking with Tim Henderson. "I mean, you're working with different people and these guys are just fantastic musicians. I said to Steve, before we started really getting into the writing, 'Look, is there any direction that we want to go in?' And he said, 'No, not at all. It's not going to be contrived. We're not going to try and go anywhere. We're just gonna write the best songs that we can. And that's what we're gonna record.' In a way, that was a real relief. I was a little concerned that some of my ideas might not work, but everything really felt natural. I found that my voice started to get a lot stronger and developed in different ways. There were a lot of things that I'd been looking for on my last recordings, like more depth of emotion, more character and identity. I felt that I was really achieving that with Iron Maiden. Steve Harris brought out a part of my voice that I couldn't find by myself. We were going through a difficult time at the start of the writing, but this is what we've come up with, a really strong album with some great songs on it, and I think that bodes well for the future."

Noted Dave on the record's guitar tones, "On *The X Factor*, we used the rhythm guitar straight into the Marshall amps turned up to 20. When we started with the lead sounds and the little melodies and stuff, we actually used some digi-tech stuff and guitar processors. You have a combination of two channels, a processed sound and the tube sound, and you can mix them together. In a way, you've got the pure sound and the processed sound. It kind of gave it a good slant. On the last three albums, we've been using computer technology for overdubbing and editing. You can drop in for half a note now—it's incredible. We want to continue using the effects but still keep the purity there. The first time we used this technology was on the *Fear of the Dark* album. It's just the future, really, and you need to keep up with the times yet still have that 1960s/1970s

Dave Wright archive

flavor. With the blues stuff like Buddy Guy and B.B. King, it's straight in and from the heart. With the stuff we're doing, we can just add that to 1990s technology."

"I think the sound of this album is our best yet," said Nicko at the time. "For the first time we really kind of got into the digital technology that's been available, and we used it. We took time making sure the sounds were right for virtually everything. Not saying we haven't in the past, but sometimes I suppose things get overlooked. I'm very happy. I think it's the best drum sound I've ever had on a studio album. We also took a lot longer with putting the actual rhythm tracks together, and then the actual guitar overdubs, rhythms and leads, and the guitars, etc. Yeah, we took a lot more time, and I think it paid off. It sounds a lot better than the stuff we've had in the past; I'm really pleased with it.

"I suppose it's more technical because of the technology applied to it," continues McBrain. "With straight analog, with the hiss, if you wanted to edit something, you had to cut the tape! So, there's a lot more stuff available. I sampled my drum tracks. We lifted the tom samples off when we were mixing and left the rest of the kit pretty much as it was. And if we hadn't had that technology available to us, it would've been back to the old way, I suppose. But having said that, it takes a different approach to make sure everything is in its right place."

A week later, on October 2, *The X Factor* showed up in shops. Oddly, the album had to be presented with two different covers. Longtime Rush artist Hugh Syme had created an Eddie so lifelike and discombobulated that it was deemed too disturbing. In fact, our newly fleshy Eddie is in the middle of a blood-dripping lobotomy recalling *Piece of Mind*, and then he's chopped at the waist, entrails hanging out, referencing *Seventh Son of a Seventh Son*. That cover is on the flip side of the booklet. "Officially" we get a distant but still-3-D Eddie on an electric chair, under a large metal X. Front or back, it's an embarrassment of design for Hugh Syme, a real negative against his legacy.

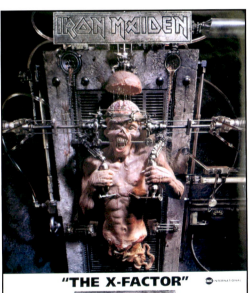

Dave Wright archive

Nicko was apparently unaware of that legacy, telling Nefarious Nick, "For the new album, we offered it to a guy named Hugh Syme, who's done artwork for I believe Aerosmith and a number of great American bands. He was very, very keen. He'd been waiting six years to get the phone call to do something like what we wanted to do, and he came up with *The X Factor* artwork. It's a model, not a painting, so it's quite a change for us, because normally the artwork is associated with our work and not with creative model making, which is still artwork or an art form. Derek is still active. We still retain his services to do the artwork on T-shirts and stuff like that."

"Not a lot of people know we'd already thought of it as the release of *Fear of the Dark*," Steve told *Hard Rock*. "We wanted to make Eddie more real. It had to look like a photograph instead of a drawing. In fact, it's not really big [holds hands about 2 feet apart]. It is true that when you look at the cover, it looks like the sculpture is much bigger. It's done in a really clever way. At first, we'd contacted different people, asking for a sample of what they could do. And then we found the right one. His work is absolutely fantastic. He looks more real, and also more scary."

Notes Blaze on the album title, "Well, it's because there was a vibe while we were in the studio. There was some kind of really good feeling and a lot of enthusiasm that was going on between us. Of course, I was enthusiastic because I was getting to sing with some people I really, really respected, and being in a top band and everything. But some of the songs and performances were a bit special, and it was a term that we used: 'Oh yeah, that's got something; that's got the X factor.' And then coincidentally that happened to be the tenth Iron Maiden studio album, so it all seemed to lean together."

The record opens with "The Sign of the Cross," which, at 11:18, is Maiden's sixth-longest song ever. After some Gregorian chanting from "The Xpression Choir" (unfortunately, Van Halen had opened their *Balance* album from earlier in the year with a similar idea), the band goes into one of their quiet intros. Soon we hear Blaze over a traditional Maiden gallop, all rich of voice and thespian, precise with his pronunciations, deliberately in a range that suits him, one lower than Bruce's.

"I suppose it's somewhere between the two, really," reflects Steve on the comparison with Bruce and indeed Paul. "It's hard to say. As far as working in the studio goes, all three were good, but sound-wise, voice-wise, I think Blaze is more earthy, if you like? It's hard to explain. They're all very different characters, but you know, Blaze's enthusiasm is second to none, really, so he was very easy to work with. We just wanted to be open-minded about it. We wanted to get the best person possible. But obviously there's a plus point about it that he's a Brit. He's the focal point of the band, he's the vocal point of the band, and he should always be the front man for the band. So, from that point of view,

Dave Wright archive

it's good he's British. There was one guy who was Norwegian, and he spoke good English, but still . . . it's one of those things. We had people from all over the world sending us stuff, and we wanted to be open-minded about it."

There are a pile of movements to the track, and they all make sense, aided and abetted by the strong melody—the song was so well regarded that after Bruce came back into Maiden, the song was retained in the set list.

"'Sign of the Cross' was one that Steve brought into rehearsal one day, that no one could play," chuckles Blaze. "I knew there was something really, really special about it, and I loved it from the moment of the quiet start on the acoustic guitar. We had to do the song in three parts and then put it all together afterwards, and we had to learn it before we went on tour. I don't think anybody would've predicted the reaction that that song had. It just went down absolutely fantastic. It's a big, long song, but it went down absolutely great on both the tours that we did. We played it many, many times.

"But it was a huge challenge because it's such an involved song, and nobody could remember how the song went. You'd get to where someone would mess up. It was the only one in all the time that I was involved with Maiden and all the songs we wrote, where we had to go, okay, we're gonna have to fuse this together. We'll record this part, we'll get that right, we'll get the conversion, now we can record this part, and then they had to put it all together afterwards. But it has such a vibe and an atmosphere."

Perhaps representing agreement across the band that they had a winner of a song on their hands, Dave's guitar solo, beginning at 8:14, quite amusingly agrees with Janick's—both are played in a bubbling waterfall of a style most associated with Gers. Although, perhaps repaying the tribute, on the next song, Janick's solo sounds somewhat like something Dave would conjure.

"Sign of the Cross" was based on the Umberto Eco novel *In the Name of the Rose* and had Steve exploring his thoughts on spirituality, which filled his thoughts increasingly through the 1990s, in the wake of his divorce and general sense of personal crisis. Steve alone gets the credit on this one, and indeed at the musical end, what we get is Maiden melody right down the middle—even the signature gallop is midpaced.

Next is "Lord of the Flies," credited to Steve and Janick, even if Blaze relates that

Dave Wright archive

"'Lord of the Flies' was one where I had an idea that I wanted to write a song about the book *Lord of the Flies*, by William Golding, and I talked about that with Steve, and he came up with some lyrics and we worked on the music together, with Janick. I thought it turned out really well."

The instrumental lead-up to the vocal allows for a cogent comparison between the original sound picture of the album and the later 2015 remaster. On the latter, Nicko's high-hat and cymbal work has been turned down and the articulation of Steve's bass work has been emphasized, while the bass tone has been cut back just a hair. Blaze's vocals seem raised as well. All told, frankly, the remaster has made the record come to life, to the point where *The X Factor* is a shockingly good-sounding Maiden album, when at the time it was summarily put down for its ragged self-production at the Barnyard.

Next is the aforementioned "Man on the Edge," a quick-paced rocker with a frantic, note-dense riff. Helping it become the hit it was is Blaze's hooky "Falling down" refrain, one of those cool choruses that want to name the song, even if the band has other ideas. Additional to Blaze's explanation above, he has said that a key turn of phrase in the song is "cannibal state," referring to the idea of the economic system chewing up its participants and spitting them out, resulting in loss of identity. Janick and Dave reprise the solo style and configuration used on "Sign of the Cross," both providing short and shredding pieces, Janick going first with one that feels more composed, like a miniature song.

"Fortunes of War" begins with one of Steve's bass intros, Blaze crooning, outside worker Michael Kenney providing keyboard washes—Kenney's main role is playing live with the band, but he is nicely credited in the liner notes of *The X Factor*. This one takes a long time to get going, and it kind of never does, due to the prominence of bass and drums on the track, Blaze there as well, but guitars firmly made secondary. Lyrically, Steve is examining the posttraumatic stress disorder (PTSD) of a soldier returning from war, the ironic title referring to the many "fortunes" the shell-shocked returning veteran now has to endure.

"To be honest with you, I have different lyrics and melodies over a period of time," explained Steve, on the subject of writing lyrics. "Mainly music I guess—lyrics is usually the last thing. It's kind of restricting sometime if you get a strong melody line. If the melody line is that strong, you have to stick to it, and you find that syllables and certain words you might want to use don't fit there, and you have to find something else. And that can be frustrating. I think it's most important that the melody is strong. I mean, that's the way we've always written anyways, since the first album. But these songs are all current, meaning that we didn't start writing till Blaze joined. We didn't want to write anything that didn't suit the new singer. Plus, I think it's important to make the new person feel part of the band. Blaze, it turned out, does write. But we may have chosen a singer that doesn't write. But we still would have preferred to wait and play to the singer's strengths, which we've done with all our singers. Blaze, I think, is like our fifth singer."

"Look for the Truth," credited to Steve, Janick, and Blaze, is a stomping, intrinsically Maidenesque track with both an anthemic "oh oh oh" football chant chorus plus a more conventional line that repeats the titling. All told, there's an element of clunkiness that reveals itself over the solo section, where Michael Kenney's keys can be heard clearly, betraying a lack of power. In the spaces, one hears that Nicko is quite loud, and you get the sense that he is trying to pound the daylights out of the song in hopes of making it pass muster.

"'Look for the Truth' is about the constant second-guessing of yourself," explains Blaze, "and the battle against my own demons and my own self-destruction. We were in Poland on the first *X Factor* tour. We'd had a really, really long overnight drive, and when we got to the hotel it was like seven in the morning, and there were already like about a hundred fans outside the hotel, and they were all singing 'Look for the Truth.' That was the song they were singing outside the hotel, and nobody could get to sleep. I'm glad I wasn't on that side of the hotel, but it was like the rest of the band were listening to them keep them awake. But I thought that was really cool, because that's another song I wrote with Janick—and one of the first ones."

"The Aftermath" follows upon "Fortunes of War," specifically addressing elements of World War I, such as the mud and the rain, the barbed wire, and the mustard gas. As well, this one's more about the futility of war, whether anything was accomplished.

Explains Blaze, "I was reading a lot of First World War poetry at the time, because I saw something that said if you really want to know about how things are in a war, don't read the historians, read the poets. And I kind of took that to heart. So, I spent some time reading the First World War poets, and that was inspired, really, from the reading I'd been doing, because of the kind of connection between people that were really young, and probably younger than me when I wrote that song, that were dying in the trenches. My grandmother came from a very large family, a family of thirteen. Six of her brothers died in the First World War, and my great-grandfather died in the First World War as well."

Musically there's a similarity here to "Look for the Truth," with the big halting chords, pregnant pauses, and spaces—that is, it's not a wall of sound. As well, the song is slow of tempo. Emphasizing the chord pattern—for better or worse—is the fact that Blaze's vocal melody often follows the riff.

Says Blaze concerning "Judgement of Heaven," "That was one of Steve's songs. It's a really good song, and there was a bit of talk at the time about that being a single. There's a lot of soul-searching in that song; the lyrics are really, really good."

Indeed, Steve is talking directly and candidly here, in fact more so than Bruce would have ever hoped for—I'm referring here to Dickinson's complaint that there was too much allegory and not enough emotion allowed in Maiden. The protagonist in the song talks directly about suicide, admitting to having those thoughts 'a dozen times or more.' He also talks very directly about both faith and fate, as well as the classic philosophical question asking if you had your life to live all over again, would you want anything to be different? The intense refection of Steve's lyric is set against a sturdy and very British-sounding riff placed on a one-and-three beat from Nicko. Later there are simple and memorable Maiden melodies set to a standard up-tempo groove.

"Blood on the World's Hands" begins bizarrely with Steve noodling on bass and not with his regular tone. Almost a bass solo, two elements evoke images of Rush: the harmonics, which sound like the intro to "Red Barchetta," and a more structured flurry of notes that sound like a part in "Natural Science." In fact, even the tone is closer to Geddy's than what we normally associate with Steve. After a full minute of this, the guys join in with pomp and circumstance, weaving a typical Renaissance-music-like Maiden melody. Blaze calls this one of his favorite vocal performances on the record. Not quite antiwar, "Blood on the World's Hands" is more antiviolence, with rape, starvation, assassination, and air raids being mentioned. By the end, the implication is that this "brutality and aggression" and "chaos" is a regular occurrence over the border, but it might be happening at home before you know it.

The mellow intros continue, with two minutes of "The Edge of Darkness" taken up with contemplative bass picking, granted with two verses getting taken care of as well. Notes Blaze, on getting to sing so contemplatively on the record (this was a celebrated Bruce trope for years—since "Hallowed," really), "Wolfsbane was very much a rock 'n' roll band, in comparison with Iron Maiden. With Maiden, the music is a lot more dynamic, and I get the chance to sing a lot more expressively. I get to sing very soft passages where the voice is almost standing on its own, which we never did in Wolfsbane, and then there are hard aggressive passages. I use more of the range of my voice. I've found another third to my voice, really, as far as my range goes. With Wolfsbane, we never toured with the intensity or the length of time as with Maiden, so that's a part of it too, learning to sing and learning to endure that."

Once the song kicks in, we're back at this very rhythmic place, the band pounding it out simply, a full ensemble version of what came before, same melody and phrasing with respect to the vocals. About halfway through, there's a shift to a different structure, more of a Maiden gallop, broken by sing-songy lead licks—singles, not twins. Come solo time, starting at about 4:20, Janick tears off one of the record's most energetic and complex leads, burbly and boisterous, followed by Dave as foil, reminding us of Maiden's legacy of singable solos.

"'I really wanted to do something about the movie *Apocalypse Now*," notes Blaze, "based around that, the book *Heart of Darkness* [Joseph Conrad], and the film. I'd been a big fan of the movie for such a long time. And being in Maiden, you have the opportunity to do something a bit more epic that didn't have to follow the rules of verse, chorus, verse, chorus, so I took that opportunity. That was one I worked on with Steve and Janick, and I was pleased with how it turned out; it's got a big atmosphere and it builds up great."

Second-to-last track "2 A.M." is one of the album's better numbers, if starkly simple. As Blaze relates, "'2 A.M.' was one of mine, taking me back to my days when I started, and I had to work a job and get home late from work." Indeed, if Steve channeled Rush earlier on the record, this is the ultimate follow-up to "Working Man," with the protagonist, just like in that song, cracking a beer and wondering what it's all about.

The X Factor closes even stronger, with "The Unbeliever" representing the best and most-progressive ideas on the record, from the mathematical verses to the softly Zeppelinesque chorus 1, from the (again) Rush-like break to chorus 2, which is essentially a form of prog that Maiden themselves have been bringing to the table since 1980.

"'The Unbeliever' is perhaps my least favorite track," Nicko told *Under the Blade*, "yet I really like it. It's funny because it's a weird timing and a weird phrasing. One minute I like it; another time I listen to it, I'm not so sure I like it. It's one of those weird tracks for me. But after the first couple of verses of the song, it opens up into a completely different dialogue and it really kind of 'gets into it,' if you like. It's a classic Steve Harris epic. But I really like 'Blood on the World's Hands' and 'Sign of the Cross.' These are all songs that I like to play live, and we actually are doing in the sets. I'm possibly leaning more towards the live performance of the album. 'Judgement of Heaven,' for instance, is a great song, and it's a shame we're not playing that live. So, I suppose my favorites would be 'Sign of the Cross,' 'Blood on the World's Hands,' 'Judgement of Heaven,' and 'The Aftermath.'"

Blaze calls "The Unbeliever" "one of the best songs Steve's ever written." If that might be hyperbole, it's at least enough to draw a level of attention to it that it deserves. Every part is interesting. Even if in true Maiden fashion, they repeat, sending this one to eight minutes, the effect is hypnotic because each one is so fresh. One could argue that "Fortunes of War" gets repetitive, but not "The Unbeliever": the writing is creative enough to sustain interest even after eight minutes.

That was it for *The X Factor*, all seventy-one minutes of it, easily Maiden's longest album to this point. But the band had fully three more tracks finished. As alluded to, the "Man on the Edge" single added "Justice of the Peace" and "I Live My Way." Both of these were used as Japanese bonus tracks, as was the third non-LPer, "Judgement Day."

"Justice of the Peace" was a knees-up rocker, as they say in England, aggressive, up tempo, with a cool "Trooper"-like trill riff that gives way to slashing chords for the riff.

An obscure modulation takes place during the chorus, and then after that the guys sound lost. "I Live My Way" begins with the obligatory endless intro before turning very heavy, with Nicko playing more double bass drum than on any other Maiden track, as well as, in spots, a novel sixteenth-note pattern on the high-hat. As with "Justice of the Peace," the production is a little rough, particularly as it pertains to the drums. "Judgement Day" roars out of the gates like a Blaze-era "Be Quick or Be Dead," but once the verse begins, any similarity ends, given the novel chord structure. Again, like the other non-LP tracks, Nicko is recorded loud, and he plays like a drunken pirate. Indeed, this is the heaviest song of the fourteen *X Factor* session tracks, from Nicko to the manic and prolonged soloing, to Blaze's singing, which sounds particularly punky, or at least low-rent NWOBHM.

"Well, I suppose it's quite a long album," figures Steve. "We had three extra songs that will end up being B-sides, and really the writing, like some of it was done with Blaze, so obviously having new input had some influence as well. And obviously being away for a while, not having written anything for a while. Also just having a new member in the band slowed things up, being more picky with what I wanted to do this time, with the sound and everything else. We wanted the drums to be more ambient, and the drum parts we wanted to be more open, so everything breathed more, so there's a lot more air and space to really concentrate on the songs. I really like 'Sign of the Cross' because it's got everything but the kitchen sink in it. I also like 'Look for the Truth' a lot, and I suppose for my own writing, 'Blood on the World's Hands.' I really like 'Man on the Edge' as well."

"I didn't think personally [that] Steve should have produced *The X Factor*," reflected Rod Smallwood years later, although, as I say, somehow just with a remaster, the record now sounds pretty darn muscular (hard to believe I find myself defending *The X Factor* against Rod!). "I thought he was doing enough writing it and everything else, all the other things he used to do. I thought it would have been a good idea to have a producer, and Steve thought if anyone knows Maiden, he does, so what's the point of hiring a producer? You just need someone to engineer. We argued long and hard, and I think I was there about eight hours.

"At the end of the day, Steve's got his side that he makes decisions on, and I've sort of got mine in terms of certain aspects in my territory. If we disagree, then if the one who wants it is still saying after hours of shouting that this is the right thing to do, we decide that if you feel so strongly about it, you must be right, and get on with it. I think any partnership's like that, isn't it? But I can't recall ever having anything even close to unpleasant. Really, we've argued things out of passion for what we believe is right for Maiden, with different takes on it. But you can't fall out over stuff like that."

Kerrang! gave *The X Factor* three Ks (out of five), with Paul Elliott writing that "a decade ago, Maiden were the definitive *Kerrang!* band, as Metallica are now. But while Metallica are still making great albums, Maiden haven't cut a classic since 1984. Let's face it, in 1995, the heat is on Iron Maiden like never before. To restore Maiden's status as Britain's biggest and hardest-hitting rock act, *The X Factor* had to be killer. Sadly, it's just average, better at least than their last two studio albums, but no match for the raw power of the 1980 debut or the blood and thunder of *The Number of the Beast*. The reasons are twofold. First, there's Blaze's voice; hearty, yet strangely flat in places like the chorus of 'Fortunes of War.' Blaze's predecessor, Bruce Dickinson, might've warbled a little too much for post-grunge taste, but he's a hard act to follow. The songs could also be better. The single, 'Man on the Edge,' is a good bit of rough-and-tumble evocative of Bayley's former band Wolfsbane, but the bulk of the album is ponderous."

The X Factor was not well received in the US either, the record stalling at #147 on *Billboard* and sales struggling to a reported 112,710 copies as of 2005. But Scandinavia loved it, as did the homeland (at least in terms of initial sales), the album rising to #8 on the British charts, with "Man on the Edge" hitting #10.

September 28 through October 9, 1995, Maiden open what was coined "The X Factour" in Israel, three shows, followed by another three dates in South Africa. It's the first time the band got to either territory, with the first Israeli date, in Jerusalem, representing Blaze's first show with the band. This is yet another parallel between Blaze's hiring and Bruce's. Both times Maiden went away to sort out the milestone, with Bruce singing for the band for the first time in October 1981 in Bologna, Italy. Also in both cases, Steve and Rod appreciated the assurance of being able to see their prospects perform live as well as hear them on full-length albums and not just audition tapes, which had necessarily been the only calling card for the hundreds of aspirants this time around.

October 14 through November 2, the X Factour rolls through Europe, with My Dying Bride signing on as support for the back half. Beginning on November 4 for a week, Adrian Smith's solo band Psycho Motel is there to warm up the crowd for the new-look Maiden.

Blaze was soon to have problems with his voice, given the heavy tour itinerary. What came to exacerbate the problem was that even though the new songs were in Blaze's range, the old songs were written by and for the Air Raid Siren. Speaking recently, and mainly about his regimen now, Bayley explains that it wasn't for lack of discipline.

"Me, the way I am is I don't drink whiskey when I'm on tour. I don't do shots, I don't do any alcohol before the concert, I don't smoke. I try to be as quiet as I can during the daytime, stay away from any conversation. Try and do what I can to keep my voice over a period of time. I'm always thinking about, it's not just five in a row—I've still got a week to do after this. And if I screw up it's gonna take weeks to recover, and I don't have the time. I love to sing. So, I'm known for my voice more than my looks, really.

"My fans come . . . it's a great feeling for me when they say, 'I love your voice' or 'Your voice sounds good' or 'Your voice sounds as good as ever.' Because my hero is Ronnie James Dio. I saw him all through his career, and he always sounded great. And I'm a fan of Eric Adams from Manowar—he's another singer that gets the ultimate respect from me because he never falters; he just sings. And I know what that takes to achieve. I don't count myself with those two guys, but it's a different mode. And that's my attitude. For me, it's a way of life, it's a philosophy, it's a way of being. It's a rich, deep connection where, at its best, I connect with my audience. And I will connect with something else—there are moments of real beauty when you manage to do that. That's my philosophy."

Back to Blaze on the *X Factor* press trail . . . "You don't realize how little you know a song until you try to sing it, then you think, 'Hang on, what are the words to that third verse?' I've had to do quite a lot of brushing up for the tour. The main thing is the music. I love their music, you know, and so a lot of the songs I've had to learn are my favorite songs anyway, so it hasn't been a chore. It's been just 'Okay, let's have a go.' And when you're in that rehearsal room with those guys cranking up 'The Trooper,' it's like, 'Fucking yes!' I like both eras, really. I really like the Di'Anno stuff because you just get straight into it. But I also like the stuff that Bruce sang, especially his later stuff, because it's really melodic, so you get a chance to show off."

November 12 through December 23, the X Factour addresses Europe more extensively, support coming from My Dying Bride throughout, with the Almighty serving as a third act for the first half. Lamented Steve at the time, "Apart from a two-year period around 1983, 1984, when maybe we were deemed as being cool, we've never been a cool, hip band, before or after that. We do what we do, and you can take us or leave us. I think a lot of people are into the band, or have been into the band, but because of the way things are with fashion and that, they're probably afraid to say so. I think some bands now are gonna disappear up their own arse if they're not careful by turning down tours, because it's not cool."

It's an interesting comment from Steve, and although one can appreciate his candid take, there are two things to point out. Maiden was definitely cool in 1980, 1981, and 1982—in fact, they were white hot. As well, not that he could know this, but surprise, surprise, Maiden would soon be cool again, the transition taking place—arguably gradually—somewhere around 2005, persisting to this day, which is a lot of years of being cool, when you add them all up. But it's perceptive of him to realize that it indeed had dropped off after 1984, although even there he's selling the band short—Maiden's reputation began to slip in 1986.

Remarked Nicko to *Under the Blade*, on the band's reduced fortunes, "There's the fact that we're playing some smaller places, and weird things keep going wrong with the stage. But I think that's the pub gig vibe: itchy power supply, dirty floors, and little holes in the stage to fall down into and that sort of crap. But we're having a great splendid time. You know, the United States at the moment sucks. As far as media exposure goes and the actual 'flavor of the month,' if you like, it's not metal at the moment. It hasn't been for the last three or four years. And so, it's reflected obviously within the general public's attitude towards the music because it's sort of been outside, you know what I mean?

"But now with the likes of UFO—they got back together last year—and Ozzy Osbourne, AC/DC, and ourselves, I think it's kind of coming back in your face. There's still a lot of good music out there, especially from these good bands that were around ten years ago. So on a health state, this kind of music just got out of a visit to the doctor's office, and I think the medicine has been prescribed and it's gonna start getting better. But in comparison to Europe, it's like miles behind. Europe wasn't as hot as it was ten years ago or even, say, six years ago, but it's definitely healthy with heavy rock."

Yes, Maiden were playing clubs.
Dave Wright archive

Into the new year (and continued industry animosity against all things heavy metal), from January 12 through February 2, 1996, Maiden perform additional European shows on the X Factour, support on some dates coming from Steve Harris's pet project Dirty Deeds. On the subject of touring with Maiden, specifically filling the shoes of Bruce Dickinson, Blaze opined at the time that "obviously, when he first left the band, he completely slagged off everything he ever did with them, so he wasn't in everybody's good books. But no, he hardly ever comes up in conversation, because everybody enjoys what we're doing now. I don't know, hardly anybody ever talks about him unless he's gone off and done something stupid, which always seems to happen. The gossip, you know, 'What's he done now?' or something like that.

"But Bruce is a really, really good singer; he did a lot of good work with the band, a lot of really great songs, and I enjoy singing those songs. I just think the best decision Bruce Dickinson ever made in my life was to leave Iron Maiden, you know? I'm just so glad he left, because it's a fucking brilliant job. It's absolutely great. I get to travel all over the world—somebody else pays for it. I get to stop into hotels, and all you have to do—get this—you put a card on the doorknob, and someone comes around and cleans your room for you! [laughs]. You don't get that at home! It's wild! And you know, at a lot of hotels, you can just phone someone up and they'll bring you food! It's great! And you get to go to a concert every night, great music, and see loads of people who really like you. So, it's an absolutely fucking brilliant job. It's not a job; it's a way of life. I don't feel like I'm going to work at all!"

Said Steve, "The songs are great onstage, even after a year playing them. Some people told me that they were much better live than on the album, and that's true. But I'd like to point out that this isn't new. Iron Maiden's main concern has always been to retranscribe in the studio what we're able to do onstage. The next album will be even stronger—you'll see. I can even tell you that it will be very different from this one. *The X Factor* can almost be considered a transition record, a bit like the teenage years of the new Iron Maiden. You only have to listen to the way Blaze sings now—it's totally different than a year ago."

On February 2, 1996, everybody keeps trying, and "Lord of the Flies" is issued as the second single from *The X Factor*, backed with covers of the Who's "My Generation" and UFO's "Doctor, Doctor," celebrating an earlier time when Maiden single-handedly transformed the art of metal covers. Metallica took the baton, but indeed it was Maiden that was the very first band to think like the fans and titillate with their cover choices, back to the likes of "Women in Uniform" and "I Got the Fire." "My Generation" doesn't exactly compute in this manner, but "Doctor Doctor" sure does.

Janick relates that what the band tends to do is go into Steve's front room and rifle through his record collection looking for tracks. Gers says that it was he who picked "Doctor, Doctor," because the band used to do it in the early days. Amusingly, Steve says they do covers for B-sides because he can't wrap his head around saying, "Okay, time to write a B-side." Because, sensibly, that just means it's a song that isn't going to be good enough to go on the album.

February 8 through April 5, 1996, the North American leg of the X Factour finds the band playing smaller venues, partly due to the continued pronounced mid-1990s backlash against traditional heavy metal. The author was on hand for the band's show at RPM in Toronto on February 11. Maiden was playing the big room, the Warehouse, which held about 2,500, while the following year, Bruce would play the small room, the Guvernment, next door, which could fit about 1,200. The venue complex is now gone, making way for condos. Support on the night came from the white-hot Fear Factory, a band that at the time was as futuristic as Maiden was archaic. A number of western dates were to be canceled due to Blaze Bayley having contracted a throat infection.

"It's not as drastic a change here in Europe as it has been in North America," groused Steve. "From what I understand, it's pretty drastic. We haven't played over there in like three years. Maybe we're in for a shock when we go over, I don't know [laughs]. But yeah, what I think is happening is healthy, because there's a lot of stuff going around. As far as I'm concerned, there's room for all of it. The only thing I've noticed is that it's become more trendy. There's a thing opened up where it's not cool to like certain bands, which I think is bullshit, because it should be about music and not fashion. But these things happen. Trends come and they go. I mean, we're still very strong in the rest of the world, really. It's mainly North America where things are a bit diminished. The single went straight into #10 in the UK, and the album's gone straight to #8, which is great. The gigs are always sold out or close to sellout."

April 11 to 18, Maiden take the X Factour to Japan for six shows. June 22 through August 17, the band plays scattered dates through Europe, mostly festivals. Support comes from Skin, Helloween, and Dirty Deeds. On August 17, Helloween's Michael Kiske issues his *Instant Clarity* album, which includes two cowrites with Adrian Smith. August 24 through September 7, Maiden take the X Factour to South America and Mexico, support coming variously from the likes of Motörhead, Skid Row, Helloween, and, in Mexico, local act Makina.

Steve Harris: "It's really a strong stage set; it's really good, based around the album artwork, metal and stuff. Eddie's obviously still there. It looks really good. I don't know, maybe I'm wrong in saying this, but I think people are getting tired of bands going out with no lights and no show and staring at their feet and looking bored. I think it's important for people to see a show, an event.

"It must be a bit strange," mused Steve on fan reaction to Blaze. "Everyone has been watching every single note he sings, but now they've accepted him. And there's not so much testing going on. Bruce never sang perfectly every night either. But that's what a year's worth of touring does. He feels a lot more confident and part of the band. It makes it exciting that we'll be doing another album soon."

"In Europe, the market is still pretty strong," explained Dave Murray, on the lay of the land for the band touring in 1995. "In fact, we found a whole new generation of fans. A lot of them were probably not even born when the first album came out. We're trying to rebuild the whole thing, in a way. It's a case of going full circle, because it seems we're back in the late 1970s / early 1980s, adjusting to theaters and clubs again. We're playing the game, and we're not fooling ourselves that it's as popular as it was. We've always been a touring band, and it's good to go back to your roots. There's always other mountains to climb. We reached the top of the last one and stuck the flag in; now we're climbing up another one. We still enjoy playing, and we give 150 percent whether it's a club or a large venue. Onstage it's like we're fighting for our life, and the music moves us that way. It's actually been quite nice because it's intimate. Playing smaller places can create a vibe, and you can re-create what you did in the early days. We're doing a world tour, and we're just playing it out to see what happens until we record the next album."

On September 2, the non-LP "Virus" is issued as a single, with a plethora of originals and covers as B-sides used throughout three different versions. This is a bit of a new thing for Maiden but not, generally speaking, for bands from the UK, where singles culture is a big deal.

As Steve told *BW&BK* at the time, "We've just been carrying on with the world tour, and during a three- or four-week break, we went in and recorded our new single. It was weird because it was a one-off thing that we'd never really done before. We had just come back from Japan, and we didn't have anything prepared. We went in completely cold, without any preconceived ideas at all. Hours later we had a song, so it seemed to have worked."

"'Virus' is very, very unusual," figures Blaze. "Out of all the songs we did, that one, the whole band, all five people, were contributing to the writing of that song. So, somebody came

Dave Wright archive

and said, 'I've got this idea,' or two people said, 'We've got this idea.' Everybody contributed and then we recorded it. In a way, we rehearsed it and rehearsed it and then put it together. Since we did that version, which is on *Best of the Beast*, then I do my own version of 'Virus.' It's my own arrangement that suits me and the band. So, we do our own version, and a version of that is on the live album. And so far, everybody that's heard that version loves it. We never played that live with Iron Maiden. So, I think that's a real plus for me, that you can never see that song live with Iron Maiden—we never played it when I was in the band. So, it's really nice when you see people singing along. They've never heard the song live before, except for with us. You see the kind of realization on people's faces—'I recognize it, but I don't know why I recognize it.' It's because they've never heard it live."

On September 23, EMI issues the aforementioned compilation *Best of the Beast*, in single-CD and two-CD versions. It's kind of a big deal, since it's the first Iron Maiden hits package ever; surprising, given the history. "Virus" is the main feature in terms of cool new things, but there's also a live with Blaze "Afraid to Shoot Strangers," plus a couple of tracks from the band's very first release, *The Soundhouse Tapes*. Of these, it's only "Virus" that is on the single-CD version. The album goes on to sell a half-million copies around the world, over 100,000 of them in Sweden alone.

Explained Steve on the cover art, "In fact, we thought about it at the beginning of the X Factour, when we found those unofficial T-shirts that some people sold at the venues. You can see the different faces of Eddie, and I found that brilliant, really good.

So, we decided to perfect the original idea, and we made official T-shirts. Derek had originally done a drawing that was completely different. So, he based himself on the T-shirt illustration to make the cover for the *Best of the Beast* album. On the one hand, we wanted Derek to make some kind of patchwork of all the previous covers, but on the other hand, we didn't want him to simply paste them together as they were originally. We wanted him to do something slightly different, a bit like a cartoon.

"We've always tried to do the best we can for the fans," continues Harris. "Having the single CD, the double CD, and the quadruple vinyl, fans can do pretty much what they want. It appeals to the collectors and the casual fans. There have been bootlegs floating around for the longest time, so we thought it would be best to clean that live stuff up. We tried to include material from across the board, but there's always certain tracks that'll be missing. It is difficult, and it's like picking a live set. We were on the road for most of the process, so Rod sort of went through it all. He'd send us out lists, and we'd go through it all. We went back and forth, changing tracks, and he'd send us cassettes to see if it flowed right. It was a team effort, but Rod was doing most of the legwork."

Countering rumors of implosion, Steve told Vincent Martin, "I said it and I'll say it again: we're not gonna split! [laughs]. No more than we're going to leave EMI. We're releasing a compilation, and that's all there is to it. It was simply the right time. I think about the very beginning, when we wanted to make it big in Britain. We were hoping to become popular throughout the country one day. We didn't even have a clue that there was a big wide world out there only waiting to listen to our music! [laughs]. Now, I don't want to make any kind of summary. I'll only say that everything's been brilliant, and that the band is still standing because we still want to record albums and get onstage. The day I'll be tired of it, when it'll be a chore to go onstage, then on that day everything will be over. I don't want to lie to myself, and I don't want to lie to the fans, although they're not as stupid as some may say."

Helping Steve with his metal cause, on June 27, 1997, Swedish retro-metal fans HammerFall issue their debut *Glory to the Brave* album. The record becomes an underground hit, as well as ground zero for a traditional heavy metal revival that sweeps Europe. The new subgenre is deemed power metal, and the likes of Rainbow, Judas Priest, and Iron Maiden are deemed the wise forefathers of the nearly "hip" new subgenre.

Dave Wright archive

Dave Wright archive

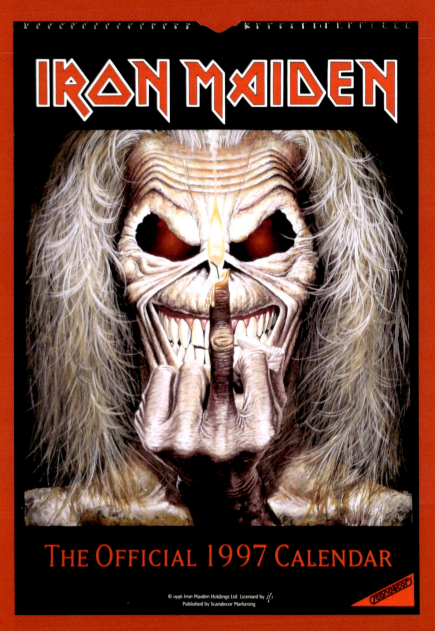

Dave Wright archive

CHAPTER 14
Skunkworks and Accident of Birth

"An alchemy of influences that we as a band think of as the best in rock music from the past 30 years."

It's hard for Bruce to be feeling any sense of Schadenfreude at Maiden not exactly shooting off the blocks with Blaze, not that he necessarily had any of that sort of ill will. Still, *The X Factor* would have affirmed the reasoning of his decision—Steve absolutely was not about reengineering the band or exhibiting any sense of rapid growth. Sure, he wanted to make good music, but it was going to be traditional Maiden music, with the handful of the band's idiosyncrasies clutched tight, fist in glove with whoever was singing.

Dickinson, on the other hand, was absolutely still about Robert Plant–level restlessness, creative yearning. One also could assume there was a desire to stay relevant to the latest music trends, as long as they were heavy, of course. I mean, Bruce is such a participator in modern life, from sport to politics to talking to fans to writing and to flying, that one could posit that he wanted to make heavy music that could attract a crowd because he likes people.

In any event, on February 19, 1996, Bruce issues his third solo album, *Skunkworks*, featuring artwork by Storm Thorgerson and, more significantly, a production credit to one Jack Endino.

"It can be a lonely road when you walk into a room and everybody moves away, saying, 'Hmm, he used to be in Iron Maiden,'" quipped Bruce at the time, speaking with Tim Henderson. "I think this is the album that is going to seize people's imagination. There's a lot on *Balls to Picasso* and *Tattooed Millionaire* that was really cool, but to read the interviews, you wouldn't really know that. When you go back and listen to some of those records, you think, 'That's quite enjoyable.' But this is a record that seems to have touched a nerve. You can hear early Deep Purple, Soundgarden, Rush, and a host of other influences. I took it as an alchemy of influences that we as a band think of as the best in rock music from the past 30 years, that we've synthesized and turned into our own.

"It's really a band effort," continued Bruce. "All the songs are written by Alex [Dickson] and myself. He is this outrageous guitarist in terms of composition and everything. He had a really clear vision of what he wanted to do with the guitars. I don't do shit on the guitar. Everything that's instrumental is written by Alex—the boy's talented. When we got Jack Endino involved, that clarified things even further. Jack is Mr. Guitar in terms of sound. He saw this album as an escape from being the godfather of grunge and just being a great producer. I listen to the record, and I still can't believe I'm on it."

Godfather of grunge indeed. Jack had produced Green River, Mudhoney, Nirvana, Soundgarden, Fluid, Gruntruck, Tad, L7, Screaming Trees, Love Battery, Afghan Whigs, even Dwarves and Blue Cheer, and certainly no one who was established British heavy metal royalty like Bruce.

Dave Wright archive

"This has nothing to do with Seattle," defended Bruce. "The only thing it has to do with Seattle is that Jack's phone number has the same area code. Jack has an amazing bullshit detector. He just won't let you get away with a cliché. So many producers market themselves as a cliché. You pay the money for the producer; you get the producer's clichés. He's not about that at all. He's a transparent producer. He tries to get rid of your clichés, whether they're vocal, lyrical, or guitar. He just sits there and goes, 'Are you happy with that?' I shy away, saying, 'Probably not.'"

Comparing Jack to the only producer Dickinson ever worked with in Maiden, Martin Birch, Bruce said, "I've got so much respect for Martin. He taught me a huge amount about singing and performing. Jack has moved me in a similar kind of way. When I worked with Martin on *Number of the Beast* and *Piece of Mind*, I was on this quantum learning curve. Doing this with Jack felt like the same thing.

"It's a kind of a reboot," continues Bruce. "There's a quote from Henry Miller that kept popping up whenever I do anything: 'All growth is an unpremeditated leap into the dark.' I was like, 'He's probably right.' If you know what's going to happen before you do your big leap, it's not growth. If you know how it's going to finish up, you're not going to find anything out. For that reason, the uncertainty that surrounds you requires a huge act of faith on the part of you as a singer, to be prepared to take a flamethrower to your past. You have patterns of behavior that have built up over the past, which you're comfortable with, that you have to smash. That takes an enormous amount of effort to put them all in the mincer and use the bits that come out."

Speaking with Mattias Reinholdsson from *The Bruce Dickinson Wellbeing Network*, Bruce compared Maiden with his new chosen path.

"Steve is not that flexible a personality; it's just the way he is, you know. He knows pretty much what he wants, and I think he tends to exclude a lot of options. He's never taken a drug in his life, he doesn't smoke, he never smoked dope, he's never taken acid or anything that would alter his possibilities. He very rarely gets drunk even, because he likes to stay in control.

"And I think that's the fundamental difference between me and him. Sometimes you have to be in control of things, and there are times when you need to be out of control. There are times when you have to let things happen, and that can be very scary for somebody who is a control freak. And that's sometimes when the best ideas happen; it's when you just take a big leap into the unknown and you don't know what's gonna happen. That can be very creative, and it can be absolute shit, but some of the best and the most exciting pieces of music have been created out there on the edge of destruction.

"But people have different interpretations of that, and, fundamentally, to me 'being on the edge' means being on the edge of actually destroying the creativity. Not being on the edge by playing fast, technically, but to try stuff that is so out there at a gig that the whole show might fall flat on its face, or it might be completely brilliant."

As for the catchy album title, Bruce told Darren Wershler in a sidebar of the same feature in our mag, *BW&BK*, "We were looking at a variety of names that dealt with space and the cosmos. We wanted something that doubled as both a band name and album name. *Skunkworks* just kind of went in a hat with a bunch of other names. It came to the top of the pile and people kept saying, 'By the way, what does it mean?' It's a great title. It doesn't matter if you know about it or not. If you discover what it's about, it's even cooler. Most think it's about skunk weed."

The short answer is that the term first applied to a configuration of workers, a can-do committee of sorts, set up within Lockheed Aviation in California, to make technological magic happen with a minimum of red tape. Out of this came the Blackbird, a Bruce favorite, and the stealth bomber. The term has now entered the lexicon to describe any sort of hotshot gathering of innovators left to prove their mettle outside the constraints of corporate bureaucracy.

"It is out of this world," explains Bruce. "It's real-life *Star Wars* stuff. The thing I love about it is that the design philosophy of the company is completely rock 'n' roll. There's a great book called *Skunkworks* by Ben Rich, and in that you will find this ridiculously colorful organization of guys basically wandering around in jeans and T-shirts, working on the most-secret projects in the free world. They have instructions that they're not allowed to spend time and money designing special components. They've got to go down to Walmart and buy parts for the stealth bomber, because the whole design philosophy is that it has to be done fast, on budget, and on time. There has to be elegant solutions, using practical means of technology.

"That's simplifying it, but that's the philosophy. The engineers have to live on the site. The rule at Skunkworks was if you were a spitting distance away from the airplane, you were too far away. If you were a draftsman or a scientist, you were literally eating your lunch under the airplane, when they were putting the rivets in the thing. Because if someone came along with a problem, you did it straightaway on the spot. It's a rock 'n' roll way of building airplanes."

As for the cover art, Bruce demurs, saying, "This is the man who created visuals for *Dark Side of the Moon* and *Houses of the Holy*. What else needs to be said? Skunkworks. It's a secret." As mentioned, Bruce tried to get a little Hipgnosis magic on his last record, but it wasn't in the budget (the company closed down in 1983, but Storm Thorgerson kept doing covers right up until his death in 2013). This time, there it is, and one can't help but think that this was part of Bruce's competitive nature, to keep current with design as well as music, to look smart.

Into the record, and one would have to say that Dickinson had succeeded. With "Space Race," although the opening compressed riff reminds one instantly of a favorite grunge trope, we're soon into a song that, sure, vaguely feels grunge of melody but is more so a form of progressive metal, in 6/4 time, and with a chorus that is pure traditional melodic metal. Bruce responds to the fecund creative challenge of the musical backtrack in kind, writing a colorful yet succinct enough missive to our audacious aggressive tendencies but ultimately our insignificance, given that there's "nothing left but burning up into the sun."

"Back from the Edge" is next, and the mandate of the impressive opener is maintained, the band coming up with a spirited straight-line modern metal rocker, snare on one and three, classy verse, classy prechorus, and truly memorable chorus, where the beat has fully relaxed for the bright lights of stadium rock. The break and subsequent solo section have us fully convinced that we're in a mature rock-songwriting place beyond anything Maiden had ever done, the magic of striking with what they struck with at the right time and place, 1982 through 1984, notwithstanding. Bruce drives home the point by layering in multiple tracks of vocals, creating a song eminently worthy of its single status, not to mention artsy production video with Bruce singing underwater and his band shot with mood lighting and quick edits.

"Back from the Edge" was issued in 7-inch vinyl format, backed with the Chris Dale–penned joke tune "I'm in a Band with an Italian Drummer," which makes good fun of Alessandro Elena, the band's "very Italian" drummer, who is in fact from Rome. Silly as the song is, it's a production tour de force with a pile of musical styles and sound effects and myriad vocal tracks, mostly goofy singing and rapid-fire spoken word. Elena himself gets in on the act, nattering away at the close.

The CD single version included "Rescue Day," "God's Not Coming Back," and "Armchair Hero," all of them non-LP. "Rescue Day" fuels the debate about whether Bruce had gone grunge. Like the character of the official record, the tempo is of that Pearl Jam vibe, and there are vaguely psychedelic melodies that reach all the way back to the Beatles. Still, it's a tight construct with thoughtful lyrics and even some slide guitar.

"God's Not Coming Back" counters with a wah-wah solo and an up-tempo punk rock riff and beat and snarly vocal to match, with Bruce poking fun at religion. There's also a nod to the screaming skills of Ian Gillan, and if one puts two and two together, the song serves as a reminder that although Ted Neely played Jesus in *Jesus Christ Superstar*, Ian played the part on the soundtrack record.

"Armchair Hero" (originally called "Share It or Lose It" and played on a portion of the *Balls to Picasso* tour) splits the difference, crashing out of the speakers as a killer metal track. There's a bit of a street vibe, but again, like many of the songs on the album, it's steered toward classic British metal by high-quality prechorus and chorus parts, topped with the Air Raid Siren at the top of his game, clearly loving that even his B-sides were songs precisely twice as good as anything Maiden had written in years, his own 1990s material with the band included.

Back to *Skunkworks*, "Inertia" is next, and the superlative modern metal continues, this one a bit like Rush in the 1990s, but again, once past the opening clean guitar and quiet bits, essentially just really well-written melodic hard rock. This one got a full-blown scripted video, with Bruce getting his head chopped off and served up *Piece of Mind* style. Again, not like anybody saw these videos, but *Skunkworks* seems to have been unjustly sunk by superficialities such as Bruce's pageboy haircut and then a similar look to his band, who came across as younger versions of this newly fashionable Dickinson. Bottom line: *Skunkworks* is vastly underrated. Put more specifically, it's the glorious actualization of the same well-meaning creative intentions splayed across *Balls to Picasso*, which failed through lack of songs and the obscure side plot of Latin percussion.

Strength to strength, "Faith" is no-nonsense metal with a biting Slash guitar tone. A harshly emotional story of love gone wrong, this one's packed with surprise prog rock musical twists, yet all of them succinct and fitting. In essence, it's GN'R crossed with Queensryche with a soaring Bruce chorus strung across it.

Back to superficialities, "Solar Confinement" sounds like Soundgarden—for about twelve seconds. Once the band kicks in, the rhythm section rocks tightly, guitars arrive and then more arrive, and we're into another one of these anthemic stadium rock choruses. No grunge to see here—please move on. Not sure what sort of alchemy Bruce is up to with the lyrics, but the images are impressive, as is the Van der Graaf Generator reference, made to feel all the more intentional by what sounds like a nod to King Crimson. Amusingly, the working title to this one was "Astral Parlour Confinement," which is only a little muddier than the final name, which at least serves the purpose of adding to the record's subtle astronomy theme.

As Bruce related to Henrik Johansson, "I love Van der Graaf Generator because they were a band that were on the edge, and although they had quite complex arrangements, they made some great sounds. And they were an incredibly depressing band—music to commit suicide to—and that's why I loved it, because it was so out there. You put Van der Graaf on, and you could clear an entire room of people, and I loved it. I love music like that. It's the same thing with other bands like Magma, these weird jazz rock bands. Arthur Brown too. There's moments of real genius in full clusters in various bits of their music, and I'm into those. I'm not into this 'vulgar display of power,' to quote a famous band. The first time you see it, it may be cool, but the second time, it's just boring."

Directly addressing the reference, Bruce explains that "yes, 'From H to He who am the only one.' It's the fundamental life force of the universe; it's what powers the stars. When I was a kid, I used to go through his lyrics with microscope. Lyric-wise I was really into Peter Hammill, Ian Anderson, and Gillan. Gillan's lyrics I thought were pretty cool, and they were very rock 'n' roll. Especially the early stuff from Deep Purple's *In Rock*. I was never particularly into Robert Plant's lyrics. They just never really got to me. I like them more now than I did then. In general, I sort of appreciate Zeppelin a bit more now than I did when I was a kid. But Peter Hammill had some really good poetical lyrics which are very cool. I'd like to write more of them in the future."

Amusingly, Bruce once said that when he was young, his dream was to be in a band with the lyrics of Van der Graaf, the energy of punk, and the "proficiency" of Deep Purple. I don't think he every arrived at the literary heights of Hammill during his first shot with Maiden, but he might have touched the hem across *Balls to Picasso* and *Skunkworks*. As for the musical end of it, even though Iron Maiden sound fairly different from Purple,

Dave Wright archive

loosely speaking you could call them a punk rock version of that band, just like you could call them a punk rock version of Priest. Incidentally, who's the *real* punk rock version of Purple? Why, that would be Ian's band Gillan. So, this framing is something somewhat shared between Bruce and Bruce's hero.

"Dreamstate" proves that a valid ballad can be crafted in this *Skunkworks* idiom. It's dark, strange and lyrically enigmatic, and sure, a little alt-metal, although again, given the conservative high-fidelity production job of Jack Endino (scrappy sound is another reason *Balls to Picasso* fizzles in comparison), it avoids direct comparisons to grunge.

"I Will Not Accept the Truth" is probably the most Rush-like song on the album, from its opening slick strafing to the dreamy Alex Lifeson strumming and the Neil Peart complication of the drums, even if Elena doesn't forget to groove. One supposes that mellow and melancholic Rush compare to quiet Soundgarden and Pearl Jam, but Bruce's big personality takes it elsewhere, through his energetic and thespian vocals to the operative timbre of his voice. Plus, as track builds upon track across *Skunkworks*, it becomes apparent that his backing band has a composite personality to match, one that is exquisitely synced to Jack's professional non-Seattle production work and even the cover art.

Next is "Inside the Machine," and the previously established alloy between alternative-hard rock writing and 1980s slickness and discipline is maintained, as is the sense of sturdy transition between sections. The song fits lyrically as well, literally reading like a description of a skunkworks.

Facetiously called "Fastgarden" during its working-title genesis, "Headswitch" indeed sounds like a variant of "Rusty Cage." What's more, "Headswitch" is a very grungy title. Still, the astronomy theme is all *Skunkworks*, even more so with Bruce's opaque narrative here, where he's describing a sort of cosmic explosion going on in the mind.

"Meltdown" charts a venomous trail of betrayal, musically, again a bit along the lines of Soundgarden-meets-Rush like so many of the album's songs—let's not forget, when we accuse something of being grungy, there are all those other bands that Bruce doesn't sound like (i.e., Nirvana, Alice in Chains, Melvins, and Mudhoney; Pearl Jam is always a wild card). What we get here is simply another smart and classy modern metal riff made only better by having Bruce's lyrics and vocals giving it guidance.

Is there such a thing as grunge melody? If so, "Octavia" reminds one of that, maybe Smashing Pumpkins or Pearl Jam. There's some of that in the oscillation between clean and dirty guitar as well, plus the slow and groovy pacing smashed by nearly constant cymbals circa "Teen Spirit."

"Innerspace" feels a little closer to classic hard rock, with a bit of an up-tempo Led Zeppelin vibe or at least something of the spirit of Jimmy Page. Lyrically, "Solar Confinement," "Headswitch," "Octavia," and "Innerspace" feel of a suite, like a bad trip, a jumble of sky and water imagery, some of it sloshing around inside the protagonist's cranium, some of it for real.

Skunkworks ends with "Strange Death in Paradise," another panoramic and thoughtful metal tune with psychedelic guitar textures and Bruce singing strongly up top. It's an enigmatic closer, epic but bravely slow of rhythm, but yet still of an expected piece with the rest of a record strong of identity, indeed true to what Bruce said about a celebration of the best hard rock from the last thirty years.

The 2005 reissue of the album added a second CD with eleven selections. There were four live tracks, one of them being Maiden's "The Prisoner." There were also the four songs associated with the "Back from the Edge" single. In the middle were even more non-LP originals. "R101" is a Led Zeppelin *III*-esque folk song with spirited percussion backing. "Re-Entry" is firmly along the same lines, but more languished, swelling with acoustic strumming, as we move from "Gallows Pole" and "Bron-Y-Aur Stomp" toward "Tangerine" and "That's the Way."

As Bruce told Henrik Johansson, "The original titles we had for them were 'Zep 1' and 'Zep 2.'" As for "R101," well, "It was a zeppelin that crashed. You are very good! Very well spotted. So, we went in and said, hey, let's do a couple of Zeppy-type songs, and so we had one little riff, which was the very Led Zeppeliny–sounding one, and then there's another one which sounds a bit more like Big Country, because I wanted to do a Celtic sort of thing."

"Americans Are Behind," by Chris Dale, is a different kettle of fish, another joke tune with Bruce nattering like he does on "I'm in a Band with an Italian Drummer."

"It's how, in my wildest dreams, I wanted it to turn out," said Bruce on the press trail for the album, speaking with Tim Henderson. Given the album, one full of potential hits and yet arguably a couple of years too late, I believe his enthusiasm was genuine, whereas a few times in the past, not so much. "I had no idea it was going to be like this. I had no idea it was going to be this good. I've often dreamed about making a record like this, but you can't describe how it can happen. It's like when we did *The Number of the Beast*; we suddenly realize that we made a record that was a classic. We'd done our Deep Purple *In Rock* in 1982. I suddenly realized that I was part of that, and it was like, Jesus Christ, how did that happen?

"That's what I think when I listen to this record. 'Is that me?' I think it's bigger than 'Air Raid Siren.' The reason the voice sounds so big is because our technique is completely subservient to content. There's no gratuitous shit or pomposity. That's one of the reasons why the vocals on the record are so powerful. When I started singing with Al, playing old Paul Rodgers and Free songs, he was kind of freaked out with my voice, because he'd never heard me sing that way before. It's not the same style as with Maiden. It's new and it's fresh and it puts everything in perspective."

Bruce confided in Mattias Reinholdsson that it was quite an uphill battle on a commercial front, not that he was surprised. On the subject of constantly being asked about reuniting with Maiden, he explains that "to an extent, that's just something that you have to try and change as much as you can and then just put up with it. Grin and go, 'Okay, that's very nice, thank you, next.' Ozzy Osbourne still has to put up with that. Ozzy Osbourne's records have all been consistently better that the Black Sabbath records since he left, and he still has to put up with people saying, 'When are you gonna join Black Sabbath again?'"

There's a reason that people keep asking, supported by the math. As Bruce explains, "Take North America for example. The new Maiden record in North America has sold 67,000 copies. In the same period, the reissued Iron Maiden back catalog has sold 400,000 copies, which means that somewhere there's a bunch of people buying all these old Maiden records. And it's interesting looking at which ones they're buying. They're all buying *Number of the Beast*, *Piece of Mind*, *Powerslave*, *Seventh Son*, and *Live After Death*. So, there must be a bunch of kids discovering that who've never ever seen Maiden.

"Effectively what that means is that there's gonna be a whole generation of kids over the next few years looking up to the old 'classic' Maiden. I don't see how they can afford to do a US tour again after this tour, because they spent so much money on it. But in the meantime, I'm a Skunkworks guy and we're just gonna be doing the whole Skunkworks thing. And we should say that this album has got an incredible reaction everywhere. In America too. I really feel that I'm back on track, headed in the right direction."

Asked by Mattias about *The X Factor*, Bruce says, "It made it so easy for people to understand why I left. It's completely clear. It's a shame, actually. Probably, in the long term, it's probably not gonna be me, but it's a bit of a shame to see Maiden go down the tubes. But they can still make the right decisions. They only have to make two or three decisions. Give up control, get a new producer, do what he says. The guy from Rage Against the Machine wants to make their next record. That would be cool, wouldn't it? Get the guy, do what he says. Just surrender."

Back to his own life as a solo artist touring on a smaller scale than he'd been accustomed to, Bruce muses that "basically the whole thing is a juggling act. I can afford to go home sometimes during a tour. I pay for myself; it's not part of the tour budget. And we're not this boring rock 'n' roll bullshit thing, where we all have to go around and pretend and follow each other round. We all have individual lives; we're all individuals. 'Oh, yeah, yeah, Bruce is off going to see the kids for the day.' Big deal. 'The boss has gone to London for the day.' It doesn't matter.

"Whereas, in Maiden there was this thing that everybody had to stick together. I was given a uniform when I joined. I was told to go and buy a pair of white boots, a pair of jeans, a black leather jacket, and a white T-shirt, and that's what I wore, that's what everybody wore, as a uniform. I was given cash, to 'immediately go and buy these sort of boots, the sort that Dave's wearing. Here's the shop where you can buy them.' That didn't last for that long, because after a while I thought, fuck this, I'm just gonna wear what I wanna wear. And by the *Powerslave* tour I was being as rebellious as I could be in terms of just disappearing and saying, 'I do not wanna play football. I'm not interested in soccer. If I wanna play soccer, I'd play soccer. If I don't wanna play soccer, I'm not gonna be put under this peer pressure shit.' Which was my position. Just being an artist or whatever. I don't see where soccer comes into this. So with Skunkworks we try to be as nontraditional as possible, which sometimes upsets some of the more traditional people that come along. But it makes for a very entertaining time."

Bruce told Mattias that "Janick still has some life left in him," but then again, "I realized that Jan has a streak of conservatism in there, and with everybody else it kind of got reinforced a bit. I'm still very good friends with Jan and everybody, so in a way that was the right decision for me to quit. If we started arguing about music, I was gonna be completely uncompromising about music; I was gonna have some really big arguments which were not gonna get resolved. Basically, the other guys didn't see the world in the same way that I did. If that was gonna be the case and if I wanna stay friends with everybody, I should just leave and take my chances. It's a much more sensible thing to do. Which brings me, of course, to Skunkworks. And Skunkworks, for me, is stepping forwards into a whole new world that actually existed, funnily enough, back in 1980, when I was in Samson. Because the Samson era of being able to jam, have freedom, and being able to just constantly create something is really back now."

Wrote *Kerrang!*'s Malcolm Dome, in his four K review of the album, "If Bruce Dickinson hasn't exactly reinvented himself on this album, he has at least taken stock of the 1990s and made a record that sits comfortably with most of the young bucks currently dominating this end of the market. And he's done the job so well that he can now face a future far more exciting than his past. You can't say that about many folks that leave successful bands and strike out on their own. What's different about *Skunkworks* as compared to Dickinson's previous solo studio efforts? For a start, this isn't a solo LP. The name Bruce Dickinson might be emblazoned across the sleeve, but this is a band effort. It has a fuller, richer, more distinctive style than any of Bruce's other non-Maiden releases. Second, he's written all of the material with Dickson, which has broadened the album's perspective considerably. The sum of these parts is an album that is tuneful, hard-hitting, complex, and intriguing. Aside from Bruce's coaxing vocals, what impresses most is Dickson's breathtaking guitar performance. The man is a modern-day hero. Imagine early 1980s Alex Lifeson jamming with Kim Thayil and Andy Cairns. And that sums up *Skunkworks*: an amalgam of Rush, Soundgarden, and Therapy?, yet with a compelling cohesion and identity."

Dome makes a number of perceptive points there. Folks this side of the pond might not get the Therapy? reference, but Dome has pretty much nailed the sound of the record, Therapy? included (man, *Kerrang!* gave those guys a lot of coverage). As well, Dome is wise to point out the band feel of the album, and more so that the guitarist and the collaborative writing shine. He also accurately points out that Bruce should be proud of the record, even if the market didn't reward him in kind.

In conversation with *Under the Blade* magazine at the time, Bruce proved again that he understood the rock landscape that Dome describes all too well.

"It's kind of somewhere between Soundgarden, Rush, and early Deep Purple, how about that?" began Bruce, reiterating his elevator pitch on the record. "That's how they described it in *Kerrang!* magazine. Very positive, I mean really positive. In England, we have a bunch of magazines like *Metal Hammer* and *Kerrang!* and everything, and basically when they review them, they give them points out of five, and we've been getting four and five out of five like across the board for the whole year. It's the best reaction to any album I've ever done of my own stuff. And I'm actually saying that as far as the singing is concerned and the lyrics and everything. If they wanted to put an album on my gravestone, they can put this one on there.

"The thing over here is that I think people love stuff that is new, and they love stuff that is fresh. When you hear this record, especially the way metal is at the moment with people saying, 'Hey, metal's over, and it's tired,' this is basically a record that kinda gets up and bites you in the ass and says, 'No, it's not old and tired.' Which is cool."

Offering what is pretty much an accurate lay of the land, something that Steve and Janick, as the chief writers in Maiden, were missing or willfully ignoring, Bruce explains that "at the end of the 1980s, there was an awful lot of bands that sucked. Heavy metal, in a way, was just waiting to get its ass kicked, because it had gotten kind of fat and boring and it kind of took things for granted. And so along comes Nirvana and Soundgarden and stuff and kicked its ass. And Soundgarden are a great heavy metal band, I think. They don't choose to call themselves a heavy metal band, but that's what they are.

"So, for me, it's kind of up to metal to get its act together and come up with more cool and interesting stuff. I mean, just think about: let's just imagine that a band like Rush had never happened. If somebody came out right now, some cool young band with *2112*, it would be absolutely huge. And you look at a band like Dream Theater with 'Pull Me Under' and stuff a few years ago. The success that they had with that proved that there's still a demand out there for really cool rock bands and really cool tracks. But there's not that many bands doing stuff that's very memorable. I mean, it comes down to songs, basically, and it comes down to singers and guitarists and stuff. And there's a lot of bands trying to be heavier than the next guy and be kind of grunty and growly and stuff. But that's not the stuff that people will listen to in five years time and say, 'Wow, that was amazing.' It's very niche oriented. You listen to all the big metal bands and they all had songs that basically had to have more mass appeal."

Bruce was wrong about that. Some of the "grunty" stuff has been accepted by a wide audience and will endure—arguably, given that metal just gets heavier and heavier, after a decade or two, Metallica, Megadeth, Slayer, Pantera, and Slipknot don't sound particularly extreme anymore.

Summing up *Skunkworks*, Bruce adds that "the lyrics are pretty introspective. There are two or three stories on there, but most of it is of personal experiences and things like that. And as far as sound is concerned, it's a three-piece instrumental band, just really slamming guitars, very melodic stuff, and it doesn't sound like anything out of the 1980s."

Years later, given some distance and accumulated rock history, Dickinson could see that some of the mixed reviews for his new direction were to be expected, if not warranted.

"*Skunkworks* was an attempt to start a band with its own style. What I was trying to do there was join together, for want of a better word, grunge or alternative, in particular, bands like Soundgarden. To me, they just sounded like a great metal band. And with the exception of dressing things up for the benefit of the press, who were busy trying to bury anything that smells of metal at that point in time, with the exception of that, I didn't see any reason they shouldn't be called a straight-out metal band. And I found it a bit annoying that metal musicians weren't somehow supposed to have access to play like that, because they were supposed to be old and traditionalists and crawl away and die in a corner.

"I didn't see any reason why I should have to do that. So, I formed the band and really did quite an intense and angry record which I'm still extremely proud of, and actually even more so now because some of [the] vitriol that was poured on it at the time has really dissolved with the passage of time. And people who at one point had poured scorn on the idea have actually turned around and said, 'Well, I rather like the record now' [laughs], which is always very pleasing but would have been much more pleasing had it happened at the time."

"I'm really proud of it," noted Chris Dale, in agreement. "I think it was a great chance for Bruce to show his voice in a different light. It's a shame it didn't sell better, but it's also kind of cool to have played on the album that was to Bruce what *The Elder* was to Kiss."

Asked for a funny memory from those days, Dale recalls that "we had some *Skunkworks* rubber ink stamps made up with the logo on. They were cool for stamping fan club letters and similar stuff. While on tour in Berlin, Bruce, in a mischievous mood, stamped our logo all over the venue's toilet areas. Unfortunately, the venue noticed and weren't too pleased. In the end Bruce owned up to it, and they gave him a sponge and bucket of soapy water to clean it up. The ex–Iron Maiden singer was reduced to toilet janitor for the afternoon. He saw the funny side and quite enjoyed his temporary change of job."

As of 2005, *Skunkworks* had sold 20,361 copies in the US, making it the worst-selling record of the Dickinson solo catalog. I alluded to the record coming too late. Perhaps more accurate is that it came too late for grunge's golden period, sort of 1991 through 1994, but it also came out in the year that was arguably the nadir, the bottom of the barrel, in terms of anybody from the heavy metal community getting a break.

So yes, grunge was in fact already kind of dead, giving way to grunge lite and a surprise pop punk thing out of California. But as we discussed, toiling away in obscurity were a bunch of bands raised on Maiden, the "power metal" people, and they'd be making some waves by the tail end of the 1990s, even though the overwhelming metal flavor of the day into the first decade of the 2000s would be the rap-metal/grunge hybrid known as nu-metal. Bruce would never have his timing right vis-à-vis the solo career, but he would eventually become a rock titan once more, surprisingly, by going back to doing what he used to do.

On May 31 and June 1, 1996, Bruce and his solo band perform two shows in Spain that will serve as material for the *Skunkworks Live Video*. Proving his worth as a musicologist, Bruce used for his intro tape some music from Hawkwind member Robert Calvert's *Captain Lockheed and the Starfighters*. Makes sense though: the record is a concept album with an aviation theme, and Dickinson hero Arthur Brown guests on the album.

In fact, noted Bruce on the show, "Right now we're just back playing our music. We're using a rather different kind of lights to your traditional heavy metal. We've basically got a Hawkwind vibe going with the lights, with the projectors we're using. So, it's really very different to the traditional average heavy metal stuff."

Generated from the tour experience is the *Skunkworks Live* EP, a four-tracker issued in Japan only. Into 1997, also through Victor in Japan, is the *Skunkworks Live* video, which eventually saw reissue as part of 2006's *Anthology* box set.

"Basically, I put *Skunkworks* to death," said Bruce in 1997, after the tour cycle—note, again, that he routinely called the band Skunkworks. "The kind of music the guys in the band were into and where they were at musically was so far away from where I wanted to be at for the new album that I decided there was no point in me wasting their time, and vice versa. They were getting into doing sort of an indie/Britpop record, and I knew that I definitely wanted to make a metal record. Skunkworks was like a Tin Machine type of thing, and it didn't work. It was too out there for a lot of people. I'm more inclined to dust off the stuff that's in the rock area. My favorite stuff is legends, sci-fi, fairy stories, dark deeds of the occult, and all of it set to soaring vocals and raunchy guitar. The truth is never clear until it clobbers you over the head, and that's what happened when I decided to make the new album."

Explains Chris Dale, "Bruce had decided to ditch the Skunkworks project, which hadn't proved as popular with fans as we'd originally hoped. He wanted to go back to good old heavy metal and realized that if anything, Alex, Alessandro, and me were going more alternative in our playing and tastes. So, he naturally renewed friendships instead with Adrian and Roy. In retrospect, I can see that he was also probably quite tired of our constantly childish behavior and our drinking and smoking habits. Fair enough. He was very nice about it all with us, and it was quite expected on our part, so there aren't any hard feelings either way. In fact, he's been really supportive of my new band, Sack Trick."

In March 1997, Bruce works on what will become his fourth solo album, *Accident of Birth*, in California. By this point, he has also recorded "Bohemian Rhapsody" with Montserrat Caballé. The song will be the leadoff track on *Friends for Life*, a record of duets, with the album released later in the year.

As Bruce told Henrik Johansson, "Monserrat has done a solo album, produced by BMG Classics in Germany, and she's taken different artists and done collaborations with them. I know there's some Swedish guys on it, there's a Belgian. I think Gino Vanelli is on it. Anyhow, my involvement with it was simply that I got a phone call from the producer, a guy called Mike Moran, who has done a lot of stuff with Queen, and he produced 'Barcelona,' that thing Montserrat did with Freddie Mercury. He asked me if I'd like to sing 'Bohemian Rhapsody' with her, with a full orchestra and a 48-voice choir. And I was like, 'Well, okay, we'll try it,' and it turned out okay. But that's about as far as it goes right now. It's not released yet. I have to say that we were having a little bit of difficulty getting precise information out of BMG Classics in Germany. They're not quite as good as rock labels are in moving quickly."

Dave Wright archive

Back to *Accident of Birth*, Bruce told Carl Begai, "I met up with Roy Z, who helped me out on the *Balls to Picasso* album, and we wrote four or five tunes, demoed them in one week, and I came home wearing a big shit eating grin playing it for people, saying, 'What do you think of this?' They were all really impressed. I called up Adrian shortly afterward and told him I was doing this metal thing and asked him if he'd be interested in playing on the album and possibly writing a couple tunes with me.

"It was like it was back when we were in Maiden," continues Bruce. "I wouldn't say we fell into old patterns of writing; I think 'Road to Hell' sounds like something we might have written back in the Maiden times, but some of the other stuff we wrote sounds much more updated and fit in well with the climate of metal in the 1990s. I think there's a lot of mileage in metal in North America at the moment because there's a pent-up demand for it. The media has just ignored it completely for the last few years. Kids aren't stupid; they know what they like, and they know what they want. They can go out and buy all the old classic rock albums. What they can't get is cool new stuff. You can go out and get any number of thrashy hard-core albums, but not classic metal that rocks. When I went into making the new album, it seemed like a really good idea to make a classic metal-sounding record with a hard-core edge, and that's what I did. I don't give a fuck about radio. If someone wants to play it on the radio, great, but I don't have any illusions about that. I imagine you might hear it on college stations or at a metal club, but that's about it."

Commenting on the more metal direction, Bruce told Henrik, "Obviously that was a conscious decision. Once I did dissolve Skunkworks there was no longer anything in the way. You commit yourself to that as long as you can, and as soon as it became obvious that it wasn't working, you just have to abandon it and start again. I think we had a situation where I think the guys weren't as committed to the idea of Skunkworks as a band as I was. Otherwise, when I suggested that we cancel the whole thing, they would have gone, 'Oh no, what a shame,' you know. But everybody went, 'Oh, okay.' Just like that [laughs]. If you feel passionately about something, you'd argue.

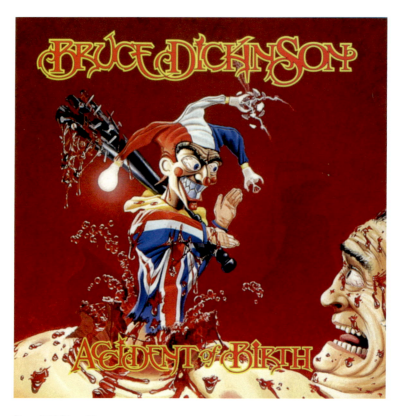

Dave Wright archive

"So, I was left last summer with no band and no songs and an album to deliver in about six months' time and a concept of Skunkworks which hadn't really caught people's imagination. I mean, people still didn't go, 'Oh, Skunkworks, that's that cool band.' They went, 'Skunkworks, that's that thing that Bruce did last year.' So, I figured that if I was gonna do a metal record, then I might as well go back to being called Bruce Dickinson, which is what everybody knows. And I went out to Los Angeles and started writing with Roy Z, and in about a week we wrote five songs and demoed them. Then I came over here and played the demos to everybody, and everybody went absolutely crazy. The demos were so good that one of the guys from the record company thought that it was already the album. And in fact, the demos are gonna be on the B-sides to the British singles."

Explained Adrian Smith, "I got involved with *Accident of Birth* in the later stages. Bruce had been writing before he got back from the States, and he was looking for another guitar player, so he gave me a ring, came around, and played me the demo, and I thought it was great. I was glad to be a part of it. Psycho Motel is definitely still happening. I just got a new singer, and we're actually halfway through doing an album right now. Once this promo tour is finished, I'll be back in the studio. When I first did stuff on my own, it was a bit of a weight to carry. When I did A.S.a.P., there was an extreme kind of reaction to me being in another band, but I wanted to do something different. If I wanted to write music that sounded like Maiden, I never would've left. I've tried a number of things that weren't particularly successful commercially, but I had a lot of fun doing them. Psycho Motel is something closer to what people expect me to do, and I think this album with Bruce is what people *really* expected.

Bruce and Adrian at the 1997 Foundations Forum. © *Tony Leonard*

"But it's not a nostalgic trip. There's something very fresh about the music, and that's why I got involved with it. From a guitar point of view, the songs are a lot of fun to play, real meat-and-potatoes guitar with that modern edge to it. Plus, I had some ideas along the same lines to begin with, before I got involved in doing the album. When Bruce and I got together to write, we just kind of picked up again like we had in the past."

On June 3, 1997, *Accident of Birth* hits the racks. Artwork is courtesy of Derek Riggs, inventor of Eddie. The idea was to create an Eddie-like mascot, in this case a mad, animated puppet named Edison.

"I came up with the concept for the artwork and everything," Bruce told Henrik. "When I got back from America, we started looking at pictures of puppets. They were thinking of trying to do a photograph for the front cover, but I said, 'No, no, no, it has to be an illustration. Who do we know that can draw monsters?' And somebody in the office said, 'What about Derek Riggs? He doesn't do anything anymore, 'cause he's finished with Maiden.' And everybody went, 'What a great idea.' So, we asked him, and he said yes. He doesn't work for Maiden anymore. I asked Rod Smallwood, the manager, and he said, 'No, no, Derek will never ever work for Maiden again.'"

"The first two were paintings, the third was digital," explains Riggs, encompassing images used both for the album and singles. "He had asked me to do a cover for him, and he had this puppet thing he wanted, a glove puppet, which I felt was a bit weird. But I wanted the money, so I did it. The puppet's wearing a Union Jack–style costume. Most of it was pretty much Bruce Dickinson's doing. I don't know about the lightbulbs. He gave me some photographs of Punch, the glove puppet, and said, 'I want something like that, with a Union Jack, and make it really horrible and evil.' So that's what we ended up with.

"I did another one where the puppet was being crucified on a cross, and the one before that was a painting, and I just . . . it was the puppet bursting out of a fat guy's stomach, which was kind of a naff idea. But I just really so hated painting at that point. I didn't want to touch them anymore. I was just starting to go over to computer design, and I didn't have enough room to do both, so I went over to computer design. It was the only reason I kept on working for a few years doing covers here and there. I was just sick of waiting for paint to dry.

"But that idea, in total, was from Bruce, not Rod," continues Derek. "He wanted me to design this puppet along certain lines. He thought he was going to create another Eddie, but it wasn't destined to work very well. I just stayed away from it. I don't know what he had in mind personality-wise for him. I mean, I never even had a personality planned out for Eddie either."

Tony Leonard Archive

Derek somewhat guesses that "what should have been the single artwork was paid for as a single artwork, but it was used as an album artwork, and they had to pay me more. They might have swapped something later for the reissue. But the paintings, the red ones, were first, and then I moved to digital, and that's where the purple one comes from. I think the idea was to introduce the puppet on a single or something and then go do the album and then crucify him on the third one. And they decided to swap them because they decided that was punchier for an album."

The picture of the puppet (named Edison due to the lightbulb hat as well as a throwback to Eddie, as in Eddie's son) clutching his bat and grinning full frontal showed up, in fact, for the original issue of the album. The same image, with green backdrop instead of red, was used for the title track's single issue. The "Man of Sorrows" single featured the crucified Edison picture, which also graced the cardboard oversleeve of the *Accident of Birth* two-CD reissue. The booklet of this reissue was fronted by the silly "Edison popping out of the fat guy's stomach" illustration—incidentally, the fat guy looks remarkably like the gent from the original *No Prayer for the Dying* cover.

Accident of Birth explodes into view with "Freak," which is grunge of title but 100 percent metal. Underneath a hellish yet artful lyric, guitars bulldoze, soaking up the sound picture. There's a groove and a doominess not unlike Kyuss, and yet like the last record, direct comparisons to anything current are subtracted by the sincere and high-fidelity production job—guitarist in the band, Roy Z, is the producer, with the guys working at Silver Cloud in Redondo Beach and Sound City in LA.

Tony Leonard archive

"Freak," like all the songs on the album but three, is credited to Bruce and Roy. "Yes, the bulk of this record is actually written by me and Roy Z, and Roy Z produced it. And the bass player and the drummer, Eddie [Casillas], and Dave [Ingraham], play with Roy all the time. So, it has a great band feel to it because three of the guys are in a band, and I didn't wanna lose that. And I've worked with Eddie and Dave before, and they're fantastic. So, it made no sense going into what looks like an old man's reunion club, because this is not an old man's reunion type of album.

"I had a lot of fun writing the lyrics, because I just went back to the idea that this album was going to be about escapism, you know, in terms of story writing and storytelling. But any good story has some kind of message behind it, you know. But there's no kind of pompous design behind the whole thing; it's just a selection of interesting little stories. I mean, some of them, I must confess, I had to construct quite an elaborate story line and then maybe only tell half of it in the lyrics. I had to do that just for my own benefit, to show that I could, you know, daydream properly."

Intro "Toltec 7 Arrival" gives way to "Star Children," a sci-fi tale that syncs conceptually with a bunch of *Skunkworks* songs. At the music end, Bruce is perfectly on point with what was established through "Freak"; namely, this simple sense of uncompromising yet somewhat conservative heavy metal represented by massive guitars.

"Taking the Queen" might be called a sister track to "Tears of the Dragon," except its loud bits are more innovative and heavier. Its waltz surge in 3/4 time is something Bruce has done before, and it allows him to explore his inner prog fan. But he stays succinct, the song soon transitioning into "Darkside of Aquarius," another combative rocker, albeit with a plaintive chorus melody that echoes the type of melancholy that would be a theme throughout the record.

"The title of the song comes from a picture I saw in a book," explains Bruce. "It was a collage that purported to show the negative side of an information technologist and how easy it would be to twist the minds of people on the internet because they don't get together and talk anymore. They do it through this medium that can be controlled. The story in the song involved fooling around with a couple of legends about the Wheel of Time found in Buddhist teachings, about how it's due to stop in 1999, according to them, at which point we'll all just fizzle away. I thought we could incorporate these ideas with some really cool tunes."

Said Adrian of the next track, "'Road to Hell' is probably what people expected with Bruce and I writing together, and maybe that's not such a bad thing, because, as Bruce mentioned, there's a demand for it from people who want something outside of the trends."

That last statement is very 1997. As alluded to, metal makers seemed to be caught in a war for their very existence. The debate eventually became full-blown, as artists such as Bruce reembraced the genre. This happened in conjunction with

The Mission, Raleigh, North Carolina, September 26, 1997. © *Tony Leonard* an eventual uptick in heavy metal activity in the late '90s—from doom to progressive death to black metal—exploding at the time. And of course, parallel to this was power metal, with HammerFall, Primal Fear, Blind Guardian, and Iced Earth celebrating their collective love for Priest, Dio, Accept, and Maiden. It was also a bit of a golden age for heavy metal magazines, which were constantly being fed new releases by the likes of Earache, Nuclear Blast, Century Media, and classic rock revivalists CMC, who had signed up both Bruce and Maiden in the States.

"Road to Hell" is in the same camp as "Freak," irresistibly groovy, with the bonus being a Thin Lizzy–like twin lead. Bruce puts a little au courant distortion on his vocals for the monotone verse, but this gives way to clean for the chorus, which, again, delivers melody but not *Skunkworks* melody, more like Teutonic metal melody. A herky-jerky video was made of the track, the band performing but captured with annoying quick edits, on a set that looked like an abandoned building.

Look to *The Best of Bruce Dickinson* for the original 1990 version of "Man of Sorrows," which comes next. Explains Bruce, "There's not a single thing on this record which is not rooted in imagination in some way, with the exception of maybe 'Man of Sorrows,' which is the only song on the album which was written about five years ago. All the other songs were written in the space of five weeks."

"No, I never even bothered presenting it," Bruce told Henrik Johansson, asked if "Man of Sorrows" was a Maiden leftover. "It was actually written for a movie that I was

Tony Leonard archive

involved with. I was involved in writing a script and we sold it to America. It was a script about Aleister Crowley, and without going into the details of what the plotline was and everything else . . . 'cause it's a good story and somebody will steal it if I tell you [laughs]. But the title song to the movie was going to be 'Man of Sorrows,' and the small boy in the church at the opening line is the young Aleister Crowley. The song is from the point of view of, you know, what makes a person want to be like that? He said in his life he wanted to be the wickedest man in the world. He wanted to be the antichrist and the beast and everything else. And the question is why? It's about what makes somebody be like that, and I went back and there was an accident in his childhood in a church, and I just put that as a starting point."

This one embodies even more kinship with "Tears of the Dragon," being a dark power ballad strong enough to make it a single, complete with narrative video featuring both Bruce and Adrian, along with the Battersea Power Station, made famous in rock by the cover of Pink Floyd's *Animals*. Bruce's spare lyric gives nothing away as to what this accident in the church might have been. In fact, other than the "Do what thou wilt" line, there's little to link it to Crowley.

The title itself is a Bible reference, the book of Isaiah, chapter 53, with the man of sorrows being Christ, who takes on the sins of mankind. But where Christ took them over and absorbed them sacrificially, so to speak, Dickinson is suggesting that Crowley took them on to amplify and emanate them. In other words, Christ is cleaning the place up, and Crowley is rarin' to make a mess. If this sounds shocking, "Road to Hell" tracks the same devilish terrain, suggesting that Christ on the cross is on his way to hell after he expires, as a sort of thanklessness for his good deeds in service of mankind. Bruce now tends to brush off his Crowley and general occult phase from earlier in life. Indeed, he's never come across as a believer in any of this, rather just an inquisitive mind who likes interesting things, a good yarn. And obviously it's served him well, with Bruce being able to encapsulate intriguing plots often and with a high level of quality—at least now, when he had gone solo.

Chemical Wedding, based on an original screenplay by Bruce Dickinson (also briefly in the film), indeed got made, emerging in the spring of 2008. It's much beyond the plot seed of "Man of Sorrows," and it's not related as such to alchemy or the Bruce Dickinson album *The Chemical Wedding*. "Man of Sorrows" was issued as the second single from *Accident of Birth*, making use of the illustration by Derek where Edison is crucified, thereby reminding us of the Christ connection.

The 2005 expanded reissue of the album includes a Spanish version of the song called "Hombre Triste," as well as orchestral and radio edit versions.

The record's title track served as the first single from the album, complete with production video shot the same day as the "Road to Hell" clip, thus a similar look

The Mission, Raleigh, North Carolina, September 26, 1997. © *Tony Leonard*

and feel. The song achieved a #54 placement on the UK charts. Derek's illustration of Edison on a green background was used for this one, which added demos plus the non-LP "Ghost of Cain," novel of riff, interesting parts but a little behaved in terms of the rhythm section performance and the production thereof.

Musically, this one's another smart, professional metal tune that graphically points to why Bruce had to get out of Maiden. *The X Factor* sounds downright doddering by comparison. And yet, it's not like this song or any others on *Accident of Birth* made a lasting impression. There's something of a lesson here that the system doesn't work. It's not exactly the travesty of, say, King's X not being superstars, but indeed, *Skunkworks* and *Accident of Birth* not being huge tells us that the artistry of the product is only one component, one duck of many that have to be placed in a row.

Proving the value of doing interviews, the value of journalism, Bruce's explanation of the lyric brings his otherwise opaque tale to light. "Accident of Birth" is about a "person" accidentally birthed onto Earth from a family who resides in hell, vomited aboveground on a day that God must have had off. His parents and siblings want him back, reminding him that aboveground he's just going to die like all the rest. But the protagonist isn't so sure his hot homeland is preferable to the world above.

"The Magician" includes a handful of references that let us know that Dickinson is once again talking about Crowley, most directly "climbed the mountain, chased the dragon." Of note, Somerset Maugham wrote a novel based on Crowley called *The Magician*, published in 1908. It's key that this track comes directly after "Accident of Birth," planting in the mind that none other than Crowley was the being coughed up out of the fires and onto solid ground. Helpfully, we now have the explanation for Aleister's life goals kind of left out of the story told in "Man of Sorrows."

At the musical end, this one has the band rocking out joyously, lightening the load left by the lyric. In fact the chorus, with Bruce offering some whoa-ohs and the catchy refrain "The Magician is my name and magic is my game" . . . well, it's almost swashbuckling.

Next is an outlier, doomy, slow, a bit Geronimo metal grunge. "'Welcome to the Pit' was a riff that I came up with and played for Bruce, and he decided he definitely wanted to do something with it," notes Adrian. "It very well could have ended up in a Psycho Motel song, because that's the kind direction we were going in." Bruce slathers on top of Adrian's primordial ooze (the opposite of a mosh pit song) yet another evil lyric that could be describing a day in the life of Aleister Crowley. In fact, there's not a single lyric across the whole record that couldn't be framed as an extrapolation or interpretation of something Crowleyesque, as expressed in his novels or poetry or experienced in his rituals and travels.

"Omega" is a sorrowful power ballad, lushly caressed by strummed acoustic guitars but then elevated by some dark riffing and then a bluesy yet stadium rock solo, a bit Guns N' Roses. Halfway through, the band breaks into a gallop that is as much evocative of Sabbath as it is of Maiden. When the band returns from the jam, they return to the doomiest theme from earlier, no more acoustic music to be heard.

As if to deliver on what was proposed with the opening salvos of "Omega," album closer "Arc of Space" stays ballad all the way through—the drums never whacked. As on both "Taking the Queen" and "Man of Sorrows," "Arc of Space" features real strings, with Rebecca Yeh playing cello and Sylvia Tsai playing violin. There are also multiple acoustic textures as well as prominent Mellotron, commandeered by Roy Z.

As alluded to, *Accident of Birth* didn't light the world on fire, selling 45,921 copies as of early 2005.

Summing up the experience, Bruce reflects that "*Accident of Birth* was, I suppose, more of a return to a traditional metal style. The way I like to describe *Accident of Birth* is that it is a good assembly of pretty much everything I've ever done in metal that was ever really any good up to that point, and it was used to the full on that record. I used every little trick, every little nuance that I needed to make that record a success. And it worked, because when it was released, very few people were making records like that."

The 2005 reissue of the record included the aforementioned "Ghost of Cain" and the three versions of "Man of Sorrows," along with fully five demos from the making of the album.

Thankfully, no changes in personnel were to take place for the extended tour regime planned for the record. Hitting the road were Bruce, Roy, and Adrian on guitars, Eddie Casillas on bass, and Dave Ingraham on drums, a lineup that would be maintained through Bruce's next album and tour cycle. April 1997 featured a week of UK dates followed by Europe and Japan in July. From October into early November, the band was in mainland Europe, followed by a week in South America, November 14 through 22.

"Adrian and I have our history," commented Bruce. "Kids are gonna show up and they'll be really, really pissed off if we don't play some Maiden songs. They're expecting us to do that, which is completely fine by me, and they'll go away satisfied."

"I have absolutely no problem with that at all," agreed Adrian. "In fact, I've always played tunes like 'Wasted Years' and 'Back in the Village.' If we can do something interesting with them, play them well, maybe add some new twist to them, it'll be great. The shows will be centered around [sic] *Accident of Birth*, of course, and the Maiden stuff will be strictly for fun. I wouldn't mind continuing to work with him. We've talked about it. I suppose it depends on how people receive this album. I had a great time making this record, and I don't see any reason why I can't do both projects."

Meanwhile, Dickinson kept building his résumé as Renaissance man, or at least king of all media, a challenge to Howard Stern. On August 1, Bruce guests on the soundtrack album for Rowan Atkinson's *Bean*, singing a rendition of Alice Cooper's "Elected," for which a music

This page and next: The air raid siren blazing a new path for himself. The Mission, Raleigh, North Carolina, September 26, 1997. © Tony Leonard

video is also produced. On August 12, he appears on comedic UK game show *Space Cadets*.

"I try not to get myself into odd press situations these days," reflected Bruce at the time. "Here's one of the strangest things. I ended up on a TV game show, a sci-fi TV game show with William Shatner [laughs]. And actually, the only reason I did it is because William Shatner was on, and I went, 'Oh my God, I can get Captain Kirk's autograph!' And I did, on one of his cue cards that had a joke about Mr. Spock. I must say I'm a little ambivalent about TV chat shows or game shows. I may end up doing one or two over here in the States, and I'll just have to see what the reaction is. I'm wary about this. I mean, I'm not going to be a celebrity of any note. I'm very wary of it; I don't see the need for it. *The Weakest Link* is one of the things they've offered me, and if Vince Neil and Sebastian Bach are going on it, I'm not going on. It's just a freak show. I can't see what the purpose is. Going on *Politically Incorrect*, okay, maybe. But *The Weakest Link*, I see no point whatsoever. Because you're kind of immediately guilty by association [laughs]. It's like here's some sad rock stars trying to revive their flagging careers. Um, don't want to be in that club."

Meanwhile as Maiden begin work on what will be their second try with Blaze, on November 24 Adrian Smith's Psycho Motel issue their second album. *Welcome to the World* features a new vocalist in Andy Makin, but bassist Gary Leiderman and bassist Mike Sturgis are still there from the first record, *State of Mind*. Old Maiden mate Dave Murray guests on guitar on a track called "With You Again," while Thin Lizzy axman Scott Gorham plays on "I'm Alive."

"Well, basically, it's just a different singer," says Adrian. "Musically it's along the same lines, classic influences, hard rock. Andy Makin, who came in, he sent me a tape, because Soli had been understandably disillusioned with the whole situation and went back to Norway. So, the management suggested getting another singer, and I listened to a lot of tapes, and Andy sent me this incredibly bad demo, recording-wise, but I could make out this great voice. It was really, really heavy, I mean, detuned like you've never heard. It was really demonic [laughs]. But I thought, this guy has a really interesting voice, so I called him up and he came down and he just blew us away. I had a few ideas, and right there we just started on new songs that he was singing, and he was incredible. He's such a musical guy, a great lyricist, and he was only twenty-four at the time, and that's Andy. And he was into the modern influences, Alice in Chains etc. But to me he sounded like a demonic Dan Reed [laughs].

"I think with Psycho Motel, I'm sort of employing things that I learned when I was a kid, which I didn't use in Iron Maiden, like Hendrix. It has a Hendrix-inspired blues tinge to it. I've always been into that. I probably practice more now than I did when I was with Maiden, because we were always on the road and never had time. But now I sit down and actually study other guitar players, just to expand a bit. I love Joe Satriani and people like that, Gary Moore as well. You can play the same old thing over and over again, but it's boring for me, not to mention boring for people who are listening to it."

As for the cover art, Adrian explains that "there's a song on the album called 'Welcome to the World,' which is about corporate greed and pollution and all this sort of stuff, what it's like for a kid coming into the world today. So, we decided to work something out in terms of a bit of a concept for the cover. So, we grabbed Dylan, my boy, and some of his pals and took them to a photo session, school uniforms, and put some gas masks on them, had a bit of fun, and came up with these pictures."

But very little was to come of the Psycho Motel franchise.

"No, nothing really happened. This is another one of the problems of doing this. It was all down to money. At the time, we're talking the late 1990s, rock was getting really, really trodden down, and they didn't hook me up with any tours. And the band was there, it was ready to go, and we did some stuff off our own back. But the financial muscle wasn't there, really. We had a deal with Castle Records, who basically reimbursed me for the money I had laid out doing the album, and that was it, really. There was no support. They thought it would sell because I was in Iron Maiden, but I mean that wasn't the case. This is what I'm talking about: breaking a band. You know yourself it takes tons of money. It just wasn't going to happen. The whole plan was wrong."

CHAPTER 15
The Chemical Wedding and Scream for Me Brazil

"Slightly worrying or very exhilarating—your choice."

Come 1998, for the first time in Bruce's solo career he was affirming a true love for the last record cycle, stating that all he wanted to do was the same thing all over again.

"It's the same lineup as the last album," Dickinson told me at the time. "Myself, Roy Z, Adrian Smith, and David Ingraham on drums and Eddie Casillas on the bass, the same guys. In fact, if you take the credits from *Accident of Birth* and just substitute the name, it's the same—same studios, same everything."

Asked if there had been any tweaks in the contribution between the two guitarists toward what would be the magnificent new record, *The Chemical Wedding*, Bruce doubles down on the similarity narrative. "In fact, there's been no subtle shifts. When you realize that 80 percent of the record was written by Roy and myself, actually 80 percent of the last record was done that way as well [laughs]. I think having Adrian join was such a big deal for other people that it sort of overshadowed things. And it's wonderful that Adrian is there—I'm not wishing to decry Adrian's contribution. But the contribution of Roy is absolutely huge. You can hear the development in the sound, just the physical sound of the way the guitars have been handled. And that's very much his growing as a producer and having the confidence to make decisions. We had discussed a sonic concept for the album, and the lyrical ideas involving William Blake and the alchemy, but it was just the idea that this album should be really heavy, just in terms of the tone of it."

January through June 1998, the guys work on what will become *The Chemical Wedding* at Sound City and Silver Cloud in LA, again, just like last time, with the record emerging on July 28. Framing the album further, Bruce explained that "having clawed my way back into some semblance of the limelight and done some tours, *Chemical Wedding* tried to take the whole process a big leap forward, really into an area that I could carve out and pretty much say that this is somewhere I've never really been before with this kind of music.

"With the solo career, there's the ability to exercise doubt, right? Because there tends to be a certainty in Maiden, which is a product of personalities within the band. So there does tend to be a certainty within Maiden, and part of it is the confidence as well that Maiden fans are Maiden fans through and through and in general will buy more or less everything that the band puts out, as long as they've done it sincerely. So, this breeds a certain sense of self-confidence that no matter what you do, it's going to be right. With my solo stuff, I have no such confidence at all. You feel that there is sort of no safety net underneath you. If you're trying to do something that is different, it can either be slightly worrying or very exhilarating—your choice.

"You know when they make concrete supports for bridges?" continues Bruce, asked if there were any tricks used to help get a bigger sound. "Well, when they do those, they have a mold that they pour the concrete into. So, we had this 15-foot-long circular tube of that stuff, and that was the bass drum. Or, more accurately, we had the bass drum at one end of it and the microphone at the other. Eddie, when he's not playing bass, he works at a building site, so he came along in his builder's truck with this huge piece of concrete molding and said, 'This is for the bass drum' [laughs]."

"And Stan Katayama, who was helping with this part of the recording, he's an engineer, he went wild! 'I have to see this!' And he stuck the microphone in there and said, 'Fucking great!' So, we tend to do things like that. After recording together, the last time, we also have tended to streamline things. For example, Dave, our drummer, his sight-reading skills, we just did away with the concept of saying, 'Hey, let's pretend we're playing in a big auditorium in front of a bunch of people.' Because we aren't. This guy has a metronome in his head, and he wrote down every single note he plays on every single drum, and he opens the page to page 1, and he sight-reads the drumming.

"I suppose you could say this is a much more contemporary album, in terms of the way it sounds," figures Bruce, although frankly, *Accident of Birth* sounded massive too. "I think what we've done on this album is extended and expanded the repertoire of *Accident of Birth*. *Accident of Birth*, I mean, what a great album, but it was also almost a summation of everything I've done up until now. This album goes beyond that. I've actually stepped into new territory. This is kind of virgin turf for me. We're really moving into the area now of taking just the sound, the raw sound of things, to new extremes."

Besides cannonizing the drums, the guys stuck fatter strings on the guitars. "Yes, that's true," says Bruce. "And that was Roy's idea. He came to me and said, 'I have this sound I can get on the guitar, but what we have to do to get it is put the skinny strings from the bass guitar, the top string, and put it on the E string of the guitar and then increase all the gauges appropriately through the rest of the scale.' Myself not being a serious guitarist, there's a bit more to it than that, because then you get into the tuning and the tensions and how not to wreck the guitar while you're playing these strings. It does wreck guitarists' hands because it's like playing high-tension cables [laughs]. So, both Adrian and Roy were getting the most-amazing sounds, even in rehearsal. I remember walking into the rehearsal studio and going, 'What is that sound?!' It's very fatiguing on the hands doing it, but I guess they both built up this kind of resistance, after two weeks of playing ten hours a day [laughs].

Martin Popoff archive

"The lyrics are kind of trippy, but it's basically a concept album about alchemy," continues Bruce, crossing over into the literary conceit of the thing—in comparison, really, *Accident of Birth* was quite conceptual as well, and so was *Skunkworks*. "But alchemy, as I was researching it, rapidly starts to feel a bit flat. After doing a couple of songs about alchemy, it's like, okay, so duh, it's a bunch of chemists trying to re-create the divine through chemistry.

"So, once you've got that out of the way, what else is there? What kept cropping up in all of the alchemical books I was reading was William Blake, who was a mystical English poet from the last century, lived 1770-ish to sort of about 1830. He was an artist and a poet, and also in many ways he was related to the alchemists. He used a lot of their imagery. One of his big heroes . . . one of his big epic poems is called *Newton*, which is dedicated to Isaac Newton, who was an alchemist, which is something that has been covered up successively by historians and scientists. Because it's not cool! For the inventor of rationalist science to be into the occult. That was his main reason for being into science, because he was interested in mysticism.

"So, one day I just decided to make this album three-dimensional. He gave it a soul and a presence. A lot of the things Blake was writing about—his imagery, his language—really struck a chord with me personally. I felt he was like a kindred spirit. Not like I was anything near as talented as him, but still I thought, wow, I understand this man and where he's coming from, and what he feels and how he sees things. I thought, well, what a wonderful muse to have for an album. So that's what the album started being about—it was an album about alchemy, inspired by the artwork and poetry of William Blake. And I thought, that's what I'm writing! Wow, this is really worth writing about; this is really worth doing! Everything just dropped into place from then and I really enjoyed it, even though it was kind of nerve racking. I didn't have a whole load of time. We had two months to write the album, two weeks to rehearse it, then six weeks to record it and then two weeks to mix it."

But don't look for a plot, says Bruce, which, again, nicely lines up with what he did on the previous two records. "No, absolutely not. I started doing that. I started trying to write stories and things like that, but as soon as I started to do that, the thing became wooden. I said to myself I have to just let go and let this thing develop, which again was kind of nerve racking. Because Roy would be there coming up with great backing tracks, and I felt like I was lagging behind. But I was just like, no, this has got to be right, I have to get the focus of the tunes and the melody right.

"I realized it was a bit like putting a stained-glass window together. You can have all the pieces of glass at your feet, but if you put them together in a hurry, you're just going to get a piece of shit. You've got to spend the time and examine each piece of glass and put it in the right place, and then you get a beautiful window. It was the same thing with this album. I had 80 percent of the pieces of it at my feet, and the last 20 percent was *my* last 20 percent that I had to put together. But I thought, if necessary, I'm going to have to wait until hell freezes over to get this right. Because that 20 percent is going to make it or break it."

"*Accident* was basically a statement that he was back," figures secret weapon Roy Z, asked to compare. "And I'm glad Bruce didn't make another one of those. Because I think we would have pissed a lot of people off. I think Bruce is artistically as pleased as he's ever been with *Chemical Wedding*. It really translated well what he felt. To me, technically,

Accident sounds really good, and there's some songs on there I just flip out over every time I hear them, but *Chemical* was more of a cohesive package. It was put together better, it was more thought out, and the sound had more depth to it, more dimension."

Speaking with *BW&BK* back in the spring of 1998, when the record was still in progress, Roy said that "everyone seems to like the song 'Chemical Wedding.' All the songs seem to be tied in, although it's not a concept album. Lyrically, Bruce is writing a lot about alchemy and English mystical folklore. As far as musically, it's pretty well the same kind of stuff we did on the last record, but we expanded our horizons. We haven't changed our style. If anything, we've gotten a little heavier. We have a more open sound, not cleaner, but metallic. There's this new tuning system that I came up with, so we're tuning a lot lower. It creates a sublow undercurrent that carries more weight. We have regular Les Pauls that have bass strings on them and stuff, just to get a lower register. It's not depressing; it's pretty much straight-ahead heavy metal, but a little more modern. Having said that, I'm always looking to improve the guitar tones."

As far as the writing sessions go, "We're all sitting in a room working out our parts. Every day, for a good eight hours we're figuring out who's doing what. We're shelling out solos, harmony guitar parts. Adrian has been involved from the word 'go.' We are hoping to write a song between the three of us. Adrian's a pleasure to work with. He's so low key, he kicks back, he lets you do your thing. At the same time, I don't tell him what to do. I suggest things to him and vice versa, so it's kind of like a camaraderie. We have a mutual respect. I know that he can play, and he knows that I can play. He's a veteran player, and I give him his space. I really don't like working with other guitarists, but if I had to, it'd be with a guy like Adrian.

"When I'm working with someone like Bruce, I'm the head consultant," continued Roy. "He calls the shots and I suggest things to him. I've helped him find his vision, and now I leave it up to him to complete his vision. With Bruce's vocals now, we're pretty much taking over where we left off, and we're moving ahead. We're not trying to repeat ourselves but expanding on what we did. Just good, heavy, solid vocals, nothing crazy or fancy. Just straight-ahead heavy metal vocals. Bruce is a great singer, great performer, and he's really easy to work with. At first when I worked with Bruce, I thought, I remember going to Long Beach Arena and being part of *Live After Death*. That's what was happening at the time when I was a kid. That music was at the forefront, and Maiden was one of the main bands. At first, I was in awe, and then after a while it's a job, and you have to do a good job."

Asked by Alex Ristic about the band being marketed fairly regularly with photos that feature just Bruce and Adrian, Roy figures, "I didn't feel pushed out. If I was working *Accident of Birth*, I would've pushed the fact that Bruce and Adrian were working together again. I wish I would've been in some of the photos and some of the other features. It was a novelty. But hopefully on this record the rest of us will get more exposure. I have no problem being more of a sideman, because my involvement is more of a supporting cast. I do a lot of things, but that's the way it's set up. You're dealing with two people who were in one of the biggest metal bands ever."

Comments Adrian, "We're trying to blend the 1990s kind of sound with more traditional metal songwriting. What we're doing is a lot of fun, and it's slightly different to what's out there. I think we're actually accomplishing something because of Roy's input and Roy's experience working with bands. It's giving it a bit of a different twist. So it always makes it interesting."

Looking across the aisle to present-day Maiden, Smith mused that "every band has its day. We had a ten-year string of peaks. Maiden right now are still selling well. They probably still sell, you know, 800,000 records. A lot of these young bands would be very happy to sell that."

In terms of the *Chemical Wedding* cover art, gone is stomach-busting evil puppet Edison, replaced by something a little more classic. Says Dickinson, "William Blake was someone I had been aware of since I was a little kid, ever since one of his paintings was used for an Atomic Rooster album cover—*Nebuchadnezzar* is the name of the picture."

Bruce is referring here to the *Death Walks Behind You* album from 1970, the image having all the more impact given the scary, uncommon heaviness of the music enclosed. Now Bruce was getting the same effect.

"So, we used a William Blake painting. We got permission from the Tate Gallery to use eight of William Blake's paintings as the cover, and throughout the booklet. So, one of them is that Atomic Rooster picture, *Nebuchadnezzar*. All of the paintings are credited with their dates as well, so people can dig them out and see what they are. The painting on the front, we actually used only about half of the painting, and it's called *The Ghost of a Flea*. Loads of people who had seen the cover have gone, 'Wow! Who did that scary monster?!' And I'm like, 'Well, William Blake.' And people go, 'Wow, that's trippy!'

"And of course, some people were trying to get me to do a computer-generated image. 'No, what you're supposed to do with a metal album . . . man, go look at all the metal albums now—it's all techno and stuff.' And I'm like, 'Uh-huh, in five years' time, are people going to be looking at all of them and going, wow, that's compelling. I want to keep looking at that? I've got a picture here that was painted two hundred years ago, and we're still looking at it, going, "Fuckin', that's cool!" Isn't that the kind of thing you want on an album cover?' [laughs]. I guess it's a difference in perception."

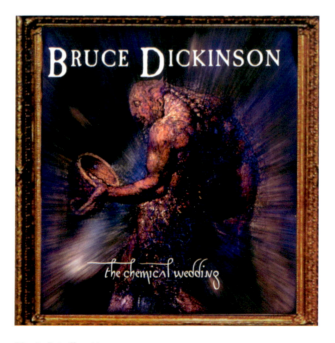

Martin Popoff archive

Into the music, and yes indeed, one instantly hears the heaviness achieved. "King in Crimson" almost collapses under its own weight before it gets going, but soon we're into a trundling shuffle that is equal parts Black Sabbath and Kyuss. True to track record, Bruce makes sure to make the chorus stronger and more anthemic—stadium rock, as it were—than the verse.

"It's not an homage to King Crimson," chuckles Bruce. "No, it's where do you think King Crimson got their name from? The King in Crimson is a reference to a character from alchemy. The King in Crimson represented the sun. But of course, I've taken some liberties with some of the concepts. It's like, okay, that King in Crimson is the sun coming up, but it's also the sun going down. When the sun goes down, you're left with night, and night is Satan, you know? And the King in Crimson is also Satan as well because Satan is the Crimson King. *In the Court of the Crimson King*—there you go [laughs]."

Next is the title track, of which Dickinson explains, "The chemical wedding is just another term for alchemy, although they called it the chymical wedding. But there's a book called *The Chemical Wedding*, which is based on alchemy, a novel that came out a while back. And I actually wrote a screenplay based on Aleister Crowley called *Chemical Wedding*, and a friend of mine, Terry Gilliam, is the editor—he actually wrote *Brazil*—and we sold it. So *Chemical Wedding* has been around for me for years. So finally, I said, thinking about alchemy, damn it, *The Chemical Wedding* is a great name for an album. And that's what got the ball rolling. I'm going to write an album about this. And then Blake cropped up, and I was like, this is really turning into something; this is a real adventure. And then so having someone read a little bit of Blake's poetry on the record came to mind. Arthur Brown is a friend of mine—you know, the Crazy World of Arthur Brown—and I thought, man, this just feels so right!"

"There is no set way," answers Roy, asked, when speaking with Mattias Reinholdsson, about his writing methodology with Bruce. "Sometimes I have a song and sometimes I have a riff. A song like 'Chemical Wedding' we worked on. The album was pretty much already written, but Bruce felt he didn't have any key song. So he came over, and we put that one together in one afternoon. I had different parts, and we moved them around. Sometimes Bruce just picks up a guitar and he'd have an idea, and we go on from there. There is never a set way it works."

As for arrangements, "Most of the time I am in working the band or I'm in working the ideas—to death. Until it works. I just keep on trying different things. There are pretty much standard arrangements you could try, and I am always trying weird ones. Hopefully one day a nice weird one will work, but most of the time they don't; it's not easy to come up with off-the-wall arrangements. Especially in metal. Because it's pretty clear how things should go. As far as orchestration and stuff, there is not a whole lot in this. On an album like *Chemical Wedding*, I would sit with it in the studio and work on one song for three days. Just coming up with parts. Different guitar or keyboard or sound effects, whatever. And try out different things. It's like a big puzzle, and you've got to figure it out. Sometimes someone will hear something in their head: 'Hey, what about if we had this in there?' Sometimes Bruce or even Adrian would come up with an idea: 'What about a part like this?' Or Dave goes, 'Let me try this on this with the drums.' So, we all talk and work together on different things.

"I have different sides," continues Roy, on his temperament as a producer. "I like to hear what everybody thinks, and work on it. I collaborate a lot with other people. I have learned over the years that there is no set way to do it. The best way to do it is not to worry about it and just make it happen. I don't really think about it; I just do it. In the beginning Bruce was there for everything, but over the years I think he trusts me more. But most of the time Bruce is there. I remember when we were doing *Accident of Birth*, he said, 'I don't like the drum sound; let's change the drum sound.' He has been more hands on in the past. But lately I think he has more trust 'cause we have done enough things together where he just says, 'Go ahead and do it, and I'll just come over and do my vocals.'

"I always feel my own pressure to do the best job that I could possibly do," reflects Roy. "But I also think as a fan, what a fan would like to hear. So, I approach it as a fan. You, yourself, as a fan, I think if you were in the studio with Bruce you would say, 'Oh no, let's try it this way!' So, I approach it as a fan. It's that simple."

Asked by Mattias about his personal producer heroes, Roy replies, "There are a few guys that I like to look into and see what they are doing. But to start from the beginning, I like the work of Martin Birch. I think it's amazing. After that, I would say Terry Date. I think his work is amazing. I got into people like Bob Ezrin that made Pink Floyd's *The Wall*. Alan Parsons. I like the mixing of Andy Wallace. I am good friends with a guy called Richie Podolor that did Steppenwolf and bands like that. But my favorite producers are guys that always can bring it together and didn't really have a sound, you know what I mean? Terry Date can do everything from old metal to new metal. I mean, Soundgarden does not sound like Deftones. I think guys like that are happening, the more old-school kind of producers. I think the new guys are more glorified engineers. Now everybody is trying to fix things on the ProTools, trying to make it perfect. To me, making it not as perfect is a lot better for the fans and for the listeners."

Over to the guitar slot, and his dovetailing with the legendary Adrian Smith, Roy says, "I grew up with Michael Schenker and Uli Jon Roth. These are my guys. I really like them. Adrian really likes Schenker; I know that. When we are working together, it's 'Schenker! Oh yeah, man!' Adrian is an amazing guitarist. Adrian writes some incredible lead lines. My role when I was playing with Bruce was more the young speed gun guy, and Adrian was more the phrasing guy. He threw in some licks too. He was picking up licks left and right. We were trying to balance it. It's boring if everyone is doing the same thing. I hope Adrian one day does a solo album with instrumentals or whatever and gets to show people, because he is amazing. Great feel. You can't figure out his timing, but it's so good. It feels so good."

"The Chemical Wedding" is similarly slow and massive to what came before, although the power chords drop away for the verse. Again, though, there's a memorable chorus on which Bruce soars into the memory banks, rich of melody, band back at full volume. It can't be said particularly that the modern metal elements from, really, all of the previous three records are entirely gone. Bruce is staying current by staying away from the power metal tropes

Martin Popoff archive

of Maiden, satisfied to be shrouded in doom, which was of course also a tone and mood inherent at the heavy end of grunge, particularly Alice in Chains, Soundgarden, and Melvins.

That said, "The Tower" borrows somewhat from "Wrathchild," not only on the bass and drums intro, but the verse chords. Again, the chorus, albeit brief, is top shelf, elevating the song before some textured guitar and slight twin-lead work lead us back to the business of another verse. There's a surprise modulation for the guitar solo, after which we're into an amusing bit of Maiden twin-lead work.

Explaining the line "And the hanged man smiles" to Henrik and Mattias of *The Bruce Dickinson Wellbeing Network*, Dickinson points out that "the hanged man always has a smile, and nobody knows why. But *he* knows. It's his own little secret. How many tarot cards are there in 'The Tower'? Lovers, the tower, sun, the moon, the priestess, the magician, the fool, the hanged man . . . going through the lyrics, there may be a few more.

"And they're all in the video," continues Bruce. "We squeezed them all in the video. The song is about fate. I was trying to think about Romeo and Juliet as the lovers and the sun and the moon and everything. You know, the star-crossed lovers doomed by fate. No matter what happens, how in love they are, it's gonna end up as a tragedy. So that's 'The Tower'. In fact, what the tower symbolizes . . . somebody who was falling out of the tower has been struck by lightning. The tower symbolizes that you can never look safe and secure and solid. It means something is gonna happen, but you don't know what."

Next up, "Killing Floor" fits the established sound picture perfectly, with its doomy Geronimo riff written by Adrian. A proggy 6/4-time signature keeps the listener on his toes, as does the surprise Renaissance music break. "Killing Floor" is also a famous 1964 Howlin' Wolf song and also the name of a heavy-blues boom band from Britain with a well-regarded self-titled debut from 1969, both factoids not lost on a musicologist like Bruce.

"Book of Thel," music by Eddie Casillas, rolls like a tank, propelled by the album's best pure heavy metal riff, again complemented by a chorus that is Guns N' Roses stadium rock, if they were from the UK and not the US. Progressive passages throughout the song make it one of the most ambitious on the album, the highlight being a big choral arrangement, followed up by one of the album's most thoughtful axe solos. "Maybe 'Book of Thel' is close to something like 'Aquarius,' because of its structure," comments Bruce. The title itself is from the 1789 William Blake poem of the same name, and it's what Arthur Brown recites elsewhere on the album.

"Gates of Urizen" offers a respite from what came before. It's a spooky power ballad, which of course gets heavy later, like pretty much any mellow Bruce Dickinson song.

Explains Bruce, generally on the record but also this theme-steeped track, "Where it all started out for me on this, I was researching a book on the history of art and alchemy, because a lot of artwork was inspired by alchemists—a lot of their processes were depicted in art. And all these Blake paintings kept cropping up, as illustrations of the sort of elemental figures featured. Because what alchemists were trying to do was to identify elemental forces in the human soul, and then try to sort of filter them out or magnify them or amplify them by using chemical processes. And that's what Blake did in his poetry and his art.

"Which brings us to 'Gates of Urizen.' This Blake poem is the story of two brothers, one called Urizen, and one called Los, and they're separated at birth for eternity, and Urizen is actually composed of the words 'your' and 'reason' put together. And one brother, called Urizen, is reasoning, he's logical, he's cold, he dead, he's ice, and he's all the elements you associate with paternalistic death—he's the guy that says you can't do that, get off the grass. And he's spends eternity in chains, freezing cold, miserable, with a long gray beard. And his brother Los—or Sol backwards—spends his life in hell, re-creating hell every single day, in the most-imaginative ways possible, because he's the imaginative, libidinous side of a personality.

"And what Blake is doing is giving us an insight into his own subconscious, and probably the subconscious of most of us as well. Because there are both these things existing. And this epic poem goes on about these horrendous agonies that these two people go through. And I use a quote at the end of one of the songs: 'What demon has formed this abominable void, this soul-shuddering vacuum? Some say it is Urizen, but unknown, abstracted, brooding secret, the dark power hid.' That's one of the lines in Blake's poem. Blake wrote *Songs of Innocence and Experience*, and the *Songs of Innocence* are so innocent, you can't believe that it's the same man. But the *Songs of Experience*, they allude to the dark side of human nature, but they're also very much in the here and now. But then there's his other stuff! There's the stuff that they keep in the backroom, as it were, that you don't get to see at school, his epic poetry, and that stuff is just mind blowing."

Relating Blake's writings to the world today, Bruce figures, "The thing is that none of this has changed from ancient times to right now. I mean Blake was one of these guys who saw . . . I won't say he saw visions, because what he saw was real for him. He had a rare gift which children sometimes have, which they lose, to actually see people who other people can't see. So, Blake at a relatively young age had a conversation with an angel in his backyard and sat down and talked to him for twenty minutes, and then came down and wrote it all down and painted a picture of the angel and got thoroughly beaten by his father for doing it.

Martin Popoff archive

"Yet, he never stopped seeing angels. In one of his letters is a conversation he had with Ezekiel in his backyard, and he said, 'I asked Ezekiel about this, that, and the other, and he told me blah blah blah,' and people said, 'Oh, a great imagination.' And he said, 'No, it's not my imagination. I saw Ezekiel and he came down and visited me.' And people thought Blake was mad, which I don't think he was. I genuinely think that he saw these people. Whether they existed or not is another question.

"But it doesn't matter," continues Bruce, ever able to ride the razor's edge between normal and paranormal. "What matters is that he saw them, and he never stopped seeing things his whole life. So, he existed in two worlds at the same time. He existed in the here and now, which he saw as being mean spirited, cruel, nasty, materialistic, and he's probably pretty correct. And he saw the other world. He had a foot in both camps.

"And that in essence is what the alchemists wanted to do. The alchemist's motto was 'As above, so below.' The macrocosm, the huge universe, was summed up in a single grain of sand. If you could look inside the atom, you could see everything that was in the universe, if you look hard enough. So, the alchemist's vision was to be able to elevate us as base metal, as lead, this useless lump of earth wandering around half asleep, doing our drudgery, our chores. We are a piece of the divine, just like everything else is, so how can we, with that knowledge, turn ourselves into union with it while we're still on Earth? So, they decided they were going to try chemistry. Or, more accurately, as a byproduct of it, they invented chemistry."

"Jerusalem" is a second ambitious ballad, a bit prog, a bit Maiden, all concept album. As usual, there's an ascension to a heavy bit over which a swaggering solo takes center stage. Comments Bruce, "The closest song to the last album is probably something like 'Jerusalem,' and it's the closest thing you'll get to a sort of progressive, epic-type metal thing. There are three titles on the albums, 'Book of Thel,' 'Gates of Urizen,' and 'Jerusalem,' which are all poems by William Blake. 'Jerusalem' actually uses the words of the poem as the lyrics. And 'Jerusalem' is also one of the most popular hymns in the English language."

Bruce recalls having to sing the hymn in school when he was a kid. "Yes, and I suppose it's worth mentioning that I added another few words of lines as well, to make up a sort of chorus and things like that. But basically, for Blake, Jerusalem was a place. He wasn't talking about somewhere in the Holy Land; he was talking about a place that you construct for yourself, or a country or a town constructs, as a sort of spiritual homeland, if you like. So, when he says, 'Can Jerusalem be built here in England's green and present land?,' he was talking about can people become aware of the divine, of the spirit that moves through the universe? That's what Blake wanted people to see in his poetry. Because in his words, God was just the supreme poet. The universe and everything we see is just an expression of his poetry, and that was it. So, there's only one god, and all religions are worshipping the same god, whether they know it or not. It's pretty farsighted for 1810."

Further framing Blake for Henrik and Mattias, Bruce explained that what he wanted to do was "alchemy, but with a soul behind it. And the more I read about Blake, even after I'd done the album, the more I realized I felt really sympathetic to his philosophy of the way he worked. And Jesus Christ, this guy had a hard life. I mean he made it hard for himself. Brutally noncompromising, you know, and so much of a fucking genius. Way beyond any of his contemporaries. They thought he was mad! They said his paintings were old-fashioned, and this is two hundred years ago. They said his paintings were boring and incomprehensible, and his poetry was mad and not even English.

"He created an entire mythology. He took his subconscious and the constant battles between Urizen and Los between his creative side, and the part of him that belonged to his father . . . the battles, the guilt, and the conflict and everything, and he took that and with that energy created a world which was both a world of vision and imagination—and a world of terror, superstition, and reality at the same time.

"I just got this really clear idea that William Blake saw everything here, and on top of it he had an overlay of ghosts, gremlins, people, and figures, and he lived in this world all the time. And if you live in that world, his poems make perfect sense, and you have to go into that world when you read his poetry. So, I thought, oh Jesus, if I can get that kind of philosophy and use it in the music.

"There's lots of references and hints all over the place," continues Bruce, as to the Blake touchstones across the album. "Blake used to do the same thing in his poems and his paintings. He would borrow, he would go along and see an exhibition and go, 'Oh, I like the hands' or something, and he would go away, go home, get his engraver's tool out, and create something because the hands fitted his vision. You know, he never did it and just copied something, like just a reproduction. He took it and he made everything his own. And that's what I tried to do on the record. I mean, I could go down the lyrics and go, 'That's mine, that's mine, and, oh, that's this and that's that.'"

"Trumpets of Jericho" makes good use of Roy Z's exploration of subcycles, with Bruce yet again suggesting that a respite is needed from the modern metal with a chorus that soars, slicing the air. His lyric is opaque, traversing time, mixing mythic and biblical imagery. As well, given the thought we know he's put into the record, he's being allegorical, the reader able to imaging how these inscrutable words apply to Blake.

But then again, "Machine Men" reminds us that we don't have to relate everything so faithfully to the main concept, this one's modern wording matching the groovy grind of the music. It's interesting to imagine what we would think if a song like this showed up on an Iron Maiden album, or, more pointedly, how it wouldn't fit, how no one in the band would write music like this. And yet, it's squarely heavy metal, and for the most part timeless in a favorable way over typical Maiden music. And then again, it's stood the test of time in terms of permeation into pop consciousness less forcefully than any tier 1 and most tier 2 Maiden songs. A debate for another time, perhaps. One amusing note: Bruce's mumbling at the beginning has him reading from the telephone directory!

The Chemical Wedding ends on a triumphant note with "The Alchemist," a slow-paced epic with a monotone riff blessed with the mystique of "Kashmir." There's also something Deep Purple about it, which almost seems underscored by the guitar solo, which slips and slides like Ritchie. Toward the tail end of this hazy trip through alchemical smoke, Bruce returns to the chorus of "Chemical Wedding" but in a different key and arrangement. It's a nice nod to a concept album trope, the recurrence of an earlier musical theme.

"'The Alchemist' started out as almost like what I would describe as reciting a shopping list of things you should do," explained Bruce to Mattias, of the very tactile lyric. "'Sulphurous and burning,' starting with 'a window to the west' in Taurus, you know. To make the philosopher's stone, you do this, you do this, you do this. It's not really a song; it's a list, right? But when I thought of Blake, I thought, he's the alchemist. So, the song is William Blake creating his vision, and as the alchemist in the chorus, what does he say? He throws the world back in people's faces. He utterly rejects it. He says he's the little hermit on the hill. You know, 'I don't need anyone else, I don't need anybody else's art, I don't need your approval, I don't care if you like me or if you don't like me. And if you're too stupid to know that, that's your problem, not mine, and I'm gonna die with a smile on my face.' Which, in fact, he did in real life. When he had no money and he had very few friends and he only had three people in the room with him, he should have been not particularly happy. But he died with this huge grin on his face, singing loudly, saying, 'You should see where I'm going—it's fantastic.'"

Those forgetting that the show has ended would be jarred by one of these mischievous false endings. After the song is over and after fully two minutes of nothing, suddenly we hear: "And all this vegetable world appeared on my left foot. As a bright sandal, formed immortal of precious stones and gold. I stooped down and bound it on. To walk forward through eternity."

Chuckles Bruce, "Oh, that's just a little tongue-in-cheek thing. When I got the tape back from Arthur, with some quotes that I asked him to read . . . I think it was in a microphone check. It was like, 'Arthur, say something into the mic.' And he said, 'And all this vegetable world appeared on my left foot.' And I was just like, that's fucking brilliant! It's so Arthur! It's just so him, because he comes up with these things that are just genius moments and then they're just gone, and you've lost them. It's usually like, 'God, Arthur, why didn't you say that with the tape recorder on?!'"

When all was said and done, you could tell that Bruce knew that with *The Chemical Wedding*, he had a winner on his hands. But interestingly, stressing the point with Mattias, he knows full well that *Skunkworks* was a winner too. Again, this just proves how on the ball Dickinson is, that as a deep and knowledgeable rock fan, he knew a good record when he heard it.

"I see similarities, only because both of them had the same type of philosophy behind them," begins Dickinson. "Neither with *Skunkworks* nor *The Chemical Wedding* am I happy to just sit down and be a Bruce Dickinson version of HammerFall. I'm not getting down on HammerFall or anything, but there are bands who are content to reproduce traditional metal that has been the same way since the end of the 1980s. The closest I ever came to that was *Accident of Birth*, which was an album which grabbed everybody and reestablished me with the metal community. Because they'd all freaked out that with *Skunkworks* I was somehow in denial, and I was rejecting metal."

"But I was like, 'Hang on; this is a heavy record.' I see a certain amount of unpredictability as being a virtue. I don't like being, as Patrick McGoohan said, 'pushed, filed, stamped, briefed, debriefed, indexed, or numbered.' 'My life is my own.' So, in that sense I can be an awkward little fucker, and it may be that, in a way, I'm almost my own worst enemy, because of that. My life would be easier if I just settled down and made predictable heavy metal records."

"But I don't regret anything I've done in the past. What businesspeople forget is that people do talk, and people realize that whatever I've done has always been an attempt to be different, or to be interesting, or to be innovative. It hasn't always worked, hasn't always connected with the general public, but if you look back over the records, I've never made a shitty record. My solo records . . . not one single record can I look back at and say, 'Ah, that record really stinks,' you know? There are some records that are better than others, but there's nothing I've looked back at and been really embarrassed by—nothing!"

Reminded by Mattias and Henrik—both big fans of *Skunkworks*—how the aggravating short-form narrative on it was "Bruce goes grunge," Dickinson again proves his deep musicologist awareness of the situation.

"Yes, I know, I know. Just imagine for a second it was a grunge album. So what?! Is a Soundgarden record a grunge album? And if they say yes, I say, 'Oh well, I'm very proud,' then, 'cause Soundgarden is a great fucking band.' If people wanna call it grunge, then it's fucking grunge. It was really exciting. It was a lot more fucking exciting than the shit that was coming out at the end of the 1980s [laughs] with big hair from out of Los Angeles! I also don't accept that heavy metal is over and done with, because all of what is exciting about this music—grunge, that is—is the influence it took from heavy metal. All these bands in Seattle had a big fucking party on New Year's Eve, Jack [Endino] told me, and all they played all night long was AC/DC, Thin Lizzy, Deep Purple, and fucking Iron Maiden.

"So somewhere, what has poisoned this whole atmosphere is the media. The media has chosen to set people at each other's throats, in terms of the fans, and it plays on the psychology of some metal fans. You know, it's not the world's best-kept secret that a lot of metal fans are quite conservative, musically. They're not incredibly open-minded to different types of things. All you have to do is have somebody going, 'Argh, he's denying metal,' and everybody leaps on a big bandwagon. It's very sad because it should not be about labels and tribalism; it should be about music. Back in the 1970s it was about music. You could have a Motörhead album and a Fleetwood Mac album sitting alongside on the same record shelf and not have a problem. And have Jaco Pastorius living alongside ZZ Top, or B.B. King, and Deep Purple.

"It's music, not marketing. I mean, one of my favorite albums is Ritchie Blackmore's *Blackmore's Night*, this acoustic medieval album that he did [at the time of Bruce's chat with the guys, Ritchie and Candice had just put out their debut, *Shadow of the Moon*]. I just happen to love that record. I got turned on to it by a bunch of people who were all metal fans who loved the record, and they made tapes of it for me. I know this German bloke who loves the record too. And he said all his friends were like, 'Argh, Blackmore, what a traitor! What a traitor—he's doing stuff with lutes and flutes and stuff.' And what's so sad is that when he did that album, he did what he has been playing and wanting to play for twenty years. You can hear it in all the early Rainbow stuff. You can hear it in 'Temple of the King.' It's exactly the same, but they've never heard that. They've spent their whole life listening to the records and never heard beyond. . . . And that makes me . . . if I didn't have people who understood what I did, then I would be tempted to take a flamethrower to the whole fucking world. I would stop making music.

"I was devastated by the *Skunkworks* thing," continues Bruce, meaning the critical and commercial indifference to it. "I was actually fucking gutted! I was on the verge of saying [that] this business is so fucked, I just don't care anymore. *Skunkworks* was a record which I tore myself apart to make, and nobody seemed to give a shit. I don't think anybody in the management really understood what was going on either, because otherwise we wouldn't have been touring with Helloween. They were totally the wrong band for Skunkworks [now meaning the band] to tour with."

Accident of Birth turned out to be the gateway drug toward *The Chemical Wedding*.

"It was actually Roy that dragged me back into some semblance, because he called up and he said, 'Listen, I've got some stuff, and it's like a metal record.' And I wasn't thrilled. I wasn't really sure that I had anything to offer. After all those years in Maiden, I'm not sure that I can do it any better than I did it the best back in 1983, 1984, you know? So I was really not sure that it's what I should be doing. Then he played me some backing tracks he'd done for what was to become *Accident of Birth*, down the phone, and I thought, there is something there. So, there I was, boom, in Los Angeles, on my own. It's kind of sunny, and I thought, let's see what happens.

"So, I went in and we came out with *Accident of Birth*, and I was like, that sounds great. And then it was like a big light went on in my head: I can do this; I know exactly what to do on this record, exactly. I don't know any of the songs yet, but I know I can write them. It was almost a huge relief that I was going to do something that I knew exactly what to do.

"And in actual fact, *Accident of Birth* is nothing new. There is nothing on *Accident of Birth* which I haven't done before, either in my solo career or in Iron Maiden or in Samson. The difference is that it all gets put together in a package where all the songs fit together. If I was a rock fan and I just wanted a great metal album, nothing complicated, no agenda, this is it. I just wanted to make an album that fucking rocked, and I guess that makes me some kind of weirdo [laughs]. Because nobody's making an album like that. 'That's brilliant, excellent; thanks Roy, good idea.'

"Then I thought, if this fails, this will be the last album I ever make. And I thought, I don't give a shit. If this is gonna be the last album I ever do, I'm gonna do the best straight heavy metal album I ever made in my life. And it was a great album, and all the reviews came in, and all of a sudden I was back up there on the Richter scale, and everything was cool.

"And I sat back and thought, wow, what do I do now?" continues Bruce. "I could do the same again, but it would be fake, it would be dull, so I can never achieve that same kind of excitement in people's minds. If I do the same thing again, people would say that that's all Bruce Dickinson can do. A few other people got caught in that trap. So, what could we do? We thought, well, let's use some modern sounds and go really heavy. Let's see how heavy we can go."

Turning to the reality of touring on a small scale, now for *The Chemical Wedding*, Bruce points out that "it's very interesting watching the way the audience reacts to the way that I'm presenting songs. You know, we can't afford a show; we're losing a significant amount of money on this tour even without a big show and stuff. So, I mean, how can I make a show of what we have? So, we just came up with the idea of using this big red light in between the amps. And I've got my book of poetry, and I get down there and the red light illuminates my face like some kind of demon, and I just read some poetry in between each song. And you know what? The first time I did it, the place was like, hush-hush—silence! And I thought, this is fucking great. It's starting to evolve into something now, and I'm thinking, this is storytelling: 'Sit down and I'll tell you a scary story.' Boom! Then the music starts. So, that's giving me ideas for presentation and possible directions in the future for the next album."

True to his established track record as a solo artist, Bruce was bursting with music during the *Chemical Wedding* sessions. As he told me back in 1998, "Here's the weird thing. There's an extra track for Japan, which Adrian and I wrote, called 'Return of the King,' which is a pretty cool track. Then I have in mind, in my greasy little mitts, a CD EP of six extra tracks, which are compiled from the last album. There's a track called 'Wicker Man,' which is a fantastic track that just never got finished, and I just finished it up."

"Wicker Man" is an excellent midmetal rocker with intriguing chord changes and Mellotron textures and is a completely different song from the composition of the same name that would bounce Bruce back into the ranks of Maiden two years later. It would see release on the two-CD version of *The Best of Bruce Dickinson* from 2001. "Return of the King" could conceivably work as a Maiden track, although the verse riff is closer to up-tempo Black Sabbath, thereby retaining Bruce's mandate of doomy heaviness, even on an energetic rocker like this. The chorus, on the other hand, feels like classic Maiden, albeit derived from Thin Lizzy.

Bruce says of "Confeos," "The best way I can describe it is an homage to Deep Purple. What happened was, we started out with this backing track, and I said, 'Gee, that sounds kind of Purpleish. Why don't we have a little bit of fun, bring in a Hammond, and tell the guy to do his best Jon Lord impression, and I'll go in and do my best Ian Gillan "I'm not worthy" voice and try and write lyrics which are appropriate?' So, it's going to be about a chick in Japan and getting drunk in a bar [laughs]. And that's what we did.

"I do this thing called Rock Radio Network over here, and I played it one night, and I said, 'We've had a mysterious tape, and we think this is Deep Purple playing back with Ritchie Blackmore—take a listen.' And it sounds so much like Purple [laughs]. That's why I sent that cryptic note to Ian. So now I wonder if they're going to start getting some emails, saying, 'I hear you're playing with Ritchie again. We heard this track. What's going on?' [laughs]."

"Confeos" is actually quite witty, although unfortunately Bruce sounds as much like Bruce as he does Ian, and the musical track is too good and original to be a straight parody, so it doesn't scribble a page full of Purple. But yes, there are the Jon Lord keys too, and the guitar solo lands upon a half-dozen Ritchie tropes. Late in the jelly jam there's a bonus keyboard solo, all Egyptian-like, after which there's a briefly shoehorned-in last Purple trope, a bit of cross-chatter among "Jon," "Ian," and "Ritchie."

"Then there's a track called 'Real World,'" says Bruce, "which is from the sessions for this album. It's actually a big anthemic kind of rock radio power rock thing. It just doesn't fit on the album—it's altogether too cheerful [laughs]. There's the Scorpions track 'The Zoo,' which we covered for CMC, which is going on a worldwide wrestling record."

If I may disagree with Bruce, "Real World" is typical *Chemical Wedding* fare, albeit almost hit single material (again, demonstrating the depth of this writing team), while "The Zoo" showed up on *ECW: Extreme Music*, issued on October 27, 1998.

"Then there's a track called 'The Midnight Jam,' which is a midnight jam, with all of us off the last album. What we did is we got lots of candles out and sat around and had a jam for about five minutes on this theme. And the lyrics . . . the idea was after the end of 'Taking the Queen,' if we'd have carried on with the same story of the destruction of the city and the burning and the desolation and lost love and devastation, what it would have sounded like. So, it's a real trippy, late-night, chill-out track."

Bruce describes "Acoustic Song" as "a little acoustic thing between me and Roy, just a pretty little song. I remember everybody freaking out. I remember calling Roy up and asking him how the mixes went on the B-sides, and he went, 'You never told me about the acoustic track! Everybody's going nuts about this stuff, that you sang on it!' And I was like, 'Oh, it was just ten minutes on the back of an envelope.' And that's always the way; you know, the quick little stuff you do, people love it."

Indeed, both these latter casually named tracks are essentially proper songs, the latter slightly more than the former. But these, as well as the Purple knockoff, offer value for money as they are produced to the end, not gratuitously long, and have enough detail and appointment to stand shoulder to shoulder with the rest of the more official material.

"I don't know honestly when any of those tracks are going to surface," noted Bruce. "We're not doing any singles in Europe, because it's a waste of time and money and everything. And actually, even when you *do* give away tracks, I think it's a waste of giveaway tracks if they are any good. I'd rather put them out as an EP so people can buy them. But not just throw them away on singles. But the Japanese are putting a single out for 'Killing Floor,' and they're going to have this Deep Purpleish thing on the back of it, and also 'Real World.'"

In that comment there are additional clues that Bruce as a solo artist wasn't lighting the world on fire. Indeed, part of what was about to transpire would have to do with Bruce learning the hard lesson that he could create art of an utmost and impressive quality, and people are going to keep asking, "When are you getting back with Maiden?"

As it turned out, *The Chemical Wedding* saw its highest chart success in Finland, a Maiden stronghold, where the record reaches #22. However, sales in the US, after seven years on the market, sat at 41,363 copies. In Sweden, the record got to #31; Germany, #41; Japan, #64; and the UK, #55. Wrapping this up, an expanded edition of the record included "Return of the King," "Real World," and "Confeos," and, as discussed, the ECW compilation and *The Best of Bruce Dickinson* would take care of the rest.

For the tour dates in support of the record, Roy Z had to bow out, only to be replaced by his guitar tech, "Guru."

"I don't know that many people who I'd like to play with who would want to do this stuff," remarked Bruce. "It's not that easy to do. To find a guitarist to do Roy's stuff is tough. I mean, for *The Chemical Wedding* tour he coached Guru. He sat down and gave him lessons for weeks and weeks and weeks of exactly how to do each bit. And when we went into rehearsals the first time with the Guru, I panicked. It wasn't Roy. But I tell you, by the time we got out on the road, after about a week on the road, it was to the point where I was like, you know, this is going great with the Guru. So, I was really proud of him; he did a great job. But that was such an exception, because he was prepared to go with exactly what Roy told him to do."

Asked by Henrik and Mattias why he's not playing, particularly, earlier solo material, Bruce said, "Oh no, I haven't even asked them to learn any new stuff. I know how hard they worked just learning the stuff they already know, so the last thing I want to do is dig out even more. . . . We were going to learn a Samson song, and then I thought, 'Oh, why don't we learn this song, and let's go in on this song?' And all of a sudden, their heads were so full of stuff. Musically, this is a very difficult set to play. There's four or five different guitar tunings in it, and there's three different types of guitar to play. If you're given a guitar, it's like, 'Shit, what kind of guitar is this? And what tuning is it in and where do I put my fingers?' I mean, it's like a real mindfuck for guitarists, this set.

"I'm not stuck in selecting the songs, but, you see, this is the first headline tour I've done in Scandinavia and Europe since 1994. So, I want people to be left in absolutely no doubt as to what it's all about. And the set as it is at the moment works great, and it's working better and better and better each night and it hasn't got to a peak yet.

"One of the problems is that we've been short of time. All the time we've been doing this whole project, we've been short of time. I've done one world tour already doing promotion. When I got back, I had ten or twelve days to rehearse for the tour with everybody. Guru had done three days in LA with the guys, and that was it! He'd been just learning his stuff at home. So, we had ten days, and three days into rehearsals I got this dreadful flu. So that was it for me singing—forget it! I went to the throat doctor, and he said, 'Okay, it's a virus, go rest, drink plenty of water, don't sing!' And I was like, 'Great!'

"I got rid of my flu one day before the tour started. The first show I was opening my mouth to sing, I hadn't sung for probably ten days, and four days earlier my voice sounded like shit. So, my rehearsals started the first night in Helsinki. That's what I mean by saying that everybody's come together so fast. To ask people to learn more material would have overloaded them completely. I mean their little brains would have been popping with material. They've just got to be able to concentrate on guitar changes, the tunings and everything else. Plus, the fact that every night we've got a different PA, every night we've got different lights, every night it's a different-sized stage. I mean, last night in Lithuania we were playing a four-thousand-seater and we had three thousand people in there, a huge stage, massive PA, big lights.

"It's really great and really cool!" continues Bruce, asked what it was like to be playing the Baltic states. "The night before [Estonia], the stage was half the size, smaller PA, but 1,200 people in a 1,400-capacity venue, and it was a great show. I mean, take a situation like Gothenburg, which was total fucking chaos. The show got moved three times on the same day—it was ludicrous. And we played in Turku in some nightclub which was like utterly bizarre! It was a great show, but it was really strange, a tiny little stage.

"And Guru has never done a tour like this! So, he's holding up really, really well. He works so hard. I mean literally, when he said that he was working 24/7—twenty-four hours, seven days a week—he wasn't joking. He really was working that hard to learn everything. And I've been trying to persuade him to loosen up a bit. I said, 'Guru, all those guitar solos'—which he learnt by the note—'if you wanna fuck with them, go ahead. Just play with them a bit, do your own thing a bit, be the Guru, you know?' I admire him so much for his determination and how hard he's worked, so I can't criticize him, 'cause he takes it so much to heart. You've got to be very gentle 'cause he knows immediately. So, you'd have to go like, 'This bit, if you did it like this, it might sound a wee bit better,' and Guru would go, 'Wow, you mean I've been doing it wrong?! Oh, God!' And he'll go out and punch himself on the head or something. 'No, no, you just try and make things better.' If ever I have to try and make a suggestion to him, I always tell him about how many fuckups I did the night before as well [laughs]. But yeah, he was the guitar tech on the album, and he was really integral to the whole team, in fact."

Emphasizing the "athletic rock" (to quote Raven) nature of the set, Dickinson says, "The thing is, it's only for certain songs. The great thing about doing it this way on the guitar is that you don't actually change the key of the guitar. With a lot of the other solutions people use to get low, fat guitar, they down-tune, dick around with the keys. But with this, you stay with the same key, and the harmonics that are being generated are just way beyond what the guitar is supposed to do."

A tantalizing possibility was reportedly in the works in the fall of 1999. It seems that in celebration of the twentieth anniversary of the New Wave of British Heavy Metal, Masa Ito from *Burrn!* magazine in Japan was setting up a festival. Samson was going to be a part of it, with the early plan being an EP of all new songs, issued on Bruce's boutique label Air Raid Records. Talk quickly moved to a full-length album. In October, Bruce had said, "Well, you know, the phone lines have been active, and Thunderstick is back with the mask and Chris is back as well, so the ingredients are all there, but nothing is certain yet. If it did happen, it would only be for a limited period, because I've got a solo record to do the next year. Well, I'll make it next year, but it won't be released until probably 2000, 'cause this millennium thing is just gonna . . . from November until like February, just forget everything, you know, because I don't think you'll get sense out of anybody during those four months [laughs]."

Bruce is referring to the "Y2K" scare, when it was imagined that all the computers will stop working and society would crash, due to coding issues with the year turning over to "00." How much carnage it would have caused will never be known, but major precautions were taken all over the world, and disaster was indeed not forthcoming.

But neither the Samson reunion nor a follow-up to *The Chemical Wedding* happened, since Bruce would soon make his return to the ranks of Maiden.

Before we get there, however, on November 2, 1999, Bruce issues his *Scream for Me Brazil* live album, the second live collection of his short solo career. "That album very nearly didn't happen at all," explains Bruce. "When we got to the first show in São Paulo, we had everything set up for the recording, and we went out for the first song, and Stan, our engineer, was in the truck and nothing was coming out of the speakers. And he was like, 'What's happened?!' And the Brazilian engineer looked at him and said, 'Hmm, I don't know; it was all working before,' and Stan said, 'We're not recording anything! What's happened?!'

"So by about the fourth song, they started getting something, and it started sounding like a band. And to this day, we don't know what happened. It was a digital desk, but basically the whole desk had completely reset itself and wiped all of its memory, which meant we had lost the first three or four songs of the set. And he told me about it at the end of the show, and it was such a brilliant show, because it was the first show in São Paulo. And I was like, 'Oh shit!'

"So fortunately, we could record one of the other concerts to fill in some of the gaps that we had. And we also had an extra show added; it was a matinee show, which was about two-thirds sold out on a Sunday, and we were leaving that evening. And that was back in São Paulo as well. So, we did two nights in São Paulo, one sold out, one about two-thirds full. So I said, well, look, seeing as we're going to do this extra show, and the mobile is in São Paulo, let's record that too, just to make sure we've covered ourselves. Because I was very suspicious of everything at this point [laughs]. But that turned out great. But we did have to muck around with the tapes. I think one of the best-sounding tracks there is actually restored from safety copies, which was 'Book of Thel.'"

As Bruce told Adrian Bromley, "Recording in Brazil just seemed like the thing to do with this record. Even Deep Purple had a live record called *Made in Japan*. Everyone who has ever gone out to make a live record has wanted to go over there and record something that was titled *Made in Japan* or something like that. I'm just included in that: a) no one's ever recorded a live record from anywhere in South America of note, and b) the audience down there is just great. The main reason you make a live record is to be able to create the best live experience possible. Brazil has some of the best live audiences I've ever encountered in my career. We did this recording over five shows, about 5,000 fans a night, and overall, it ended up being that we played in front of 20,000 people."

Publicity shot sent out with *Scream for Me Brazil*.
Tony Leonard archive

Continues Bruce, "With that extra matinee show, we were able to record the first three songs properly and add them to the recording that we had done the previous night. That pretty much helped solidify our set, though I think the song 'The Tower' is from a show in Rio de Janeiro, and 'Chemical Wedding' is from a small town, Vinhedo, a couple [of] hours outside São Paulo. We didn't change much within the set that we had homed in on all these months of playing. Why change the songs we had become so good at playing? A record of the best of what you've got? We did a few extra tracks at the end of each show, but funnily enough, the songs didn't get included on the disc. The extra tracks were 'Jerusalem' and 'Taking the Queen.'

"We also excluded any Iron Maiden stuff that we had recorded too. That was my decision. I wanted to keep the two things separate because I am going to continue making solo records and I think it is important to keep a very strong line between both things. I think that it's fair to everybody, both Maiden and my own fans. I think I share a fan base with both, so it was an important decision."

Asked by Bromley to name his favorite live album, Dickinson responds with "Oh my God. It has to be Deep Purple's *Made in Japan*. That record, to me, is the best live record of all time, because there is no other record at all that just captures the ecstasy of a rock 'n' roll gig from a musician's point of view than that record. I'm not a big fan of live records where the audience is the loudest thing, like you're in a bathroom. I can get a bad sound like that any time of the week. Roy Z mixed this record, while I helped. And we aimed to have the record sound from the perspective of what it sounds like on stage to us. Rather than standing in the middle of the audience, with this record, you're standing on the stage with us.

"I really wanted to do this record," continues Bruce. "I always have since I started out with the solo career. Had I not joined back with Iron Maiden, I would have done the South American tour, and some form of a tour in North America, taken some time off,

Martin Popoff archive

and gone back to do the next studio album. Then I would've gone out on tour with the background of those three albums of material, including the new one, and I would've recorded something live. With me rejoining Maiden, that kind of preempted that. I really thought I'd better do a live record now, because the band is just so hot, and the audience is right there. I felt a real need to document this, not only out of respect for the musicians who I've been working with on the last two projects, but also because this is their record too. I'm glad I got the opportunity to do this, and I'm excited with the end result."

I was as guilty as the next guy about bringing up rumors of Bruce reconciling with Steve (my chat with Bruce was a little before Adrian Bromley's, before this news had broken). On *The X Factor*, Bruce smartly answers, "I don't wish to comment on any of that. I don't want to be negative, because it's really none of my business. We're all going off and trying to do the best we can."

About the possibility of at least playing some gigs with Maiden, Bruce figures, "I really think the whole deal with all of this boils down to me and Steve. That's it. There's no friction anywhere else, I don't think. We share the same manager [laughs]. We're both with Rod Smallwood. I mean, we sit and talk about this in the pub and things like that. And people say, 'Are you getting back together with the band?' And I say, 'Look, you want me to get up there tomorrow and sing a Maiden set? Hang on, let me go find my boots.' Not a problem. And it would be great. I could walk onstage with them, and we could do a concert tomorrow night and it would be absolutely fucking mega!

"But I don't think that's quite the point. For some of the people involved, there's more to it than that. Well, there's two things here: a live situation and a record. One question is, Will anything ever happen again ever under any circumstance? The other one is that could something happen live? And that would be great; it would just be like a really cool laugh. As for records, I'm not really sure how that would or could happen. I don't know if that could work at all, because I'm making records now [sighs] . . . I'm making records now that . . . the way I would put it is, we make records in very, very different ways now [laughs]. So, I guess what I'm saying is, I'm not sure how we would close the gap between the way I work and the way Steve works now.

"But having said that, there's no reason at all if he wanted to go have some fun, you know, in addition to the fun he's having now, and do some shows; sure, fuck it, yes. But I'm perfectly happy with what I'm doing at the moment musically. But if he said, 'Would you like to go and sing a few Maiden tunes?,' I'd be like, 'Yes, I'd love to. And you don't have to fire anybody or anything else like that. I'll go onstage; we'll do half a dozen songs, and we'll go have a drink.' But it's not as simple as all that. There are all kinds of complexities and things which I'm not going to go into. Because I made a great record and I'm going out promoting it, and really, that's where my life is at right now. That's my future. This record is my future."

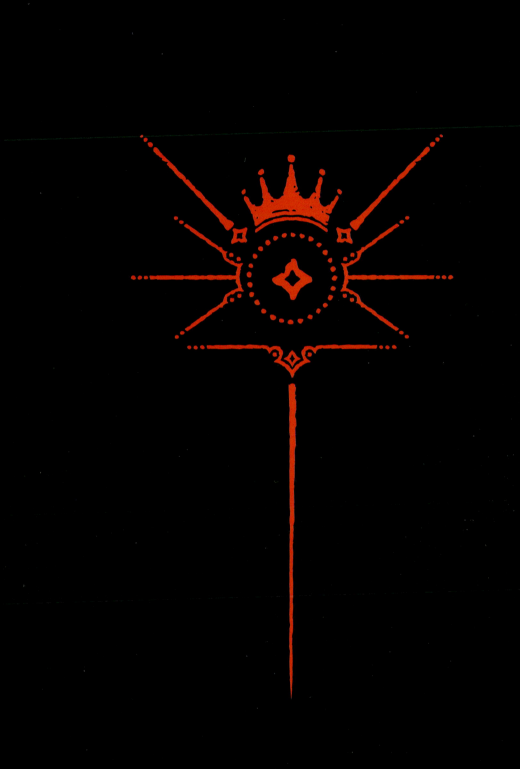

CHAPTER 16
Virtual XI and the Return of Bruce

"Where am I? What do I do now?"

Back in the land of Maiden, not only are Steve and crew—like Bruce—not doing great guns on the live front, but the records aren't all that hot either. At least Bruce could say that he was making some of the best music of his entire career, a notion that still stands today, despite the strength of Maiden's records in the 2000s and 2010s.

From late 1997 into January 1998, Maiden worked on what will become *Virtual XI*, again at Steve's own Barnyard Studios on his property in Essex, England.

Recalls Blaze on the sessions, "When we recorded *The X Factor*, we recorded to digital tape; we used sixty-four-track digital tape. The desk would fail, or one of the tape machines would fail, and it would take a week to fix; all of that we would have to get through. But now, with this studio we used, a lot of it has been refitted, a lot of different technology, everything was working, and we spent a lot less time on technical problems. Because we recorded direct to hard drive on this album and then used tape as the backup. So, we had virtual tracks. With Soundscape, any time we had a bug, we'd phone them up, they'd email it to us, and we'd download it off the internet and carry on recording. We were right there, even though the microphone I use is probably ten years old, because that's what we like to use to bring out the sound of my voice.

"But we're still using the most up-to-date stuff to get the best representation. And I found it really exciting to be working with the cutting-edge technology. I really got the feeling that technology is coming of age. Now it's a tool you can use without too much training. Now it's not getting in the way of the music. It's more like, 'Oh well, we'll use it, and it helps.' So, it was good. A lot of the guide vocals we did, we kept as the main vocals for the finished recording. And what we did as well, we didn't rehearse as much for this album. For this album we got together the arrangement for the bass and drums and started recording.

"But that left the three of us kind of in the wilderness," continues Bayley. "We'd think, 'Well, God, but what are the chords? How many choruses are there? What is the verse?' So, we'd be like writing notes down, 'Is it C? B? All right, you give me the nod when we start the chords.' It was like that, really. But that gave it a bit of a spontaneous edge. So, we had a great vibe. It was very much like you do live; a different hall every night, you walk out, you don't know what the sound is, you don't know what you can hear, it's kind of a muddle that you have to work out. And it was like that in the studio. 'Where am I? What do I do now?' It added excitement to it."

"We started writing early last year," Steve told our mag *BW&BK*. "We went into my Barnyard Studios around July, and we finished mixing in late January. This one's a bit special. There are only eight songs on it, so they're all long, which gives us the opportunity to really stretch out musically. The songs are a variety of topics from the virtual reality in the opening track through to a sad but powerful closing track written by Blaze and Janick about the Falklands War. There's also a track inspired by the *Braveheart* and *Rob Roy* films, which is about the Scottish clans struggling for freedom. When I wrote the music, it had a Celtic flavor, which is why I wrote the lyrics about the clans."

On the resulting low number of songs to make the record, Dave explained to *Hard Roxx* that "we had 12 tracks altogether, but it was just a question of time. We thought about doing a double album, but we had just done *Best of the Beast*, and we had the eight tracks that had continuity running through them to make one album. When you get 73 and 75 minutes on a CD, people try to pack them out to the full amount, which is what we did on *The X Factor*. We wanted to bring it down to make it more concise, but eight tracks was all we could get on, because the length of some of them are nine and ten minutes long."

Meanwhile, pre-Bruce legend at the mic, Paul Di'Anno, is keeping busy with his cottage industry career, issuing in 1998 two albums, *New Live & Rare* from Killers and *Feel My Pain* from the Battlezone configuration, which essentially is just Paul and guitarist John Wiggins from the original band. Like Bruce, like Halford with Fight, and like Priest with *Jugulator*, Paul is going for a harder-edged sound here, piling upon an old-school frame bricks of speed metal, thrash, and hard core. Budgets aren't high in the heavy metal bush league, and it shows.

On March 9, "The Angel and the Gambler" is released as an advance single from the forthcoming *Virtual XI*. It is issued in two digipak parts with various live and video tracks as well as a maxi single and a 7-inch. There's the audacious full-length 9:56 version launched as a single, but also an edit, which pares the track down to 6:05. The song would get to #18 in the UK charts, with Finland's #3 placement being the most favorable result. Two weeks hence, on March 23, 1998, *Virtual XI*, the second Maiden studio album featuring Blaze Bayley on vocals, is issued.

Offers Blaze further in terms of the framing of the record, he figures that "the difference between *Virtual XI* and *The X Factor* is that with *The X Factor* I had just joined the band. We had been writing together and were recording the album, but we hadn't actually played live together—no touring at all. And the record was successful, the tour was very successful, and I had a lot of support and encouragement from fans all over the world. All that experience really made me feel . . . you know, I had a lot of confidence going into *Virtual XI*. There was a really good vibe. *Virtual XI* has a very positive sound compared to *The X Factor*, and I think that reflects the feelings in the band at the moment, whereas *The X Factor* I think is a very dark album, introspective in many ways and heavy in the sense that you really have to listen to that album quite a few times to get the most out of it.

"*Virtual XI* is more immediate. As well, because I'd done a whole world tour and survived, I think my vocals are a lot better and my voice is a lot stronger. I knew my way around the studio a lot better. I think that all goes to make a lot more positive record. It was all very natural. Whatever ideas you've got, you get together with different people, and you just see how it would go. I worked mostly with Steve, a bit more on than on the last one, but also with Janick.

"But nobody sits down and says, 'We've got to write a hit single.' Nobody says, 'We've got to write a song nine minutes long.' Whatever the ideas are, you just take them wherever you feel they're going to be natural. Whatever the flow is, that's where you go. And it's worked out very good for us. Wherever the song goes, if you feel it's sharp and aggressive and you've said everything in three minutes, you know, that's it. So be it. And if with another song you want to set a whole mood and tell a story and it's ten minutes long, then that's okay too. You're not restricted, and I think that's the most important thing."

Specifically in terms of the sound picture, Blaze offers that "I thought the bass was a lot lower on this album. If anything, there's more guitars, and the vocals are much better in terms of the mix. So I thought it was more of a guitar-oriented mix. We spent too long, actually, in the studio, recording *The X Factor*. I thought it lacked a little bit because of that. The production on *Virtual XI* is vital, a bit easier to listen to, because it was a bit more rough and ready. There wasn't so much time spent going around in circles and ending up in the same place."

Things went pear shaped with *Virtual XI* when it came to the album cover. Melvyn Grant was tasked with the brief to reference both video gaming and World Cup soccer along with his Eddie. The guys had gaming on the mind, with the impending release of *Ed Hunter*, so there was that ill-fitted concept, tied further to the album with the song "Futureal." As well, the 1998 World Cup was on, and we all know how much Steve loves his football, with Maiden being famous for getting kitted out and playing other bands or industry people on the road.

"If I hadn't have done this, I would have wanted to be a professional soccer player," explained Steve. "The beauty of this, though, is that I've been able to do the music, and I've also been able to play in charity soccer games and play with very famous players. I've actually played at Wembley, so I've really had the best of both worlds. I've been very lucky. Otherwise, Nicko's a keen golfer, Dave also. Although he's also taken up tennis as well, which is cool, because I love tennis too. Blaze really is not so much a sporty person. I mean, he'll get on the football pitch and have a go, but he's more into working out,

Dave Wright archive

doing weights and stuff. But I suppose I'm the most passionate one. I'm soccer mad, really. But when I'm at home, I really don't go out much. When you think about it, when you're on tour, you're out most of the time. When you're home, you just want to be home and do normal things. I'm pretty boring. I'll go to a restaurant or go to a movie. I very rarely go to clubs, unless I'm going to see a band in particular, but that's not very often, really. I've got four kids, so I tend to stay home a lot. But I go see soccer, and I play soccer every week when I'm at home."

In conversation with Bob Nalbandian, Steve further explains his love for the sport. "Over the last couple years in particular, more and more young kids are getting into soccer. Not so much in the US, but in the rest of the world, people are soccer mad! Especially in places like Italy, Spain, and South America. We headlined the Monsters of Rock festival on our last tour, and when we played São Paulo, I would wear Brazil's soccer shirt, and when we were in Argentina, we would wear the Argentina jersey. The fans over there give us loads of shirts because they know how much we're into soccer, and the fans get so into it. So, we thought it would be great if we could tie the two together. It's our eleventh album, the World Cup is coming up, and we're totally into soccer. So, to tie in with *Virtual XI*, we have the five members of the band and the eleven is made up of six international soccer players. It's great fun, and it's brilliant for me because of my love for soccer."

Dave Wright archive

The request put to Grant for football on the sleeve came later in the process, but there it is, tucked into the left. We also see the first of a slightly altered band name logo, with the extenders on the letters, "R," "M," and "N" (twice) clipped off, making it just slightly worse for no good reason, not to mention the fact that its sort of mottled fill-in color makes it hard to discern in the cover art.

The titling also confounds, with the *XI* put in a circle. Capping off the dog's breakfast is an Eddie that doesn't look like Eddie, given the vampire widow's peak hair and the bulbous forehead. This has been a problem all along, no matter who is drawing Eddie. Whether it's by deliberate design or lack of caring or lack of skill, this presumably single character, however set upon by circumstance, looks fundamentally like a different person across the albums, in fact starting right with the debut album over to *Killers*.

There was also a limited 3-D edition of the cover. But don't ask Nicko to see it, because as Blaze told me back in 1998, he'd given his away. "Nicko is a very generous person," laughs Bayley. "He's so generous that he just can't stop giving everything away. A classic example, for the new album there's a limited edition with the 3-D cover, and they're very hard to get hold of. Nicko had three of these, and in the studio today, he was saying, 'Hey, do you have one of those covers with the 3-D?' And I said, 'Yeah, I've got one.' And he said, 'Because I haven't got one.' And I said, 'Yeah, I have one because I got it from the record company.' I just kind of said 'cause I was on a promotional tour [laughs]. So, he's really one of the warmest, most generous people to be with."

The images within the booklet include screen grabs from the band's new video game *Ed Hunter*, but as Steve mentioned, there's also a shot of the guys in soccer uniforms—and not only the band members, but a bunch of other guys, a jarring, sort of distracting thing to see in an official CD booklet.

"The bodies are real, but the pictures were taken individually," explained Dave to George Koroneos of *Life in a Bungalow*, with respect to the botched cut-and-paste job, further turning the CD booklet into a comedy of errors. "The computer graphics were laid out on a green background, but all the bodies are real. Except there is one shot of me that isn't my body, but it is my head, because I never made it to the photo shoot." And it's not even any sort of Maiden team . . . "No, that football team . . . all the players are professional players. They were approached with the concept and thought it was a good idea. It would have been virtually impossible to get all those guys together. So, they went to the studio and had their individual photos taken. They were computer manipulated so that some of the faces were changed to protect the innocent."

"I am not as fanatical as Steve," Janick told *Hard Roxx*. "I play once a week, but I don't support a team. I don't think Steve goes to see the Hammers every week. I come from Hartlepool, and every Saturday when that result comes through, I am a praying for a result. But usually, we don't get it. Dave's a Spurs supporter."

Promo poster. *Dave Wright archive*

"Football fans and Maiden fans are very similar, similar passions and chants," continues Gers. "The bands and teams that you support when you were ten, the chances are that you when you are eighty, you will still support them because there is that loyalty there. When you support a football team, you want them to win, and when they do, you become ecstatic, which is a bit like a gig. You get the same feelings. It's like playing in the FA Cup for us every night.

"This links in with the World Cup. Normally when we release an album, we have a big press event to announce it is coming. And when they came to us and said they were thinking about playing a few games of football around Europe and linking it in with the press, Dave and I saw that there would be a party after the game, we thought, yes! We play a bit as well. We get on and play twenty minutes and it's fun. I'm a keeper, but I cannot play in that position in case I damage my hands, so I play somewhere behind the front two. Paul Mariner's the goalkeeper. I remember turning up at Hammersmith Odeon, to see Iron Maiden when Bruce was in the band, and I remember the door bursting open and hearing him, saying, 'I'm here.' As he came into the room. He had three scarves on, three hats, and an Iron Maiden T-shirt. We took him to the party afterwards and he had a great time. Paul used to come and see us in the Gillan days. He used to be well into it."

Adds Dave, "Nicko was taken out against Rainbow, so he doesn't play anymore. He just cheers from the sidelines with Blaze. He had a serious injury. Yesterday we played our first game against some radio and TV guys, and it was a very clean game because to take out one of the musicians I don't think would be very good. You have to strike a balance, but it got a bit serious against Rainbow, and Nicko did his back in."

Past the pitch and into the album, *Virtual XI* opens with "Futureal," a succinct and swift rocker with the band's trademark sense of sing-songy melody most famously exemplified on "The Number of the Beast." Issued as a single on July 28, four months after the launch of the album, the song was deemed good enough to be one of five Blaze-era tracks to live on in the set list after Bruce came back. It is also on the *Edward the Great* compilation from 2002 as the only track from *Virtual IX* (*The X Factor* was represented by "Man on the Edge"). The picture sleeve for the single featured Eddie rendered in full CGI rather than illustration, and he's looking very much like the Eddie from *Somewhere in Time*, the long previous record with a future-technology theme.

Explains Blaze, "'Futureal' I enjoy doing. It's a song that I worked on very, very closely with Steve Harris, with the lyrics and the music. Steve had said, 'Oh, I've got this fast idea; I wonder if you've got anything to go with this?' And we worked on it together. I had these lyrics that I'd been working on based around paranoia. They say that if people are after you, then you're not really paranoid. If everybody is out to get you, then you're not paranoid. That's what the lyric is about. And I said, 'Well, let's try this,' and that was it; it turned into 'Futureal.' And it came out fantastic and was a set opener. Live it's just great. When I include it in my own set, it's so much fun to do."

Indeed, Blaze included a rendition of "Futureal" on his solo live album, *As Live as It Gets* from 2003, the record also including Blaze and his band rocking their way through "Sign of the Cross," "Virus," and "When Two Worlds Collide." Steve is the one who ties the sparse lyric to modern technology, claiming that it's about being trapped in a state of virtual reality. Truth is, the lyric can be read both ways, due to its minimal and inscrutable wording.

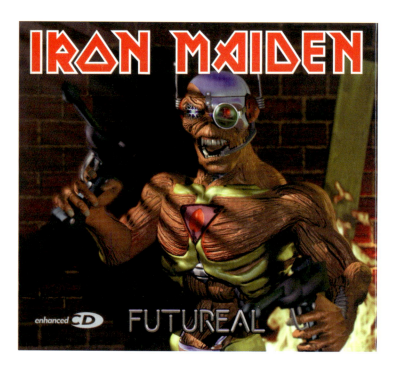

Dave Wright archive

Noted Dave at the time on the subject of lyrical inspiration, "We always try to stretch ourselves and try to push ourselves musically. We may go to Turkey and get inspired there. There's still is a lot of ground to cover. We can also go back and try old stuff again. Like the sci-fi stuff or even some political things. You can actually revisit some of that and expand on it. There is a lot of life in those songs. It's not just getting up onstage, drinking and singing about my baby. That's all good, but we like to go a little bit deeper. So, when the fans read the lyrics, it's kind of like reading a story. They may actually learn something from it."

And yet, Dave knows as well that Maiden is conservative. "I think every band has their own way of doing things, but with Maiden, you know what to expect. There is this deep-rooted style that has been written in concrete and carved into stone. Fans know the identity of the band, and they know what they're going to get. Bands that change their sound drastically still draw the crowds, so maybe it takes the fans a little bit of time to get their heads around the new music. Kind of like the Monty Python saying, 'And now for something completely different.'"

"The Angel and the Gambler" is the subject of a famous row between Steve and Rod, Steve winning the argument to make the song the first single from the record, against Rod's wishes. The production video for the track has so much going on that one comes away fully entertained and also distracted away from the song's pedestrian nature.

Indeed, "The Angel and the Gambler" attracted a fair bit of stick for its piercing simple keyboard part, along with a chorus repeated too many times, although it's a bit of a grower, especially with its bonus southerny prechorus. But the space alien video is fun stuff. It's amusing to poke at, given how far computer animation has come since, but all told there's lots to hold interest. The band is cheery and energetic in their faux-live footage, and there's a story line akin to the "Stranger in a Strange Land" single sleeve / *Somewhere in Time* narrative with Blaze in a long coat bellying up to a cyber bar. Thankfully, so as not to wear us out with sugary visual confection, the short version of the song is used for the video clip.

Remarked Steve, "'The Angel and the Gambler,' when I came up with that song idea, I put it on a mini tape recorder while I was driving down the motorway, the M4 to Wales, and I distinctly remember saying to myself, 'This reminds me of the Who meets UFO.' So, I just took it in that direction. It has a real 1970s feel to it rhythm-wise.

"It's like a love/hate thing, really," continued Steve, on the subject of wearing the producer hat for the record. "I do enjoy it, but it's a lot of hard work. I suppose I kind of coproduced the earlier albums and arranged the songs. In a way, I'm very glad I worked with Martin Birch on the previous albums because I learned a lot from it. I also mixed the two live albums, *A Real Live One* and *A Real Dead One*, because Martin decided to leave. So, I had to hire an engineer, and fortunately I had some experience in the studio."

But of course, Steve is most known as a legendary bassist. "I do get a lot of people saying that I've influenced them, which obviously is very flattering. But the truth is, I'm really more interested in trying to write great songs. Maybe it's because I'm a bass player and I write a lot of the music. I grew up listening to a lot of different bass players like Chris Squire and John Entwistle. Also, Martin Turner from Wishbone Ash and Rinus Gerritsen from Golden Earring were both a very big influence on me. If you listen to some early Golden Earring records, you can really hear the influence!"

As for the single sleeve used for "The Angel and the Gambler," well, the cheapness theme is maintained, with a thrown-together collage of plastic Eddie parts, dice, and

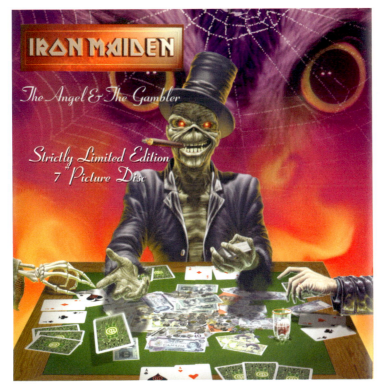

Dave Wright archive

gaudy logo text. Besides the aforementioned CD single versions (Maiden including video for the first time), the 7-inch kept it simple, with a live version of "Blood on the World's Hands" from the previous album as the flip.

Next, one of Blaze's favorite vocal performances with Maiden is on "Lightning Strikes Twice," with Bayley saying that "my voice is really powerful there." Dave Murray gets his first credit on a Blaze-era album, following up a second and last on "When Two Worlds Collide." Says Bayley, "Dave Murray is an absolute diamond, a fantastic guitar player of the highest caliber, an incredible blues player. He's got such a sense for the blues. What we do sometimes in rehearsals is when we're warming up, we just jam through a blues—Nicko, Dave, and I. We just have a great time. But he's a really warm, genuine person.

"Janick's a great player too," continues Blaze, asked for his impression of the rest of the guys, "and great sense of humor, really, really good fun. Steve, he's really good fun as well. He's really focused on the band. The reason I think Steve and I get on so well is that it's all about not compromising the music or the artwork or anything to do with the band, putting in that effort. And he doesn't like fancy food. If we're traveling business, he'll ask what's on the menu in economy."

"Lightning Strikes Twice" has a number of different phases, but the verse riff is in a distinctive, hard-hitting 3/4 format, after a 3/4 intro, after an initial 3/4 verse without full band. Most of the song, however, is a groovy, up-tempo 4/4 almost jam, part chorus, part solo section. In fact, once this cranks up, the band never return to the intro verse structure. Amusingly, Steve calls this a song of optimism and hope, but other than the "maybe lightning strikes twice" sentiment, it's all storm clouds.

Next is "The Clansman," which is probably the most famed song from the Blaze era, exemplified by it being firmly embraced by the band after Bruce came back. The song is typical long-form Maiden, and a galloper. Keyboards, played by Steve, are fairly prominent, but mainly as a wash, a texture—Harris says he was looking for an orchestral effect, which is also the case with "Don't Look to the Eyes of a Stranger."

Notes Blaze, "We used mostly keyboards to do those strings sounds. We just thought, you know, as a sort of embellishment, as a bit of backing, really. Steve was producing the album, and in places he thought this is a good place to use keyboards to produce certain sounds. There's some flexibility there. Obviously, the main focus is on guitar, bass, drums, and vocals, but you're under the microscope when you're in the studio, really, and sometimes it's good to have different sounds in there.

"It says a lot and it's a very complete song," reflects Blaze further on "The Clansman," "from the early parts of the song where I think it does create the mood of someone who is feeling pretty desolate and alone and wondering what to do with their lives. I really think it captures the idea of making a decision to fight and stuff like that."

The 1998 *Maiden Hell!* Bruce-era promo sampler. *Martin Popoff archive*

The theme here, of course, is all William Wallace and *Braveheart* and Scottish history, with the climactic moment being those repeated calls for "Freedom!" At nine minutes, there's time for the mood-setting mellow intro (with clean guitar) and then reflective respites along the way.

"I have an affinity with that song," continues Blaze, "because it's about freedom and it's about independence, and I feel when I'm singing that song that, partly, it's my story as well. I've been in these situations where I've been on different labels, I've made huge sacrifices, I've failed many, many times. I've had to start from nothing three times over. And to stand on the stage singing loud and proud, 'Freedom!,' and to be free and to be independent, is something very special for me. So, I often include that song in the set, and I really enjoy doing it."

As Blaze told Jimmy Kay, "I remember Steve Harris coming into the studio with a bit of paper, and he said, 'What do you think of this idea?' And he just sang it to me, very quiet, and played it very quiet. And I said, amazing, absolutely, that's fantastic. And that was 'The Clansman.' It went from just that little acoustic thing and a bit of an idea to where we rehearsed it all together. There was a real magic about it. Because of the subject of the song... you know, there were a lot of things against Maiden at that time. A lot of promoters had lost confidence, CD sales were down at that time. And to be singing that song, and the spirit of that song being about freedom and holding on and knuckling down, not changing direction, not doing anything like that, really staying true to yourself—that was really special. And you could never predict the impact of that song live. It was just fantastic."

Moving on, "'When Two Worlds Collide,' I had the opportunity to work with Dave Murray," says Blaze. "We started working on the idea, got it to where it was pretty good, then we took it along to Steve and then finished it off with him, which was great."

On the subject of lyric writing in general, Bayley told me, "I keep writing all the time. When I'm on tour, if I get any flashes of inspiration, any little ideas, or if I see something interesting in the news or there's something happening in science that gets me, or a really cool movie I like about an interesting subject, I'll jot those ideas down. There are quite a few ideas I didn't get to use on this album, I'm sure subjects I'll be looking at for the next record. But I like 'Two Worlds Collide' because of writing with Dave, and I like the subject of that as well, a meteor or something like that colliding with the earth, wiping out humanity like it did the dinosaurs. Will anybody survive? What kind of pain would you have to endure?" Of note, Steve always saw in this song the idea of the two rock 'n' roll worlds Blaze has operated in; namely, feisty baby band (the hungry wolf) and now besieged Maiden (the buffalo set upon by wolves).

As we've discussed, part of the growing impatience with Maiden songs is the repeated use of mellow intros, and often played mostly on bass. "The Educated Fool" gives us yet another of these. As well, if and when fans complained about Blaze on record, it was always easier to point to songs like these where he's singing at the low end of his range. So first off, too far up high and he has a problem—this is where the main complaints came: in a live situation where he had to do Bruce songs. But on "The Educated Fool," he's forced into that zone where he's barely pushing air. It's the part of the range usually given to Keith Richards or Joe Perry—or Nicky Wire in the Manic Street Preachers, for that matter—when you are trying not to ask too much of the second banana. Bottom line: Blaze has a really interesting voice, with some barrel-chested richness, but he's best exerting himself, and in the proximity of the top of his own range, not Bruce's.

Remarks Bayley, "You've got the start of 'Educated Fool,' which has a real swing to it, almost like a waltz kind of tempo. It's such an unusual rhythm, but it's great fun to sing something like that. But the lyrics are pretty dark. I'm so lucky as a vocalist. I'm unlimited in what I can do with Maiden, given the styles of the songs. You can encompass just about everything."

"Don't Look to the Eyes of a Stranger" is ponderous and proggy but also rife with pickup parts. As Dave told George Koroneos, "'Eyes of a Stranger' was a big production, and songs like 'Clansman' incorporated a lot of little things as well, like a track for chimes here and there. We used a lot of computer technology on this album. With virtual tracks, you can have as many tracks as you'd like to play with. We used that to try to bring the sound of Maiden into the new millennium and to get the album sounding really modern. We laid the drum tracks down, but this time we kept a lot of the original stuff with guitar and bass because they felt really good with the track. We used a lot of keyboards, and the rest was the same except we have thousands of tracks available."

Keyboard padding is prominent, and the chorus (basically the title) is hammered out too many times. Late in the sequence there's double-time jamming, powerless upon plonky bass. If there's a positive, like so many songs across *Virtual XI*, there's tasty guitar soloing, much to entertain the student of this corner or crease of a composition. The song's ridiculously punctuated ending may as well be called a microcosm of, or metaphor for, everything that's wrong with *Virtual XI*: lousy ideas.

Commendably, at the lyric end, despite the title, Steve is not playing the streetwise snob about academics. Rather, he's reflecting on his own life and lamenting that the older and wiser he's supposed to be, the less he feels he knows the answers as to what really matters. If Bruce left because the lyrics were too removed from reality, he'd definitely raise an eyebrow now about how introspective and honest about his failings Steve has become in print with Bruce away.

Virtual XI closes on a strong note with somber ballad "Como Estais Amigos," Blaze explaining to *Kerrang!*'s Paul Elliott that "I was in Buenos Aires, and I saw the memorial for the soldiers who died in the Falklands War. It seemed unreal. How could you possibly have a war with these people? They're so generous. It just reminded me that it's politicians who start wars, not ordinary people. I found it very moving. If I wasn't in a band, I can't imagine how I would've had the opportunity to be in Argentina to look at that memorial. A guy I went to school with died in that war too. It's not a political song. It's about me and my feelings. It's about people."

Back to the discussion about Blaze's singing, here he's in his element, sonorous, weighty, and operatic like Messiah Marcolin in Candlemass and Memento Mori. It is on performances like this that Blaze matches and arguably exceeds Bruce, not only in material voice but perhaps even feeling, soul, decisions pertaining to what he does with his voice. Again, one need only look to the rock-solid Blaze solo catalog to see what a fine singer Blaze is, given the chance.

And that's the end of the record, which is pretty interesting because, as mentioned by Dave, there are only eight songs, the fewest of any Maiden album, granted clocking in a fairly robust fifty-three minutes. Says Bayley, "We had lots of ideas, and we couldn't fit them all on it. But what we did was just record eight, so we have nothing in the vaults. We have live tracks for B-sides. We just thought we'd get these songs together because we thought they'd make the best record." So yes, there's not even any Japanese bonus tracks, let alone CD single or EP oddities.

Sales of *Virtual XI* through the first seven years of release, more than its effective life cycle, sat at 65,243 copies, making it the worst-selling Iron Maiden album of all time. Part of the fault falls to the flat writing, but we mustn't forget that metal in general was in the doldrums.

Reviews were mostly negative too, which rankled Steve. "We've always been made to feel like outsiders," groused Harris, speaking with Paul Elliott. "And it still feels like it's us against the world. I suppose at times you feel like you're up against everything. Every time we do an album, we have to prove ourselves again. But in a weird way, that works for you, because you fight even harder to show people you can still cut it. It gives you an edge. It's funny. You don't tend to remember the good reviews, but the bad ones you do. It's the bad ones that fire you up and make you think, 'Fuck 'em, we'll show 'em.' It gives you a bit of an attitude again. It's a challenge. Luckily enough, we never have to worry about the media too much because we have a hard-core following behind us. It's not as big a following as we had in the mid-1980s, but the fans have always made up their own minds, rather than believe everything they read about us."

He then relates a story about a visit to the *Kerrang!* offices just after the previous album, *The X Factor*, had gotten a duff notice in the magazine. "When I came in, I was really wound up. I just spent a year of my life working silly hours doing this album—which I still love, and I don't give a fuck what anyone says—and some wanker has completely dismissed it in one sentence. I feel like he was having a joke at our expense. Another time I might've laughed at it, but I thought it was out of order. I wanted to see if he'd say it to my face. He could've been built like a brick shithouse and beat me to a pulp, but I had to have a word. It just ain't right.

"You know me, that ain't my style. I felt bad afterwards. I thought, fuck, I'm glad he wasn't there, because I probably would have fucking whacked him or at least got him against a wall or done something stupid. And that gets you nowhere. I'm not a violent person, but I was wound up. I'd been through a divorce as well. I was going through hell anyway. But I've got to be honest, it still annoys you. Constructive criticism's okay. It's just when it gets personal, you feel like giving them a slap, but you can't."

"I don't know; I think over a million copies," answered Blaze at the time, when I asked what he thought worldwide sales had gotten to of the first one, *The X Factor*. "It sold better than what people expected; that's what I'll say. Because at the start of that record, people were saying, well, isn't metal dead? Because grunge came along. So I kept saying, well, from where I'm standing, in the center of this stage, playing in front of thousands of people every night, well, no it's not. The number of albums that I'm signing when we're doing these things and the fans that are hanging around, it's not dead, now that metal is the alternative to alternative.

"You know, bands like Maiden, they've just become one of the world's biggest cult bands. We went through that whole thing, we had great reaction—especially in Canada, the response was just fantastic—and we'd come out the other side of it and made what we all think is a great record, really positive, right? And even already in the first few weeks, *Virtual XI*'s almost outsold *The X Factor* worldwide. Plus, we're in the charts all over Europe, the album and a single, and that just adds to it; people really are interested in this music. And we're planning a great big tour in the US, probably called Metal Mania, and coming up to Canada as well. You'll probably find out before me what other bands are included. Me, I'm just in the band. They stamp my passport, put me on a tour bus, and point me to the stage—that's about it."

Chapter 16

Summing up years later (and contradicting himself), Blaze admitted, "I think *The X Factor* is my favorite. I love both albums. They're very special because of the time we worked on them and the songs we wrote together. But I think *The X Factor* is my favorite just because we spent more time rehearsing, writing, living with the songs. On *Virtual XI* we didn't quite have so much time to spend on the writing as perhaps we would have liked. So, I thought perhaps there were a couple of things that maybe got rushed. But there are a couple of great songs on *The X Factor*; it's one of those that is a real grower."

"I enjoy them; I think they're fine," says Janick, asked for his take on the two Blaze records. "I enjoy them for what they were. Bruce did not want to do it anymore. So, it was a question of not carrying on. I had worked with him in a solo capacity, and I worked with him on two Maiden albums, and then he decided to leave, which was a shock to me. And then we got together, and it was a question of, well, what are we going to do? We tried every singer out that we could, but nobody matched what we wanted. And when Blaze came in, he gave 120 percent; he gave more than he had had, and with a very different voice from Bruce. And he was very professional in his attitude. We went out and did some great gigs, and we did some very good albums. But over the tours, he tried to sing Bruce's songs and it was very hard, because Bruce has a higher voice. And eventually that hurt his voice and now he's gone on to do solo stuff, and I wish him all the best and I hope he does very well."

Before we lose Blaze, however, there's gigging that got done. April 26 through May 30, 1998, the *Virtual XI* tour moves through Europe, with Helloween and Dirty Deeds as support. June 26 through August 4, the band hit the US, with support coming from

SDSU Open Air Theatre, San Diego, California, August 4, 1998. © *Tom Wallace*

Dio, W.A.S.P., and Dirty Deeds on this Metal Mania '98 package Blaze alluded to. A number of late July and early August dates had to be canceled due to Blaze's "pollen allergies," later understood to be problems with his voice crapping out. Despite the presence of Dio on the bill, arguably worthy of being coheadliner, the venues were small, reflecting the reduced fortunes of the band in the Blaze era and, again, metal's standing in the wider world of rock as a whole.

As Dave told Koroneos, "There are a lot of people—a lot of critics out there—that are claiming that rock is dead, but on this tour, we have been playing to a lot of people. We've had shows with like 8,000 people, and it's been a really healthy turnout. On the last tour, we were testing the waters because the whole metal scene had taken a really big dive. We wanted to tour America, but the promoters weren't interested in doing bigger venues. We went on a club tour—except for LA, New York, and Chicago, where we played theaters—which was just an introduction of Blaze Bayley to the American public, and that went really well. This time around, we felt that we could justify playing bigger venues, and we had the belief that if you build it, the fans will come. They did and they have.

"There's a new generation of fans out there," continues Murray. "We get a few fans from the 1980s, and they tend to stand in the back, but you get the young kids up in the front. The reaction is the same—they're really into the music and sing all the lyrics. We have a special interaction between the band and the audience. You can put us in a small club or you can put us in a stadium, and we're still going to enjoy ourselves. You have to get that across to the audience so they're out there responding to that with their fists in the air and just let go. The music moves you, and you can absorb it, and it's been working really good that way."

Asked by George if he misses playing stadium shows, Dave says, "We are doing a couple of them on this tour, but it's basically, 'If you can fill them, we'll then do them.' We prefer playing packed-out theaters than playing to half-empty arenas. I look back at those times, in the mid-1980s when the band would play 20,000-seat arenas every night, but that was the peak of our band's career. To continue, you sometimes have to take a step back to walk forward. However, we still try to make every gig an event, something special.

"We are now part of CMC/BMG in America," continues Dave—both Maiden and Bruce were with the classic-rock-loving upstart derisively called Cheese Metal Cemetery. "But we are still on EMI in the rest of the world. BMG has been a very supportive label for the band, and they've got a lot of other great bands from Deep Purple to Yes to Motörhead. They are a very good label, and the album is in stores. BMG is much more of a family label, and they pay attention to the bands, promote the bands. We've got a good relationship, and they are a great bunch of guys.

"If it were all to end tomorrow, I would feel very satisfied with everything I've accomplished personally," muses Dave. "I've been very happy, and it's been a very rewarding career. So, if I were to die tomorrow, I'd just go, 'Hey, it's been brilliant.' When you make an album and you go on tour with it and you take a year off, you have time to recharge, and everything becomes fresh and new again. There is always more to do. We've got more ground to cover, but the main thing is the fans. As long as they are buying the albums and coming to the gigs, we are going to keep on rolling. And as long as the fans are still around, we will keep doing what we love doing.

"There are a lot of bands still around—Sabbath; Emerson, Lake & Palmer; Yes—all those guys are still out there doing their thing, and they are doing it for the love of it. I don't think it's a monetary thing. There is this adrenaline rush that comes from going onstage in front of all those people. It's something that boxers can relate to. George Foreman is in his fifties and he's still fighting. It's the whole buildup of going out there and playing in front of adoring fans. It's an intangible feeling."

Similarly reflective about where the band found themselves at the time, Steve figured, "All I can say is that we are very lucky. We're still very strong in most countries all over the world. If our popularity in one country goes down a bit, it goes up in another country, so we're not relying on one country in particular to keep up our popularity. Whereas some bands rely heavily on success in Japan, we're not in that position, fortunately. Our last album sold well over a million copies worldwide, but a lot of people here in the States thought we'd just vanished. That's why touring for us is very important. And we don't really make money touring—we pretty much break even.

"To be honest, there were a couple of times it came across my mind," admitted Harris, asked by Bob Nalbandian if he ever thought of hanging it up. "But it'd only last a few hours before I'd realize that I didn't really mean it. I think it has more to do with your frame of mind and what's going on around you rather than what's actually happening with the band. I just love it too much to ever want to give it up!"

SDSU Open Air Theatre, San Diego, California, August 4, 1998. © *Tom Wallace*

"He's fitted in great," remarked Nicko, gamely plumping for Blaze in conversation with *Hard Roxx*'s Alan Holloway. "He's got such a fiery personality towards the whole entity of Maiden, which is a great deal of being in this band. You've got to live it; it's not just a job. He's very focused. It still takes me a little bit of getting used to even today when we play the older stuff. The songs that we do now that Bruce would sing, it's as though we've written them with Blaze. Not the arrangement, but in the actual phrasing of the notes. Blaze doesn't have the high voice. He's quite baritone, and I find it hard sometimes because I expect to hear a certain note ascending rather than descending. But he has fitted in really well, and he has brought some great songs into the band and a lot of energy."

Commenting on the two Blaze records, he says, "I think they are very strong. The last album was very reminiscent to me of the *Somewhere in Time* era. There were a lot of epic songs on there with dark content. The new one, *Virtual XI*, is probably one of the most simple albums in terms of content that I've ever made with Iron Maiden. I don't think there is anything you can compare *Virtual XI* to. It's most definitely the straightest album Iron Maiden have ever made."

Asked about any sort of extraneous plans, McBrain divulges, "Not right now, no. Sure, I have an ambition one day to do a solo album and go on tour with my own project, but right now I don't have to do that. I'm fulfilled with Iron Maiden. I am a lot older than I was fifteen years ago, but it is still a challenge, as it was when I first joined the band. It's my life, and I'm very comfortable with being in this band. When somebody turns around and says, 'I want to do a solo album' . . . as soon as somebody mentions a fucking solo album, they are not happy. Not fulfilling what they really want to do. What they should be doing is fulfilling the role in the band."

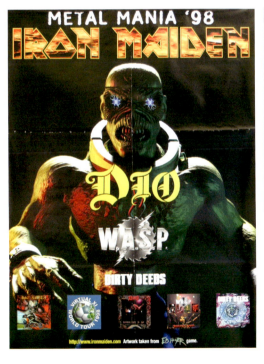

A couple of tour posters. *Dave Wright archive*

CHAPTER 16

Three weeks before the tour began, the heavy metal world was rocked by the car accident death of Cozy Powell. "I knew Cozy pretty well," says Nicko. "We were road mates as we didn't keep in touch when we weren't working. When we'd run into each other on the road, we would have a bit of a laugh and a drink. I was very, very sad when I heard about the accident. We have lost another great. And I suppose there are not very many of us heavy players left now."

On August 7 and 9, Maiden played two shows in Mexico, with Janick remarking to *Hard Roxx*'s Matthew Honey, "As a person, you grow, and your opinions change on certain things. In this band, you go on tour, and you travel around the world, and it *is* around the world. You go to South America, Moscow, and find yourself standing in the Kremlin or end up doing PR in Seoul or Mexico. You meet so many different people and you kind of suck it all in, and a year later you regurgitate it because it is organic, and you grow with it. It doesn't mean you're going to become a Mexican band, but you will have feelings that will come out based on what you have done in the last year. But we are not going to turn into a Mexican band, are we Dave? Arriba, arriba arriba!

"I cannot understand this 'rock is dead' attitude," continued Janick. "When I started in 1970, listening to rock music and playing it, people told me it was old-fashioned music and Deep Purple and Led Zeppelin got totally slagged off—even Led Zeppelin *IV* got slagged off. Then it's 1979 and the New Wave of British Heavy Metal, and within a year even *that* was supposed to have been dead. I was with Gillan at the time, and we played Donington. Rock was dead and there were 50,000–60,000 people there. In 1992 we played Donington with Iron Maiden, and they said rock was dead there in 1988 and there were 100,000 people there. It's 1998, and people are saying the same stuff—'It's old-fashioned, it's finished, guitar music is done'—and we're still doing it.

"I think that if you stick to your guns and do what you believe in, you will be successful. We're a cult band and I love that. That is all I ever wanted when I first started listening to music. Wherever Maiden go, they have this cult feel about them. I think it's because of Eddie being on all the covers. I think rock is meant to be like that. It's not meant to be like the Bon Jovi thing where you break through and can iron to it on Radio One. I'm not knocking that as long as they believe in what they do. The Spice Girls—God bless them."

On the subject of staying on the straight and narrow when playing live, Janick told Matthew that "we are all very down to earth and have our act together and are very conscientious about the concerts. I have been the kid who has saved up all his money to go and see a band—and it does cost a lot of money—and they come on, have an argument, get pissed, and fall about the stage, and you just feel ripped off. So, I am aware that when we come on, you have to give everything, and that gig is an important gig. I don't go on drunk, and I know Dave doesn't. You can party after it. If you go and tour for six months, you cannot party every night. I have never needed drugs to play. I've never needed anything. I just won't do it. I have been in bands with the guy who's said, 'I cannot go on without my two bottles of wine or a sniff of this.' When I first started playing, when I was 15, everybody was doing it, and I said no. If I'm going to do it, I am going to do it straight. And I've kept to that. I think I was pissed once on a New Year's Eve and that feeling of not being in control, I went to play a riff and I was doing it but it was not my hands. I thought I don't like this. I drank a lot afterwards, though."

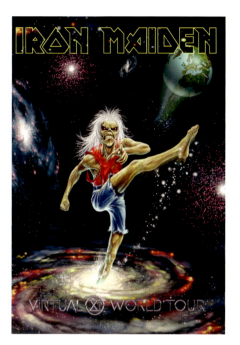

Booklet for the world tour. *Dave Wright archive*

September 4 through October 15, 1998, the *Virtual XI* tour returns to Europe, again with the same support acts, Helloween and Dirty Deeds. On September 28, "Futureal" is launched as a single, and then from October 17 through 26, the band performs eight UK shows in the UK, with Dirty Deeds providing continued support.

The fall of 1998 also marked a major remaster program for Maiden, with Dave commenting that "I just heard yesterday, or the day before, that every one of our albums has gone Top 40 in the UK—every one of them. That says something there. This is reaching out to the old fans. They'll probably say, 'Let's get these remasters. They've got all this info and other stuff.' Plus, you've got new fans as well that are just logging on. All you can do, really, is go by your gut feeling and release stuff that you feel truly justifies the band. I mean, a lot of effort has gone into this. There's lots of new stuff on the CDs. We don't feel like we'll be ripping the kids off or anything like that."

A plastic "Ed Head" was issued on December 7. This was a molded Eddie head that pivoted open to reveal the 12 albums along with an *In Profile* interview disc. Eddie's eyes lit up red. The package came with a certificate of authenticity and was issued in a numbered limited edition of 25,000.

November 18 through 22, The *Virtual XI* tour hits Japan, while from December 2 through 12, with Helloween and local act Raimundos, Maiden play South America, with the concluding Monsters of Rock show on December 12 in Buenos Aires being Blaze's last show with the band.

Into 1999, at 6:00 p.m. on February 10 at the band's website, it is announced that Adrian Smith and Bruce Dickinson have rejoined Iron Maiden.

"We all got together at Rod's house, which is in Brighton, the south coast of England," explained Bruce, in our mag here in Canada, *Brave Words & Bloody Knuckles*. "I've been bumping into the guys in the band for the last six years, socially anyhow. Janick and I have always been best friends, but none of us have ever spoke about a reunion, because we always thought it was off-limits basically. Because they had their career and were doing great; I had my career and was very happy with that. At some point, obviously, they had made the decision that Blaze was going to, you know, leave, and I don't know anything about that, or the circumstances or anything at all. Nor do I really wish to know; it's none of my business.

"Rod called me and said, 'Look, how do you feel about getting back together?' And I said, 'Well, let's all meet up and talk about it.' I had always indicated that getting together and doing something live would just be a blast, and then I'd always said that I'd think about anything further in the light of people's commitment of doing things in terms of making records. See how we would work together and stuff like that. When we had the meetings, I was just knocked out over how far people wanted to just go balls out to get a great producer, get a great sound, and just put Maiden back as the best heavy metal band in the world, bar none.

"I feel very grateful," continues Dickinson, "but a lot of it had to do with the fact that myself and Adrian and Roy were making terrific records. That has an awful lot to do with it. Also, so many fans have stuck by Maiden as well over the period. Obviously, we share a lot of those fans. I'm not stopping doing solo records. Nor does anyone in Maiden now want me to stop doing solo records. But my solo career, in terms of live performance, was never going to attain the same kind of numbers and arena status and everything else that Maiden did. That was just kind of common sense.

Dave Wright archive

"But that's just the way it is, unfortunately. I guess if I plugged away at it for another five years, I could build up as a kind of theater circuit, you know what I'm saying? But the point is, I can still make interesting solo records and things like that. And I can still tour with the greatest heavy metal band in the world, in my opinion, which is Iron Maiden. And all the more so, because the whole lineup is now complete. In fact, it's more than complete. It's bigger and better than it ever was because we are with three guitarists. We really have the opportunity to do something that people haven't done. I can't remember the last time a band had three guitarists."

Dave Wright archive

In a later chat, Bruce reiterated the point about having gone away and proved himself, fleshing out a point that we all understood but dared not utter. In fact, in the same *BW&BK* piece I *did* utter, writing a sort of open letter to Iron Maiden, making the point that Bruce creatively had just been killing it, while Maiden was busy propping itself with a cane. The awareness here from Dickinson is clear—we know he knows.

"I'm not going into Maiden world with some problem getting my head through doorways," explained Bruce. "I'm not going in there going, 'I did this, and I did that; look how cool my records are.' I'm going in there as a singer to work with everybody and make the best damn Maiden record that I can. And it's very much the same attitude as on the first Maiden record I did. In fact, it's very bizarre; the attitude in the band is closest to *The Number of the Beast*. It's astonishing how similar the vibe is what it was like just before we started writing *Number of the Beast*. It was like, 'Anything goes; everybody will listen to anything from everybody.'

"And that's all I ask, really, is that I'm going to try and be creative and do my best for the Maiden guys. I don't really see any difference in the way I would write. I write a song with the guy I write the song with. I've written with Janick already and it sounds great. There are some songs off of *Accident of Birth* which would fit straight on a Maiden record. And there's one or two songs off of *The Chemical Wedding*, especially like one of the extra tracks, 'Return of the King,' that would fit right on a Maiden record. So, it could very well be that songs of that sort of ilk may appear. Of course, they will sound a lot more like Maiden when Maiden actually record them. I'm not too worried and I'm not trying to second-guess it or be overly concerned about it."

Continued Bruce in the February 1999 chat, "We're going off at the beginning of March, and we're going to be writing together. That will be ongoing through the whole year. By the time we come to record the record, we should have pretty half-decent material. Certainly, there is a big, big determination from everybody that any of the criticisms that got thrown at the last couple of Maiden records will definitely not be thrown at this one. The album will absolutely take no prisoners, and we will do whatever is required to make this one of the greatest Maiden albums ever.

"I think that what you have to say here is that this does not affect my ability to do interesting solo records and stuff like that. But what it does do is create the opportunity for Iron Maiden to come back, firing on more cylinders than it ever had before. Even when I was with the band in the 1980s, the buzz is now much bigger. There are so many bands and so little content these days in music. Generally, that's my impression. And Maiden is one of the last bands that can really cut it. This is not a bunch of sad old gits getting together. This is a very, very potent little unit that we're putting back together here. I don't think there is a band in the world who would like to go on after us.

"There's no intention of this being short-lived, no intention whatsoever," continues Bruce (and as we know, this played out as stated, whereas the continuation of the solo career, not so much—there's been only one additional solo album in the twenty years since these musings).

"When we had our meeting, which I have to say was absolutely fantastic, I had a hangover for three days after," chuckles Bruce. "We went down to the pub and had a great time. We all made a joke about all the things the press have been all over, like the feud between me and Steve. The first thing I said to Steve was that I'm definitely not making a country-and-western album, and we both laughed. This idea of a feud is a load of shit. My only reservation was, let's make sure we do everything right to make the right record, and everybody was unanimous that this was what they wanted to do. There was no question about any compromise whatsoever. That was my question and answer. Steve's only question was 'Hey, you're not going to run away after the tour this summer?' I was like, 'I want to be in this. I want to put the band back together so it can be bigger than it ever was.' When you leave something, obviously, you grit your teeth and say, 'You know, I've left it. And I have to leave it all behind.' There's that element of determination: damn the torpedoes; let's make a gap between the band I was in and my new future and the rest of it. It's just human nature. It's just the way human beings do it.

"But actually, it was like, I walked out of one door and said good night and walked in the next and said good morning. Nothing's changed at all. It's incredible. People said to me . . . when we did the photo session with Ross Halfin, people were wandering around going, 'It seems like these guys have been together forever.' I think the whole thing will take it by storm; I really do. People are not going to believe how many people are going to come out of the woodwork and see this. I'm overwhelmed with the reaction. And all I can say is that my intention—and I'm sure everybody in the band's intention—is not just to live up to expectations but to exceed them."

"Sometimes you have to kick yourself up the ass to do things," pondered an also-returning Adrian, always the calm presence. In that respect he's in line with Dave, really, although Dave adds, as a bonus, a level of "just glad to be here" amusement to his musings.

"You know, I think Bruce and I have both been on a bit of a journey the last few years. I'm so happy I'm back in Maiden, to be honest with you. That doesn't mean it's the end of me doing anything else. It's nice to be back playing with the guys, but we're not married, you know what I mean? We're all our own guys with our own lives. But yes, I'm very proud of the solo albums I've done. I just wish they would have been marketed differently, to be honest with you. And I think sometimes having a whole band is confusing.

"We have the benefit of hindsight," continues Adrian. "I've made five albums since being out of the band, and I played with a lot of different people. There's a lot of things I want to inject into the structure of Maiden. You've got the benefit of experience, but you're young enough to do it. I think there's a niche for us now. It's the turn of the decade, and people

Dave Wright archive

want to listen to something different. There's a kind of freshness to it. And we're pretty confident that we can make a great studio album. That's what it's all about. It's going forward. I've been out of the band eight, nine years, and coming back I've got a fresh perspective on it. New energy, more so than the later years with the band when I was a bit jaded, and I was stuck in the album/tour/album/tour syndrome. We aim to keep the essence of Maiden. We're getting a producer in to try and capture us at our best, which is when we play live. We want to capture that on the album and come up with a bunch of great songs. It's going to be Maiden, but very focused. Capture what it's all about."

"Oh, it was fine," chuckled another Bruce compatriot, Roy Z, on the new circumstance. "Whenever you're working with someone like Bruce or Rob Halford, you're just along for the ride. Just the opportunity to work with musicians of this caliber, it's cool. I wasn't bummed at all. I was really pleased. I was happy for them and the music that was going to come out of it. For about two minutes there was talk of me producing, but it wasn't going to work out because I was too close to Bruce. It wasn't a negative thing; it was more like, 'Hey, that's Bruce's guy.' But I think just having them all back together will really raise the quality. I've just got my head down to the ground. I really like working with metal; I always have. Right now, my friends call me the Resurrector, because I'm going to be getting all the metal bands back together and fueled up and ready to go again. And I'm really glad Bruce wants to keep making records, because as an artist, he can keep fulfilled. Because whenever you're in a band with that many members, it's really difficult to do exactly what you want."

"I left Iron Maiden not by choice," says Blaze. "I was fired. They said it wasn't good enough. And I said, 'Well, is Bruce coming back?' And they said yes. And I think what was happening at the time was the worldwide CD sales had gone down, and EMI had closed all of their manufacturing facilities around the world. The record business was shrinking. Partnerships were starting to call, and record companies were working together in partnerships. Really, I think it was more of a business decision that Bruce came back at the time.

"And yeah, I was just gutted by that. I think it took me about four years, really, before I kind of accepted what had happened. And I think, really, if things had been slightly different, then it would've been very difficult for Bruce to come back. Because the songs that I was working on at the time, the ideas for what I thought would be the third Iron Maiden album, I really thought that that would be it. That third album would really show fans that we were serious, and that this lineup would work. But I didn't get the chance to make that third album."

Our magazine, *Brave Words & Bloody Knuckles*, had received and published a report (February 1999 issue) that at the end, especially in South America, the guys were barely talking to Blaze and were traveling on separate vans. The fans were complaining about Blaze's delivery of the earlier Bruce material, with the band even experimenting with playing only Blaze-era songs. Even Janick said, "I can't take it anymore!"

"It was a question that had come up every year since I left," Bruce told Mick Wall. "Plus me and Adrian were playing together and writing together again, and it wasn't just me they invited back; it was both of us. Finally, Rod took me aside and said, 'How do you feel about putting it back together again?' I said, 'Well, there's a couple of things that concern me, but 90 percent are things that I think are massive opportunities.' The main thing was whether we would in fact be making a real state-of-the-art record and not just a comeback album. In other words, if we were back together, then potentially Iron Maiden is looking at nothing less than being the best heavy metal band in the world again. I really wasn't prepared to compromise on the idea.

"It was strange," continued Bruce, asked by Mick about seeing Steve again. "I think we were both a bit nervous. But as soon as we walked in the room, we gave each other a big hug and it all evaporated. Literally. Like 'Boof!' Gone. And we both just chatted away. He said, 'I'm still not sure exactly why you left.' He said it a couple of times, and then he said, 'But that doesn't matter to me now.' And I went, 'Oh, but it *does* matter!' And so, I told him like, 'This is why I left.' I can't remember exactly what I said, but at the end, I said, 'Does that make any sense?' And he went, 'Well, yeah.' I thought, okay, well, then that's all right then. And then of course we all ended up going down the pub. One thing led to another, and we all woke up with thick heads the next day.

"It certainly wasn't anything to do with money," continues Bruce. "If money was the only motivation, we'd probably all have retired years ago. It's not about the money for Maiden at this point. It's about living the dream again. Steve didn't want to see this as some sort of comeback, either. To him this was like just the next step in Iron Maiden. And that's exactly how it should be. How it is."

To be sure, it wasn't *only* about the money, but money would have played a significant part. As did fame and ego. Giddy excitement about creative heights to be conquered . . . not so much. Bruce would have been rightly wary about the band's potential, given the classy music he had been crafting with mere minor leaguers, and given how across two records, Steve was proving himself stuck with rules-laden, old-maid Maiden music of diminishing returns. No, this was substantially both about money and missing the limelight.

On February 20, 1999, Global Entertainment Corp completes the sale of $30 million in securitized bonds for Iron Maiden, secured by cash flow from future album royalties. The bonds are sold to a single institutional investor. On more of a headbanging note, on May 18, Anthrax side project Stormtroopers of Death issue their *Bigger Than the Devil* album, the front cover of which is a parody of *The Number of the Beast*. Anthrax had toured extensively with Maiden both in Europe and North America, back in 1990 and 1991. Paul Di'Anno is staying out of trouble as well, issuing *Beyond the Maiden: The Best of*, as well as *The Masters*.

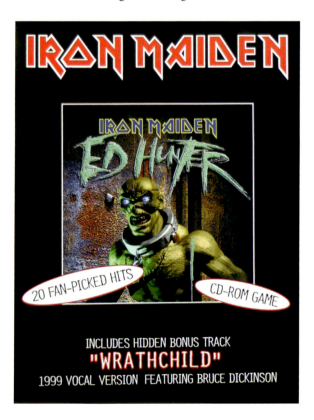

Dave Wright archive

In May 1999, the band issues their first video game, *Ed Hunter*, in two-CD form with compilation album. The game is instantly deemed underwhelming, but it and the hits pack, and all the buzz about Bruce, have set the band up well for what was to come. Which was... early July, Maiden set up shop in Saint John, New Brunswick, to rehearse for their upcoming *Ed Hunter* tour dates.

Asked by Bob Nalbandian about *Ed Hunter*, in the works before he was gone, Blaze told him that "Iron Maiden was planning on doing a video game for a long time, but with this band, we always want everything to be the best quality and the best representation we can have for our fans. The technology didn't really exist to do justice for an Iron Maiden fan until now. We were approached by a company in England, and they had a few ideas, and a couple of the guys who were working there were actually huge fans of the band, so they had a really good handle straightaway of what an Iron Maiden game should be about, featuring Eddie. We had some meetings with them, and I had a real strong idea for the story where each album cover is a level of the game.

"So, the first couple albums is in the streets, which we turned into a whole virtual environment so you can walk around the streets and encounter all the different characters. And the *Powerslave* cover we turned into a whole 3-D environment where you can walk into the pyramids, and you also get to go into the future and enter the torture chamber on *The X Factor*. The album covers are brought to life into a 3-D environment, and Eddie is a 100,000-hologram character, which is more than the T-Rex in *Jurassic Park*. The game is titled *Ed Hunter* because you're hunting down Eddie. The idea is the heads of the five members of the band have been chopped off, and you gotta go and find them! [laughs]. At the same time, you're trying to survive Eddie, because he's trying to stop you from getting to the next level."

Added Steve, "The idea is to make Eddie weaker, basically, because you can't really kill him; you can just make him weaker. It's brilliant, really. I mean, I would buy it just for the graphics alone. It's like actually walking into the album cover and wandering about!"

As Dave told George Koroneos, "In the game, *Ed Hunter*, you are going to be chasing Eddie throughout time and space, kind of like *Doom*, except each of the Iron Maiden

A couple of publicity photos for the game. *Dave Wright archive*

albums are going to be three-dimensional levels. Take an album like *Somewhere in Time*, and you're running after Eddie in a futuristic world with all these space-age cars. With *Powerslave*, you're going back to Egyptian times, and there will be pyramids everywhere and a ton of sand. The first level, you're running through the back alleys and subways of England chasing after Eddie and follow him through each level until you get to *Virtual XI*. I gather there is one level where you will have to put 3-D glasses on to play. There is also going to be instrumental Maiden music throughout the game and will tie the level in with that particular album. Check it out on PC and Playstation."

July 11 through August 8, Maiden—now with Bruce and Adrian—take the *Ed Hunter* tour to North America. Support for the opening Canadian dates comes from Voivod, followed by Clutch and Monster Magnet, with select concluding shows featuring nu metalers System of a Down and Puya as support. Three July shows would go on despite Adrian's absence to attend his father's funeral. Later on, three shows saw cancellation due to Dave breaking a finger.

As Janick told David Lee Wilson at the time, asked about touring a video game, "I don't think that it's been done before, but we will tour on anything! We love touring. It just gives us an excuse to go out on tour. And since we have this band together, it's great to get out on tour rather than to record straightaway. It gets the band all bedded in and confident, especially with the three-guitar thing. I just think that it was a great idea, and I love playing live so it gets me out playing. The last tour that we did, we went out in January, and we finished in December, at the end of the year, so we did a full year and took a little bit of time off and that is when this thing happened, and we decided it would be great to get out there and tour again. To me, this is what this band is about. The prerequisite of Iron Maiden is to have a touring band. That is the exciting thing."

Janick was looking forward to an Iron Maiden that for the first time would feature three guitarists—himself, Dave, and Adrian. When Lee points out that the songs thus far had been written in a two-guitar configuration, he says, "That is true. But every album there is a lot of guitars that are overdubbed. A lot of higher octaves, lower octaves, harmonies sometimes, even three-part harmonies. Sometimes with harmonies, there is a guitar underlying everything, and when you play live you have to decide which ones you are going to use and which ones you are not going to use, and sometimes you have to leave quite a bit out. From that respect, we try to do a lot of things from the album that normally would have to be left out."

Which is a great point: now moving forward, two guitars would be able to execute the harmony, and one guitar could provide the crunch of the underlying riff, the stacked power chords. Thundering under would be Steve and Nicko, who previously had to carry the load alone any time the guys wanted to fire off a twin lead.

Continues Janick, "Also, we have added a lot more to it. On some of the songs we have detuned down to D on one guitar, so it is the Maiden sound with a down-tuned D underneath it, and it adds fatness to it. They are only subtle changes, and only to make the band sound bigger and louder. On some of them we are doing three-part harmonies, and there are some solos where we are doing joint solos. So it's kind of like what we would call in the studio an ADT, where you would have one solo on one side and another solo on the other side. And sometimes it's only a millisecond behind, and it's kind of like double-tracking. So, we have done a bit of that.

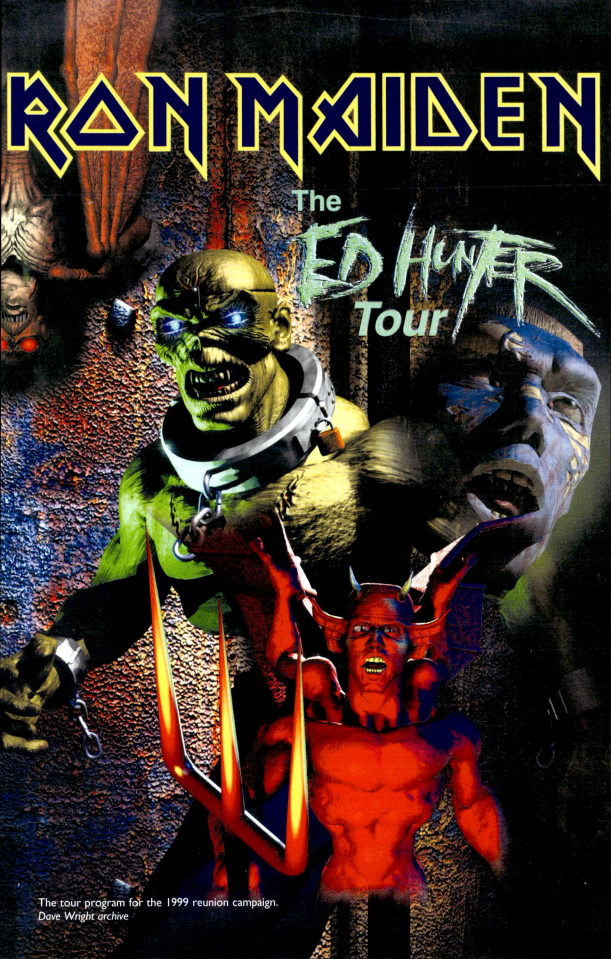

The tour program for the 1999 reunion campaign.
Dave Wright archive

CHAPTER 16

"It has been very creative, what we have done. We got together on a couple of days and went through every song and said, 'How can we improve this song as opposed to just sticking another guitar on it?' I think that the maturity of each of us and the musical ability of each of us means that we don't have to get everything all equal and become all excited about who is going to get the solos and stuff. We can use the best bit of what we have in the songs, and the songs sound better.

"Offstage, I can't tell you [what it sounds like] because I am not out there, but onstage I can hear everything. I can hear all three different guitars and all the different stuff. I can hear the three-part harmonies and all the underneath stuff, and that is exactly what we wanted to do. The only other band that really does that is Lynyrd Skynyrd, but that is more of a country rock band. I have never heard a band this heavy do it. I think we have enough themes and threads going through the tunes where we can have that guitar and really feel that we have made the band heavier and more colorful."

Commenting on the set list for the tour, Janick explains that "the songs that were chosen were from the poll that we put on the internet. The kids chose twenty songs that particular week, and we put them on *Ed Hunter*, and when we decided to tour, we thought that the first argument or the first problem that we are going to have is 'Who is picking the songs?' So, we decided that we would do the *Ed Hunter* set. We leave off one or two and change it around a little bit, but that was it! One argument straight out the window. Solos are worked out amongst ourselves so that everyone has a solo here and there, and I think that each of us is big enough to accept that we are each a different type of guitarist."

Asked by Wilson about the band's position in the heavy metal pantheon, Gers says, "I don't feel that we belong to any genre of music. Bruce would disagree with me on this, but to me it's just music. People talk about heavy metal coming back. To me it's just music, and I don't categorize music. I have never categorized music, and I don't think that you should. I think that media people do, and they have to in order to write about it, but to me it is either good music or bad music. When I listen to something I think, 'Hey, that's really good.' I don't think, 'That is heavy metal, so I like it.' I don't see it in those terms. A good song is a good song if it is a good slow song or a good fast song.

"What I think happened to heavy metal was that a lot of the younger bands thought that if they just play real loud and noisy, that is heavy metal—but it's not heavy metal! Go back and listen—it is not. You have lost melody and you have singers who growl. There is nothing wrong with that—bless the people who do it, and I wish them luck—but to me, the three great singers that I listened to when I was a kid all had melody. Plant and Ian Gillan and Paul Rodgers—those guys all had melody. All the other guys like Anderson and Jagger have all got melody in their voice too.

"The moment that heavy metal kind of fucked itself up was when it lost the melody, and it stopped making songs and only made riffs. Give a riff to Jimmy Page and he would give you a melody back. Give a riff to Tony Iommi and he would come out with something like 'Iron Man' with an incredible riff and a powerful melody. Give it to some of these younger bands and it would be 'gurgle blech!' Some kids might hook into that and get the physical aggression, but I want aggression, but I also want colors. That's what Led Zeppelin and Free had: color. I want to have color, and I don't want to have somebody screaming down the back of my neck. Having Bruce back is brilliant because he is one of the best singers there is, and I feel that we are on top of our game."

September 9 through October 1, the *Ed Hunter* tour moves to Europe, with Megadeth as support. Chuckles the Air Raid Siren, back in his plush-lined box, but a box all the same, "I've been out there getting my hands dirty for the last six years! You want grassroots? I've been living with the fucking worms! I've been 'round all the clubs in America and Europe, I've done fanzines . . . I thought my last two solo albums were pretty fucking good, frankly, but I realized that in the big, bad world of commerce, nobody gives a fuck! I was clawing my way from gig to gig. Maiden were in the clubs as well. Well, whoop-de-doo. You put the two of us together and you do 50,000 people!"

On September 6, Bruce has a scare in the air. This was still during his early piloting days (famously, Bruce would soon be flying jet airliners, as celebrated in the music documentary *Flight 666*).

As he explained to Henrik Johansson, "It was in Greenland. Well, there was actually nothing wrong with the airplane, or with the engine. What happened was a malfunction in the fire detection system in the engine. We got a light in the cockpit indicating that we had an engine fire on the left engine, which is an emergency. So, I shut down the engine, the 'fire' went out, and we landed in Greenland on the right engine. And then we went out and inspected everything and went, 'Okay, there's obviously no fire.'

"But you can't take any chances whatsoever with this kind of airplane, and having a fire in the engine at 23,000 feet in the middle of the Atlantic, it's not a very good idea, because what happens if you get a fire is not very pretty. But that's the training—if you have an engine fire light, then you switch off the engine, you switch off the fuel to that engine, and the fire goes out. And what happened in fact was that it was one loose wire that caused the false indication, and we found it as soon as we took the engine apart to inspect it. So, we continued on to Iceland, and I had to take a scheduled flight to Paris, because we'd lost some time, and I had press all day, the following day. So, whilst it was in Iceland, the engineers there gave it a thorough inspection and said everything was fine. So, I flew it down to Scotland and then on to Luton the next day and then to Rotterdam and then flew it to Hamburg the day before yesterday and then up here to Stockholm, and everything's fine."

As if it was all meant to be, the Iron Maiden reunion happened in conjunction with the crashing of relations with the US record company CMC, both with Bruce as a solo artist and with the Blaze-era Maiden.

"I'm not with CMC anymore," explained Bruce, true to form, speaking as if his solo career would still run parallel. "What happened there was, we had the tour booked and we were all ready to go and we were all excited. It was entirely down to the fact that they wouldn't come up with any tour support for the album (meaning, here, *The Chemical Wedding*). I went, 'Let's imagine I underwrite the tour loss myself. Would you put some money into a promotion at active rock radio to support the tour, then?' They said, 'We don't want to do that either.' The emails were flowing freely. There were some pretty vitriolic emails floating back and forth between Sanctuary Management central and CMC.

"I mean, I think everybody went into CMC thinking that it was going to deliver what it promised. It talked it up that it was going to bring metal back. And what they actually were interested in doing was servicing the existing metal audience and turning a profit on that—and then doing it again and again and again. I was just so disappointed because I went, 'You've got one of the best metal albums at least of the year, with *Chemical Wedding*.

And probably one of the best albums I've ever made in my whole life. And you're saying, 'Here's some money—go do another one. Yeah, that was cool; do another one like that.' So, I'm not with them anymore, and neither is Maiden."

And so the break just got clean, with Bruce and the boys all set to make a new record together, with the stakes raised, and a better label situation commensurate with the excitement around the reunion.

Acknowledging in a backhand way what the fans knew, that he was currently the only Maiden guy who had a clue, Bruce says, "People ask, 'Are you going to pick the songs?' And I say, 'We'll pick the best songs.' In a sense, if I ended up writing ten songs and none of them got on the record, the way the band is at the moment, the reason why they didn't get on is because there are ten better songs. And I'm fine with that. I know that everybody is thinking about that one point: make a great record. Not 'I want to get my songs on this record.' Which is fucking wonderful: Iron Maiden make a great record. That's what it should be like."

Bruce also makes clear an earlier point, that Maiden getting back together for a new record in the year 2000 is just a great story.

"We put tickets on sale in Stockholm a couple of days ago, and we did 9,500 in the first day. It freaked the promoter out, because when Maiden played there last summer, he expected five thousand and they got eight thousand. He was like, 'Jesus, where are all these metal people coming from?' But now, he puts it on sale, and he does nine and a half the first day. Whoa! I played in Stockholm last year as well, and there was like a thousand people. So, the sum of the parts is much greater than all the individual bits put together with Maiden. It always has been, but this just makes it blindingly obvious. In the States, we're doing only a dozen shows this summer, to basically plug two things: the *Ed Hunter* video game and also demonstrate to people, lest they have forgotten, what Iron Maiden coming at you full force looks like. Because there aren't many bands like us around anymore. There's nobody that has three people that leap around like me, Steve, and Janick onstage simultaneously.

"So, we're going to have a blast," promises Bruce. "The first time around, there's a lot of stress. Now the only stress is going to be 'We've got to write that killer song.' Once we've done it, once we're in there, we just focus in. Our ability to concentrate is actually much better now than it was back then. You can cut out all the crap and go, 'The stage is the thing—I think I'll stay in bed all day because I have to be onstage for two hours.' That's it."

When the idea is put to him that it's partially because of *The Chemical Wedding* that both Bruce and Adrian are coming back as a package, and that they are coming back as coleaders in a sense, Bruce says, "I must confess—people do say that, and I have to say they're wrong. I'm very proud of it and I think it's a great record, but from the point of view of Steve, I don't think he's ever been coerced in his life. He's not that kind of guy.

"Steve and I are doing this because we want to do it. I put it this way: most people in their lifetime never get the chance to be the best in the world with anything. And I've been really lucky. I've been in a band who had been the undisputed best metal band in the world for a period of time in the 1980s. I've just been given the opportunity to do it again, and I'm not turning it down. Within the bounds of human decency, I'm going to do whatever it takes, because it's there—it's all there. We can do it. We're young enough, good God. It makes us laugh when we get mentioned in the same breath as Judas Priest.

Excuse me, I was in high school listening to Judas Priest. We've got ten or fifteen years on those guys. Which is not to say they're old fucks and they're washed up—they're not. But the kind of stuff that we're doing requires a kind of physical intensity, which we can still pull out. Actually, we're probably better capable of putting it out now, because we're hungry. And now we're not taking this for granted. Plus, I think this time around we'll all enjoy it a lot more."

Indeed, what would ensue is one of the most remarkable second acts in heavy metal history. Iron Maiden would spend the 2000s and the 2010s clawing themselves back . . . and beyond. Record after record would be effusively embraced by a cult headbanging fan base that would grow alarmingly fast into a jean jacket army resembling the troops of old. What's even more impressive, hundreds of shows around the world would be consistently packed out. Impressive still further, the guys would suddenly tap some sort of fountain of youth, turning in almost ecstatically inspiring shows, the predictable feedback loop resulting in even-stronger ticket sales. Thus ends our tale of a Maiden in trouble, while the door opens for a tale of a Maiden resurrected. In that spirit, stay tuned for book III of our trilogy, in which we celebrate the near Deadhead-level sense of community that marks the Iron Maiden of the new millennium.

CHAPTER 17
Brave New World and Rock in Rio

"We suddenly appear to be the hippest thing on the planet."

As Iron Maiden wrapped up their *Ed Hunter* tour just into October 1999, headbangers were bracing for the end of the world. "Y2K" was supposed to bring down Western civilization not because of the rantings of some doomsday cult, but because computers were supposed to go berserk trying to process the switchover from 99 to 00. I've never for a moment thought it was a false alarm, or, more stupidly, a hoax or conspiracy theory. Rather, months and even years of preparation, hard work, and ingenuity were applied to the problem, the end result being that on May 29, 2000, Iron Maiden could serve up on a platter *Brave New World*, the first Maiden studio collection with Bruce Dickinson at the helm since 1992's *Fear of the Dark*. Also back was guitarist Adrian Smith, and with no one let go, Maiden became a six-headed beast with three guitarists set to conquer the world by land, sea, and air for years to come.

The band wet the whistles of the Maiden faithful through the aforementioned short summer and fall tour of 1999. This was after the unceremonious sacking of previous lead singer Blaze Bayley. But now the guys had to prove that they were not satisfied to tour venues that were only gradually getting bigger. To avoid being derided as a nostalgia act on a victory lap, Steve Harris and his survivors of the New Wave of British Heavy Metal, in the winter of 2000, set upon the task of delivering new music, music designed to make the next tour soar with relevance and then . . . well, it was up to Steve and manager Rod Smallwood (always with a mischievous glint in his eye) over pints to figure out what was next after that.

Speaking of Rod, on April 8, 2000, *Billboard* reports that Sanctuary has acquired Castle Music for £46 million.

"When I signed with Maiden, I didn't really want to manage anybody else," explains Rod. "I aspire to be like Peter Grant, just one band and do it and do it well and enjoy it. Just the fact that I'm in partnership with Andy Taylor, who I was at college with, and we've been partners a long time, since way before Maiden, then the expenditure was actually led by what Maiden needed. We needed a reliable travel agency, so we bought one and changed it to our travel agency. We wanted John Jackson, our agent, to be in a good situation, so we brought him in 1984 and started the company around him. Sanctuary was named after a Maiden song in 1979, when I wanted to rename the company. I looked at the titles we got, and 'Sanctuary' seemed to be ideal: 'Let's have a sanctuary away from the crap,' you know. There's no question that the company was built to make sure that everything that Maiden got was the best it could be, really. It sort of went on from there and on and on.

"What happens," continues Smallwood, "is if you get good people there to fill certain functions, what happens when they're not working? They've got to have something else to do. So, you start bringing the things in. That develops, and so you start getting little satellite things around the core. They're taking care of aspects of Maiden, but others are taking care of aspects of other things. Then it's all 'We should grow,' and we thought actual property rights was the place to be. So, we went into TV and then gradually we thought the company were able to acquire a company like Castle. It just so happened that Castle . . . we'd done a deal with Castle for the Maiden catalog for North America a few years before, when this wasn't even a twinkle in our eye, so to say. When we took it away from Capitol and put it with Castle. Because we would purchase Castle, obviously we ended up owning the Maiden catalog in North America. The band were absolutely fuckin' delighted. Now they would definitely be well looked after."

But business aside, there was a record to deliver. Maiden fans weren't going to let the boys rest on their laurels, especially when the latest offerings from the band had been somewhat suspect. We were restless for the guys to get their mojo back.

"I think it is an immediate song; that's why it's the first single," enthused Maiden guitarist Janick Gers, on the band's next spot of news—namely, the first volley from *Brave New World*, a little something called "The Wicker Man," issued two weeks before the album proper. "That's the first thing we wrote together. Adrian came in with the riff and it just felt great, like all the other stuff coming through after that. And it's good because Adrian had just come back, and it was great to get that off his back, and he felt more comfortable after that. And that was even before we did the *Ed Hunter* tour."

Dave Wright archive

Adds Adrian, who along with Janick and Dave Murray completes the novel three-guitar army Maiden now was, "I was glad to get that out of the way, because then I thought, you know, this is going to work. So that was the first song we actually recorded. We set up in this big warehouse in Portugal, and it was the first song we actually played together."

"Steve is having a major kind of progressive moment on this album," mused Bruce, no longer wary over the whole concept after an impressive bank of solo albums that found him squarely more relevant that Maiden in the 1990s. "But the thrust of almost everything he's done has been that. I confess, I was pretty apprehensive about some of it. But I went with it out of respect. And I'd go, 'Well, you know what? He went with "Wicker Man," and he went with my stuff, you know, and he threw himself into it, so I'm just gonna go for it on his songs.'"

What Bruce is referring to there is the sense of brotherhood satisfaction he felt with "The Wicker Man" being picked as lead single, in fact *advance* single. Steve wrote the lyrics to fully seven of the tracks spread across the sixty-seven-minute panorama of the new album, with Bruce penning "Brave New World" and "The Wicker Man." Second track on the record, "Ghost of the Navigator," would see a cocredit between Bruce and Steve, the two parties previously most at loggerheads over the direction of the band.

Continues Dickinson, "As we started doing 'Nomad,' I thought, I don't know if this could work. I was worried about 'Nomad,' and it worked fucking brilliantly, so I happily ate my words. We never dared to be that loose on a record before. So, I think it's a marvelous record. I have to say that I was wondering through it, 'I think this is the right thing to do.' But there's always a bit of 'I hope it works; I hope people get it.' But at the end of the whole record, I got it. We put the album tracks down, and twelve days later Nick [Nicko McBrain, drummer[goes off on a plane to Florida playing golf. The next time we see him, he's heard the record for the first time, and he just grabs ahold of me and starts kissing me. I'm like, 'Well, I gather you like it?' He was just freaking out at how good it was, and because we had been so close to it, it was great to see that from somebody that had also been involved with the record and then heard it all finished. So I think it's a really outstanding record, and I think most of the people who listen to it get that too, even though they've only listened to it very briefly and haven't had a chance to pull it apart in any great depth. But the important thing is actually the initial reaction to it."

One of Bruce's demands with respect to returning to the band was that they work with a real producer. That sort of happened, and I say sort of for three reasons: (1) Steve still coproduced, (2) the resulting album doesn't sound particularly "extensively produced," and (3) Kevin Shirley was not a famed producer, particularly, more of an engineer laddering up to this post.

Once things got underway, a pattern emerged, as Bruce told Jerry Ewing. "When we were recording the album, we were all living in the same apartments, all five of us, Nicko having gone back to Miami. I'd pop in the studio every day and hang out with Steve and Kev, and it would get to the end of the session, about eight, and Steve would go home, and me and Kev would go out to the pub and have a pint. Then Jan would pop in about nine o'clock and have a beer, and then we'd go home and go to bed. And that would happen every single day. Once every two weeks, Steve would come out for a beer. Otherwise, he'd sit in his room all night on the internet. And before the internet, he would sit in his room with his video machine and watch videos. That's what he does. People read too much into it. Yes, we are different people, and yes we do get along. If we didn't get along, then this record wouldn't be anything like as good as it is. I couldn't face being in a band with Steve if I didn't get on with him and respect him.

"I think it's the best-sounding Maiden record," said Bruce at the time, pleased with the choice of Shirley. "And it has nothing to do with technology at all. It has to do totally with the fact that Kevin insisted on recording the band live on the basis of what he heard at the Hammerstein Ballroom. It sounded fantastic. He's like, why do you want to do anything else? Why do you want to talk about recording any other way?

"So that's what he did. And we looked for a studio that was going to be able to deliver all of what we needed, a place where we could get a huge drum sound and also have the guitarists all playing together live, have me putting my vocals down live, and we could all look each other in the eye as we were doing it. We found this place in Paris that had just worked brilliantly, and we rehearsed the tracks as we were doing a gig and then went in there and recorded the whole thing live. It took about twelve days to record all the stuff, about a track a day. We did four, five, six passes on each song and then spent the next six weeks basically sitting on our ass waiting for Kevin to work his way through all the six passes on the drums, and then on the bass, and then on the guitars, and then on the vocals. I came back in after six weeks or so and went, 'Okay, great, it's time for pain and suffering, time to do the lead vocals.' Kevin said, 'No, you're done, you've done it all.'"

There was the thought that maybe Roy Z would be brought in to produce. After all, he had gotten excellent results with Bruce's solo albums.

"It was mentioned in a production capacity," confirms Janick. "And nothing against Roy, but we wanted somebody to come in from outside. We did not want it to sound like Bruce's solo album; that would be silly. We sound like we sound. You can manufacture a sound like that, and you can do it with any band that you want, but that's not what we sound like. We want somebody to capture our sound with the three guitars. And that's what Kevin did. He came in and he did not really add anything to it other than his ability to collect the sounds. It's a different album. All the guitars sound the same these days, with too much bottom end, and the drums have a certain sound, and that's what sells on radio. So, he came in and captured our sound, and that's the hardest thing to do.

"Gillan were never captured in the studio like they were live," continues Gers, referencing his biggest pre-Maiden band. "It's very difficult to capture the live essence of a band, and I think Kevin did that. I must admit, I worked with a lot of producers, including the Gillan stuff, and I never got along with any of them. In fact, we nearly came to blows with some of them. But Kevin has this ability to make you pay attention to what you're doing, and in fact it makes you play better; you get a vibe."

Dave Murray Nicko McBrain Adrian Smith Steve Harris Bruce Dickinson
Janick Gers

Dave Wright archive

On the subject of Steve coproducing, Janick figures, "It's always difficult bringing someone different in. Steve has this concept and this direction he wants to go. And it's very important we don't get diverted from our direction too much; otherwise, we won't be us anymore. And that's why he's there to make sure that doesn't happen. But I think they got on fairly well."

Asked about rumors that "scratch" guitar parts were used, meaning sort of parts that the guitarists didn't think would be used, or first passes, or bits rescued from the cutting-room floor, Gers says, "Yes, there's an element of truth in some of that. There's a lot of stuff I would have changed. You see, the studio is quite a small studio, and if you want to play live, you can't plug in the amps. So, we had a great live feel, but in order to go back in and recapture that live feel, we had to scrap everything and go from scratch. So, there is an element of truth in that. From my point of view anyway."

"You need a strong personality," adds Adrian, further on Kevin, "which he has, and you need technical know-how, which he has. It's sort of a rare combination. He would come and see us live, and he would come to rehearsals and listen to each one of us individually, and he really got it down and had a plan. But him and Steve spent a couple of days together sparring. He did have a strong personality, so if you let him, he would bully you a little bit. So, you had to come back and get in his face a little bit. But once that all got out of the way, we were fine. There is that crackle of energy when you are in the room together and you want to do well. It was a bit of a departure, really. It's different from the way we normally work, or different from the way things were done when I was in the band before. We tried really to do a lot of it live. When we decided on Kevin Shirley, we liked what he had done, so when he suggested we do most of it in a live environment, we had to respect that because he's done such great stuff.

"So, he found us a studio where we could all set up and have lots of eye contact and keep the spontaneity in the song. Obviously, with the technology the way it is today, there are certain things you can do to enhance it. So, it's not like we went in there and just bashed it out. It took two or three months to do. But we did as much live as we could, and yet make it sound like a studio album. I like the progressive element on it. I think it's something we do well, something I think we're comfortable doing, and something that a lot of bands aren't doing these days. We could have gone detuned and surreal and tried to make it really heavy, but there's no point. I think we've gone off in a direction that really serves us. We've found a niche. Songs like 'The Navigator,' 'Brave New World,' they're great live as well. I think the album sounds heavy, but we didn't overkill it with overdubs and stuff like that."

"The key thing is, is that everybody's writing with everybody else on this album," Bruce told Tim Henderson. "And that's by far and away the most important thing. Be cool, chill out, and be relaxed and go with the flow of the whole thing. It's so obvious it's a band. It's got the vintage Maiden classic sound. That sound has never sounded better than it does in this incarnation. Mainly because of Kevin Shirley, but also because we were persuaded to do the record live, and it makes a huge difference. Between Kevin and that, the attitude comes across. It's like sitting in a rehearsal room with Iron Maiden. We do actually sound like that.

"The other difference is we're a little bit wiser. And we're all a little more self-aware of our likes, dislikes, and little foibles. Therefore, writing the record and recording it, both Steve and I were conscious of all the ways that we could really wind each other up.

And we didn't. So, it's kind of a grown-up record. I was in for the long haul, and strangely, we suddenly appear to be the hippest thing on the planet. You can tell I was obviously having a good time during rehearsals, because me and Jan were paralyzed every night after rehearsal. We'd come back in and go out and do that Belgian beer thing. It's like 8.5 percent, you know. And there ain't nothing else to do, so we would just go out to the blues club until four. It's dangerous, you know; it's tough out there, I'll tell you."

For the cover art of *Brave New World*, Maiden went with a classy image of a dystopian metropolis by digital artist Steve Stone. Hovering in the clouds above the futuristic world is Eddie, drawn by returning friend and nemesis of the band Derek Riggs. The vibe matches that of the Aldous Huxley novel from which the record gets its name. The cool blue unity of the cover is maintained by the sober logo presented in white, and the tiny yellow text used for the title. All told, it's a huge step uptown from *The X Factor* and *Virtual XI*.

"I was doing an illustration for 'Wicker Man,'" explains Derek, with respect to the album's much-anticipated and surprisingly punky first single. "This face was in the clouds; it was in the smoke. But 'Wicker Man,' where they burn the fellow, I designed this thing that looks a bit like a church, with people inside it, all being burned. But the band didn't like it. The manager liked it; he got it. The band didn't like it. Bruce started bullshitting about it. And I turned around and told Bruce that he was talking bullshit. 'It's not about this and it's not about that,' and I said, 'Excuse me, I know a bit more about ancient religion than you do, mate.' And the manager said he wanted to see a version every day, and I don't work like that. And then he starts going, 'Oh, I don't like this, and I don't like the grass and I don't like the sky.'

Dave Wright archive

CHAPTER 17

"I just turned around said, 'Look, forget it, I'm not doing this.' So, they paid for the artwork, and they used the Eddie in the sky on that thing. And that was my contribution to the cover. I just don't work like that. 'It's not finished, you know? It's an unfinished picture. It's a picture in progress. What part of this don't you understand?' 'Oh, I don't like the grass.' 'Yeah, but there's three hundred figures to go on top of the grass. Hello?!' If somebody comes back on you like that all the time, it stops being fun after around about a week.

"But yes, the album itself was going to be called *Wicker Man*," continues Derek, "and then they started messing about again. I was trying to say, 'Can I just finish this?' I was just so pissed off by then. They were just being stupid. Like I say, Bruce was talking bollocks and Steve was going on a bit, and then they decided that they didn't like the Eddie, so I just said, 'Forget it; I'm not going to finish it.' And they did a 3-D model of a city."

Bruce kind of had a point. To be sure, there was an impressive and creepy old English horror movie called *The Wicker Man*, to which Bruce's solo version of the song more closely adhered. With this lyric, there's a real struggle to align it with the film, although the superlative Mark Wilkinson cover art for the single does so pretty directly.

Then there's the official video. To quote EMI's press materials, "Accompanying the infectious fury of 'The Wicker Man' is an equally arresting video, directed by Dean Karr, based on the 1973 erotic/horror movie masterpiece of the same name, and shot in Sheldon Pit, California, during two particularly mud-splattered torrential night shoots. Karr, a man whose credits include the likes of Marilyn Manson, Cypress Hill, and the Deftones, it transpires, is a lifelong Maiden fan."

Remarked Bruce, "Dean is the hottest video director in America, bar none, and he is a huge Maiden freak. He actually sent us a handwritten note asking if he could do the Maiden video before he'd heard any of the music at all. He got the note and a show reel via a friend to Dave Murray, who passed it on to our manager, Rod, at a party on New Year's Eve. It's a good job he was sober at the time. Dean just really wanted to do it because he is such a big fan of the band."

But the actual making of the video was like a scene out of *Apocalypse Now*. "I walked onto the video set," explained Bruce to Phil Alexander, "and just sank into this mud bath right up to my waist. Everyone else thought I was just arsing around, walking around on my knees or something. Then they realized I wasn't moving. So, they sent these two guys to drag me out of the mud, and of course they got stuck. Everything that could've gone wrong pretty much did during the filming of this video. There were several *Spinal Tap* moments. You've got to laugh about the whole thing. The idea was to come out here and get a bit of sun. We were meant to be shooting for two all-night sessions, so we should've been able to relax in the day. Instead, on the first night's shooting, I was up for twenty-five hours. To make matters more interesting, it was about 2°C on the video set. We had freezing rain and windstorms on top of that, along with 2 inches of rain on the ground.

Dave Wright archive

"Building an entire Wicker Man on the set was another saga. We had to burn the Wicker Man the first night in the middle of the storm because we only had a permit for that night. The one enduring moment was when all these video people were running around with megaphones going, 'We're going to burn the Wicker Man! Stand by for the burning! We don't have long to get the shot!' These two guys were on this big hydraulic arm with 12 gallons of rubber cement, which they were meant to pour on the Wicker Man so it would burn equally. Among all the running about, there was this plaintive little cry from 30 feet up in the air: 'Has anybody got a spanner?' They needed a spanner to open the cans of rubber cement. It was just one of those moments where you couldn't help laughing at these people. I think it was around then that we had another hailstorm."

At the music end, "The Wicker Man" kicks off with bare, spare guitar, like a combination of "China Grove" and "Running Wild." Soon the band tucks in and the intro riff is maintained. It's key that Adrian is in the writing of this one, because the song hits right between the eyes. But soon Maiden melodies arrive, for a rich prechorus and then the "Your time will come" chorus proper, which takes place at half time and with a highly melodic and latticelike lead—if it's twinned at all, it's in unison.

Recalls Bruce, "I remember Kevin was mixing 'Wicker Man' and Steve just sat there, not saying a word. And I looked at him and said, 'It sounds fucking great.' And Steve went, 'Yeah, yeah, sure.' He goes, 'I'm still listening. He hasn't done anything wrong yet.' 'What do you mean he hasn't done anything bloody wrong?! Tell me it sounds great.' And he said, 'I'll tell you when it's finished.'"

As Dickinson explained to Phil Alexander from *Metal Hammer*, "By the end of the first day in the studio with Kevin Shirley, we had this track pretty much down. At certain points in the past, people scurried off to their little bolt holes. This time it was different. Everyone stayed in touch and saw the songs through. We developed it together. So, you see three people on the song credits, which is unusual for Maiden. Everybody's been grown up about it. I'm sure people will read between the lines this time around all over again."

Noted Steve, on patching up relations with Bruce, "He'll probably say the same about me, but he's a lot more amenable now. Everybody's noticed that he's a happier person. Whether it's to do with his personal life, I don't know. He wasn't very happy at home when he was in Maiden back then, and that kind of stuff affects you. Maybe we should've spoken to him a bit more, I dunno. We've never ever had a punch-up. All the stuff that was said was because of the fact that we didn't talk to each other. There were loads of comments flying around and people trying to wind us up. To be honest, when we sat down together, we did have some stuff to resolve. I was a bit worried because I thought, Are we going to be dealing with the same old thing we had to deal with? To be honest, we haven't had to. It's been very different."

Dickinson really wanted "The Wicker Man" to be a headbanging, crowd participation song, and he got his wish. As a trivia note, there's a radio version with a different chorus featuring a smattering of altered words, but yes, it is curious that there's such a strong repetitive chorus that doesn't mention the Wicker Man. In fact, those words occur only once in the song, and as part of a kind of throwaway line.

The single was issued in all manner of formats with various B-sides, with the shortest, most common edition featuring two Blaze-era tracks live with Bruce; namely, "Futureal" and "Man on the Edge." For cover art, this one featured a memorable live shot of the band with Bruce holding a torch. The Wicker Man looms in shadow behind the heavy metal army that is Maiden in the 2000s.

CHAPTER 17

All told, this was a successful but somewhat expected way for Maiden to open the record, with an immediate track and a brief one, the second shortest on the album. What is fresh, however, is that the song is not a full-on speed metal onslaught with twin leads afire in front of a wall of drums. The relaxed feel, with the band in no hurry to impress, demonstrates a sense of swagger, maturity even.

Next is "Ghost of the Navigator," music by Janick, whose writing for the band is so Maiden-like, it's almost fated

Dave Wright archive

that he should join, which took place at this point now ten years earlier. As with the fortuitously similar state of mind lyrically between Bruce and Steve, Janick and Dave are of singular purpose, and then Adrian can play with their dreaminess of melody with ease as well, joining them in their world willingly and often.

Lyrically we're in the realm of "Rime of the Ancient Mariner" or Homer's *The Odyssey*. An old seafarer seems resigned to the doom of his final voyage, beckoned by the sirens to join ghosts who can appreciate his plight. It's an epic tale heavy with drama, but it keeps to under seven minutes and is riffy enough, despite a slow build.

And the title track does much the same, specifically with its slow build, its overt melody, and its progressive movements. In essence, demonstrating bravery, "Brave New World" is framed like a ballad—and when the opening structure is repeated with full band and high speed later, it still feels ballad-like. There's also a time-honored Maiden gallop, but all told, only three tracks in, a huge chunk of this album is sounding like *The X Factor* and *Virtual XI* with a different singer and a little more spring in its step, a sense of optimism, driven by the new career circumstance but also by Kevin Shirley.

Like both tracks thus far, "Brave New World" places us in a timeless realm of struggle, and more so than timeless, more like historical, back at least a couple of hundred years and easily much further back to the Dark Ages. And again, like in "The Wicker Man," this lyric is of a surprising topic not linked to its legendary title. But more lasting than any pontification over the words, all of a sudden we have two huge, memorable choruses on the record, with "In a brave new world" living up to the standard set by "Your time will come."

Even though there's not much about the 1932 Aldous Huxley book to "Brave New World," Bruce did indeed ponder the book when writing the song. As well, he tied in something he had read about swans going extinct in Japan and nobody caring, using the image because it shows the residual effects of the type of political landscape depicted by Huxley. Apparently, the discussion Bruce had with these people in Japan revealed the idea that it was good enough to have these swans preserved as pictures in books, a virtual reality of sorts, again, one dynamic of a brave new world.

One interesting wrinkle with this song is that the words "brave new world" had already showed up in an Iron Maiden song—namely, "Stranger in a Strange Land"—where Dickinson ruminates, "No brave new world, no brave new world."

Next is "Blood Brothers," which finds Steve reflecting upon the recent death of his father, addressing him personally but then reflecting upon the wider world and the meaning of life, including life beyond death. This is set to a sort of full-band Celtic ballad, very percussive, very Maiden, with prominent bass and even keyboards.

"Other people were worried by 'Blood Brothers,' which never worried me for an instant," chuckled Bruce, speaking with Jerry Ewing. "I loved it. I was like, 'Hang on, where's me flute?' Steve wrote the whole song from start to finish and then handed it over to me to sing it, and I was like, 'How far on one leg do you want me to stand?' I loved it. Even the register that it's written in is very Ian Anderson, but it was such a blast. I love that song. But yes, we had a hoot recording the album. When we were doing it live, the ten or twelve days we actually spent doing the thing was one of the most inspirational periods I've spent in the last ten years, just watching it come together.

"There are moments that are very close to the bone in terms of Steve's sentiments," Bruce told Phil Alexander, addressing this song. "He's really opened up. 'Blood Brothers' is about Steve's relationship with his father, who died very suddenly in the middle of a Maiden tour, and his continuing relationship with him after his death. That's the kind of depth there is to a lot of the stuff on the album."

But as Alexander—one of our best—points out, Steve demurred on getting too personal, which is a microcosm or metaphor for his personality in general within the Maiden dynamic, particularly his relationship with Bruce. "Er, yeah, in 'Blood Brothers,' there's a line that mentions my father. But that song's about everything bar the kitchen sink, really. Life, death, war, the whole lot. But yeah, it's heartfelt and it's one of my better moments."

Dave Wright archive

The song soon became a poignant moment at Maiden shows, with fans singing along, even linked arm in arm, joined by their shared love of Maiden and metal. Given the lyric, the song served well as one to dedicate from the stage to various plights. For example, in 2010 on the *Final Frontier* tour, the band's performance of "Blood Brothers" was dedicated to Ronnie James Dio, gone too soon from stomach cancer, on May 16, 2010. Later, the song was dedicated to victims of the earthquakes in Christchurch and Japan and victims of the mass shooting in Norway, as well those affected by political upheaval in Libya and Egypt.

CHAPTER 17

"Blood Brothers" is followed, sensibly, by a short and quick-paced rocker that gets down to business immediately. "The Mercenary" is based loosely on the movie *Predator*, but despite the oblique references, it's another worthy addition to the band's war chest of war songs.

With "Dream of Mirrors" we're back to the proggy Maiden of the Blaze era, and, in fact, Blaze figures in the penning of this one, a track that Steve says is one of his favorites because it's a bit like "The Clansman."

Explains Bayley, "Well, 'Dream of Mirrors,' I worked closely with Steve on. And when I left the band, he said, 'You know what? I really like this

Dave Wright archive

song. I'd like to keep it. I would like to use this in the future.' And I said, well, fine. So, we did a small deal where he could use that for Maiden. There's another few songs on there I was part of too, but it just came out great. *Brave New World* is a fantastic album. The production, the vocals from Bruce . . . everything on *Brave New World* is amazing. Absolutely fantastic the way it came out."

Of note, Blaze's own first post–Iron Maiden album, *Silicon Messiah*, hit the shops a week before *Brave New World* did. And it's a barnstormer, self-assured, professional, objectively better or at least as good as the record the mother ship was proposing.

"The first album, we wanted to make sure we had the recording all worked out," explains Bayley on his new solo joint. "I didn't want to spend too long in the studio; I wanted to keep that down. We wanted enough time to do a good job but not enough time to go up our own ass. So, we did that, and we had a bit more time with getting the band together, a bit more time writing songs, everything. There were a few ideas that were hanging around for a while—with *Silicon Messiah*, there was quite a lot of writing time, about six months, and we were really happy with the results.

"We're a metal band, really," continues Blaze, comparing it with his pre-Maiden firecracker of an act. "Wolfsbane was much more of a rock 'n' roll metal band, a little bit on the wild side, with the kind of lineup we had and the way we arranged our songs. We had just much more of a rock 'n' roll, happy-go-lucky kind of style, a bit more punky, I suppose. Maiden are of course a bit more . . . they're kind of on their own, really. They're one of the great heavy metal bands of all time, and they have their own style. They are traditional and have their own sound. But Blaze, the band, we wanted to do something that had two guitars and used those guitars effectively in the arrangements. And it's something that has power, really, power and emotion. We've got just more of a heavier edge; we're more metal than Maiden, just by virtue of not having keyboards, and our sound is more guitar based. It's definitely about getting those two guitars right up in the mix, just trying to get that powerful guitar sound over.

"I've just learned so much, both from the Wolfsbane days and from when I joined Maiden," continues Bayley. "It's like learning another half of my voice. And the great experience I had from those days and making those albums, I've carried that over into my own music, and it's worked out great so far. I feel that I'm singing better than ever. I sound like I feel, and I waste a lot less energy trying to get the results that I want. I feel that I've tapped into it more; the singing that I'm doing is a lot more emotional and connected from a power and energy point of view. I've managed to combine those things, and I feel pretty good about it."

Before Maiden would get another record out, Blaze, moving from strength to strength, would crank out *Tenth Dimension*, issued on January 15, 2002. Through action and not words, Bayley was quickly establishing a reputation for records that were every bit as creditable as the albums this book celebrates, be that the Maiden records proper or the side projects we will talk about from Bruce, Adrian, and Steve.

"*Tenth Dimension* we recorded a lot more quickly because we just didn't have the time because of tour commitments and everything like that. But we had more time in the studio. And I think that's a much, much-bigger production, with a couple of epic songs. We kept the first album, *Silicon Messiah*, very straightforward and as simple as we could, and then on *Tenth Dimension*, it's a whole concept album. I wrote a short story and based all the lyrics around that short story, a tale of a scientist who makes a discovery, and basically the government wants to steal that and use it as a weapon of mass destruction, whereas he wants to use it for the benefit of mankind."

For his part, Adrian has affirmed in interviews that "Dream of Mirrors" has its origins in the *Virtual XI* sessions, along with "Mercenary" and "The Nomad." Steve says that "Blood Brothers" was started at that point as well. "Dream of Mirrors" is a track that is laden with some of this record's most magic musical moments. Arguably, its lengthy mellow intro is the richest and best integrated in terms of its links to the loud bits to come. Indeed, when the band comes in—somewhere between a crash and an amble—there's lots of soul, with that passion applied to stout-of-heart prechorus and chorus passages. Again, arguably, both the "I only dream in black and white" and "The dream is true" refrains are a couple of the hookiest, most poignant passages on the album. All told, despite a speedy metal rave late in the song, this one's another "loud" ballad, but it's one of the most mature of these that the band would ever manage.

Of course, "Dream of Mirrors" had to be followed by another rocker, and "The Fallen Angel" fits the bill, with Nicko and Steve building a sprightly gallop, accentuated by prominent and distorted bass. Bruce underscores the melodies of the guitars by singing mostly in unison with the riffing.

At the lyric end, Steve gets completely specific, with the first utterance out of Bruce being "Azazel." But that's the last proper name we hear, as we join the guys on a bit of a demon-studded Old Testament sermon concerning the end of the world.

"The Fallen Angel" represents the second and last writing credit on the album for Adrian, after opener "The Wicker Man." Defends Smith, "The worst thing is if you enter into something like this and you have very fixed ideas about what it should be like and who should get credit for what. At the end of the day, it's all about making a great album. If you get sidetracked into politics, as you can, that can be detrimental and cause a lot of stress. If it rocks, great—it doesn't matter who writes it."

"I think everybody added to the album, and that's the way it came out," seconds Janick. "It was definitely a band effort. That's just the way it came out. I mean, there's stuff that didn't get on the album as well that we had ready. Adrian had a lot of stuff as well that we didn't use."

Is "The Nomad" this record's "Loch Ness"? By that, I'm referring to the long progressive track on 2005's *Angel of Retribution*, Judas Priest's first album back with Rob, for which

Dave Wright archive

the band was pilloried (the song, not the whole album!). The "Nomad" track is a long song about a nomad, with a chorus that begins, "Nomad!" Comparisons with "Loch Ness" are inevitable, as are comparisons with "Quest for Fire," the first Maiden song where we could see our heroes visibly grasping for straws.

Defends Bruce, good-naturedly (but then again, at the time he had to be), "In this world of ever-increasing shallowness, in the land of the blind, the one-eyed man is king. It's true, isn't it? So suddenly for people to look at Maiden again, oh my God, what a revelation, a nine-minute song. Oh, good God, Arabian and Eastern rhythms; oh boy, that's never been done before [laughs]."

Speaking with Jerry Ewing, he was more candid (but sold by quote's end), saying, "I sat there thinking about some of the longer songs, like 'The Nomad,' because when we were going in and doing the writing and preproduction, and Steve came in with 'The Nomad' and a couple of other longer ones, I was like, 'I hope these work.' Because I could hear them in the raw state and was going, I hope this doesn't sound too pompous and overblown. It only takes one song to blow the album. But I kept schtum and went with it. And it's turned out fucking great. 'Nomad' is one of the highlights, totally superb."

If there's justification for fan impatience with the music on this one, it's because Maiden have already applied Middle Eastern tonalities to a handful of Middle Eastern–themed songs, and by this point it's all a little predictable. Still, it's a rocking, grinding track, quite solid save for the chorus. Nor does the mellow jam add much. All told, really, the attuned Maiden fan's ear is offended mostly by the chorus, where there's a sense of stepping in it, again, clutching at straws with another one of these "occupational" songs, a sort of "These are the people in your neighborhood," if I may quote Sesame Street.

"Out of the Silent Planet" lifts its title from the famous C. S. Lewis book of 1938, but the lyrics are universal enough to reveal a message about an environmentally degrading world. Indeed, the references lean closer to 1956 sci-fi film *Forbidden Planet*, while Bruce has framed the story as being about aliens who destroy their own world and now are coming for ours, a topic being discussed today, with the über rich musing about moving to Mars. Musically the song is framed upon a beat from Nicko that places the snare whack on four only, in any given verse bar. Into the chorus and we have a standard Maiden gallop with twin leads, Nicko punctuating the pattern with busy bass drums. This one sits in the midrange duration-wise, and with Maiden that usually means it could have benefited from an edit down to four minutes.

This one saw issue as a single, on October 23, 2000, again with cracking artwork by Mark Wilkinson. As B-sides, we got live tracks from the recent *Ed Hunter* reunion tour with Bruce and Adrian; namely, "Wasted Years" and "Aces High." Included on the CD version was the video for the song, which featured the band performing it live on the European leg of the new album's touring cycle—oddly, the song was rarely played live, despite it being a single.

Dave Wright archive

If Dave Murray might be castigated for "The Nomad," he's redeemed himself on his second and last credit on the album. "The Thin Line between Love and Hate" is arguably the finest song on *Brave New World*, if only for the fact that melodically it is so fresh for Maiden, not so much come chorus time but most definitely for the punk rock 'n' rolling verse riff, killer on its own but greatly enhanced by Bruce's edgy, low-register vocal, one in which he doubles with himself. To be sure, the song falls to pieces barely a third in, becoming a sort of long goodbye mixing the chorus with soloing and mellow bits, and mostly instrumental. The band could have busted it into two, and I kind of wish they did—those first three minutes constitute some of the greatest writing the band would conjure across all of the 2000s and 2010s, again, if only due to how unexpected it is. But yes, to be fair, each of the records moving forward tends to rise to this challenge, giving us at least one track that is both heavy and smartly outside expected Maiden tropes.

As the lingering goodbye fades, that's it for *Brave New World*, a reunion record comprising sixty-seven minutes of music spread over a tidy ten tracks, seven of them over six minutes long.

Wrote Tim Henderson at the time, in his review of the album, "Life must feel good in the Maiden camp. Remarkably, some are saying that *Brave New World* is Iron Maiden's finest output to date. Pretty strong sentiments to compare a bunch of ol' blokes' output at present with some of the finest heavy metal created, *Powerslave*, *Piece*, *Seventh Son*, and *Beast* to name a few. Sitting with pint in hand and with plenty of repeated listens, I'm in awe. This album wrestles *every* comeback to the ground: Aerosmith, Priest, Purple, Kiss, Ozzy, Sabbath, Page/Plant, whoever. This is the real deal, from start to finish. And the funny thing is, the first single, 'The Wicker Man,' is far from representing the full feeling of this record, although it grows over time with its anthemic qualities. A definite show-opener. In one-word, *Brave New World* is mature, a record created by experience itself, the six-piece far from weathered by the sands of time. Maiden have made great albums in the past, but with *Brave New World* the whole unit is aligned in synch with fascinating results. At the very end of the record, producer Kevin Shirley includes McBrain's in-studio comment, 'Oh, I fucking missed it,' regarding some miscue. These lads have far from missed it. And Steve, whatever was going through yer head when you hired Blaze, you're now mostly forgiven by providing us a *Brave New World* to focus on. Thank you."

Wrote Paul Schwartz, for the highly respected but squarely extreme metal-focused *Chronicles of Chaos*, "As I was disgusted enough on first listen to not be able to finish the entirety of *Brave New World* past track six, I have since given it repeated spins now totaling in excess of 20. I have 'lived' with this record, and as an Iron Maiden fan. In the words of the album's final song, there is a thin line between love and hate, and Iron Maiden's comeback with Bruce Dickinson—back and happily exercising the air-raid siren—exemplifies perfectly how possible it is to love and hate the same group of musicians, to differing degrees, over nearly 70(!) minutes of music.

"It feels strange to advise a band with years of experience behind them—and, we assume, megatons of talent still in them—about arrangement and song selection, but at a rough estimate I'd say Maiden could've cut *Brave New World* down to about half (discarding the fat of inadequate songs and unnecessary repetitions) and come out with a better and eminently more listenable album.

"You see, *Brave New World*'s greatest asset is that it is Iron Maiden who made it. The musicianship and melodic sensibility are present and correct, and Bruce Dickinson, though maybe not 'as' spectacular as on certain past releases, is nonetheless still in possession of some of the finest lungs in the metal world. Many other bands (see current Century Media and Nuclear Blast rosters for details) would probably have performed this record a lot worse, more obviously exposing its considerable shortcoming. However, we shouldn't lose sight of the fact that Maiden have released an album which, by their standards, is verging on the diabolically bad and not just merely the so-so level witnessed in Bruce's final early 1990s days with the band. The weakness of *Brave New World* is hard to understand considering the high quality and sheer metalness of Dickinson's last solo offering, 1998's *The Chemical Wedding*. I hope the band collectively remember that for next time. Honestly speaking though, I don't think Maiden will ever again make an album that I will feel the need to own."

Malcolm Dome, in his review for the influential *Metal Hammer*, stated that "what we have here is a clarion call to arms, a rousing resurrection that suddenly brings sharply into focus what some of us have been saying for the past few months: heavy metal is back, bigger, bolder, brighter, and better than for years. What you first must bear in mind is that the clear-eyed production, courtesy of Kevin Shirley, has accentuated the band's obvious hunger. Perhaps not since the days of *Number of the Beast*, when Bruce Dickinson first rid himself of that ludicrous posturing Bruce Bruce stage name and threw in his lot with Harris'[s] Marauders, have the band had so much to prove. And their appetite and desire here are equal to the occasion and demands. You really feel them biting into opener 'The Wicker Man,' that trademark galloping chorus thankfully backed up by a sense of the six riding once again towards the sound of cannon fire rather than shying away from meeting the menace of complacency head on—and this is one of the album's weakest tracks! All of which means this is easily the best Iron Maiden album in years. Certainly, the most important metal album in eons. 'Have you ever thought the future is the past?' sings Dickinson on 'Dream of Mirrors.' True, because once again we can proclaim Maiden's supremacy, just like the old days."

"This kind of music—metal, hard rock, or whatever you want to call it—has suffered from the death of a thousand cuts in recent years," reflected Bruce, in the record bio for *Brave New World*, sent out to the press at the time, including Dome, Henderson, and of course the author. "It's had to go underground again, and it's about time someone dragged it back out into the daylight. That's where Maiden come in. I feel that this will be a very important and successful time for Maiden. You can sense that this kind of music is coming back, and when it comes to playing it, there are very few bands that can live with Maiden when we're on form. And right now, we are on form. A listen to the album will tell you that. A lot of people have pointed out that this album has a really classy edge. It's still Maiden, but it's got hooks and it's got really adventurous songs. A few people have told us that the closest band they can compare it to is Queen. That's incredibly flattering. I think people will be genuinely surprised by this record. Whichever way you approach it, it's got loads of integrity and it sounds fucking great. To me it sounds like the best Iron Maiden record you ever heard."

Added Steve, "It's pretty strange right now because there are so many different types of Maiden fans out there. With musicians that like Maiden, it's quite strange for us to deal with things. I suppose it was the same with us when we started this band, because we all looked up to our heroes and all that. That doesn't stop it being a bit strange when people look up to you."

CHAPTER 17

All of us at *Brave Words & Bloody Knuckles*, Tim included, would downplay our enthusiasm for the record somewhat over time, but back in 2000, with the close relationship we had with the band, it was hard to contain our glee. And truth be told, well, two things: (1) it was just as much about how on fire the band was live now with Bruce back, which swings the narrative decisively positive, and (2) even more positive, some of the reservation for the record came in light of comparing it with even-better records the band was going to get up to moving forward, which is also a positive to bestow upon the narrative.

"I don't have any complaints about that album," mused Bruce, later, similarly with a bit of distance. "I thought it was excellent for what it was, for when it was. It did a great job, and it was a terrific precursor to the next record. To follow on from *Brave New World*, we wanted to do something that was sufficiently different where people might sit back and go, 'Wow, they've really done a good job on this one.' Because nobody expected *Brave New World* to be as good as it was, so it was nice when we sort of quietly sat down and looked around and said, 'Not too bad, is it chaps?' I think *Brave New World* is a great record. I think it's a great Maiden album. I won't say there are no flaws, because there are a few which I'll keep to myself, in the same way there are a few flaws on every album I've done, some more than others. I'm the last person to turn around and say an album is perfection, because if there was, I don't think there would be any point in continuing making them. But in general, it's an excellent Iron Maiden album, certainly one of my top four Iron Maiden albums."

When I spoke to Adrian on the same day as Bruce back in 2003, he told me that *Brave New World* "had some good songs on it. I always felt that we never did ourselves a favor with the production of it. We never flatter ourselves with production. It's one of my little bug bears. I think it could have sounded a little more . . . I think I would like to do it slightly different. But if the six of us sat down, you'd get six different mixes. That's what a band's all about: it's compromise. As long as it's good and the songs come across, that's all you can hope for. Like I say, if you get six guys in the band, Nicko would mix more drums, you know what I mean? Like *Piece of Mind* is kind of dry, but it's real. It depends on your philosophy of recording. Whether you think the band should sound like they're in a room playing or whether they're in a huge arena. We'd just come back together. I had been out of the band for eight years, and Bruce had been out for six. We came back together for *Brave New World*, and there were already four songs left over from the previous album, so we really only did six new songs. So creatively there really wasn't a lot of room for me or Bruce on that."

Brave New World didn't set the world on fire sales-wise, but to be fair, the album was issued at the beginning of the downloading wars, specifically the dispute between Metallica and Napster, which kicked off with a lawsuit two months previous. Still, that's no excuse, with physical product still enjoying ubiquity for years to come. As of 2008, the album had shifted 307,000 copies in the US. But then again, Iron Maiden is famously a band belonging to the whole world, including countries other rock stars can't even pronounce. Still, there was a bevy of gold certifications, including Canada (for sales of over 50,000 copies), Brazil (100,000), UK (100,000), and Germany (150,000). Both Finland and Sweden punched well above weight, with 16,000 copies sold in Finland (population 5.5 million) and a whopping 40,000 copies in Sweden, a country with a population of ten million. As for the charts, bright spots included the UK (#7), Germany (#3), Italy (#3), and Sweden (#1). On *Billboard* in the US, *Brave New World* got to a #39 placement.

Dave Wright archive

CHAPTER 17

The first leg of the *Brave New World* tour was a European one, with support coming, variously, from Dirty Deeds, the Almighty, Slayer, Entombed, and Spiritual Beggars; this took place from July 1 to 24. June 20 marked the release date of Ayreon's *Universal Migrator Part 2: Flight of the Migrator* concept album, which includes a track called "Into the Black Hole," on which Bruce provides lead vocals.

As Bruce told Dmitry Epstein, this was a one-off. "I'm not going to be doing anything with Arjen. I did one track with him; he's a very talented guy. I was thinking to do some writing with him, possibly doing an album project, but what happened was this all got out into the internet because he released details of it, either through email or something to his fan club. And all of a sudden it all was released, that I was doing an album with Arjen. So, I asked him; I said, 'This is not true; is it you who put everything out; there's no professionalism.' And he mailed me back saying, 'Oh no, no, no, I'd never do anything like that.' But I found out that actually he did it. So, I don't have any plans to do anything with Arjen. He's talented, he has his own career, and I wish him all the success."

Three mid-July Maiden dates had to be canceled, due to Janick falling off the stage at the Metal 2000 Festival in Mannheim, Germany, on July 8, at which Dream Theater and Motörhead were on the bill as support. Gers sustained a head injury after he fell 10 feet to the floor of the venue. He was knocked unconscious and also sprained his back and was bleeding from his head, while also suffering additional bruising. His head wound resulted in six stitches applied at the local hospital.

Two out of three ain't bad. San Diego Sports Arena, San Diego, California, September 12, 2000. © Tom Wallace

Steve issued a statement directly after, writing, "We are always very disappointed when we are forced to cancel shows in this way, but we are also relieved that Janick is recovering, as it was a serious fall. We were all very concerned for him when he was taken away in the ambulance. Right now, all we can say is sorry to our fans in Germany, Bulgaria, and Greece, but I'm sure they can understand the reason and will also wish Janick a quick recovery."

Speaking with Valerie Potter from Metal-Is, Steve added more detail concerning the mishap. "He's all right. Well, he's not 100 percent all right, but he's getting better day by day. He was pretty bad. I suppose it could've been worse in a way. He had quite a few stitches in a cut on his left eyebrow and a cracked collarbone. He had a concussion and unbelievable bruising. He looked like somebody had painted him! Luckily enough, he doesn't remember any of it. He only remembers waking up in the ambulance and hearing us do 'Hallowed' and was thinking, 'I should be playing my solo on this!' That's what he said, yeah!

"Thing was, when they took him off on the stretcher, we thought maybe he wasn't too bad because although he was covered in claret everywhere, I could see the cut was above the eye and you always bleed badly from a cut there anyway. He was waving to us, but he doesn't remember any of that. I never saw it happen because I was right on the catwalk on the other side. I heard one of the guitars go off, but I thought the gear had packed up. Then Bruce said about stopping the show, and first and foremost in my head was that someone had been hurt in the audience, because the paramedics were going over. And then of course as I ran over the other side and looked over and it was dear old Jan.

"It didn't look too good because he was laying [sic] on his back covered in blood. He wasn't moving too much. That was during 'Number of the Beast' and we decided to carry on and do that song again, and then do 'Hallowed' and then we didn't bother doing 'Sanctuary.' And it felt weird, I must admit, doing them. But with 14,000 people in the audience, we thought we couldn't just stop. I suppose because it was old stuff we were playing in the encores; we could get by doing it with the two guitar players. But that's why we had to pull the other three shows—Essen, Sofia, and Athens—because he plays a lot of key parts on the new material. And there's no way we could've done it with two guitars."

Typically, six *Brave New World* selections were played on the campaign for the album, but that would drop to only "Brave New World" on the *Dance of Death* tour, nothing on the following tour, but then sporadic usage later on, typically "The Wicker Man," "Ghost of the Navigator," and "Blood Brothers."

Dave Wright archive

August 1 through September 24, the campaign shifts to North America. Also, on the bill at this point were Entombed for the opening Canadian dates, Queensryche for the remainder, and Halford throughout. All bands were part of the Sanctuary stable, to varying degrees.

Noted manager Rod Smallwood at the time, "You don't agree on every detail every day. We work very much as a team. I think the fact that I've always viewed it very much the same way as Steve in the beginning, and obviously as the band changed, with Bruce coming in, that we all tended to see things pretty much the same way. I've had fights with Steve over the set list. There's one tour in America a few years back that I just kept going at it all the way through the tour [laughs]. But at the end of the day, the set is what the guys want to do. I mean, I'll put my viewpoint in of what's working best, but it's not a big deal. Putting the stage set together, I'll take it to a certain point, at which point it's a good time for the band to get together and take a look at it, and then we'll look at it together and make some adjustments. I think one of the reasons we've been able to move along so well is that we all have pretty much the same feel for what Iron Maiden should be. We all feel privileged to work for a thing called Iron Maiden. Everyone has got a different job to do, whether it's sound man, manager, band; we all work for this thing, and we all want the best for it. So, I think you have to take it from an Iron Maiden perspective, not an individual perspective."

Steve had a treat for his family planned, telling Valerie Potter, "I'm flying to some shows with Bruce, but I'm taking the family out for about five weeks during the school holidays, so that will be good. When I told them I was going to use a tour bus or a motor home, they were totally excited about that. Because they love being on the bus. They don't get off on flying around everywhere. It's a good vibe, isn't it, I suppose, an adventure? As it's a summer tour, we'll probably stay out of town on campsites and stuff like that. It'll be fun.

San Diego Sports Arena, San Diego, California, September 12, 2000. © *Tom Wallace*

"I enjoy the gigs as much as I've ever done, but the traveling becomes a bit tiresome, I've got to say. Being away from the family is the hardest part, but the fact that they will be out with me in the States makes it fine. It's not easy, touring. That's the thing, I think. If the band ever knocks it on the head, it's because of that, because we're fed up with being away from our homes and families. But once we've had a bit of time off and recharged the batteries, I think everyone will probably be itching to get out there again. But who knows? Maybe they won't. They might feel, 'I could get used to this, being at home!' We'll see."

Midtour, on August 8, Halford issue their debut album, *Resurrection*. Bruce Dickinson cowrites and sings on the album highlight, "The One You Love to Hate." Noted Bruce as the opus was being assembled, "I've heard some of the back tracks. Obviously, I did a track with Rob on it, and I heard some of the demos and I heard one of the songs called 'Silent Scream,' which is just fucking awesome. The whole album is like classic *Screaming for Vengeance*–era Priest. Brilliant. His singing is amazing, so I think it'd be a really positive move for him. It will be pretty good for the audience too. I think they'd love it, in the absence of Priest from the marketplace."

As Bruce told Dmitry Epstein, "'The One You Love to Hate' was a song that Roy and I wrote for my solo album, and we went, 'Ah, that's a cool song, and for next solo album we must record that one.' Then Roy got the job with Rob Halford, and I forget whether it was me or whether it was him who said, 'Why don't we do "The One You Love to Hate" as a little duet? That will be funny and ironic and everything; it'll be cool.'"

We've heard from Blaze, but on August 29, Maiden belter from the first two records Paul Di'Anno returned with an all-new batch of songs called *Nomad*. Mused the Beast at the time on calling the record *Nomad*, "I spent a lot of time in the States, in Texas and LA and wherever. At the moment, I'm sometimes in England, but most of the time I'm back in Brazil, in Sao Paulo. In England I'm in Salisbury, near Stonehenge. But I just seem to not be able to settle down anywhere. I move around the world, as they say, here and there, meet many different sorts of people, get ideas. Some of the things I see around the world, I'm not very happy about. Musically, we wanted something that is heavy but not hard core. I suppose it's just heavy metal for 2000. We don't try to sound like the old stuff; I don't believe in that. As a musician you should go forward with the times. It's not as heavy as what we did before with Battlezone.

"As for my singing, this is very strange, because going into that Battlezone album, it was a lot heavier. I don't know, I keep finding this . . . there's some sort of a rage inside of me, and sometimes it comes up. I don't know if I'm an angry young man anymore, but as I'm getting older, I'm finding that I'm more pissed off [laughs]. One thing I do know, it's as I'm getting older, my voice is getting better and better. I'm very happy with that. It just seems to be getting easier, and I don't do anything to take care of my voice in any way, shape, or form, to be quite honest with you [laughs]. I wish I did. I still smoke cigarettes, so I don't really take much care of it. All I know is if you can't do it in the first place, you shouldn't be doing it at all.

"They're not very happy ones, are they?" laughs Paul, asked about the lyrics on the record. "I don't know, there just seems to be a lot of shit going on in the world. Certain places you go to see, I can't stand seeing poverty and racism. You just become more and more aware of it. I mean, there are a lot of other people who say the same things on the subjects that I do, but it means a lot to me, so it comes from me and I'm pretty happy about writing about it. My life has changed quite a bit."

Paul says that when it came to the vocals, he'd lay it down in one or two takes. "I've just done eight tracks in two days over the weekend for my punk album. I'm pretty fast. I mean, if you can't get it the first or second time, you should just leave it. I couldn't see myself being one of those people who would be in the studio for two years making a record. I'd probably commit suicide. But we were pretty lucky because me and Paulo [Turin, guitars] were sort of swapping tapes. We'd send each other music, and I took care of the lyrics. And when it came down to rehearsals, we were pretty much there. We rehearsed for about five days. The guys got all the music together in about three days, four days, and then they recorded for about a week and a bit and then I came in, in Brazil, for about four days, I think. I did all my vocals in one and a half days, and then I thought, oh shit, I can do better than that, and I went in and did them again."

But Paul wanted to end his nomadic lifestyle, as well as clear up legal troubles that had him unable to enter the US.

"I'm probably going to be going back to Brazil for good, either towards the end of next year or maybe early in the year after. I've got my girlfriend down there, a family and stuff, so I've got to go back for that. Plus, it's a hell of a lot warmer than England. And we've got some of our roots from Brazil in the first place. I absolutely love it. I speak Portuguese only a little [laughs]. The thing is, I'm so bloody lazy. I can get away with it. It's okay. But once my girlfriend and me are together, she speaks bloody English! And it gets on my bloody nerves. She was thrown into the deep end and couldn't speak any English at all, and now she's been working in the States for a year, and she's had to learn. She is practicing her English, but she should be teaching me Portuguese.

"We've got a few little business ventures on the go," continues Di'Anno, torn, it seems. "There's a little hotel and pub thing we run here in Salisbury. I've got the restaurant franchise, so I do a lot of restauranteuring and stuff like that. So, we've got that one and plans for another one. I want to try to open up a restaurant in Brazil. Me and Paulo have some good ideas for the internet. But we're basically going to try to get some government help on that. We want to set up . . . well, we're going to have to start in Sao Paulo and then spread to other cities, for people sixteen to fifty-five, to educate them, get them IT-trained so they have a better chance at getting a job. Because there's no welfare in Brazil. If you've got no money, you die, basically. So, we're trying to get them computer-literate or at least trained up and literate to give them a chance to get them out of the ghettos and the favelas.

"We're trying to give something back. Paulo and I had this idea to set up and then encourage them, so give them something like $25 a month. I know it doesn't sound like a lot, but it's a hell of a lot of money in Brazil. So obviously to do that, we've got to put in vast amounts of our own money, something like a couple of million bucks each, and then see if we can persuade the government to back us up with the rest of it. Out of all the South American countries, Brazil is probably one of the best and most lenient, but not always [laughs]. There's a hell of a battle there, and it's going to start on a small scale, but if we can get them interested, then they might put it in most cities. I don't know how the hell you're going to do it, but we have to work it out that so many people can come, maybe twenty-five people a day at various levels. There's a hell of a job there. We're still trying to work out the logistics of it."

On making a living as a singer and recording artist across all these different band configurations, Paul figures, "Obviously you've got bills to pay, mortgages to pay, kids to feed, and clothes and stuff like that, and a family to look after. So that's all been done okay, but that's not really the important thing at the end of the day, is it? The important thing is you've got a chance of getting up and doing something onstage. You've done everything and you are now just basically showing off a little bit, aren't you? That's the most important thing to me, the actual playing. Everything else is a bonus. But I've been able to feed and clothe my children. And my mother and stepfather have a really nice house. I've got a nice place and all that stuff; I've got a couple of Harleys; I'm quite happy. Times get a little bit tough now and again, but then again, I've done a couple of stupid business ventures which weren't too smart [laughs]. No, I've got loads of plans for more production and engineering work. But I'm not ready to give up playing live yet."

Asked if playing live is more satisfying than writing, Paul says, "No, no, no, it's the two coming together. The one thing I really don't like is being stuck in the studio. But going on tour, oh God, I've done that for years, but I love it, getting to meet lots of people. And the writing, it gets the anger and stuff out of me onto paper. That's good, very cleansing sometimes. Apart from that, I absolutely adore playing, and never more so than when I get back to Brazil as well.

"I'll tell you what; not nearly a day goes by when I'm not nearly in tears down there. Because the way they are towards me and the way I am towards them . . . we're probably the second-biggest band to come out of Brazil, apart from Sepultura. And it's nice to see the country getting some more recognition apart from football, which is absolutely wonderful. But I'll tell you, it's a whole different thing. There's fans and there's *fans*. But it's very, very emotionally draining at the best of times to be onstage and give everything you've got. But it's even more so once I'm back in Brazil. Because they know they've got me anytime, anyplace that they want me, because I have such a big love for all the guys. It's almost like a one-to-one basis with every one of all of them. It's absolutely fantastic. I am so, so happy. When I get off the plane in Sao Paulo, I truly get down and say, 'Okay, I'm home.'"

On November 21, 2001, Di'Anno issued *Killers Live at the Whiskey*. Also this year is *Cessation of Hostilities*, a box set of all of Paul's three studio albums with Battlezone. The trio is also repackaged for a box in 2008, at that point called *The Fight Goes On*. Explained Paul, "We rerecorded 'Children of Madness' for the last Battlezone album, and we sort of made it a bit more how it should be. But unfortunately, over these last six months or so, Battlezone has just come to a complete dead halt. There's some personal stuff going on with one of the boys. I won't say who, but they got a little bit fed up with me and Paulo, like, 'What's going on with this solo stuff?' There are some petty jealousies going on there, and I said, oh, sod that, I ain't having all that. So that's out the window, and the bass player is now playing in the punk band with me [laughs], and he's happy to do that, and me and Paulo will just carry on with the solo stuff."

Back in Maiden world, on September 23 *Billboard* magazine celebrates Sanctuary Group's twenty-fifth anniversary with typical in-depth coverage and congratulatory notices from a multitude of businesses associated with the company. This is a busy time of dealmaking for the company that would have its consequences later on.

Maiden's novel triple-guitar attack. San Diego Sports Arena, San Diego, California, September 12, 2000. © Tom Wallace

October 19 through 29, the *Brave New World* tour hits Japan. Janick "Crazy Legs" Gers is his typical self, a ball of energy second only to Bruce, who isn't encumbered with a guitar. "There isn't much to it," Janick said, when, backstage at the Toronto stop, I asked about his stage presence. "If I feel good and I feel comfortable, I move around. If I can't, I can't. I'm feeling pretty good, but I'm still recovering from my fall. I guess I won't be too mobile tonight." Offered Adrian, "Maybe just a shimmy!" Janick: "Yeah, I'll be shimmying. It's a bit like this [sticks his toe out]. I'm afraid the spirit is willing, but the flesh is weak [laughs]." Commenting on his playing versus the other guys, he figures, "We're all different. It depends how you look at it. It's hard to talk about yourself. Dave has a very smooth sound, and Adrian is very rhythmic. I'm maybe a bit more rackety, off the wall."

November 2 through 10, Maiden and Halford play a handful of European dates as part of a package called Metal 2000. Offered Bruce, "In the 1980s, the Monsters of Rock thing was a series of celebratory metal festivals, kind of like Ozzfest but, you know, nobody gave a shit if it was like Lollapalooza at all. Metal festivals for fans. We're calling it Metal 2000 because everybody was getting bent out of shape. They're like, 'Monsters of Rock? There aren't too many monsters of rock left.' So, we said, well, let's just call it Metal 2000. That's pretty clear, isn't it? Nobody can bitch about that. It's a pretty blue-collar kind of name, it's not subtle, it doesn't have overtones of supermodels or any bullshit like that. It's just straight down the line and pretty primitive. Metal 2000 leaves you in no doubt what it's all about. I don't know where Korn fit into all that, but never mind."

On December 4, Eagle Vision issued for their *Classic Albums* DVD series an edition examining 1982's *The Number of the Beast*. Into the new year, January 6 through 19, Maiden play two UK shows at Shepherd's Bush Empire before flying to Mexico for a performance, followed by three South American dates. Halford and Queensryche support on the Mexican date, with Halford alone continuing on to South America. On January 19, the band plays (and records) the show that will become the *Rock in Rio* live album.

On February 6, 2001, Paul Di'Anno issued *The Beast: Live*, explaining, "My old band Killers and me have agreed to do a little reunion tour. And we've just been in rehearsals last week, and it's going really good. Yes, Killers, we've all stayed friends and stuff, but I didn't see any . . . there's a time you have to walk away from it. Things were getting a little bit stale. They like to play this sort of old-style music, and I've never really been a big lover of that. I came from punk and then Iron Maiden."

Back in the Maiden camp, 2001 was a bit of a year off. But Bruce emerged in February 2002 to talk with our magazine's Tim Henderson about . . . toys! Namely, the Todd McFarlane Eddie, issued in May 2002. "I'm doing some strange things," begins Bruce. "I went to a toy fair yesterday, and having seen the toys, you know, I can understand. They're not really toys. I mean I went 'round the showrooms when I saw the full-size originals of all the things that Todd does, and they're pretty awesome. The *Spawn* stuff is amazing, and in the backroom he's got like the 'adult' collection, which is all the H. R. Giger stuff. So, I'm like, 'umm.' It's pretty serious business, one or two of the things he does.

"I was blown away, to be honest with you, when I heard we were doing an action figure," continues Dickinson, "and we were doing it with this guy Todd McFarlane, and people were making a big deal about it. I was like, 'I don't know who this guy is.' So, I did a bit of poking around, and as soon as I heard he was Marvel Comics and then I saw some of his art, I thought, 'Wow, this guy's really awesome.' There's something really there about this guy and the way he comes across; he comes across as such an ordinary guy that you know he's not. He makes out like he is 'Oh yeah, it's just something I do, and blah, blah, blah,' but there's something . . . 'How do you come up with all this twisted stuff?' 'Oh just, you know, messin' around.' And I'm like, 'Yeah, right.'"

San Diego Sports Arena, San Diego, California, September 12, 2000. © *Tom Wallace*

CHAPTER 17

As most boys his age won't admit, Bruce played with dolls. "Oh totally, we had GI Joe [laughs], but we didn't call it GI Joe; we called it Action Man. It was exactly the same—it was the guy with big muscles and no dick. When I was a kid, I spent, I suppose, a large part of my youth fighting war games with little lead soldiers and stuff and refighting the Battle of Waterloo endlessly. This is like a twelve-year-old. I had entire armies painted up and all manner of things. I had fleets of Greek battleships, you know, triremes and biremes and things like that. Actually, I've still got them. It's just a fascination for kids, and when I did it, it was all kind of quaint. It was so underground; people were making all their own stuff, or they were converting little plastic soldiers like you'd get in a multibuy, buy a hundred soldiers for two bucks or something, little Chinese things. People were converting those into things to play war games with and coming up with their own rules and stuff.

"And then you had Dungeons & Dragons, and of course in England at the moment you've got this thing, Warhammer, which is an equivalent to the thing. It's like fantasy armies and it's gone very kind of sci-fi, and in a sense a bit corporate in the background because it's all organized and they have chains of shops, and they have tournaments. It's the same basic idea; it's a strategy game. It's kind of like chess but without the dry academic thing. There's a bit more humor involved.

"But then that's what kids are interested in; not so much war, but the idea of combat. Males in general like competition of some kind. I was a pretty geeky kind of a kid, you know. I wasn't a brilliant kind of sports jock, but I still would have liked to get it on with somebody. You know, you would prove yourself. Guys want to prove themselves. It's kind of a biological thing, in some way. And if you're not Muhammad Ali, then maybe you can do it with your brain. Maybe you do play chess or maybe you play war games or whatever. Or you fence. You try and prove yourself; you try and butt heads against some other guy and find out what he's made of and find out also what you're made of. You know, it's natural.

"Anyway, I said to Todd, 'I've got some fuckin' great ideas for action figures for you' [laughs]. I got quite a buzz yesterday, I must say. I must confess to being cautious about it, because it's one thing for marketing people to love something and say, 'Yeah, yeah, isn't it a perfect match?' Maiden's thing is music, and whilst Eddie is a big part of the band and everything else, without the music Eddie would be a very different creature. If you took Eddie separately to Iron Maiden, I suppose he could have his own career. But it would be a very, very different kind of Eddie to the one we have at the moment, if he actually had to have a career, you know, rather than just appear every couple of years in a different guise on album sleeves. So, I'm very wary of what the fans' reaction is gonna be. At least some of it is fairly easy to gauge, because if they don't like the stuff then they're not going to go and buy it. Todd's take on the whole thing is, you know, he's done the first one, the *Killers* one, and it's pretty much . . . it's just, it's gone. It's gone like crazy. So, he's doing 'The Trooper' one, and with each incarnation, if it sells, then we'll do another one. But it's going to be a kind of organic growth. There's no plan to do, 'Oh yeah, let's do a range of twelve of them' or something. We'll just do them one at a time."

At the time, Bruce and the guys had only recently discovered that their dear old drummer Clive Burr—*Iron Maiden, Killers, The Number of the Beast*—was suffering from multiple sclerosis. They quickly got it together to do some benefit gigs, three nights at the Brixton Academy in March, and raised a significant amount of money for a new Clive Burr Multiple Sclerosis Trust Fund.

"We'd already asked Clive if he was okay with the idea of us doing a charity show for him, and he said yeah. It leaked out two or three weeks before it should have. People were telling me that it had been posted, so we figured we'd better release the information. But yeah, it's a really shitty thing to happen, and there's not a lot you can say about it other than the fact that we are going to try and raise some money to help him pay for some treatment and/or alleviation of the symptoms of the disease. I see things that have happened to friends of mine. I don't have that many people who are close to me who I have lost over the years. It makes you think about life and what a cool thing it is."

Added Paul Di'Anno in a statement, "Get well, Clive. I am very sad indeed to hear about Clive's current health condition. And I really hope and pray that there will be a major improvement for him soon. I have always admired Clive as a wonderful person and also as a brilliant drummer too. During my early career, I shared some of my very best times alongside Clive, and I have nothing other than good memories of him. Clive, you can fight this, so hang on in there, mate, and if there's anything at all I can do, just call me and I'll be there."

Noted Nicko, speaking with Ray Van Horn Jr., "It's so sad that I see this friend of mine. He can hardly hold a cup of tea, much less a pair of sticks, and that's pretty bad in itself. We want to try and help get Clive through a better quality of life, and by us making an awareness, our fans are only too generous to step up every time. Doing those shows was great. We got a chance to actually say, 'Look, this is for you, Clive.'"

On the live show in general, Nick added that "we have always been and always will, with whatever time God has blessed us with, to just carry on and do these wonderful tours, go out with something very special, because the fans, to us, they're the special people. When we think about putting a stage show together, we spend a lot of money, and sometimes it's not enough; we think we need to do this and the management will go, 'You can't do that; it's ridiculously expensive!,' and we go, 'So what?' To be honest, we don't really make a lot of money when we go on tour, because we put it into the show; I mean, sure, we make merchandise and stuff, but we put a lot of money into our shows

Nicko, tail end of the North American campaign, San Diego, California, September 12, 2000, before the band jets off to Japan. © *Tom Wallace*

because we believe our fans deserve that. It's the way we've always done that. We pride ourselves not only for putting out great music—that's the essence, number one—but secondly is great lights, having a fantastic lighting array onstage, and then you've got the theme of the gigs."

"Clive had really dropped off the radar screen," continues Bruce. "And it was one of those things that, I suppose up till about five years ago, he was always kind of around as it were. He lives over on the other side of London, and I'd bump into somebody in the pub, and they'd say, 'I saw Clive the other day and he was drumming or doing something.' And I went, 'Oh, cool.' And you just knew that he was around. And then he just disappeared, and people kept asking me if I had seen Clive, and I didn't know what he was doing. I don't know when he found out about this disease. If I did know anything else, I'd be a bit reluctant to start talking about his personal life. He must be feeling a bit ambivalent about this thing because, yes, we're helping him out, but at the same time he's getting his problems splattered all over the papers. I haven't spoken to him about it. I would really like to get together with him and have a chat about things and find out how he's doing. But that hasn't happened."

During his time away from Maiden, Bruce had been working as a pilot, but . . . "I *was*, but the airline I was flying with went bust December 14, so . . ." Remember, this chat with Bruce took place five months after the terrorist attacks of 9/11, and the debate was on about security in the skies. Explains Bruce, "I mean, the crazy thing is that last year in fact was the safest year for flying since records began. That is including the deliberate crashing of those airliners and the American crash that happened shortly afterwards. Including all of that, including the loss of life and everything, it was still the safest year for air travel since records began. Less people and less airplanes crashed than ever before. Nobody's interested in that fact.

"In the States, people still seem to be, at least in the press, extremely twitchy about things. I think in Europe the feeling is that we've had all the security measures that the US are now implementing in Europe for many years. We're also used to having terrorism. We've had numerous hijacks in the UK. We've had various people try to blow up large parts of the city over the course of the last few years, quite recently in fact, so we're used to it. It doesn't really affect the way we go about our daily business. Nobody changes what they do because there's a bomb threat, other than 'Oh, there's a bomb threat; I better take the alternative route to work.' That's it. Or 'Oh, a bomb's gone off; oh well, it's all over now,' and we go back to work.

"It's not numbness necessarily; it's just a sense of, well, hang on a minute; if you throw up your hands and panic and run around like a headless chicken any time some psycho decides to make his little bid for glory, then you let them win. You cannot let the terrorists win. The terrorists' only weapon, really, other than a bomb, which tragically might kill a few people, most of these things, if they kill people, kill a handful of people in a very localized area, but it seems like they've blown up half the country from the impact they make. The thing is, so you reduce the impact they make by refusing to be affected by it. Other than to say, 'Excuse me, is that your bag there?' on the train. People need to be a bit more vigilant and switched on about things.

"Thank God they didn't go with this thing of having pilots wandering around toting guns in the cockpit. I had visions of Wyatt Earp flying me from LA to New York. Now you don't even need to smuggle a gun onto an airplane [laughs]. Let alone the idea of a pilot actually going psychotic with a weapon. Actually, there were far more instances of pilots becoming incapacitated or pilots becoming mentally ill or something else like that, than there ever are of people hijacking airplanes. Having all these guns on airplanes makes me extremely nervous. I'm not in favor of guns on airplanes, or anywhere near airplanes.

"I was stuck here on September 11. I was here in New York when it all went down [as noted, the author conducted a phone interview with Bruce that day]. I was stuck here for four or five days. I got out on the Saturday and on the Monday or the Tuesday I flew 230 people to Turkey in a 757. That was my first job, and that was on the day when Osama went, 'All Muslims stay away from airports and airplanes.' I went to work, flying for this airline I was flying for, and flew to Turkey. You just get on and go and do it. We were a charter flight for holidaymakers, so unless this terrorist had booked his holiday well in advance . . . It does obviously cross your mind, but you have to have a sense of proportion about it and balance the security aspects and the paranoia with reality. Anyway, somebody once said to me, 'What do you do?' and I thought, 'What day is it?' It's nice because when I do have big chunks of time off, hopefully I can go and grab myself a part-time job doing what I love. It's good."

On March 11, 2002, Iron Maiden issued their "Run to the Hills" single, in two parts with various live tracks as B-sides. Proceeds earned went to the Clive Burr Multiple Sclerosis Trust Fund, courtesy of EMI and music publisher BMG. This was followed by the shows at the Brixton Academy, March 19, 20, and 21, also in support of Clive.

Busy week it was, for on March 25, Maiden issued a live album called *Rock in Rio*, which served as the ultimate celebration of the reunion with Bruce and Adrian, through the inclusion of six *Brave New World* tracks; namely, "The Wicker Man," "Ghost of the

Note Steve's football jersey, which is *Brave New World* themed but nonetheless ties us back to the aesthetic of *Virtual XI*. San Diego Sports Arena, San Diego, California, September 12, 2000. © *Tom Wallace*

Navigator," and "Brave New World" (as first, second, and third selections on the nearly two-hour double album), along with "Blood Bothers," "The Mercenary," and "Dream of Mirrors."

"Well, basically it's the *Brave New World* tour," explained Bruce. "That's it; if you saw that tour, that's what it is. And I mean, this is one concert in its entirety with nothing added, no overdubs, no fooling around with it. It's just been mixed, that's it. Which makes it different to all the other live albums we've ever done. I mean, the one we really have to live up to, of course, is *Live After Death*. Because that is the one by general agreement that, far and away, is the biggest, the most popular, the one that everybody seems to regard as the classic Maiden live album. I actually think that this one, *Rock in Rio*, stands a chance of displacing it, or if not that, at least matching it. And from a personal viewpoint, I think my performance on this is vastly superior to *Live After Death*. I haven't listened to the originals for years [laughs]. The arrangements wouldn't have changed at all, but the way we played them might have. I mean, if anything's happened, it's happened by a process of osmosis, just gradually. We were so lucky on this one because this particular concert, *Rock in Rio*, it was broadcast live to 100 million people the same night we recorded it. So, people who doubt my word on this, all they have to do is go and avail themselves of the many bootlegs [laughs] and listen to the TV mix, and you'll see that ain't nothing been changed. It just sounds a shitload better [laughs]."

Steve, however, had to step in to settle what was a bit of an internet row over folks doubting Bruce. "Let's get one thing straight," wrote Steve in a statement. "Bruce is *not* a liar. There are *no* overdubs on this live album. While it was being mixed in New York

The ever-athletic Janick, September 12, 2000. © *Tom Wallace*

by Kevin Shirley and myself, Bruce was in London, to my knowledge, or wherever he was. It's not an issue, except to say that he could not overdub anything if he wasn't there!

"What *has* happened is that I made an executive decision to cut and paste with a computer to put back in his *live* on the night vocals into parts where he was getting the audience to sing on some choruses on some lines on their own. The reason I did this is because in the cold light of day, it sounds better with him back in there because sometimes the audience were either out of time or not quite loud enough. So, I simply cut out parts of his vocal on the line before and pasted it into the next line, which was possible because it was a repetitive part. I find it amazing that people would question this band's integrity and indeed to go as far as to accuse someone of being a liar. Supposed fans like that we don't want. As far as I'm concerned, we're better off without people like that. If you don't like what I've done with the album, don't buy it. Simple! Steve Harris, 18th of March 2002."

On the increasingly debated concept of releasing physical product, Bruce reflected that "I think it proves, in a sense, that . . . there's been so much doom and gloom caused by this whole MP3 and Napster and everything else, that it's nice to have a band like us where the fans do actually go out, and whether they download MP3s or not, they still go out and buy the stuff, and it's good to do good stuff that's worth buying. I have to say that the *Rock in Rio* live album is something I'm extremely proud of. I mean, we've had five live albums, haven't we? I've lost count. We had a flurry of live albums, none of which were particularly distinguished. *Live One*, *Dead One*, and *Live at Donington* I haven't listened to in any great depth 'cause I didn't think they were that great. *Live After Death* is the one that everybody picks and says, 'Hey that's the classic live album,' and up to now I'm not going to disagree.

"But I think this one's really cool, and it's worth having a listen to because the band is just so fucking good on it. The attitude when we go out onstage and everything else is like a sports team. We go out and kick the hell out of the opposition, except the opposition isn't there. We're not trying to beat up our audience, but there is some invisible barrier that we want to bust through live. And Kevin Shirley's done a great mix. It's the best audience in the world. It is far and away the best audience in the world, this Brazilian audience, 250,000 people. It's a great-sounding record. It really is like you're there, and you are there because it's one entire show. There are no overdubs; it's not been fucked with in any way at all. I believe the only thing we had to do—and I heard this from another journalist who'd interviewed Kevin Shirley—was he had to move the audience's singing because with the size of the venue there was a huge time delay. The audience was singing along, but by the time it got to the microphone they were singing out of time with the band. By the miracle of ProTools, he managed to get the audience singing in time. Otherwise, the audience was so loud it would have

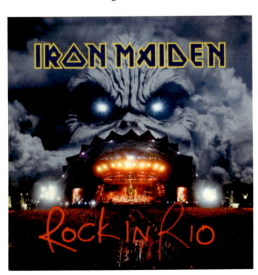

Dave Wright archive

been pretty confusing, with the audience singing out of time but with all the right words. But there's been no altering of any guitars or vocals or anything like that, no redoing of anything. It's one complete concert—pretty cool."

"A South American crowd knows every single lyric of every single song," Shirley told *Mix* magazine. "What used to be a problem with 300,000 people, where you have all these delay towers all the way down the field, was that you'd have this long delay thing. So, I just went into ProTools and found a snare crack on all the delay towers and shifted all the delay towers in time. All of a sudden, you have 300,000 people singing in time with the track, and it's phenomenal. For the 5.1, it's outrageous. The band barely features; the audience is just spine-tingling."

In terms of interesting wrinkles, Bruce says, "There's a bunch of songs on there that they haven't heard live anyway—'Blood Brothers' and 'The Clansman' and things like that are just spine-tingling stuff. So, no apologies whatsoever for doing this record 'cause it really is a worthwhile listen."

As for the art, "There's a lenticular sleeve that's going to be out in a limited edition. Now in Canada, I believe, you're going to be lucky enough to get ahold of it. But in America, of course, Sony are like, 'We don't know about this lenticular sleeve.' But it's great; what happens is as you look at the *Rock in Rio* front on, and you see, you know, the audience and the stage and the band and then you move it like that, and Eddie comes up 'Arrgh' and the stage is his mouth. It looks great."

"The Rock in Rio festival was a huge production," summed up Steve, in the press materials, "and as the recording facilities were already there, we had the opportunity to record the event, which was Maiden's biggest headlining show ever. Kevin Shirley came down to the show to oversee the recording, and we then returned to New York to put together all the parts. The crowd was absolutely amazing and at times nearly drowned out the band with their singing. The show was an unforgettable experience. And I want to thank all the fans who were at the show. It was a fantastic way to finish the tour, and I'm really pleased with the final result as it really captures the atmosphere of the night."

On June 12, 2002, *Rock in Rio* emerges as a two-DVD package, which Bruce wondered, back in February, whether it would ever get done.

"Oh, Christ yes. I mean, you know Steve—he's Mr. Picky. I was there in the office when he downloaded some files for them to send, just some extras, and he'd done it in such kind of fidelity that it was taking ages to download. They were really having problems and they were tearing their hair out going, 'Why the fuck does he have to do it in full bloody detailed maximum color broadcast mode? It's only a fucking thumbnail thing that's going to be on there, blah, blah blah.' It's because it's Steve, and it's got to be absolutely the dog's bollocks [laughs]. But he's been tearing his hair out by the roots to get this together. It's a huge undertaking.

"He's basically set himself up with Final Cut Pro, which is a more user-friendly version of Avid, Avid being a fairly advanced editing software. I've spoken to professional video guys that have gone, 'Oh yeah, Final Cut Pro's really easy; yeah, it only took me about a year to get the hang of it.' Basically, he's been doing this since last summer, nonstop pretty much, on his own, and he's had all kinds of screw-ups, technical snafus, some of which are to do with the transfer of the data. But anyway, to cut a long story short, as I understand it, the bits that he's finishing up now are the offstage footage of the band. So, the bulk of everything else is more or less together, but he's been working extremely hard on it."

Sounds like a lot of blood, sweat, and tears for what is supposed to be downtime. "Yeah, this is one of the problems. We haven't actually stopped. I certainly haven't bloody stopped. I've got three and a half weeks of promo that I've just done, I've got another two weeks of promo and then I'm going to rehearsal and will be doing fucking three gigs. I'm like, 'Hello?!' So anyway, I think Steve is going to take some time off. There will be a record next year; I'm pretty sure of that. But he really does need to take a break; he was supposed to have twelve months off. He wanted twelve clear months off, and he's had nothing like that. But with my twelve months off, I was like, 'Okay, I have twelve months off, but I could do a couple of bits and bobs during it.' But suddenly this year has gone absolutely crazy, pretty much from the word 'go.' February and March in particular are going to be nuts, but I sort of knew that when I started the year."

The guy Bruce replaced the first time was keeping busy as well, although (ahem, predictably) not opening internet schools all over Brazil. On June 28, 2002, Blake Publishing issued *The Beast*, Paul Di'Anno's autobiography, a frightening and yet charming book, and beautifully appointed, unlike most of his records, which are on tiny labels.

"Obviously I have to use a ghostwriter," Paul told me ten months earlier. "I haven't got bloody time or patience for that. What it is, is a friend of ours called Dale Webb, he came down to where I live the other day, and we did about five and a half hours of straight talking. And he was like, 'Well, about another three or four of them should do it,' and I'm like, 'Fuckin' 'ell, you've got to be kidding me!' [laughs]. It won't be the complete story. I think it will be up to probably about three or four years ago. But hey, there could be room for another one. John Blake Publishing here in England have done loads and loads of books and are quite well respected. They've done a lot of books about gangsters, all this true-life-crime stuff. So, I thought, ah, they might not want to hear too much about the music. So, it's about some of the other things I've gotten up to, interesting things from the seamier side of life [laughs], which is actually good because I've sort of exorcized the demons now. I'm pretty much a completely changed person."

The year 2002 closes off with a few notable events in Maiden's inner and outer orbit. On August 29, Di'Anno sees the release of *Screaming Blue Murder: The Very Best of Paul Di'Anno*. On October 23, skateboard video game *Tony Hawk's Proskater 4* features Eddie as an unlockable character. Also included in the game is the song "The Number of the Beast." The next day, Dream Theater, a Maiden support act in the past, perform *The Number of the Beast* album in its entirety at a show in Paris. An additional connection with Maiden is the fact that Kevin Shirley has worked extensively with both bands.

On November 4, EMI issues the band's third compilation, a sixteen-tracker called *Edward the Great*. On November 16, EMI issues the *Eddie's Archive* box set. It consists of a two-CD early live package called *Beast Over Hammersmith*, a two-CD package called *BBC Archives*, and a third two-CD package called *Best of the B'Sides*.

Dave Wright archive

CHAPTER 17

As Rod Smallwood explained to Tim Henderson, "The *Archive*, the box set, we've been meaning to do for about three years. It was going to be a twenty-fifth anniversary, something from the inception of the band up until last year. So, we've been thinking about doing it, but the target was last year. Really, the greatest hits; it was actually the label that came to us and said, 'Look, there's all these young bands out there; we see how much they're influenced by you and into you.' Whether it's Sum 41 or the old Smashing Pumpkins guys or Papa Roach, you name it, it seems that very many popular bands grew up with Maiden and Eddie and the whole thing.

"They [EMI] thought it'd be great as an introduction to the band, a very simple introduction. *Best of the Beast* was a double album with forty tracks. They want us to do a single, easy introduction. We made it clear to the fans that this is not a fan item. The only thing the fans would want from it, really, assuming they've got everything on there, which they probably have, is the artwork. We're putting that on our website for a free download anyway, so they can get the artwork. It's not for the fans—the box set is for the fans. The greatest hits is—there was a good idea from EMI—if we could introduce Maiden metal to more people, then fuckin' great, you know, why not? We want to play to as many people as we can next year, and if this softens up some new fans to us, then great. I don't think there's any harm at all."

This was all part and parcel of Sanctuary's busy hive of activity at the time, a period that included the acquisition of Trinifold Group, managers of Judas Priest, and the Who, as well as Jimmy Page and Robert Plant.

Asked by Henderson at what point Sanctuary will stop hoovering up businesses, Rod chuckles, "When we've got all our favorite bands. I mean, we've got, from the rock

Dave goes kerrang. San Diego Sports Arena, San Diego, California, September 12, 2000. © *Tom Wallace*

side, Maiden, Priest, Guns N' Roses, Plant & Page, and the Who, and then Ray Davies, of course. And then the catalog side with Motörhead, Black Sabbath, and the Kinks. A lot of my favorite music we're getting involved with, which is fantastic. It's like being a kid in a sweet shop, actually. You know, we just love all the music.

"It's a good move from our point of view. I've known Bill Curbishley for a long time, and he's very good, obviously. We're just in the final days of signing a couple more situations with some more great acts. It's not a matter that they can't handle it; it's just a matter of that they understand how the business is developing. I think our model is good, with how we can supply 360-degree services to an artist. We've got very developed DVD capabilities, both in creating them and marketing them worldwide. We did the Maiden DVD outside North America and got #1 in practically every market in the world. Back here, we've got the studios, we've got the mobiles, we've got the DVD mastering, etc. We've got international offices and we've got a very good team. On managing, we've got the production department, the travel departments, a developing sponsorship end. We work well as a team and managing as a team. We've got a lot of things at our disposal, at our fingertips, really. We can concentrate on the creative end and let the functions run through the group."

But not much has changed in terms of Rod's hands-on approach. "Not at all. We go to the bar about half past six every day and talk about what we're doing. At Sanctuary, we just do things a bit different. We are very careful about who joins the company; we want people that we can look in the eye. You know, what we've been like for years. Nothing's changed at all. Just bigger. More offices and more acts, but the ethics haven't changed at all. And certainly, the music we're into—and into dealing with—hasn't changed."

On December 17, the *Rock in Rio* DVD, having gone gold a month earlier, receives its platinum certification. This all clears the plate for Smallwood and the Maiden guys to get down to business in early 2003 on a follow-up to *Brave New World*. And while the record would serve as merely another fine collection—no waves made yet again—the tide would start to turn in terms of the band's live side of the business. In 2003, or certainly over the ensuing eighteen months, evidenced by shows getting bigger and buzzier every tour out, Iron Maiden would become legitimate classic rock royalty, never to look back.

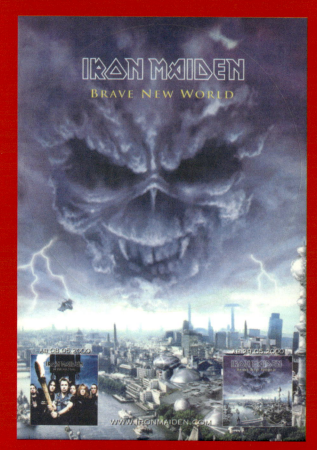

Martin Popoff archive

Dave Wright archive

CHAPTER 18
Dance of Death and *Death on the Road*

"A bit darker, more ominous."

As Maiden rolled into 2003, there was a sense from industry watchers on the outside that Rod and Steve really had a handle on the band's career, backing up the reissuing and the celebration of nostalgia with new music and then getting onstage and pushing that new music hard into the memory circuits of the 'Edbangers.

Proud of their legacy but proud of adding to it, in January and February 2003 the band worked on what would become *Dance of Death*, at Sarm West Studios in London. Noted Adrian, comparing the new proposal with *Brave New World*, "I think we approached them in the same way, same producer, Kevin Shirley. He likes to work; he's a young guy but he's more of an old-school producer. He likes to record the band live and do multiple takes and just pick the best takes. Sometimes we keep some vocals, mostly keep the guitars. It's not a building-block process like we used to do. It's much more of a spontaneous thing. We usually do a song a day, and we record from sort of lunchtime until early evening. During that time, we'll do maybe eight or ten takes of a song. Usually, the first take's the best one, but we usually do it over and over again and then usually come back to the first one. We just keep going to see if we can get a better one. I cowrote a lot of stuff, with Steve. And I don't usually write with Steve; I usually write with Bruce. Bruce and I wrote a lot of stuff for the album, but it didn't make it onto the album. It was probably a little bit more slow and heavy kind of rock, and this one is quite an energetic album. But yes, I obviously cowrote quite a few songs. There's quite a bit of my personality on there."

While Maiden were toiling away, churning out live takes, trying essentially to make a lamp of individual fireflies, as it were, this thing called "power metal" was entering a mature phase. Gamma Ray, Blind Guardian, and HammerFall were keeping alive the type of music Maiden helped invent, and delivering it to younger audiences. So was the original "baby Iron Maiden," Helloween. On February 25, a new baby Maiden emerged, with Dragonforce—oddly and importantly, from the UK—issuing their debut album *Valley of the Damned*, which soon has critics calling them Iron Maiden on speed, in much the same manner that Helloween in the 1980s were seen as a sort of new and improved version of a band perhaps not so secure on the throne in 1986–87.

As well, on March 25 Blaze Bayley's band Blaze issue their live album, *As Live as It Gets*. Along with songs from the Blaze catalog (2000's *Silicon Messiah* and 2002's *Tenth Dimension*), there are a handful of selections from his time with Maiden. Not to be outdone, on August 15 Paul Di'Anno issues a twenty-five-track concert DVD called *The Beast in the East*.

Before the second Maiden album of the 2000s would hit the shops, from May 23 through July 12 the boys embark on the Give Me Ed . . . 'til I'm Dead tour, in Europe, supported, variously, by Stray, Murder Dolls, and Arch Enemy. Arch Enemy's Michael

Amott had already toured with Maiden, as part of his stoner rock band Spiritual Beggars. The set list featured one song, "Wildest Dreams," from the forthcoming studio album. Again, what we see is smart management here, with Smallwood hammering hard on all fronts: with new music forthcoming, there was license to relive the past, again, pedal to the metal everywhere, Maiden ubiquitous. And so, on June 2, EMI issues a two-DVD set called *Visions of the Beast*, a collection of forty-seven promotion videos, just as the band takes the show stateside. July 21 through August 30, the Give Me Ed . . . 'til I'm Dead tour moves to North America, with Dio and Motörhead reprising their roles as support.

Remarked Bruce Dickinson, on the state of his career, speaking with the author at the Toronto stop on the North American leg, "I'm taking, musically speaking, one project at a time. I mean, certainly with going from six years of really intense solo activity, which I nearly lost my shirt, quite literally, financially, and was right on the ropes after a couple of records, to coming back, pulling myself up, and getting back to where I actually had a career as a solo artist again, and then rejoining Maiden in the middle of it, and getting chucked back into the frying pan and *Brave New World*, and then the tour, two tours, and then this album."

And ticket sales had been brisk. "Yes, pretty much sold out in Quebec City, which is really interesting, because what was funny was that the promoter thought we were going to get about one-third the people we actually got. Shows how in touch they are with what's going on in the world. So yeah, we just played to 700,000 people in twenty-eight days. And it's interesting, the Rolling Stones were here and did this free gig, and we outsold them in Scandinavia—the Stones.

"So musically it's been pretty busy," continued Dickinson. "And in some ways, I'm sort of looking for an antidote to the musical side of things. Because the musical side of it is changing now. Maiden is becoming—and I don't know if it's becoming it in North America, but certainly outside of North America—we're becoming like a heavy metal Rolling Stones. It really is, where the live side is very divorced from the album side. Our two biggest tours now, we haven't had a record. We haven't had a bloody record out! So, getting your head around that, that somehow the band has acquired this iconic status by which it seems to do less and yet gets bigger [laughs]; it's difficult to get your head around. And I can't think of myself as a fossil or an icon or that sort of thing; it's just impossible. I don't want to think of myself in that way. So, I simply avoid the issue

Dave Wright archive

altogether and go do something else. I go work for an airline company and fly airplanes as an ordinary Joe, get a suit and tie on, and sit in the front, lock the door, and fly people around for ten hours a day, and they never see me."

As we're going out the door from the dressing room, Bruce mentions going into town for cortisone shots in his knee, in his shoulder, and in his back. His driver says, "We've got to pick up Lemmy on the way. He's in a stripper bar" [as mentioned, Motörhead is on the bill, as is Dio]. I note that it's five o'clock in the afternoon, a couple hours before the band goes on, and she says, "He's been there since 10:30 in the morning!"

Wrote Sean Palmerston in his review of the show that Bruce was to put on that night in Toronto's 16,000-capacity outdoor shed, "This triple bill was made for old-school metalheads. Motörhead kicked things off, storming the stage early and sending the crowd scrambling for their seats. Ploughing through classics like 'No Class,' 'Metropolis,' and 'Killed by Death,' the trio played deafeningly loud and left everyone with a lust for more after a fantastic encore of 'Ace of Spades' and the ultimate closer 'Overkill.' Dio had a lot to live up to and failed miserably. While the 63-year-old warbler still has a hell of a voice, even his honed chops couldn't lift a lifeless, limp performance by the rest of his band. The end of Dio's set couldn't arrive quickly enough, especially knowing Iron Maiden was up next.

"And up they were. This was the Maiden set I have always dreamed of. This show was nearly perfect. With a set depicting their mascot Eddie throughout his different incarnations, they opened with five straight songs from their peak: 'Number of the Beast,' 'The Trooper,' 'Die with Your Boots On,' 'Revelations,' and 'Hallowed Be Thy Name.' You couldn't have asked for a better beginning, and they just built on it. Playing before the largest crowd they've had in Toronto in more than a decade—at least 12,000—the band made good use of their allotted time and wowed the crowd. Upcoming single 'Wildest Dreams' was the only new song; its 'Wicker Man'–style intensity shows promise for the upcoming album. The rest of the show was classic after classic. Vocalist Bruce Dickinson had the crowd eating out of the palm of his hand and was in fine form, except during '2 Minutes to Midnight,' when he was busy kicking beach balls into the crowd. His exuberance and the band's surprise at the warm reception Toronto gave in return supercharged their performance and made it the best metal show I have seen in Canada this year."

Then it was time. On September 1, the band issues "Wildest Dreams" as an advance single, in 7-inch, CD, and DVD formats. Oddities across the four different pieces of product include a jam called "Pass the Jam" and an orchestral mix of "Blood Brothers." The following week, on September 8, the band issues *Dance of Death*, the second studio album since Bruce and Adrian had rejoined.

"To be honest, I would say it was more or less identical," Bruce told me, on the process of crafting the new record. "The only difference, I guess, is that we were really comfortable with the way we were working, and we were used to it from the last record. So, we were pretty delighted, really, to be able to work in the same way, doing things live, rehearsing and doing it live, and that was it. The writing is divvied up fairly equally. Everybody in the band now, basically, if we all had a mind and we all had long enough, we could write three albums between the six of us. So, there's no shortage of material. So, what you have to do is everybody, pretty much, just chill out and sort of go with the flow. It's not like everybody sits there and votes songs in and out and all the rest of it. We more or less take turns, and people go with what is their best stuff. And by and large, if it's a song where you think, this one is pretty cool, play it to everybody, and you go, 'Oh, that's okay,' then it's the next guy's turn."

The "Wildest Dreams" green-vinyl 7-inch and DVD issues. *Dave Wright archive*

Bruce says that the guys would bring ideas to the band in very rudimentary form. "Oh no, I mean raw," he asserts. "As raw as you like. You'd strum a guitar or hum some melody. I mean, the songs are all a collaboration anyway. Sometimes there is no drum machine or anything. Sometimes it's just bass and guitar, and you just do the drums in your head. Me and Adrian had two or three songs left over that we thought were pretty cool. On the other hand, we had one or two unfinished songs that turned into songs. So, we were quite happy. It's all divvied up fairly equally."

Voiced Nicko, in conversation with Carl Begai on a press day in Germany for our mag *BW&BK*, before the album was made available to the public, "The last one, although we had a great time doing it, Kevin Shirley really went to town on the sound. He mixed it rhythm section heavy; the guitars were there but they were down in the middle of the mix. On this album there's much more of a live vibe. Each song on *Brave New World* was mixed on a standard of sound. On the new album we were a little more picky; this song needs more of that, this song needs less of that, this song needs more of that than the one before it. Each song has a different flavor to it.

"If you're a Maiden fan, there's something on this new album for everyone," continued McBrain. "I think the fans can take it as a retrospective history of the music of the band because whether you like *Killers* or *Number of the Beast* or *Seventh Son* the best, there's something in there for you. We never really preconceive our ideas; we don't go in and look at the previous album and say, 'Oh, we had that sort of song, and it went over well; let's do it again.' *Brave New World* was a very mature album, I think, and that was refreshing for us, but this time we decided to try and make the album as live as we could. We did four or five passes of each song, and we'd piece things together if someone fucked up, which I did quite a lot [laughs]. We didn't ProTool it, though. The essence of everything you hear, apart from the guitar solos, are overdubs. We recorded this album in a very traditional Maiden manner, including plenty of red wine. But yeah, there's four big epic songs like on *Brave New World*, but there are also a couple of really quick ones—not as quick as 'Wrathchild' though—like 'Wildest Dreams' and 'Rainmaker,' but we didn't write those songs with the idea of a single in mind. That's just the way they came out.

"Prior to our having three guitars, 90 percent of all our albums featured tracked guitars," continues McBrain. "With the rhythm tracks, the guitars would be doubled, and that would carry through underneath the solos because we only had two guitars, which meant that when we played live, there would be some holes in the sound. With an extra guitar player, we're getting to re-create the old songs live, to really fill things out with harmony rhythms and things. On *Brave New World* and the new album, we had the extra guitar to fill the blanks, which meant a lot less grief for everybody. And when it came down to doing solos, there was no bickering about, 'Oh, he's done two and he's done three and I 'aven't done one yet.' It was more of a 'Come on then, do the solo, you wrote the bloody song.' 'No, you do it 'cos yours sounds better,' which is a great thing about this band now."

"I think it's a more consistent album than *Brave New World*," said Adrian at the time. "This one obviously has a lot more scope. But we always have little disagreements. Nicko in particular had a little disagreement with Steve [laughs] about the drum parts to a song. But it's good because it shows that people care about what they're doing. They had pretty much a face-to-face about it [makes a gesture with his hands 3 inches apart]. Everybody else around just left, and I kept one eye just in case. But it stopped there. But generally, if someone's written a song, I tried to respect what they want. If someone brings a song in, they get a little bit of leeway to say, 'Well, it goes like this and this.' Unless I really think it could be better, then I say so. I think before, I wouldn't say anything, but now I don't hold my tongue. If I really feel something, I say it; I think we're all a bit more like that. So, the end product is better and surer to what we all feel. It's not always easy to criticize someone else's work. You don't like it when people do it to you, but it's better out than in. I think we can all take criticism a bit better. We're a bit older. When you're young I think you take it a bit more personally.

"But to be honest, we never write more than we need. We finished 11 songs; there are 11 songs in the album. We didn't start things and, halfway through, discard them. Once we're sitting down, two or three of us, and we think we have something really good, it usually makes it to the album. There's quite a lot of stuff that Bruce and I wrote that we didn't use."

Among himself, Dave, and Janick, Adrian estimates, "I think it's pretty much even Steven; maybe me a bit more than the other guys, but they did more on the last album. I'm talking about songwriting. Solo-wise, the thing about us is that we all play differently. I can show Janick one of my riffs, but no matter how many times I show it to him, he can't play it the same as me, and I can't play his stuff the same as him. So, there's a little bit of move in the songs, so that adds a bit of a flavor to it. Rather than if Janick just overdubbed his guitar four times, you've got the three of us, and it just means a bit more and it comes out more natural sounding."

True to the guys' collective description of the process, Kevin Shirley would record multiple takes of songs, four, five, even nine or ten in a day, with everybody playing at once. He would then sift through them and use as much of a great take—one thing he is looking for is an "air of confidence"—as he could, but splice in bits from other takes, using ProTools HD, subsequent to transferring the recordings from the analog Studer twenty-four-track (at 96 kHz, 24 bit!). As always, the band isn't playing to a click track, so there is, as he calls it, "push and pull." Digital is used only for editing, not manipulation of the performances, to maintain that human Who-like feel. Still, there's no rule that everything has to be a live take—Kevin Shirley lives up to his taskmaster reputation and asks for all sorts of extra solos, as well as extra isolated vocals from Bruce after everybody's assumed they were done.

After recording, Kevin takes the album to New York to get mastered, with George Marino, the most famous name in mastering. Controversy ensues. Marino didn't like the sound of the album at all, particularly the bottom end, and he did some deep-tissue massage on the tapes to make the bass warmer. At this point Kevin is questioning himself, and he sends the results back to Steve, who instantly says that it doesn't sound like Maiden at all, nor does it sound like the mixes he had heard in the studio.

What happens next, as Kevin explains, is that "the album is mastered from a CD that I made for Steve. It's not ideal [laughs], but that's what the master was at the end of the day. I had this really old Apogee digital converter that I used to just smash the crap out of it, to put it on a CD for him to play in his car. And then I printed all the other, you know, half-inch and 96K versions, and he just loved the crunching of whatever that . . . that horrible converter was [laughs]. So at the end of the day, I think he went to Tim Young and he said, 'Just transfer it off the CD. That's how I like it sounding; that's how I want it to sound.'"

Officially, Kevin is credited as sole producer of the album, with a coproduction credit going to Steve. He is also written in stone as having "recorded, engineered and mixed" the album, with Drew Griffiths also getting an engineering credit and Brad Spence listed as assistant. George Marino is not in the credits, with the mastering credit going to Tim Young, working at Metropolis Mastering in London.

Before we take a look at the music, we have to stare dumbfounded at the cover art. *Dance of Death* features a clumsy CGI-marred image that looks like a hasty lift of an idea from Kubrick's *Eyes Wide Shut*. The image goes uncredited, because artist Dave Patchett (of Cathedral album cover fame) was none too pleased that an unfinished version he had shown Steve turned out to be enough for Harris, who said, essentially, 'Thanks, we're done here; this is what we are using.' Patchett requested to have his name removed from the project as a disavowal, and subsequently, predictably, the image was panned as amateurish. Again, who knows what Patchett would have done, but it emphatically still needed work, he felt (well, we do know what he would have done—the Cathedral covers are some of the best in the business). Versions with just Eddie and none of the wonky extra figures could be seen on promotional materials, although it's unclear if it would have gone that way.

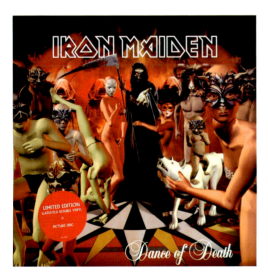

Dave Wright archive

But there's another story that goes like this. Patchett had drawn something up with Eddie and some monks. Rod thought the scene looked too empty, and then hired a company from Oregon to do a photo shoot with some people in masks. The results of the shoot are handed over to someone who worked at the Maiden website, who sticks the half-naked masked figures into Patchett's art, using a program called Poser. Apparently Patchett gamely tried to work with it, to smooth out the textures, but he didn't like the results and then asked that he be disassociated with the thing.

As Bruce told me, in the cover's defense, "The album art, for which we have been given such a caning on the website, it's completely deliberate. People are complaining that it's been computer-generated—yeah. It looks weird and uncoordinated—yeah. And it's been deliberately done that way. It's designed to be unnerving and unsettling. It's not supposed to be nice. It's not supposed to be Manowar. It's not supposed to be any of these, like, death to false-metal bands, which Maiden is not part of, never has been. And therefore, it's fair to completely distinguish Maiden from all of those bands. And if we lose a few fans because of the artwork, it will be a shame, but tough. Because the album art in itself is as much of a statement about the nature of the record. The record itself is heavy as fuck, but it sort of draws a little line in the sand, saying, look, it doesn't always have to be about this. We don't always have to have a big snarling, slavering Eddie exactly the same on every single album cover."

With a "1, 2, 1, 2, 3, 4!," *Dance of Death* is off to the races, opening with "Wildest Dreams," a strangely melodic and simple rocker, quick of pace, more about chord washes than riffs. As well, Nicko stands out, for good and bad, the good being that he's typically groovy Nicko, the bad being that he has his way and we hear it over and over again, same ride cymbal patterns, same "sink the basketball" fills, started at the same early place in the bar. The song's spontaneous feel seems to be for a reason. Notes Adrian, who cowrites the song with Steve, "For something like 'Wildest Dreams,' the first song on the album, that takes a couple of hours, just to bang it out, a little demo, a few chords, and you've got the song there, straightforward. I kind of run across the spectrum. It's sort of a cross between 'Number of the Beast' and 'Run to the Hills,' that kind of up, driving sort of riff. I played it to Steve, and he said, 'That would make a great single.' And he wrote the words, and there you have it; it happened pretty quick."

Adds Bruce, "'Wildest Dreams' is about living your life the way you want to live it. And you can too, you know, if you just want to visualize your dream. It's up tempo, fairly optimistic, I'm going to live my life and do what I want to do."

Figures Janick, "It's one of the shorter, snappier songs on the album. There are some quite diverse, thematic songs in there, that are quite prog oriented, but this one is short and snappy and to the point, pure rock 'n' roll."

The video for the track, directed by Howard Greenhalgh, is fully 3-D computer animated, looking rudimentary by today's standards. Notes Bruce, "When we first heard that Howard was looking to do a fully animated video, we were very excited as we were familiar with his previous work. We saw the first sketches and we knew right away that Howard had got the right feel for what the track needed, loads of energy and movement to complement the song. And we didn't have to appear live in the video! When you first see it, you think, 'Hell really looks cool.' Then you look closer, and you think, 'Actually, maybe not!'"

Stills from the clip were used for the various single issues of the track, working surprisingly well in this context, given the muted steely coloring used through the apocalyptic landscape of the originating video. "Wildest Dreams" was premiered live on the preceding Give Me Ed . . . 'til I'm Dead tour, and discerning Maiden fans were concerned for the future, finding the song, well, middling. But then again, first singles for Maiden—"Holy Smoke," "Can I Play with Madness," "Flight of Icarus," "Be Quick or Be Dead," "Man on the Edge," "Wasted Years"—are often not indicative of what the ensuing record is going to sound like, and indeed, this turned out to be another anomaly, belying its odd Smith/Harris penning.

"Rainmaker" comes next, and it's also the next single from the album. Bruce's lyric—Dickinson says that the intro riff made him think about raindrops—nicely ties images of an actual drought with the idea of rain as redemption, not only of the land but of psychological hardship.

"Rainmaker" colored-vinyl 7-inch. *Dave Wright archive*

Unsurprisingly it's also the second-shortest track from the album, after "Wildest Dreams," with every song going forward clocking in at over five minutes. This one finds Maiden still in a chord-centric zone, like "Holy Smoke," but it's much more familiar melodically. Plus, the twin leads are back, something that had been in decline starting with *Fear of the Dark*, really.

"I come up with some riffs and ideas, but Steve is such a proficient writer," explains Dave Murray, music writer of this one plus one other, "Age of Innocence," on the album. "I've done a couple of things with Bruce, where I would have the chords and Bruce would just go and put the lyrics straight on. But I would say 90 percent of the time I would be sitting down with Steve and sharing an idea, and he would develop it. Something like the track 'Brave New World,' that came out of a little riff, and Steve had a big chorus and some other things. So, it's like you go in with a little piece of the jigsaw puzzle, and the other guys fit the pieces in and complete it. 'Rainmaker' was really enjoyable, because of sitting down and playing the intro and working some stuff out with Steve. We had the instrumental bit already done, and we played the thing for Bruce, and he came out with the lyrics, pretty much there, already written, in his head [laughs]. So, it's a collaboration, and I think it's the same with the other guys—Janick with Steve, Bruce, and Adrian—it's basically that collaboration. And the good thing is there hasn't really been any shortage of material. Everybody's got stuff in the can. So, it's basically getting the strongest songs that are going to make the album. So, when you come forward with something, you've got to be pretty positive that this is going to work for the band."

"No More Lies," credited solely to Steve, features a lyric that is fatalistic like "Hallowed Be Thy Name," only here it sounds like the protagonist is about to go into battle, sure of his death. Steve keeps it intriguingly universal, and the repetitious exhortation of "No more lies!" offers an indication that the generals are painting a rosy picture. Both the intro and the outro are integral and enhancing features, as is the use of strings. The chorus is novel with its percussive military rhythm, and as a bonus there's a three-guitar trade-off of solos just like the old southern rock guys used to do it, most notably Lynyrd Skynyrd. The structure of the song feels very Blaze era, especially toward something like "The Educated Fool."

"Shit, this is great stuff, you know?" chuckles Bruce, in conversation with the author, addressing the next track on the album. "It's a classic Maiden record; it's got all the classic sounds. The riff on 'Montségur,' as soon as it kicks in, you think, oh shit, I'm listening to a Maiden record. Lyrically 'Montségur' is pretty cool, but it's a pretty straightforward medieval story of Catholic persecution and everything else, a medieval siege and stuff. It's a fascinating story. I like 'Face in the Sand' and also 'Journeyman' and 'Rainmaker,' but, if you like, they're the less obvious lyrics."

This one starts heavy and hard immediately, the band executing a shuffle gallop similar to that of "Losfer Words" from *Powerslave*. When the riff starts, the band goes into one of their novel "sweet and sour" melodies, which then goes sturdily Maiden, and third, very sour, very Celtic. It's an oscillation between minor and major keys that works well here, with that third passage sounding both martial and progressive rock. Keeping things lively is another round of hand-to-hand combat between the three guitarists, the "duellists," which is the name of another song that uses this riff 'n' rhythm structure.

Bruce's lyric can be classed as one of his denunciations of Christian hypocrisy. In this real tale, the pope goes to war with the Cathars, a breakaway Christian sect, who hole up at one of their strongholds, Montségur, in fact the seat and head of the Cathars, circa the 1230s, high up in the Pyrenees. The end result is a siege, after which, on March 16, 1244, approximately 220 Cathars are captured and burned alive. There is also talk that the day before, a cabal of Cathars slipped away before the razing of the place, escaping with esoteric knowledge and possibly the Holy Grail, or at least knowledge as to its whereabouts. This slice of exotic French history went down well, of course, in France, which has long been one of Maiden's strongest territories—indeed, Bruce speaks French to crowds at shows in France as well as Quebec, another huge territory for Maiden.

One could place "Montségur" somewhere between "Sign of the Cross" and "Holy Smoke," with Dickinson condemning religion more so through the fact of its history lesson rather than first-person vilification. But this is all comfort food for the fans, Bruce offering another concise history, sending the curious to their computers for elucidation on the origins of the flowery name of the song.

Next comes the title track, which came to be a bit polarizing, separating the committed fans from those with a lower tolerance. "Dance of Death" is pure indulgent Maiden, very Celtic and dare I say clichéd, drawing from "Fear of the Dark," "Fortunes of War," and "The Clansman." The lyrics are a muddle of a mystery, with connections to the cover art but also the Everglades, and therefore sort of deep-woods voodoo, a chafe against the urban, sexual vibe of the front cover and indeed the eerie photography of the guys inside the booklet. Was it all a dream, this dancing—and prancing!—with the dead? That certainly clears up the incongruity of our protagonist being in Florida.

"There is a lot of melody on the record," Bruce explained to me, in what is an eye-winked rationalization of the "stepping in it" music of songs like this. "There's a lot of storytelling on the record. In fact, 'Dance of Death' could almost be on a Jethro Tull / Ian Anderson album, sitting by the fireside smoking his pipe, as he starts off: 'Let me tell you a story.' And I love that. I thought, wow, this is great; this is what Maiden should be doing. This is how to take Maiden forward in a way that so many other bands can't touch this. They can't even go near what we're trying to do at the moment, because they could never hack it. They could never manage to walk the fine line between doing it and carrying it off and falling off and the absurd and *Spinal Tap*. Because that's the line you walk all the time with this music."

"Bruce agrees with me that there is more melody on this album," affirms Adrian. "There's always a lot of melody on a Maiden album, probably more than a lot of metal bands. Sometimes I don't even think we're a metal band, because there are folk influences and all sorts of things, Celtic influences. Steve has a knack, a talent, for coming up with melodies. Whether it's more melodic than the last one, I don't really know."

"Gates of Tomorrow" seems to be one of the *Dance of Death* songs least beloved by fans. Fronted by a long "From Here to Eternity"–like intro (note the bass arpeggios) that doesn't make sense given what follows, once the verse starts, Dickinson doubles himself over a milquetoast melody.

There's much speculation what Bruce is on about, whether it's religion or the allure of the internet (Bruce often chides Steve for being, essentially, "caught in the web"), with some proposing that it's a dig at Metallica and their suing of Napster over downloading. Bruce curiously had it in for Metallica, saying that Maiden would never do a "black album" and exhorting from the stage to go ahead, record the show and even illegally download it, as long as you also buy the album. There's a twin-lead section before the solo, set to an all-new melody that sounds a bit like "22 Acacia Avenue." After the solo, Bruce sings a few lines atop this structure, before the bands careen back into the sturdy half-time chorus of the song. After that, the guy brings us full circle with a full-band retelling of the song's intro.

Come "New Frontier," the band opens the show with a slashing chord sequence that sounds like the verses of "Holy Smoke." But then Bruce starts singing, way up the register over obtuse melodies (compare with "The Clairvoyant," at least the intro) that give way to something more comforting come the prechorus and chorus. Nicko's lyric expresses reservations over cloning, scientists "playing God," as in the classic *Frankenstein* story.

"I wrote the song with some help from Adrian—my first one," says a proud Nicko, indeed bringing his one and only (to this date) songwriting contribution to Maiden. "We were listening to the final version in the control room, and it was great. The other guys were like, 'That's it, innit? Fuckin' about time too; it's only taken you twenty years!' [laughs]."

As McBrain explains in the press materials for the album, "I wrote the verse riff on the bass guitar [Nicko plays finger style, i.e., without a pick]. That's like Steve does it; I took a leaf out of Mr. Harris's book and wrote some lyrics, which I presented to the band. Adrian helped me with the bridge and chorus, and we kind of collaborated on that part of the tune. I had to sit there in front of Steve, with his acoustic bass—he had his electric bass—and show him the bass line. And then he went, 'Yeah, do you want to do the bass on the tune then?' I said, 'Well, you ain't playing the drums, that's for sure, mate!' [laughs]."

Added Steve, "I think everybody was a little surprised with Nicko coming with an idea, because it's twenty years he's been with the band now, and it's the first time he's actually come in with anything. When he showed me the bass line, I thought, well, it sounds just like me. He says, 'Well, what do you bleedin' expect after twenty years playing with you?' So, I thought, okay, fair enough. It is just amazing, really, that there's no drum solo in it, I suppose. I mean, he was really quite straight. In other songs, we're actually trying to get him to play straight. On his own one he's playing straight naturally anyway. Reason with that what you will, really. Good song, though."

"He plays bass really well," muses Adrian. "He plays a lot like Steve [laughs]. It's probably because he's been listening to him for so many years. And he had this riff, and I said, 'That's great; let's work on that,' and I added some bits to it."

"It's got the Maiden stamp on it," says Dave. "Nicko came up with this great idea, and if you Maidenize it and start playing the song . . . it just bloomed," to which Nicko added, "If it wasn't worth it, it wouldn't have made the album."

Next is "Paschendale," another one of what are many, many Maiden songs about war, this one World War I. Performing it live, Bruce reinforced the lyric by dressing in the uniform of a British infantryman.

As Dickinson told me, "This is a more emotional album and personal record than *Brave New World*. It's also less dark in many ways. Even though some of the songs are about some pretty black subjects, it doesn't paint human beings . . . there's always somewhere in there a glimmer of hope; there's always a message. Like the song 'Paschendale,' which is a ten-minute extravaganza—we haven't written a song like this since 'Rime of the Ancient Mariner.' Adrian and Steve wrote it, and it's an absolute masterpiece and will be stunning live. It's about a World War I slaughter, the Battle of Paschendale, which I think is the first or the second battle of Ypres—I'm not too up on that particular aspect of World War I history [the Battle of Passchendaele is the Third Battle of Ypres, fought on the western front from July to November 1917]. The atmosphere of it, I mean, the song, as in 'Dance of Death,' as in so many of the songs, is just chock-full of atmosphere and emotive sounds and guitars and pictures. As soon as you hear the song . . . I sat there and listened to the guitar, and you can close your eyes and sort of see the shells and see the lights and the barbed wire and the star shells illuminating the trenches."

Promo postcard and sticker. *Dave Wright archive*

Just as "Montségur" is in possession of resonance for fans in France, "Paschendale" has meaning for punters from Canada, given how integral Canadian soldiers were in this campaign. In fact, the Canadian Corps were credited with the capture of Passchendaele, after British and French forces were diverted to hotspots in Italy (there would still be a Fourth and Fifth Battle of Ypres).

Adds Adrian, when I asked about his reputation as the writer of the more rock 'n' rollsy material the band does, "I suppose people might have thought that. I'm '2 Minutes to Midnight' and 'Flight of Icarus,' all that stuff. But there's actually a song on this album that is one of the longest songs we've ever done, 'Paschendale,' which is one of my ideas, whereas in the past I was kind of focused in on the shorter stuff. I thought, well, I'll have a go at writing something a bit longer. And it was very difficult [laughs]. It took me sort of like five days to get the music together."

"Paschendale" represents another opportunity to use strings on the album (orchestration by Jeff Bova), which are heard most prevalently here and on album closer "Journeyman." Kevin has stated that there are also French horns, orchestral percussion, and tubular bells on the track. There are also whispers, signifying the souls of dead soldiers, plus a hawk's cry, representing the call of a warrior to the warrior's resting place, and a boys choir, representing the lost innocence of these soldiers, many of which, Steve points out, are all but eighteen years old.

Adrian recalls playing the musical roughs for Steve, who loved it instantly, immediately tucking in and writing reams of lyrics for it. He says they had the song fairly fleshed out by the end of the day.

Comments Harris, "What Adrian came up [with] kind of inspired the lyrics, really, for the First World War theme, Paschendale, which is the place that was the frontline trenches and stuff. It's just a very atmospheric song. It's heavy but moody, and also, I think, a little sad. Adrian really surpassed himself. I think it's a great song. He has done great songs in the past, but I really think this is gonna be something that is going to be an epic onstage, without a doubt." Adds Dave on playing it live, "'Paschendale' is a monumental track. Musically there's a lot of stuff going on in there, so you have to really knuckle down."

As Adrian alludes to, this is his first epic—but it won't be the last. This represents another example of something that happens with Maiden in the 2000s, this concept of all of them becoming more similar as writers as the catalog builds. Bruce and Steve have always famously been nearly indistinguishable from each other as lyricists, gravitating to weirdly similar subject matter. But now Adrian is writing epics and Nicko is writing a song. Dave, well, he's always been virtually indistinguishable as anything other than the core soul of Maiden. And over time, albeit, frankly, quite a bit right from the beginning, Janick, with very different roots, in White Spirit and Gillan, he's so significantly poured right into the soul of Maiden as Dave has always been, indeed, as Steve has always been as a music writer as well. It's just one big, six-headed beast leaning into the wind, arriving at a single place: Maidenness.

But back to "Paschendale," this is a track with the guitars way forward in the mix, and when Steve takes any sort of central role, usually in the quiet bits, this is a song where we really hear his Wishbone Ash influence, notable in his counterpoint to what the guitars are doing.

"Face in the Sand" has the band making use once again of orchestration, but the most pertinent fact about this one is that Nicko is playing double bass drums, albeit at a slow and steady tempo, and in 6/8 time. Kevin had a hard time getting a good take of this, but as day turned to night, he felt he had enough by the fifth and sixth time through.

At the lyric end, this one's about war and, subtly, terrorism, still fresh in everybody's minds after 9/11—indeed, a more horrific reading of "No More Lies" might paint the protagonist not as a soldier but a suicide bomber. And then there's the middle ground: situated among rational, necessary, and even humane and moral war and acts of terrorism, there's war at the hands of dictators, not exactly state-sanctioned terrorism, but institutional atrocities of war that veer close to lone-wolf terrorism.

"Age of Innocence" represents Dave's second songwriting credit on *Dance of Death*, Murray turning in a grinding up-tempo rocker, tempered in the extreme by a chorus that could have sat comfortably on Bruce's semi-hair-metal solo album, *Tattooed Millionaire*.

When Dave writes, he would often work up his demos complete with drum machine. "Oh yeah, absolutely. I do, and I know Adrian does as well, and Janick did on *Dance of Death*. Basically, it's a fun thing; you're sitting at home, you've got a drum thing going, and you put on some riffs. And it does inspire you. You try and get a chorus type of sequence going, which is a good thing, a verse, some melodies. And especially now, with the computer stuff, it's made things a lot easier. But at the end of the day, the idea has to be solid. But it's a fun little thing to do at home, and I'm sure people have stuff that wouldn't even make the band, but it's nice to have. But it's fun if you've got a few hours to kill and you're playing and something pops out."

Lyrically, Steve begins this one as a standard screed against politicians, speaking on behalf of the working man, who pays for everything and, if he's unlucky to be born at the wrong time, gets sent off to war as a bonus. But the last two-thirds of the song are very specifically about crime in Britain, how punishment is too lax and how the victims suffer unduly.

Closing *Dance of Death* is "Journeyman," a rare acoustic ballad for the band, albeit midtempo, backed by full drums. There's also electric bass, albeit behaved and properly soft of bass tone rather than signature clacky and note dense—Steve on a tear, as it were. At the chorus, which finds the band switching to a minor key, Bruce belts it out as he would on any given Maiden rocker. Carrying the tune throughout, as much as the acoustic guitars, are perennial strings placed high in the mix.

"Journeyman" was written on acoustic guitar, but an electric version was tried first. Nicko then suggested that they try an unplugged version, joking that Kevin tried to claim the idea for himself, suggesting, no, they should try an "acoustic" version. The guys then called down to the local guitar shop to send around a bunch of acoustic guitars. They then played the song back against the electric version, and Steve said, "There was no comparison," noting that they could keep the "power ballad" version for a B-side or something.

The electric version of "Journeyman" can indeed be officially experienced, given its inclusion on the *No More Lies–Dance of Death Souvenir EP*, issued March 29, 2004, in a box, which included a free sweatband, the item framed as a thank-you to fans. There's not a heap of difference from the album version of "Journeyman"; at the verses, there's polite, clean electric strumming, although the choruses do feature power chords, making the song a power ballad. Also included is the album version of "No More Lies," an orchestral version of "Paschendale" (essentially the same, with the orchestration more audible and the guitars turned down), plus "Age of Innocence . . . How Old?," which is the album version's music with Bruce wiped and Nicko added, McBrain oscillating between ersatz alternate lyrics, song commentary, and unrelated muttered musings on the mundane and Maiden.

Back to *Dance of Death*, "I love 'Journeyman,'" says Bruce. "It's one of my favorite songs on the album. It's just about life; it's about choices. It's about the choices you make and the consequences of those choices and creative issues. It's melancholy in a funny sort of way, but it's an uplifting kind of melancholy. It's the sort of thing, on a really rainy day, when you stare out the window, a kind of day like this, when you stare at the clouds and sometimes you think, I think I'm going to go be a rock star or I think I'm going to go do this; I'm going to go and wrestle tigers. But that's a game I've completely abandoned playing. I never really used to do it that much anyway. But as I go on, I find that spending time looking back and wishing is a real waste of your time when you could be spending the time actually doing. Or even better, not doing [laughs]. Just chilling out.

"We knew that we could do a better record," continues Bruce. "And actually we've put down the markers on this record, the indicators, of two or three potential directions in which the band could go on the next record. And if people want to sit down and listen to 'Journeyman' and 'Rainmaker' and 'Paschendale,' you could think, well, there's three potential directions right there."

Two years after issue, US sales had stalled at 138,904 copies; however, in the unique world of Maiden, that wasn't the most important thing. As we've alluded to, the band was becoming a formidable economic proposition as a live band once again. Also, the album tallied significant sales in markets all around the world, amassing gold certifications in Argentina and Brazil to the south and Finland and Sweden to the north, and also hitting gold, for sales of over 100,000 copies, both in Germany and the UK. Notably, Canada sat this one out. Additionally, the album got to either #1, #2, or #3 on the charts in a dozen countries around the world.

Offering a summation for Mitch Lafon, here at the end of our album analysis, Dave figures, "*Brave New World* is the lighter of the two. I mean, there's heavy stuff on there, but there's a lot of melody. I think it hearkened back a little bit to an 1980s feel. It had a type of *Piece of Mind* / *Powerslave* color to the album. *Dance of Death* is a bit darker and moodier. And probably, as well, *Dance of Death* was a more complex album, in the intensity and the playing. But it didn't start out that way; that's just the way it evolved in the studio. So yes, a bit darker, more ominous in places. But it was done specifically to kind of create a mood. 'Dance of Death,' the track itself, and like 'Paschendale,' there are a lot of things going on there. 'Paschendale' is a real kind of vibe and groove track, a lot of intricate things there. Where probably the whole of *Brave New World* was a bit lighter, more melodic.

"We've gone from strength to strength with *Dance of Death*. The creativity is there and we're having fun playing, so this is definitely not a farewell tour! We spent six weeks doing that album. You get in there and do it quick, which is a great way to do an album. When you first get it home, you play the album to death—in the car, in the bath, everywhere—but now I don't listen to it all the time. But when I do hear it, I'm very satisfied. It's a strong stand-up album with a lot of depth both lyrically and musically. I think it's a big album. When you put it on the first time, it's like, 'Wow!' And the more you play it, it grows on you. We're very proud of the album, and it's one of the strongest albums we've ever done. But obviously time will tell. It's in the hands of the fans, and it's their opinion that matters most."

As Dave said, at this point *Dance of Death* was done and dusted and turned over to the fans for their assessment. Wrote Carl Begai in his review of the album for our mag, "If you're a Maiden fan, then the new album will not disappoint. In the spirit of *Brave New World*, it is an album of epic songs, anthems, and shorter burst of brilliance, often predictable, staying true to the Iron Maiden legacy that was built with the success of albums like *Number of the Beast*, *Powerslave*, *Seventh Son of a Seventh Son*, and *Brave New World*. In a year of high-profile releases, *Dance of Death* is sure to be near the top of the 'hit' list when 2003 finally draws to a close, as it lacks the rhetoric and controversy used to try and sell albums like Queensryche's *Tribe* and Metallica's *St. Anger*.

"It's fair to call *Dance of Death* business as usual, but it also has a charm that *Brave New World* does not. There is a warmth to the new songs that the last album didn't have, sounding somehow less calculated, possessing a fly-by-the-seat-of-yer-pants vibe similar to that of *Number of the Beast*. The first two tracks, 'Wildest Dreams' and 'Rainmaker,' are short and to the point in the spirit of classic 1980s Maiden, reeling us in with hooks after singalong choruses before giving us a typical yet very welcome Steve Harris tune in 'No More Lies.' And from there the band is off and running, doing what they do best, a devil-may-care smile plastered on Eddie's face."

Assessed Tim Henderson, "Aside from producer Kevin Shirley's excellent online updates, the follow-up to *Brave New World* was locked up tighter than Fort Knox. Not a peep has been leaked aside from the band's live airing of the leadoff cut / first single,

'Wildest Dreams,' an unmemorable 1970s-inspired Status Quo / Slade anthem. But then with virtually every snapshot in time indicating where leader/bassist Steve Harris's head is at, the band consistently fire on all cylinders. Trouble is that the vehicle is in need of an oil change. *Dance of Death* is undeniably classic Maiden. And Sanctuary knows if it ain't broke, don't fix it. But that's the problem. Aside from the orchestral bits that are peppered throughout the record, the writing template remains a constant. And there's just way too much meat on the bone. Chop the record down by a third and release the follow-up in late 2004, not 2006. Never thought I'd see myself complaining about the length of a Maiden record, but in this case the UK heroes dilute the overall appeal of *Dance of Death* by filling the mother up and the cup spilleth over. If you want epic, you've got it—nine cuts over five minutes plus, six of them over six minutes plus. The event gets extremely tiring."

"Within the *BW&BK* camp, I was in the minority with regard to *Brave New World*," begins Mark Gromen, offering yet a third opinion for *Brave Words & Bloody Knuckles*, "feeling it was not a thrilling return to form, but rather a staid helping of the same old (choose your favorite derogative noun). In terms of the Maiden community at large, a feeling of déjà vu surrounds me that once again I will be outnumbered. The inclusion of classical orchestration is bound to be a hot-button issue, but rest assured, this ain't *S&M* or Kiss *Symphony*. Given Maiden's penchant for playing live, several of the more structured bits are probably off-limits on tour, as they'd require samples/tapes, and the Brits have always prided themselves on being able to reproduce the feel and scope of any original on stage.

"The upbeat stuff is truly augmented by the introduction of these diverse elements, and the initial trio are full-speed racers. A simple, repetitive, 'No More Lies' (my favorite) is classic Maiden, built around a stirring guitar solo (actually three, one from each guitarist, melded into a single section). The daft bookends of an opening 'Wildest Dreams' and the acoustic-begun finale 'Journeyman' belied the tasty inner filling. The dynamic title cut teases the listener, with ambitions of running off with its folky/orchestral mix, but fear not. Make no mistake, this is a guitar-oriented album! The Nicko McBrain–penned 'New Frontier' rides an anti-cloning sentiment, while the World War I epic 'Paschendale' is painted with lush, lyrical strokes. While there might not be a standout on first listen (time might prove otherwise), it's a fairly consistent platter. Can't remember when I felt that way about these old sots!"

From October 19 through November 28, 2003, the *Dance of Death* tour begins proper, with a fairly extensive European leg, supported at first by Gamma Ray. Again, perpetuating the pattern of playing with friends, Maiden already knew Gamma Ray's Kai Hansen from shows conducted with Helloween in the late 1980s. Plus the band was now on their second of three albums that they would do with Sanctuary Records. As well, Derek Riggs had been doing Gamma Ray's cover art, using his early days' new digital style. This role was soon usurped by Hervé Monjeaud, also an Iron Maiden illustrator, who promptly gave the band an Eddie-like monster of a mascot.

On November 24, "Rainmaker" emerges as a single, in CD and DVD formats. "More Tea Vicar" is another impromptu jam, and "Dance of Death" is presented in orchestral version format. December 1 through 21, the *Dance of Death* tour hits England, with UK gold-certified emo band Funeral for a Friend in tow; the last two dates are rescheduled European stops. Into the new year, January 11 through 17, Maiden perform four shows in South America, followed by a short North American leg to close out the month—brief, given that the band had just visited in the summer. Main support comes from Arch Enemy, with indie Priest-alikes Cage jumping on for the concluding two LA stops.

"It's a different world now, a different approach," mused Maiden manager Rod Smallwood at the time, on the business of touring. "You know, in the early days, when Peter Grant and Don Arden were out, it was the Wild West. It was the early business. Things have changed a lot. I'm sure there were cash deals in those days, but they would be well hidden, I'm sure. But that was the way of the world at that time. I've been fortunate; I've been with Maiden since the very beginning, and certainly since *Number of the Beast*, it's run as a very professional organization. It is different. My management style, I probably get more involved in the creative issues than most of the others, in terms of the artwork and the stage set, and I still write all the bios and everything, so I guess it's different that way.

"But certainly, you've got to give credit to Peter Grant [laughs]. He was a great manager. But you don't tend to think of that. There are no rules out there, and one of the great things about music is that there aren't rules. You have certain codes of behavior you try to stick by, and integrity and things, and you take it from there. But I think everyone has got their own style and their own fortés. I mean, if it was a band based on radio, I'd probably be useless because I never listen to radio, because I don't like listening to stuff I'm being force-fed. If I want new things, I'll go out and find new things. I mean, one of the great things about the web now is that you can actually choose what you're going to hear. And so, if you're a radio band, it would be quite tough, because you're not something that I'm that into."

The day prior to beginning the North American campaign, Dave spoke to Mitch Lafon, eager to get the show on the road. "The crowd up there is absolutely fantastic," touted Dave, speaking specifically of Montreal. "There's a very European vibe to it, and the reaction from the fans is amazing. We've been playing Montreal for quite a few years, and every time we go back, it's always a pleasure. The reaction from the kids is spectacular. We've had a chance to come up there in the beautiful summer. Now, we'll have a chance to suffer with everyone else at minus 40 C. But obviously, once you get onstage and you get the show underway, it's going to be great!

"When we came in the summer, it was the Give Me Ed tour, which was the 'best of,' but this tour is based on *Dance of Death*. We'll be playing half a dozen songs from the new album, so it's a whole different theme, different lights, different show, different everything, really. We've completely changed the script. Every time we've toured it's been on the focus or strength of the new album. We could be like a cabaret band and just go out and do our old songs all the time, but the strength of Maiden has been about always moving forward. The only way to do that is to go out with the new material, and we're not afraid to do that. The reaction has been great. The fans know both the old songs and the new songs.

"You spend a few weeks rehearsing, but you have to take it out onstage in front of a live audience, and that changes the pace of everything. But we're well settled into it with the songs. This is one of the most theatrical things we've ever put together visually, with the props and things going on. But the songs translate to the stage very well. 'Dance of Death' itself starts off very moody and melancholy, but it gets very heavy. There's a lot of light and shade. We don't go out onstage for nearly two hours and bang bang bang. There's a lot of subtle quiet things happening. Yet there's a lot of very up-tempo fast things. The set itself changes pace and shape.

"Maiden have always shined best in an arena," continues Murray. "Obviously, we've played in clubs and stuff, but you just get a backline. The whole Maiden experience is the backdrop and the whole production. It also gives you space to move around. The thing with Maiden is that when we play the bigger places, it kind of shines through. Still, we could go out with just a backline, no thrills, frills, nothing, but I think the fans expect more. It's an interaction between the band and the audience. Bruce goes a long way to talking to them and getting them involved. There's a wonderful feedback. The Iron Maiden experience is an event.

"Once we finish this tour, we're going to take some time off," divulged Dave. "We won't be doing much till 2005. We've been everywhere twice on this tour. We need a break; we need to rest. We'll definitely be coming back out again in 2005. There's going to be another album as well, maybe 2006. We've been documenting and videotaping this tour, so something may be coming out from this tour. There was this thing on the internet that suggested that we were going to continue touring, but not for eight or nine months' stretches or go everywhere. Obviously, we're not getting any younger, but we can still get around everywhere. However, it's going to be [high-]quality shows rather than quantity. We'll be coming out with a big tour and everything, but it's a case of we need to ease our foot off the accelerator a little bit. We have no intentions of a farewell tour—we will be continuing."

From February 5 through 8, Maiden concluded the *Dance of Death* tour in Japan, bringing Arch Enemy along. As Dave indicated, the band had been planning a break, but a period of pretty substantial activity would take place for the balance of 2004 and the first few months of 2005. Following are a few dates notable on the Maiden calendar during the ensuing stretch of downtime, excepting Bruce and the release of *Tyranny of Souls*, which we will look at in its own chapter.

Before the year is out, on November 9, 2004, EMI issues a DVD called *The History of Iron Maiden Part 1: The Early Days*, but into the new year, it's up to others to celebrate the band's accomplishments. DRZ Records issues *World's Only Female Tribute to Iron Maiden*, the debut album from the Iron Maidens, cover art courtesy of Derek Riggs. The Iron Maidens would go on to be a regular and beloved touring act for years. On October 11, 2005, an all-star tribute album called *Numbers from the Beast* is issued, on Rykodisc. Vocalists guesting on the record consist of Joe Lynn Turner, John Bush, Ripper Owens, Lemmy, Mark Slaughter, Chris Jericho, Dee Snider, Robin McAuley, Chuck Billy, Jeff Scott Soto, and Paul Di'Anno. Also in 2005, Clive Burr's signature white drum kit is donated to the Hard Rock Cafe in London.

Back in Maidenland, on January 3, 2005, "The Number of the Beast" is issued as a single, with various live and video versions of the track as B-sides. On January 14, *The History of Iron Maiden Part 1: The Early Days* receives its gold and platinum certifications on the same day. On February 18, *Brave New World* achieves gold certification in the UK, while additionally, by this point, the album reaches sales of 282,460 in the US. Of note, a SoundScan tally of the 1980s catalog since the SoundScan era began on May 25, 1991, to this point, roughly fourteen years later, revealed sales of 2.4 million units for Maiden across the catalog. An analysis of the numbers shows that every Iron Maiden album from the 1980s outsold, essentially by a 2:1 margin, every record from the 1990s and 2000s, save for *Fear of the Dark*, which sat at sales of 421,786 as of February 2005.

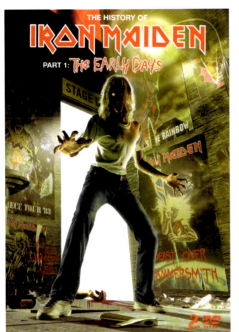 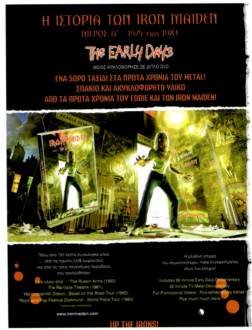

Dave Wright archive

Back to work, May 28 through July 9, Maiden conduct the European leg of their Eddie Rips up the World tour, the theme being songs from the first four albums only, with the stage set inspired by the band's recently released *Early Days* DVD. Support comes from the likes of speedy Maiden-alikes Dragonforce as well as Mastodon, Within Temptation, and Dream Theater.

Reflected Dave at the time, "What we've tried to do is stick to our guns, written the music, played the music the way we've wanted to. We've never really followed any trends or fashions. We basically stayed true to ourselves, and I think that's one of the values of the band, that we haven't gone commercial. We've just written songs that have come out naturally, really. And basically, you do that over a period of time, taking the band around the world. Really from the peripheral, looking from the outside in, it looks a bit different. But there's a lot of hard work that goes on behind the scenes. But hopefully, you know, we've done a lot of albums now and quite a few tours, and hopefully the songs will stand the test of time. At the moment we're out playing the early stuff, so that's one of the proven factors, the foundation. A band is only as strong as the songs are. But I guess, really, it's up to the rest of the world to justify it and say how they stand. It's basically up to the individual, how they perceive it."

Addressing the band's use of keyboards onstage, Dave explains that "in the studio, I think Steve does a lot of the keyboards. And then there's a guy, in fact, Steve's roadie, Mike Kenney—he's the guy that does behind the scenes when we're playing live. If there's any keyboards, he'll be behind the stacks and playing it back there. In fact, we used to bring him up in the 1980s, bring him up on a riser, for a feature piece. I can't remember what song it was now, but he would kind of rise up from behind the stacks, doing his kind of *Phantom of the Opera* thing. Then he would go back down again [laughs]. But now I subscribe to keyboards. I think it makes things a bit more musical and adds more dynamic and a bit of warmth to the whole thing."

On June 21, the *Visions of the Beast* video received its gold and platinum certifications on the same day. Two weeks later, on July 5, *The Essential Iron Maiden*, a twenty-seven-track compilation over two CDs, is issued.

At this point Rod takes yet another victory lap, offering a sermon on heavy metal history up to this point, and Maiden's place in it.

"The way I see it, Maiden have had a huge influence over the last twenty-five years. Many of the bands now are heavily influenced by Maiden, but many bands were heavily influenced by Sabbath prior to that. No question Sabbath was the first. I mean, to me the first heavy metal was the Kinks' 'You Really Got Me.' You go from there into the period of Sabbath, Purple, Zeppelin. Zeppelin never wanted to be called a metal band, but let's face it, anybody into metal is definitely into Led Zeppelin. And they were what you would call the godfathers of all that, Sabbath obviously at the very heavy end, Purple at the musical end, which is probably the wrong way of putting it. They're into playing, and the musicianship is pretty astounding. And then you've got Zeppelin, who were unique anyway.

"And they were all British bands. It was pretty much a British start to these things, and it just continued through, I think right the way through the last, what? Thirty-five years? The British bands have had a pretty different angle on the whole thing. They've always been based more on the playing and the songs, longer songs as well. American bands have tended to go a different route. There are exceptions. I mean, something like Metallica would fit well with the British bands, whereas a band like Mötley Crüe wouldn't. And Def Leppard would fit well with the American bands, but Iron Maiden wouldn't. And there are different strains of it. I think you have to look through the history at different sections of it. I mean, you had the great first three, and following from that you had, starting off in the early 1970s, Judas Priest, UFO, Scorpions, and then really Maiden was by themselves in a way. Maiden came through the early 1980s, contemporary with Def Leppard, but Def Leppard aren't necessarily viewed as a metal band, although I've got a lot of time for them.

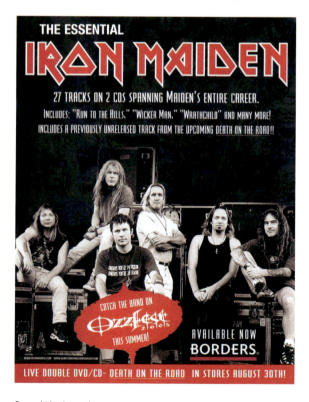

Dave Wright archive

"So Maiden were kind of isolated, although they were with the New Wave of British Heavy Metal, which was a ground surge of metal bands at the time. And we went on in the early 1980s to great international success, and then following that, there was Metallica, Megadeth, Anthrax, those sorts of bands, followed of course by the grunge scene and then the nu-metal scene, all which went away in a relatively short period but left their legacies, like, for example, Nirvana.

"So how we fit in that was, we were probably one of the steps along the way. And I think Maiden is as valid as Sabbath, in what they've done. I think Maiden brought new things into it. We did a lot for . . . you know, just things like the value for fans in terms of merchandising. I don't think there was a lot of that around, to the level it was, in the early 1980s. I think Maiden put a bit of a stamp on that, in terms of making sure the kids got real value and some great-looking stuff. And the across-the-board musicianship. But I think all the bands I've mentioned have been terrific musicians."

From July 15 through August 20, the Eddie Rips Up the World tour hits North America, with the band as part of Ozzfest. Black Sabbath is the headliner on the night.

Assessed Bruce, "Certainly with Maiden, we looked at Ozzfest as being an opportunity to really go and grab a much-younger audience. It's very difficult for us to get access to a younger audience, frankly. Because the shed-type shows, they've got age limits, they've got age restrictions, they've got all the bullshit about restricted-access seating and everything else like that. The kind of audience we want to play to is the audience we play to in Europe, which is primarily kids. Ozzfest is that audience, so what we want to do is go and play to that audience—that is the reason we're doing Ozzfest. For whatever reason, I think metal as a community seems a bit more organized in Europe in general than it is in the States. In the States it's kind of responsive to radio and things like that. It's difficult to get people out en masse in sufficient quantities and at the right place at the right time. So, to get a bunch of kids out to go and see Maiden, it seems to be quite difficult. So Ozzfest represents a great opportunity for us to try and knock people back a couple of paces and have people go, 'Geez, this is Maiden.'"

At an Ozzfest date in Devore, California, on August 20, Bruce Dickinson's ongoing spat with Ozzy's wife and manager, Sharon Osbourne, comes to a head with "the Eggfest Incident," in which, mysteriously, eggs are thrown at Bruce and the band onstage while they are performing "The Trooper," amid other attempts to sabotage the band's set. It is rumored that it is an organized and orchestrated response to Bruce bad-mouthing Ozzy Osbourne for using a teleprompter.

From August 25 through September 2, 2005, the band closes out the Eddie Rips up the World tour with four dates in the UK, the last dedicated to the Clive Burr MS Trust Fund. Support at this show comes from Steve Harris's pet project Voodoo Six (featuring Rob Halford's nephew Nigel) and Pig Iron, featuring legendary Iron Maiden employee Dave Pattenden (now former Pig Iron, working for Banger Films) and industry mogul and all-around metal swami Hugh Gilmour.

As the last leg starts hopping, *Visions of the Beast* goes double platinum; "The Trooper" is issued as a single, with various live and video versions of the track as B-sides. More pertinently, on August 29, EMI delivers a double-CD live album called *Death on the Road*.

What's remarkable about *Death on the Road* is that it's the document of a single show, at the Westfalenhallen in Dortmund, Germany, from November 24, 2003. The sound is gorgeous and explosive, and the performances are spirited, especially "The Trooper," which Nicko roars through like a lion, as does Bruce, ducking nothing or very little. There's also "Can I Play with Madness," early in the sequence, which begins and ends with an a cappella "Can I Play with Agnes." Most obscure is Blaze-era track "Lord of the Flies," once more, Nicko willing it into the memory circuits of the fans through his enthusiasm. The band's previous record is represented only by "Brave New World," but then again, that album was more than well covered by the previous live record, *Rock in Rio*.

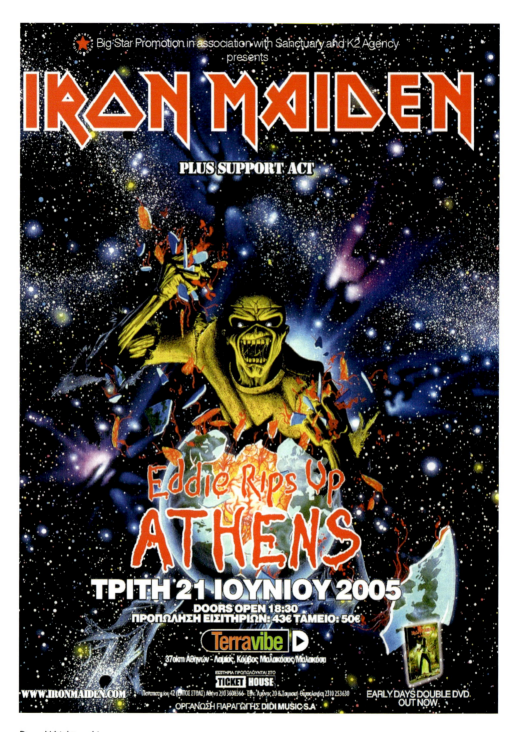

Dave Wright archive

From *Dance of Death*, we get "Wildest Dreams," "Dance of Death," "Rainmaker," "Paschendale," "No More Lies," and "Journeyman," the latter authentic to the original—that is, acoustic—but now with crowd participation that warms the cockles. The record races to a close with impossibly swift versions of "Number of the Beast" and "Run to the Hills" and out we go, exiting the Westfalenhallen.

Five months after the CD version, *Death on the Road* was issued as a mammoth three-DVD package that included a lengthy documentary on the making of *Dance of Death*, a "life on the road" documentary, fan interviews, and videos for "Wildest Dreams" and "Rainmaker," plus photo and artwork galleries.

Mused Nicko, speaking with Carl Begai on the happy state of the band at this juncture, "Bruce, since he's been back, he's changed completely. He needed to do what he had to do, and then he realized he missed it. I still, to this day, don't forgive him for the way he left Maiden, but I'm glad he did it because he had to. I've told him that, and he understands it. But he's come back and he's a new man. What we have now is very special. We're all really, really excited about being in this band. We all have our differences of opinion on certain things, whether it's sound or a song or whatever—you're always going to have that—but there's no grief about it. There's a lot of history on the new album; primary for me, like I say, is that I've written a tune [laughs]. We're still like we were when I first joined the band, but I think we're more shell-shocked in that we've got more than we had, and we had it all then.

"It's difficult to explain the essence of it all," Nicko continues. "I'd have to write a book. It comes down to teamwork though—no one man makes this band. Okay, this is Steve Harris's band—take him out of the picture and you wouldn't have Iron Maiden. I talked to him about that once, and he was like, 'Fuck off with ye; o' course ye'd get a new bass player if I left,' and I was like, 'Ye've gotta be friggin' jokin'; piss off 'Arry!' He's not vain; he's not thinking, 'I'm the man.' I'll never play with another bass player, and I know he'll never play with another drummer [laughs]. Don't get me wrong; I'm not setting you up because we're doing this interview. This is the way people are in this band."

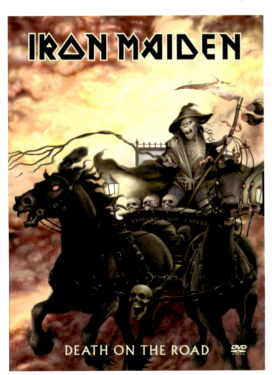

Dave Wright archive

CHAPTER 19
The Best of Bruce Dickinson and Tyranny of Souls

"I wanted to write about the beauty of technology."

Back in the 1990s, the Air Raid Siren essentially howled alone, out on his own path—many paths—as a solo artist, both during and after his blaze-out with a Maiden already crashing in flames creatively. But in the 2000s, Bruce stayed faithful to the machine, issuing only one solo album over the span of twenty years.

Then again to kick off the new millennium (well, sort of, September 25, 2001), there was *The Best of Bruce Dickinson*, a two-CD spread of anthologizing that for half its width and girth summarized the action-packed solo catalog proper and then, for the other half, treated the fans to all the rarities along the way.

The album also featured two brand-new songs in album opener "Broken" and "Silver Wings" later in the sequence. "Broken" found Bruce straddling his Maidenness, given the song's strong melody, its twin lead, and the singalong "whoa whoa" section, with his grinding, groovy guise that was part and parcel of *Accident of Birth* and *The Chemical Wedding*. "Silver Wings" starts in the same vein and then turns into a bare-bones sort of speed metal, almost punky given its nearly D-beat rhythm. But again, there's a twin lead and some tricky fills, keeping the affair upscale.

"Initially there was only supposed to be one new song," Bruce told me at the time. "I went out to write this one song, which turned out to be 'Broken,' with Roy Z. And in the process, we were playing around with old demos, and I had heard this other backing track that we had, and said, 'That sounds like Maiden, 1985 style.' And he said yeah, yeah, yeah. And I said, 'Go on, I'll write some lyrics and I'll put a tune to it.' So, I did, and we all just had a hoot putting the demo down, and we were laughing and drinking beer and I said, 'Come on, let's put it on the record.' And he said, 'No, we can't do that; we'll get in trouble' [laughs]. And I said, 'No we won't. I'll take it to London, and I'll see what everybody thinks about it before we do anything.' So, I played them this thing and I said to Rod, Maiden's manager, I said, 'What do you think, man?' And he said, 'I think it sounds fantastic!' So, I said, 'So we can put it on the record then?' And he said, 'Oh yeah!' And so 'Silver Wings' is pretty much Iron Maiden 'Aces High' style, done by me and Roy. But yes, the other track, 'Broken,' was conceived, I suppose, as a fairly catchy four-minute song done along the lines of *Chemical Wedding*."

Among the highlights from the regular catalog, there's "The Tower," one of a handful of classics from the best record Bruce ever made, *The Chemical Wedding*.

"Yes, and the one thing I remember about 'The Tower' is doing the video. Doing the video involved trying to get as many different tarot card images as we could, and we were really running out of time. So, one of the things I did was hang upside down for about ten minutes in a straitjacket dressed as the Hanged Man, hanging by one leg, which is extraordinarily uncomfortable. And it's very galling that none of the shots actually made the movie [laughs].

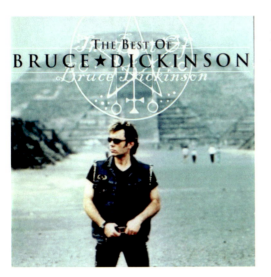

Martin Popoff archive

And the other thing I did is I nearly break both my arms hurling myself from one side to the other side, in a straitjacket again, in a darkened room just by torchlight while being filmed, like a madman in a padded cell. We couldn't get any padding, so we just did it without. I've still got the bruises."

Also included is non-LP track "Wicker Man," a tribal and yet proggy and even grungy song not to be confused with the Maiden song of the same name.

"Right. It's not an alternate version— it's a completely different song. The original title for the Iron Maiden 'Wicker Man' song was 'Your Time Will Come.' Nobody was really that keen on that title, and Steve then had picked out of the line I had written, 'The shadow over the wicker man is rising up again,' and said, 'Wow, why don't we call it "The Wicker Man"?' At which point I thought, oh man, it's going to be 'Bring Your Daughter . . . to the Slaughter' all over again, but then I said, 'Okay, I see it does make sense.' Because 'The Wicker Man' gave us a cover, it gave us a look to the album, it gave us a stage show, all from this movie. So, it was a good choice, a good decision. But the song that appears on my album, on CD 2, is a completely different song, written and recorded at the time of *Accident of Birth*."

As well, Bruce does a bit of mansplaining on the record. Rather than regular liner notes, Bruce says, "What there is, is a short story done in monkish handwriting, four pages on parchment, the allegorical story of 'Bring Your Daughter . . . to the Slaughter.' And I also did my own biography for the album, sort of like an open letter, and they've actually reprinted that biography along the bottom of all the pages of the artwork."

Even though a single-CD version of the album was eventually issued, Bruce said at the time that "at the moment, all the copies that have been produced anywhere in the world are all going to have the second CD. So, nobody who goes out in the first couple of months is going to get a single-CD copy. There's probably enough for CD 3 and even CD 4 kicking around. This is just a sampling of the stuff. There may be more to come, but I'll have to make another record first."

The original plan, as Bruce explained to Dmitry Epstein, was to issue only the rarities CD. "Yes, CD 2 of *The Best of* set was going to be called *Catacombs* and was going to be a collection of unreleased songs and rarities. It went back and turned into *The Best of* album by adding another CD which has two new songs on it and a lot of remastered tracks from the previous studio albums. So, this *The Best of* album includes what would have been called *Catacombs*.

Asked by Epstein why we are seeing this record now, Bruce explains that "it's a nice quiet time for Iron Maiden, and I'll be releasing a new solo album next year, so this is a really good time for the managing of my solo career, which is going quite well. I had a whole lot of new potential fans after the last Iron Maiden record, and it was a success, so this is a good chance to get my material out to them, and also to keep existing fans happy with some unreleased and some rare material and also some brand-new material."

Amusingly, Dmitry brings up that the chorus of "Broken" is all about being *not* broken. Why, then, call the song "Broken"? "Because it's more interesting," laughs Dickinson. "And if there's a song called 'Broken,' people think, 'Why broken?' And they find it's 'not broken.' I mean, there's an expression in England: 'Never let the bastards grind you down.'"

Talking future plans then—this is the interview I had with Bruce literally late morning of 9/11—Bruce says that there were no plans to tour the compilation. "Even if there was a big demand, I have no band at the moment [laughs]. They are scattered to the four winds. The plans are, as soon as I can get ahold of Roy and dig him out of the bunker he's in with Rob Halford making *his* new album [laughs], then early next year we'll start. Lyrically, I'm keeping that under wraps [laughs]. Musically what's going on, I'm keeping that under wraps too. And late next year we'll be on with Maiden. There will be a record with Maiden, and then touring in 2003."

Adds Adrian Smith, same subject, "I mean, I've been involved in his last three albums. Obviously, we're very involved with Iron Maiden full time right now. But Bruce has plans to do some solo stuff next year. If he rang me up and said he wanted me to do a bit of writing or play on a couple of tracks, that would be fine. As for going off on tour for six months or something, I don't know. When Bruce joined, we kind of gravitated a bit towards each other. He was very keen to write, and I used to stand around playing riffs all the time and we used to get together and write a lot. I guess we do have a chemistry. Bruce is a great songwriter and writes great lyrics, and I think it's one of those proven things. A guitarist and singer [snaps his fingers]—it just works together. You sit down as a guitarist and try to write and all of a sudden you have a million riffs. You sit down with a singer, and it focuses things immediately."

Surprisingly, Adrian would not be part of Bruce's next—and last, to date—solo album, remarking after the fact, "Personally, I mean, Roy Z had a lot to do with those albums. He produced and he played guitar, and to be fair, he wrote most of the songs with Bruce. I really loved playing those songs, and I chipped in with a few myself. I enjoyed more the guitar-playing aspect of it. I'm happy just doing what I'm doing right now [with Maiden]. I don't feel the need to do more. Maybe I can get into songwriting or something, but that's another minefield, writing songs for other people. It's a whole 'nother can of worms, something I might do in the future. I might do something more instrumentally based just for myself and maybe put that out. But before, I had more ambition, where I wanted to do some solo stuff. But I don't really have that anymore, to be honest. I don't know if Bruce is going to do one. I certainly don't have a yearning to do it like I used to. I've kind of done solo albums, I've done albums with Bruce, I've done all that stuff; I don't really feel the need to do it. I don't know the way Bruce feels about it."

Bruce, as it turns out, had one more in him. But at this juncture, that was it for Bruce's solo career for a long time, although one spot of Dickinson-centric news took place the following year, 2002, when the BBC's *Bruce Dickinson's Friday Rock Show* hits the airwaves, with Bruce becoming a well-known radio personality over the years, leading to Dickinson's appearance in various documentaries for the broadcaster. On a related project Bruce gets involved with, in 2005 he hosts the Discovery Channel's *Flying Heavy Metal*, a five-episode documentary on aviation.

"I'm not going out for nine months touring, forget it," mused Bruce at the time, on finding balance between rock 'n' roll and these other pursuits. "You know, I've got a life inside music, and I've got a life outside music. And actually, I rather like both of them. And, put it this way, when I'm seventy years old, my life outside music is the one that's going to sustain me for the rest of my life. And let's pull it back a little bit. In five years, when I'm fifty years old, my life outside music is going to be the one that I care about. Not my life inside music. It's going to be my kids, my family, whatever. So this is a way of transferring from one to the other. I love the idea of going out and doing a tour for two weeks and then just saying, okay, we won't do anything for four or five months, and we'll go play somewhere else for two weeks. Hey, let's go to the East Coast for two weeks, boom, boom, done! And in fact, it's taking the whole thing back to . . . I mean, other bands do it, actually, mainly punk bands, to be honest with you, bands like Bad Religion and people like that. You know, they all have full-time jobs as university lecturers. They get together and plan their holidays and they say, 'Let's go on the road for a month! Yeah!' I think it's a fucking great idea."

The next couple of years had Bruce stalking stages with Maiden, but then Judas Priest reunited with Rob Halford, and Roy Z was suddenly free to work with Bruce again on solo material.

I asked Bruce how privy he had been to the return of the Metal God to the Priesthood, a reunion that resulted in a new record called *Angel of Retribution*, issued March 1, 2005, and a permanent reinstatement of Rob to the fold.

"Oh, I wasn't," replies the Air Raid Siren, next king-to-be in the line of metal royalty after Halford. "Only that it was blindingly obvious that that was eventually what was going to happen—or either or both of them were going to fall apart. In some respects, Halford's solo career was doing great up to a point, and then there was the last record, and this tour that he suddenly went off on. Everything just seemed to fall apart. And for *Crucible*, I know that Roy had a lot of advice for that record that was ignored. And Roy was like, well, at the end of the day, it's not his record; it's Rob Halford's record and whoever was advising Rob at the time. So, he just had to go with that. It was a shame, because it would have been nice to see Rob do another record as good as the first one. But we'll see what happens now that Priest is back together. I hope they do a great record. But yeah, oh God, that kind of sank our collaboration, actually, the Halford project, in many ways. Because it tied Roy up for an incredibly long period of time, and it really burnt him out as well—actually the second one. It's one thing making a record, and it's another thing having to be a politician at the same time."

Bruce Dickinson's sixth solo album, *Tyranny of Souls*, recorded at Castle Oaks, Calabasas, California, and Signature Sound in San Diego, California, saw issue through Sanctuary Records on May 23, 2005. On the front of the thing, building on the favorable reception afforded the cover art of *The Chemical Wedding*, Bruce went with a classic picture once again, a demon depiction from Renaissance artist Hans Memling from circa 1485 called *The Mouth of Leviathan*.

"Oh, nothing ties into the cover," says Bruce. "No, the cover is the cover because it looks scary. By and large the album is a scary heavy metal album. I thought, 'Well, we could try to be clever, we could try to be this, we could try to be that.' I thought, 'No, don't try and be too clever; just put a cover with a great title that sounds scary.' So, *Tyranny of Souls* was the title just because I thought it was a great title. The actual track itself, of

CHAPTER 19

course, was written for the Three Tremors project (the aborted project band that was to feature Bruce, Rob Halford, and Geoff Tate). Ironically, it's a track which is really not that related to the overall subject matter of the album. I don't give a shit. I just thought, 'I want a title that sounds really cool.' I just think the name *Tyranny of Souls* sounds really cool, and when I was looking at artwork, which Hugh Gilmour, the art director, selected a whole bunch of potential paintings to use, subjects to use, I just looked at that particular picture and I thought, 'Yeah, that looks like a tyranny of souls to me.'"

Martin Popoff archive

Warned guitarist and producer Roy Z, in conversation with Tim Henderson, concerning the impending release of *Tyranny of Souls*, "We just finished up Bruce's new album, and I can tell ya, it fuckin' smokes. All I can tell you is that it's everything people expect and more, because the album just smokes. It's on fire. It has a lot of raw energy, power, and great storytelling. Bruce is a great storyteller. There's some crushing stuff, but there is some real emotional stuff as well. Bruce has never sounded better in my mind."

As to what took him so long—after all, *The Chemical Wedding* was seven years ago—Bruce said, "I've been a chicken. A complete chicken. And then when circumstances conspired to say, 'Well, even if you wanted to make a solo album at this point, you couldn't,' because of timing and Roy's availability and blah, blah, blah, I must confess to being secretly relieved because I really didn't know how I was going to follow up *Chemical Wedding*. When I joined Maiden and we did *Brave New World*, I thought, 'Wow, thank God that was a really good record, because now I don't have to follow up *Chemical Wedding* for a while.' 'Cause I thought, 'Shit, how am I going to follow this record up?' It was such a great album. I put so much of myself into that album. I didn't know that there were any more bits of myself I could dig out. I thought whatever album I put out now has got to be really good, so I was terrified. I thought I had to find some way into the process of writing this album.

"As usual, it's just some act of complete random irrationality," continues Bruce, on how events transpired to make the record happen. "It was one of those late-night phone calls from Roy Z. He phoned me up; this is in between the European and little American tour that we did. We did the American tour where we did the Hammerstein Ballroom in LA, Canadian tour in the winter, not last winter but the winter before. So, shortly before we started that tour, Roy called me up and said, 'Look, I've got all these guitar tracks sitting around on CD and they're really cool; lemme play you a couple.'

"So, he played me a couple, and I immediately, like within about two minutes, wrote down the tune and the chorus for 'Navigate the Seas of the Sun' and 'River of No Return.' And I said, 'Roy, let me stop you there.' I said, 'I've got these two songs; one is called 'Navigate the Seas of the Sun' and this one is called 'River of No Return,' and you have to send me the rest of the songs on CD and we're going to make this record, because I just know we are now. I've just got the fiddle vibe, and I just know it's going to be great, but send me the songs.'

"And he said, 'Do you want me to put rough drums, like drum machine on the songs?' I went, 'No, no, no, just send me the raw guitars with nothing on it at all; no bass, no keyboards, no rhythm, no click track, nothing.' And so I got a CD of a bunch of untitled raw guitars. I went off to America, and I just used to walk 'round the hotel lobbies and coffee shops with a pair of headphones on, daydreaming with a big notepad, writing down words and humming things to myself. After about ten days of that, I phoned Roy again and said, 'Roy, look, I've got most of the tunes in my head, so you go ahead and put drums on the following tracks.' This is without Roy hearing any of the songs. So, I said, 'Just do the drums, and when I get back to LA, I'll sing you the songs.' So, he did that, with this guy Dave Moreno, who did just an amazing job on the drums. So, we're putting drums onto the guitars, not the other way around. We didn't change the guitars; we put the drums onto the guitars.

"Then I went back, and I said, 'I expect you want to hear what the songs sound like, Z.' So I sang the songs for him, or just the rough melody, la, la, la, la, la; I didn't have all the words yet, and I went, 'Okay, that's great, that'll work, that'll work, that'll work,' and we had two or three bits that we had to change on the drums, just for the rhythms, just so it fitted more with the words, and that was mainly on 'Kill Devil Hill.' I said, 'Great, well, you tweak those, and I'll go off to Japan for another couple of weeks, do a tour, and I'll finish all the songs up, write the rest of the words, and then I'll come back home. We've got the guitars down—well, we've got some guitar—we've got the drums, so we'll put the lead vocals down. We don't need the bass. If there is any, then that's a bonus.'"

And then, bang, bang, Bruce had a new record called *Tyranny of Souls* that opens with "Mars Within (Intro)," a minute and a half smudge of soundtrack audio in which Bruce invokes Professor Bernard Quatermass of BBC science fiction TV fame.

"*Quatermass and the Pit*, a Hammer classic, is a very inspirational movie for me," Bruce told *Terrorizer* magazine. "Nigel Kneale is one of my big inspirations. I just watched *The Stone Tape*. I've got all the Quatermass TV series and all the movies, but *Quatermass and the Pit* for me sums up so much of Nigel Kneale's thing about the human condition and about the need for man to survive by his own wits. It's what the heart and soul of this album's about."

This leads into UFO tale "Abduction," a straight-line heavy metal chugger with twin-lead appointments and a ripping solo from Roy. Next is the jackhammer of "Soul Intruders," which, come verse time, goes into a similar staccato chug as the track before it.

"It's never one-way," Z says, with respect to how these songs got written. "Obviously Bruce is a very accomplished songwriter, but this time we collaborated right down the line. To be honest with you, it's going to be a record that people are going to talk about for a while. It's serious. I really enjoy the record a lot, and the songs are really strong. I brought in Stan [Katayama] to help; he's always on the Bruce records, and he worked with me on the Priest. I brought Stan in to help me mix the Priest record, 'cause I was tired, man. He was in England with me for about a month."

Katayama is credited with the mix as well as corecorder of the drums, which are played by the aforementioned David Moreno. Roy did all the guitars and bass on "Power of the Sun" and "Believil." Ray "Geezer" Burke plays the bass on "Mars Within (Intro)," "Kill Devil Hill," "Navigate the Seas of the Sun," "River of No Return," "Devil on a Hog," and "A Tyranny of Souls." Juan Perez plays bass on "Abduction" and Soul Intruders," while all keyboards are credited to Maestro Mistheria.

"Kill Devil Hill" is named for the town (Kill Devil Hills, North Carolina) that included the site where the Wright brothers first demonstrated powered flight. This ties in nicely with Bruce's second career, and the lyric is steered mystically so that it fits the concept established by the preceding tracks. The song is a mix between dreamy mellow music and a sort of doomy waltz structure.

Next is "Navigate the Seas of the Sun," which is arguably the greatest ballad Bruce ever wrote, exquisitely hooky, lush, and acoustic. As Dickinson told *Terrorizer*, "'Navigate the Seas of the Sun' is about carrying on, to go and not return, to raise families, to colonize. 'River of No Return' is the same deal, but it's a spaceship on which two people are sent out. They're partners, but there's a guilty secret, and as they go on through eternity, the secret pushes them apart. It's an allegory of lousy relationships.

"I watch loads of old sci-fi movies, and when I started writing this album, I had an idea that I wanted to write about the beauty of technology; the beauty of well-crafted machinery and engineering, and the idea of space, literally 'the final frontier' and 'we boldly go' and all that. It's kinda what we're here for. Mankind is here to carry on, to survive, and we're not gonna survive if we stay on this ball of rock forever. The only way we're going to survive is by technology—that's our future. Mankind is destined to survive; we must keep that in vision, all of us. We mustn't regress to this idea that we must stand still in our muddy boots and eke out a living until finally this ball of rock dissolves when the sun burns out. We're bigger than that."

"River of No Return" is another gorgeous ballad, albeit with a heavy chorus and a pulsing midpaced rhythm. There's a detectable up-ratchet in Bruce's songwriting abilities on this record—look no further than the elegant break on this one, and the deft arranging throughout.

"The album is all about the songs," says Bruce, but then amusingly switching gears. "I mean, it's guitar and vocals—that is what the heart and soul of everything is. So that's what happened. In the meantime, I fell offstage in Los Angeles and screwed up all the muscles in my chest. Then about a week later in Japan, all the muscles in my lower back went on the opposite side, which my osteopathphysio-whatever in England said, 'Oh yeah, well that's generally what happens. You screw up one side of your body, and then the other side goes out in sympathy.' So, I ended up doing the lead vocals hobbling back to Los Angeles after Japan, after the Japanese tour, and I was there for about ten days. I did all the lead vocals, but we did have to have a bed by the microphone so I could lie down in between takes [laughs]. Really sad. Can you imagine me not being able to get around? I was cursing and swearing. I mean literally I couldn't walk. I could walk about 100 yards and then I had to go have a sit-down and a rest. All the muscles in my lower back were just ripped. Can you imagine me not being able to get around?

"We didn't use a studio; we did it all in ProTools in Roy's kitchen [laughs]. So nobody knew what was going on because nobody knew. I'd just go 'round to Roy's house, and he was there with all his ProTools rig all set up, and he did all the guitars in his room. Everything gets done in his house except the drums; he did the drums in the studio with Dave. And that was it, really; nobody knew what was going on. I don't think even my management knew what was going on. I said, 'Oh, I'm just going to go over there, and I'll be back soon.' And then all of a sudden, I said, 'Okay, it's done, it's finished, it's mixed, here it is,' and everybody that listened to it went, 'Jesus, wow, what a record.'

"And you know what? I am so delirious with having done this album on ProTools. It's such a different way of working for me. You know, the idea that you could make a record, leave it for eight months, [then] come back to it, and it still sounds fresh and untouched, and then complete it and still keep the energy was amazing. I don't think you could do that with analog. Analog, of course, has many advantages because of its limitations. It makes you focus on the immediate performance, which is good. I wonder whether a generation that is brought up on digital and ProTools will have the same set of performance skills, if you like, as the generation that was brought up on analog.

"But that's no concern of mine, in a sense, because when I perform and we're doing ProTools, I pretend like it's tape. I pretend that you only have one chance to get this right. But the truth is, once you've done your performance you can actually sit back and relax and go, 'Wow, now we can listen to it and do what we like with it,' which is really cool. The other good thing about ProTools is that you don't lose anything in terms of magic moments, a mix that has a magic moment to it. You can recall that at any time and say, 'What was it about when we did the demos that was just so cool?' And you can listen to them, there it is, on the hard disc. And you can then go back into your main mix and say, 'Well, let's make the main mix sound more like the demos.' You know, so you can do fantastic things."

Back to the track list, next is "Power of the Sun," another rocker, this one with a covert and scurrying vibe that nonetheless gives way to strident half-time passages and smoother full-speed sections for the twin-lead passage and for the choruses.

"It's quite a philosophical record in a way," Bruce told Tim Henderson. "Yeah, like I say, I wrote the record about our need to carry on discovering things. In the big picture of mankind, here I am past my mid-forties with three kids that are growing up in the world and I'm thinking, 'They're gonna have kids and then they are gonna get to their forties; then they're gonna have kids.' This big process keeps going on and on and on. What does it mean? What in God's name does it all mean? Why are we here? Are we just here to sort of, like sheep, to just eat the grass and walk around and get eaten by wolves? Or are we here to discover great things and to move forward and move on and eventually to leave this planet and go somewhere else? What is the end point of it all?

"The only answer that I can come up with is that there isn't an end point. The end point is just existence; it's carrying on, that's what we're supposed to do. We're supposed to carry on and discover things. Maybe one day we'll discover that there is an end point. But discovering the end point would be way too boring. As I started thinking about that, writing for some of the songs and thinking of all the little manifestations of that that came off it, we needed something for this little intro piece at the beginning."

Hence the aforementioned "Mars Within (Intro)" . . . "Yes, which sort of sums up, if there was a sci-fi movie that summed up the philosophy of the record, what would it be? And I went, *Quatermass and the Pit* from 1958, the Nigel Kneale Hammer movie. Absolute science fiction masterpiece. So that's why the little voices say, 'Professor Quatermass, where are you?' In the movie this brainy professor always comes to the aid of mankind and, just with rigorous scientific logic, solves what appear to be insoluble spiritual problems. So, he cuts through religion and superstition and the occult and stuff like that and actually discovers far-deeper, more-profound insights which come about because of the reality of the science behind what's going on."

"Devil on a Hog" is a no-nonsense rocker at the verses, but it just might contain the most hummable and loveable chorus of Bruce's solo career. At the lyric end, there's a "Space Truckin'" vibe to Dickinson's playful, oblique imagery.

"Believil" is a big, bad doom monster with light and shade like the mother of all apocalyptic heavy metal, "Black Sabbath" by Black Sabbath. Then we're into "A Tyranny of Souls" to close things out, similarly a big, slow doom, perfect for a last track, given

Bruce's explanation that it really doesn't integrate into his cosmic story line concerning man and his mastery of technology, and the sense of spirituality that mastery entails, especially if at some future point it goes quantum and interstellar.

All told, as alluded to, the record went smoothly thanks to technology as well as the camaraderie between the duo doing most everything.

"Bruce is like my big brother," reflects Roy. "That's how I look at it—he's my big brother. I look up to him in different aspects. I love him and I love his family. That's it, man. To work with him, it's like cutting butter. It's nothin'—it's not even work."

As for whether this relationship might have him working for the mother ship, Iron Maiden, one day, Roy demurs. "You know what, man? I don't know. And that's the kind of subject where I go, 'Pfffttt!' At this point I don't know if it's a good idea. I think now, working with Priest, I like to stay with one in each genre. You know what I mean? It's hard to not work with Rob and with Bruce, 'cause they are the top singers in their style. I'm trying to keep it one in each style. Now that I've worked for Priest . . . I'm not saying I'll never work with anybody; I'm just saying it's harder to be doing those. To work on those mammoth records like that, it takes a lot out of me. Plus, Steve, I think he's doing a great job, and personally I don't even think I'd want to get in there, because I think what they are doing is great. They don't need me."

"I would reciprocate," says Bruce, told by Tim Henderson what Roy said. "His big brother? Okay. I would say I'm not that much bigger than him [laughs]. I would say we're about the same. I'd say Roy is like . . . he's kind of like a soul brother because there is like a psychic link between the two of us. When he plays me music, I just know what he's thinking, and he knows what I'm thinking. I can't put a finger on that, or whatever.

"I would just love him to succeed in his own right, just as an artist, as Roy Z, just because what he does is so beautiful, and people need to hear it. It was very sad when Mercury had a deal with him and they really dropped the ball, but they kind of drop the ball with everything. Tribe of Gypsies, some of their stuff was just unbelievable. I felt very, very passionately about that band—it really deserved a shot. I don't know where it is at the moment. I know he's doing some new stuff, and we'll just have to see where it leads, really. It's difficult for him and it's difficult for record labels to get a handle on it, because as Roy Z, he's actually more well known now as a guitarist with me and as a producer.

"But hopefully people will be hearing what he does and thinking, 'Wow, what a great guitar player.' What might happen, which really would be great—and my fingers will be crossed anyway—was if somebody like *Guitar Player* magazine or something like that just picks up on what a fucking awesome guitarist he is, and just presents him as 'Roy Z: The New Guitar Guru.' And if they champion him—all right, it might be Roy Z and His Tribe of Gypsies, rather than Tribe of Gypsies—it would be an excuse for him to get out and showcase the band and get into it that way. You need a way in, in this day and age, to get into people's heads that they can understand. So perhaps that could be a way in. I really hope so, and I really hope that somebody that is looking after him has a sense of vision about what he is really capable of."

Bruce's way in in 2005 was through the renewed fame and exposure he had as singer for Iron Maiden, a formidable touring act and a band not shy about writing new songs. And record sales, as we've mentioned, tended to add up to something substantial for a panworld phenomenon like Maiden. "Yeah, I mean we still get gold records and stuff like that in Europe, but I think the States would be pretty difficult. Although, having said that, the records are still selling. We're still selling a million albums when we put a new record out, which is pretty good for a band of our vintage."

In June, Dickinson's solo catalog saw reissue in expanded form, and then a year later, Sanctuary issued a three-DVD box set called *Anthology*. With the compilation and all of this, Bruce's solo years were laid bare for all to see, all the official records, all the behind-the-curtains songs (and jokes), plus all the visuals.

Mused Bruce at the time, looking at his two music jobs, "I'd say, if you like my solo record, go tell your friends and go buy some copies and just enjoy it for what it is, and if you like the Iron Maiden records and the way we make them and everything else, then simply enjoy them. And if you don't, then there is no need to go around and dis them. They are what they are, Maiden is what it is; it's not gonna go changing any time soon. That is the nature of the beast, that's what we all accepted when we joined, when we rejoined Maiden. It's both Maiden's strength and some people see it as a weakness. But you can look at it from both ends. I don't see any reason why people need to turn one record into a weapon against another one. Just enjoy the records for what they are."

But as pertains the solo career, "I actually quite like being a cult phenomenon," affirms Bruce. "I'd be very happy if the cult phenomenon gets to be a little bit of a bigger cult phenomenon, but, you know, one of the advantages of being a cult phenomenon is that people understand what you do, and they look at it and they analyze it and pick it apart and stuff. In that respect it's quite nice 'cause I can do things that have some content and some depth that people will actually notice.

"I don't have the huge support network of major record labels and companies and all the rest of it behind me," answers Bruce, as to why he isn't a bigger commercial success. "And also, because I think I step back from doing all the sort of cliché things that might make you a bit more acceptable. In addition, as soon as you step back into Iron Maiden, stepping away from Iron Maiden, it makes it difficult if you're not touring and all that kind of stuff as well.

"But I'm actually very pleased the way that *Tyranny of Souls* has been received," continues Bruce. "We're getting amazing reviews over here in Europe and covers and all kinds of things. There's a lot of support. I mean, everybody here at the record company, certainly in the UK, is really behind the record and they really love it. The reaction in Germany has been astonishing. We've got front covers in all the major magazines in Germany, and it's 'Album of the Year' in one of them. I just did a front cover here for *Terrorizer*, and *Kerrang!* are even giving it a great review.

"Plus, I think the fact that Maiden are doing Ozzfest, the fact that it's coming out on the eve of a Maiden tour and there is basically nothing else that people can buy that's Maidenish, other than this album, it seems that the record label have got their shit together. We might yet be quite surprised. They're doing a huge repackaging of all the old stuff, which should actually be going in the shops, not that I'm bitter about the fact that it should have been in there when it first came out, but hey, better late than never.

"Although it was always difficult because, actually, my records in the past were always in direct competition with Iron Maiden records, when I wasn't in Iron Maiden. I was still managed by Sanctuary. It was a difficult scenario and situation, I think. It was the sort of thing whereas an artist, how much priority are you going to get? And the answer was, not a huge amount. So, it was a difficult problem and one that was difficult to resolve.

CHAPTER 19

At the same time, I felt that it was better to remain within the fold of all the people that I knew, that supported me, rather than, as it were, going out and declaring war on everything Sanctuary and Iron Maiden and blah, blah, blah, out of a sort of spite, if you like. There seemed no point in doing that, because I'm not sure that you would necessarily . . . what you would end up with is having a big fight which nobody was going to win. Nobody wins in that scenario. Much better to work with the people you have who are all working under difficult circumstances anyway. But yes, there are so many people who are unaware of the fact that I've had a record out since *Tattooed Millionaire* [laughs]."

When all is said and done, Dickinson's heart was in the right place.

"The essence is that I'm a great believer that if you keep on doing good things, good things will eventually happen," chuckles Bruce. "And I think that this could be a really good turning point. I just sense a really good time now for a bit of a sea change, a bit of a turnaround in terms of the profile of my solo stuff. Without taking away from Iron Maiden and things like that, this album, I think, has got a lot of things that people are going to really love, and it's a gateway into previous albums for people that haven't investigated the previous albums. Like I say, the previous albums are all rereleased, or repromoted rather, with extra tracks and so on and so forth. There's a big promotion gonna go on with all of that. And of course, touring with Iron Maiden, if you want something new to buy, then this is the only Iron Maiden new-type thing that you can get your hands on. So it's perfect timing. Steve's got a copy of the album, and I think he really likes it [laughs]."

CHAPTER 20
A Matter of Life and Death and *Flight 666*

"We carry on, and when we feel it's finished, we stop."

Now firmly reestablished as one of the top heavy metal bands in the world, mining catalog and creating catalog anew, Maiden look to make their third record with Bruce and Adrian back, writing in late 2005 and then breaking for Christmas.

"As usual, we allowed ourselves just a few weeks," notes Steve in the official "making of" video, with regard to the penning of the songs. "A quick scramble, the pressure of writing, which seems to get the best out of us. We allow ourselves a couple weeks to get the songs together. For me, personally, I don't know if the rest of the guys feel the same way, but I feel a lot of pressure when we're writing. And it was about two months from start to finish, recording and mixing. That's like, unbelievable, just so quick. Ridiculous, really." When Nicko remarks that the end result is "pretty progressive," Steve qualifies with "If you think prog, people start thinking all kinds of weird things. But to me it's more 1970s-influence progressive, which is a different thing from 1990s or kind of 'now' progressive."

On February 6, *Death on the Road*, previously issued as a live CD, sees release as a two-DVD package of the live concert plus extras, and then the following month and into April, the band works on what will become *A Matter of Life and Death*, recording it at Sarm West Studios in London—Eddie sculptures placed prominently—finishing the task two months early, despite Kevin taking the time to film much of the proceedings. Working titles for the album included *The Legacy* and *The Pilgrim*, both names of songs on the record, but then the guys decided on . . . that mouthful, which is a cliché to boot.

"We had other titles, but this one stuck," explains Janick. "We didn't have a title when we were making the album. Often a song will present itself. On the last album, 'Dance of Death' presented itself as a title track. On this album, nothing really presented itself as a title track. Maybe 'The Legacy' would have been okay, but it would've felt like the last album, calling it *The Legacy* after a song on the album. That was mentioned but pushed to the back. So, *A Matter of Life and Death* came out, and we thought, well, that was quite cool, plus there wasn't a song on it called that. *The Legacy* wasn't really bandied about; it was just mentioned. It's not something where we all sat down and said *The Legacy* would be great. As we did the song, someone said—I can't even remember who it was—that would be a good title. We thought about it for a couple of days, and I personally thought that the title sounds like it's going to be your last album, which it definitely doesn't feel like. I mean production-wise there are so many songs in the band, we're very happy working together, and so I don't think it was the right title. *A Matter of Life and Death* was put forth, and it just sounded right.

"This was the quickest, definitely," continues Janick, on the making of the record. "Because the other ones were really similar in time. But this was quick for the very reason that, on the last album, Kevin Shirley wasn't fully happy with the mix that went out. He wanted a slightly different mix. And that's because he had done a mix, and everyone, well, Steve, had felt he was happy with it, and then he'd done another one, and he was happy with both, and then there was a bit of an argument about which one was going to go out.

"And for this one what he did was actually recorded then mixed, which we've never done before. We would always record all the songs live, go and do that, and then go overdub what we need to overdub, and then they'd take everything away, they'd bring it back, and they'd re-EQ everything and then do a remix, which is the basic mix. And that's how we'd do albums. That's how we've done them for the last twenty years.

"Well, what Kevin's idea was on this one, which I suppose gives him a little bit more control, is, as we went along, we mixed it. So, as we were finishing the overdubs for the guitar or vocals or whatever needed doing, as we finished that track and went on to the next track, he would finish the mix at the same time. Which sounds a bit strange, but it actually works fantastically well, because once you pull the whole thing down and you have to put it all back up again, it never sounds the same. Even though the computer says it does, it never does, so when we add it up, which is literally sprinkling the fairy dust on, he would put the mix together and that was it. And you know, he basically did the mix as we were overdubbing it. Once we did overdubs, it was complete."

On May 26, longtime Maiden and Sanctuary financial guru (and Sanctuary cofounder) Andy Taylor leaves Sanctuary Group after a period of poor results. This is a time of turmoil for the company after rapid growth through acquisition. Remember as well, we are fully into the era of downloads at this point, and the death knell is on for physical product, or at least the significant bulk of it. Streaming is not an issue yet—this is the interim period, where the challenge is to get music files onto one's hard drive (or even burned onto recordable CDs) as cheaply as possible, and in the eyes and ears of many music consumers, ideally for free. Into September, Sanctuary Management goes through another restructuring, notably, with longtime executive Merck Mercuriadis forecasted to be leaving the company shortly. This indeed takes place on October 31, with Merck then founding publicly funded music IP company Hipgnosis Songs Limited after twenty years with Sanctuary, his last post as Sanctuary CEO. Both Morrissey and Guns N' Roses migrate over to the new company with Merck.

On August 14, 2006, "The Reincarnation of Benjamin Breeg," backed with a BBC Radio 1 version of "Hallowed Be Thy Name," is issued as an advance single from the forthcoming *A Matter of Life and Death*. In total, there is a CD version, a promo version, and a 10-inch clear-vinyl version, all with different track listings. The single hits #1 both in the Swedish and Finnish charts as Maiden mania mounts.

Reflects Janick, "We figured we wouldn't get any airplay anyhow, with radio play or any particular . . . I mean, we're not a band that gets airplay. In fact, they would go out of their way to avoid playing us, even if we had a #1 single. So, worrying about whether they could play it on the radio went out the window. We figured, let's just put this song out, with this great riff that sort of states where we are. It's a hard-edged song, and the content was pretty incredible, the Benjamin Breeg idea. Great lyric, fantastic riff, so we figured we'd put that out as a taster for the album. We weren't looking from a commercial point of view. It was, this was what Iron Maiden was about."

For an album cover, the band went to longtime Maiden fan and comic book artist Tim Bradstreet, famed for *Hellblazer* and *Punisher*. Bradstreet worked in conjunction with Peacock Design UK, who were responsible for the classy, understated inner booklet art (lyrics with individual black-and-white band member portraits by Simon Fowler), and colorist Grant Goleash.

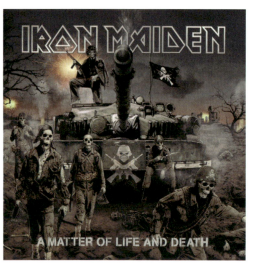

Dave Wright archive

"That particular thing was very striking," comments Janick. "With *Dance of Death*, the basis of the album cover was a very similar thing to a mockup that we had, and we just liked it right away; it had a Kubrickesque feel about it, *Dance of Death*. And this one, a lot of the songs were about war and soldiers, truth and lies, people who'd been to war, what it was like, touching on some of the themes, some of the issues of the day. It was an apt title, and the cover just seemed to go with it. It just seemed to leap out of the page, as it were, and it just felt right."

Eddie is pictured standing atop a Korean War–era tank. In front is a collection of five skeleton soldiers, making it six total, matching the number of members in Iron Maiden. Let's not forget that the original inspiration for Eddie was a shrunken death's head that was perched atop a tank. There's a logo flying a flag of crossed guns and a simple Ed head. This is also painted on the front of the tank and fills the back cover of the CD packaging (originally the plan was a picture of Eddie shot in the back). Bradstreet took his cue from the lyrics on the album, which addressed war with a frequency higher than the band's already high preponderance on all things martial.

As is the case with many Maiden moments, it's hard to tell from the cover whether Eddie is with us or against us, a hero or a villain, the latter suggested by the pirate imagery. As well, what are his powers, and are they temporal or netherworldly? After all, his machine gun and tank are very real, yet his soldiers are a paranormal force. Whatever the case, there's a confidence in his pose, and what is ensured is that wherever he's going, there's gonna be trouble.

The record would hit the shops on August 25 and enter the *Billboard* charts at #9, making it the first Maiden album to enter in the Top 10 on the strength of 56,000 units sold in the first week. "To me, it's got a natural progression to it," explained Gers, setting the scene. "The songs are slightly longer; they're more thematic. When we come to an album, it's a point in time. It's where you're at at that particular moment. I enjoyed *Dance of Death*; it's a great album. You know, I hate it when bands come along and go, 'This is the best thing we've ever done.' Well, what about the last one? And they always go, 'Oh man, this is better than the last one!' They do this all the time. I don't think that way. I was really pleased with *Dance of Death*, and I'm very happy with *A Matter of Life and Death*. Because it's a progression from it. It's pretty much down to a different stage, a different page, down a new avenue. Longer songs, it's a little bit deeper, and there's a lot of subtlety in the framework of the words and the vocal ideas, I think. And I think it's just a really interesting departure for the band, and I'm very proud of it."

The album opens with "Different World," Maiden predictably going with a short, direct, up-tempo number. There's riff, but not when Bruce is singing—there it's a rootsy chord pattern and clacky bass. Noted Adrian, "Actually, it's kind of a riff I had, but I had it in a totally different format and played it to Steve, and he straightened out the time. It was in like 7/4 before, I think. And we straightened it out to a 4/4. I think it was the first thing we worked on."

"Different World" in CD single and DVD single formats. *Dave Wright archive*

Remarked Steve, speaking with Dom Lawson, "It wasn't intentional when we sat down and wrote it, but as soon as it was finished, we thought 'Thin Lizzy!' It's a tribute to them, in a way. Obviously, it sounds like Maiden, but it just conjured up that Thin Lizzy vibe." Hard to figure where or how this manifests, but one might point to Bruce's measured vocal on what masquerades as the song's chorus.

But what stands out most is the vitality of the mix.

"Well, you know, the thing with mixes is, it's like a painting," explains Janick, elaborating on what he said earlier with respect to the novel methodology upon which *A Matter of Life and Death* was built. "Once it's finished, it's purely down to the individual. And that's where I stay well away from it. Because that's like, you throw purple into a pool and the whole pool changes. If you bring the high end up, it affects the guitars. You bring the snare drum up, other things disappear; so you bring them up so the snare drum disappears a bit. And someone might like their guitar slightly louder, someone wants it quieter, someone wants the drums up. You really have to say, 'Hang on a minute; who is going to do this mix? Because who's got the hearing? Is that what we want to hear?' Because everyone has a slight variation; it might just be tiny, but everyone has a slight variation on how they want the songs to sound. Including the producer.

"So again, yes, we do all of the songs live first, and then we go back and overdub the first one, add exactly what we needed on it; we did the solos or whatever. And then Kevin mixed it. So, he was doing it as we were going along. And that actually saved about a month from the album. Because instead of taking them away and bringing them back up again and starting mixes one at a time, he's done, he's finished it. You've got to be a very clever engineer to do that, to understand what the band is about to do that. And that's the kind of producer Kevin is. He's very hands on, very particular about his sound. He's always thinking about how to separate the guitars and make them sound subtly . . . interweave them with each other so that they can enhance the song. And it worked great, and I think the album sounds very fresh and spontaneous.

"You have different kinds of producer," continues Gers. "You have guys like Mutt Lange who are fantastic producers but have a sound of their own, that they bring to the band. Well, we don't need that; we have a sound. We don't want to sound like anybody else. We sound like us, and you have producers like Kevin who try to capture the sound we have and put it in the digital domain. You would think that that is an easy thing to do, but go and ask Martin Birch, who is a very similar kind of producer; it's a very difficult thing. You've got a band in the studio, and to collect the sound on a tape or in the digital domain and have it sound as vibrant and exciting as good as it actually does in the room, that's a very difficult thing to do.

"So, this is where I think Kevin is good, because he can collect our sound and not interfere with it too much, because we are what we are. We're not changing. We don't want the guitars to sound sort of like a 2006 grunge band. That's not what we sound like. We sound like Maiden guitars, good, strong, powerful, aggressive, where you can hear the note in the guitar sound, not a processed sound. It has to be real; all those guitars sound real. You know, that's his forte. He gets a good sound in the studio."

"Different World" got the full video treatment, again, as with "Wildest Dreams," computer-animated under the watchful eye of director Howard Greenhalgh.

Noted animation director Ian Bird, speaking with *Digit* magazine, "The treatment from Howard was extremely detailed—almost a film script—and required a very narrative-led piece which gave us enormous scope to work with. We needed to present a grim and dark vision of the world and create scenes that would hold the viewer as a real action thriller would do."

Added Greenhalgh, "The brief was to create a future world that would—courtesy of Eddie—destroy itself. I referenced stylistic movies such as *Metropolis* and *Soylent Green* but stressed that we had to create a contemporary version of these, not simply emulate them. I hadn't originally intended Bruce to be the star of the video, but the animators thought they could deliver him as the protagonist, and I think it really helps the audience—fans—to engage with the story line, and I'm sure Bruce had a laugh when he saw his awesome agility—although he's one hell of an athlete in real life. The guys at Sanctuary gave us enormous freedom to go with it. This kind of confidence is very rare in these controlling days within our industry. They wanted the next step from 'Wildest Dreams'—the previous promo from Ian and his team—and Bird Studios has pulled off a miracle to deliver so much in so little time. Not just a small step, in my opinion they jumped a whole staircase."

Which sounds very much like what Derek Riggs always had to contend with. In other words, this is rock 'n' roll—everything runs a little chaotic and seat-of-the-pants, even when it's the uncommonly capable Rod Smallwood running the ship.

Next, weirdly, "These Colours Don't Run" is structured very much like "Different World," with relaxed melodic chording at the verses, surrounded by moderate attempts at riffing. Overall, of it across both tracks, Nicko is doing exactly what Nicko does,

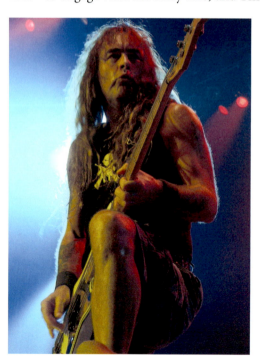

Tweeter Center, Camden, New Jersey, October 7, 2006. © Ray Van Horn Jr.

tumbling into each new bar after a short fill and further signaling through variations in high-hat or ride cymbal work (or both). Bruce's vocals are stunning for the second track in a row, powerful and often high up his range. Midway, there's a key change en route to a new musical section serving as a bed to soloing. There's also a "whoa whoa" crowd participation bit, as the band winds down toward the same quiet bit used as intro music nearly seven minutes ago.

Said Steve on the band's making of video, "I went and got the version together first and worked out all the melodies and everything, and then Bruce came in and wrote the lyrics based around the melodies." Added Adrian, "Again I had that riff—it was going to be like our big ballad—when it starts slow. But then of course it gets fast, as we tend to do. And it went into another anthemic chorus."

Lyrically, this is our first overt war song, with the title referring to the patriotism and courage that any country claims in the heat of battle. "That song was an effort to put a human face on people who go out and fight wars," Bruce told Dom Lawson. "They call it 'peacekeeping,' but these people put themselves in harm's way. And whether or not you agree with the reasons why they're doing it, they're just doing their job. Some of the new songs are quite angry. It's just the times we're living in."

The title of the song, however, came from the Ozzfest incident in San Bernardino from the previous year, in which Sharon Osbourne was said to have tried to sabotage Iron Maiden's set. At one point, during Maiden's most patriotic display live (i.e., "The Trooper"), someone came onstage waving an American flag, to which Bruce replied, "This is a British flag, and these colors don't fucking run."

Reflects Bruce, in the band's making of video, "When I was a kid, it was all about the Cold War and the four-minute warning, and we were all going to get dissolved into some radioactive cinder. There's a few other things now. There's, you know, terrorist fundamentalists and dirty bombs and droughts and global warming and bird flu. I've been in one or two war zones. There's two things; one is, you can't believe the depth of barbarity that people will stoop to. But the other thing is the way people bounce back. It's the way that people survive and live and continue. But we're not like 'new men' and all that kind of stuff—we're blokes. Wars and battles and struggles and things like that strike a chord. It obviously refers to the colors of a flag, and certain things you do are not negotiable. Certain areas of morality are not negotiable. The song itself is done from the point of view of being a soldier. And what it actually means. All these people are heroes. All of them. Whether they wanted to be or not. They did it because their loyalty to their sort of band of brothers, as it were, was nonnegotiable."

"Everything that's going around definitely affects and influences your writing, without a doubt," adds Steve. "I think it's just a reflection of what's going on. It's topical, I suppose. I just think you've got to be open-minded with what's happening. We're not trying to be preaching about one thing, one way or the other. It's just observing; that's what we're doing. Devil on one shoulder, angel on the other. Which route, which part, do the people take? That's always been an interest."

Next is "Brighter Than a Thousand Suns," a massive Maiden achievement, from Bruce's lyric, which charts the invention of the nuclear bomb with much poetry, to the heaving, novel riff and its transition to a melodic yet dark chorus, memorable and sturdy. Suddenly there's mellow, moody music, but it fits too. Adrian, working with Steve, deserves much credit for this one, for the musical structure here is wholly fresh for Maiden—even the punky fast part veers away from clichés, except for it being a late-arriving fast part.

The title comes from comments made by scientists watching the nuclear detonation testing in the deserts of New Mexico. The Robert referenced is of course Dr. Robert Oppenheimer, chief scientist on the so-called Manhattan Project (previously addressed in a Rush song of that name). Again, Bruce's lyric is top shelf, Dickinson mixing the science ($E = mc^2$) with the use of the bomb in war, while also mixing damnation here on the material plane with damnation of a traditionally religious ilk.

"'Brighter Than a Thousand Suns' is about the Manhattan Project," explains Bruce, "which is one of the most banal titles for one of the most terrifying projects ever undertaken in human history. Which is building a destructive weapon that could encompass the destruction of all human life on Earth. The incredible concept that you could play God. The bomb is as close as we've ever gotten to, you know, breaking worlds, to destroying worlds. The scientist that saw the first bomb go off said it was brighter than a thousand suns. The idea that human beings could bring about their own total destruction totally changed the way people thought."

Chuckles Steve, "Bruce's lyric, he wrote specifically to the melody lines. I kind of got me own way a little bit more in this album, I suppose, or whatever. But it's a strong lyric and the melody is still intact. So, I'm pleased."

"I don't know; I couldn't separate them," remarks Janick, asked by the author to contrast Steve with Bruce as lyric writers. "I find Steve writes very simple, and, well, I find them hard hitting. I find he's very honest. And he does it in a very simplistic manner, to get his point across. And Bruce probably goes the other way. It's not as simplistic, his lyrics. And I love both ways. I've worked with Bruce in the past many, many times, and I love his lyrics as well. Steve's very precise in his enunciation, and he knows exactly how he wants the words to be said. You know, you can hear the nuances in the words. You have a certain way to say each word, which will link everything together. He's very, very particular about that."

"The Pilgrim" begins with an awkward and folky intro but then gets quick and dependable very fast, with verse, with prechorus, and with chorus. There are a few Middle Eastern tones, which tend to lean the vibe toward a desert pilgrimage, even as Steve's words deftly keep it universal, albeit very Christian. Still, all told, despite the unproductive intro, this is another resounding Maiden victory, more than anything because of the swelled-chest NWOBHM passion of the verse music but also the attention-keeping effect of varied rhythms throughout. Again, the band can't resist wrapping the song in a neat red bow, reprising the intro music for the conclusion of this tidy enough five-minute rocker.

Tweeter Center, Camden, New Jersey, October 7, 2006. © Ray Van Horn Jr.

The lyric on this one comes from Steve, placed on music by Janick, who explains that "Steve has these ideas and these theories. He makes me shiver sometimes with his lyrics. With 'Pilgrim,' I took a load of ideas in, and I think that music took him along to a sort of Arabic feel in the parts, took him where that came with the music. That content too . . . it's always interesting about Steve. As I've said, I find him really very honest. You'd have to read the lyrics yourself and read into them what you get. I'm very sensitive about explaining what lyrics mean.

"Because there's a lot of poetic license to lyrics. I used to hang out with Ian Gillan, and I used to ask him about lyrics, and I'd get the answer I didn't want, really. I made my own mind up about what the lyrics meant to me, and it didn't mean that to him, but that didn't mean to me that's what it didn't mean. It means what it means to you. The same when John Lennon wrote that stuff about Paul McCartney, slagging him off and whatnot. And years later, Lennon said, 'You know what? It wasn't about Paul. When I look at it and read it, it was about me.' I think that's the thing with lyrics; you can write something, and you think you know what you're writing about, and someone else views it totally different and understands it possibly more than you did when you wrote it. So, I never delve too deeply into that. I get feelings from it, which is more important to me."

Musically, "The Pilgrim" is not showy, yet it has integrity; in other words, it's quietly effective, again, despite being undermined by—almost hidden behind—its incompatible intro music.

Turns out Janick had presented Steve with "a mixture of two parts of two different songs." Says Steve, "I just took the two sort of strongest elements of Jan's ideas and put them together, made the one song. Wrote the words and it turned out to be a dark horse, that one. I wasn't sure to start with how strong it was going to be, but it turned out really good. It's more about actually going to America, on the Mayflower, that kind of vibe. It's not one specific era, but it's kind of based originally on that."

"The Longest Day" begins with a bunch of verses arranged quietly, as a sort of intro, followed by a soaring full-band prechorus with further uplift to the chorus proper, which is performed over a rhythm slower than the pre.

Says Bruce, "'The Longest Day' is about the D-day landings, about how humanity can get through something that awful. You read some of the eyewitness accounts, and it's terrifying. Beyond belief what people did on that day. I wanted to make the words sound like the actions. And it does sound like throbbing engines chugging, you know, through a cold gray sea."

The song is eight minutes long, and just past the halfway point we get a complex musical passage that is entirely new for the song. This grooving passage continues as a bed for gorgeous Thin Lizzy–like twin leads before the guys collapse into another run at the impassioned chorus before, locked to format, the song ends with a refrain of the intro music. All told, the rootsiness of this one—notwithstanding the quick-picked break at the 4:30 mark—speaks to a style that feels like a cross between late 1980s Maiden and Bruce's last two solo albums, *The Chemical Wedding* and *Tyranny of Souls*.

"Out of the Shadows" feels even more so like a Bruce Dickinson solo song, one of his dark ballads integral to one of his themed records. Essentially what we get is the full power ballad band version of "Journeyman," an updated "Prodigal Son" as it were, even more so given the lyric along those lines or indeed the *Seventh Son of a Seventh Son* concept. Bruce has said the song is about being born, when, for a moment, you are "king for a day," and this from previously not even ever existing. This one is a welcome arrival right here in the middle of the album, after a war chest of songs arranged similarly.

With respect to the music, Steve says that the song is mostly Bruce's, although he helped with the melody line for the verse. Nicko admits to having much trouble nailing the drum part, and he actually figured it out through the programming of it on a drum machine.

"We did a lot of takes on the 'Out of the Shadows' thing, but I think the rest were pretty quick," notes Janick. "We tend to not do more than three. If we don't get it on the first one, then we'll have another go. If we don't get it on the second one, we'll have one more go, and then that will be it. But it has to be pretty . . . I mean, more often than not, you go back and the first one was the one. Very rarely will we do a lot of takes. I mean, we rehearse them up in a studio before we go to the studio, so we're ready. We have them down live when we go into the main studio to record. And then we separate the instruments so we can turn everything up and get the sounds you want, because this was the problem before. You're in one big studio, and you turn the guitar up, and you want to bring the snare up, and then you bring the guitar with it.

"You need that separation, which is why we recorded at Sarm in Notting Hill," continues Gers. "You can separate the band, where you can see each other, through the glass. So, you are effectively playing together, and you can see Steve and you can get that groove—you get that thing going where you can feel each other. To me, that's on the album. You can feel that.

"A lot of bands, what they do is they get the rhythm track out, and they put on a drum machine timer, metronome, and they play with the time, and they redo the guitars. You know, I've done that in the past, and you lose something. You lose what Maiden have. You go to see bands, and the record sounds brilliant, and you see them live and the live sound just doesn't have it; 98 percent of the bands now live don't sound like the record. That's fine, but it doesn't sound like the record. It doesn't happen with us because it's us playing live on the record. Do you see what I'm saying?

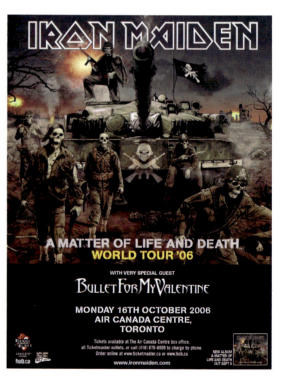

Dave Wright archive

"Whether that's in vogue at the moment . . . you go see a band live, and their record is very heavily, heavily produced. The guitars have that in-your-face guitar sound, but it's not a real guitar sound. It's sort of manufactured. And you go see them live; they don't sound like that. You must've seen that over the years. And there's nothing wrong with that—good luck and God bless them—and that's what they do. But we don't do that. We're looking for guitar sounds that are real, that have an earthy sound, that are authentic, with an old Marshall sound.

"People might say, well, that's an older sound. But you know, I'm not looking for the button you press that sounds like Jimmy Page. I've been in the studio and watched people and they're looking for the Jimmy Page button. Jimmy Page doesn't have a button. He plugs an amp in, and he moves the mics around until he finds a sound he likes. You can get a little processor where you press Jimmy Page or whoever, Jimi Hendrix or Ritchie Blackmore, and press them buttons, and you're supposed to get a sound like them. But we don't do that. We go in and we move the mics around and we look for the sound. It's a very, very different way of doing it. I'm not knocking the other way; it's just our way."

Next comes advance single, "The Reincarnation of Benjamin Breeg," one of the band's finest songs of the 2000s—music by Dave—and a bold choice for single, given its length, resolute pacing, and idiosyncratic titling. Again, as Steve would work with Janick, he took three ideas that Dave had suggested, and worked them into a coherent and cohesive song. This one presents an example of a long intro sequence that works, with an important chunk of the lyrics taking place before the band crashes in with the song's authoritative and leaded riff structure after a good two minutes of quiet. Even though there is essentially no chorus, parts and passages are kept to a minimum, all the better to concentrate on the hypnotic headbang of the song's exquisite root riff, one that frames verses of plain and passionate chord progressions.

The 10-inch vinyl issue of "The Reincarnation of Benjamin Breeg." *Dave Wright archive*

As Steve told Dom Lawson, "It's very different for us. It's very riffy. The intro has an almost nursery rhyme eerincss. Sometimes you try to create a mood. Everyone's going to ask who Benjamin Breeg is, but you'll just have to find out for yourself!

"Five years ago, we were thinking about possibly retiring at this point," continues Steve, pondering with Dom the band's future. "But now we're at this stage and there's no way! Why should we? I don't know why, but I always had it in my head that we'd do fifteen studio albums, so we've got at least one more to go!"

At the lyric end, Steve's written a universal story where one could say that Benjamin Breeg is actually Eddie, reflecting on the life of hardship done to him and then hardship inflicted on others. Immediately we are drawn in by Bruce confiding intimately, "Let me tell you about my life." We're instantly paying attention, as Bruce sits us down for story time, a tale thankfully devoid of showy props, leaving only pathos.

As for who Benjamin Breeg is or was, the band has kept mum, going so far as to throw up a smokescreen in the form of a short-lived website elaborating on his fictional past. The artwork for the single issue shows Eddie digging up an old grave. The gravestone contains a message in Romanian, which translated into English reads "Here lies a man about whom not much is known." The look of the artwork is very King Diamond, as is the tall tale about Breeg's identity as an orphaned child, born in 1939, growing up to become a tombstone engraver who paints mysterious paintings based on his nightmares, and then a writer of occult books.

"For the Greater Good of God," both music and lyrics by Steve, addresses a soldier's relationship with religion, as Steve says, "topical," given Islamic terrorism, which would seem to be on his mind given the reference to "bodies in the sand." But then again, there's reference to the cross, which is enough to conjure memories of all the wars fought in the name of Christianity. This emotional, personal, and lengthy bank of lyrics very much feels like the work of Harris, indeed something that Bruce might struggle with when it comes to the singing (as Dickinson says, "I do sound a bit like Cat Stevens at the beginning, but hey, how ironic is that?"). It tilts Steve's way as well, given the deep religious overtones, with Steve saying that it simply poses the question, saying that he's nether proreligion nor antireligion in his beliefs.

The song also bears many of Steve's trademarks at the music end, given its rich soaking in Maiden melodies, some of them quite Celtic, evoking the memory of the pair of Blaze-era albums. Arguably, the song is a bit long, with lots of rings 'round both the prechorus and the chorus, both passages anthemic to be sure, but pretty familiar as Maiden tropes.

There's a telling exchange on the electronic press kit for the record, in which we get to hear the push and pull that takes place when a strong-willed vocalist like Bruce often has to voice words written by the band's boss bassist.

"People tend to ask that question a lot," begins Steve. "What do you come up with first, this and that? Nine times out of ten with me it's a melody, and I'll fit a lyric to it. We've had this debate many times, whereas you will go in with a lyric, and he doesn't like to stick his lyric to a particular melody. Whereas I work usually the other way around. I think the melody is the most important thing."

"I see the melody as being infinitely changeable to fit the drama that goes with the words," counters Bruce. "Steve and I, I suppose, over the years, we actually more or less sort of agree to disagree, and sort of see each other's point of view on the lyrics versus melodies."

"I usually try to pin him down," reflects Steve. "If I feel I've got a really strong melody, I'll try and pin him down even to the syllables to what he's writing. My argument is that, you know, the first time people hear a melody, they don't know the lyric."

In an allusion to fans around the world who don't have English as their primary language, Steve adds that "they wouldn't know what the lyric was. It's the melody that they go with." Picking up on this, and moving away from the discussion about vocal melody, Bruce makes an interesting point about how he does things. "As far as I'm concerned, I write in English, and if it's difficult for foreigners to understand, that's just tough. Maybe they don't get the nuances and things like that. But then I'm not singing for them. I'm singing for me." In effect what Bruce is saying is that, sure, he's singing for himself, but he's also going to assume fluency in English upon his listeners. Plus, given the man's intellectual curiosity and his high regard for Maiden fans, he also likely sees his high literary presentation as a chance for folks from Brazil and Greece to brush up on their English. In other words, not only is it a fool's game to dumb down his words for greater comprehension, but working at an admirable front edge of high-mindedness is just, well, good for everybody in the long run.

Moving on, "Lord of Light" feels of a set with the preceding track, dripping in Maiden melody, same kind of intro, again the lyric mixing religion with violence, the Lord of Light being Lucifer. "We're trying to be a bit more even-handed about this notion of heaven and hell," laughs Bruce, speaking on the EPK. "Maybe the guy downstairs got a rough deal. Maybe he should go upstairs and ask for his money back."

At the music end, this is Adrian writing like Steve or Janick—namely, toeing the party line, evocative somewhat of his work on "22 Acacia Avenue." As Adrian jokes, the band had refused to do gallops for a couple of albums but that the time was nigh that they gave the fans another, in the spirit of "The Trooper" or "The Evil That Men Do."

Smith's parts on "Lord of Light" are played on his Gibson Les Paul Goldtop, "the first guitar I ever bought," as he told Kevin Shirley, who was filming the sessions. "I bought this guitar when I was about seventeen years old. It cost me £235. I worked on a building site for the summer to buy this, and I'm still using it. Still probably the best guitar here. It's a Les Paul that's been mucked about a bit; it's been cut around. It's probably worth a lot more than I paid for it, but I will never sell it."

Noted Dave on this day of show-and-tell, "This is a Fender Stratocaster, Fender Stratocruiser, that's custom-made by Fender, who very kindly put this together for a couple of quid [laughs]. But I've had it for quite a few years, many years. It's been on a couple of albums and a couple of tours, and it's a good stock working guitar." As for Steve's bass warmed up for the track, white with a West Manchester FC sticker, "It's a very

Tweeter Center, Camden, New Jersey, October 7, 2006.
© Ray Van Horn Jr.

special guitar. It's been used on every Iron Maiden album. It's been about three different colors. It started out as white when I first got it, then it was black, then it was blue, and now it's the best color it could be."

Nicko gets in on the action too, pointing out, "Oh, this is the *Beast* snare drum. This drum I bought at Manny's music, in 1975. It's thirty years old, this snare drum. I brought out my snare drum on this record, out of retirement. And it's sitting right there on this album—and it sounds lovely."

A Matter of Life and Death closes with a progressive epic from Janick. Celtic, pomp rocking, strafed with acoustics and overt keyboards, "The Legacy" even features a part that sounds like a lift from Black Sabbath's "Under the Sun," among the sprinkling of other slightly gratuitous weirdness. But lo and behold, Steve validates all of the pomp and circus pants of the song's many movements by a deeply philosophical lyric, maybe the best of the album, and also a summation of so many of the ideas touched on throughout the songs that precede it on the record. As Janick has explained, he had been aiming to make a song that was more orchestral, with multiple themes taking the place of a rote chorus. For his part, Steve played the role of steward of melodies, sorting some out to be used as guitar melodies and some as vocal melodies, with the opening mellow sequence inspired by something Genesis might do.

This is one for the committed Maiden fan, a member of the loyal legion who wants to surrender to all things Maiden. As a reward for such loyalty, Bruce gives it his all. "The kind of singing that I do is very physical," chuckles Bruce, a happenstance that is so evident on this thespian performance. "It makes a lot of racket and uses a lot of muscles, and I'm a sweat bucket. So, I go out there and come in after a vocal performance, and I'm sort of pretty drenched." Adds Janick, "Bruce has an incredible voice. You know, the things he can sing . . . he never ceases to amaze me. Some of the singing he does in 'Legacy' for instance, really right up there. And he never misses a note. Absolutely stunning voice. Whatever you ask Bruce to do, he goes out and does it."

Recalls Nicko in the making of doc, "It's funny, on the last day when we recorded the Janick song, 'The Legacy,' which is the last track on the record, he said, 'You know, do you realize something? We haven't had an argument, have we?' I went, 'No, it's incredible. All these years.' Every album, even before Janick joined the band, from 1983, we'd have an argument about something. He says, 'Is there something wrong with you, Nick?'"

"Because every album we have a blazing row," adds Steve, "always about the same thing. Because he'll work something out in rehearsal, and then basically, you know, he'll change it. But I can never make out whatever it was, because he couldn't remember it, or just because he's like that and just wants to stick a little bit in there, like drummers do."

What Nicko and Steve are referring to is how the methodology surrounding the making of *A Matter of Life and Death* generated this sort of silver lining. Because they'd knock off a song at a time and then place it on the shelf completed, there was no creative license for Nicko to rejig his parts over the space of days or weeks.

"Yes, this time, because we had it recorded down and that was it, there wasn't that change," continues Harris. "There wasn't those arguments going on, because we would learn it and that's how we rehearsed it and that's what worked. We didn't actually have a row. We were all talking about it, what's happened. We got to the end of the recording, he's going back to sunny Florida, and we're like, well, what happened there, then? And we've been together so long, we have a blinding row and it's all got done and dusted and forgotten by the next day. It always happens, but this time it didn't. So, I don't know."

And then Bruce sticks up for McBrain, saying, "If I was to pick a Man of the Match award, I'd pick Nicko. Although everybody's played spectacularly. I think the drums on the album, the sound of it, the playing, his performance is just outstanding."

Explains Janick on his second composition on the record, "Obviously we all bring a lot of songs in. But I had about an hour's worth of material, and 'The Legacy' was one of them. And it was a song I felt quite strongly about. It came about because somebody was very ill in the political world, who everybody sensed was a man of peace. There was this whole media onslaught of this man of peace, and the Middle East was never going to be the same again, because he was ill or whatever. And I actually read some of the history in the background, and it was completely the opposite. You know, half the problems in the Middle East were created by this person. I won't say who it was. It made me realize that we had been fed a lot of lies, and it made me realize that there's a lot of untruths spoken, that come across as truths. So, when you ask to look into it, and read about it, and read the in-depth stuff about it, you find out the complete and utter opposite. It's completely the opposite. It felt like a bit of a fairy story to me—that's where the idea came from in the beginning.

"And I took that to Steve, and he took it away and took it somewhere else, which is what he does. It's still about truth and lies, it's still about people being lied to, the promises made that never materialized, and it became a song about soldiers coming back from the war—'The Legacy' came from that. So basically, I took that to Steve, and Steve had this great idea and took it elsewhere. Which, in these politically sensitive times, it's probably a great idea.

"There isn't really a theme," continues Janick, addressing the record as a whole. "What kind of happens is, we write about what we feel and what we see. You know, I think we're at an age where we see what's going on in the world, listen to the media, and try to make sense of what's happening. It came out from that. You regurgitate things, because we travel a lot and we've seen a lot. You know, I've been to Israel. I've been to the top of Masada. I've wandered around Jerusalem, and those ideas come out. I like to think we have a little bit of depth about us, and we're not just writing silly songs about death. It's deeper than that. We're kind of like a boy's own band. We deal with issues. If you go out and have a few drinks and a chat with your friends, you'll probably talk about politics, you'll probably talk about football and a little bit about religion and the paranormal—all those things are there. And they are interesting things to talk about. You'll find them in our songs, scattered around. There will be history here and there, all sorts of interesting things, and I think that's one of the good things about Maiden. It can send you off somewhere, and you can discover new things."

As for the acoustic passages in "The Legacy," Janick told me that "pretty much it is 'as is.' The song I brought in was as it is. I don't think anything changed. The acoustics on 'Legacy' I did myself because I knew exactly what I needed to do. So, there was no reason to get Adrian and Dave to sit with me and do it, because I put one down and added a few bits and pieces here and there and built the guitars up a bit. But we did most of the song live. For the beginning piece, me and Steve did it separately. We put those down with a separate feel. So, things like that, I would do that, or Adrian might go back and add a harmony or something, that we didn't do live, that he would pop in. We might put a two-part harmony on, or he might shove a three-part harmony on one of his songs, like a third part. So there are things like that that are done quite often—you just go and pop them on.

"It's more about textures," continues Gers. "I'm not out there to prove that I can be the fastest in the West anymore. I'm looking at textures. There is a lot of playing where one of us will do all of the playing, until we come to do it live, and then we will share the solo. If there are certain harmonies and stuff, I would do it myself, because I know the harmonies. There are a lot of textures there on this album. I think everyone's playing on it is great. It's a spontaneous, live-in-feeling album, and I think it's vibrant. It really feels like this is a band that is happening now. You know, I think a lot of people look back and say this is a band who happened in the 1980s, still making albums. But in Europe and the rest of the world, we're a band that is happening now, right this second. We've got fourteen countries with our album #1 in Europe at the moment, and it's fantastic. We're very proud of this album, I think the playing on it is great, I think the songwriting is great, Bruce's singing is great, and Nicko's drumming is fantastic throughout the album. I really feel like we're happening at this moment. We're a band of now, not a band of yesterday."

Noted Dave on the band's harmony guitars, specifically how the band approaches them live, "When the material is put together and we go over the stuff in the studio, on the album, every note's got to be perfect, and when we play live, we approach it the same way. It's like three-part harmonies now. There are harmonies that weren't on the album, because now we have three players. But basically, you stick to the harmony parts, and you stick to the riffs and the chords, the real structure of the song. And I guess with a solo thing, that's when you can actually mess around. Because you're playing four or five shows a week, there is a little leeway; you don't have to be so structured and play the same solo every night. But as far as harmonies go, they will basically be the same as you hear them on the album."

Prompted to contrast *A Matter of Life and Death* with *Brave New World* and *Dance of Death*, Janick ventures that "well, you make an album, wherever you are at, at that time, you make an album. You have ideas and things you experience and see around that album, and I think all the albums have a different feel to them, with Iron Maiden. People say they all sound the same—I've heard that—but they don't. If you go back and listen to the first album and *Somewhere in Time*, they're totally different, and if you listen to this album and *Seventh Son*, completely different. If you listen to *Brave New World* and *Dance of Death*, they're completely different. We have a certain sound—it sounds like Iron Maiden—but each album to me is very, very different. *Piece of Mind* is nothing like this one, or *Brave New World*, or *Dance of Death*."

"To me, they progress, and they travel different avenues, which is what a band is supposed to do. You're supposed to stretch themes and stretch ideas. You know, hopefully we're one of the few bands where we can write the nine-minute songs. One, we've got the musical skills to incorporate into a song of nine minutes, and two, we can extend a theme and a lyric until we think it's finished. We don't have to do it in three minutes because the record company only wanted a three-minute song, or the radio station would only play a song of three minutes. It's not like that. We write the song until we feel it's finished. We carry on, and when we feel it's finished, we stop."

"People ask us, 'Where do you come up with this stuff?'" says Nicko, summing up the new album in conversation with Ray Van Horn Jr. "It's all about life experiences from what people have gone through since the last record or ten years ago, how their lives have changed and how the world's changed. Is this new record political? No, not really, but it's kind of political science, if you like. Later on you can go back to a song and go and it'll mean something to you. I'm not saying it's religious, but it certainly can change lives and also be reflective, right or wrong.

"If you don't like it, too bad!" chuckles Nicko, on the subject of Maiden's longer and longer songs, it seems, each year. "It's not a very good attitude, I know. If you said, well, let's write a four-minute piece of music and you get to the four minutes and you've haven't reached the freaking chorus yet, what's going to go, then? It's as if you want to write a single for the radio; Iron Maiden can't do that unless it's 'Wrathchild' at two and a half, three minutes, that just happened to be that. It wasn't written as a three-minute piece of music to be a single. What happens is when the music is written, it goes through its natural progression of here's a verse, here's a chorus, here's a bridge, here's a tag. There's no set theory to it. It just happens to be how it is, and if it's a long song, then it's a long song. It is what it is, you know? Why's the sky blue? You can't really say there's a reason for a song being seven minutes or seventeen minutes. It's a piece of art.

"I think it's like an old pair of shoes," adds Nicko, happy to have Bruce Dickinson back in the band now for a third record in a row. "You can wear those shoes forever, and you'll think, 'I'll go out and buy a new pair of shoes,' and you go away, and you do your thing, you strut your stuff, and then later on you put your old shoes on and go, 'Gosh, that's comfy!' You get a comfort zone, and I think what happened was there was a lot of experiences that we all lived with. What I think happens is an emotional thing, personally, and then the musical things after that. The fact is that once Bruce came back, we made a couple of great records, but this one has basically surpassed everything else we've done, I think. It's like putting on that old pair of shoes again, and you've changed your socks and maybe new shoelaces on the boots! When Bruce came back, we all knew this is where we should've been, not to take anything away from Blaze—the four years and two tours and records we had together, they were great times. I love the man. He was a fantastic guy, a different singer than Bruce, different rules that just didn't work out at the end of the day. What possessed the band and made them want to do what they did in the 1980s was back when Bruce came back, that passion and fire, going out and doing the best writing that we could and making the best records."

Nicko's in there somewhere! Tweeter Center, Camden, New Jersey, October 7, 2006. © Ray Van Horn Jr.

A Matter of Life and Death would go gold in seven countries (however, not reaching that plateau in the US), with Finland particularly on board, sending the record platinum at 30,000 copies. The heaviest hitters in terms of volume sold were the UK and Germany, where the album went gold for sales of over 100,000 copies. As further testimony to the band's global reach, the fans in pretty much any country that had a pop chart pushed the album to single digits, including a clutch of #1s.

CHAPTER 20

Wrote the esteemed Adrien Begrand, one of today's most respected metal tastemakers, in his review for *Popmatters*, "At the end of a very contentious 2005 Ozzfest that had the band stealing the show on a nightly basis, the boys in Maiden went head to head with Sharon Osbourne on the last night of the summer tour, the band performing while being pelted with eggs and having their power cut by the woman and her minions. Professionals that they are, they valiantly kept a cool head amidst such childish antics and the publicity that followed, and that same defiant determination has carried over onto their fourteenth studio album, *A Matter of Life and Death*.

"A dark, raw, muscular 70-plus-minute epic, it's their most focused record since 1988's *Seventh Son of a Seventh Son*, one that eschews crowd-pleasing anthems in favor of massive, sprawling compositions that, while unlikely to win many new fans, will certainly please the old ones to no end. It's the sound of a bunch of wily veterans discovering another gear, and on this record, it's full throttle all the way.

"Musically, *A Matter of Life and Death* benefits from its simplicity," continues Begrand, "the band sticking to its strengths, their oft-duplicated formula still managing to sound fresh. 'The Pilgrim' possesses an old-school swagger that hearkens back to the band's early days, Dickinson is in terrific form on the galloping 'Lord of Light,' and the acoustic-tinged ballad 'Out of the Shadows' is reminiscent of both 1981's *Killers* album and Dickinson's much-loved solo tune 'Tears of the Dragon.'

"Most compelling is the enigmatic 'The Reincarnation of Benjamin Breeg,' which, after a two-minute intro that borders on Jethro Tull at its most tedious, launches into one of the biggest, [most-]muscular Maiden riffs in recent memory. Incredibly, the trio of guitarists stick to the riff, Harris keeps his bass low (as opposed to his usual upper-register melodies), and McBrain, who delivers one of his best performances to date on the album, shows great restraint on drums. The loose, jam-like feel of the song is a significant departure from the band's usual tendency to complicate things, and accordingly, it sounds surprisingly fresh.

"Producer Kevin Shirley has brought an air of spontaneity to the last three Iron Maiden albums, and the immediacy is palpable on *A Matter of Life and Death*, the punchy, unmastered mix suiting the live-off-the-floor music perfectly. It's not unlike Killing Joke's recent *Hosannas from the Basements of Hell*, in that neither album attempts to reinvent the wheel, each band content with delivering a product that will make their legions of fans happy; consequently, both records are roaring successes. The six members of Iron Maiden might all be in their fifties, but the second wind they've discovered during these last seven years is something to behold, a testament to the ageless quality of their music and heavy metal in general."

The author saw this artwork in progress at Derek's house in York, Pennsylvania, while writing *Run for Cover: The Art of Derek Riggs*. Tweeter Center, Camden, New Jersey, October 7, 2006. © Ray Van Horn Jr.

"Scream for me, Garden State!" Tweeter Center, Camden, New Jersey, October 7, 2006. © Ray Van Horn Jr.

From October 4 through 21, 2006, Maiden open their A Matter of Touring tour (informally deemed so—these things are fluid, with the tail end called *A Matter of the Beast*) with eleven North American dates, support coming from Bullet for My Valentine. For a stage set, the guys go with a grim World War I motif, with trenches, sandbags, barbed wire, searchlights, and a tank.

The band makes the (mostly) fan-angering decision to perform the new record in its entirety. Defended Bruce, "When you've got an album this good, it's really important that you do something bold. If we can go out and do a whole album of brand-new material, I think that we can give ourselves a pat on the back. Everyone will have heard the album up front, and the songs will really come to life. I think it could be extraordinary. *Brave New World* and *Dance of Death* were both good records. But they weren't anywhere near as good as this one! This one is *Dance of Death* without the effort. This whole album feels effortless. It's like driving a big gas-guzzling motorcar. You just put your foot down and there's limitless power under the bonnet."

Truth be told, despite the element of "being fed what's good for you," all seventy minutes of it, and indeed to kick off the show no less, the hits eventually came. By show's end, the band had essentially overdelivered, pleasing themselves, the fans who wanted the headbanging classics, and indeed those—of which there were many—who had seen so many Maiden shows; this must have been a welcome happenstance, one they knew would not be happening ever again following this tour cycle.

A week into the tour, *A Matter of Life and Death* receives its gold certification in the UK. Then, as a special presentation on-site in Toronto just before the band's Air Canada Centre show (author in attendance), the band receives from EMI honcho Deane Cameron (an industry legend in Canada, deceased from a heart attack on May 16, 2019, at the age of sixty-five) the Canadian (CRIA) triple-platinum certification for *Number of the Beast* plus double-platinum certifications for *Piece of Mind*, *Powerslave*, and *Live after Death*. Canadian gold was awarded for *Brave New World*, *A Matter of Life and Death*, and the *Edward the Great* compilation. Also bestowed upon the boys was an amalgamate award for over two million records sold in Canada since inception of the band.

Backstage after the show were myself and Tim Henderson and possibly another gent or two from our magazine, as well as Sum 41's Deryck Whibley and Keith Sharp from influential Canadian music mag *Music Express*. Also clinking pints was the crew from Banger Films, who would, years later, bring to the world a fine documentary on Iron Maiden called *Flight 666*.

CHAPTER 20

From October 25 through 31, Maiden played five dates in Japan, with Steve's daughter, Lauren Harris, supporting. From November 9 through December 8, the guys took their A Matter of Touring tour to mainland Europe, with support coming from Trivium and, once again, Lauren Harris. No record at this point, Harris would issue, in June 2008, an album called *Calm before the Storm*, produced by Tommy McWilliams (multi-instrumentalist in the band) and Steve, who also plays bass on four tracks and chips in with backing vocals as well.

Remarked Adrian on the band's overseas business, "In Europe we definitely get wider coverage. Some of the festivals we did in Germany, I mean, we play with all sorts of bands. So, we have to go out there and fight for the audience a little bit. Because there are people out there seeing the Cardigans and Los Lobos [laughs]. But by the end of the night, on some occasions, the place is rockin', so we feel good about that. But I guess if you stick it out long enough, you become classic rock, don't you [laughs]? If you stay alive long enough. I think a lot of the metal bands came up the hard way, a lot of roadwork. Certainly, with us it wasn't based around radio, so there's always been a bit more substance to it, I think. Nowadays it seems like it's just a conveyor belt of bands, high turnover; it's just so quick. People do albums in a short space of time, computerized. Bands like us are sort of a rarity, bands that actually play and do it the hard way."

On November 3, Yahoo! reported the surreal news that Rod Smallwood was leaving Sanctuary . . . and taking Maiden with him! It was stated that he would remain as a consultant to the company for a six-month period but manage Maiden under the new umbrella, Phantom Music Management. Explained Rod, "It's obviously a bit of a wrench leaving Sanctuary after all these years, but at this time in my career and with the band's ever-increasing international stature, it makes total sense for me to concentrate on developing the band's huge potential in the many areas of what is now a very complex and time-consuming business."

As the tour moves from mainland Europe to the UK, "Different World" sees issue in a number of formats, highlight being the inclusion of the band's "Hocus Pocus" cover. This is the infamous heavy metal classic with yodeling from Dutch prog band Focus, issued in Europe in 1971 but known to the world through wider distribution in 1973. The guys chicken out on the yodeling, but it is of no mind, since hearing Bruce warble would only distract from Nicko's greatest drum performance ever, across the likes of Streetwalkers or Pat Travers or Trust, let alone Maiden—if only he'd unleash the beast like this on his own material.

Iconic Steve stance, New Jersey, October 7, 2006. © Ray Van Horn Jr.

Custom shirt designs for Norway, 2006, and Dubai, 2007, along with the artwork Derek first painted for the cover of *Run for Cover: The Art of Derek Riggs*, with text by the author. *Dave Wright archive*

Speaking of yodelers (!), the most unruly of ex-Maiden member—namely, Paul Di'Anno—finds himself busy at this time with records out in 2006, albeit of an archival nature. His fine *Nomad* album from 2002 is expanded and reissued as *The Living Dead*. Also from Paul in 2006 is *The Maiden Years: The Classics*.

On the renaming of *Nomad*, Di'Anno told me that "the song itself was such a powerful song. And every time I work with people, they keep saying to me, 'Oh God, you must be almost suicidal' [laughs]. Which is not really true. But it's a good song; in some ways I seem to be the living dead—I'm always constantly on tour and I'm always tired.

"The album is a lot heavier," chuckled Paul. "Which is what we've been trying to get to for quite some time. I just, I write, and whatever I write, I'll try to use. Believe me, there are a lot of songs I just throw away. It seemed like a good idea at the time, but you go back the next day, and it's not that good. I just do what I can. I can't just write stuff that sounds like what I've done before. I'm trying to move on with each album. On this album there are some sort of thinly disguised politics [laughs], struggle and stuff like that. The song 'The Living Dead' speaks for itself. You know, I travel all around the world and see things which I really think, in this day and age, should not even be existing, people hungry, starving, no money. The lyrical content of 'The Living Dead' is basically, you sort of just close your eyes to it and be numb to the rest of the world because there is so much going on, and you sort of hide from it. 'POV 2005' is about point of view, racism, Nazism. 'Mad Man in the Attic' . . . I travel a lot; I go back to Brazil and see so much of what is going on there. It's like, lock me away, I don't want to see it. It's gone crazy, what you see around the world. You just come home and lock yourself away—you want to be the crazy guy [laughs]."

Into the following year, on August 7, 2007, Di'Anno issues *Iron Maiden Days & Evil Nights*. The covers album features five Iron Maiden songs and seven by other bands.

Back in Maiden's world, the schedule is light. March 9 through 17, the guys play four dates in Dubai, Greece, Serbia, and India. June 2 through 24, they close out A Matter of Touring with a second short leg of Europe to address festival season. Strictly speaking, by this time the guys were doing *A Matter of the Beast*, where they celebrated the twenty-fifth anniversary of *The Number of the Beast* by playing about half the record, while also trimming back the number of selections from the current album. Lauren Harris supports through to the end. Also, this year, Adrian Smith signs up to endorse Jackson guitars, which represents his first such deal in fifteen years.

CHAPTER 20

On February 6, 2008, EMI issues Iron Maiden's landmark 1985 live album *Live After Death* on DVD. It had already been issued, pretty much simultaneous to the double-LP release, as a visual back in the 1980s, first on VHS and VHS rival at the time Betamax (by Sony), as well as VHD and Laserdisc. But that was it until now, with the label adding to this new DVD issue an hour-long documentary on the band called *The History of Iron Maiden, Part 2: Live After Death*, plus a "Behind the Iron Curtain" feature and assorted other bits.

Otherwise not that big a deal, the DVD issue was in fact part of a larger campaign that saw the band mount a campaign called the Somewhere Back in Time tour, where the set list comprised 1980s classics only, essentially becoming a celebration of the *Live After Death* album.

Wrote Dom Lawson in our magazine, *Brave Words & Bloody Knuckles*, in a major feature on the occasion, "We've been heading towards this somewhat inevitable destination for some time. When Bruce Dickinson and Adrian Smith returned to the Iron Maiden fold at the dawn of the century, enough excitement was generated to propel the band forward for several years, through the triumphant return of *Brave New World*, the strident consolidation of *Dance of Death*, the chrome-plated nostalgia of *The Early Years* DVD, and subsequent archive-plundering live shows and onto the towering, progressive behemoth of *A Matter of Life and Death* . . . and the remarkably successful, album-dominated tour that followed.

"As unstoppable and irresistible as they've ever been, Iron Maiden find themselves in the unique position of being a band that can revisit their illustrious past while still maintaining their status as a band with plenty of creative juice left in the tank. But throughout the renewed glory of the last few years, we've always been heading inexorably to this point; to the none-more-long-awaited release of *Live After Death* on DVD and the impending thrills and spills of the Somewhere Back in Time tour worldwide jaunt. A timely return to the most celebrated era in Maiden history and a legacy-defining live album and video beloved of innumerable Maiden acolytes around the world—scream for me, metalheads!—this is an exciting time for anyone who has ever heard or watched *Live After Death*. This is an exciting time, period. Even Adrian Smith—always the coolest and least excitable member of Iron Maiden—is happy to admit that there's something special going on right now.

"Not just a visually enhanced rebirth for the *Live After Death* video itself, but a veritable treasure trove of cherishable

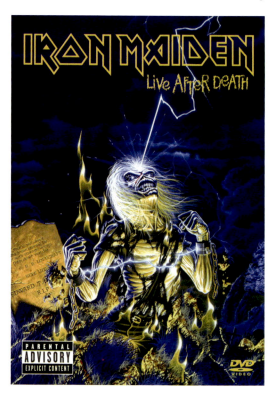

Dave Wright archive

Maiden artifacts—including the fantastic 'Behind the Iron Curtain' documentary and some seldom seen live footage from the band's first Rock in Rio performance—this has been a long time coming and, despite some surprisingly low-key packaging, you would have to have several screws loose to be disappointed by the reality of the thing. Apart from anything else, it's incredible to witness how immense and straightforwardly thrilling *Live After Death* sounds after all these years, whether you're making the walls shake with Kevin Shirley's new 5.1 Surround Sound Mix or simply treating your ears to the seminal original version."

"The original hasn't been touched at all," Adrian told Dom. "We were going to do a remastering and remixing with Kevin, and do the whole treatment on it, and I suppose we could have tarted it up, but really, it's a statement of where we were in the mid-1980s, so in the end we didn't mess around with it. I don't know if people have still got video players, so it's a good thing that it's finally out on DVD. Once you've seen DVD, you don't really want to go back to video, do you? [laughs]. There's all the extra stuff on there too."

From February 1 through 15, Maiden embarked on the first leg of the Somewhere Back in Time tour, playing India, Australia, and Japan, with support by Lauren Harris plus local bands in each market (Lauren Harris indeed supports right through to the tour's conclusion in April the following year).

Wrote Dom Lawson, gleefully anticipating the tour back in early 2008, "As Iron Maiden embark on this year's Somewhere Back on Tour [note: alternate moniker], their popularity is at an all-time high. And what a tour this promises to be. Not just revisiting the phenomenal, eye-mangling glory of the *Powerslave* stage set, with its Egyptian theme

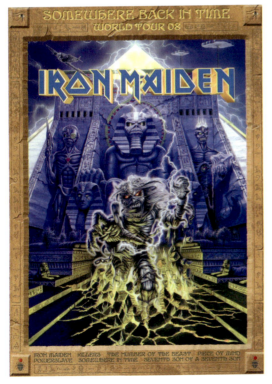

A 2008 Somewhere Back in Time tour shirt along with the tour program. *Dave Wright archive*

and Eddie-as-mummy shtick, but also revisiting numerous songs from what is arguably the band's most important and revered creative period. Earlier albums might have a certain romance about them, but for the discerning metal fan it's *Powerslave*, *Somewhere in Time*, and *Seventh Son of a Seventh Son* that represent the most significant peak in Maiden's evolution as songwriters and musicians. Smith is happy to admit that Maiden will be peeling off many cherished classics on the coming dates."

"The songs pick themselves, don't they?" chuckled Smith, asked about the set by Lawson. "It's basically all the songs from those albums that we've played live. There are no songs that we haven't played live before, so it was just a case of putting them in order. I can't say if there are any surprises. Actually, there are a couple of things that surprised me. We're playing a couple of songs that I didn't think were going to work, but they sounded so fresh and really rocking when we rehearsed them, so that was great to hear. When we rehearsed, we pretty much ran through the songs that we were familiar with, and then we had a go at the ones that we haven't played for a while, and really, we just played them! It was incredible. We basically got them right the first time. There were a few little mistakes here and there, but it all sounded really fresh. It sounded great.

"We've done so much before, with stage sets and everything else," continues Smith. "It's just a case of getting all the bits together. I don't have anything to do with that side of things. I know it has been a massive project for the management, the production side of things, but in the end we're the ones that have to go out there and play the songs! We just concentrate on playing the music. We've got a production team who work on the stage sets. They recruit people as they need to, the set designers and the lighting engineers. We have a blueprint for what we want, on every tour, and we all know what that is, the dimensions and so on. But I do appreciate the contribution everyone else makes to enable us to do it. It's going to look fantastic. It's very dramatic. I don't think there are too many bands that go in for this kind of thing anymore. It's great fun, and Maiden fans come to the gigs expecting to see something. They want a bit of razzmatazz, don't they?"

"Iron Maiden also now have their very own Boeing 757 jet," notes Dom. "A plan conceived by Bruce Dickinson and the band's management team, 'Ed Force One' will be transporting band, crew, and equipment around the world, occasionally piloted by Dickinson himself; now a qualified airline pilot and sometime employee of Astraeus Airlines, who, in turn, have provided the plane and the necessary expertise to get the whole idea, quite literally, off the ground. Touring the world, playing to sell-out crowds, and traveling in your own customized jumbo jet . . . it really doesn't get much better than that, surely?"

"You'll have to ask me in a couple of months," answers Smith, "because it's really an unknown quantity to me. We've had our own little plane for a while in Europe. It sounds very decadent, but it's actually cheaper than renting out loads of hotels. It works out quite nice. But having a dirty great big plane for the crew and the band and everything else? To be honest, I was skeptical to start with. I tend to keep a low profile, and I don't like too much razzmatazz. I don't mind a bit onstage, but I think most of us are a bit more humble than that offstage. We like to keep ourselves to ourselves. We're not Jack Daniels–swigging madmen anymore. There'll be no Jacuzzis on the plane. It's just a practical thing. I don't think we'd be able to play places like Australia without this plane, so that's a plus straightaway."

This of course went off according to plan, with a significant byproduct of the concept being the documentary footage shot of the tour, which would turn into the film *Iron Maiden: Flight 666*.

The Heavy MTL festival, Parc-Drapeau, Montreal, Quebec, Canada, June 21, 2008. © *Patryk Pigeon*

"It's very unique, isn't it?" Smith remarks, concerning the good graces the band find themselves experiencing. "I suppose that if you hang around long enough, things will happen. It's nice now. We can tour when we want. We all have families and lives away from the band, which is great because when we do come together, we really appreciate what we've got. It's a nice balance, and while we've got that it keeps everything very strong and very fresh. There's no reason why we can't carry on for a few more years yet. We don't feel any older. We'll know when to stop when the time's right."

From February 19 through March 12, Maiden kicked off a Latin and South American tour with a date at the Forum in Inglewood, California, before heading into Mexico. Stuck in the middle of that, March 4 marks the release date for horror movie *The Chemical Wedding*, screenplay by Bruce. Bruce also plays two roles in the film, which is based on his album of the same name. As well, on May 12 EMI issues a single-CD compilation called *Somewhere Back in Time: The Best of 1980–1989*. Paul Di'Anno–era tracks are represented in live form, with Bruce Dickinson handling the vocal chores.

From May 14 through June 21, the Somewhere Back in Time tour moves to North America, while on May 17, Maiden take over an issue of influential industry magazine *Billboard*. Even the *Billboard* masthead is recast in the signature Iron Maiden font. Bruce tells the magazine that his favorite Iron Maiden songs of all time, in order, are "Rime of the Ancient Mariner," "Moonchild," "Run to the Hills," "The Number of the Beast," and "Paschendale." From June 27 through August 19, the Somewhere Back in Time tour rolls on, this being an extensive European leg with various festival dates.

The nineteenth edition of the celebrated Wacken Open Air heavy metal festival runs from July 30 to August 2, 2008, with Iron Maiden performing on July 31, representing pretty much the biggest band ever to play the fest. By the close of the gathering, Maiden is already playing in Greece, where Adrian has one of his Jackson guitars stolen.

The Heavy MTL festival, Parc-Drapeau, Montreal, Quebec, Canada, June 21, 2008. © *Patryk Pigeon*

Six months go by before the band picks up their weapons again. From February 10 through 22, 2009, Maiden took the Somewhere Back in Time tour to Serbia, Dubai in the UAE (for the second time, the Desert Rock Festival), India, and New Zealand. February 25 through April 9, the tour visits Latin America for the second time, including the band's most extensive blanketing of South America ever. Again, as alluded to, this is commandeering their own airliner, which allows for the gear to come with the band and crew at the same time—this logistical improvement is instrumental in the guys being able to get to some of these places. On March 15, Maiden play São Paulo, recording the highest attendance figure for a nonfestival Maiden show ever, at 63,000 happy 'Edbangers.

As Janick told Bryan Reesman, "We've had tremendous support in South America for years and years now. Back in the 1990s we did all those big gigs, and even when Bruce left we used to play there a lot. We always try to go there because the kids are so supportive. We want to play to people, and there are people there who want to listen to us, so we'll travel wherever. It's always a thrill to go somewhere different because there may be some people that haven't seen us before, and that's part of the fun of being in a band. It's very exciting for us to travel around. I love going to different places."

"I feel like in America we're spoiled because we get so many tours," continues Gers, "whereas someone in Japan or South America doesn't get to see some of these bands as often as we do, and therefore they are much more passionate in their support for bands. I would assume that Japan has many, many tours. I had been there before Maiden with other bands. They have lots of tours there. South America is more difficult to tour. We took a plane because it's more difficult to carry the gear there. You have to hop around certain areas. With the gear in the plane, we can go to places like Ecuador which we couldn't go to before. It's impossible to get the gear in through customs and get it out again. There's a lot of paperwork involved. You can spend six months setting up a tour like that. The logistics are quite frightening, really. I don't even get involved in it, but we have people working on those tours like a year before. It's quite difficult to tour there, and you have to have a fan base that is definitely going to come, because the promoter has to risk his money putting a band on. If he puts the band on and nobody turns up, he's in big trouble. You have to have a big following to start with. You can't just go there and expect everybody to turn up."

Parc-Drapeau, Montreal, Quebec, Canada, June 21, 2008. This is the last North American show before an extensive European campaign. © *Patryk Pigeon*

The Heavy MTL festival, Parc-Drapeau, Montreal, Quebec, Canada, June 21, 2008.
© *Patryk Pigeon*

Janick gives Reesman an interesting answer when asked if Maiden make more money on merchandising than anything else. "I wouldn't know," reflects Gers. "What we tend to do is cross-collateralize any merchandise. It might take two million quid to set a tour up, so you need that money up front, and I don't think any bank is going to lend you it. If you want to set a tour up, you need two million quid or whatever it costs to get the tour on the road and actually pay for it. When we're out playing, we cross-collateralize stuff. I couldn't tell you the figures—I haven't got a clue. But to set up a tour of the magnitude that we do costs an arm and a leg. We're constantly investing in what we use. We want the best lights. We've got eight trucks on the road. We've got to have the biggest stage possible. We take huge Eddies, and that stuff has to be carried from country to country. Either we use the plane, which has to be paid for, or we use eight, nine, or ten trucks. It all goes into making the band work."

The global heavy metal pageant that was the Somewhere Back in Time tour was captured sumptuously and professionally by Sam Dunn and Scot McFadyen and the rest of the crew at Banger Films, who, in conjunction with the band, issue a documentary called *Flight 666*, which celebrates the Somewhere Back in Time world tour, on which the band, crew, and equipment all travel on one airliner, part of the time piloted by Bruce Dickinson. As mentioned, the band calls the converted Boeing 757-200 Ed Force One.

"It was a little bit of a difficult decision," Nicko told Camille Dodero of the *Village Voice*, with respect to consenting to the movie. "There were two or three of us in the band—myself included—that had a bit of trepidation about it because we have always been private people. When we're on stage, that's our domain. But we've never been a band who searched out paparazzi and would want to go to nightclubs where we'd know we could get our picture in *OK* magazine or *People* magazine. We've always shied away from that kind of limelight. And having a camera crew 24/7 in your face for seven, eight weeks was not our idea of being private. So, it was discussed, and there were mumblings and grumblings and moans and groans all over the place. And finally, we kind of relented and thought, 'It is such a historical event. And it is something we've never done before. And it should be something that could make a great piece of film.' So, we all kind of agreed.

"I have to be honest though," continues Nicko. "There were times over those seven or eight weeks when the film crew boys were out with us on the airplane that they got into trouble, verbally, with none more so than my good self. I actually threatened to throw them off the plane while it was in the air one time [laughs]. But what happened when we all sat back and watched the roughs of this film just before Christmas, I was gobsmacked. And I thought, 'My Lord, these two guys, Scotty McFadyen and Sammy Dunn, they did such a great job.' And those moments when you thought, 'I don't want to do this. I don't want these guys here. I don't want them in the dressing room,' yadda yah, the moans and groans, were all worthwhile, because it all came out so well. And they are so much a part of our family now. I think the proof is in the finished product."

Asked by Camille about a highlight moment in the movie for him, Nicko says, "There's a shot of a guy holding my drumstick, and he just starts crying. That shot . . . it's funny, because when I first saw it, I says, 'Is he kind of crying because he got my drumstick? Or is he crying because he didn't get Dave's pick and he only got my drumstick?' [laughs]. Or is he crying because he's a Nicko McBrain fan? Oh no! He's crying because the show is finished, and this guy's just had such an immense time.

"It pulled a string in my heart and I'm going, 'Look at the passion in these people.' I don't get to see that from the stage. I don't even think the band realized that this is going on after we've left the stage. But that kid, the crying man . . . I did actually get to meet him, this year when we went back. But that memory really struck home with me: the true power of the music of Iron Maiden, what it means to an immense amount of people around the world. And that really does humble me."

Flight 666 played theatrically, but there was also a hardback DVD version (issued May 22 in the UK and June 9 in North America), which adds a seventeen-track bonus DVD, described as "the whole live set with a track filmed in each of 16 different cities." There was also an attendant two-CD album version containing the same songs as the bonus DVD (i.e., every song coming from the 1980s version of the band with Bruce, save for "Iron Maiden" from the debut, which featured Paul Di'Anno, and "Fear of the Dark" from the 1990s).

The DVD version of *Flight 666* was a rousing success, selling platinum in the US pretty much instantly for sales of over 100,000 units. As well, perhaps partially given that the movie was a product of a pronounced Canadian success story in music documentary filmmaking, Banger Films, *Flight 666* went five times platinum in Canada, for sales of over 50,000 copies, with the album version also doing well in that territory, certifying as gold. Australia, perhaps in part due to the band kicking off the tour there with fully six shows (after a lone inaugural date in India), also stepped up to the counter, sending the movie platinum for sales of over 15,000 copies. In celebration of what was a flash two-year victory lap for the band, Adrian goes fishing, on August 25 making the cover of *Angler's Mail* magazine.

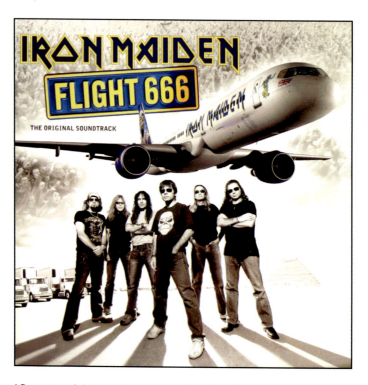

LP version of the soundtrack to the film. *Dave Wright archive*

Live shots on this page and next two are from the Tweeter Center show in New Jersey. © *Ray Van Horn Jr.*; memorabilia on page 497, *Martin Popoff archive*

CHAPTER 21
The Final Frontier and *En Vivo!*

"Cigars were still smoking in the ashtray."

In October 2009, Iron Maiden conducted writing sessions for what would be their fifteenth album, with Janick revealing to the BBC on November 2 that they'd essentially done what they could do in advance of the recording sessions to take place early into the new year.

The guys set for themselves the usual challenge, creating an environment in which they were to work fast to generate the material. As Steve remarked in the electronic press materials for the album, "Personally I always feel a lot of pressure. I can't quite work out whether I need to have that pressure to psych yourself up into a frenzy to come up with the goods, or whether it's just the way it is. I'm not really quite sure. There's this little black cloud that sits there for three or four weeks. And then when the album is ready to go out and rehearse, the songs are all arranged and written; then the cloud tends to go away."

"It was a little bit intense, actually," added Bruce. "Because we turned up in Paris and we had two weeks, basically, to put the record together. Which wasn't enough time. But we got through about seven songs, seven and a bit, that we could sort of play through start to finish. There was number eight, which Steve was working on, which we didn't get to hear until the studio, which was 'When the Wild Wind Blows,' which is like eleven minutes' worth. There was what turned out to be called 'The Alchemist' that didn't have a title at the time. Because all I had was a demo. I was gonna go and write some words to it, en route, as it were, so that was another one. And then we had 'The Man Who Would Be King,' which we were working on. We were gonna try and get through the very last day of rehearsals, and then Janick cut his hand on a door, really badly, gashed all his finger and stuff. So we went, 'Oh well, let's go home then.'"

Bruce underscored this method further in conversation with *The Aquarian*. "We don't allow ourselves too long, because if you allow yourself six months to write, you'll take six months. So, we tend to put ourselves under a bit of pressure. And it is a bit of pressure; I certainly feel it anyway. A little black cloud goes away when you know you've got enough songs and you've got good material. It just makes you feel a bit anxious because you know you've got to come up with good stuff. But that's always been a good thing, a positive. It's almost like going through a weird stage when you're doing it, because you do feel sort of an anxiety. I, in particular, I can't really sleep properly when I'm writing. Too many ideas flying about all over the place, so I don't really sleep very well. But once the writing's done, you feel this massive pressure cloud go away. Once we've got enough songs, we stop. We've always done that, because there's no point in really working on stuff that you can't record. We don't really give ourselves enough time to do that, and we don't want to do that. We just want to record an album and go on tour with it."

"We walked in there, and Adrian had quite a few ideas," continues Dave, on the Paris sessions. "I had some ideas. So, it was a process, once we were in the studio, like where do we start? And Steve has always been at the helm, and kind of steering the ship in a way. We just locked into . . . was 'Avalon' the first track we worked on? Which was one of the more complex songs on the album. So that took us a little while to get going, really, because of the different changes and just creating the atmosphere, the vibe that Adrian had on the demo—we kind of wanted to re-create that.

"So, it was kind of a slow kickoff. But once we got moving, we came out of Paris, three weeks later, with probably about 60 to 70 percent of the album basically there. Not 100 percent. But enough to go into the studio in the Bahamas and have something of substance to start recording. And after that it was basically up to Nicko to absorb that and capture the feel, which he's done majestically with the drumming. Because there's a lot of stuff going on here. So, once he got that down, that was it. But basically, the foundation was made in Paris."

As Steve told Jon Wiederhorn, "We wrote the album in Paris when it was pissing down rain and cold, so we didn't even want to go outside, and we focused on what we were doing. And then we recorded in the Bahamas, which we hadn't done since 1986. So that was good as well. We all felt good. We toured for a while for the last record, and we did the film as well, so the time passed quickly. We took some time off to spend with our families, and before we knew it, it was time to make another record. And the fact that we were all in the same room as well kept the vibe strong. Kevin Shirley put all the equipment in the other room to keep it separate, and we had a fantastic headphone system rigged up. For the first time—and it made a big difference—we could all be in the same room; that meant we could all communicate better, which was fun. It was pretty well live. It worked really good because we could see each other when we were playing. We'd definitely record like that again. There were no scratch tracks or anything. We did the songs live and then we added bits on top as well. For some songs we did a few more takes than others, but then we did some tracks in just one or two takes, which helped keep things sounding really fresh. Some of the songs are very proggy, especially the ones toward the end of the album. It's weird because you talk about one song, and it doesn't really represent what's on the rest of the album. It's so diverse, which I think is good. It's one of the things that makes the album enjoyable for me."

"I would say my first and foremost goal was to finish the record without keeling over dead!" chuckled Nicko, in conversation with Joe Bosso. "In all seriousness though, we rehearsed seven tracks in Paris before we went to record them. Three of the other ones we had the sketches for, but we had to work them up once we got in the studio. For me, the big expectation was working on the three songs that we didn't rehearse; I wanted to get their vibe as quickly as I could and really nail them without taking a whole lot of time. In terms of figuring out the progressions on the album, it was very much like it was in the old days. It was us together in one room going, 'Okay, how are we going to get from this bit to that bit?' It was natural, a band working as one. We were all looking at one another and communicating and feeling at home, if you like."

After Paris came Compass Point Studios in Nassau, the Bahamas, this being the studio that birthed *Back in Black* as well as *Powerslave*. "Frankly, it was weird," mused Bruce, on the EPK. "The studio was like Mary Celeste, you know? Cigars were still smoking in the ashtray. Unfinished beers from 1983 still there. The carpet was the same. They still hadn't fixed a little piece of shuttering that was missing out of the slat in the window. I mean, it was bizarre. It was identical to 1983."

"And then I walked into the studio itself," seconds Nicko, "and [sings a song] a Dr. Who scenario. It was the TARDIS, the Time Machine, all the same pictures on the wall, all the same smoke stains on the ceiling. They had the very same pool tablecloth that they had twenty-five years ago. It was a great experience, because it was literally going back in time for me."

Remarks Dave, "I loved stepping back into there. It's good, because there'd been so much change in all our lives and all these many years, it was nice to step back into something twenty-five-odd years ago and actually see that this remained perfectly, you know, as it was back then. So, there was a real comfort zone there. And the room just has a huge magic about it. But it was great to go somewhere familiar. Because we've recorded albums all over the world, so it takes a little while to settle in. This was immediate; we felt at home straightaway."

Getting into the mechanics of assembling the record, Janick says, "I really enjoyed it, because what we did is we got the amps . . . well, the speakers, we put elsewhere. We had headphones, a big headphone setup—we used helicopter headphones, which were tremendous. So, it felt like we were playing live. But because of the overspills, normally you can't have that feeling. But because the gear was so far away, it didn't matter. We'd all get in the same studio together. I think that makes a huge difference to the sound, because if you're playing together and you're looking at each other and you're feeling each other, the spontaneity that you have between each other works within the music and it comes out different. When we're in with Nick, you can feel his presence and his power, and that added to the songs. And we can see Bruce in the little box in the same room; he kept popping his head out and talking."

"Actually, I never had the joys of a vocal booth in the studio before," remarks Bruce. "Which is this funny little thing that looks like a cross between a Swiss mountain chalet and a phone booth. But it wasn't a very comfortable place to sing in, frankly. They had the three guitarists all sat down in chairs, but their equipment was, you know, a couple hundred feet away, buried in offices and things like that all around the building."

"The equipment there isn't very good, but the actual room is great," Adrian told Richard Bienstock. "The thing is, it's important for us to be able to see one another while

A couple of gear ads from 2009. *Dave Wright archive*

we're recording, and a lot of newer studios aren't set up for that, because today everything is tracked separately. But at Compass it was possible for us all to stand in the same room and play and then have the amps off in a different room. And it turned out great. Steve likes that real raw sound. And he and Kevin, they don't like people going back and tidying things up. They say, 'Let's just record a lot of stuff and then we'll put a track together.' I think if I'd had complete freedom, I'd have probably made things more polished sounding. But those two kind of keep you at arm's length. So, it's a little like making a movie: you do your performance and you're out of there."

"We're more wise to the ways of recording," Steve explained to Wiederhorn. "I'm a lot more knowledgeable and confident when we're in the studio now. I know more what I want and how to get it now as opposed to then. We're just more experienced. If we don't know what we're doing by now, we never will. I love the technology that's around today. I think it's amazing what you can do these days. And it's amazing you can fit so much information on a small hard drive and carry it about. All those years ago we obviously had to worry about taking all those big reels of tape. It was a nightmare, really. And if you wanted to cut something, you had to splice it by hand with a razor. It was pretty scary."

Bourbon Street, Baltimore, Maryland, December 23, 2010. © Dave Wright

The Final Frontier turned out to be one of the last records to be recorded at Compass, with the band hard at work (and play) from January 11 through March 1. An official statement from the studio's website reads: "Compass Point Studios™ ceased operations in Nassau as of the end of September 2010 because of a series of incidents . . . socio-political-based happenings which made it untenable to continue doing public business in The Bahamas. Those involved in the historical operation of Compass Point will continue their work within the music business, just as always before . . . simply not in The Bahamas."

Other reports spoke of an uptick in crime and unrest. Now there's a café there, with much of the control-room recording equipment (plus sound baffles and even tympani!) still on-site, locked behind heavy wood doors swollen shut by the heat and humidity.

In other news, in the months leading up to the release of the new album, on April 1 Paul Di'Anno issues *The Early Iron Maiden Songbook*. Meanwhile, in March, Maiden go through some additional vocal work and mixing for *The Final Frontier* in Malibu, California. On March 4, the office announces some upcoming tour dates for North America and Europe. A couple of months, hence, on May 16, 2010, Maiden lose their dear friend Ronnie James Dio to cancer. Maiden was scheduled to play some dates with the re-formed Black Sabbath, renamed Heaven & Hell, but now that was an opportunity sadly not to be. Finally, on May 28, after eight years on the air, the BBC's *Bruce Dickinson's Friday Rock Show* airs its final episode.

With respect to the mastering of the album, Bruce was asked by Patrick Slevin of *The Aquarian* if what we had here was a similar situation to that of *A Matter of Life and*

Death, which Dickinson said "was mastered, but it was pretty flat. It's the same with this one too. It's just that these days, I think mastering, dare I say it, is kind of . . . I'm not saying you don't need it, because sometimes you do to get the levels the same and stuff like that. When you work in a digital format and you've got your mixes sounding just how you want, then you don't really need a great deal of tweaking. Well, we don't. Some artists might, but we don't. And that's what we've found more and more lately, really, that we don't need any tweaking at all. When things are tweaked, they affect everything across the board, and it tends to mess with the mixes.

"I'm not going to say in the future that we're not going to master, but the last couple of albums have been fairly flat. Because they're dynamic enough anyway in the mixes, so we don't really want anything messing with it. We did try different things, different frequencies, and this and that. But it didn't sound better, really. Sounded different, but it wasn't better [laughs]. Also, the live sound of Iron Maiden is really what you want to capture in the studio. You spend a long time capturing all that and getting it just how you want it, and if someone else comes and puts a frequency across it and it affects the whole mix . . . sometimes it sounds good, and you let people try these things, because you want to be open-minded about it. But if it doesn't make it sound better, then what's the point?"

Dave Wright archive

On June 8, the band issues the track "El Dorado" as a free download advance single from the forthcoming studio album. The song eventually garners the band their first Grammy Award, in the Best Metal Performance category of 2011. Also on this day, the band announces the full track listing of the album and reveals the record's cover art. June 9 through July 20, Maiden conduct the first leg of their world tour in support of *The Final Frontier*, in North America, with Dream Theater supporting at all shows except for Winnipeg.

Tim Henderson talked to Rod Smallwood in March about the outsized attention that Maiden had always paid to Canada, this jaunt being no exception, with the band spending two weeks in the Great White North from late June into July. "Maiden has always enjoyed going to new places," mused Rod. "It's exciting and keeps you fresh. I recall very vividly the *Powerslave* tour when we were still on tour buses. We rehearsed and played in Halifax, Nova Scotia, and played eleven cities, including Sudbury and Regina, all in hockey stadiums, right across Canada in one go. We kidnapped a journalist—how are you, Mitch?—and he ended up in Sudbury thinking he was just going to our hotel bar in Toronto! I particularly remember waking up and looking out of the window at dawn as we climbed the Rockies. Wow! On the tour before, we played in Chicoutimi. I remember the T-shirts they had made for us: First Chicoutimi, Then the World! Great times. And they were right."

As for where in Canada the flame for Maiden burns brightest, "It would have to be Quebec City," picks Rod, "close run by Montreal. Sorry, guys, but these are such amazing, passionate, *loud* audiences. Not that the rest aren't great, but Quebec province is right up there with Mexico City and South America. It's also where we headlined our first big shows in North America. We were playing to six thousand fans a night there, when we were still supporting in America! We never ever supported anyone ever in eastern Canada; we started in clubs, then small halls, then big halls, and then very big halls. It really was a remarkably smooth transition thanks to the loyalty of our fans and the word of mouth they created on Maiden. And the Beavers are from Montreal—yes, you know who you are.

The Bell Centre, Montreal, Quebec, Canada, July 7, 2010. © *Patryk Pigeon*

"The scenery is magnificent, of course," continues Rod. "I have visited Whistler, BC, a few times with my wife, Kathy, and our kids. Even if snow now seems to be a bit of a problem nowadays! But any country is really made by its people, and Canadians generally I think have a similar outlook to us and of course generally like a few beers too. We are very comfortable anywhere in Canada. Food-wise in the early days, we couldn't wait to get to Canada for the HP Sauce, a vital ingredient of any tour, which at the time you could not get in America. Very important to add to Baked Beans a La Murray! All my direct family live there: my parents live on Vancouver Island and sister, niece, and nephew in Edmonton, so I get out to both a bit more often than the other guys. So, I guess I am a bit Canadian, which meant I was very pleased when Canada won hockey gold a few days ago. I used to go and see Gretzky and the Oilers at Northlands in the mid-1980s, when my sister moved there, and I still follow them. You may remember an event shirt from that time with Eddie in Oilers colors with the number 999 on his back."

To reiterate, these North American shows are all happening before the album is in the shops—only "El Dorado" from the record is part of the set list—but soon it was time for another teaser. On July 13, EMI releases what would be the only video from *The Final Frontier*, for the opening track, "Satellite 15 . . . The Final Frontier." Warned Bruce, speaking with *The Aquarian*, "There are some unusual things going on on the album. I think the opening song . . . I won't say it's going to shock people, but it's quite different. We'll see. You can get ten people in a pub discussing Iron Maiden songs, and they'll have ten different ideas about this and that anyway. It's a very interesting album, quite diverse, and there's a lot going on. It's a long album, hour and a quarter. I think it's a pretty rich darn album; it's pretty different. But we don't really analyze it until we start speaking to journalists, to be honest."

Then it's on to Europe for more dates, July 30 through August 21 constituting a second leg of the current campaign, including the 21st Wacken Open Air festival, August 4 to 7, featuring Alice Cooper, Iron Maiden, Mötley Crüe, and Slayer as the most-high-profile acts. But by the last night of Wacken, Maiden are already at Sonisphere in Stockholm, Sweden, along with Wacken compatriots Alice, Mötley, and Slayer, plus Iggy & the Stooges and HammerFall.

"We did the Sonisphere gig in Stockholm, and it was torrential rain all day," Janick told Bryan Reesman. "The minute we went on, it stopped, and the sun came out. Then we finished and it thundered and lightninged again. It was unbelievable. Our crew were just drenched all day. When we landed in Finland the next day, there was a plane on its side on the runway. Our tour manager said, 'Hey, I ordered a crew plane just like that!' Then we went, 'Really?' Bruce asked, 'How many seats do you have?' The tour manager went, 'Thirty. That's a thirty-seater right there.' What had happened is a tornado or something similar came through, and it just literally ripped half the trees out and turned the crew's plane over. Luckily the crew weren't on it.

"We went up to the stadium, where there were two huge stages. Mötley Crüe and Alice Cooper were playing there as well, and Mötley Crüe's stage literally got bent in half. It was unbelievable; the scaffolding was just snapped in half. It all happened in ten minutes. Our gear was completely kaput. The tarpaulin above the stage cracked, and the water came down on the mixing desk. It was bedlam. Iggy Pop went on to do an acoustic set for a couple of numbers. Alice Cooper went on about an hour and a half late, and then I think we went on about two hours late. We got the job done. There were a lot of kids there, and canceling would not have been the thing to do. We went out with half the PA and half the lights and very little monitors on stage because the mixing desk was kaput. We did a great gig and had good fun."

The Bell Centre, Montreal, Quebec, Canada, July 7, 2010. © Patryk Pigeon

CHAPTER 21

The Bell Centre, Montreal, Quebec, Canada, July 7, 2010. © *Patryk Pigeon*

From August 13 through 18, 2010, Iron Maiden issued their fifteenth studio album, *The Final Frontier*, staggering the release worldwide over five days. Eddie grins out of the cover art almost unrecognizably, and then to boot, what exactly he is up to is a mystery as well. The meticulously crafted illustration is by longtime Maiden artist Melvyn Grant, with the overall design stewarded by the Peacock team.

"The Eddie on this one has been sort of percolating for a while," explained Bruce, in the EPK. "Because in actual fact, I thought up the title of the album on the last tour. I said, 'You know, we should call the album *The Final Frontier*. It has a kind of ring to it about . . . you know.' And Steve's like, 'Yeah, kinda cool.' And I said, 'We could sort of revisit space, but not like *Somewhere in Time*.' So then when we came out, we had the song 'The Final Frontier' that Steve had written, and Adrian, and we were still going somewhere with the idea of Eddie.

"So, we started out with, okay, Eddie as kind of alien, as a starting point. Now we don't want an H. R. Giger version of Eddie, but we also wanted a kind of sci-fi component to it. And we wanted a kind of Marvel comic look to it, you know, a *Forbidden Planet*–type moment. Because I think that gives it a kind of timeless quality, as opposed to just a gross-out slasher sci-fi thing with blood and everything else. It gives it a bit more class if you make it a bit more cartoony and make it your own.

"So, we then got into sketches and there were lots of sketches going forward and back, being emailed to us all, with myself and Steve making comments. I remember typing—I couldn't believe it—'Yeah, I think the left eye needs to be a bit more drippy, and I think we need more destruction on the brain' and things like that. 'The fangs are a bit too extended. You need to retract the fangs a bit. He should look like he's feeling this.' And I'm thinking, What are you saying? Just, what is in your head?"

As for the title itself, Bruce told *Kerrang!*, "People will think it's a Trekkie-type thing, won't they? We knew when we picked it that it would wind a few people up. I actually came up with the title before we'd written any songs. There are songs about war and the state of the economy. It's about that feeling of uncertainty." But the main talk of the time revolved around Steve's curious comment about how fifteen studio albums sounded like a nice, neat number in terms of knocking it on its head, hence *The Final Frontier* serving as the band's final album.

"The space theme is there for the artwork," cautions Steve, "but lyrically there are all sorts of different things going on. Each song tells an individual short story, really, as always with our stuff apart from *Seventh Son of a Seventh Son*, which was a concept album. All our other albums have been short stories."

Asked by Jon Wiederhorn about the title and any intended ties to *Star Trek*'s famed line, "Space, the final frontier," Steve figures, "I wouldn't say I was a massive fan, but I've always liked *Star Trek*. I don't think any of us are Trekkies as such, but we all like the show. Personally, I'm more into something like *Lord of the Rings*, but I also like *Star Wars* and other sci-fi as well, anything that's exciting and takes you on a bit of a journey. Bruce had the title before we even started the album. And when it worked on the first song, I felt, 'Well, this totally ties in.' It gave us a bit of a direction. I suppose he was being a bit tongue in cheek, but we all thought that was sort of funny."

LP version of *The Final Frontier*. Dave Wright archive

The CD booklet offers additional visual gems. The first page features a straight-on Eddie shot that itself would have been worthy of taking the front cover. Then there's an illustration of a sort of mine stamped El Dorado. There's a series of nine pencil sketches of additional Eddie concepts, again, each highly creative and ghoulish, each potentially a cover art idea in the making, and all by Melvyn Grant, who created the front cover. On the last page, there's a silhouetted John McMurtrie band shot done somewhat in the style of the *Brave New World* pictures. On the back of the CD tray, there's a simplified, monochromatic Eddie logo that recalls the basic military Eddie from *A Matter of Life and Death*.

The record opens with one of the most bizarre and extended intros of the band's long career of often-awkward intros. This one is so oddball that it gets a name, one that is suitably messy, with the leadoff track getting the title "Satellite 15 . . . The Final Frontier" and weighing in at 8:40, even if the eventual song is rock 'n' rollsy and definitely not the sort of thing that should run that long.

"That's just something I recorded in my studio," explained Adrian, to Richard Bienstock of *Guitar World*. "I did it rather quickly. I thought it was an interesting, kinda futuristic-sounding thing. Steve picked it out and started getting all these ideas, like a 'lost in space' kind of vibe, and he said, 'Yeah, we should use that.' I thought when we got to the studio, we'd rerecord it. But he just lifted it straight off my computer, really. I did it in about five minutes with a cheap little drum machine [laughs]. But after the shock of the first thing, the next four or so tracks are pretty straightforward. And then it gets a bit more complicated, to say the least."

"The beginning part was mainly Adrian's idea," affirmed Steve, speaking with Jon Wiederhorn. "And to me, it really had the feel of film theme music. It's very dramatic, very sci-fi, and we just went from there, really. We put it together and went into the second part of the song. It felt really good. I was really excited about it when that was together. And Adrian was kind of surprised with what I did with it, because he didn't anticipate it being like that. But I was very excited because it basically gave us everything. It gave us an intro, it set the tone for the album, and it gave us imagery as well to work with."

The song was issued as a single without the intro, at 4:05, plus as a video, slightly longer, at 5:08. "Once we had the second part of the song," says Steve, "we knew that would be a good . . . well, not really a single, because we don't have singles anymore, but we knew that it would make a good promo. So, we got some ideas together, and we were really pleased with it. The company Darkside Films that did it were really, really good. I knew them anyway. They did the interface for *Visions of the Beast*. That was really good, but since then they've come along and done so much other really interesting stuff. I just thought they would be a really good choice, and I knew what they were capable of. And the main guy there, Andy Bishop, I knew him personally as well, so it made it an easy choice."

Amusingly, "The Final Frontier" is an opener in the spirit of "The Wicker Man," "Wildest Dreams," and "Different World" that is earthy, straightforward, not that fast or flashy. It's a different ethic here in the 2000s from the "Aces High" and "Tailgunner" ploy, one used by so many metal bands (i.e., over the top) from the top. Despite the tuneful and groovy roots rock chord pattern, lyrically the song is downright horrific, as an astronaut contemplates his last moments stranded in space without contact, ruing the fact that he won't be able to say goodbye to his family but somewhat consoled in that he's lived ten lifetimes and would do it all again the same way if he had the chance.

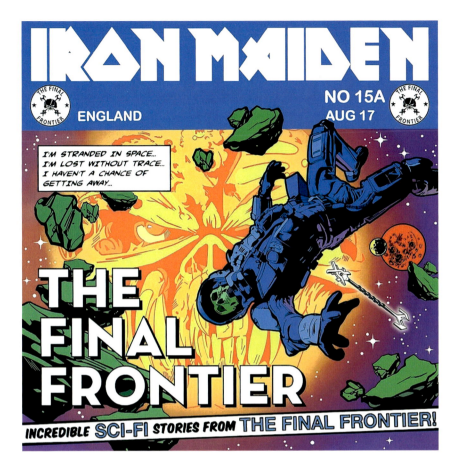

Dave Wright archive

The guitar solo portion of the show is demonstrative of the contrast between Adrian and Dave, with Smith taking the first burbly and note-dense solo, and Dave the lyrical and fluid second part. Then it's back into more turns of the simple chorus as soloing continues behind Bruce.

Almost Monty Pythonesque, "Satellite 15 . . . The Final Frontier" ends with a big bashing windup—which we immediately hear again as the opening salvo of "El Dorado" and then . . . "El Dorado" ends with a third round of this exact same thing. But back to the beginning, as this twice-clanged pile of noise fades, we hear Nicko on hi-hat accompanied by a "Barracuda"-like gallop from the guitars. Then we're into a sterling single choice every bit as good as "Benjamin Breeg," "El Dorado" being a heavy and low-slung rocker evocative of "The Evil That Men Do" or "Flight of Icarus" in its gravitas. It's a Maiden gallop, to be sure, but the band and producer Shirley conspire to make it uncommonly thick sounding for Maiden.

"It's about greed and drawing people in, basically," says Bruce of the lyric, speaking with Patrick Slevin. "Imploring them to sort of do whatever and giving them the once-over afterwards. It's about that, loosely. A lot of people that have heard the album—press and people who have heard it—think that there's some sort of concept or something, but there isn't really. There are only two or three songs around that sort of subject. It's actually quite a diverse album. There's not really one song—'El Dorado' or any other song. You can use any song as a lead, a taste. That's what we do; we put out a taste, but it doesn't really represent the rest of the album at all. There's not really any other song that's like that on the album."

"El Dorado" is credited to Adrian, Steve, and Bruce. In fact, Steve is credited on every track of the album, and this for the fourth time, following *Killers*, *Brave New World*, and *A Matter of Life and Death*. As Adrian has hinted, this is now not so much because Harris is bringing in songs on his own more frequently, but, rather, reflecting his deep-tissue massage or songs brought in by others, often in the mysterious realms of vocal melodies and arranging, the latter of which with Maiden doesn't mean instrumental textures as much as it might with other bands, but rather the sequencing and frequency of parts.

Noted Bruce on writing credits, "It's not about keeping people happy; it's just about getting really good songs and whatever combination of writers does that. We don't write twenty songs and use ten; if we've got enough, we stop. There are always lots of bits and pieces flying around, but basically we just use whatever we think is strong at the time. There's no fixed plan of who's writing with who or anything like that. It just worked out this time as well as the last album that I wrote more stuff with Adrian, purely because we were the first ones to get together, really, and it just sort of stemmed from there. It doesn't always work like that, and it probably won't necessarily work like that in the future."

Further on the message of the song, a response to the economic crash of 2008 and 2009, Bruce told *Kerrang!* that it's "a cynical lyric about the economic crap that's been happening. It seemed a bit like a perfect storm; people were borrowing money like crazy. I thought, 'This is really going to screw people up,' and sure enough, we're all in deep doo-doo! And that's what 'El Dorado' is about; it's about selling somebody the myth that 'the streets are paved with gold' and them asking, 'Where do I sign up?'"

The title itself refers to the Spanish legend of the "Lost City of Gold," presumably located in the Andes. The song was issued as a free mp3 download but then came out as a physical CD single, fronted with excellent '50s-styled EC Comics–influenced art by Anthony Dry. Fourth time's a charm: "El Dorado" won the 2011 Grammy for Best Metal Performance after two previous nominations, for "Fear of the Dark (live)" in 1994 and "The Wicker Man" in 2001. Betraying his bad taste in music (!), Steve thought this was the least deserving of the band's three nominations—"El Dorado" is clearly the best track of the four (in this writer's opinion, of course!).

Roll into "Mother of Mercy," and again the student of production is hit with the impression that the heft of "El Dorado" was no fluke—again, this song trundles like a Sherman tank, with "Flight of Icarus" once more coming to mind. Indeed, as the record builds, it becomes clear than Kevin Shirley has turned in the warmest, fattest, richest production job the band pretty much has ever been blessed with. This comes from the treatment of the guitars, to be sure, but most pertinently the bass, with Steve's hard surface sound put aside for something more conventional. Lyrically, this one is a brutal indictment of war and a God that would allow such physical and psychological carnage. A soldier in the dark awaits his doom while contemplating his life and what's left of it, very much like the astronaut from "The Final Frontier."

Strength to strength, "Coming Home" deepens the emotional well as a sort of follow-up to "Blood Brothers" and "Wasted Years," songs that connect with the crowd through a combination of hook and lyric sentiment. Here Bruce speaks of returning

Limited-edition CD. *Dave Wright archive*

home through flight. He doesn't say he's flying the plane, but we implicitly think that, especially with the memory of *Flight 666* so fresh in mind. Through the images conjured by the words "Albion's land" and "thunderbird" and a dozen other lofty phrasings, Dickinson pushes the song universally, philosophically, and timelessly, even though we very clearly get a song that is about air travel. What is also whip-smart about the lyric is that it can be read as the musings of a space traveler, with recurrent reflections similar to those of actual astronauts about how with such dramatic distance, one realizes how insignificant "borders that divide earthbound tribes" really are.

Noted Adrian, responding to the description of the song by Richard Bienstock as "outside the box for Iron Maiden as well, almost a full-on ballad," "We had a song on the last album called 'Out of the Shadows,' which was kind of a similar thing, and Bruce was great on it. He actually does those kinds of ballads really well. So, this time I had an idea for something like that, and I could just hear him singing it."

In this writer's opinion, "Coming Home" is the greatest near ballad Maiden has ever crafted. It's stuffed with memorable melodies, somewhat indicative of Bruce's solo stuff at its best. Heck, even the intro is mournfully beautiful, and uncommonly synergistic with what comes very soon, and that is the first gorgeous verse. Despite being nearly six minutes long, there aren't a lot of parts, the band having the good sense to know that they had a clutch of magic moments here, and that revisitations to them would be welcome and not in the least bit fatiguing.

Next comes a fast-paced rocker, and the shortest song on the album. "The Alchemist" has Bruce recounting a tale he knows well, that of the world's most famous alchemist, John Dee, and his right-hand man, Edward Kelley, perhaps the world's second-most-famed alchemist. At the concrete end of the narrative, there's the wife swapping, the burning of Dee's library, the peering into the black mirror. But Bruce also spends much time on the mystical, closing the story with a vow by Dr. Dee to return and reinvigorate intellectual thought to the benefits of alchemy.

"It's just a rock 'n' roll tune," Janick told Bryan Reesman. "I brought in about an hour's worth of material, as everybody else does. They all bring loads of stuff in. That was a rock 'n' roller I brought in because I thought there might be a few long songs on it, so I thought I'd bring a short, more straight-ahead power rocker in. I had a few different things, probably a lot more progressive things in there, but that was just one that was on the side that everybody seemed to get off on. Steve found a melody for it, Bruce wrote some lyrics, and it just seemed to work. I obviously end up with lots of songs and ideas sitting about, but the most important thing is that it all fits together and has a theme running through it. It works well musically, and sometimes something that's really good doesn't make this album, but it's put on the back burner for perhaps something else. You never know."

Next is "Isle of Avalon," a lengthy tale concerning the legendary locale of Arthurian legend dating from medieval times. Of Welsh origin, the isle is often surmised as Glastonbury tor, and there are similar legends in Irish lore. King Arthur's Excalibur sword was said to have been forged there, and it is also considered his final resting place. The word "Avalon" is associated with fruit trees, and in Irish lore moving more toward apples. In Steve's lyric, fruit is used more in the abstract, and he refers much more often to corn and in fact ritual around the corn harvest as well as Mother Earth and fertility

The Bell Centre, Montreal, Quebec, Canada, July 7, 2010. © *Patryk Pigeon*

rites. Annwyn is also mentioned, this name referring to the Welsh "otherworld," and all told, there's a sense of famine and war to the dramatic telling at the hand of Steve.

At the music end, this is one that fans were less happy with. At nine minutes, too much of the track is singing over intro-styled music, with the up-tempo portion featuring somewhat pedestrian chording and attendant unremarkable vocal melodies—it's all a bit too barroom rock 'n' roll for a tale of this levity. More creatively out on a limb is the proggy middle core—Rush comes to mind, a rare thing with Maiden—but then it's back to refrains of the other bits.

Explained Adrian, penner of the track, on the EPK, "Steve is coproducer as well, so you've got two guys in the driving seat, and they're very different about how they do things. It's always difficult. I really enjoyed the writing process. The recording is always a bit painful; it can be. But I really enjoy sitting in a room playing—it's great. But, you know, having demoed a lot of the things, it's two sides of when you demo songs. You get a bit close to them and you get used to hearing them a certain way, and you want to follow it through. And there's one thing I wanted to do on the album, is I really wanted to pursue the way I thought they should be. And I did that as much as I could.

"But at the end of the day, you know, I didn't produce it. So, there's always that; it can get a bit tense in the studio. With six, seven guys, you've been in there a few hours, and you've been flogging away at a song. You've got to be tactful sometimes. Some people are more tactful than others. It's all part of the chemistry. And if you don't have, you know, disagreements, it wouldn't be a breathing band, but that's what it is. So, there's a bit of give and take. But all I can do and say is, you know, you just give it everything you can. And the way we record these days is, it's a bit like making a movie. You do your takes, you do your best, and then it's up to the guys who are really mixing the album.

"I've got a sensitive ear or something, for tuning as well," continued Smith, further expressing a vague sense of dissatisfaction with the process. "I get like, I can hear stuff that's out of tune, and no one can hear it but me. I don't know, but I'm really . . . tuning is one of my things. And with three guitars, the intonation of the guitars, even if you're playing the same riff, the same notes, sometimes they don't blend. And I really wanted, on this album, to try and make sure that they blended as well as they could. It's easy to say, oh yeah, it sounds all right, but you've got to stick your neck out a little bit somewhat, even if it gets chopped off."

"Starblind" is another long one among many on the second half of the track sequence, but it's a corker, due to the dual purpose of the music and the lyric. First, at the lyric end, this is Bruce at his action-packed and philosophical best, assaulting the listener with every dynamic that death might bring, from the nihilistic and atheistic to the cosmic, and then, most intriguingly, sort of religion based, but malevolently so. The music is simple but steeped in Maiden melodic tradition, providing a sturdy, dependable frame for Bruce to rapidly deliver a dizzying array of images, all of them about the ultimate transition. There are also keyboard washes, this helping smooth over a halting rhythm section, and then it's back to the verses, which almost swing.

Remarked Janick on the record's next track, "The Talisman," speaking with Metal Pirate Radio, "It was just an idea that we put together; it had a very kind of like sea shanty beginning, like an old chap sitting on a seawall telling a story. And it's got a really good vibe to it. It's about somebody trying to get somewhere and not quite making it, somebody who sees a vision but doesn't quite get there."

More specifically, Steve's story charts a phalanx of refugee immigrant boats (by the tenfold, meaning, ostensibly, at least ten!) heading west, with a number of them lashed by storms and lost, and some of the survivors arriving half starved, dying of thirst and of scurvy. All throughout, it's a talisman that keeps them alive. In typical celebrated Maiden fashion, the lyric feels like it could refer to any desperate migration but is rendered specifically timeless so one can view it in light of more-recent tragic news stories, notably boats crossing the Mediterranean from the Middle East and North Africa to Europe. At the music end, what we get is a spirited Maiden gallop, up tempo, regal, passionate of chorus. The song clocks in at nine minutes, but essentially it's a classic Maiden barnstormer preceded by nearly three minutes of intro. The harsh reality is that—take a poll—to a man, most every Maiden fan would have said just forget the mellow bit and give us the rest of this classic *Piece of Mind*–like rocker.

Added Janick, speaking with Bryan Reesman, "The beginning of 'The Talisman' has a folkie Celtic approach to it. There are a lot of Celtic melodies. One track off of *Virtual XI*, 'The Clansman,' is also a very Celtic song. We did that with Bruce on one of the tours. 'Dance of Death' has a similar kind of feel to it. There are a lot of those kind of Celtic folk elements. Steve's quite heavily influenced by Jethro Tull and Ian Anderson, and people like that, as I am too. I grew up with that stuff, and the rest of the band did too, so there's an element of that in our music. I grew up listening to a band called Lindisfarne, who have a very folkie element, and I used to love their stuff. They were quite a big band in the early 1970s in England. Some of it was really edgy stuff. Bruce and I were brought up on that stuff. That's all in there."

Next is another lengthy number, but structured like many of them so as not to sound too onerous or overstay its welcome. Again, fronted by a long intro, "The Man Who Would Be King" then gets down to rocking, Dave turning in a working man's music track onto which subtle but storied Maiden vocal melodies are placed. A gorgeous suite of instrumental passages blesses the song from deep within, and then we're out with a short full-band mellow section. Once more, the construction is unassailable *except* for the mechanism of the intro, which is too long, goes onto a big pile across the catalog, and is too similar to many other mellow Maiden buildups. Steve's lyric is inscrutable but seems to tell the story of a man of stature self-exiling into the desert, for multiple transgressions, including murder. There's a vague biblical feel, which is the case with so many of both Steve's and Bruce's timeless, epic lyrics. I'm sure one day we'll see seminary school master's and PhD theses on the theology of Iron Maiden, but I am unaware of any of these papers in existence right now (nor does that sound like a fun read).

The Final Frontier closes with "When the Wild Wind Blows," which loosely follows the plot of the famed and bleak 1986 animated feature *When the Wind Blows*. An elderly couple stoically prepares for the fallout of nuclear war with the then Soviet Union. However, at the end of Steve's story, the couple commits suicide to avoid the worst of it, not knowing that what has happened has been an earthquake and not the dropping of an atomic bomb.

Explained Steve, in conversation with Jon Wiederhorn, "Writing is always the hardest part. Recording is sort of academic, to a certain degree. We approached 'When the Wild Wind Blows' in a slightly different way. Basically, I wanted to try something where the guys didn't know much of what they were playing much before we did it. We just learned parts and then did them, and we saw where it went to a certain degree, or how many

Dave stretches the art of heavy metal guitar. The Bell Centre, Montreal, Quebec, Canada, July 7, 2010. © *Patryk Pigeon*

parts we did. Nobody knew which order they were coming in, and nobody except me knew where I wanted to take it. So, I just thought it was good to play with a bit of spontaneity like that. We got some really interesting takes for that. I said to the lads, 'I hope you don't mind indulging me with this, because I want to try something different.' And they were like, 'Mm, okay, that sounds ominous, but sure.' And we did it and it worked out really well, so everyone was pleased."

Musically, this one can be a little weak in parts, relying on Celtic tropes and rhythms and tempos from the Blaze era. It's certainly one of the "trips" on the record, with its meandering twin leads spinning a cocoon around the listener. To be sure, the relentless melancholy of the melodies matches the horrible story, so there's a connect, but all told, Maiden have been to this place many times, and the discerning listener is all too aware of that fact.

"That was one of the songs we did in the studio," explained Nicko at the time. "When Steve brought the song in, he showed it to us, gave the guitarists the chord progressions and everything. I could tell right off it was something special. Because of the kind of song it is, though, I looked at 'arry and said, 'What do you want from the drums, busy or straight?' And he said, 'Let's have it straight. We need some real groove on this track.' That's all he needed to say. I told him, 'Let me have what you're playing on the bass,' and we worked that part out. Then we went for the second part, then we had the segue breakdown, and it went from there. When we finished recording the song, I turned to Steve and said, 'Next to "Hallowed Be Thy Name," I think this is the best song you've ever written.' And he went, 'Nahhh!' And I said, 'To me it is.' That's how I feel—I think it's just immense. The funny thing is, there wasn't a lot of preparation for that song or any of the other ones, really. It was just learn it, feel it, and play it. That's what we did on this record. It was true to its form, without a lot of contrived pieces. And there's even a couple of mistakes on it, to boot, which I think is great."

Commented Dave to *Billboard*, "The rhythm's a little bit different from what we've done before, and there's lots of melodies. It's a big song. We learned it in sections just because it was such a complex arrangement, but it sounds quite natural."

And after nearly seventy-seven minutes, essentially the limit of a single compact disc, Iron Maiden's fifteenth studio album came to a shudder of a close.

"With *The Final Frontier*, it wasn't as if we regressed," mused Nicko, summing up, speaking with *Music Radar*. "We took a lot of our history and revisited it in certain ways. Take our album *A Matter of Life and Death*, for example: that's a very adventurous record that uses elements from late 1960s and early 1970s underground progressive rock. So now we've kind of stepped back into that territory and carried it further, way beyond anything we've ever done before. It's filled with epic songs, but it doesn't just go on and on for the sake of it. There's ideas and real heart on it. We felt everything we were playing. That's what makes a band a real band and a record a real record—the amount of feeling you put into what you do."

We're all guilty—band and fan alike—of being a little off base when we throw around the word "progressive" to describe Iron Maiden at eight minutes. In the majority of cases, what is really happening is some mixture of long intros, extra verses, an extant instrumental passage or two, a long guitar solo section and then another, and a more than average number of rounds of chorus. In a word, what we really mean is unedited. I rankle at using that word, however, because it implies that paring these songs down would make them unarguably better, or subtly different, that better versions of the songs would be shorter. Maybe sometimes, maybe not, and maybe personally I have my scissors out for certain things (i.e., the intros) and not others (pretty much everything else). But of course, there is no right answer.

"Notwithstanding the fact that it's got all these little proggy-type influences and it's gone a little folky vocally, I think it's a much-harder-edged record," said Bruce, on the EPK. "It's more direct is the word I would use. I think *A Matter of Life and Death* . . . I mean, it's a great record, but this sounds simpler. The songs seem to connect more directly. Certainly the vocals, there's really no or minimal double tracking, and I think there are hardly any backing vocals on there at all. So, in the main it's a single voice on virtually all the tracks. Given that, I think Kevin did a fantastic job on recording the voice; he did a great job of capturing it. A song like 'Talisman,' for example, where it's one voice for the whole thing, and there's this bloody racket going on underneath it, it's really cool that he's managed to capture it and have it sit there in the track, so it sits on top of everything. The mix is good—[I] like the mix. What's to say, really? It sounds like us."

Pondering whether it indeed was "the final frontier," Bruce ventured, "We don't know. I mean, we genuinely don't know. And that's why we liked calling it *The Final Frontier*. Because we knew that people would ask that question. And we knew we couldn't give them a straight answer. In fact, the straighter answer is we don't know. And it's not that there is an intention to not do another album. But it's two and a half, three years away. I don't know. Will this be the last tour? Well, we're going to be touring next year anyway. But we'll see how we feel. You just live, live for every gig, every tour, this album. You don't try and project to the next ten years. Screw it. Just think as far as next week, and that'll all be good. You can try and plan and predict and things like that, but the universe will still throw curveballs, volcanoes will erupt, airplanes will stop. Whilst you can hope for the best, you may as well just stay in the here and now and be nice to people. It's the best you can do."

Speaking of "best you can do," *The Final Frontier* did rather well in the marketplace, at least in terms of Iron Maiden's unique business model in this new era when the idea of physical product has become antiquated. The short-lived era of downloading music files was by this point passing by and showing in the rearview mirror, and the sensible way to get music was now streaming. Nonetheless, Maiden sold a half-million copies of *The Final Frontier* around the world, led by platinum sales for over 100,000 copies both in the UK and Germany. France, Canada, and Italy all sent the record gold for sales of over 50,000, 40,000, and 30,000 copies, respectively, while the record did brisk business in the rest of Europe as well. Chart numbers mean less, but the album hit #1 in a couple of dozen countries and, most significantly, #4 in the US, which is the band's highest placement ever.

For a review of the album at our website BraveWords.com, boss of us "Metal" Tim Henderson turned to eminent Maiden watcher Dom Lawson, who wrote, "It is, of course, the more overtly progressive and extravagant end of Maiden's recent output that has bred the most dissent from hardcore fans who, despite all the nostalgia tours and chances to hear those hallowed old songs, will not be satisfied until Martin Birch is brought out of retirement and Eddie heads back to 'Acacia Avenue.' But this album is not intended to placate anyone but the men who created it, and with songs like 'Isle of Avalon' and 'Where the Wild Wind Blows,' Maiden are proudly proclaiming the bloody-minded determination that has enabled them to survive with dignity intact after so many years of active service.

"'Isle of Avalon' is plainly Adrian Smith's baby, with its chiming, left-of-centre chords and tantalizing, slow build-up, but it's also a sublime demonstration of Dickinson's ageless vocal skills, as its colossal chorus erupts amid lengthy passages of elegant but forceful progressive metal that seem almost to mock the notion that Maiden have ever been stuck in a rut. Similarly, 'When the Wild Wind Blows,' a Steve Harris composition from the opening seconds to a beautifully pitched denouement, contains enough familiar traits during its deceptively smart 11-minute duration to provide a link with the past while still pushing Maiden forward into atmospheric and harmonic territory that is as new to the band as it will be to the fans.

"With comparable acts of bravery being played out during the trippy surges of 'Starblind,' the bold pirates' tale of 'The Talisman,' and the gorgeous tangential shifts and dynamic flashes of 'The Man Who Would Be King,' this is a long way from sounding like a closing chapter in a grand saga. Instead, for all the rumours at the time of this being the last Maiden album and other such speculative balderdash, *The Final Frontier* sounds like a stepping-stone to a few more years of business as usual, yet more creative endeavours to come. Maiden gigs would remain a celebration of the past and present, but fittingly for an album adorned with such galaxy-bound imagery, this is a thrilling and deeply satisfying glimpse into a brave new future for the people's metal band."

And if I may add anything to that beautifully expressed treatise, *The Final Frontier* reinforces the fact that if the band isn't particularly changing its spots at the musical end, Steve and Bruce continue to grow at a vigorous pace as lyricists, to the point where a few records into the 2000s now, we can safely say that Maiden have been criminally underrated in this department—the silver lining of these "unedited" songs is that such languished soundtracks allow for lots of vivid Maiden poetry, reams and reams of verse, prechorus, and chorus bits that deliberately and deftly straddle the line between the specific and abstract. And often the guys offer a bit of both, with an anchoring in the specific, usually through the dropping of a couple of proper names, serving as metaphor for the fans to ponder the universality of the story being told.

Back to some rapid-fire Maiden timelining at this juncture, August 17, 2010, Adrian provides lead vocals on "Reach Out" on *Guitars, Beers & Tears*, a solo album by Bad Company's Dave "Bucket" Colwell. On September 16, Bruce is hired on by the now-defunct Astraeus airline as marketing director. Into the new year, February 11 through April 17, 2011, the third leg of Maiden's tour for *The Final Frontier* is primarily an Asian and South American one and is (somewhat informally) called the *Around the World in 66 Days* tour. Meanwhile, while one Maiden singer is up onstage in front of thousands, on March 11 Paul Di'Anno is sent to jail for welfare fraud, serving two months of a nine-month sentence. On May 6, Ian Gillan, and Tony Iommi issued their "Who Cares" charity single. Drummer of choice is Nicko. The next month, Bruce is featured in a UK Civil Aviation Authority video explaining aircraft-loading safety—in May 2012 he will start an airline maintenance business based in Wales called Cardiff Aviation Ltd. Then, on the nineteenth, Queen Mary College presents Dickinson with an honorary music doctorate.

From May 28 through August 6, 2011, the fourth and final leg of Maiden's tour in support of *The Final Frontier* is an intensive European one. There's some product issued in conjunction: on June 6, EMI issues a two-CD compilation called *From Fear to Eternity: The Best of 1990–2010*, which reaches #86 on *Billboard*. Blaze Bayley–era tracks are represented in live form, with Bruce Dickinson handling the vocal chores. Speaking of Bruce, on September 25 metalcore band Rise to Remain issue their debut album, *City of Vultures*. The band's lead singer is Bruce Dickinson's firstborn son, Austin. On December 10, Bruce shares the stage with Jethro Tull's Ian Anderson and Justin Hayward from the Moody Blues at Canterbury Rocks, helping to raise funds for the renovation of the local cathedral. Meanwhile, back at the drum stool, October 31 through November 18, 2011, Nicko goes on a drum clinic tour of sorts, sponsored by drum company Premier. Called "An Evening with Nicko," the tour encompasses seven dates each in Germany and the UK.

The biggest news, however, comes on March 23 of the following year, when Maiden issue a live album and DVD called *En Vivo!* Writes Aaron Small, for our website BraveWords.com, "Digitally filmed just over a year ago on April 10, 2011, *En Vivo!* is Iron Maiden at their finest. Feeding off of 50,000 ecstatic fans in Santiago, Chile, during the *Final Frontier* world tour, the band delivers a magnificent 17-song set, captured by an astonishing 22 HD cameras and a flying octocam that provides aerial scenes. Both full-screen and split-screen shots are utilized to allow for maximum exposure, resulting in the viewer being glued to the screen. Fifty-three-year-old front man Bruce Dickinson runs and jumps across the massive stage with the agility of a man half his age, all while belting out an impeccable vocal performance. And to the sheer delight of the diehard crowd inside Estadio Nacional, not one but two Eddies appear during the two-hour set. And that's only disc one."

The *En Vivo!* album will forever be distinguished in the catalog as the live record that celebrates *The Final Frontier*. Among a smattering of old hits, the 2000s is represented by "Dance of Death," "The Wicker Man," and "Blood Brothers," plus fully six tracks from the most recent record, totaling forty minutes.

On May 11, 2012, *En Vivo!* receives its gold and platinum certification on the same day. Noted Nicko at the time, on the band's continuing enthusiasm for all things Maiden, "Steve and I lock into what we do. Having three guitar players gives us a fuller sound, and they're all fantastic players. Sometimes I think they're almost too polite when it comes to splitting up the solos. We have a great time. After all these years, there are no egos in this band. Our competition is in-house. When we go in to make a record, we don't talk about the last record and what we're going to do the same or what we're going to do differently. Our favorite album is the one we're working on now."

A 2010 concert T-shirt, along with two from 2011, with the Japanese shirt representing a gig that got canceled. *Dave Wright archive*

CHAPTER 21

On the heels of *The Number of the Beast* being named in an HMV survey as the public's favorite British album issued during Queen Elizabeth's sixty years on the throne thus far, from June 21 through August 18, 2012, Maiden embarked on the Maiden England tour, covering the US and Canada. Support comes from Alice Cooper. Mused Steve at the time, speaking with John Doran, "I don't know about ten years, but I think we've certainly got another five years in us, but it's hard to say. As you get older it gets doubly hard to keep yourself fit and in shape. We do work really hard on doing that. It's important to us. We'd be selling ourselves and everyone else short if we didn't, so we do look after ourselves. It does get tougher. I don't play football much anymore, but I play a lot of tennis."

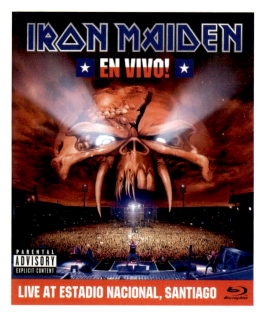

The Blu-ray version of the live album.
Dave Wright archive

"Conquer more shores?" questioned Rod. "I don't know. I think we've pretty well conquered what we expected to and wanted to. We certainly don't intend to start trying to get radio. It'd be a real shame to get radio now, wouldn't it? Embarrassing. We'll make a record that can't get on air, can't get on

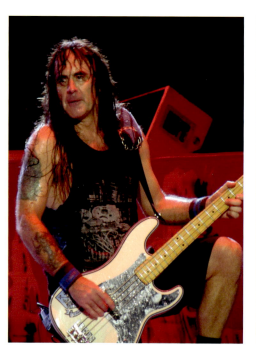

Molson Amphitheater, Toronto, Ontario, July 13, 2012. © Bill Baran

radio, for sure. We don't really give a fuck about radio, to be honest. You can quote me on that. It's not in our terms of reference, really. We're never played, and it's never supported us. We wouldn't let people present our shows in the past that didn't play us. Who cares? It doesn't matter. You know, we've done fifty million albums, and we've probably kept, of any band, a closer relation with the fans, probably than there's ever been in some respects worldwide. The kids have got an immense amount of affection and respect for Maiden. Why should we care about radio? It comes and it goes and changes its mind every three minutes. Sort of inappropriate, really [laughs]."

"Inside this 53-year-old exterior is a 17-year-old," mused Bruce, speaking with the BBC's *HARDtalk*. "That's the core of why you do this thing. When you're a kid and you experience something that makes you feel, 'Wow, walking on air.' The first song you write, the first experiences, you have to ring-fence those and guard them against the cynicism of the world, because the world eats into people and destroys those hopes and dreams. And it's those things that people call childish. Those are the things, actually, that motivate us and that keep our creativity precious; that's what's inside people, and they lose it at their peril."

Continuing on with our Maiden calendar (of note, this was a band that actually printed calendars regularly!), on January 9, 2012, Blaze Bayley, after years with his well-regarded Blaze configuration, re-forms Wolfsbane, the band that he was in before landing the Maiden gig, issuing a new album called *Wolfsbane Save the World*. On February 2, the man Blaze replaced and then replaced Blaze—namely, Bruce—at the invitation of

Molson Amphitheater, Toronto, Ontario, July 13, 2012. © *Bill Baran*

the captain, spends three nights on a British nuclear submarine. On August 28, 2012, video game *Rock Band Blitz* is issued, which includes a playable version of "The Wicker Man." On October 10, Bruce gives a motivational speech (and sings!) as one of the keynote speakers at an IBM conference in Stockholm. Five days later, EMI kicks off a chronological vinyl picture disc reissue campaign, the first releases being *Iron Maiden* and *Killers*. Into 2013, on March 25 EMI reissues in expanded form 1989's *Maiden England* as *Maiden England '88*. The set was originally available as a VHS but is now issued in CD, DVD, and two-LP vinyl formats. Shortly thereafter, on April 9, Maiden start brewing their very own Trooper premium beer.

However, not all is a cause for celebration. On April 8, British prime minister, and Maiden nemesis, Margaret "Iron Lady" Thatcher dies at the age of eighty-seven. Previous to this, on March 12, beloved Maiden drummer Clive Burr, longtime sufferer from multiple sclerosis, dies peacefully in his sleep at the age of fifty-six.

"Clive and I used to share a room together," recalls Adrian Smith. "He was a great guy. He was a very funny guy. He was . . . let's say, he embraced the rock 'n' roll lifestyle maybe a little too much. And that's why he ended up leaving the band. Because he was a great drummer and a great guy, but it just got a bit much for him. So, we had to make a change. So that was very sad. And I know Bruce has said subsequently—and I think he said it at the time—'I wish we had more time, taken some time off, so he could've sorted himself out.' We just didn't have the time. Because we would finish one tour and go straight into another one. That's just the way you had to do it then—tour, tour, tour. And the same thing happened with Paul Di'Anno. It's tough. And it nearly happened to me. It can get on top of you. Young guy, you're out there and you've got to perform every night. And mentally it can be quite tough, because you have a lot of downtime as well, sitting around and thinking about stuff in your hotel room. And of course, you end up drinking too much and that spirals—this is what happens. It's a funny old life, you know? It doesn't suit everybody."

Molson Amphitheater, Toronto, Ontario, July 13, 2012. © *Trevor Shaikin*

Molson Amphitheater, Toronto, Ontario, July 13, 2012. © *Trevor Shaikin*

Clockwise from above: Paul and band, Rio de Janeiro, April 18, 2013. © Daniel Croce; Paul in 2001. © Dave Wright; Dave and Adrian, Toronto, 2012. © Trevor Shaikin; another shot of Paul in Brazil. © Daniel Croce; and finally, ticket stub. Dave Wright archive

Toronto show, 2012. From the top, shots 1 and 4 © Trevor Shaikin; and shots 2, 3, and 5 © Bill Baran

CHAPTER 22
Primal Rock Rebellion and British Lion

"I like the new-style metal with the big heavy riffs and de-tuned guitars."

It's no secret that in Maiden, Adrian Smith is sort of second to Bruce Dickinson in musical restlessness and occasional concern with the process and result of making music with the band. Adrian has given us a record with A.S.a.P. and two with Psycho Motel, and on January 2, 2012, his new side project—Smith had definitely not left Maiden—Primal Rock Rebellion, issued a new single, "I See Lights," as a free download. This was followed by the release of a music video on the band's website on January 26 for a second track from the finished full-length album, this song called "No Place Like Home."

Then it was time for the record, which arrived in shops on February 27, 2012. *Awoken Broken* surprised fans with its aggressive and actorly vocals from Adrian's coworker Mikee Goodman. At the guitar end, Smith upholds the harsh alternative-tribal-metal ethic put forth by Goodman, making a pile of noise, and also handling all bass duties and some backup vocals, while Dan Foord takes care of the drumming.

According to a press release from the band's label, respected extreme-metal midsizer Spinefarm, "Primal Rock Rebellion is the meeting of different minds, different mentalities, and different musical backgrounds, but the end result is very much a cohesive, self-produced whole . . . albeit one that reflects the individual talents of the musicians involved: Adrian provides the guitars, the bass, and the advanced songwriting skills, the sense of drama, of light and shade, of music designed to stir the senses, all of them. Right from the start, it's been very much a labour of love."

Stated Adrian, "It was great working at my own pace and in my own studio with no time constraints. I think during the making of this album, I went around the world twice with Maiden, working on the project in between. In the process, it allowed for a bit more of an experimental approach." Added Goodman, "Adrian inspired me in many ways. I learnt the importance and the power of choruses in songs. Adrian also gave me a lot more belief in myself melodically. I think we pulled each other out of our comfort zones, creating something fresh and exciting along the way. We coproduced the album together, and the whole recording process was very relaxed—no deadlines, just honing the songs naturally as we recorded them, a new experience for both of us."

"It just kind of evolved, really," explained Smith, to Mitch Lafon, for our site BraveWords.com. "I met Mikee Goodman five or six years ago. I saw him playing in a band called SikTh and I was quite impressed. I ended up writing with him, but I didn't know that it was going to turn into an album. If anything, it was more his solo album to start with, with me producing and writing, but then it became more of a joint project. It just sort of grew, really. It's pretty much 50/50. When I first met Mikee, I had a couple of songs. The first was 'Savage World' and I had 'Search for Bliss.' They're

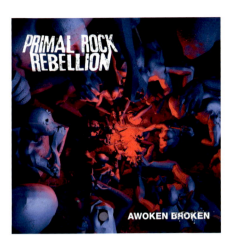

Martin Popoff archive

both on the album. I had those roughly demoed, and I wanted to see what Mikee would come up with. I thought what he came up with was really interesting. He's not your conventional singer, and I just thought his vocal approach was kind of interesting. I thought there might be something in it, so we pursued it.

"It has a life of its own," continues Smith. "I had two songs and then we didn't do anything for almost a year. I went out on tour with Maiden and then we did another couple of songs. Then I went off again. So, this was a few years in the making. It was only after we had done those initial four songs that we got some good reactions from people. We initially wanted to do an EP, but then we got the go-ahead from the record company to do a whole album. We then had to sit down and write another six or eight songs. That's pretty much how the body of the album came together.

"It's new territory for Mikee. When I saw him in his previous band, he took care of the more extreme kind of vocals, and they had another guy take care of the more melodic vocals. I think Mikee wanted to possibly do something more melodic. I definitely did. I like the new-style metal with the big heavy riffs and de-tuned guitars. I like to hear some melody in the stuff I listen to, so that was the idea—to make heavy music with anthemic memorable choruses . . . make it musical. It pulled Mikee in a different direction and encouraged him to sing more melodically and write melodies. He can actually write good melodies. That's not what he grew up listening to, because he's a bit younger than me. He probably grew up listening to Korn and Pantera. Whereas I come from Purple, Sabbath, and the Beatles. So, we have different musical backgrounds and that makes for an interesting mix."

Indeed, the record achieves what Adrian says there, massive, stone-carved riffing upon slow and rumbling structures, but with sophisticated melodies that remind one of Killing Joke or Tool. Mikee sings in a bewildering array of guises (see "Savage World" for some of this sense of experimentation), while Adrian finds himself comfortable in this alternative, at times dissonant "spookycore" world. Bottom line; if you have a predilection for angsty modern metal, then you should dig this, given its top-shelf reeling and roiling in that realm. But Goodman provides further provocation: Primal Rock Rebellion polarized listeners in no small part due to Mikee's vocals, which, song after song, become the center of attention to the point of distraction. The guy is hugely versatile and thespian, no question, but as a listener, you have to be inclined to accept a singer you aren't familiar with emoting this relentlessly.

Continuing his chat with Lafon, Smith explains that "these days, I seem to be able to sit down and come up with something. We spent a couple of weeks and came up with a song a day. With technology today, you start writing and recording it as well. So, you start off with a rough draft and build the track from there, right from the writing stage, and if you want to change anything, you just edit it. When we worked it was pretty fast."

CHAPTER 22

Asked by Mitch to contrast it with his other quite modern metal project, Smith figures that "in Psycho Motel there were two different singers involved on two different albums, and we decamped to a studio. But the way we did Primal Rock, I have a studio at home, so I can work when I like and how I like, which is great. Mikee has a studio, so we work separately and together. I would say that's the main difference. And Psycho Motel was more of a band—you had a drummer, bass player, guitar—where[as] Primal Rock is just me and Mikee, although we did get Dan Foord [also, from SikTh] to play drums."

Although a second record never happened, at the time, unsurprisingly, Adrian was more optimistic about continuing the thing. "Mikee and I are friends, and we live nearby each other. There's a possibility that we might do something in the future. I enjoy working with him, but Mikee has gotten into making videos now. We've done two videos ['No Place Like Home' and 'No Friendly Neighbour'], and he's working on the third one. He's a really creative guy."

In fact, Goodman would fully direct a fourth video from the album, for the track "Tortured Tone," which was issued on October 12, 2012, well after the record had run its course in the press and public consciousness.

But despite all the visual promotional items, there were limitations to the project, says Adrian. "It was never the intention to make it a touring band. There's not a band as such. We'd have to find members, and to re-create the album live would take a little bit of doing, so there are no plans at the moment. I'm always at my happiest when I'm working and being creative, writing songs or doing something. So, I'll definitely be doing some stuff in the future, and I definitely don't see why Mikee and I can't do something as well. Primal Rock has got its direction now, and I think it's a strong direction, so it would be interesting to see where that direction leads, but that will always pretty heavy. Although some of the stuff on the Primal Rock album is quite off the wall. You've got songs like 'Mirror and the Moon,' which I had a little bass riff, and Mikee liked it and put some words to it and it came out really unusual. I think that's what you can say about the album: there's nothing quite like it out there. I like my music with passion and power always, and a bit of melody as well. Anything like that I'm into, but who knows what the future holds? I would certainly think we'd do some more Primal Rock stuff."

"Listening to this album is like being given an auditory tour of the world as seen through the eyes of the insane," writes Sarah (no last name given), in her 7.5/10 review of the album for Scene Point Blank. "It at first presents a thick, abrasive façade that repulses and repels, but as you begin to understand it more, you discover that it's frequently punctuated by moments of sweet lucidity. Or just imagine Mikee Goodman screwing your brain with nothing but his voice and, well, you will get more or less the same effect. Man's got a fucking weird voice is what I'm getting at. *Awoken Broken* is likely to please even minimally broad-minded fans of both SikTh and Iron Maiden. Any fans that don't mind the artists stepping a little bit outside of their original styles will appreciate their combined talents at work on this album. Granted, at its heart, it's still a big, dumb hard rock album, but it's certainly on the upper tier thereof. In fact, the only reservation I really have with the band is that I honestly doubt they have another album of completely original material in them. Regardless, for now, Primal Rock Rebellion have undeniably delivered something memorable."

Adds *Metal Assault*'s Aniruddh "Andrew" Bansal, who gave the album 9/10, "To start with, it doesn't sound like Iron Maiden and undoubtedly takes the Maiden fan in me by surprise. Right from its opening track, 'No Friendly Neighbour,' it's relatively modern and groovy as compared to anything Smith has done with Maiden. But importantly, the track has the stamp of Smith's songwriting all over it, and the same can be said about all of the 12 tracks on this album. Mikee Goodman's crisp vocals give aggression and power to the music, while Smith's lead guitar work provides it the exotic touch that makes it a winning combination.

"The musical styles vary within the album, from song to song. On one side of the spectrum, tunes like 'No Friendly Neighbour,' 'I See Lights,' 'Tortured Tone,' and 'Search for Bliss'[s] showcase the melodic and exotic side of Smith's musicianship, and on the other side we have straight-up hard rock tunes such as 'No Place Like Home,' 'Savage World,' 'White Sheet Robes,' and a couple others that are all about the groove. Each song varies from the others in terms of tempo as well, making the album all the more interesting.

"But my favorite track is most definitely 'Bright as a Fire.' The longest track on the album, it moves along brilliantly, and the complete range of Goodman's vocals and Smith's musicianship is evident on this tune. I'm also a huge fan of the closing track, 'Mirror and the Moon,' simply because of Smith's outstanding guitar work on the tune. Besides Goodman's vocals, the backing vocals on some of the tracks are also very well done, and they enrich the overall sound even further.

"On the whole, it's an ambitious move by Adrian Smith to write music of this kind, and although I instantly found a sizable portion of the album to my liking, hard-core Iron Maiden fans might take some time to get used to it. I love Iron Maiden as much as anyone else on this planet does, but I have no doubt in my mind that I appreciate this release a lot more than the latest Iron Maiden album, *The Final Frontier*, an album that left me hugely disappointed as a Maiden fan. I just hope that more Primal Rock Rebellion albums are released in the near future, and it's not just a one-off like some of Smith's past projects."

It was.

But not so with Steve Harris's British Lion joint—there, as of mid-2020, we have two records, along with another singer to debate, with respect to how much we can relate.

Similar to what Adrian went through, Steve says, "It's been a long time in the making." This of course refers to the man's first album—Is it a solo album? Is this a band?—*British Lion*, apparently under the "act" name Steve Harris. The record emerged on September 25, 2012, through EMI, wrapped in a cover that featured a cool pewter lion's head and rich grayish greens surrounding it.

"It goes back years," explained Steve, speaking with Tim Henderson. "It goes back with guys I've known for a long time, so it's not a project with people I didn't know. It goes back to sort of 1990s, really. There was a band. I was trying to help them at the time, and I renamed the thing British Lion. I was producing them, managing them; I wrote some songs with them, which nobody knew about. Not even a couple of guys in the band knew I was involved in that way. And it all imploded unfortunately.

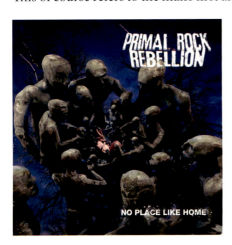

Martin Popoff archive

CHAPTER 22

"But I just thought from that point on, someday I've got to do something with this because I thought some of those songs were so strong that they need to see the light of day. So that was it, really. So, the singer from that band, Richie Taylor, I kept in touch with him, Grahame Leslie, the guitar player also, and then we got together with David Hawkins, the guitar player I met through Richie, and we started working on some other songs, and it developed from there, really.

Dave Wright archive

"But it's taken forever and a day to actually finally come out. The fourth song, I think, 'Us against the World,' is probably the most Maiden sounding; it's got like the harmony guitars and sound that Maiden use. There's a bit of harmony guitars on 'A World Without Heaven' that sound Maideny to me. But most of the other stuff, really, I don't think sounds like Maiden. Of course, my bass playing is what it is; that's what it says on the tin. I did try a few different things out with different songs which I don't normally get the chance to do with Maiden.

"When we do Maiden, it's a whole different thing. You know, I prefer working like that, where you book off one period of time. But this was done in bits and pieces, different times, but I've tried different sounds with different songs, and I think it's worked really good. But I still think it sounds like me. I didn't really try to distance myself from anything. It was just approaching the songs how I felt they should be approached. And the songs are sort of organic. That's the word everyone uses these days, but it very naturally came together. Although it wasn't natural recording it sometimes. But I think the end result is a very cohesive album. It doesn't feel like a bits-and-pieces album to me at all. Because I've always worked with Maiden like you've got periods of time, this has proved to me now that you can go the completely different scenic route around and then still come out with a great result."

The end result is a record that is modern, like Adrian's, but more melancholy than angry, more smoothly textured and melodic. Richard Taylor has a sweetly clean voice, and his style is one where he sings comfortably, rather than pushing a lot of air through exertion. Like Adrian's record, there's a strong percussive undercarriage, but all told, this is much more Maiden-like of somber tone, just with all the edges rounded off.

"I don't know what people are expecting, but it's probably not this," warned Steve, speaking with *Classic Rock*. "The album has been coming together over a ridiculously long time, but we've managed to keep it a secret and that's been kinda fun. The guys have been waiting very patiently for years for me, and it's been frustrating at time[s], but what can I do? I'm so busy with Maiden. People have already said to me, 'Are you going to do this instead of Maiden?' and I'm like, 'Of course not!' Maiden is always going to be the priority, always has been and always will be, but it's interesting and exciting to try new things."

Circo Voador, Rio de Janeiro, Brazil, November 9, 2018. © *Daniel Croce*

As for the music, Steve ventures that "what I think and what other people will think might be two different things, but I'd say it's more mainstream rock than metal, very British sounding, very 1970s influenced and quite commercial, but good commercial. There's all kinds of stuff going on, with nods to the Who and UFO and some classic British rock bands, but it's not the progressive rock album some might be expecting.

"There's quite a nostalgic feel to the album in places. The older you get, the more nostalgic you are: you become more aware of your own mortality and start thinking weird and wonderful things . . . especially when you've had a few pints of Guinness! Truthfully, I don't know what kind of reaction it's going to get. And that's quite exciting for me. Even with Maiden I don't have expectations, and this is a very different thing: this is stepping outside that safe Maiden bubble and finding out what's going on in the real world.

"British Lion isn't that different from early Maiden material, essentially, in the style of songwriting at least," explained Steve, speaking with John Doran from The Quietus. "But there is one way in which it is very different. Part of Iron Maiden's success is that they appeal to the imagination, and even if the songs are set in a real-life situation like during World War I or ancient Egypt, they are primarily about escapist fantasy and using your imagination. On *British Lion*, you seem to be dealing with the day-to-day struggles of life. Richard wears his heart on his

Circo Voador, Rio de Janeiro, Brazil, November 9, 2018. © *Daniel Croce*

sleeve a little bit more than I do. I do sing about some of these things sometimes, but I tend to disguise them in little stories. I think if you dive in a little deeper with Maiden, that stuff is there but maybe it's more obvious to me. British Lion is a little bit more open in the lyrics, like the Who were. You'll understand 'Us Against the World' if you support a sports team. It's the vibe you get that makes you feel invincible. It's a really strong and powerful feeling that can inspire you to fight and get through things even when it feels like everything is against you."

Wrote Ryan Drever in his review of the album for *Drowned in Sound*, "Perhaps the most glaring fault is that Taylor's lacklustre vocals simply aren't strong enough to make any kind of impact. On 'This Is My God' and 'Lost Worlds,' his listless crooning makes Chris Cornell sound like Tom Araya, and the accompanying paint-it-by-numbers 'hard rock' does nothing to lift it any higher. The only really powerful moments come from the Maiden-esque leanings of the likes of 'Us Against the World,' the intro of which, with indulgent and instantly recognizable twin guitars, could raise a thousand studded fists in any given corner of the world.

"But again, it's instantly rendered flaccid by Taylor's ball-less Paul Rodgers impression. The same goes for 'A World Without Heaven,' which, brimming with some of Harris's signature flourishes, is easily one of the strongest on offer, with a pounding, riff-heavy backbone worth its weight in silky solos and almost channels the stargazing fantasy metal of '80s Sabbath—which again, you either love or loathe.

"It's a redundant thought, but by this point, you start to wonder what work the mighty Dio (R.I.P.) or, inevitably, Bruce Dickinson, might have made of these same tracks. Because it's not so much that the bare bones are so unworkable, it's just that there appears to have been little to no effort made to drive this album beyond its members' classic-rock influences or to make it stand tall on its own merits as a unique and instantly recognizable piece of original work. *British Lion* is not far-removed enough from Maiden musically to herald an exciting new chapter in Harris'[s] career, nor is it strong enough to challenge any other contenders in the genre, old or new. Again, it's almost painful to cast it off, but it would be safe to say that this is a piece of work suited purely for curious diehards. But fuck it, you can always go and listen to *Powerslave*."

British Lion have had a novel touring history. They didn't get down to business right away but played a bunch of summer dates in 2014 and 2015. Then it's been a few small tours all the way up until and just after the release of the second album, usually, again, in the summers or the November/December time frame. All told, it's been pretty commendable of Steve, getting out there on the small scale and taking it to the masses.

Indeed, a second album arrived, after more fits and starts, on January 17, 2020. The band was now clearly called British Lion, and the album had a name, specifically *The Burning*,

Circo Voador, Rio de Janeiro, Brazil, November 9, 2018. © Daniel Croce

with a classy album cover that built upon the image of the debut. When I say fits and starts, it's more like cart before the horse, with the band playing the new songs live long before the album would be issued, through sub-EMI label Parlophone internationally, Explorer1 in the States, and Warner Music in Japan. There would be dates as far back as 2018, with the album slated to come out soon, although that was not to be.

In fact, I spoke to Steve about the situation at the time—on October 3, 2018, to be exact—and then again, over a year later, the week after the second record saw the light of day.

"I'm just loving playing in small places," reflected Harris. "I'm really enjoying doing something different, and it's obviously very different than what I do with Maiden—it's rock rather than metal. We've been doing it for a few years now, and the more I do it, the more I enjoy it. We've put in quite a few shows in Europe already, but apart from a cruise ship that we played last year, we've not played on terra firma outside of Europe. So now, coming to do shows in Canada, South America, and Japan is fantastic. Well, not only for me, but for the guys in the band, because some of them have never been to some of these countries. Although we did do the first couple of British Lion videos in Canada. They were done basically in Banff and Vancouver. But they haven't really been to the other side of Canada. So, at the end of the day, it's great for them. Plus, it's great for me, and great to see them enjoy themselves and do things for the first time. It's always nice to see that in people. Now I'm back to places, countries, and cities I've been to many times before, but I haven't played the small venues."

Contrasting the British Lion sound with that of Maiden, Steve said that "it's just more rock rather than metal, really. But then I grew up being influenced by rock anyway, UFO, Thin Lizzy, the Who, Wishbone Ash. The first album was intended to be like that. You know, some people complained about the production, but it was meant to sound retro—that was on purpose. This new album will be different; it's now a few years later, and the sound has evolved over a period of time, as well as from playing a lot live together. But the first album was intended to be like that—it was meant to have that kind of 1970s vibe to it."

Steve is of course one of Iron Maiden's two overwhelmingly dominant lyricists, but with British Lion, he essentially cedes that territory. "Yes, a lot of the lyrics are actually written by Richard. I mean, I do help him along the line with some bits and pieces here and there, but a lot of the time it's his stuff; it's a different approach and a bit more personal. I mean, if I do personal stuff with Maiden, I tend to disguise it in other things, in other topics. So, this is a little bit more open. For example, 'Eyes of the Young' is about, you know, the way I grew up, but it's also about my father as well, so it's a bit more personal. But overall, yeah, I think if people come see it live, they'll see that there's a passion there and we just enjoy it. We just have fun. That's what it's all about really—having fun."

Steve further expressed contentment with how British Lion takes him back to his experience with getting the mighty Maiden off the ground. "Yes, it's basically going back to how I used to feel, I suppose, when I was struggling with Maiden to try and get noticed. It was a challenge. Everyone's trying to push . . . with any new band, you're trying to get noticed and go out and fight for everything. And that's the kind of feeling I get now. It gives me that freedom. I really enjoy it. I still enjoy playing with Maiden and playing massive venues and all that business, but I love playing clubs as well—always have done. It's been thirty or more years since I've played clubs like I've done with British Lion. And some of the clubs I'm going to do now on the upcoming tour I've never ever played, because we sort of bypassed a lot of them. Whenever I play, whether it be big or small festivals, indoor, outdoor, you know, I still give 110 percent whether I'm with Maiden or British Lion. Plus, it gives me a chance to meet more fans as well. Because with Maiden you tend to go straight off to the next city after the show or whatever, and it's almost impossible to do that. But with British Lion it's a different thing; it's a bit more personal, and you're up close and personal at the show as well.

Martin Popoff archive

"I always used to say it's called bums on seats," continued Harris, still fighting, still healthy of rock 'n' roll attitude. "You've got to try and get people in. You've got to try and entice people into sort of checking you out. It's not easy to do that with anything these days. It's not easy to get people to come along to a show or convince people of what you're doing. Sometimes it takes a long time for the penny to drop, and it was no different than with Maiden in that sense. We played clubs and stuff in the UK for four or five years before we really started getting noticed and taking off. But I'm not trying to be a worldwide successful band with British Lion—that's not necessarily the purpose, really. It's just having fun, playing clubs, and doing it all for the right reasons. Still, it's a challenge and I do enjoy that."

In 2018, Steve framed the upcoming second British Lion album as "more live and vibrant. I think the songs are really powerful. There's some on the first album that are really powerful too, but this is kind of more as we are now—it's five or six years further down the line. It's different in a positive way. So yeah, it's a lot more live sounding. We've done it more kind of live in the studio, one-or-two-takes type of thing, with the backing tracks. A strong track is one called 'Spit Fire,' and we'll be playing that and some other stuff off the forthcoming album. It's a strong album. It's really hard to be objective about stuff when you're just sort of working on it. I don't know if there's anything particularly experimental or proggy on there. 'Elysium' has got a different flavor to it, strong catchy melodies, and a different vibe—powerful track but in a different way.

"There's not really time for anything else, to be honest," Harris said, near the end of that first British Lion chat. "It's tough to juggle all this stuff right now without thinking about something else. I think another project might kill me off [laughs]. But having said that, I am enjoying it. I'm loving what I'm doing in both bands. I love going to different regions with both projects, so I don't really think there's room for another one even if I wanted to do another one, to be honest. Also, I don't feel like doing another one. I'm fulfilled in what I'm doing in both projects right now."

Flash forward to 2020, long delayed, *The Burning*, a.k.a. the second British Lion record, was finally here. Said Steve now, of what now suddenly had a name and was physical product, "It's quite different to the first album purely because we've been touring for like about the last seven or eight years with the same lineup. There's a few different people playing on the album, but obviously, all five that we're touring with now are on there as well—the second album is just the unit that has been touring for the last seven years. And it makes a massive difference.

Maxwell's, Waterloo, Ontario, Canada, November 2, 2018.
© Franc Potvin

We've been playing together all that time, we've done shows all around the world, traveled a lot together, and just done a lot of good shows together in Europe and Canada, South America, Japan, and now we're touring the US for the first time. So really, we're turning into quite a nice tight unit, and it shows on this album, I think."

And very guitary as well, with dual axes clanging along in disciplined lockstep over the exacting rhythms of Steve and drummer Simon Dawson, who, compared to Nicko, Steve says, "uses a lot less drums for a start, and I can actually see him [laughs]."

Continues Harris with regard to guitarists David Hawkins and Grahame Leslie, "Just different styles; in the same way that all three Maiden guitar players have different styles from each other. Dave Hawkins is younger than the rest of us, so maybe he's got some different influences going on there, including sort of 1980s American ones, while Grahame is more rock, the Who and UFO and the like."

Asked to compare to the Maiden guys, Steve figures, "I don't think either of them sound like anybody in particular, but Dave Hawkins leans possibly towards Adrian, purely because he tends to work out his solos like Adrian does. It's good to work with different people doing different stuff, although it's all rock, as far as I'm concerned."

With a few keyboard bits, as it turns out. "Yeah, I play the keyboards on this album, just purely because it was easier. I was there to do it, and David was fine with that. First album, David did all the keys. Well, there wasn't a load of keys on the first album anyway. But I mean, Dave is a far better player than I am. But it's just purely, I was there, around, and able to do it, and it wasn't really difficult stuff. It's just kind of what we call wash, to add a bit of ambience or atmosphere. But I don't ever profess to be a good keyboard player, really [laughs]. I do what's necessary in the studio, and then someone else does it live anyway."

Up top, like the first time, there's Richard Taylor, who sings, once again, clearly, cleanly, and melodically. Really, loads of the persona of the band come from Richard, to the point where *The Burning* could pass for a Richard Taylor solo album. Hard to explain, but there's his lyrics, plus his prominence in the mix, over songs that are pretty straightforward, kind of like blue-collar Maiden, focused, less eccentric than Maiden, more like a general-access NWOBHM band crossed with UFO or Thin Lizzy, as it were.

Maxwell's, Waterloo, Ontario, Canada, November 2, 2018.
© Franc Potvin

Explains Harris, "Richard's stuff, really, is coming from his upbringing, and the fact that he had a tough time and ended up being in . . . one prime example of that is 'Land of the Perfect People,' which, he was an orphan, and basically the orphanage he was at, it was run by the Taylor family, and they basically ended up moving from there, and they took him and they adopted him. So, he had quite a tough upbringing, and I think a lot of that's come out, which is really good, because it's emotional and it's powerful and it's real. A lot of it is him getting stuff out. As a vocalist, he's got his own unique sound, really. But he's definitely more of a rock singer rather than a metal singer. Everyone's got different influences, and all those things end up coming into the pot somehow or other. It's just part and parcel of working with different people and getting different reactions."

British Lion vocalist Richard Taylor. Maxwell's, Waterloo, Ontario, Canada, November 2, 2018. © Franc Potvin

Steve provides lyrics on "Spit Fire," which is, he explains, "basically about my father, when he was in the war. All the kids were basically evacuated, to get away from London, out of the war zone. So, he was moved out to the countryside, and it's about that. He was evacuated, funny enough, to Suffolk, where some of the band now is based; Simon, our drummer, is in Suffolk, and so is Richard and David Hawkins."

Back to the tightness and forward mass of the record, Steve says that the core narrative was laying it down live in the studio. "We just went in and played live as a band, recorded most of it like that, and then just added a couple of little embellishments on top, very little, really. That was the idea, was to do it as live as possible. We had been playing some of those songs live for a while anyway, so they were the really easy ones, and those just went straight off. But the other ones we hadn't played live yet; we needed to get them sounding like the same sort of vibe. So, we just worked them up in rehearsal and got up and did them. Plus, Tony Newton did a great job at production, you know, capturing the essence of what we were doing live. It's not the easiest thing in the world to get a band to sound live, and he did a fantastic job, and pat on the back for that. Maiden does the same, really—we try to re-create what we do live. I think it's the best way you can be, rather than the other way around [laughs]."

Asked why he does British Lion in the first place, Steve figures, "It's mainly because I enjoy working with these guys. I think they're really good people, and I think they deserve a real good shot. But not only that, I just love playing small gigs. I love playing all the different size of gigs, actually, but it's a challenge. I love playing with Maiden and I enjoy traveling, and whether it's being on a nice plane or on a bus or whatever, it doesn't matter. It's not a chore for me. I just enjoy it all. I never get fed up with playing or touring. And we get on great. I don't really care about material things. I think the way we travel around in a bus is great for them and it's great for me. It is what it is. We play something like the one tonight, and there's no shower, and you just deal with it. But I've always been like that; it doesn't cause problems in that sort of respect. I'm used to touring more than they are, but I mean, they've all toured at some point, although they've never toured the States before, so that's fun to do with them."

All told, *The Burning* was a tougher yet still-melodic record compared to the debut, definitely punchier and more steeped in band chemistry, which, as it turns out, makes perfect sense, given its forging in the crucible of live shows.

Reviews were more favorable this time versus the debut, but curiously, they invariably gravitated to debate about the vocals—as I've said, very much in concert with my opinion about Primal Rock Rebellion, British Lion is very much about Richard Taylor's world.

Wrote *Kerrang!*'s George Garner, astutely, "Be it the frenetic, quick-fire tangle of notes on the title track and 'Bible Black,' or the rolling groove of 'Spit Fire,' the first impression gleaned from *The Burning* is that British Lion have become a much, much heavier proposition than they were eight years ago. This comes courtesy not only of the magisterial clang 'n' clank of Steve's trademark rattling bass, but also the deft crunch of the album's production.

"Yet that's only part of the story here. Elsewhere, British Lion exhibit a real and welcome appreciation of experimentation and quietude. Kudos in this respect should go to guitarists David Hawkins and Grahame Leslie. 'Father Lucifer' captures them Alter-Bridging the gap between classic rock, metal, and alt-rock, while 'Land of the Perfect People' sports a delicate intro that's almost evocative of Fleetwood Mac in their prime.

"These signs of growth are obvious throughout. The band's debut was rather a baptism of fire for singer Richard Taylor, who had to weather some predictable yet redundant criticisms comparing him to Bruce Dickinson from Steve's 'other' band. He sings like he has a point to prove throughout *The Burning*. A telling sign of the front man's burgeoning confidence comes on 'Elysium,' a song that boasts a killer chorus but an even better final passage, as he belts out a series of absolutely massive, sustained notes over a swelling choral section. Equally impressive is his ability to extract emotion from a song. Whether he's communing with lost souls on 'Lightning' or offering a consolatory ear on closer 'Native Son,' he often brings a moving sense of fragility to the fore. Clearly, this particular lion has more at its disposal than claws alone."

Maiden expert and *Brave Words* compatriot Dom Lawson, in his review for *Louder Sound*, was similarly pleased with the results: "In truth, the first British Lion record didn't exactly set the world alight, despite being pretty damn good. A stoically straightforward and melody-driven hard rock record, it was full of great songs and moments of gritty flash, with Harris's finger-powered rumble dominating the sonic background and vocalist Richard Taylor's engaging croon leading from the front."

"If there was a downside, it was that a slightly vexed and muddy production ensured that the album was an acquired

Maxwell's, Waterloo, Ontario, Canada, November 2, 2018. © Franc Potvin

taste and, despite widespread great reviews, wasn't as celebrated as you might imagine a Steve Harris side-project might be. Fortunately, *The Burning* sounds vastly more punchy and powerful than its predecessor, while also giving the distinct impression that British Lion have evolved into a fiery and character-ful ensemble with a strong identity of their own. We are still firmly in traditional rock territory here, and Harris's love of UFO and Golden Earring remains as cheerfully conspicuous as ever. But thanks to a brighter, breezier sound and unmistakable hints of looseness and swagger, everything from the briskly uplifting title track to the brooding hulk of 'Bible Black' sparkles with freshness and weirdly youthful vigour.

"While many contemporary classic-rock bands seem fixated on reproducing the aesthetic specifics of bygone eras, songs like motoring opener 'City of Fallen Angels' and preview single 'Lightning' clearly favor timelessness over nostalgia. Similarly, melancholy closer 'Native Son' wears its prog influences with pride and dares to saunter down a more restrained, acoustic path. But the sum of those parts is simply an irresistibly downbeat rock ballad, worthy of any era you care to mention.

"It may be significant that Harris's bass is less domineering second time out: his absurdly nimble fingers still propel the songs along, augmenting everything with those trademark chords and flourishes, but never muddying the sonic waters with a surfeit of rumbling bottom end. Meanwhile, Taylor sings with unfussy aplomb throughout, clearly thrilled to be part of such an honest, unpretentious enterprise, and blessed with a generous helping of brilliant songs to sing."

Again, one wonders what we are to glean from this British Lion idea. Bottom line is that like Adrian with both Psycho Motel and Primal Rock Rebellion, and like Bruce with his solo career, what we have is the refreshing happenstance to work with people who are not Iron Maiden members, resulting in albums that take us away from the half-dozen to dozen things that must be on an Iron Maiden record. The result is always, strangely, something that sounds more like the work of "adults," for better and for worse, the better being obvious, the worse being the subject of debate, how much we want to hear of the personal, of angst, of emotion, from these guys, and most notably, the guys who are not the Iron Maiden members.

CHAPTER 23
The Book of Souls and The Book of Souls: Live Chapter

"Because I'm old-school, this is a triple album."

As 'Arry and his light brigade rolled on through the 2010s, it became more and more apparent that the band had entered another realm, one built equally by the regular enough release of creditable new music, and the celebration of the singular institution that was Maiden's form of British metal—old and new but old styled—that the band took to stages all over the world.

From May 27, 2013, through to August 4, 2013, there was a second leg of the Maiden England World Tour that was entirely European. The theme for this tour was approximately a reconsideration of the band's late 1980s output, underscored by the use of a stage show that celebrated the surreal and chilly album cover of *Seventh Son of a Seventh Son* and a clutch of songs from that record, and also *Somewhere in Time*.

Rod Smallwood would have been perceptive enough to realize that the *Seventh Son* album had been rising in fans' estimations over the years past its cold reception at the time, to the point where for Maiden fans of a certain second-generation vintage, it's now considered a masterpiece. So, this was hammered home, along with the hits and nothing newer than "Fear of the Dark." In fact, really, the old hits outweighed any attempt at re-creating *Seventh Son*, but at least Rod proposed an extra dimension to the thing to keep us interested.

From September 3 through 17, the Maiden England tour goes back to America for seven dates, plus one show in Mexico City. From September 20 through October 2, another leg of the campaign takes in South America, with the show at the National Stadium in Santiago, Chile, being the largest concert ever in that country by a British band, with 60,105 fans attending the show. Slayer supports at all but one of these dates, a case of tidy poetic justice, really, given that Slayer has experienced the same kind of "welcoming into the wider fold" late in their career that Maiden had enjoyed.

Meanwhile, while all this is going on, Bruce "polymath" Dickinson was seeing his airline maintenance business Cardiff Aviation expand to between sixty and seventy employees. Into 2014, he purchases a Fokker Dr1 replica and joins the Great War Display Team and does reenactments of World War I air battles at air shows in the UK. In December 2014, TeamRock Radio acquires a bunch of old Bruce Dickinson radio shows, now that he's quit that, and begins reairing them. In other Maiden microphone news this year, Blaze Bayley issues a DVD called *Live in Prague* while also collaborating with John Steel on a studio album called *Freedom*. Paul Di'Anno also enjoys the release of a DVD, called *The Beast Arises*, while on July 29 of the following year, he has a new band called Architects of Chaoz putting out a first studio album titled *The League of Shadows*, followed by a tour of Brazil, where Di'Anno is adored.

Unused (and hence backward) Trooper beer decal. *Martin Popoff archive*

And the whole family can celebrate in style with a tipple: as of May 2014, Iron Maiden's Trooper beer has notched sales of 2.5 million pints across forty countries. (I have an empty bottle in my display case, across from another empty of Motörhead's Road Crew, which is sitting on top of the fridge. Although I notice, also in my display case, my years-old bottle of American Dog's American Light Lager is full—better do something about that before it explodes.)

The final leg of the Maiden England campaign, May 27 through July 5, is a European one once again. Support for the band in 2014 comes from Anthrax, plus once again Slayer, as well as Ghost, who are the closest thing we get in the modern age to a new Iron Maiden, unless we go more conventionally power metal with the likes of Dragonforce and Sabaton.

Just as Maiden got down to begin work on what would be their sixteenth studio album, the band learned of the shocking suicide death of comic and acting legend Robin Williams, on August 14, 2014—the sad news would manifest in a song on the album called "Tears of a Clown." Maiden would record at Guillaume Tell Studios, Paris (last and first used by the band for *Brave New World*), once again with Kevin Shirley herding the cats, beginning in September, the guys completing the lion's share of the work in December.

"Basically, we knew it was a good studio," remarked Steve, speaking with Patrick Prince. "We felt comfortable there before. We knew the engineer there. We really like the sound in the room. And Bruce wanted to be somewhere that was close to the UK, and that was the obvious choice. It had nothing to do with the vibe of an album. When we make a new album, it doesn't matter where it is. Even if we recorded somewhere before, it makes no difference to a new album, really."

This time the guys nixed the idea of a pressure cooker writing session before recording, with the result being that the guys brought in only roughs that they had kicking around, which ostensibly helped contribute to a live and spontaneous feel to the proceedings.

"Normally we would go into rehearsal where we would write and rehearse it, and then we'd go and record afterward somewhere else," continued Steve. "But this time we did it all in one place, so it was good because we'd write and rehearse a song and then put it straight down. Which makes a lot more sense, really, in a lot of ways. I mean, we actually really enjoyed it like that. But I think most people know that studios are so ridiculously expensive that most bands would rehearse in a rehearsal room first, and that was normal. This time around we decided to go straight in there, and partly because there was going to be another band rehearsing in the rehearsal room. We thought, we can't be somewhere where we'd write a new album and have someone else listening to what we were doing next door, you know [laughs]. So, we decided to go straight into the studio, which is more private. It worked great. I think when we do another album, we'll do the same thing again."

Air Canada Centre, Toronto, Ontario, April 3, 2016. © *Trevor Shaikin*

On the subject of "another album," Steve told Patrick, "I've been quoted as saying that it would be nice to do fifteen studio albums. I remember saying that, and we've done our sixteenth one, which is great. But to be honest, we didn't know our career would be this long, no. In the early days we were just trying to do what everybody else does, which is to play for as many people as possible and make records. And that's all we can ask for, really. The fact that we've had such a long career is amazing, that we're still doing it. I think we're all very lucky to be able to say that we're still out there doing it. We've always had a very positive attitude."

While assembling the record, Steve suffers the death of a close friend as well as a family member and thus is not represented in the writing on every song, which had been the case now for two albums in a row. Rather, Bruce gets two sole credits, also sharing credit 50/50 with Adrian on two tracks, "Speed of Light" and "Death or Glory," which were two of the first songs whacked together for use on the record.

Recounted Nicko on the sessions, looking back almost a year later, in conversation with Tim Henderson, "I think Bruce got together with Adrian and Steve at that time. In fact, 'Empire of the Clouds' was just a dream earlier last year, and Bruce I think had already written 'If Eternity Should Fail' on his own. I believe 'Speed of Light,' 'The Great Unknown,' and 'Shadows of the Valley' were all ready to go. So, by the time Kevin had gotten to the studio, we were ready to do four songs. It was a magical moment because going into the room to just rehearse didn't have that character it has—and it had—when you light up the desk and go into record mode (i.e., putting all the Apple gear, lights, and mics on, the isolation room and all of that). As soon as Kevin got there, the kind of clinical feel of the control room was completely changed. We were like, this is what it's all about. This is what I remembered from fifteen years ago. The studio is slightly different now. They've lowered the stage. It was an old vaudeville theater that used to have stage productions. It had a big old pipe onstage. They've since cut that down and put in some isolation rooms, with one on stage right where Steve puts his gear. On *Brave New World*, he was in the fire escape going out of the building. It was a brilliant change, and the vibe is much better.

"By the time we got through five songs, no one was watching the clock," continues McBrain, on the length of the record, which required it to be two CDs, a bona fide double album. "I think it was about five songs in when we realized we kind of had some very long songs here. I mean, 'The Red and the Black' is more than thirteen minutes long, almost as long as 'Rime of the Ancient Mariner.' Then we have a couple coming in at ten and twelve minutes, and of course Bruce's opus. At that point, we were like, we haven't even yet finished writing, as we were only half a dozen songs in. I think it was at this time that Bruce turned around and uttered something about a double album. We all just shrugged it off and got on with it. In the past, we have always done it the way we want anyway. We have never been, 'Let's write a single.' Not to say there aren't single-worthy songs on the album, as most definitely 'Tears of a Clown' or 'Death or Glory' could be the next singles. But, to have that choice from a double album is great, and it's still only eleven songs. To me, because I'm old-school, this is a triple album. But, nowadays, with technology the way it is, it's a double album.

"In the end, we just got on with it and had the best time with it that we could," continues Nicko. "This was the best vibe we have ever had making a record, and we have always had great times making a record in the studio, because that's where we love to be. That said, it doesn't touch being in a live situation. We make great records, but in the end, we are a live band. That's where we really breathe the essence of Iron Maiden. This album we wanted to try and create more of a live feel, which is what we did. We sat around the studio with headphones on, oftentimes around my drums playing—dare I say it—acoustic electrically, like we were set up to do a show. Then we literally just pushed the record button.

"It was really fresh. By the time you learn the first song, you put it to bed. When you learn the second, you play the first one again. By the time you get to the last song, you might have played the first, second, and third songs a few times, but there is a lot going on and it's overkill. It's good to get it down."

Explained Dave of the process, speaking with Rob Laing, "On previous albums we've usually gone into a rehearsal room for maybe a couple of weeks and maybe have four or five songs under our belts. This time we went in there with a blank page and a bunch of ideas. It was a really fun experience because it keeps you on your toes. You have to be really sharp. We're scribbling guitar chords down, melodies and harmonies, changes . . . basically we were flying by the seat of our pants because we never knew what was coming next. But it was wonderful how things kept flowing. We stopped there, but there were probably some other things that were floating around; otherwise, we would have been in for three or four albums!"

Once the album is done, its release is delayed while Bruce receives both chemotherapy and radiation therapy for cancer of the tongue. Said Steve at the time, reassuringly, "Bruce's situation, he's a very positive person and felt he can get through this. And I think that attitude helps in all kinds of situations. It's important." On May 15, 2015, doctors say that Bruce's cancer scare is over, while Nicko celebrates the life he's managed to live through by quitting drinking.

Air Canada Centre, Toronto, Ontario, April 3, 2016. © *Trevor Shaikin*

"I cried," answered Nicko, when asked by Tim Henderson how he reacted when he'd heard the news about Bruce. "When I was told, I literally cried. I'm an emotional guy and I said fuck it, I just cried. I started questioning mortality. My brother, my friend, the guy I have known longer than thirty-three years—lived and played with this guy for half of my life. Bruce was very positive, and I knew if anyone was going to beat it, it would be Bruce. But never did I question that the band might be gone. The first thought was that my God, my friend is sick. Throat cancer? Listening back to the record, how could he have had throat cancer singing like that? Well, turns out it was behind his tongue and didn't affect his vocals. The great news is he has come out of this amazingly. He is in remission, and the way his oncologist treated him they haven't destroyed his vocals chords. They've managed to keep them intact. His taste buds are coming back, but he can't taste sugar. I said, well you never really took a lot of sugar in [laughs]. He said he could put ten spoonfuls of sugar in his coffee and he wouldn't taste it.

"So, this is his recovery, and this is why we aren't touring until next year," continued McBrain. "We have to give Bruce his time to let his body heal. Don't get me wrong, as he is not going to slow down—he runs even faster than he did two years ago. I mean, he is learning to fly 747 systems in December; he just doesn't stop. After talking with him about how well he had researched that particular disease, I thought wow, this man is really in a good position. There are good times and there are bad times. Once the treatment kicked in, he lost a lot weight, because you don't eat, you don't take stuff down well.

"I really didn't take it well at first. But I put it in prayer, and I think those prayers were answered, along with the prayers of millions of other people. I'm just amazed because the timing is so weird, as we had just made the best record we have ever made, in my opinion. Someone asked, 'Even better than *Number of the Beast*?' I said, 'For our age, definitely.' Going back to Bruce, you start to ask yourself how you can help to ease the burden. But with Bruce, you just have to step back and let him get on with his family and kids."

Air Canada Centre, Toronto, Ontario, April 3, 2016. © *Trevor Shaikin*

When Tim reminds him that the metal community was still mourning the loss of Ronnie James Dio, Nicko says, "Yeah, it was stomach cancer that took Ronnie. With Bruce, it was a tumor the size of a golf ball, and he doesn't even play golf! That's me [laughs]! I love the man, and I would take a bullet for him. My analogy is, I have a love affair with five guys, and the sex is the music. I know it's a weird analogy to make, but Steve had a dream, and five other guys are living it."

On August 14, "Speed of Light" is issued as an advance single and music video from the forthcoming *The Book of Souls*, which hits the shops on September 4, a heckuva cool Eddie glaring out at us from the racks, courtesy of the ever-capable Mark Wilkinson, scribbler of the fantastic sleeve for "The Wicker Man" among others. More of Wilkinson's very best work for the band occurs throughout the booklet, with the gorgeous mandala-like artwork printed on the actual discs being done by Anthony Dry. There's even a custom "Maya" font that was created by Jorge Letona put to use for the song titles, with Julie Wilkinson doing the Mayan codex drawings. Mayan scholar Simon Martin was consulted for historical accuracy. All of this was put together by Stuart Crouch Creative, who pretty much, right here, have designed the best art package of Maiden's long career.

So yes, we once had Eddie out of Egypt; well, now Eddie emerges from Mayan myth, as depicted on the title track from the album and throughout the album's sumptuously colored booklet (of souls). As a final touch, the band went back to their original logo (i.e., with the four descending letters), this for the first time since *The X Factor* twenty years previous—not a big difference, although it's something. And then again, it's not exactly original because it's not red and white.

The Book of Souls begins with an intro not of Steve thrumming and strumming his bass, but of Bruce over keyboards done in Roy Z's bedroom. Indeed, this song was slated for a proposed solo album from Bruce and is further distinguished in that direction through its rendering in drop-D tuning, a first for Maiden. But once "If Eternity Should Fail" kicks in, what we get is a regular, meat-and-potatoes musical track that sounds like something Steve or Janick or Dave might write. Bruce's lyric fits well the record's light conceptual throughline around souls and death and fate and eternity, and indeed the Mayan vibe of the title track and the cover and booklet art. As is often the case with Bruce, there's a malevolent knife thrust at the end, which wakes us up after a long bank of lyrics that are more on the spiritual end of things. It's an odd way to open the album though; namely, with a lengthy song that is midpaced and without much going on, other than the long intro, the long outro, and a fast bit just for fun.

"We've always done what we wanted to do right from the first album, so there's no difference there," shrugs Steve, asked by Patrick Prince about opening the album with an eight-minute song. "It's just that we do have difficulty writing short songs these days. I don't know why that is. It's just the way it evolved. There's no real reason besides the fact that we do have all kinds of influences, some of them being prog kind of stuff. But we're not trying specifically to be like anything other than just writing what the songs we feel are right at the time. We never really know what we're going to write next, which is part of the excitement when we go in and do a new album. No battle plan; we just go in and do it and what comes out comes out. It's only afterward, when we do interviews, that we try to analyze it. We don't analyze what we do. We just do it."

Limited-edition CD issue. *Dave Wright archive*

Speaking of fast bit, "Speed of Light" is a barnstormer, groovy yet quick, with a grand stadium rock chorus. Bruce likened the track to something that could have fit comfortably on *Burn* by Deep Purple, a band everybody in Maiden appreciated greatly. As an homage, Dickinson peels off a classic Ian Gillan scream to open the proceedings. Adrian pens the music to this one, rocket-launching it forward while Nicko settles in, driving it ably with short collapsing fills regularly dropping us into the next bar. As Smith explained to Rob Laing, "I thought I'd try writing shorter songs, like '2 Minutes to Midnight' and 'Can I Play with Madness,' with just Bruce and I [*sic*]. We haven't done that since I've been back in the band. Maybe with 'Wicker Man' we did it. So that was different. He came over before we started recording, and we wrote 'Speed of Light' and 'Death or Glory.'"

Further on "Speed of Light," Adrian explains, "That is a lead scale I'd been messing around with. I've sort of rediscovered the pentatonic scale, and I was listening to a lot of really good players, and I noticed a lot of them were using these scales, even Eric Johnson and people like that. But if you do them in a certain way, they can sound really good and really to the point. So, I was messing around with that, and it's a variation on a pattern; I got that little riff out of it."

Once more, Bruce is on about humanity's insignificance against time and space, writing astronomically and cosmically (and a bit like a Russian cosmist!) like he did all over *Skunkworks*. Of note, further to this idea of insignificance is the subnarrative of the album being about civilizations that disappear, whether it's Mayan civilization or ours right now. Are we going to kill the planet with overpopulation and pollution? Maybe so, but those are things we can control. An additional message is the idea that we can forget controlling larger forces such as planets and stars and supernovas just going about their business mutating.

One more thing, on top of all the quick-paced and quick-witted Maiden excitement of "Speed of Light," Kevin Shirley shows up and makes the guitars molten, aided and abetted by Steve being super-fat of bass with zero articulation—the result is a confident power and, oddly, the opportunity for the listener to revel in the rhythmic sixth sense of Nicko.

"'Speed of Light' was done on the first take," says McBrain. "There are a couple of drum errors in there, but I left them. People critiqued us and asked us why we left mistakes in there. Well, that's because it's the way we are. We aren't overly clinical. I missed a couple of sixteenth notes on the last chorus. Plus, the intro was not exactly the drum fill I wanted to do, which is what I rehearsed prior to recording it. But when we went in and had the red light on, it had such a vibe and dynamic feel to it—the whole track—and it speeds up a little bit, but it's got this fucking live feel, and we decided to keep that. We all critiqued every track that we recorded as a band, and that's the first time that has ever happened. You know, we have all been in different combinations in the control room listening to what we have just done, and a lot of the time it would be Steve as the driving force—and he still is—of what stays and what goes, but this time we all contributed to what stayed, what went, and what we would redo."

As for how it actually all kicks off from a song construction point of view, Nicko says, "I bruised the shit out of my legs because I would play with a pair of sticks on my knees, the lot of us sitting in a semicircle playing acoustically, very lightly. I wouldn't play on my drum set, because I'm too fucking loud [laughs]. We get what we call a sketch of the album—like an artist who has sketches. It's basically a blueprint.

Chapter 23

Then, I sit on the drum kit and put my rhythm to it. Now, nine times out of ten, it's what is needed. Then, perhaps 1 percent of the time, there may be a particular drum groove that Steve would like me to play, like a particular four-bar section or something like that."

As mentioned, "Speed of Light" was issued as an advance single and as a video. Directed by Llexi Leon, known for the comic book series Eternal Descent, the video is like an amusing medley celebrating Eddie's appearance in video games. In it we see the development of the genre, linked by wicked graphics of a very modern-day cyber Eddie shooting through cosmic tunnels.

Adrian is the penner of "The Great Unknown," onto which Steve places a very generalized lyric about how violent and horrible the world can be. There's an element of deep Maiden soulfulness to this one, which necessarily (but somewhat ironically) takes us to the heart of the two Blaze-era albums. In other words, there's a call to solitude and contemplation even though most of the song is grinding metal. Perhaps helping take us there, again, weirdly into the heart of Britain in turmoil is the fact that this is Steve at his most pessimistic, which is essentially how he spent the Blaze years—no fault to the new lead singer, who just happened to be around him at the time.

And we're kind of in that place again with "The Red and the Black," this time more so through the music. Steve writes this one, but it sounds like something Janick would do, with its overt Celticness. The standout feature to the song is how fast the words come, Steve joking that Bruce was a bit ticked off with him, given what he was asked to do, namely and gamely articulate this mouthful of words, which incidentally had to be voiced quite high up the register.

Air Canada Centre, Toronto, Ontario, April 3, 2016. © *Trevor Shaikin*

The title of the song instantly recalls Blue Öyster Cult, who have a famous song called that from back in 1973, itself a nod to Stendhal's book of the same name from 1830. The colors historically have referred to colors of military uniforms but also to alchemical workings. There's a little bit of John Dee to this one and also some Nostradamus, but Steve ventures past that, referring to "the blackjack king and the red queen." He also relates these colors to "fate and hypocrisy" and brings in a few oblique gambling references. But just like the song before it, there's a general message emanating that the world is in anguish, and the most obvious reason is armed conflict.

Opinions were and remain divided on *The Book of Souls*, and "The Red and the Black" was indeed one for the detractors—the "whoa-oh" chorus is a bit grating, and, all told, at 13:33, there are way too many go-rounds of the song's handful of musical parts, none of which are particularly novel.

"When the River Runs Deep" corrects boldly, offering an odd, gutted guitar sound; a quick arrival at the action; and a weird stack of melodies once we're there. We have Adrian on music this time, with Steve sticking on a lyric that reads like a rueful look at his own band's legacy. The sentiment seems to be that we signed our life away, and that in itself sealed Maiden's fate. Now it was time to execute, take some chances, go boldly. Quite intriguing is the sentiment that once one's work is done, then it's time to sit next to it and simply watch to see if and to what extent it stands the test of time. Almost as a metaphor for the idea is Bruce's slightly lower-in-register vocal, where very appropriately it sounds like he's ruminating over Steve's words in poignant agreement.

Next comes the title track, another long one, slow and Egypto, music by Janick, lyrics by Steve. No surprise that this one ties closest to the Mayan theme of the artwork, with Steve all on about the kings, their relationship to the gods, and their pomp and circumstance, along with a bit of human sacrifice. Steve intimated that his piqued interest in Mayan culture was similar to what happened back in the *Powerslave* era with Egyptian history. Additionally, though, he liked the Mayan preoccupation with souls and life after death, a pliable and amorphous enough area of study that permeates everything on the album, making it conceptual by proxy (i.e., without hitting the 'Edbanger over the 'ed with it).

Detractors again bristled at the song's length, plus the idea of another look-in at Middle Eastern tonalities, which sort of seems like a regular recurrence when the well runs dry. Keyboard washes don't help the cause either, and the jump up to a fast part sounds a little too uncomfortably close to "Losfer Words" from *Powerslave*. Steve himself realized this, amusingly saying that it gets a pass because it came from Janick, who of course wasn't in the band in 1984. As well, he mused that stealing from yourself isn't something that should be considered egregious or out of bounds. Plus, it's in a different key.

"There is a lot of back-end groove on this record," Nicko told Tim Henderson, on this one, "and I would adjust accordingly. 'Book of Souls' is kind of like my Bonham tribute—it's almost 'Kashmir'-ish, Bonhamesque. I said to the guys that I wanted to make that whole section how I think Bonham would have played it. And when it came to sitting in the circle in the control room critiquing the recordings, there was no anger, no 'You should have played it this way or that way.' Everybody was wide open to each other's thoughts about the particular piece of music we just made.

"And with ProTools, if you make a mistake, you can go back and clean it up. But we are old-school. We want it to be exactly what we play. We've taken songs where we have recorded three or four bits of the song, and we take the best parts of it. A big argument went down years ago when this technology became available, because I said it's cheating. Kevin mentioned that it's not cheating because I actually played it. It's not like we constructed and compiled something that has not been played. We've just taken the best bits of that verse and stuck it on that chorus. Then it became okay with me. When you are not disciplined at playing with a click track, it's really difficult. Iron Maiden's whole essence is based on emotion. Live is a different beast. I would speed up all the time onstage, and Adrian would be like, 'I can't play to that' [laughs]. But, in the studio we would make sure that the drum track is solid. It's the hardest thing to redo or drop a drum track. When your drums are singing, especially when you hit a cymbal, it has a natural decay to it, making it impossible to edit unless you redo it with the exact power that you originally hit it. So, at the end of the day, we just go and play it again. The drums are the focal point at the very beginning of every track. When I say 'beginning,' I mean when we have played it, recorded it, and listen back to critique. The drums are key."

"Death or Glory" rocks along atop a solid shuffle from Nicko. Adrian provides a note-dense, acrobatic riff that collapses into relaxed chording come verse time, perfect for the tight, high-speed shuffle from Nicko, with Steve going for a nonarticulated bass-as-bass accompaniment. Bruce's lyric is about World War I triplane dogfighting, Dickinson reminding us that sometimes these planes go down when the actual person flying them, as well as the gunner, actually get shot, against the popular conception (gleaned from war footage and reenactment in war movies) that it's more so a case of the plane being disabled. This one and "Speed of Light" were written early, by Adrian and Bruce without Steve, with the expressed aim at having a few succinct rockers on the album.

The intro to "Shadows of the Valley" sounds very much like that of "Wasted Years," and then, amusingly, the next song on *Somewhere in Time* after "Wasted Years"; namely, "Sea of Madness" is quickly name-checked. And then once we're into the verses, well, there's a marked "Alexander the Great" vibe! Which all contributes to the idea that this is just another song of Maiden tropes stacked upon each other, with Janick writing deep into his mean median averageness of what it means to be a galloping, stage-cavorting songwriter in Steve's army of British historians. At the lyric end, this one is very much adjacent to the theme of crossing over, accompanied by the ominous image of a raven glancing overhead and squawking as an old man wanders aimlessly through the mist.

"Tears of a Clown" finds Steve, quite surprisingly, writing a song in tribute to actor and comedian Robin Williams, who, as we've discussed, committed suicide in 2014, shocking and saddening millions around the world. Bruce calls this one his favorite song on the album, and indeed, lyric aside, it's a stirring heavy metal rocker, music courtesy of Adrian, big "Heaven and Hell" beat provided by Nicko, who further distinguishes himself during the proggy bits as well as the fills, which are some of Nicko's best ever. Speaking of "Heaven and Hell," Adrian turns in a wah-wah-drenched solo just like Tony might, followed by a lyrical display of runs from Dave, ethereal, artful. The phrase "tears of a clown" was used as a title of a famous Smokey Robinson song, the image being derived from a clown named Canio in Italian opera *Pagliacci*.

"The Man of Sorrows" finds Dave turning in something quite novel for Maiden, novel for its overall quite-chaotic construction, and novel for its one passage, which finds Bruce singing a sort of lone verse over a one-note riff. This never returns, save for use as a bed for soloing. Most of the rest of the song is essentially chorus, and chorus of a very melodic Maiden ilk.

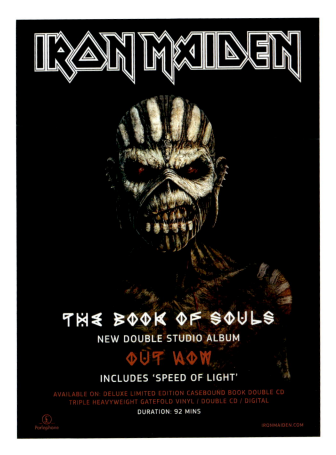

Dave Wright archive

But it is this reprise of the one-note structure for the solo section that represents the highlight of the whole record, at least in this writer's opinion. It is preceded by a bit of nice Thin Lizzy tribute and then Dave soloing, still over the melodic mélange. Then this structure appears, and Adrian rips off a searing solo indicative of his fine work all over the album (and maybe indicative of what John Sykes might do)—again, arguably, this is the greatest Iron Maiden album of them all in terms of Adrian Smith's contribution as a guitar soloist. But we're not done there. After a lapse into the song's morose keyboard-washed chorus for a bit, then Janick gets a turn, again over this irresistible one-note riff. And while Gers is doing his thing, Nicko is busy raising the interest level even further with big tom rhythms and cool, errant cymbal stabs. It's a thing of beauty, and the whole thing, a combination of the mundane (that chorus) and the innovative . . . it's just odd and surprising, a cool addition (and addiction) to the record.

At the lyric end, Steve is giving us a very sad lyric about loneliness, the death of dreams, and the general sense of depression and futility that results. Essentially and somewhat remarkably, it's a carry-on from "Tears of the Clown" and even "Shadows of the Valley," all three by Steve, all ending in deaths, and deaths that are met with some degree of peace.

The Book of Souls ends with Iron Maiden's longest song ever, the eighteen-minute "Empire of the Clouds" coming completely and utterly from the mind of Bruce.

CHAPTER 23

"He was working on it for about a month on his own," Adrian told Rob Laing. "Every single day we'd be in the studio blasting out stuff, and he'd be in the soundproof glass booth playing piano, like Beethoven with his ear to the piano, concocting this masterpiece. I think he wrote every single note in it. We interpreted it and we did it in sections. Kevin and Bruce would be in the control room and say, 'That's too bluesy; can you make it a bit more classical sounding?' He recorded all the piano from start to finish, and then we played along to that. Then I think they put on all the orchestration afterwards. It's a bit of a story on its own, that one."

As Nicko told Tim Henderson, "With 'Empire,' I really worked with Bruce on the different dynamics and timing. I knew it was gonna be tough because it's a nine-beat groove—it's the SOS signal. Bruce was adamant that I do what I feel like, and I tried some massive triplet fills but it didn't need it. Now, when I listen back, I wish I had put some triplets in starting at the top and going all the way down the kit. I kinda second-guessed that, but when we were doing it, there is kind of a long section where there is an accent that goes from the top down, and I did one, but Bruce and I thought it was a bit too much—less is best.

"So, we really communicated together with that whole section. There is also a section in the middle where it's this sweeping arpeggio, which is meant to signal when the airships are coming out of the sky and realizing they were going down. They didn't know they were going to explode—hopefully not—but they did. So, we had to come up with a way to musically interpret grinding metal. I suggested we put some gongs in it and some voices, some orchestral parts, but they were muted in the background for effect. I love the way Kevin, Bruce, and Steve constructed these sounds. They put a military snare at the beginning of it. That song, out of any of them, is where I had a lot of input on how

Air Canada Centre, Toronto, Ontario, April 3, 2016. © *Trevor Shaikin*

we were going to interpret and drive the band through these parts. It was really a joy, because I had learned the story of the song prior to actually hearing the music. So, my input from the percussive side was easily 90 percent. I just went with it. We would listen back to the sections I recorded, and I would either speed it up where needed or ease up on the back end."

"What enabled the song to happen was winning a piano in a raffle about three years ago," Bruce told Steven Hyden. "So, I started playing it, or fooling around—'playing' is too strong a word. You come up with ideas, atmospheric ideas initially, because I couldn't really string more than a few notes together. I had ideas of trying to use it as an introduction to a song about air warfare in the First World War, which is obviously a very bloodthirsty and brutal affair. But at the same time, I started off using dawn patrols, where you get these moments of calmness. It wasn't modern blood in the trenches and the horrible mess of humanity. This is quite a civilized way of starting out your day, culminating in the most appalling violence, people being burned to death and just awful stuff."

Elsewhere Bruce has said that the song "Death and Glory" sort of took care of the World War I idea, and he decided to change the topic for this proposed epic to end all epics.

"So, I wanted to write a song and start off with a very atmospheric, beautiful, but kind of ominous storm," continued Bruce. "I just chipped away at it every day. Steve is working with everybody else on all the other tracks; I'll just hunker down and work on this every night. We'd finish in the studio about six o'clock, 6:30, and I'd stay till about nine or 9:30, just playing piano over and over and over again, trying to get the words down, and then the arrangement down, and then working on the little bits and links and things. That's how it was. It just came together, piece by piece by piece. Five-minute songs kind of write themselves because they are very simple. Intro, verse, bridge, chorus, verse, bridge, chorus, link bit, guitar solo, guitar solo—it's just a pretty simple concept. Ever since *Piece of Mind*, it's always been pretty straightforward. But the problem is because they're quite simple in that respect, it's also very easy to become formulaic. And after a period of time of knowing how to write a song like that, it's almost dishonest to do a bunch of songs like that. It's like shooting fish in a barrel."

Hyden breaches the topic of Bruce doing all this in the midst of a serious confrontation with his own mortality. "Oh yeah, absolutely," says Bruce. "I didn't go to the doctor for about six weeks until I finished the record." Asked how he coped, Bruce answered, "Oh, you know, like an ostrich. Head in sand, or head in backside, whichever you wanna choose. I thought maybe I should get this looked at, but until I get confirmation that this is something that's not very nice, just chill out and keep singing. I mean, I made a dramatic recovery, and bouncing around, everyone turns around and says, 'Wow, you look great.' Some of them look surprised and some of them look relieved, which is nice. But for me, the big thing is there's still some things that are healing up, and some of the systems are still coming back online, you know? Things like mucus membranes start to get back to work again; salivary glands come back and functioning normal, which is great. All this stuff is coming back. So, I'm just in the process now of getting those things back online. I'm running around, jumping around; everything else is working just fine for me now. I've got about three months now before I start getting into the window where I want to be singing two or three times a week to start gently bringing my voice back online, working it, working it, working it, because it still needs time to heal up internally."

CHAPTER 23

Air Canada Centre, Toronto, Ontario, April 3, 2016. © *Trevor Shaikin*

"Empire of the Clouds" is about the R101 airship disaster on October 5, 1930, in which a British airship, planned to be the world's biggest aircraft, crashed in France on its inaugural outing overseas (not its maiden voyage, but its first attempt at crossing the channel), killing forty-eight of its fifty-four passengers. As a talisman helping him write the story, Bruce had with him a tankard from the ship that said, "Welcome aboard from the airship crew," and a pocket watch from one of the survivors. The words "We're down, lads," reproduced in the lyrics, were said to have been the last thing the survivors heard from the crew as they leapt to the ground from the rear of the ship.

Explained Bruce at a spoken-word event in Montreal, "I had built the airship, the R101, when I was six or seven old, from one of the plastic kits. Maybe I was a bit older. No, I was pretty young when I built it. And the kit had the mast and everything else. In actual fact, the R101 was a sister ship. Don't know if you know this, but the R100 flew to Canada and back—successfully. And spent a whole week touring around Canada and had a mast built for it, for the Empire of the Clouds, at St-Hubert, just down the road."

At the close of the song, we get the line "Eight and forty souls, who came to die in France," and, more poignantly, two lines previous, "The empire of the clouds may rest in peace." Given that Bruce's very life was up in the air at this point, this could have been (and still could be) the last we hear from Bruce on an Iron Maiden studio album. As well, for the rest of the band, the weight of performing on the longest Iron Maiden song ever, and one written entirely by Bruce, as the last song on the record no less, could not have been lost on them, given Bruce's diagnosis.

As for how *The Book of Souls* did out there in the marketplace, indicative of Maiden's continued growing legendary status or entrenchment in the pop culture fabric, the record sold more copies in the UK and the US than its predecessor, *The Final Frontier*, and this in an era where all physical sales were on a relentless march into the crapper. The last stats had *The Final Frontier* cresting at 44,385 copies in the UK, with the new one selling over 60,000. In the US, first-week sales for the new one were 74,000 versus 63,000 for its predecessor. This marked the sixth time in a row that first-week sales for a Maiden record went up, again, against a tsunami of an industry trend away from physical product. Five months in, the album had notched 148,000 in sales, and one wonders if this had something to do with the packaging being the best of the band's long career. Chart positions were high, as was to be expected, but accolades from the establishment press were truly surprising, with *Classic Rock*, *Metal Hammer*, and *Loudwire* all calling the record the best of the year by anybody.

Wrote Jeremy Ulrey in his review of the album for *Metal Injection*, "Often it's more that time flies by so fast you didn't even realize that years had gone by since a certain event occurred. But the half-decade interim since Iron Maiden's last LP, 2010's *The Final Frontier*, has conversely seemed like a real eternity. It may be that *Final Frontier* 'didn't count' for many fans, as it received a wildly mixed reception, some praising its fidelity to the kind of long-form, epic songwriting that the band made their bones with in the 1980s, while others found it bloated and lacking in memorable hooks. And when the track listing for this year's *Book of Souls* was revealed, there were similarly equal amounts of anticipation and trepidation: did the band learn from the mistakes of the last album or, conversely, would they be able to build on its strengths? *The Book of Souls* offers a textbook example of how a band's previous album can effectively set fan's [sic] expectations for the follow-up before a single note of new music has been heard by the public."

CHAPTER 23

"Empire of the Clouds" picture disc. *Dave Wright archive*

After a smart and detailed track-by-track analysis, Ulrey ends with "It would be futile to itemize every single thing that's great about the album, but lest this sound like a critical fanboy ball-washing, let's end by coming back down to Earth a little bit. 'Empire of the Clouds' is certainly an ambitious way to close out *Book of Souls,* 18 minutes of cinematic grandeur that, with its heavy reliance on Dickinson's own piano playing, somewhat recalls old Emerson, Lake & Palmer crossed with the operatic sensibilities of Queen. But it's also symptomatic of a certain amount of unchecked bloat that occasionally permeates the album. 'If Eternity Should Fail,' while an overall great song, could have easily wrapped up two minutes earlier without losing anything of substance. Conversely, the title track actually concludes with a flurry of interesting ideas but takes its time leading up to them. And 'Empire of the Clouds,' which would have made a stellar song pared down to nine or ten minutes, sags a bit under its own weight at a full 18. It's the old *Lord of the Rings* ending where everyone keeps saying goodbye, but no one really wants to leave.

"But hey, that's the academic in me talking. By and large *The Book of Souls* looms over the Maiden catalogue like a cocky monolith, essentially daring us to posit our traditional favorites as superior to its heft and might. Whether it is entirely consistent enough to successfully contend against the leaner 1980s albums is debatable, but the fact that the band is even attempting something of this scope and accomplishment is a wonder to behold. There's been a lot of handwringing over whether any of the younger metal bands will ever be able to draw the kind of festival-headlining crowds that longer-in-the-tooth bands like Maiden and Judas Priest enjoy even in their senior years. Well, let those bands put forth an album of this weight and we'll talk."

Air Canada Centre, Toronto, Ontario, April 3, 2016. © Trevor Shaikin

From February 24 through March 8, 2016, the first leg of the *Book of Souls* tour takes in the US, Mexico, and Central America. Once again, Bruce is piloting Ed Force One, only now the band has upgraded to a Boeing 747-400 jumbo jet. Bruce had spent some time training for the occasion in late 2015, and in October of that year, performing as guest speaker at Aviation Week's MRO Europe Conference in London. The stated plan called for the jetting of 12 tons of equipment and personnel a total of 88,500 kilometers, covering thirty-five countries in six of seven continents.

"My goodness, it's great," reflected Nicko, speaking with Tim Henderson at the time. "But it's never been about mainstream thinking in Iron Maiden. It's always been our way. As we have progressed, and people look back on the career of Maiden, they are amazed that we have done this with very little press. We have become, dare I say it, a household name. I have met older people right here in this restaurant, ladies in their seventies and older, who say, 'You are the drummer for Iron Maiden! I love your restaurant. How many people are you playing for at your next show?' I answer, 'Oh, thank you, and 70,000 people in Chile next week.' So, it has become like that. It's being respected. We have always made the best records that we can, and I will quote Janick and say, 'If we ever become a parody of ourselves, then that's it.' I've quoted Jan on that because when he first said it, I thought it was very true. We'll never rest back on our laurels of past accomplishments. This album shows it. There is still life left in us old guys yet! Maybe the drummer is stringing along a bit, but he is still the best-looking bloke in the band [laughs]. The success of Iron Maiden is that we love to do what we do together. That really is the whole essence of it.

"You know, this band has always had class, panache, in whatever we do," continues McBrain. "Primarily, we are very selfish—we do what we want to do. We love to do this stuff together, the way we do it. We've been very, very blessed, in terms of our success and the way management works with us. It's not just us six guys; it's Rod and Andy and a bunch of other people behind the scenes. All the people in the office who take care of the press,

CHAPTER 23

our accountant, all back in London. All these people are part of the Iron Maiden family. I mean, you hear this said all the time, but this is something different—it really is. We may do things the way we want to do it, but it's done properly. We don't rip the fans off; we don't charge a ton of money for T-shirts. Sometimes we have to charge a few bob more because concessions take a chunk of that. So, yeah, we make a very good living from touring, because you certainly don't make money on albums anymore, at least not like you used to."

And that reference above to his restaurant? Well, this is Rock 'N Roll Ribs, Nicko's joint in Coral Springs, Florida, about thirty minutes outside Fort Lauderdale.

"Yeah, this restaurant, it's not just Maiden fans coming in," laughs Nicko. "There are a lot of people who come from all over the place. In fact, there was a family that just came in today from Brazil to listen to *Book of Souls*. The restaurant has the same principles that Iron Maiden was built on—from the people that I have working with me, all the way down to the cleanliness of the restaurant. I love ribs, and long story short, a chef friend of mine, who was one-third partner of this restaurant when we started, made these ribs for me one night, and they were the best ribs I have ever had in my life. He taught me how to make his BBQ sauce, and I made some variations of it. One day we were at my place cooking up some ribs, and I used my sauce. My friends were all over him how my sauce was better than his.

"So, we got talking, and someone suggested we open a rib joint called Rock 'N Roll Ribs, and it just stuck. This was all the way back in 2004. It took a few years to get things together, but here we are. With all my world touring with Iron Maiden, going to all these fine eating establishments, having good wine and good food, clean environment, not too pricey . . . it was born from all of these experiences. So, we started the restaurant and taught the chef how to make the sauce. We don't use molasses as it's too expensive; we use fructose. The signature dish is the baby backs. We smoke the ribs, chicken, and pulled pork. We also have a hamburger that is to die for. The french fries are hand-cut, blanched, not frozen—totally fresh. People just love it. We have our own potato salad, which is my recipe. We have been doing much better this year, and it continues to grow. I couldn't wish for a better crew working for me. People often ask me if I'm going to open another one. Yeah, I would like to, but my main focus right now is on *Book of Souls* and the tour."

Back to that tour, March 11 through 26, the second leg takes in South America, followed by two weeks in the US and Canada, at the close of which, on April 16, "Empire of the Clouds" is issued as a single for Record Store Day. It emerges as a 12-inch picture disc single, limited to 5,500 copies. April 20 through 26, the band plays two shows in Japan and two shows in China, followed by two shows in New Zealand and five shows in Australia over the course of April 29 to May 14. From May 18 to 21, the band plays Cape Town and Johannesburg in South Africa. May 27 through August 4 represents dates throughout Europe, most poignant for Bruce being the eastern European ones—Bruce is credited as the producer of *Scream for Me Sarajevo*, a documentary about his tour in that country, under siege in 1994. After seven months off, April 22 through May 28, 2017, the band does Europe once more, followed by two months back in Canada and the US.

Martin Popoff archive

Air Canada Centre, Toronto, Ontario, April 3, 2016.
© *Trevor Shaikin*

CHAPTER 23

I think it's important at this juncture that we check in with old Maiden kicking post Blaze Bayley. Why? Well, in what can only be described as a swift and remarkable career rehabilitation for the ex-Maiden man, the guy immediately dusted himself off and built for himself a catalog of high quality. In 2016, Bayley issued the more-than-well-regarded *Infinite Entanglement* record. And then on March 1, 2017, he suddenly had *Endure and Survive, Infinite Entanglement Part II*, an album equal in scope and execution to anything his other band had been up to.

To quote a piece I wrote at the time, Bayley made two records with Iron Maiden before getting sent back to the minors, a realm he travels with pride, in metal communion directly with his own fans, whom he addresses with military precision and a high level of respect that is mutual, if not returned tenfold. The vocals are legion, rich, and deep in experience, and the writing is of utmost quality, across eightish records of post–*Virtual XI* solo material—Bruce Dickinson, no slouch with the solo records himself, must surely be proud.

"What I'm able to do for the first time," Bayley told me, on the verge of his upcoming intensive month in Canada and the US, "is bring my own band with me, that I've played with on the *Infinite Entanglement* album and the new album, *Endure and Survive*. They've done four tours with me across Europe, and now this is the first chance I've been able to take them to the rest of the world. So, I'm very, very excited about that. We're all coming over, and it will be a set with a couple of my songs from the Maiden era, a Wolfsbane song and some of my solo stuff, but of course material from the two new albums, from *Infinite Entanglement* and this year's *Endure and Survive*. I'm very excited about it."

Essentially Blaze—in the tradition of Ritchie Blackmore swallowing up Elf back in 1975!—had absorbed a band called Absolva, and the synergy between the two solitudes produced a package of pure metal might between the eyes, but also o'er top, a sound that is very British, oddly, the mélange of musics across the two *Infinite Entanglement* installments sounding like a cross among Maiden, mainland power metal, and Skyclad.

"They were a support band once, years and years ago, and we got along and we kind of kept in touch," says Blaze. "And then Chris Appleton, the guitarist, I was doing my acoustic show, and he said, 'Well, if you ever want to do anything full metal, or do some writing . . .' And I got in the mood to do another full metal album, and we got together and wrote some songs and it started to work out. And then I wanted to do my greatest-hits tour, my *Soundtracks of My Life*, and then I had a *Silicon Messiah* anniversary tour that I wanted to do, and I rereleased *Silicon Messiah* on vinyl and CD and did a proper tour to go with it, and the guys did that.

"We just kind of built a rapport there," continued Blaze. "And the material that we came up with when we started writing the new album, *Infinite Entanglement*, I thought was really good, and I just wanted to keep it together after that. And it's worked really, really well. It's so nice to work with the same people. I've really enjoyed over the last few years working with a lot of different musicians, but it's nice to be in a situation where we're taking the same show everywhere in the world, all the places that we played. There's a real strength to that, because there's a kind of telepathy to what you do if you go long enough. And I think that's where the real, real emotions and the passion can come out. You're much less worried about getting things right and more focused on the performance of making it come to life."

As for the band's regal brand of conceptual music, so incredibly suitable to Bayley's Shakespearean voice and precise enunciation using that rich tool, Bayley figured, "It's just metal. Well, I don't even think of it as metal; to be honest, I think of it as music. It just comes out. I *am* metal. So, anything I do, it just turns out that way. It's not by choice. I make music and it turns out metal. So that's the classification if you want to put one—it's metal.

"And metal has the values of the traditional British heavy metal, of being a machine. Rock 'n' roll is maybe dead on the side of the road, choking on a sandwich and a bottle of Jack Daniels at age twenty-seven, but metal goes on forever, as a machine. And that's the difference, I suppose. Where[as] maybe the rock 'n' roll guys want to have a party at the end of each show and see what available women there are, in metal we are trying to perform each show to the absolute best of our ability and look forward to the next show. The reason that I do what I do is because I love to sing. And the most precious thing to me is to be able to sing well for fans that support me. I'm completely independent. There's no big record label. I am the record label: Blaze Bayley Recordings. I'm absolutely tiny, but every record that I make is my own, and they all belong to me. Everything I've done since Iron Maiden, apart from one thing, is all my own. So, I'm very, very lucky to be in the situation that I'm completely independent. And the reason that I'm able to do that is because I have the support of so many loyal fans in different parts of the world that preorder my albums and come and see me on tour. They make it possible for me to live my dream of being a professional heavy metal singer."

Further on his master plan, Blaze told me that "what I did was, I said, right, I want to do three albums, because this is a story that is in three parts. It is the beginning, the journey, and the conclusion. So, I want each one to come out on or around March 1. So, first of March 2016, first of March 2017, and first of March 2018. I am a working-class, ordinary person that is used to going to work, doing my work, and finishing my work. And I have very poor respect for people who say, 'Well, when I feel it's done, when I'm in the mood . . .' I don't like that. All the fun part, the inspiration, and the writing the songs, you've got to catch those moments, but making the album and getting it all together—that's work, and it's working hard and getting it done. And I am the record company, so I set my own deadlines. When you are on someone else's label, they tell you when your album can come out. It doesn't matter who you are. 'Well, sorry, your album can't come out that week because Elton John's releasing that week.' So given that I am Blaze Bayley Recordings, if I say it comes out on March 1, 2018, so it does."

True to his word, in 2018 we got *The Redemption of William Black – Infinite Entanglement Part III*, and then in 2019 there was *Live in France*, on both CD and DVD, followed by *Live in Czech* the following year. This is why Blaze deserves some space in this book. If you didn't know better (i.e., which was the legendary titan act of heavy metal and who was "working class"), you certainly wouldn't have been able to tell by the two bands' respective catalogs. Fact is, Blaze has been producing as much great music in the 2000s as has Maiden, and that's why we should care, even if we leave him now for the duration of the book.

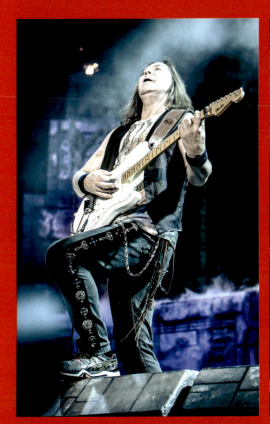

These four pages, Budweiser Stage, Toronto, Ontario, July 15, 2017. Supporting on the night was Ghost. © *Dave McDonald*

Chapter 23

In other Maiden front-man news, on October 19, 2017, HarperCollins publishes Bruce's memoirs, smartly titled, *What Does This Button Do?*, with a mischievous front cover to match.

"There're a lot of personal details that I deliberately didn't go into because I didn't want the book to turn into some sort of bizarre public therapy session," Bruce told *Revolver*'s J Bennett. "And also, because a lot of things to do with family—births, marriages, deaths—if you write about that stuff, you start impinging on a lot of other people's personal space that's not actually to do with you. Whilst it might be good for gossip magazines and things like that, it doesn't advance the narrative of the story."

Turns out Bruce wrote up 170,000 words' worth of stuff that got pared back to 105,000 words, and all of it longhand handwriting, rather than on computer, and even more amusing, a lot of it down the pub.

"Quite a bit of it, yeah. I'd just take my little notepad, go have a couple of beers, and write about 1,200 words at a time. I was giggling to myself as I was doing it. I wrote it on trains, on planes, in hotel rooms—and in pubs. The one place I hardly ever wrote it was at home. I find it very difficult to do any kind of work when I'm home. I do stuff everywhere else, but when I get home, I don't do anything."

Asked by Bennett if he thought Steve would read the book, Bruce says, "I don't know. I hope so. The thing with Steve and I is that we started out not quite understanding each other. But over the course of thirty years, we've just about got to an understanding [laughs]. I think it's the same with everyone in the band, which is why I liken it to being a band of brothers. I don't mean we're all united and fighting together on the same side and all that bollocks. Most brothers aren't like that. Most brothers fight like hell. If they're really brothers, the fact that they came out of the same organism is random. The organism that birthed us is Iron Maiden, and we've actually grown into each other's company over the years. We weren't joined at the hip, despite what press releases would have you believe."

And then, sadly, in our last bit of news about a former Iron Maiden front man, on October 29, 2017, Paul Di'Anno performs, singing from a wheelchair, "Wrathchild" and "Iron Maiden" during the encore of the show by female Iron Maiden tribute band the Iron Maidens. At this writing, Paul's health is quite grave, and his mobility severely limiting to his activity. If we are to remember the lovable rogue, it should be through his autobiography *The Beast*, which sure gives Bruce's a run for its money in terms of high entertainment.

Back on the big stage, on November 17, 2017, Iron Maiden issue *The Book of Souls: Live Chapter*. Produced by Steve and Tony Newton, this is the band's first live album since *Beast Over Hammersmith* not to have the hands of Kevin Shirley on it. True to Maiden's modus operandi, the package is a mammoth two-CD set that is the one place where you get to celebrate the band's most current songs, never to be heard from again, in many cases. In that spirit, we get "If Eternity Should Fail," "Speed of Light," "Death or Glory," "The Red and the Black," "The Great Unknown," and "The Book of Souls" before the boys take us out with four old hits along with, surprisingly, "Blood Brothers" from *Brave New World*.

Budweiser Stage, Toronto, Ontario, August 9, 2019. © Dave McDonald

Air Canada Centre, Toronto, Ontario, April 3, 2016. © *Martin Popoff*

Air Canada Centre, Toronto, Ontario, April 3, 2016. © *Trevor Shaikin*

In March 2018, Nicko, as a famous Jaguar auto enthusiast, following upon an XKR-S having been built to his specifications in 2012, has a Land Rover Classic Works customized Jaguar built for him. In the same year, McBrain launches a musical instrument store in Manchester called Drum One. From May 26 through to August 11, 2018, Iron Maiden conduct the first leg of their Legacy of the Beast tour. From July 18 through September 30, 2019, the Legacy of the Beast tour goes to North America, closing off with three dates in Mexico, all in Mexico City. From October 4 through 15, the band plays five dates in South America. These are the last shows that Iron Maiden would play in advance of the shutdown of concert touring worldwide due to the COVID-19 coronavirus epidemic. Support across the expanse of the Legacy of the Beast shows comes from the likes of Killswitch Engage, Sabaton, Gojira, Rhapsody of Fire, the Raven Age, Tremonti, and Fozzy.

Also in 2019, Bruce is declared an honorary citizen of Sarajevo, receiving the Sixth April Award for performing there under siege as a solo artist in 1994 and then making a documentary of the tour. Into the new year, Maiden helped us in our virus containment lockdown by delivering the booze: on March 7, 2020, we got Fear of the Dark, a 4.5 percent ABV English stout, and Trooper IPA, a 4.3 percent ABV India pale ale, followed on April 24 with Trooper Sun and Steel, a sake-infused brew.

At this point, Bruce and his kids were hit with some horrible news. Already divorced from his wife of twenty-nine years, Paddy Bowen, in November 2019, on May 18 of this year, it was reported that Paddy, mother of the couple's three children, Austin, Griffin, and Kia, was found dead at her home in Chiswick, North London. No cause of death was given, with Bruce saying that "this is a terrible tragedy which appears to be a tragic accident."

But the Maiden camp was ever optimistic about the future. Proclaimed Rod Smallwood in an update: "I hope you and your loved ones are staying safe and well, wherever you may be, and my continued thanks to you all for bearing with us so patiently. Due to the continuing health issues worldwide around COVID-19 we regretfully inform you that Iron Maiden will now not be playing any concerts until June 2021. However, we are now in a position to give you details of our touring plans in respect to those shows we had hoped to play this year.

"Firstly, we are very pleased to tell you that we've managed to reschedule all our European own shows on the Legacy of the Beast tour for June/July 2021 with the exception of Moscow, St. Petersburg, Weert, and Zurich, which unfortunately we have been unable to re-arrange in this period.

"To consolidate the tour routing, as you can see, we have added two further shows in Arnhem and Antwerp. We are in the process of inviting back all the Special Guests and supports who were due to play with us this year. Where any band is unable to commit to this due to their own rescheduling situations, we will look at finding other suitable acts of equivalent stature.

"Rearranging the headline festival dates has unfortunately not been possible. This is mainly because we already had an extremely busy year lined up for 2021 and, as I'm sure you can imagine, a great deal of forward planning has already gone on and there's only so much we can do within the timeline and logistics already in place. The band enjoy playing at festivals so please be assured we will get back to as many of these as we can at another time.

Budweiser Stage, Toronto, Ontario, August 9, 2019. © Dave McDonald

"In respect of what should have been the opening leg of the 2020 tour starting on May 1 in Perth, Australia, and visiting New Zealand, the Philippines, Japan, Dubai, and Israel, we are currently working on a possible return to as many of these countries as we can, in some guise, in the first half of 2022; more news on that will follow at the appropriate time. The band are all fine and send you guys their best wishes. They are very much looking forward to getting back on-stage next year and seeing you all, so, please, continue to take care of yourselves and stay *smart*."

But there was a wily omission in all that claptrap, because the internet was all abuzz with rumors that in utter secrecy, the band had in fact finished a new album. Again, that is something Rod didn't bother to tell us, crafty bugger. In fact, the clue, or slight slip, or whatever you want to call it . . . well, that came from Kevin Shirley!

As it turned out, due to the ongoing worldwide epidemic, the band wouldn't play live again all the way up to May 22, 2022. But fortunately for the fans, rumors of a new studio album proved true, and by that point the record was well in hand—six months young—and fully assimilated by the Maiden army, who were ready to rock again after two years of Eddieless lockdown.

Budweiser Stage, Toronto, Ontario, August 9, 2019. © *Dave McDonald*

This page and the following four:
Budweiser Stage, Toronto, Ontario,
August 9, 2019. © *Dave McDonald*

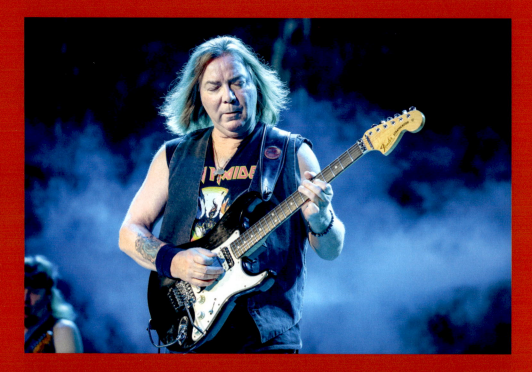

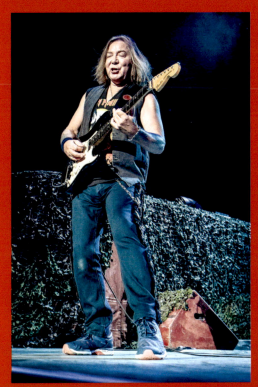

CHAPTER 23

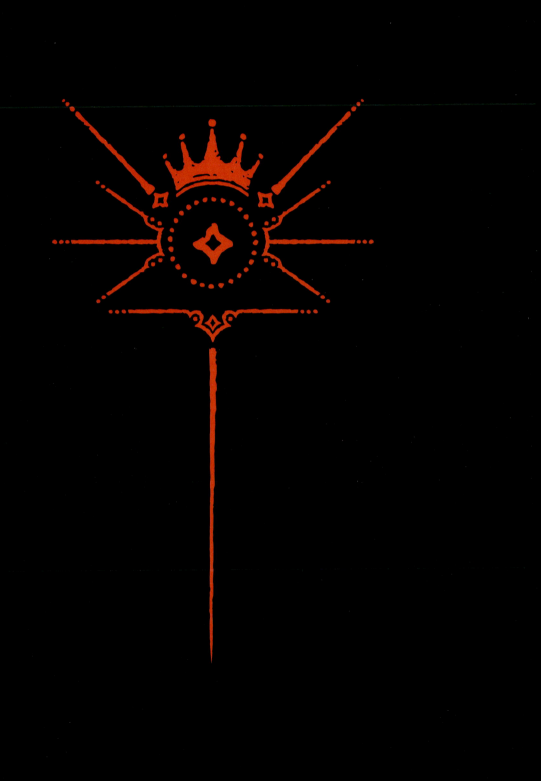

CHAPTER 24
Senjutsu

"I don't know if you know, but that song was over 12 minutes long."

On August 9, 2020, the Maiden guys found themselves grieving the loss of producer Martin Birch, who had done fully ten albums with the band and even gone exclusive with them for the back half of his career.

"Oh God, I love that man," begins Nicko, speaking with the author a year after we'd lost "the Headmaster" at the age of seventy-one. "I'll never forget the first time I first met Martin, when he was doing *Number of the Beast* and I went to the studio, and I met up with all the boys. And then when were rehearsing in Nassau, Martin came down to visit with us before he went over to the studio to get everything set up for us. He said to me, 'Right, dear boy, what is your favorite snare drum sound? What snare drum sound would you like me to get?' I went, 'That is easy. Alex Van Halen, please' [laughs]. And he turned around and went, 'Who?' [laughs]. He was joking, of course. Anyway, 'Who?' No, I love Alex's sound; that is my all-time favorite snare drum sound. 'So, if you can get my snare sounding like . . .' and I use a 402 Ludwig Super Classic, or Supraphonic. And so, I said, 'Get the snare drum that Alex uses, the Bonham snare.' Of course, you know, John Bonham is famous for that sound as well. But I was really, at that time, in love with Alex's snare. That was one great memory.

"And the other memories of Martin, with the drum sounds, were just, every time I would set that big kit of mine up in the studio, he went, 'Do you expect me to mic the lot of those drums up? Can you get rid of a couple of them for me?' [laughs]. I'm like, 'No! You've got all those widdly knobs in there. You get on with it.' Oh, we had so much fun. He was one of a kind. And sorely missed. Because he basically had retired after all the Purple stuff he did and all the other bands that he worked with. He kind of came back out for us, and he stayed with us for many years, doing those records for us.

"One nice story I'll just tell you very briefly," continues Nicko. "We were recording the backtracks for *Somewhere in Time*, the last album we did in Nassau, of the three. And we went out . . . we used to go to this club called Club Waterloo, which is still there, in the Bahamas, in Nassau. What we used to do is, we had this custom. We'd do the first track and then we'd go out to celebrate. We start up at the Traveller's Rest and we end up at the Waterloo till five or six in the morning. Nine times out of ten we wouldn't work the next day because we were all so hung over. But this particular night [laughs], I think we'd finished five tracks off the record, and we went, 'Well, that's half an album—let's go celebrate.'

"So, we're in the Waterloo club one night, and we're getting ready to go home, and our techs and stuff are driving us. None of us were driving. Although we did a couple of times. We go, 'Where's Martin?' So, we sent a search party out for him, to look for him, because this bar was outdoors and there was a big lake and lovely places to sit and look at the moonlight, on the lake, whatever [laughs]. So Martin is standing . . . I think he had a G&T

or whatever he had in his hand, talking to a tree. Having a full conversation, I might add, with the tree. And we said, 'Martin, you're boring the life out of it. We've got to go home.' He didn't want to leave. He had this whole conversation going with the tree. Beautiful. So that sums up some of the crazy stuff we used to get up to back in the 1980s."

Equally crazy, on November 30, 2020, Adrian Smith became a published author, issuing *Monsters of River Rock: My Life as Iron Maiden's Compulsive Angler*, all 304 pages of it, through BMG Books.

As Smith explained to Jimmy Kay, "It's primarily a fishing book. But it's not overly technical. A lot of these stories, a lot of fishing stories and what happened around the fishing, traveling to and from the fishing, sometimes the fishing and the music literally crossed lines. Like when Maiden were doing the *Powerslave* album in Bahamas, at Compass Point Studios. I always take my fishing rod wherever I go, so I had some time off. I was fishing outside the studio, in the Caribbean. I cast out and I got tangled up with another line—it turned out to be Robert Palmer, you know, from 'Addicted to Love,' that guy. Who comes running out of his balcony and told me off [laughs]. The book's full of stories like that. And then of course he was there when I was in the studio recording the solo to 'Powerslave.' So, all these things happen on my travels. When I actually got the book, the physical copy, I was surprised there was so much music content in there. I would say it's 30 percent private stuff about me personal, and then music stories, stories about how we wrote certain songs, situations we found ourselves in in the studio, as well as fishing and travel stories, of course. But that's it, really. I've got good feedback from people who actually aren't anglers, but having said that, there are a couple of hard-core—for want of a better word—chapters about fishing for the hard-core fishermen."

As for why he took up fishing, Adrian notes that "as I said in the beginning in the book, there's a Billy Connolly quote: 'Fishing is meditation.' So in other words, you're concentrating so much on the fishing, you forget everything else. And that's the idea—it *is* relaxing. It empties your mind. Fishing is meditation with a punch line. You know, you've got the excitement of occasionally catching a good fish. I do fishing to kind of get away and clear my mind, really, from work."

Specifically concerning Canada, much of Adrian's experience is out west, Kamloops, British Columbia, for example. However, Steve has family in Quebec, from his wife's side. "I've done a lot of fishing in the Montreal area, in the St. Lawrence, and I've done a little bit of fishing in Toronto. Last time we played down in Toronto, I think it's the Molson Amphitheatre, the lake there, I went out for a sound check, and after the sound check I took my rod and wandered along the bank. There were fans everywhere, but I ended up . . . I had sort of a UV mask that I pulled up, and I just went fishing in among the fans, and they didn't know who I was."

Jimmy also asked Adrian about legendary guitar master Eddie Van Halen, who had passed on October 6, just shortly before their interview. "Very sad, very sad," reflected Smith. "I mean, probably him and Jimi Hendrix, certainly in my lifetime, had the biggest effect on the electric guitar. I loved his playing, although when he came out, I'd already been playing five or six years. If I'd been starting out when I heard him, I would've just stopped, like 99 percent of the other guitarists did [laughs]. But yeah, he was fantastic. I would've loved to have met him. I came close a couple of times, but I never met him. And I love his guitar sound. If I've got a guitar and an amp and I'm just trying to get a sound, I would probably use him as a reference point."

Scotiabank Centre, Toronto, Ontario, October 11, 2022. © Dave McDonald

On March 26, 2021, Adrian added a new duo album to his canon, issuing *Smith/Kotzen*, featuring his collaboration with funky, bluesy guitar wizard Richie Kotzen. "Richie and I started working together a couple of years ago," explains Smith. "We'd been jamming, as we'd been friends for a few years before that. We both share a love for classic rock and bluesy rock, so we decided to get together and start writing some songs, and it went from there. Pretty much everything on the album is handled between Richie and myself, including the production. We had developed a really strong idea of how we wanted it to sound, and I'm very pleased with how it turned out. There's a lot of cool songs on there that we are really happy with."

"We had a very fluid process in writing," notes Kotzen. "Sometimes Adrian would send me a riff, and I would immediately hear some kind of melody or a vocal idea. And sometimes it was the other way 'round, so it was a kind of circular motion. We'd get together whenever we could and throw some ideas around and it just evolved, which was great because there was no pressure and nothing other than just a natural course, and I think the record really speaks for that."

But surprise, surprise, smack in the middle of the coronavirus pandemic, Maiden are busying themselves with what would become their seventeenth album, *Senjutsu*, which roughly translates to "tactics and strategies." The band would be back again at Guillaume Tell in Paris, with Kevin Shirley dialing in the sounds, rough, wild, and analog in outcome even if technology is unapologetically a huge part of the process. "We ended up jumping in with Kevin in 2000 on *Brave New World*, and I don't agree with some of the critics I see about Kevin's sound. Kevin is a genius—he's brilliant. There's no question about it. For proof there's *A Matter of Life and Death*—listen to that album."

The process was loose, even by Maiden standards. The boys arrived with a few ideas but would often find themselves playing pinball while Steve locked himself away and wrote another song. The tape was constantly rolling, with the songs being captured on the fly. In the middle of the proceedings, Bruce tore his Achilles tendon, requiring him to finish the project in pain and in a big plastic healing boot while propped up on crutches. This was all with a tour looming once the cake was baked. The boot phase was followed by two weeks of rehab and then learning to walk again.

"We chose to record at Guillaume Tell Studio in France again as the place has such a relaxed vibe," notes Steve, in an official statement. "The setup there is perfect for our needs; the building used to be a cinema and has a really high ceiling so there's a great acoustic sound. We recorded this album in the same way we did *The Book of Souls* in that we'd write a song, rehearse it, and then put it down together straightaway while it was all fresh in our minds. There's some very complex songs on this album, which took a lot of hard work to get them exactly as we wanted them to sound, so the process was at times very challenging, but Kevin is great at capturing the essence of the band, and I think it was worth the effort!"

Added Bruce, "We're all really excited about this album. We recorded it back in early 2019 during a break in the Legacy tour, so we could maximize our touring yet still have a long setup period before release to prepare great album art and something special as a video. Of course, the pandemic delayed things more—so much for the best-laid plans—or should that be 'strategies'?! The songs are very varied, and some of them are quite long. There's also one or two songs which sound pretty different to our usual style, and I think Maiden fans will be surprised—in a good way, I hope!"

"The album was recorded in 2019," explains Adrian, in an official posting. "We were excited about it. We wanted to get it out to the fans. You know, we all enjoyed being in Paris. The studio's familiar territory. We worked there before. We did two albums there. It's got a nice big live room that we can set up and play live, like we like to. And it's just convenient and comfortable, you know, to start working there. I really enjoy it, actually. We holed up in one of my favorite hotels, go there and have a swim every morning, keep fit. Got my music gear in the room, got my ProTools. I can record, I can practice and do what I like, no distractions. And you can go to the studio, come home, it's great. There's great restaurants in Paris and there's plenty to do. I can go fishing if I want, get a bottle of wine, got my lakes there, absolutely love it.

"But of course, the priority is the album," continues Smith. "It came together pretty easily. We didn't rehearse before we went into the studio. We haven't done that on the last couple of albums—we go straight in the studio. I mean, I had quite a lot of stuff prepared, in demo form, fairly advanced demos, from start to finish. About four songs, as well as a ton of other ideas. Steve brought in stuff; you know, he'd have something on an iPhone or something, just an idea that he wanted to expand, so we'd work on that. So, we'd go in in the morning, work on what we were looking to record on that day, and by the end of the day we had something. Some of Steve's songs, the longer songs, we did in parts. We never actually played the song the whole way through. But some of the shorter ones, like 'Writing on the Wall' and 'Days of Future Past,' we managed to do them pretty much together. Yeah, the album's got several different slight departures musically."

The cover art for *Senjutsu*, issued on September 3, 2021, features what is arguably the greatest Eddie of all time, elegantly brought to life by the legendary Mark Wilkinson, back again after doing *The Book of Souls* (but not *The Final Frontier*). Wilkinson was

Limited-edition CD issue. *Dave Wright archive*

careful not to load Eddie up with too many layers or make use of a traditional samurai helmet, which would have covered too much of Eddie's battle-scared visage and the war-paint motif the illustrator imagined for our hero.

"One thing that really makes me excited about this album," figures McBrain, "is the imagery, Eddie. You've got *Senjutsu* Eddie, and on the inner sleeve, you know, Eddie the archer. And you've got a nasty-looking Eddie on the back of the cover, who kinda frightens me. It's almost as bad as the *Book of Souls* Eddie, the one we had with all the teeth and stuff—very evil looking. But the imagery just lends itself to all that Japanese culture and of course samurais. Look here, got one on my arm, huh? I've got a samurai, and he's a Yakuza samurai. He's got tattoos on his tattoos. But yeah, I love it, I love it. And I think that inspired Steve. Maybe it's that first track that made him think about that, the concept of senjutsu."

On the subject of Eddie's travels and travails throughout the years, Adrian Smith has arrived at a philosophical place. "I could see the good things about it. I mean at first, we had these monsters running onstage and banging into you when you're trying to play. Our manager used to take us around to radio stations in the early days, in America and in Canada, and he used to wear like an Eddie mask and go in and start growling at everybody. I'd be like, oh my God. But people remembered it. They remember you. No matter what you do, it always comes back to the music. You can attract as much attention as you like; if the music's not good, then it's not gonna happen. But luckily, people liked our music too. But Eddie has definitely attracted attention over the years, and that's what you gotta have. We're just musicians. We like to just get up and play our music, record, and then sort of stay out of the spotlight. So, Eddie enables us to do that. He's on the album covers and people are interested in him. So that suits me fine, these days."

"But yeah, it's very interesting," continues Nicko. "Because, you know, when Steve first came up with the lyrics on the tune, I think he was thinking about Sun Tzu's *The Art of War*. But it means inner . . . I take it to mean inner strength and tactics. So, it kind of lends itself either way. There's various ways you can translate that. But it suits us because we do write songs about war and the futility of war. And not political, by the way. I don't think we've ever been a political band and we never will be. But yeah, I think it sums it up."

The album opens with a swirling, tribal title track clocking in at over eight minutes, music by Adrian, lyrics by Steve. "Senjutsu" is like a war dance, a call to arms. Parts are kept to a sensible minimum, and Nicko's crashing and bashing is pretty much continuous, as Bruce brings Celtic melody come chorus time.

Explains Smith, "I was inspired by those amazing Japanese drums, the Kodo drums. You see the guys, whole groups of them playing these amazing drum patterns. I just thought that'd be a really dramatic way to start a song. So, I just kind of dreamed it up on my ProTools, digital sort of recording. And then the music just kind of flowed. The whole thing sounded very epic, very atmospheric. So, I played it to Steve, and he suggested the title and making it about maybe a city under siege—it was conflict; it was drama. We actually put that down off my demo, and Nicko played along with it on his own, and then we put the rest of the stuff on it. That's how that was recorded. But it turned out great. I think that's gonna be a good live song."

As Bruce told *Kerrang!*'s Nick Ruskell, "I looked at the lyrics and I thought, 'This sounds like someone's been binge-watching *Game of Thrones*!' There's northern people coming down from the grasslands, there's a wall, and they've got to protect the wall at all costs. I said, 'Are you talking about the Great Wall of China here? In which case we're mixing our metaphors a lot.' And Steve went, 'No, not the Great Wall of China. It's just a wall.' It doesn't matter, really—it's a good story, and a great vocal to sing on."

"Well, it features primarily the best-looking bloke in the band—come on!," chuckles Nicko. "It kicks off and the first thing you hear is a massive like, boom, you know, and all this tinkly-winkly fairy stuff going on behind it. The idea when he wrote the tune, I visualized the Japanese Kodo drums. They're kind of like our marching bands going into battle with the snare drummer and a flute and fife. The Japanese lads would have these big, massive Kodo drums. So that was where it originated. And they had this rhythm for it, which developed into the whole opening rhythm track. It's a fantastic album opener because it's totally different for Maiden. I don't recall us ever having a track like that. I love the melodies within the tune.

"The actual framework rhythm doesn't change very much," continues Nicko, again, indeed surprising, given the song's duration. "There's slightly different bass drum parts that go in there and triplet fills and stuff, but it's a cracking opener. And I was very surprised when I heard that track when Steve sent me a copy three months ago, because I hadn't heard it in over two years. Can you imagine that being the first song opening live?! With the whole massive, big drum feel? Oh, I should get up front with the Kodo drums. No, I think it's a brilliant album opener."

Nicko's on to something there, and he runs with it. "Yeah, I don't think I can do . . . I thought about this. I talked to 'Arry about it months ago, 'Oh, it'd be nice to have a Kodo.' And he goes, 'Yeah, it would be cool.' But maybe Bruce could do it. Because if I did it, I would have to do it behind my drum set, up on the riser, if we did that, right? But I've got to go from the boom boom boom, because it's one, two, two, and three. So, I couldn't get the third one, because the guitar starts going [sings it]. A little bit of a shaky time. Unless I did the whole thing with the drum set at the front of the stage. Who knows, boys and girls? My drum company wouldn't like that, because I'd have to have two sets of drums, one up on the front and one up on the back [laughs]."

Total Guitar calls "Stratego" "one of the more succinct offerings, using the same power chord to minor sixth shifts heard on some of the group's classic 1980s material," with Janick telling the magazine's Amit Sharma, "I wrote a lot of the music for this one, and Steve brought his melodies in. It's a basic rock 'n' roll track with some extra creativity thrown in." Adds Adrian, "That power chord to minor sixth shift is very dark sounding and always very effective. It sets up a mood and away you go! It defines the sound of the song, with that element of discordance to it."

The track features a tight gallop from Nicko and Steve with gorgeous succinct fills from McBrain, across the song's five-minute duration. Only Janick solos, for thirty seconds, with Gers turning in a disorienting but elegant piece of sculpted music. Steve specifically mentions the art of war in this one, but the imagery is left abstract. Still, a theme is building. "Stratego" was issued as the album's second single, released two weeks in advance of the album.

Issued as the first single was "The Writing on the Wall," fully a month and a half before the album, breaking the internet, as they say. The song has been called everything from heavy southern rock to classic rock. Comparisons were made to Bon Jovi's "Wanted Dead or Alive," but also noticed were additional Celtic vibes as well as the keyboards.

"Some people say it sounds a bit country," adds Adrian. "No, I don't think that. I think it sounds maybe a bit folky when you think old English folk music. Maybe when it went to America, it got translated into country. And you add that little bit of blues to that. It's sort of a concoction of styles. But there's a flavor to it. I would say it's more folk based, 'Writing on the Wall.'"

As for the song's penning, "Usually I have the idea of a song musically pretty much start to finish. Maybe I'll have a title. 'Writing on the Wall,' I had the title. I wasn't familiar with the story of 'Writing on the Wall.' It's a common expression, you know, 'The writing's on the wall.' Something's gonna happen, usually bad, you know. But I played the song to Bruce, he liked it, and I said, 'What about "Writing on the Wall" as a title?' And he said, 'Yeah, we can do Belshazzar's Feast.' And I said, 'What's that?' So he had the whole story of that. So we managed to incorporate that in the lyrics, which was great, you know, really made the song."

'Writing on the Wall' actually wasn't that easy to record, although it's a simple song. We kept doing it, and for some reason it wasn't sounding great. We had a break, and I went outside and walked around the streets of Paris, just praying we could get this song right. Because I thought it'd be good if we could get it down. But we just couldn't get it. It was something to do with the intonation on the guitars, because the way the chords go, it's very simple, but it has to be . . . it has to ring, and it has to resonate. And we just couldn't get it. But went back, we had a break, took a deep breath, came back, and we knocked it out, so it came out really well and it ended up being the first single."

Dave and Janick solo on "The Writing on the Wall," but between them is Adrian, taking a stretch. "As far as playing solos, when I first joined the band, I used to work my solos out," notes Smith. "I didn't quite have the confidence to just kind of let go. I'm a bit more spontaneous these days. We started off doing the solos, and I would be out in the control room and Kevin and Steve would be producing what I'm doing. And we did it all like that. I did feel like I was under a bit too much pressure, though, and perhaps want to go with something I wasn't happy with. I was too close to it. So, I said to them, 'Look, I'm going to go off and do them all on my own.' So, I went upstairs and there's another studio upstairs. And I know how to work recording gear, so I just did my solos again. And I think we ended up mostly using what I did the first time around. It's amazing—perspective is a great thing. It's very difficult to retain your perspective when you're that close to recording. But 'Writing on the Wall,' yeah, a few people have commented on that. I think that's the first time I've ever done a solo of that length on a Maiden album. When normally Jan, Dave, and I would do sixteen bars and that's it. That's all we've ever done. At least I'm pretty sure that's all I've ever done. So thought, well, I'm gonna write myself a nice solo. It must've been my birthday or something. I thought I'd write, you know, do a thirty-two-bar solo, which was a bit of a challenge. But you know, something different. I try to do something different on every album."

As Bruce told *Kerrang!* regarding the highly narrative animated production video, the band wanted "something epic that people would not expect us to do, because we haven't done a video that's worth talking about for a long time. I said to Rod, 'Have you seen the video for "Deutschland" by Rammstein?' That, to me, is a groundbreaking video. That's astonishing. Now, I'm not suggesting we do that, because we're not Rammstein. But think of what we could do that would have the equivalent impact for us. So, I wrote a storyboard for the vid, tweaked it a little bit, and gave it a happy ending. Well, kind of

Scotiabank Centre, Toronto, Ontario, October 11, 2022. © Dave McDonald

a happy ending—Adam and Eve start again, but with Eddie going, 'I'll still get you in the end.'" Mark Andrews and Andrew Gordon, former Pixar folks, were enlisted to take the idea to fruition, and the result is a visual that adds a whole new layer to the song, in fact flipping the script and making the Maiden song something analogous to soundtrack music, easier done when there's not much metal dynamism.

"Lost in a Lost World"—9:31 and credited to Steve alone—starts with lush acoustic guitars, keyboard washes, and fancy backing vocals. Things crank up at the two-minute mark, and there are enough spaces in Nicko's chunky rhythm where one can rest and ponder the production palette of *Senjutsu*. It's a funny debate. Everything sounds crisp and vibrant, but there's also something old-school about it. There's nothing to complain about, and yet, many Maiden fans continue to complain. Actually, there's one thing to complain about: those shrill, high, piercing keyboard tones. But other than that, one has to surmise that if Maiden went for a flash modern Andy Sneap Judas Priest / Accept / Saxon sound, we'd be complaining that things are too machine-like and perfect.

"Oh, I gave him $30 before I left, to make sure I'm up in front," cracks Nicko, asked to characterize what Kevin Shirley brought to the project. "Yeah, he was a cheap night out that night. Well, the one thing I love about the whole of this album is sonically, each track is different. It's got a different EQ, it's got a little bit different compression on the snare drum, and it's got a little bit different sounds to the bass. Some of the guitar solos are brighter; some are not. Not because they're not mixed, but because it's mixed within the song. It's not just everything goes up. To reiterate, there's the mix for 'Senjutsu.' Right? Let's do 'Stratego' next. And it's not, 'We'll just leave everything there and maybe just pull the solo up and put Bruce's vocal harmonies higher.' It's not like that. Every track had its own place, in terms of sonically. And I think Kevin is just . . . and Steve because Steve comixed it with Kevin. I can't just sum it up. I think the performances, from all my bandmates, are like superb. They're just magic. Steve's bass playing . . . I mean, I'm blessed to still be able to do what I do with this band and be their drummer, but they have all excelled themselves absolutely. And of course Kevin has put the old man up there nice in the mix, and I love it. I think the drums sound fantastic. Certainly, if I had a criticism, some of the cymbal sounds are a little bit too compressed. They don't sing enough. They fade a little bit quick. But that's only my thing. And that's not all the tracks. That's just in a couple of places. So sonically, yeah, he's done me an A+, without a doubt. He's made me sound really good [laughs]."

Next on disc 1 of this double-CD journey is "Days of Future Past," with music by Adrian and lyrics by Bruce, reflecting Bruce's ol' solo career back in action. At 4:03, it's the album's shortest track, and unrelated to that, it's the personal fave of this writer, passionate of melody, sung soaring by Bruce, half-time chorus grooved deep by Nicko. There's but twenty seconds of soloing, by Adrian, slow then rapid-fire but musical and resolving.

Recalls Adrian, "'Days of Future Past,' now, that title was in my head, because I had the music to the song. Gotta do this song. It's a great title for a song. So, it was nagging me. Moody Blues did an album called *Days of Future Passed*, but they spelled 'passed' PASSED, whereas ours is PAST, so we didn't worry too much about that. Again, I just came to Bruce and said, 'I've got this idea for a . . . I've got the music and I've got the title; where do we go from there?' So, he made it about somebody wandering the earth, somebody who is immortal, and the ups and downs of being immortal [laughs]. Usually, I approach Bruce with the music and maybe a few melody ideas or a title or something, just to spark him off.

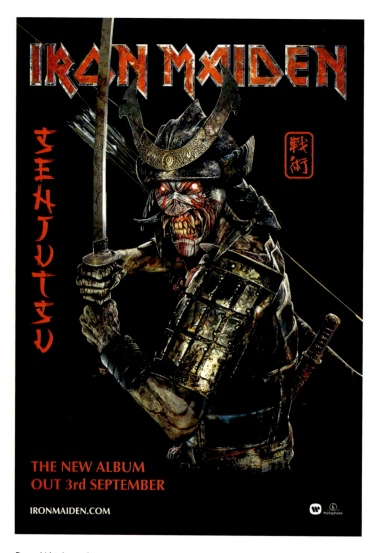

Dave Wright archive

"'Days of Future Past' is a bit more of a modern take. It's probably the shortest song on the album. There's some longer pieces, like I said, very intricate. You know, the fans of all the Maiden epics will be happy with that, I'm sure. So, there's a few different styles on the album. It's very dramatic. I don't see why this wouldn't translate really well. You know, certainly as an album, sonically, I think it's one of the best things we've done. I'm really happy with the mix. I was knocked out. I didn't listen to it for a long time, and I listened to it a few months ago and it was absolutely fantastic. I think it will be great in the live situation."

Commented Adrian to *Total Guitar*, "The riff that comes in at 30 seconds feels very fresh and youthful. It uses the E position on the seventh fret and then you use one finger to play a C bass note, then down to the A. It's almost a Spanish flamenco thing if you play it on acoustic with a bossa nova rhythm, but then you plug into a Marshall and play it differently, it sounds like a rock song! I like that E chord with the movement underneath."

Closing disc 1 is "The Time Machine," which opens with one of the band's much-maligned dreary, mellow intros, featuring vocals, clean arpeggiated guitar, bass, and Nicko tinkling. Then we're into a creative and proggy verse section, sophisticated of chord change and vocal melody. Later we have a soulful chorus section and a typical Celtic-tinged Maiden gallop.

"It's a good question," ponders McBrain, asked to contrast the lyrical styles of Dickinson and Harris, with Steve writing this one to music by Janick. "They both have the same kind of moral issues, with what they both tend to write about. There's some lyrics that Steve writes where you go, 'Well, what's he on about?,' but in most of Steve's lyrics, there are stories within the lyrics. Bruce is very surreal in some of the things that he writes. But the two of them, they're on the same page. But, you know, Steve would be on page 9 and Bruce would be on page 10. When I say the same page, that's what I mean—they're on each side [laughs], facing pages. So yeah, it's really interesting. And this is the nice thing, because when Steve writes a song and he writes all the words, you know you're going to get a story. But Bruce, like with 'Writing on the Wall,' for instance, what's that about? What's he mean? What's going on? Whereas with Harry, I think you'll find you get what's on the can."

All three guitarists solo on "The Time Machine," first Adrian, then Dave, and then the penner of the track, Janick, with Adrian playing aggressively over a thorny, geometric structure but Dave and Janick playing melodically over sympathetic happy chords.

"Janick has definitely got a certain flavor to his playing," figures Nicko. "Then you've got Davey Murray, who is like, he's got these arpeggios he plays which are just totally little trills, and quick-offs that he plays. He's unique. There's no one else who can do it like Dave Murray. He has a very, very special feel to his solos. Now, he's very close to Janick, whereas Adrian, in the middle, on the other hand, has a completely different way of approaching his solo. He has more of a melodic style of playing within the song structure. What I mean by that is he plays melodies across his solo.

"Janick has this kind of flair where it's a bit more frantic, but when you listen to it and you analyze it back and he's precise. He's a Ritchie Blackmore; he's the Ritchie Blackmore soloist in the band. That's his favorite guitar player. Plus, he does his slinging the guitar around his neck and slinging it up in the air and whatnot. So, you have these three different characters of players. I mean, 'Writing on the Wall' is a classic example. That's Dave Murray at his bluesy, wonderful best, pulling a little Paul Kossoff there, a little bit of Gary Moore; there's these wonderful influences that Davey has playing that solo. It's very, very moving. And then you get the Adrian solo, after the little middle eight section, and Adrian's got that melody. You know when Adrian plays a solo, he's got a structure. It's kind of like a rhythm guitar player playing the solo. That's the only way I can make sense of that. And then you've got Jan, who flies off and does these incredible, quick, trilly things, you know, loads of trills. Sometimes people think he's messy. Sometimes live he is. Sometimes live I am [laughs]. But when you listen to the work on the album—stunning. But when Jan writes with Steve, we're off, we go running off. It's like, 'What comes next after the eighteenth bar? What meter are we going to?'"

Disc 2 begins with "Darkest Hour," pretty much a straight-up Maiden ballad, a vehicle for soloing from all three guys and powerful vocals from Bruce, past sixty at the time of recording. "My second-favorite song on the album, funnily enough," says Nicko, "and that's also related to war. 'Time Machine' to a certain degree, also 'Death of the Celts.'

Janick ponders his next move. Scotiabank Centre, Toronto, Ontario, October 11, 2022. © *Dave McDonald*

Samurai Eddie looks on in approval. Scotiabank Centre, Toronto, Ontario, October 11, 2022. © *Dave McDonald*

There's all these flavors. 'Darkest Hour' is the best ballad Bruce has ever written, with Adrian. And when Janick rings in, it's kind of 'Dance of Death.' It's got these beautiful little motifs that Janick has written into that song at the end on the chorus."

Explains Adrian, "Again, I had the music. It was a ballad idea, a very kind of atmospheric ballad. I mean, Bruce does those songs great. And again, I had a title, 'Darkest Hour.' And I had that for years. I've always wanted to do a so-called Darkest Hour. It just so happened that year, the Winston Churchill film came out. So, I told Bruce I had the idea, played him the music, and told him the title, and then Bruce went from there and finished the lyrics and the melodies on that."

Then we're into this remarkable trio of long songs to end this long album, each of them written by Steve and Steve alone. Asked why Steve tends to write this way these days, Nicko figures, "Because, really, they're compositions. Any piece of music is a composition, if you like, but he writes a story within the music. Now people go, 'Why does it always have to have a slow intro? And then that same outro and then another slow bit?' It's telling the story with the music. You know, when we do the songs, we finish them and we go sit in the studio, in the control room with Kevin, and we listen. We're critiquing; everyone is critiquing each other's work, which is beautiful. The last few albums, that's what we do. We sit in the studio, and we go, 'Steve, is that bass line right?' Or I missed the bass drum part or the snare whack and it's not right. So, you critique each other. We listen to the track and go, 'That's brilliant, but can we maybe find a second verse? The first part of the second verse wasn't as good as it could've been?' Right?

"And Kevin will sit around and go, 'Here, I don't know if you know, but that song was over twelve minutes long.' And we're like, 'No, can't be!' You know, you're hearing a song, and the clock doesn't lie. And he points to the timer on the desk, and we're like, 'So what? It's twelve minutes frickin' long! Why are you telling us? What does that got to do with anything?' The thing is Steve, when he writes a piece of music, he has a complete sketch in his mind of where it's going with all these different lovely different harmonies. Plus, we've got . . . he is very considerate of three guitar players in the band. And he writes for one solo from that man, one from that man, and one from that man. And maybe if it's that good, he'll go one from that, no, that's going to two, that's going to two, and that's going to two, and he'll pick and swap. And as they're doing their solos, the track is building. And it's a beautiful way . . . I love the way Steve composes. I don't think he's an earthling. I think he's from another world. Because he comes up with these insane melodies and he's just a genius, absolutely."

"Death of the Celts" indeed begins with a long, quiet intro as promised, over two minutes of it, before swirling into view in 3/4 time. More musical passages unfold and unfurl in 3/4 and then there's a punctuation mark, after which we're into a hammering Maiden gallop in regular 4/4, featuring cheery Celtic scale climbing, like Celtic knot work. There's another brand-new musical motif, featuring prominent keyboard washes, after which the 3/4 feel finally returns, but only mellow and moody like the intro, a bookending with the same music.

Next is "The Parchment" at almost thirteen minutes, although it gets going after a mere minute of intro. Once again there's pervasive keyboards—Steve is the only credited keyboardist on the album—again in a sort of shrill high zone, albeit delicate in the mix.

Remarks Nicko, "Any time Steve comes in with a song, I go, 'Oh shit, what now?' [laughs]. 'What time are we going to be playing in halfway through the song?' No, I love

Scotiabank Centre, Toronto, Ontario, October 11, 2022. © Dave McDonald

Scotiabank Centre, Toronto, Ontario, October 11, 2022. © Dave McDonald

it. Steve is the challenge. I always get super excited when Steve goes, 'I've got a song I've written on me own.' And I go, right, I know it's going to be epic. Because those songs Steve writes primarily on his own are always, always very structured, with beautiful melodies and parts. When he came up with 'The Parchment,' I thought, oh my, that reminds me of 'The Red and the Black,' where we've got all these different guitar motif lines of melody and then you've got another one, and you've got eight bars of that and sixteen bars of that and then three solos—stunning, absolutely stunning. But pretty much you've got '1, 2, 3, 4; all right, see you at the end' throughout. Pretty straight, not too difficult of a song."

"This one has that Egyptian feel to it," Janick told *Total Guitar*. "With Maiden, we love the imagery that comes through the music. We can take people places, and that's the great thing about music and playing guitar. You think about what you're playing and how you can transport the listener. That's something magical."

Indeed, there are two important points made there: "The Parchment" is definitely heavy on the Egyptian or Moroccan tonalities, and it's also surprisingly straightforward, all soberly midpaced and 4/4, save for a double-time rave-up near the end. For sure, this one ascribes to Nicko's description of Steve paying tribute to his guitar army, with fully five solo sections.

Closing out *Senjutsu*—eighty-two minutes, so not egregious, albeit only ten songs—is "Hell on Earth," at eleven minutes plus. This is an up-tempo Celtic Maiden romp, a sprightly gallop, featuring an amusing slight slow-down for the solo section at the six-minute mark and additional surprises as the song progresses stridently to conclusion.

"This is such a thematic end to the album," notes Janick, "with so much power. It's very cinematic, and I love how all the guitars interact with each other. It's heavy, but it has so much soul to it. It's an album we can be proud of. I can't sit here and tell you this is the best album we've ever done. That would be stupid. But I'm very proud of it—as proud as I am of any Maiden album."

Scotiabank Centre, Toronto, Ontario, October 11, 2022. © Dave McDonald

Scotiabank Centre, Toronto, Ontario, October 11, 2022. © Dave McDonald

"It's about the shit state of the Earth," Bruce told *Kerrang!* "It's almost nostalgic for something other than the situation we find ourselves in right now. It was all written pre-COVID and lockdown and everything else, but seeing the way the world is going, how things are depersonalised and trivialized. There's now so much choice; you don't know what to do with yourself."

Commenting on the stacking of three long Steve Harris solo compositions at the end, Nicko told me, "You know, you could say, 'Why isn't "Senjutsu" the closing track?' And I think the way that Kevin and Bruce . . . Bruce was there towards the very end. Kevin was also submixing us as we were playing the tracks. Normally what we used to do is we used to record the tracks, put all the songs together, then you take the master tracks and go into the studio in a mixing suite. But Kevin, since *Brave New World*, was mixing as he goes. And he's kind of gotten very good at that. So, I think what happens is, when you sit back and look at all your tracks, you leave them one after another and you go, 'How shall we structure the album? What should we open with? What should we have in the middle?'

"It's not like doing a gig, where you go, 'Opening, well, bam, thank you ma'am, fast song straight up, whatever, bring it a bit down for the new set and then crack it up for the end.' But the album, I think they'd come up with it because it felt right. Those songs in the running order felt right. One thing I think I'd like to mention before you cut me off—I'm going on yapping too long—if you think about it, 'Hell on Earth,' right? It's the close of the album. Terrific track. And I think it's probably one of the only tracks—or the only album—where we had a track fade out on the very last track of an album. I may be wrong. If I am, boys and girls, send your answers on a postcard and then I'll throw it in a bin.

"But you know, you've got a structure. It could've been a list. There's no rhyme or reason behind the fact that, yeah, people say, well, Steve wrote the last three songs and put them on the album. No, it's not that. It's just that that was, you know, 'Death of the Celts' is followed by 'The Parchment,' which is out of the three, the longest song, but it's got more melody. It's got a slower pace. It's not a high-tempoed song. And then you've got 'Hell on Earth.' It makes sense—those three songs work well together."

It would be pointless to go over the dozens of reviews of the album, the dozens of chart positions, and the sales figures across dozens of countries surrounding *Senjutsu* (one notable bright spot concerning the latter would be silver status in the UK, for physical sales of 60,000 copies). Fact is that everybody with a platform talked about it, and as with every Maiden album, opinions started high and polite and then quietly were revised downward over time. After absorption, *Senjutsu* is as hotly debated as brilliant all the way down to crap in lockstep with any of the band's recent albums, most notably *The Final Frontier* and *The Book of Souls*. After all is said and done, consensus has it that *Brave New World* and *A Matter of Life and Death* represent the best Maiden's brought in the 2000s, although this writer would go with *A Matter of Life and Death* and *The Final Frontier*.

Before touring in support of *Senjutsu* commenced, Bruce put himself out there on another one of his spoken-work campaigns. Billed as An Evening with Bruce Dickinson, the tour began January 17, 2022, in Ft. Lauderdale, Florida, and ended March 30 in Kitchener, Ontario, Canada.

Scotiabank Centre, Toronto, Ontario, October 11, 2022. © Dave McDonald

Bruce rockin' the man bun. Scotiabank Centre, Toronto, Ontario, October 11, 2022. © Dave McDonald

In Montreal, Dickinson gave an insightful answer as to why he quit Maiden back in 1993. "Wow, nearly twenty years ago," reflected the Air Raid Siren. "Shit, there you go; how time flies when you're having fun. Well, honestly, I was just as surprised as everybody else. And I don't think people really believed that at the time. But you know, you just have to have a change-around in your life sometimes. And I just thought that if I stayed with Maiden forever, all I would learn about was what was life like within Maiden. And in order to learn about what it was like outside Maiden, you have to leave. Because unless you left, nobody would take anything you did seriously. It would always be like, 'Oh, bless him, he's doing a solo record. It's not very important, really. Let him have his fun, and then he can go back to being in Maiden.' I hated that, right? So, I thought, well, fuck it, I'll just leave. And then what happens if your career doesn't work out? Well, that's God or fate saying, maybe that's the best. Maybe better that you do that now and do something else with your life than just sit there in some weird fantasy world and end up just grumpy in the end."

He also divulged some info on the machinations behind a follow-up to *The Tyranny of Souls*. "It's only been fourteen years since the last solo album—fourteen years. So problem is, when I did the last chunk of writing for the solo album, that was before the *Book of Souls* tour, obviously. So that was 2015, 2014, or something. And then 2015 we made the album. In 2016, I had throat cancer. In 2017 we played catch-up for all the shit we didn't have a chance to do before. And then 2018, '19, this stupid old pandemic decided to fuck everybody up. There was nothing you could do there. So, the idea was, the solo album should've been done like four or five years ago. But it wasn't for obvious reasons. So now we are revisiting it. And so now when I get done with these spoken-word shows, I'm going back to LA and we're going to work on it for three weeks, and then I'm going to be working with Maiden, and Roy is going to be working with the instrumental parts. So eventually, hopefully, this year or early next year we should have it finished. When it's going to come out, that's another question."

Scotiabank Centre, Toronto, Ontario, October 11, 2022. © Dave McDonald

Y'know, possibly the best Eddie yet. © Dave McDonald

"Next year, mate," was Nicko's promise in the fall of 2021, on the subject of putting Maiden back on the road. "We still owe Legacy part 3, which was canceled due to unpopular demand [laughs]. We all know why. But we're scheduled to go out next June. So, I'm looking forward to that. I know that all the guys are absolute chomping at the bit. But we're going to make it next year."

True to McBrain's word, Maiden fired up the machine again on May 22, 2022, performing in Croatia, two and a half years after their last prepandemic show in Santiago, Chile. Shows opened with "Senjutsu," "Stratego," and "The Writing on the Wall" before transitioning over to the hits. Somewhat surprisingly, two lengthy Blaze-era songs, "Sign of the Cross" and "The Clansman," were part of the festivities. Supporting on the tour most regularly were Airbourne, Within Temptation, and Lord of the Lost. Also warming up the Maiden faithful on occasion were the Hellacopters, Sabaton, Shinedown, Powerwolf, Avatar, Mastodon, and Trivium.

Into 2023, Rod and the guys put together what they were calling the Future Past World tour. Featured most heavily were the new album, *Senjutsu*, and 1986's *Somewhere in Time*, with most of the internet chatter revolving around "Alexander the Great" getting played for the first time.

...

There's an incredible optimism around the band at this juncture, since their legend seems to grow and grow each year without limit. Bruce's cancer scare aside—touch wood (I literally did that)—the guys are all healthy and athletic, as is to be expected by the rabid throngs long spoiled at having witnessed for decades the most vigorously delivered shows across all of heavy metal history. Whether it continues this way—and whether we see an eighteenth Iron Maiden studio album—is still somewhere off in the future past, caught somewhere in time. For now, the band continues to gulp at the fountain of youth, and by all accounts, that energy has transferred to the band's headbanging minions, with each and every member of the crowd effusive and inspired that Iron Maiden still lives.

This page and the following two, © Dave McDonald

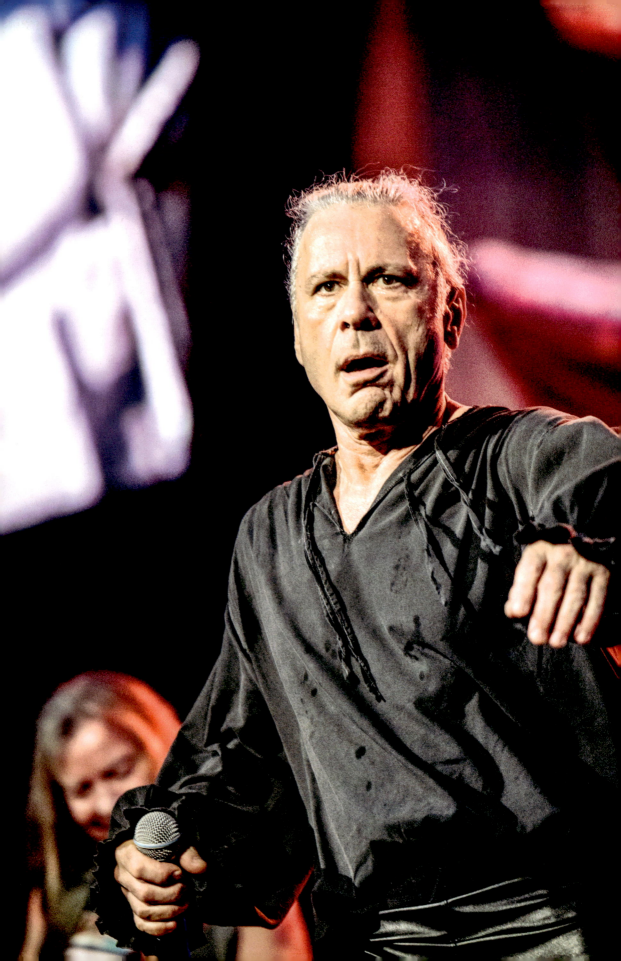

EPILOGUE

As we went to press with this book, Bruce Dickinson surprised the heavy metal world with a new solo album called *The Mandrake Project*, complete with comic book tie-in and tour. The occasion turned out to be a boisterous and blessed way to finish this weighty tome, because, in this writer's opinion anyway, it's the very best record of the Bruce canon, eclipsing even *The Chemical Wedding*.

To be sure, the majority of the Bruce Dickinson solo catalogue is beloved by Maiden fans, but *The Chemical Wedding* has always held a special place. And yet *The Mandrake Project* seems to shake the shackles of a signature albeit detectably "youthful" heavy metal sound that is shared by *The Chemical Wedding*, the record before it, *Accident of Birth*, and the one after it, *Tyranny of Souls*.

"I think you can definitely hear some links and a continuation," counters Bruce, in conversation with the author, two months prior to the release date of *The Mandrake Project*, namely March 1, 2024. "I would say that this album starts as if *Tyranny of Souls* and then *The Chemical Wedding* met one dark night and had a love child—that's this album. But we started on this record and seven years went by, from when we first started writing the songs to when we got back together after COVID and all the other weird stuff that went on. So, the love child had grown up. And the first thing we did, Roy Z and myself, was write two brand-new songs, which actually open the record. And what that did is that gave us a new lease on life to look at all the other songs again. Now the other stuff didn't feel stale. It was like, okay, we're going to reinvent the songs that we already invented once already, but let's look at them with fresh eyes and fresh ears and see where we go with it."

There's a sense that *The Mandrake Project* is more universal in comparison to the rest of the canon, through texture, through conservative production, through recurring and surprising steps away from the heavy metal rulebook. In essence, it feels like the work of a mature artist confident and comfortable with his memories of his favorite hard rock—and even progressive rock—records from the '70s and '80s.

"Yeah, in the good sense of the word, this is like a grownup record," agrees Bruce. "It's like metal for grownups because it has such an emotional range. And this is the most number of Bruce songs that have ever been on one of my solo records. For example, 'Resurrection Men' and 'Fingers in the Wounds,' those are songs where all the melodic bits, as in, you know, the verse, the chorus, the opening riff—I wrote all of that. And 'Mistress of Mercy,' that was all written on a Drop D acoustic."

What Bruce is referring to there is the fact that since the second album, he's essentially been collaborating on the writing of the songs with crucial solo band guitarist and producer Roy Z. The distinction he's making is that he's generated much of the music this time, writing on guitar and piano.

"It's all a continuous progression," offers Z. "We keep going and we keep growing. I agree with what you are saying. The music reflects our ages, I suppose, even though Bruce is ten years older than me. But it's a constant progression of moving into other realms of things that we like. There are also a lot of 'firsts.' It's the first time that Bruce is playing guitar. It's the first time that Bruce is playing percussion. Of course, he's written all the lyrics, although I came up with a couple titles. I'd say about 80% of it was done in 2012; most of this, or the foundation, was written and recorded back then. We went and did drums over at Signature Sound in San Diego, where we like to do our drums these days. And we ended up using only ten tracks. There are other tracks that were left off, which are also really good and hopefully those will see the light of day. But yeah, there's actually one track on there called 'Sonata (Immortal Beloved)' that started in 2002."

Regarding the production of the album, Roy explains that, "Oddly enough, it's all in there. I used the same tools that I used before, on, say *Chemical* and *Tyranny*, but I used them in a different way. Production-wise, I wanted to keep our brand and sound. I didn't want to take the caramel out of the Coca Cola, if you know what I mean. I wanted to make sure we had our sound and so that's always there. The odd thing is this is the first time that I was the only bass player on the record. And that was only because Bruce really liked my bass playing, and said, 'Just keep that bass, please.' And I'm like, 'No problem, Bruce.' But my main philosophy for production is to make the artist's vision happen."

"All of that really," answers Roy, asked about watching Bruce write music. "I would have my musical bits, but there will be times where he'd just grab a guitar or a keyboard and just go for it. And I love that, just being spontaneous and being able to do stuff like that with Bruce. For some reason, our Creator gave us the ability to do that together without trying. I'm not exactly sure when Bruce picked up a guitar, because since I've known him, he's had a guitar. The keyboard thing was a new thing at that time, in 2012."

It must have taken patience having such a strident and accomplished record sit mostly done for a dozen years with no pay-off. "Well, it's no secret he's the lead singer in one of the biggest hard rock/heavy metal bands of all time," shrugs Z. "And so, we constantly had to work around those schedules. And also, we had COVID, the whole pandemic thing, right? And that slowed us in our tracks. But here we are and I'm speaking to you, Martin [laughs]."

Asked about if 2012 means 2012, or if in fact the sessions were spread over time in bits and pieces, Roy says, "No, 2012 was really concentrated, and then, as I say, unfortunately our plans got derailed a bit. I was really looking forward to having Uli Jon Roth play with us because he was keen on being on the album back in 2012. And so, he said, 'Leave some space for me.' You know, that's Uli. And then I left some space. That's why there's not that much guitar on there, to be honest. But then I filled in what was needed."

The album begins with "Afterglow of Ragnarok," issued as the album's first advance single back on November 30, 2023. Befitting of its title, it's got a triumphant almost Viking metal riff at the verse, but the chorus brings an element of anthemic stadium rock hook-making that persists throughout the album, strengthening the songs. An elaborate, acted video was crafter for the song, and the heft inside of the lyric ("A story written by Bruce Dickinson & Tony Lee") reminds us that the album is being extended into the comic book domain.

Bruce frames the song as being "growly and very heavy, with a very dense kind of sound," with Roy adding that, "it's one of the last two songs that made this record, along with 'Many Doors to Hell.' I just felt that we were missing those elements, and so those were kind of like my babies, and then Bruce took over and did the words and melodies and stuff. It was just a gut feeling that we needed those two extra, newer songs. Because we were covering so much other ground on the other songs, as a producer, I just wanted to give it a fresh coat of paint. 'Afterglow of Ragnarok' was, to me, a nod to the *Chemical Wedding* sound, because I'm using the same tunings and a lot of the same sounds that I used on that record. I thought that was needed. I have my bag or my bucket of tricks and sounds that I use exclusively for the Bruce solo situation, and I thought some of that was missing."

"Many Doors to Hell" continues the world-beating musicality heard on the chorus of the first song, with Dickinson sounding relaxed and mainstream, nothing to prove, comfortable in his skin. Muses Bruce, "Yes, I mean, 'Many Doors' I loved because it was like, hey man, this is like a conventional, Scorpions-y song with a big chorus and everything. And I thought, man, that's fun, because that's gonna be the only song on the record like that."

"Rain on the Graves" instantly took this writer back to Deep Purple song "Vincent Price" and indeed Bruce's own Ian Gillan parody track "Confeos." This one also got advance single and full-on production video treatment, being released to the world on January 24, 2024.

"'Confeos,' yeah, we had fun with that," chuckles Bruce. "But with 'Rain on the Graves,' I thought, okay, what are we doing in this song? Answer is, we're channeling a bit of Robert Johnson, a bit of like a really dirtied-up Fleetwood Mac, and with my tongue firmly in my cheek, I'm going okay, we're gonna raise the ghost of Screaming Lord Sutch—here we go. You know, with that big crazy organ chord in the middle of it."

"Now, the chorus to 'Rain on the Graves,' not the melody, but I scribbled those words down in a churchyard, looking at the grave of William Wordsworth. It was pissing down with rain, and I was at his granite tombstone. It's this weird place in the Lake District where he lived and wrote his poems and I remember thinking about the melancholy of it all. What does he think underneath? Maybe he's gonna get up one day. They have like a cage over his grave. Is that to keep him in or is that to keep us out? And I wrote down, 'There is rain on the graves.' And that was it. I thought, I don't know what I'm gonna do with that. One day I'll use it. That was like 2003 or 2004."

"When Roy and I were writing what turned into that song, it just started out as, 'Hey Z, why don't we try something like an early Fleetwood Mac vibe?' I say early; I'm talking like 'Green Manalishi,' 'Oh Well,' that sort of stuff, the Peter Green stuff. And I said, 'But let's twist it; we're gonna heavy it up.' But more in a kind of rock 'n' roll way, not in a heavy metal way. And I'd gotten this idea of, you know, maybe we revisit the Crossroads, with the devil."

"So he came up with this heavy riff," continues Bruce, "and you could see the 'Green Manalishi' influence there. And then I said, well, let's just go real simple, just straight in with the vocal. And I thought, what would happen if I sang a tiny bit like, let's say, Johnny Cash? It doesn't sound like Johnny Cash at all, but in my mind, I'm thinking that. It's not the big operatic stuff. I'm gonna meet the devil in a graveyard and the devil is gonna say stuff to me. And he's gonna say, 'What are you doing here? And don't lie because I'll know.'"

"So, I wrote the first bits of a verse and sang that and we thought we had a really cool little vibe. Where do we go for the chorus? And I said, 'Okay, Z, what's gonna sound really good is a big chorus chord.' And we got the right key and the right note and that's what came out: 'There is rain on the grave!' and set to the same tempo. And it just works.

I was like, 'Z, I do believe we've got something here.' And then when Mistheria came in and did the keyboards, he just put in this crazy, discordant chord and I was like, 'That's genius!' Because that is straight back to Screaming Lord Sutch getting out of his coffin, you know, in the '60s, that kind of sound."

Adds Roy, "'Rain on the Graves' was Bruce's idea, and we just ran with it. It was like our version of 'The Devil Went Down to Georgia' meets 'Thriller.' Bruce and I have a lot of things in common musically, but another thing we have in common is the Hammer Horror stuff. I grew up being a fan of that and so did he and so there's a bit of that in the video and the song as well."

"Resurrection Men" is one of the creative highlights on the album, featuring soaring vocals and an obtuse vocal melody at the verse. But it's the stunning Ennio Morricone-type intro that really raises eyebrows, serving as a metaphor for this record's ambitions.

"That's me playing the Dick Dale surf guitar," laughs Bruce. "I wrote the song up until the crazy stoner Geezer Butler bass bit—that's all Roy. But the first bit of it, the verse and the chorus and the intro, I did. And then I found the tremolo button. I went, 'Hey, whoa, this is cool!' I said, 'Look, if Quentin Tarantino was gonna do an intro to this song, it might sound like this.' And I played that sort of spaghetti western intro and then said, 'And now we have to put bongos on it.'"

On this one, we see the influence on Bruce of the English novelist, occult philosopher, and comic book legend Alan Moore.

"As far as I'm concerned, Alan Moore… is the guy a genius? Yeah, probably. Is he out of his mind? Yeah, probably. But most geniuses are. *Watchmen* is just such a monster book. I've read it half a dozen times now, and every time I read it, I'm like, oh, I didn't see that before. So, my intention when I did the comic was always to aspire to something dark and, eventually, a little bit philosophical like that. Because you've still got to have a great story, you've still got to entertain people, you've still got to have the great art to go with it."

"But yeah, that was the intention. And that changed, because in 2014, the comic was one episode, which was almost just a promotional item: that going to be the idea. But it was going to be an excuse for some stories within the album. Fast-forward seven years, in lock down, I'd been twiddling my thumbs and coming up with crazy ideas. And the comic had grown and grown and grown until eventually I went, you know what, I really don't need to limit what I write musically to fit the straitjacket. I've got this story, and it can live on its own. It's got links with the album. So, for example, 'Resurrection Men,' you go, 'Oh, who the hell are the resurrection men?' Well, the answer is they're Dr. Acropolis and Professor Lazarus because it's what they do. They take people at the point of death, and they bottle their soul and then bring it back. So, they are the resurrection men. And there are a few nods in there to Hawkwind as well, in some of the lyrics to 'Resurrection Men.' But I can't give it away because there's gonna be an episode two. But yes, there are some subtle links to Hawkwind within the comic story."

Asked if he'd ever consider novelizing the comic book, Bruce says, "No, I would never do that. I mean, that's the whole point about comics is you can do things with comics that you can't do the same way in a novel. I would write the novel in a completely different way to the way I've written the comic. The thing with a novel is, often you're going down a timeline. A novel tends to be more linear, but a comic is freed from that. You can have the flashbacks and you can also have absolutely out-there, crazy changes of scene, changes of world, changes of dimension. I mean, look at Alan Moore and

EPILOGUE

Watchmen. You know, one minute you're in Manhattan; next minute you're on Mars. And you go, 'Yeah, that's cool; that makes sense.' I mean, it's just a different medium."

"Fingers in the Wounds" is arguably one of the most Goth rock songs Bruce has ever done. But in its distance from heavy metal, and in its piano plunking and keyboard textures, it's another one that contributes to the argument that Bruce is creating a major late-in-life statement here.

As Dickinson explains, "All the songs were written on acoustic guitar or a keyboard and then transferred. The riff to 'Fingers in the Wounds' was written on my crummy little keyboard at home, the verse and all the rest of it. And then I said to Z, 'This is the riff, this is the verse, blah, blah, blah, stick it on guitar.' And then when Mistheria came in with the keyboards I said, 'Now, can you do big, almost Europe-style keyboards, big washes of keyboards? Yeah, come on!' I've never done that on a record before and it wops you in the face, that song. Wow! And then we go into Moroccan roll territory, with that 'Kashmir'-like break in the middle, which people just go, 'What?!' [laughs]. I love that we do that on this record and surprise people, ambush them with music—it's great."

Asked if there's a Van der Graaf Generator vibe ebbing and flowing across this song and the wider album, Bruce says, "Sure, well, Peter Hammill is a huge childhood influence. I've always wanted to do an album of covers of all my weird influences. And update those artists' versions with my take and our modern band. I mean, there are several Van der Graaf songs that I would love to cover."

Commenting on the preponderance of keyboards on this song, Roy says, "That's the element that Mistheria brings in. We'll suggest things to him, but I kid you not, he'll give us a hundred tracks of him just doing different things. And then it's up to us to decipher what's gonna go in there and what's not. This is on the masters. We send him a stereo track of the master and then he sends us, I don't know, 50, 80, 100 different things [laughs]. And we have to go through it, really. This happened for *Tyranny of Souls* too; we had to do the same thing. He sends more than enough. So, it's up to Bruce and I to sift through it and say, 'Okay, this is what I feel we need in this bit, this is what I feel you should do in this bit.' And we go back and forth until we both kind of agree. At the end of the day, like I say, my job is to make the artist's vision happen. And if my artist is happy, then I'm happy."

"But yeah, I've been working with Mistheria since 2002," continues Z, "and he's just a brilliant musician and composer. And just over-the-top; I mean, anything you can imagine to be done on a keyboard—and then some—he can do it. He plays the keytar as well, and he can play it like Yngwie Malmsteen if he wants to. You know, he can make it sound like a guitar. But the atmosphere that he brings every time was essential, really, to giving *The Mandrake Project* that extra dimension."

Next is "Eternity Has Failed," which is in fact the original version of the song adopted and adapted for Iron Maiden as "If Eternity Should Fail," featured prominently as the opening track on 2015's *The Book of Souls*. "It was written in 2012, originally, for this album," points out Roy. "And then I guess Bruce played it for the office and played it for Steve and they decided to do a reverse 'Bring Your Daughter to the Slaughter'-type move [laughs]. Because we did it first, you know? And yeah, our version is our version and Maiden's version is their version."

As soon as "Mistress of Mercy" kicks in, the knowing Bruce fan is instantly taken back to the opening track on *Accident of Birth*. This is a combative, no-nonsense alternative metal raver, although, yet again, the clouds part for the chorus.

EPILOGUE

Notes Roy, "I remember Bruce saying, 'Hey Z, we need a little bit of this.' And he goes, 'You remember when we had the song "Freak?"' And he goes, 'Well, I've got one,' and then he just started riffing out. And also, the middle bit, I said, 'Hey, let's throw a little bit of Argent in there,' you know? We're both fans of Argent."

Drummer Dave Moreno gets to shine on this one, bashing away, loading this hefty song up with groove.

"For sure; Dave is our foundation," explains Z. "He's our rock. He plays like a lot of my favorite drummers, and I think some of Bruce's favorite drummers. I've known Dave since he was like 13 years old, which is a long time. But you hear John Bonham and Cozy Powell in him, the drummers that we feel we needed for this record; he was there for us, He can play Latin, he can do anything. He's well educated on the drums. But we actually did pre-production with him. Bruce and I literally went through every drum hit before we went to the big studio to record and that was cool to do that. Because I had never done that with Bruce before, where we worked with the drummer together and went in and literally broke down every bit on the drums that we needed for each composition. And we're happy that we did because the end result is what it is. I'm really proud to say that we did not use any drum replacement or drum samples. That's all real drums. And I'm so glad Bruce and I did that with Dave. I'm so fortunate that I have a musical partner that has an open mind."

So, in terms of beats, licks, fills and other percussion decisions, the ideas at the drum end are… "a combination of all three of us. Bruce can hold his own on the drum kit—I've jammed with him!"

"Face in the Mirror" is the closest thing to a traditional ballad on the album, although typical of Bruce's tenor and tone, it's dark and moody, epic, and very English.

"Sure, but what even is a ballad?" counters Dickinson. "I guess it's just a song without a loud bit. Okay, 'Face in the Mirror' is kind of folky, but folky and not as hokey, if you like [laughs]. It's certainly not a cheerful song. It's a melancholy song about alcoholism. And there but for the grace of God go all of us, you know? You could say 'Tears of the Dragon,' yeah, okay, that's what you might describe as a ballad. 'Gypsy Road' on the first album, *Tattooed Millionaire*, yeah, that's just straightforward. 'Gypsy Road' is like, 'What territory are we in here?' 'You're in Jon Bon Jovi town!' But of course, everything on this album is removed miles away from that."

And check out that guitar solo! "Yeah, I played guitar on that song. Roy actually kept my one-finger guitar solo on it. So that's me playing the one-finger guitar solo. Maybe I used two; I can't remember."

"That's a first," reiterates Roy. "That was cool because I pushed him. He didn't want to do it. And I'm like, 'Come on, no, this is your solo record, man. Let's do stuff that you've never done before. So, here's the guitar. Let's go for it.' And he was upset. He was upset at me. But now, as they say in England, he's chuffed because he can hear himself do a guitar solo on one of his records. I back him on the bass, and it was just a lot of fun. And he did it in one take. It's interesting for somebody that doesn't play guitar all the time for them to do a solo, especially as a singer, because he was singing through the guitar, and I really like that—he's vocalizing on that solo. It's a nicely composed solo and it's fresh; it's not like somebody on YouTube, learning how to play guitar."

And the surprises across the terrain of *The Mandrake Project* continue. In isolation, "Shadow of the Gods" isn't a particularly out-of-character Bruce Dickinson composition. But sequenced here second to last, it contributes to the idea that the back half of the album is uncommonly quiet, again, Bruce breaking the template for what we expect from one of his typically headbanging records.

"Again, is it a ballad?" questions Bruce. "Well, it starts out and you think it might be that, but then it turns into something else. And oh, then it turns into something else. And then at the end it's like the kitchen sink: choruses and everything and layers and choirs. The songs are all quite different."

"'Shadow of the Gods' was one of my babies," adds Z. "It's sort of my homage to Brian May, really."

Still, on a Bruce Dickinson solo record, a song like this can't help but becoming a vocal showcase, and in that light, I asked Roy what it was like to record Bruce, in contrast to Rob Halford, who Roy has produced many times as well.

"To be honest, there's quite a difference but a similarity at the same time," begins Z. "They both come from working-class backgrounds in England and so they're both hard workers; they really work on their craft. They're both equally talented as singers, but of course unique. one to the other. And I'm glad that they're friends. Because that helped me a lot when I worked with Rob. Rob trusted me to work with him because I'd worked with Bruce and vice versa."

"But I have some funny Rob stories," adds Z, "where I would come up with some vocal ideas, which I don't do with Bruce at all. Whereas Rob, he'd be like, 'Just go for one.' 'What are you talking about?!' 'Like, just go for one,' and I'd sing into the mic. He's like, 'Oh, I love that, Z. Keep that, but put that on the left side and put me on the right side.' We'd have that kind of thing and go through lyrics together and stuff."

"Whereas with Bruce, I don't really get involved on his melodies, for the most part, not really. I might come up with some titles, like 'Shadow of the Gods' or 'Sonata (Immortal Beloved),' but for the most part, he's writing all the bits that he wants to have. Whereas with Rob, Rob wants that extra, because he's used to working with Ken and Glenn. He's used to that trio, which is a whole different dynamic. I was blessed enough to do a Priest record; what an experience, to do *Angel of Retribution* and to really watch those guys in action. I was like, wow, I'm getting a masterclass here, on the chemistry of Judas Priest."

As for the hours these guys keep, Roy says, "Mornings. They're both morning people. Again, those working-class values. You want to get cracking no later than 11 in the morning, ten, sometimes earlier. We would be done by five or six every day with Bruce. And I like that, because then you can go have supper with your family and have family time."

The Mandrake Project closes with "Sonata (Immortal Beloved)," another long and hypnotic song, steeped in English sounds, again, almost Gothic, as in generations past and even, somewhat, in the spirit of Goth rock. To reiterate, there's a bravery and freshness to the idea and choice that fully the last 21 minute of this remarkable album are quite pensive.

"I really liked my slide work on there," ventures Roy, asked for his favorite guitar bits across the album. "I mean, I like everything that was done on there, but 'Sonata,' the last solo, was really difficult for me, and Bruce really helped me through that. I had a broken finger on my right hand, and my whole arm would swell up and that took a lot of effort and a lot of work. To get through that was tremendous for me because I was starting to… not doubt myself but feel a little bit inept by my physical state, not being able to play. I mean, look at this finger (shows me his hand); the finger is still broken [laughs]. But just to get through that moment with Bruce's help meant a lot."

EPILOGUE

The first thing that Dickinson thinks about when asked about this strident, ten-minute epic is how not particularly produced it is.

"Well, yes, key for me is that technical perfection is overrated, and emotional impact is everything. Roy and I record everything and although we call some song a demo—'Yeah, we're gonna do a demo'—there's nothing there that can't go straight on the real thing if it's good enough or if it's authentic enough or real enough, if it's a moment in time that you really can't repeat again."

"So, the last song, 'Sonata,' is like 25 years old. One evening, Roy went in, and for the hell of it, without any project in mind, without going in specifically to write a song, he was just inspired to write, riffing around Beethoven's 'Moonlight Sonata' after going to see the movie, *Immortal Beloved*. So, he stayed up all night, put together this ten-minute thing that was basically an ambient wash of things. He played it to me later and said, 'What do you think? You know, I don't know what you'd do with it. Is it cool?' And I went, 'Yeah! But it's not the sort of stuff that we we've done in the past. I'm not sure where it goes, what to do with it. But screw it. You know what? Let me go in the studio.'"

"And I don't do this very often, in fact, hardly ever. I used to do it a lot when I was younger. I said, 'Let's go in and I'll just make something up. And it might be rubbish, in which case we'll give up.' But I went in and just dropped into improv mode. So, stream of consciousness, I closed my eyes and thought, 'Where am I in this song?' Answer is, I'm in a dark forest where nothing will live. I sing 'I see the frozen eyes' and you hear the hesitation in that first verse, which, by the way, is one take, stream of consciousness. And the reason it's so hesitant and has that plaintive quality is because I can't sing loud, because I don't know what I'm going to say next. And because I'm in the dark forest, and I'm lost, and I'm looking around and searching, it's there, that's it, it's the performance. So, the idea then is don't improve it. Don't make it in time. Don't do that because you destroy it. And 80 percent of that song is the first take; it's made up on the spot, including the spoken word and everything."

"And then we rediscovered the song," continues Bruce. "Roy put it on a CD for me along with all the other various bits and bobs of ideas. And I was like, 'Blimey, wow, what's this? Oh, I think I remember this—God.' And my wife was like, 'That's the most incredible thing I've ever heard you sing. That's beautiful. It's sad, but wow. Emotional.' I go, 'So you think it's okay then?' She went, 'Um, that's going on the record, isn't it?!' 'Well, I don't know.' She's like, 'What, are you mad?!' So, 'Okay, okay, we should put it on then.'"

"We didn't really have to, but we added drums, real drums, over the top of the drum machine, but didn't get rid of the drum machine. Because the drum machine is essential—it's part of the sound. Somehow it makes you… when you hear the drum machine, it actually makes me feel almost lonely. Because it's a machine; there's no emotion to it or anything. Then the drums kick in. I'm okay with it now, but at the time, I thought that the added drums were too much. It's now too much like heavy rock music. This song needs to breathe and needs to be sparse and spare. Like I say, I'm okay with it now, but that's the worry we had, that it would destroy the fragility of it."

In the end, "Sonata (Immortal Beloved)" turns out to be a thoughtful way to end the record, an easing into a future of… what? No one knows. As I write this, there's been minimal news in the Maiden camp. Bruce details for me an ambitious remix and reissue program for his solo catalogue, and already announced is an upcoming solo tour. But

EPILOGUE

what a poignant and searching way to end this record and in fact this mammoth book, with a contemplation on loneliness and life on the wane. What I get from 'Sonata (Immortal Beloved)' that as we age—and as Bruce and the guys in Maiden age—systematically, one by one, piece by piece, everything is taken away.

"Well, thank you," reflects Bruce. "I mean, yes, 'Sonata' is as epic as you would want. As I went on about earlier, I wouldn't describe it as a ballad. It's more a kind of a walking poem. It's like a twisted version of *Sleeping Beauty* with narrative and tragedy and everything. I think it's beautiful and, as you put it, poignant, and heavily emotional and has a really profound effect on people. Not everybody, I guess, but most people that listen to the album, I'd say 50 percent of them namecheck that song as being something that really affected them and they thought was extraordinary, and made them, you know, sad or melancholy or whatever. So that's amazing. I think in the modern world, records are done stylistically in quite a similar fashion; an album won't vary too much within its own confines. Well, this one does, and yet I think it really holds together as an identity. I wish I could say that we did that deliberately [laughs]. But to do a record that moves people, properly, on a journey from one emotional state to another, that's something that you aspire to your entire career."

Post-production, myself and Schiffer Publishing respectfully acknowledge the death, on October 21, 2024, of Paul "Paul Di'Anno" Andrews. The Iron Maiden singer died at his home in Salsbury at the age of 66.

The last time I spoke with Paul was on July 16, 2024, and as always, he was witty, intelligent, accommodating and staying positive and cheerful despite his ongoing health problems. Always busy, and always wanting to give a piece of himself to his fans around the world, he had acknowledged that he needed to step back from touring and focus on mending himself, as well as get a monumental history book he was writing finished.

It must be said that Paul's death didn't come as a shock, although we all stupidly assumed even serious issues with his extremities and mobility could be dealt with. As he patiently explained to me, he was very pleased with the care he was getting in Croatia.

As soon as the news hit, there was a deluge of grief and tributes across the internet, demonstrating the respect Iron Maiden fans have for those milestone first two albums Paul was a part of, as well as the love fans had for this cuddly bear of a legend.

Again, on behalf of myself and the Schiffer Publishing team, we honor Paul and all that he accomplished across a long career, decades in fact, regularly making new music and, as importantly, giving Iron Maiden fans so much of his time and energy and happy disposition even when it was obvious he was struggling.

Martin Popoff

DISCOGRAPHY

A few notes on process: for tidiness's sake, quote marks around songs are not used, although I did use them in the notes section. Writing credits are not added to the tracks as shown in the live material. Records get side 1 / side 2 designation up to the end of the vinyl age (I would call *No Prayer for the Dying* the band's first CD-era album). You'll note that we've included solo material, with the level of detail commensurate with how deeply it's discussed in the book. Specifically, the Maiden, Bruce solo, Primal Rock Rebellion, and British Lion catalogs get equal level of detail, and it drops down from there. Compilations get no detail because who cares, other than Bruce's, which offers a pile of rarities; hence, we've rewarded it with a full showing.

Iron Maiden

Studio Albums

Iron Maiden
April 14, 1980; producer, Will Malone

Side 1:
1. Prowler (Harris), 3:55
2. Remember Tomorrow (Harris, Di'Anno), 5:27
3. Running Free (Harris, Di'Anno), 3:16
4. Phantom of the Opera (Harris), 7:20

Side 2:
1. Transylvania (Harris), 4:05
2. Strange World (Harris), 5:45
3. Charlotte the Harlot (Murray), 4:12
4. Iron Maiden (Harris), 3:35

Notes: US issue adds "Sanctuary" (Harris, Murray, Di'Anno). Personnel on the album are Paul Di'Anno, Dave Murray, Dennis Stratton, Steve Harris, and Clive Burr. Additional during this era is "Burning Ambition" (Harris) and the aforementioned "Sanctuary," as well as "Invasion" and Skyhooks cover "Women in Uniform." Previous to *Iron Maiden*, there is of course an independent single / short EP called *The Soundhouse Tapes*, featuring "Iron Maiden" (4:01), "Invasion" (3:07), and "Prowler" (4:20).

Killers
February 2, 1981; producer, Martin Birch

Side 1:
1. The Ides of March (Harris), 1:48
2. Wrathchild (Harris), 2:54
3. Murders in the Rue Morgue (Harris), 4:14
4. Another Life (Harris), 3:22
5. Innocent Exile (Harris), 3:50

Side 2:
1. Killers (Harris, Di'Anno), 4:58
2. Twilight Zone (Murray, Harris), 2:33
3. Prodigal Son (Harris), 6:05
4. Purgatory (Harris), 3:18
5. Drifter (Harris), 4:47

Notes: Guitarist Derek Stratton is replaced by Adrian Smith. There are no non-LP originals or covers issued during the *Killers* era.

The Number of the Beast
March 22, 1982; producer, Martin Birch

Side 1:
1. Invaders (Harris), 3:20
2. Children of the Damned (Harris), 4:34
3. The Prisoner (Smith, Harris), 5:34
4. 22 Acacia Avenue (Smith, Harris), 6:34

Side 2:
1. The Number of the Beast (Harris), 4:25
2. Run to the Hills (Harris), 3:50
3. Gangland (Burr, Smith), 3:46
4. Hallowed Be Thy Name (Harris), 7:08

Notes: Lead vocalist Paul Di'Anno is replaced by Bruce Dickinson. The only additional non-LP-era track during this era is "Total Eclipse."

Piece of Mind
May 16, 1983; producer, Martin Birch

Side 1:
1. Where Eagles Dare (Harris), 6:08
2. Revelations (Dickinson), 6:51
3. Flight of Icarus (Smith, Dickinson), 3:49
4. Die with Your Boots On (Smith, Dickinson, Harris), 5:22

Side 2:
1. The Trooper (Harris), 4:10
2. Still Life (Murray, Harris), 4:37
3. Quest for Fire (Harris), 3:40
4. Sun and Steel (Smith, Dickinson), 3:25
5. To Tame a Land (Harris), 7:26

Notes: Drummer Clive Burr is replaced by Nicko McBrain. New non-LP tracks during this era are Montrose cover "I Got the Fire" and Jethro Tull cover "Cross-Eyed Mary."

Powerslave
September 3, 1984; producer, Martin Birch

Side 1:
1. Aces High (Harris), 4:31
2. 2 Minutes to Midnight (Smith, Dickinson), 6:04
3. Losfer Words (Big 'Orra) (Harris), 4:12
4. The Duellists (Harris), 6:07

Side 2:
1. Back in the Village (Smith, Dickinson), 5:03
2. Powerslave (Dickinson), 7:10
3. Rime of the Ancient Mariner (Harris), 13:40

Notes: New non-LP tracks during this era are Beckett cover "Rainbow's Gold," recorded "argument" "Mission from 'Arry" (Harris, McBrain), and Nektar cover "King of Twilight."

Somewhere in Time
September 29, 1986; producer, Martin Birch

Side 1:
1. Caught Somewhere in Time (Harris), 7:22
2. Wasted Years (Smith), 5:06
3. Sea of Madness (Smith), 5:42
4. Heaven Can Wait (Harris), 7:24

Side 2:
1. The Loneliness of the Long Distance Runner (Harris), 6:31
2. Stranger in a Strange Land (Smith), 5:43
3. Deja-Vu (Murray, Harris), 4:55
4. Alexander the Great (Harris), 8:35

Notes: Non-LP extras at this time are "Sheriff of Huddersfield" (Iron Maiden) and early Adrian Smith project songs "Reach Out," "Juanita," and "That Girl."

Seventh Son of a Seventh Son
April 11, 1988; producer, Martin Birch

Side 1:
1. Moonchild (Smith, Dickinson), 5:39
2. Infinite Dreams (Harris), 6:09
3. Can I Play with Madness (Smith, Dickinson, Harris), 3:31
4. The Evil That Men Do (Smith, Dickinson, Harris), 4:34

Side 2:
1. Seventh Son of a Seventh Son (Harris), 9:53
2. The Prophecy (Murray, Harris), 5:05
3. The Clairvoyant (Harris), 4:27
4. Only the Good Die Young (Harris, Dickinson), 4:42

Notes: Non-LP extras at this time are "Black Bart Blues" (Harris, Dickinson) and a cover of Thin Lizzy's "Massacre."

No Prayer for the Dying
October 1, 1990; producer, Martin Birch

1. Tailgunner (Dickinson, Harris), 4:13
2. Holy Smoke (Dickinson, Harris), 3:47
3. No Prayer for the Dying (Harris), 4:22
4. Public Enema Number One (Dickinson, Murray), 4:03
5. Fates Warning (Harris, Murray), 4:09
6. The Assassin (Harris), 4:16
7. Run Silent Run Deep (Dickinson, Harris), 4:34
8. Hooks in You (Dickinson, Smith), 4:06
9. Bring Your Daughter . . . to the Slaughter (Dickinson), 4:42
10. Mother Russia (Harris), 5:30

Notes: Bruce Dickinson, vocals; Dave Murray, guitar; Janick Gers, guitar; Steve Harris, bass; Nicko McBrain, drums. US bonus track is "Listen with Nicko! Part XI." The 1995 reissue adds four covers and features different cover art.

Fear of the Dark
May 11, 1992; producers, Martin Birch and Steve Harris

1. Be Quick or Be Dead (Dickinson, Gers), 3:21
2. From Here to Eternity (Harris), 3:35
3. Afraid to Shoot Strangers (Harris), 6:52
4. Fear Is the Key (Dickinson, Gers), 5:30
5. Childhood's End (Harris), 4:41
6. Wasting Love (Dickinson, Gers), 5:46
7. The Fugitive (Harris), 4:52
8. Chains of Misery (Dickinson, Murray), 3:33
9. The Apparition (Harris, Gers), 3:55
10. Judas Be My Guide (Dickinson, Murray), 3:06
11. Weekend Warrior (Harrison, Gers), 5:37
12. Fear of the Dark (Harris), 7:16

Notes: Band personnel same as previous record. The 1995 reissue adds seven bonus tracks.

The X Factor
October 2, 1995; producers, Steve Harris and Nigel Green

1. Sign of the Cross (Harris), 11:18
2. Lord of the Flies (Harris, Gers), 5:04
3. Man on the Edge (Bayley, Gers), 4:13
4. Fortunes of War (Harris), 7:24
5. Look for the Truth (Bayley, Gers, Harris), 5:10
6. The Aftermath (Bayley, Harris, Gers), 6:21
7. Judgement of Heaven (Harris), 5:12
8. Blood on the World's Hands (Harris), 5:58
9. The Edge of Darkness (Bayley, Harris, Gers), 6:39
10 2 A.M. (Bayley, Gers, Harris), 5:38
11. The Unbeliever (Harris, Gers), 8:10

Notes: Blaze Bayley replaces Bruce Dickinson as lead singer. Japanese issue included three bonus tracks, all new originals; namely, "Justice of the Peace," "I Live My Way," and "Judgement Day."

Virtual XI
March 23, 1998; producers, Steve Harris and Nigel Green

1. Futureal (Bayley, Harris), 3:00
2. The Angel and the Gambler (Harris), 9:51
3. Lightning Strikes Twice (Harris, Murray), 4:49
4. The Clansman (Harris), 9:06
5. When Two Worlds Collide (Bayley, Harris, Murray), 6:13
6. The Educated Fool (Harris), 6:46
7. Don't Look to the Eyes of a Stranger (Harris), 8:04
8. Como Estais Amigos (Bayley, Gers), 5:26

Brave New World
May 29, 2000; producer, Kevin Shirley, coproduced by Steve Harris

1. The Wicker Man (Smith, Harris, Dickinson), 4:35
2. Ghost of the Navigator (Gers, Harris, Dickinson), 6:50
3. Brave New World (Murray, Harris, Dickinson), 6:18
4. Blood Brothers (Harris), 7:14
5. The Mercenary (Gers, Harris), 4:42
6. Dream of Mirrors (Gers, Harris), 9:21
7. The Fallen Angel (Smith, Harris), 4:00
8. The Nomad (Murray, Harris), 9:06
9. Out of the Silent Planet (Gers, Harris, Dickinson), 6:25
10. The Thin Line between Love & Hate (Murray, Harris), 8:26

Notes: Bruce Dickinson replaces Blaze Bayley on vocals. Adrian Smith returns, making the band a six-piece: Bruce Dickinson (vocals), Adrian Smith (guitars), Dave Murray (guitars), Janick Gers (guitars), Steve Harris (bass), and Nicko McBrain (drums).

Dance of Death
September 8, 2003; producer, Kevin Shirley, coproduced by Steve Harris

1. Wildest Dreams (Smith, Harris), 3:52
2. Rainmaker (Murray, Harris, Dickinson), 3:48
3. No More Lies (Harris), 7:21
4. Montségur (Gers, Harris, Dickinson), 5:50
5. Dance of Death (Gers, Harris), 8:36
6. Gates of Tomorrow (Gers, Harris, Dickinson), 5:12
7. New Frontier (McBrain, Smith, Dickinson), 5:04
8. Paschendale (Smith, Harris), 8:27
9. Face in the Sand (Smith, Harris, Dickinson), 6:31
10. Age of Innocence (Murray, Harris), 6:10
11. Journeyman (Smith, Harris, Dickinson), 7:06

Notes: Other than alternate versions, the only non-LP songs from this era are jam tracks "More Tea Vicar" (Iron Maiden) and "Pass the Jam" (Iron Maiden).

A Matter of Life and Death
August 25, 2006; producer, Kevin Shirley, coproduced by Steve Harris

1. Different World (Smith, Harris), 4:17
2. These Colours Don't Run (Smith, Harris, Dickinson), 6:52
3. Brighter Than a Thousand Suns (Smith, Harris, Dickinson), 8:44
4. The Pilgrim (Gers, Harris), 5:07
5. The Longest Day (Smith, Harris, Dickinson), 7:48
6. Out of the Shadows (Harris, Dickinson), 5:36
7. The Reincarnation of Benjamin Breeg (Murray, Harris), 7:21
8. For the Greater Good of God (Harris), 9:24
9. Lord of Light (Smith, Harris, Dickinson), 7:23
10. The Legacy (Gers, Harris), 9:20

The Final Frontier
August 13, 2010; producer, Kevin Shirley, coproduced by Steve Harris

1. Satellite 15 . . . The Final Frontier (Smith, Harris), 8:40
2. El Dorado (Smith, Harris, Dickinson), 6:49
3. Mother of Mercy (Smith, Harris), 5:20
4. Coming Home (Smith, Harris, Dickinson), 5:52
5. The Alchemist (Gers, Harris, Dickinson), 4:29
6. Isle of Avalon (Smith, Harris), 9:06
7. Starblind (Smith, Harris, Dickinson), 7:48
8. The Talisman (Gers, Harris), 9:03
9. The Man Who Would Be King (Murray, Harris), 8:28
10. When the Wild Wind Blows (Harris), 10:59

The Book of Souls
September 4, 2015; producer, Kevin Shirley, coproduced by Steve Harris

CD 1:
1. If Eternity Should Fail (Dickinson), 8:28
2. Speed of Light (Smith, Dickinson), 5:01
3. The Great Unknown (Smith, Harris), 6:37
4. The Red and the Black (Harris), 13:33
5. When the River Runs Deep (Smith Harris), 5:52
6. The Book of Souls (Gers, Harris), 10:27

CD 2:
1, Death or Glory (Smith, Dickinson), 5:13
2. Shadows of the Valley (Gers, Harris), 7:32
3. Tears of a Clown (Smith, Harris), 4:59
4. The Man of Sorrows (Murray, Harris), 6:28
5. Empire of the Clouds (Dickinson), 18:01

Senjutsu
September 3, 2021; producer, Kevin Shirley

CD 1:
1. Senjutsu (Smith, Harris), 8:20
2. Stratego (Gers, Harris), 4:59
3. The Writing on the Wall (Smith, Dickinson), 6:13
4. Lost in a Lost World (Harris), 9:31
5. Days of Future Past (Smith, Dickinson), 4:03
6. The Time Machine (Gers, Harris), 7:09

CD 2:
1. Darkest Hour (Smith, Dickinson), 7:20
2. Death of the Celts (Harris), 10:20
3. The Parchment (Harris), 12:39
4. Hell on Earth (Harris), 11:19

Live Albums

Maiden Japan
September 14, 1981; producers, Iron Maiden and Doug Hall

Side 1:
1. Running Free (2:48)
2. Remember Tomorrow (5:27)

Side 2:
1. Wrathchild (2:52)
2. Killers (4:39)
3. Innocent Exile (3:44)

Notes: A live EP. Nine months earlier, there had been the Japan-only *Live!! + One* EP. Variants exist, but the "anchor" version, as it were, is the American, as listed above.

Live After Death
October 14, 1985; producer, Martin Birch

Side 1:
1. Churchill's Speech (intro) (1:09)
2. Aces High (4:07)
3. 2 Minutes to Midnight (5:52)
4. The Trooper (3:59)
5. Revelations (5:59)
6. Flight of Icarus (3:21)

Side 2:
1. Rime of the Ancient Mariner (13:03)
2. Powerslave (7:06)
3. The Number of the Beast (4:48)

Side 3:
1. Hallowed Be Thy Name (7:17)
2. Iron Maiden (4:11)
3. Run to the Hills (3:52)
4. Running Free (8:16)

Side 4:
1. Wrathchild (2:54)
2. 22 Acacia Avenue (6:04)
3. Children of the Damned (4:19)
4. Die with Your Boots On (4:51)
5. Phantom of the Opera (7:01)

Notes: A double live album, in gatefold sleeve; the band's first official full-length live album

A Real Live One
March 22, 1993; producer, Steve Harris

1. Be Quick or Be Dead (3:17)
2. From Here to Eternity (4:20)
3. Can I Play with Madness (4:42)
4. Wasting Love (5:48)
5. Tailgunner (4:09)
6. The Evil That Men Do (5:26)
7. Afraid to Shoot Strangers (6:48)
8. Bring Your Daughter . . . to the Slaughter (5:18)
9. Heaven Can Wait (7:29)
10. The Clairvoyant (4:30)
11. Fear of the Dark (7:11)

Notes: A live album featuring songs from 1986's *Somewhere in Time* through 1992's *Fear of the Dark*

A Real Dead One
October 18, 1993; producer, Steve Harris

1. The Number of the Beast (4:55)
2. The Trooper (3:55)
3. Prowler (4:16)
4. Transylvania (4:26)
5. Remember Tomorrow (5:53)
6. Where Eagles Dare (4:49)
7. Sanctuary (4:53)
8. Running Free (3:49)
9. Run to the Hills (3:58)
10. 2 Minutes to Midnight (5:37)
11. Iron Maiden (5:25)
12. Hallowed Be Thy Name (7:52)

Notes: A live album featuring songs from 1980's *Iron Maiden* through 1984's *Powerslave*

Live at Donington
November 8, 1993; producer, Steve Harris

CD 1:
1. Be Quick or Be Dead (3:53)
2. The Number of the Beast (4:54)
3. Wrathchild (2:54)
4. From Here to Eternity (4:44)
5. Can I Play with Madness (3:33)
6. Wasting Love (5:37)
7. Tailgunner (4:08)
8. The Evil That Men Do (7:58)
9. Afraid to Shoot Strangers (6:52)
10. Fear of the Dark (7:11)

CD 2:
1. Bring Your Daughter . . . to the Slaughter (6:17)
2. The Clairvoyant (4:22)
3. Heaven Can Wait (7:20)
4. Run to the Hills (3:56)
5. 2 Minutes to Midnight (5:38)
6. Iron Maiden (8:15)
7. Hallowed Be Thy Name (7:28)
8. The Trooper (3:53)
9. Sanctuary (5:18)
10. Running Free (7:54)

Notes: A live album capturing the band's performance at Monsters of Rock, Donington Park, August 22, 1992. Not issued in the US until October 1998. Also issued as a VHS video.

Rock in Rio
March 25, 2002; producer, Kevin Shirley

CD 1:
1. Arthur's Farewell (1:55)
2. The Wicker Man (4:41)
3. Ghost of the Navigator (6:48)
4. Brave New World (6:06)
5. Wrathchild (3:05)
6. 2 Minutes to Midnight (6:26)
7. Blood Brothers (7:15)
8. Sign of the Cross (10:49)
9. The Mercenary (4:42)
10. The Trooper (4:33)

CD 2:
1. Dream of Mirrors (9:37)
2. The Clansman (9:19)
3. The Evil That Men Do (4:40)
4. Fear of the Dark (7:40)
5. Iron Maiden (5:51)
6. The Number of the Beast (5:00)
7. Hallowed be Thy Name (7:23)
8. Sanctuary (5:17)
9. Run to the Hills (4:59)

Notes: Recorded at the Rock in Rio festival, January 19, 2001

BBC Archives
November 4, 2002; producer, Tony Wilson

CD 1:
1. Iron Maiden (3:46)
2. Running Free (3:10)
3. Transylvania (4:03)
4. Sanctuary (3:45)
5. Wrathchild (3:32)
6. Run to the Hills (5:36)
7. Children of the Damned (4:48)
8. The Number of the Beast (5:29)
9. 22 Acacia Avenue (6:36)
10. Transylvania (6:20)
11. The Prisoner (5:50)
12. Hallowed Be Thy Name (7:37)
13. Phantom of the Opera (7:02)
14. Iron Maiden (4:58)

CD 2:
1. Prowler (4:27)
2. Remember Tomorrow (5:59)
3. Killers (4:43)
4. Running Free (3:53)
5. Transylvania (4:49)
6. Iron Maiden (4:56)
7. Moonchild (5:43)
8. Wrathchild (3:00)
9. Infinite Dreams (5:51)
10. The Trooper (4:05)
11. Seventh Son of a Seventh Son (10:27)
12. The Number of the Beast (4:43)
13. Hallowed Be Thy Name (7:10)
14. Iron Maiden (6:01)

Notes: Archival live album featuring performances from BBC Radio 1 *Friday Rock Show*, November 14, 1979, Reading Festival, August 28, 1982, Reading Festival, August 23, 1980, and Monsters of Rock, Donington, August 20, 1988

Beast Over Hammersmith
November 4, 2002; producers, Doug Hall and Steve Harris

CD 1:
1. Murders in the Rue Morgue (4:32)
2. Wrathchild (3:31)
3. Run to the Hills (4:20)
4. Children of the Damned (4:38)
5. The Number of the Beast (5:08)
6. Another Life (3:45)
7. Killers (5:47)
8. 22 Acacia Avenue (6:56)
9. Total Eclipse (4:14)

CD 2:
1. Transylvania (5:51)
2. The Prisoner (5:49)
3. Hallowed Be Thy Name (7:31)
4. Phantom of the Opera (6:53)
5. Iron Maiden (4:20)
6. Sanctuary (4:13)
7. Drifter (9:19)
8. Running Free (3:44)
9. Prowler (5:00)

Notes: Archival live album from March 20, 1982, at the Hammersmith Odeon

Death on the Road
August 29, 2005; producer, Kevin Shirley

CD 1:
1. Wildest Dreams (4:52)
2. Wrathchild (2:49)
3. Can I Play with Madness (3:30)
4. The Trooper (4:12)
5. Dance of Death (9:23)
6. Rainmaker (4:02)
7. Brave New World (6:10)
8. Paschendale (10:18)
9. Lord of the Flies (5:04)

CD 2:
1. No More Lies (7:50)
2. Hallowed Be Thy Name (7:32)
3. Fear of the Dark (7:28)
4. Iron Maiden (4:50)
5. Journeyman (7:03)
6. The Number of the Beast (4:58)
7. Run to the Hills (4:24)

Notes: Recorded at the Westfalenhallen, Dortmund, Germany, November 24, 2003

Flight 666
May 22, 2009; producer, Kevin Shirley

CD 1:
1. Churchill's Speech (0:43)
2. Aces High (4:49)
3. 2 Minutes to Midnight (5:57)
4. Revelations (6:28)
5. The Trooper (4:01)
6. Wasted Years (5:07)
7. The Number of the Beast (5:07)
8. Can I Play with Madness (3:36)
9. Rime of the Ancient Mariner (13:41)

CD 2:
1. Powerslave (7:28)
2. Heaven Can Wait (7:35)
3. Run to the Hills (3:59)
4. Fear of the Dark (7:32)

Notes: The soundtrack to the Banger Films documentary of the same name

En Vivo!
March 23, 2012; producer, Kevin Shirley

CD 1:
1. Satellite 15 (4:36)
2. The Final Frontier (4:10)
3. El Dorado (5:52)
4. 2 Minutes to Midnight (5:50)
5. The Talisman (8:45)
6. Coming Home (5:57)
7. Dance of Death (9:03)
8. The Trooper (3:59)
9. The Wicker Man (5:06)

CD 2:
1. Blood Brothers (7:04)
2. When the Wild Wind Blows (10:37)
3. The Evil That Men Do (4:17)
4. Fear of the Dark (7:30)
5. Iron Maiden (5:08)
6. The Number of the Beast (4:57)
7. Hallowed Be Thy Name (7:28)
8. Running Free (7:57)

Notes: Recorded at the Estadio Nacional in Santiago, Chile, April 10, 2011

Maiden England '88
March 25, 2013; producer, Martin Birch

CD 1:
1. Moonchild (6:23)
2. The Evil That Men Do (4:18)
3. The Prisoner (6:00)
4. Still Life (4:32)
5. Die with Your Boots On (5:19)
6. Infinite Dreams (5:53)
7. Killers (4:57)
8. Can I Play with Madness (3:25)
9. Heaven Can Wait (7:43)
10. Wasted Years (5:06)

CD 2:
1. The Clairvoyant (4:30)
2. Seventh Son of a Seventh Son (10:08)
3. The Number of the Beast (4:47)
4. Hallowed Be Thy Name (7:21)
5. Iron Maiden (5:11)
6. Run To the Hills (4:01)
7. Running Free (5:33)
8. Sanctuary (5:24)

Notes: Expanded reissue of CD issued in 1994 and video issued in 1989. Also released on DVD and vinyl.

The Book of Souls: Live Chapter
November 17, 2017; producer, Tony Newton

CD 1:
1. If Eternity Should Fail (7:46)
2. Speed of Light (5:08)
3. Wrathchild (2:59)
4. Children of the Damned (5:14)
5. Death or Glory (5:15)
6. The Red and the Black (13:17)
7. The Trooper (4:05)
8. Powerslave (7:31)

CD 2:
1. The Great Unknown (6:50)
2. The Book of Souls (10:49)
3. Fear of the Dark (7:34)
4. Iron Maiden (6:05)
5. The Number of the Beast (5:06)
6. Blood Brothers (7:35)
7. Wasted Years (5:38)

Nights of the Legacy, Legacy of the Beast: Live in Mexico City
November 20, 2020; producer, Tony Newton

CD 1:
1. Churchill's Speech (0:38)
2. Aces High (4:58)
3. Where Eagles Dare (5:12)
4. 2 Minutes to Midnight (5:54)
5. The Clansman (9:16)
6. The Trooper (4:02)
7. Revelations (6:32)
8. For the Greater Good of God (9:23)
9. The Wicker Man (4:43)

CD 2:
1. Sign of the Cross (11:00)
2. Flight of Icarus (3:43)
3. Fear of the Dark (7:46)
4. The Number of the Beast (4:59)
5. Iron Maiden (5:30)
6. The Evil That Men Do (4:25)
7. Hallowed Be Thy Name (7:38)
8. Run To the Hills (5:07)

Notes: Recorded at the Palacio de los Deportes in Mexico City, September 27–30, 2019

Compilations

Best of the Beast (September 23, 1996)
Ed Hunter (May 17, 1999)
Edward the Great (November 4, 2002)
Eddie's Archive (November 4, 2002)
The Essential Iron Maiden (July 5, 2005)
Somewhere Back in Time: The Best of 1980–1989 (May 12, 2008)
From Fear to Eternity: The Best of 1990–2010 (June 6, 2011)

Bruce Dickinson

Tattooed Millionaire
May 8, 1990; producer, Chris Tsangarides

1. Son of a Gun (Dickinson, Gers), 5:55
2. Tattooed Millionaire (Dickinson, Gers), 4:28
3. Born in '58 (Dickinson, Gers), 3:40
4. Hell on Wheels (Dickinson, Gers), 3:39)
5. Gypsy Road (Dickinson, Gers), 4:02
6. Dive! Dive! Dive! (Dickinson, Gers), 4:41
7. All the Young Dudes (Bowie), 3:50
8. Lickin' the Gun (Dickinson, Gers), 3:17
9. Zulu Lulu (Dickinson, Gers), 3:28
10. No Lies (Dickinson), 6:17

Notes: Bruce Dickinson, vocals; Janick Gers, guitar; Andy Carr, bass; Fabio Del Rio, drums. There's a Sony Legacy edition from 2002 with five bonus tracks and a 2005 expanded edition with a second CD comprising eleven bonus tracks. Original 1990 issue was widely available on vinyl.

Balls to Picasso
June 3, 1994; producer, Shay Baby

1. Cyclops (Dickinson, Z), 7:58
2. Hell No (Dickinson, Z), 5:11
3. Gods of War (Dickinson, Z), 5:02
4. 1000 Points of Light (Dickinson, Z), 4:25
5. Laughing in the Hiding Bush (Dickinson, Z, Austin Dickinson), 4:20
6. Change of Heart (Dickinson, Z), 4:58
7. Shoot All the Clowns (Dickinson, Z), 4:24
8. Fire (Dickinson, Z, Casillas), 4:30
9. Sacred Cowboys (Dickinson, Z), 3:53
10. Tears of the Dragon (Dickinson), 6:24

Notes: Bruce Dickinson, vocals; Roy Z, guitar; Eddie Casillas, bass; David Ingraham, drums; Doug van Booven, percussion. Drums on "Tears of the Dragon," Dickie Fliszar; additional vocals, Dean Ortego; percussion on "Shoot All the Clowns," Mario Aguilar. There's a 2005 expanded edition with a second CD comprising sixteen bonus tracks.

Alive in Studio A
March 1995; producers, Spencer May and Bruce Dickinson

CD 1:
1. Cyclops (7:15)
2. Shoot All the Clowns (4:55)
3. Son of a Gun (5:44)
4. Tears of the Dragon (6:27)
5. 1000 Points of Light (3:53)
6. Sacred Cowboys (3:56)
7. Tattooed Millionaire (3:55)
8. Born in '58 (3:23)
9. Fire (4:57)
10. Change of Heart (4:39)
11. Hell No (5:11)
12. Laughing in the Hiding Bush (4:08)

CD 2:
1. Cyclops (7:54)
2. 1000 Points of Light (4:02)
3. Born in '58 (3:15)
4. Gods of War (5:10)
5. Change of Heart (4:29)
6. Laughing in the Hiding Bush (3:51)
7. Hell No (6:02)
8. Tears of the Dragon (6:19)
9. Shoot All the Clowns (5:06)
10. Sacred Cowboys (4:17)
11. Son of a Gun (5:41)
12. Tattooed Millionaire (6:17)

Notes: Bruce Dickinson, vocals; Alex Dickson, guitar; Chris Dale, bass; Alessandro Elena, drums. Disc 1 is live at Metropolis studios; disc 2 is live at the Marquee club in London.

Skunkworks
February 19, 1996; producer, Jack Endino

1. Space Race (Dickinson, Dickson), 3:47
2. Back from the Edge (Dickinson, Dickson), 4:17
3. Inertia (Dickinson, Dickson), 3:04
4. Faith (Dickinson, Dickson), 3:35
5. Solar Confinement (Dickinson, Dickson), 3:20
6. Dreamstate (Dickinson, Dickson), 3:50
7. I Will Not Accept the Truth (Dickinson, Dickson), 3:45
8. Inside the Machine (Dickinson, Dickson), 3:28
9. Headswitch (Dickinson, Dickson), 2:14
10. Meltdown (Dickinson, Dickson), 4:35
11. Octavia (Dickinson, Dickson), 3:15
12. Innerspace (Dickinson, Dickson, Dale), 3:31
13. Strange Death in Paradise (Dickinson, Dickson), 4:50

Notes: Bruce Dickinson, vocals; Alex Dickson, guitar; Chris Dale, bass; Alessandro Elena, drums. There's a 2005 expanded edition with a second CD comprising eleven bonus tracks.

Accident of Birth
May 14, 1997; producer, Roy Z

1. Freak (Dickinson, Roy Z), 4:15
2. Toltec 7 Arrival (Dickinson, Roy Z), 0:37
3. Starchildren (Dickinson, Roy Z), 4:17
4. Taking the Queen (Dickinson, Roy Z), 4:49
5. Darkside of Aquarius (Dickinson, Roy Z), 6:42
6. Road to Hell (Dickinson, Smith), 3:57
7. Man of Sorrows (Dickinson), 5:20
8. Accident of Birth (Dickinson, Roy Z), 4:23
9. The Magician (Dickinson, Roy Z), 3:54
10. Welcome to the Pit (Dickinson, Smith), 4:43
11. Omega (Dickinson, Roy Z), 6:23
12. Arc of Space (Dickinson, Roy Z), 4:18

Notes: Bruce Dickinson, vocals; Adrian Smith, guitar; Roy Z, guitar; Eddie Casillas, bass; David Ingaham, drums. Sylvia Tsai and Rebecca Yeh provide strings on "Taking the Queen," "Man of Sorrows," and "Arc of Space." Richard Baker plays piano on "Man of Sorrows."

The Chemical Wedding
September 15, 1998; producer, Roy Z

1. King in Crimson (Dickinson, Roy Z), 4:43
2. Chemical Wedding (Dickinson, Roy Z), 4:06
3. The Tower (Dickinson, Roy Z), 4:45
4. Killing Floor (Dickinson, Smith), 4:29
5. Book of Thel (Dickinson, Roy Z, Casillas), 8:13
6. Gates of Urizen (Dickinson, Roy Z), 4:25
7. Jerusalem (Dickinson, Roy Z, William Blake), 6:42
8. Trumpets of Jericho (Dickinson, Roy Z), 5:59
9. Machine Men (Dickinson, Smith), 5:41
10. The Alchemist (Dickinson, Roy Z), 8:27

Notes: Same band personnel as previous album, which is a first for Bruce's solo career. Guest vocals by Arthur Brown on "Book of Thel," "Jerusalem," and after the close of "The Alchemist." Greg Schultz provides keyboards on "Killing Floor."

Scream for Me Brazil
November 2, 1999; producer, Roy Z

1. Trumpets of Jericho (6:25)
2. King in Crimson (4:56)
3. Chemical Wedding (4:33)
4. Gates of Urizen (4:20)
5. Killing Floor (4:11)
6. Book of Thel (8:26)
7. Tears of the Dragon (8:06)
8. Laughing in the Hiding Bush (4:01)
9. Accident of Birth (4:18)
10. The Tower (7:41)
11. Darkside of Aquarius (7:32)
12. Road to Hell (4:58)

Notes: Bruce Dickinson, vocals; Roy Z, guitar; Adrian Smith, guitar; Eddie Casillas, bass; David Ingraham, drums. Recorded live in São Paulo, Brazil, April 25, 1999.

The Best of Bruce Dickinson
September 25, 2001; producers, Roy Z, Jack Endino, and Shay Baby

CD 1:
1. Broken (Z, Dickinson), 4:00
2. Tattooed Millionaire (Gers, Dickinson), 4:25
3. Laughing in the Hiding Bush (live) (Z, Austin Dickinson, Dickinson), 4:09
4. Tears of the Dragon (Dickinson), 6:19
5. The Tower (Z, Dickinson), 4:43
6. Born in '58 (Gers, Dickinson), 3:36
7. Accident of Birth (Z, Dickinson), 4:28
8. Silver Wings (Z, Dickinson), 4:16
9. Darkside of Aquarius (Z, Dickinson), 6:50
10. Chemical Wedding (Z, Dickinson), 4:05
11. Back from the Edge (Dickson, Dickinson), 4:16
12. Road to Hell (Smith, Dickinson), 3:58
13. Book of Thel (live) (Z, Casillas, Dickinson), 8:27

CD 2:
1. Bring Your Daughter . . . to the Slaughter (Dickinson), 5:00
2. Darkness Be My Friend (Dickinson), 2:00
3. Wicker Man (Z, Dickinson), 4:40
4. Real World (Z, Dickinson), 3:55
5. Acoustic Song (Z, Dickinson), 4:23
6. No Way Out . . . Continued (Baker, Crichton, Dickinson), 5:18
7. Midnight Jam (Z, Smith, Dickinson), 5:11
8. Man of Sorrows (Dickinson), 5:15
9. Ballad of Mutt (Gers, Dickinson), 3:33
10. Re-Entry (Dickson, Dickinson), 4:03
11. I'm in a Band with an Italian Drummer (Dale), 3:52
12. Jerusalem (live) (Z, Dickinson), 6:43
13. The Voice of Crube (Dickinson, discussing the tracks), 13:45
14. Dracula (Siviter, Siviter), 3:45

Notes: Issued both in single-CD and two-CD formats. Disc 1 of the two-CD version comprises mostly album tracks, while disc 2 is mostly rarities. Various lineups.

Tyranny of Souls
May 23, 2005; producer, Roy Z

1. Mars Within (Intro) 1:30
2. Abduction 3:52
3. Soul Intruders 3:54
4. Kill Devil Hill 5:09
5. Navigate the Seas of the Sun 5:53
6. River of No Return 5:15
7. Power of the Sun 3:31
8. Devil on a Hog 4:03
9. Believil 4:52
10. A Tyranny of Souls 5:54

Notes: All songs written by Roy Z and Bruce Dickinson. Band personnel consists of Bruce Dickinson (vocals), Roy Z (guitars, bass), Maestro Mistheria (keyboards), Ray "Geezer" Burke (bass), Juan Perez (bass) and Dave Moreno (drums). Japanese bonus track is "Eternal."

The Mandrake Project
March 1, 2024; producer, Roy Z

1. Afterglow of Ragnarok 5:45
2. Many Doors to Hell 4:48
3. Rain on the Graves 5:05
4. Resurrection Men 6:24
5. Fingers in the Wounds 3:39
6. Eternity Has Failed 6:59
7. Mistress of Mercy 5:08
8. Face in the Mirror 4:08
9. Shadow of the Gods 7:02; Sonata (Immortal Beloved) 9:51

Notes: All songs written by Roy Z and Bruce Dickinson. Band personnel consists of Bruce Dickinson (vocals, guitars), Roy Z (guitars, bass), Maestro Mistheria (keyboards) and Dave Moreno (drums). As part of the extended Bruce Dickinson discography, there is also a three-DVD video set called *Anthology*, issued June 19, 2006, plus a 3CD box set called *Alive*, issued May 23, 2005.

Primal Rock Rebellion

Awoken Broken
February 27, 2012; producers, Adrian Smith and Mikee Goodman

1. No Friendly Neighbour (4:53)
2. No Place Like Home (3:06)
3. I See Lights (4:59)
4. Bright as a Fire (6:21)
5. Savage World (3:38)
6. Tortured Tone (5:08)
7. White Sheet Robes (5:16)
8. As Tears Come Falling from the Sky (0:47)
9. Awoken Broken (4:58)
10. Search for Bliss (4:13)
11. Snake Ladders (4:43)
12. Mirror and the Moon (5:04)

Notes: All songs written by Adrian Smith and Mikee Goodman. Band personnel consists of Mikee Goodman (lead vocals), Adrian Smith (guitar, bass, vocals) and Dan "Loord" Foord (drums, percussion). Additional personnel: Mark Clayden (bass on "I See Lights"), Tarin Kerry (backing vocals), and Abi Fry (viola). Japanese bonus tracks are "Scientist" and "Mooncusser."

Steve Harris / British Lion

Steve Harris / British Lion
September 24, 2012; producer, Steve Harris, assisted by Richard Taylor and David Hawkins

1. This Is My God (4:57)
2. Lost Worlds (4:58)
3. Karma Killer (5:29)
4. Us Against the World (4:12)
5. The Chosen Ones (6:27)
6. A World Without Heaven (7:02)
7. Judas (4:58)
8. Eyes of the Young (5:25)
9. These Are the Hands (4:28)
10. The Lesson (4:15)

Notes: All songs written by Steve Harris, David Hawkins, and Richard Taylor except "The Chosen Ones" (Hawkins, Taylor), "A World Without Heaven" (Fitzgibbon, Harris, Leslie, Liederman, Roberts, Taylor), and "Eyes of the Young (Harris, Leslie, Roberts, Taylor). Band personnel consists of Richard Taylor (lead vocals), Steve Harris (bass), David Hawkins (guitars, keyboards), Grahame Leslie (guitars), Barry Fitzgibbon (guitars), Simon Dawson (drums), Ian Roberts (drums), and Richard Cook (drums).

The Burning
January 17, 2020; producer, Steve Harris

1. City of Fallen Angels (5:21)
2. The Burning (5:15)
3. Father Lucifer (4:38)
4. Elysium (5:11)
5. Lightning (5:50)
6. Last Chance (6:06)
7. Legend (4:07)
8. Spit Fire (6:20)
9. Land of the Perfect People (4:52)
10. Bible Black (6:33)
11. Native Son (6:04)

Notes: Band consists of Richard Taylor (vocals), David Hawkins (guitars), Grahame Leslie (guitars), Steve Harris (bass, keyboards), and Simon Dawson (drums).

Adrian Smith

A.S.a.P.: *Silver and Gold* (1989)
Psycho Motel: *State of Mind* (1995)
Psycho Motel: *Welcome to the World* (1997)
Smith/Kotzen: *Smith/Kotzen* (2021)

Paul Di'Anno

Di'Anno: *Di'Anno* (1984)
Paul Di'Anno's Battlezone: *Fighting Back* (1986)
Paul Di'Anno's Battlezone: *Children of Madness* (1987)
Killers: *Assault on South America* (issued in 1994 as *South American Assault Live* [1990])
Praying Mantis, Paul Di'Anno and Dennis Stratton: *Live at Last* (1990)
Killers: *Murder One* (1992)
Killers: *Menace to Society* (1994)
Killers: *South American Assault Live* (1994)
Paul Di'Anno and Dennis Stratton: *The Original Iron Men* (1995)
Paul Di'Anno and Dennis Stratton: *The Original Iron Men 2* (1996)
Paul Di'Anno and Dennis Stratton: *As Hard as Iron* (compilation, 1996)
Paul Di'Anno: *The World's First Iron Man* (1997)
Killers: *Live* (1997)
Killers: *New Live & Rare* (1998)
Paul Di'Anno's Battlezone: *Feel My Pain* (1998)
Paul Di'Anno: *Beyond the Maiden* (compilation, 1999)
The Almighty Inbredz: *The Almighty Inbredz* (1999)

Paul Di'Anno: *The Masters* (compilation, 1999)
Di'Anno: *Nomad* (2000)
Paul Di'Anno: *The Beast* (2001)
Paul Di'Anno's Battlezone: *Cessation of Hostilities* (2001)
Killers: *Killers Live at the Whiskey* (2001)
Killers: *Screaming Blue Murder: The Very Best of Paul Di'Anno's Killers* (2002)
Paul Di'Anno: *The Living Dead* (2006)
Paul Di'Anno: *The Maiden Years: The Classics* (2006)
Paul Di'Anno: *Iron Maiden Days & Evil Nights* (2007)
Paul Di'Anno's Battlezone: *The Fight Goes On* (2008)
Paul Di'Anno: *Wrathchild: The Anthology* (2012)
Architects of Chaoz: *The League of Shadows* (2015)
Paul Di'Anno: *Hell over Waltrop: Live in Germany* (2020)

Blaze Bayley

Blaze: *Silicon Messiah* (2000)
Blaze: *Tenth Dimension* (2002)
Blaze: *As Live as It Gets* (2003)
Blaze: *Blood & Belief* (2004)
Blaze Bayley: *Alive in Poland* (2007)
Blaze Bayley: *The Man Who Would Not Die* (2008)
Blaze Bayley: *Best of* (2008)
Blaze Bayley: *The Night That Will Not Die* (2009)
Blaze Bayley: *Promise and Terror* (2010)
Blaze Bayley: *The King of Metal* (2012)
Blaze Bayley: *Soundtracks of My Life* (2013)
Blaze Bayley: *Live in Prague* (2014)
Blaze Bayley: *Infinite Entanglement* (2016)
Blaze Bayley: *Endure and Survive: Infinite Entanglement Part II* (2017)
Blaze Bayley: *The Redemption of William Black: Infinite Entanglement Part III* (2018)
Blaze Bayley: *December Wind: Classical Acoustic with Thomas Zwijsen* (2018)
Blaze Bayley: *Live in France* (2019)
Blaze Bayley: *Live in Czech* (2020)
Blaze Bayley: *War within Me* (2021)
Blaze Bayley: *Damaged Strange Different and Live* (2023)

SOURCES

Interviews with the Author

Bayley, Blaze. April 1998.
Bayley, Blaze. April 7, 2003.
Bayley, Blaze. October 19, 2014.
Bayley, Blaze. August 6, 2017.
Bayley, Blaze. October 3, 2017.
Birch, Paul. 2009.
Bushell, Garry. 2010.
Byford, Biff. October 11, 2011.
Collen, Phil. July 28, 2011.
Cox, Jess. 1998.
Dawson, Steve. January 6, 2012.
Di'Anno, Paul. November 19, 2000.
Di'Anno, Paul. October 15, 2001.
Di'Anno, Paul. April 21, 2006.
Dickinson, Bruce. July 30, 1998.
Dickinson, Bruce. September 11, 2001.
Dickinson, Bruce. February 10, 2002.
Dickinson, Bruce. August 3, 2003.
Dickinson, Bruce. January 18, 2024.
Gers, Janick. August 1, 2000.
Glockler, Nigel. September 15, 2013.
Gorham, Scott. February 11, 2009.
Harris, Steve. October 13, 1995.
Harris, Steve, October 3, 2018.
Kay, Neal. 2010.
McBrain, Nicko, September 10, 2021
McCoy, John, October 18, 2006.
Murray, Dave. August 2005.
Quinn, Paul. 2009.
Riddles, Kevin. 2010.
Riggs, Derek. December 13, 2005.
Riggs, Derek. March 23, 2006.
Riggs, Derek. April 7, 2006.
Riggs, Derek. April 8, 2006.
Slagel, Brian. July 24, 2017.
Smallwood, Rod. October 2005.

Smith, Adrian. August 1, 2000.
Snider, Dee. August 1, 2006.
Stratton, Dennis. 2010.
Tatler, Brian. 2010.
Tsangarides, Chris. February 15, 2006.
Tucker, John. 2010.
Tucker, Mick. 2010.
Ulrich, Lars. September 4, 2008.
Z, Roy, January 6, 2000.
Z, Roy. February 2, 2024.

Articles

Alexander, Phil. "To Live and Fry in LA." *Kerrang!* 795 (April 1, 2000).
Andrews, Rob. "Iron Maiden: Armed and Ready." *Hit Parader* 243 (December 1984).
An Evening with Bruce Dickinson. MTelus, Montreal, QC. March 23, 2022.Arnopp, Jason. "Running Man." *Kerrang!* 387 (April 1992).
Arnopp, Jason. "The Darkest Hour." *Kerrang!* 441 (May 1, 1993).
Arnopp, Jason. "Handle with Scare." *Kerrang!* 388 (April 18, 1992).
Bansal, Aniruddh. "Andrew." *Awoken Broken* record review. *Metal Assault*, April 19, 2012.
Begai, Carl. "Bruce Dickinson: 'Welcome Back to a Scary Metal Record!'" *Brave Words & Bloody Knuckles* 17 (April/May 1997).
Begai, Carl. "Iron Maiden: Do You Wanna Dance?" *Brave Words & Bloody Knuckles* 73 (October 2003).
Begrand, Adrien. *A Matter of Live and Death* record review. *Popmatters*, September 5, 2006.
Bennett, J. "Bruce Dickinson on Life of Metal, Mischief, Fighting with Iron Maiden 'Brothers.'" *Revolver*, October 31, 2017.
Bienstock, Richard. "Iron Maiden Guitarists Discuss *The Final Frontier*." *Guitar World*, December 2010.
Bonutto, Dante. "Bruce on the Loose!" *Kerrang!* 25 (September 23–October 6, 1982).
Bonutto, Dante. "Metal Makes Magic Mayhem!" *Kerrang!* 25 (September 23–October 6, 1982).
Bonutto, Dante. *Piece of Mind* record review. *Kerrang!* 42 (May 19–June 2, 1983).
Bosso, Joe. "Iron Maiden's Nicko McBrain on New Album *The Final Frontier*." *Musicradar* August 16, 2010.
Bromley, Adrian. "Bruce Dickinson: Still Screaming." *Rip n' Tear* 2 (1999).
"Bruce Dickinson: 'When the Magic's There, You've Got to Do It.'" *Terrorizer* 132 (June 2005).
Collingwood, Chris. "Stab Your Back." *Sounds* May 10, 1980.
Cummings, Winston. "Quest of Honor." *Hit Parader* 259 (April 1986).
Dabin, Grégory. "Interview with Clive Burr." *Rock Hard*, November 2002.
"*Dance of Death* EPK." EMI Records, 2003.
Dodero, Camille. "Interview: Iron Maiden Drummer Nicko McBrain on Flight 666." *Village Voice*, June 12, 2009.

Dome, Malcolm. *Brave New World* record review. *Metal Hammer*, June 2000.

Dome, Malcolm. "Iron Maiden / Praying Mantis / Diamond Head, Lyceum, London." *Record Mirror*, February 16, 1980.

Dome, Malcolm. *Skunkworks* record review. *Kerrang!* 585 (February 24, 1996).

Doran, John. "Iron Lion Scion: Steve Harris Interviewed." *The Quietus*, October 15, 2012.

Drever, Ryan. *British Lion* record review. *Drowned in Sound*, September 18, 2012.

"Dr." Wieder. "Great Moments in Metal: Iron Maiden." *Metal*, April 1988.

Dumatray, Henry. Bruce Dickinson interview. *Hard Force* 2 (June 1992).

Dumatray, Henry. Steve Harris interview. *Hard Force* 33 (September 1990).

Dunn, Sam. Interviews with Bruce Dickinson, Ashley Goodall, Steve Harris, Neal Kay, Adrian Smith, Dennis Stratton, John Tucker. 2009–10.

Elliott, Paul. "Street Fighting Men." *Kerrang!* 693 (April 4, 1998).

Elliott, Paul. *The X Factor* record review. *Kerrang!* 564 (September 23, 1995).

Epstein, Dmitry. "Interview with Bruce Dickinson." *Let It Rock*, October 2001.

Ewing, Jerry. "Meet the New Band . . ." *Metal Hammer*, June 2000.

"*The Final Frontier* EPK." EMI Records, 2010.

Garner, George. *The Burning* record review. *Kerrang!*, January 9, 2020.

Gromen, Mark. *Dance of Death* record review. *Brave Words & Bloody Knuckles* 73 (October 2003).

Harris, Steve "Selwyn." "Maiden Bananas (Oops! I Mean Bahamas)." *Kerrang!* 42 (May 19–June 2, 1983).

Henderson, "Metal" Tim. "Iron Maiden: A "Dark" Return for the Masters of 'Fear'-ful Metal!" *M.E.A.T.* 32A (June 1992).

Henderson, "Metal" Tim. "Iron Maiden's Nicko McBrain." BraveWords.com, November 5, 2015.

Henderson, Tim. "Banging Heads in Britain!" *Brave Words & Bloody Knuckles* 9 (August/September 1995).

Henderson, Tim. "*Brave New World*: "This First Look!" *Brave Words & Bloody Knuckles* 40 (June 2000).

Henderson, Tim. "Bruce Dickinson: Stealth Bombers, Blackbirds, and Space Family Robinson!?!" *Brave Words & Bloody Knuckles* 12 (April/May 1996).

Henderson, Tim. "Bruce Dickinson: Sweet Emotion." *Brave Words & Bloody Knuckles* 1, no. 4 (August/September 1994).

Henderson, Tim. "Hallowed Be Thy Name!" *Brave Words & Bloody Knuckles* 41 (July 2000).

Henderson, Tim. "Iron Maiden Do or Die: Have They Done It?" *Brave Words & Bloody Knuckles* 10 (November/December 1995).

Henderson, Tim. "Iron Maiden: The Man behind Eddie's Mask!" *Brave Words & Bloody Knuckles* 66 (January 2003).

Henderson, Tim. "Iron Maiden Manager Rod Smallwood Talks Canada: Loud Audiences, Scenery, Hockey, HP Sauce, and Beavers Eh!" BraveWords.com, March 7, 2010.

Henderson, Tim. "Iron Maiden's Dave Murray." *Brave Words & Bloody Knuckles* 12 (April/May 1996).

Henderson, Tim. "No Rest for the Wicked!" *Brave Words & Blood Knuckles* 59 (May 2002).

Henderson, Tim. "Psycho Motel: No Vacancy!" *Brave Words & Bloody Knuckles* 23 (April/May 1998).

Henderson, Tim. Rod Smallwood interview. *Brave Words & Bloody Knuckles*, 2005.

Holloway, Alan. "Nicko's Virtual Reality." *Hard Roxx* 38 (December, 1998).

Honey, Mathew. "Iron Maiden." *Hard Roxx* 31 (May 1998).

Hotten, Jon. "Clever Dick of All Trades." *Kerrang!* 285 (April 14, 1990).

Hyden, Steven. "Q&A: Iron Maiden's Bruce Dickinson on Beating Cancer and Late-Career Stagnation." *Grantland*, September 4, 2015.

"Interview with Janick Gers." *Talking Metal Pirate Radio*, episode #5 (August 2010).

"Interview with Kevin Shirley." *Mix*, 2002.

"Interview with Steve Harris." *Classic Rock*, August 2012.

"Interviews with Adrian Smith." Iron Maiden YouTube channel, August 13, 24, and 31, 2021.

"Iron Maiden." *Brave Words & Bloody Knuckles* 29 (April 1999).

"Iron Maiden: A Behind-the-Scenes Look at the 'Different World' video" (as quoted from *Digit*). BraveWords.com, November 2, 2006.

"Iron Maiden: Cyber-Eddie!" *Brave Words & Bloody Knuckles* 22 (February/March 1998).

"Iron Maiden, Rod Smallwood Part Ways with Sanctuary." Yahoo!, November 3, 2006.

"Iron Maiden: 'This Is Not a Reunion!'" *Brave Words & Bloody Knuckles* 31 (June 1999).

Irwin, Colin. "Eddie, the Maiden and the Rue Morgue." *Melody Maker*, April 4, 1981.

Jeffries, Neil. *No Prayer for the Dying* record review. *Kerrang!* 309 (September 29, 1990).

Johansson, Henrik, and Mattias Reinholdsson. "Interviews with Chris Dale, Bruce Dickinson and Roy Z." *The Bruce Dickinson Wellbeing Network*.

Kay, Jimmy. "Interviews with Blaze Bayley, Paul Di'Anno, Steve 'Loopy' Newhouse, Doug Sampson, Adrian Smith, Dennis Stratton and Thunderstick." *Metal Voice*.

Killers record review. *Billboard*, May 30, 1981.

Koroneos, George. "Interview with Dave Murray." *Life in a Bungalow* 8 (Winter 1998).

Lafon, Mitch. "In Conversation with Iron Maiden's Dave Murray." BraveWords.com, January 19, 2004.

Lafon, Mitch. "Iron Maiden's Adrian Smith Talks Primal Rock Rebellion." BraveWords.com, July 12, 2012.

Lageat, Philippe. "Interview with Paul Di'Anno." *Rock Hard* 39 (December 2004).

Lageat, Philippe, and Olivier Rouhet. "Iron Maiden: Eddie's Fantastic Adventure." *Hard Rock* 17 (October 1996).

Laing, Rob (*Total Guitar*, guitarist). "Interview: Iron Maiden's Adrian Smith and Dave Murray on *The Book of Souls*." *Musicradar*, August 14, 2015.

Lawson, Dom. *The Burning* record review. *Louder Sound*, January 17, 2020.

Lawson, Dom. "Iron Maiden: Travelers in Time." *Brave Words & Bloody Knuckles*, January 2008.

Lawson, Dom. "Iron Maiden's Bruce Dickinson" (as quoted from *Kerrang!*). BraveWords.com, June 29, 2006.

Marc. Bruce Dickinson interview. *Hard Force* 6 (April 1987).

"The Making of *A Matter of Life and Death*." EMI Records, 2006.

Martin, Vincent. "Iron Maiden: Inside the Belly of the Beast." *H Le Mag* 2 (October 1996).

Masters, Drew. "M.E.A.T.'s Choice Cut of the Month: Iron Maiden." *M.E.A.T.* 17 (October 1990).

Millar, Robbi. Iron Maiden / Praying Mantis concert review. *Juke*, December 5, 1981.

Millar, Robbi. *Live After Death* record review. *Sounds*, October 12, 1985.

Montague, Sarah. "HARDtalk Interview with Bruce Dickinson." BBC, May 29, 2012.

Nalbandian, Bob. "Interview with Steve Harris and Blaze Bayley." *Shockwaves*, 1998.

Nefarious Nick. Bruce Dickinson interview. *Under the Blade* 9 (1996).

Nefarious Nick. Nicko McBrain interview. *Under the Blade* 9 (1996).

Newton, Steve. "Bruce Dickinson Says It Would Be Unthinkable to Do an Iron Maiden Album without Martin Birch." *Georgia Straight*, 1983.

Newton, Steve. "Iron Maiden: 'Platinum Headbangers' in Vancouver." *Georgia Straight*, 1984.

Newton, Steve. "Iron Maiden's Clive Burr." *Georgia Straight*, July 9–16, 1982.

Palmerston, Sean. "Iron Maiden / Dio / Motörhead, Molson Canadian Amphitheatre, Toronto, ON, August 3, 2003." *Exclaim*, August 3, 2003, and September 1, 2003.

Potter, Valerie. "Conquering the Brave New World." *Metal-Is*, July 28, 2000.

Prince, Patrick. "Iron Maiden Continue to Naturally Expand Sound." *Goldmine*, September 15, 2015.

Ravin' Pestos. Interview with Bruce Dickinson. *Hard Rock* 108 (November 1993).

Reesman, Bryan. "Iron Maiden's Janick Gers Talks Festivals, Fish and *The Final Frontier*." *Attention Deficit Delerium*, August 17, 2010.

Ristic, Alex. "Iron Maiden: (Re) Master Blasters." *Brave Words & Bloody Knuckles* 26 (November/December 1998).

Ruskell, Nick. "The Way of the Samurai: Uncover the Secrets of Iron Maiden's New Album, *Senjutsu*." *Kerrang!*, July 21, 2021.

Sarah. *Awoken Broken* record review. *Scene Point Blank*, July 19, 2012.

Saupiquet, Nelly. "The Big Sleep." *Hard Rock* 21 (May 1986).

Saupiquet, Nelly. "Steve Harris & Dave Murray." *Hard Rock* 26 (October 1986).

Schwarz, Paul. *Brave New World* record review. *Chronicles of Chaos*, October 25, 2000.

Secher, Andy. "Iron Maiden: Exclusive Steve Harris Interview." *Hit Parader* 231 (December 1983).

Sharma, Amit. "Iron Maiden's Adrian Smith and Janick Gers on *Senjutsu*, Track by Track." *Total Guitar*, October 22, 2021.

Sharp, Keith. "Iron Maiden: Adding a Bit of Character." *Music Express* 69 (June 1983).

Sharp, Keith. "Maiden Drummer Beats 'Looney' Tag." *Music Express* 73 (November 1983).

Simmons, Sylvie. "Interview with Bruce Dickinson." *Hard Force* 17 (April 1988).

Simmons, Sylvie. "Last of the Summer Whine." *Sounds*, September 26, 1981.

The Sledge. "Bruce Dickinson: Tattooed Millionaire." *M.E.A.T.* 11 (April 1990).

Slevin, Patrick. "Interview with Iron Maiden: Conquered Earth; Next, *The Final Frontier*." *The Aquarian*, July 8, 2010.

Smith/Kotzen press release. *BMG Music*, January 26, 2021.

Smith, Monty. *The Number of the Beast* record review. *New Musical Express*, April 3, 1982.

"Stop the Presses: Bruce Dickinson Studio Report!!!" *Brave Words & Bloody Knuckles* 23 (April/May 1998).

Sutherland, Jon. "Iron Maiden: Eddie's Lobotomy and Other Inside Stuff from Iron Maiden's Steve Harris." *Record Review* 7, no. 4 (August 1983).

Sutherland, Jon. *The Number of the Beast* record review. *Record Review*, August 1982.

Thiollay, Pierre. "Interview with Steve Harris." *Enfer* 42 (November 1986).

Touchard, Philippe. "Interview with Bruce Dickinson." *Enfer* 17 (October 1984).

Ulrey, Jeremy. *The Book of Souls* record review. *Metal Injection*, September 10, 2015.

Van Horn, Ray, Jr. "Iron Maiden: Riding High with Benny Breeg." *Caustic Truths*, 2006.

Wall, Mick. "Portuguese Maiden O'War." *Kerrang!* 306 (September 8, 1990).

Wall, Mick. "Prayer Meeting." *Kerrang!* 307 (September 15, 1990).

Wall, Mick. "Running Free." *Guitar Legends*.

Wiederhorn, Jon. "Steve Harris: *The Final Frontier* Won't Be Iron Maiden's Swan Song." *Noisecreep*, September 2, 2010.

Wilding, Philip. "Tattooed Millionaire" single review. *Kerrang!* 285 (April 14, 1990).

Wilson, David Lee. "Interview with Janick Gers." *Metal Rules*, July 1999.

ACKNOWLEDGMENTS

Thanks to all of the above writers who had the good sense to talk to the Maiden guys when you could. Thank you also to my photographer buddies who helped make this book come alive; namely, Bill Baran, Rudy Childs, Daniel Croce, Rich Galbraith, Wolfgang Guerster, Tony Leonard, Dave McDonald, Patryk Pigeon, Franc Potvin, Trevor Shaikin, Ray Van Horn Jr., Tom Wallace, Rod Dysinger, and Dave Wright.

This book is dedicated to Hendrix Henderson.

AUTHOR BIOGRAPHY AND BIBLIOGRAPHY

At approximately 7,900 (with over 7,000 appearing in his books), Martin has unofficially written more record reviews than anybody in the history of music writing across all genres. Additionally, Martin has penned approximately 120 books on hard rock, heavy metal, classic rock, prog, punk, and record collecting. He was editor in chief of the now-retired *Brave Words & Bloody Knuckles*, Canada's foremost heavy metal publication for fourteen years, and has also contributed to *Revolver, Guitar World, Goldmine, Record Collector*, BraveWords.com, lollipop.com, and hardradio.com, with many record label band bios and liner notes to his credit as well.

Additionally, Martin has been a regular contractor to Banger Films, having worked for two years as researcher on the award-winning documentary *Rush: Beyond the Lighted Stage*, on the writing and research team for the eleven-episode *Metal Evolution*, and on the ten-episode *Rock Icons*, both for VH1 Classic. Additionally, Martin is the writer of the original metal genre chart used in *Metal: A Headbanger's Journey* and throughout the *Metal Evolution* episodes.

Then there's his audio podcast, *History in Five Songs with Martin Popoff*, and the YouTube channel he runs with Marco D'Auria, *The Contrarians*. The community of guest analysts seen on *The Contrarians* has provided the pool of speakers used across the pages of this very book. Martin currently resides in Toronto and can be reached through martinp@inforamp.net or martinpopoff.com.

...

2024
Hallowed Be Thy Name: The Iron Maiden Bible
Led Zeppelin: A Visual Biography
Honesty Is No Excuse: Thin Lizzy on Record
Van Halen at 50
Pictures at Eleven: Robert Plant Album by Album
Perfect Water: The Rebel Imaginos

2023
Kiss at 50
Dominance and Submission: The Blue Öyster Cult Canon
The Who and Quadrophenia
Wild Mood Swings: Disintegrating the Cure Album by Album
AC/DC at 50

2022
Pink Floyd and The Dark Side of the Moon: 50 Years
Killing the Dragon: Dio in the '90s and 2000s
Feed My Frankenstein: Alice Cooper, the Solo Years
Easy Action: The Original Alice Cooper Band
Lively Arts: The Damned Deconstructed
Yes: A Visual Biography II; 1982–2022
Bowie @ 75
Dream Evil: Dio in the '80s
Judas Priest: A Visual Biography
UFO: A Visual Biography

2021
Hawkwind: A Visual Biography
Loud 'n' Proud: Fifty Years of Nazareth
Yes: A Visual Biography
Uriah Heep: A Visual Biography
Driven: Rush in the '90s and "In the End"
Flaming Telepaths: Imaginos Expanded and Specified
Rebel Rouser: A Sweet User Manual

2020
The Fortune: On the Rocks with Angel
Van Halen: A Visual Biography
Limelight: Rush in the '80s
Thin Lizzy: A Visual Biography
Empire of the Clouds: Iron Maiden in the 2000s
Blue Öyster Cult: A Visual Biography
Anthem: Rush in the '70s
Denim and Leather: Saxon's First Ten Years
Black Funeral: Into the Coven with Mercyful Fate

2019
Satisfaction: 10 Albums That Changed My Life
Holy Smoke: Iron Maiden in the '90s
Sensitive to Light: The Rainbow Story
Where Eagles Dare: Iron Maiden in the '80s
Aces High: The Top 250 Heavy Metal Songs of the '80s
Judas Priest: Turbo 'til Now
Born Again! Black Sabbath in the Eighties and Nineties

2018
Riff Raff: The Top 250 Heavy Metal Songs of the '70s
Lettin' Go: UFO in the '80s and '90s
Queen: Album by Album
Unchained: A Van Halen User Manual
Iron Maiden: Album by Album
Sabotage! Black Sabbath in the Seventies
Welcome to My Nightmare: 50 Years of Alice Cooper
Judas Priest: Decade of Domination
Popoff Archive, 6: American Power Metal
Popoff Archive, 5: European Power Metal
The Clash: All the Albums, All the Songs

2017
Led Zeppelin: All the Albums, All the Songs
AC/DC: Album by Album
Lights Out: Surviving the '70s with UFO
Tornado of Souls: Thrash's Titanic Clash
Caught in a Mosh: The Golden Era of Thrash
Rush: Album by Album
Beer Drinkers and Hell Raisers: The Rise of Motörhead
Metal Collector: Gathered Tales from Headbangers
Hit the Lights: The Birth of Thrash
Popoff Archive, 4: Classic Rock
Popoff Archive, 3: Hair Metal

2016
Popoff Archive, 2: Progressive Rock
Popoff Archive, 1: Doom Metal
Rock the Nation: Montrose, Gamma, and Ronnie Redefined
Punk Tees: The Punk Revolution in 125 T-shirts
Metal Heart: Aiming High with Accept
Ramones at 40
Time and a Word: The Yes Story

2015
Kickstart My Heart: A Mötley Crüe Day-by-Day
This Means War: The Sunset Years of the NWOBHM
Wheels of Steel: The Explosive Early Years of the NWOBHM
Swords and Tequila: Riot's Classic First Decade
Who Invented Heavy Metal?
Sail Away: Whitesnake's Fantastic Voyage

2014
Live Magnetic Air: The Unlikely Saga of the Superlative Max Webster
Steal Away the Night: An Ozzy Osbourne Day-by-Day
The Big Book of Hair Metal
Sweating Bullets: The Deth and Rebirth of Megadeth
Smokin' Valves: A Headbanger's Guide to 900 NWOBHM Records

2013
The Art of Metal (coedited with Malcolm Dome)
2 Minutes to Midnight: An Iron Maiden Day-by-Day
Metallica: The Complete Illustrated History
Rush: The Illustrated History
Ye Olde Metal: 1979
Scorpions: Top of the Bill (updated and reissued as *Wind of Change: The Scorpions Story* in 2016)

2012
Epic Ted Nugent
Fade to Black: Hard Rock Cover Art of the Vinyl Age
It's Getting Dangerous: Thin Lizzy, 81–12
We Will Be Strong: Thin Lizzy, 76–81
Fighting My Way Back: Thin Lizzy, 69–76
The Deep Purple Royal Family: Chain of Events, '80s–'11
The Deep Purple Royal Family: Chain of Events through '79 (reissued as *The Deep Purple Family Year by Year*)

2011
Black Sabbath FAQ: The Collector's Guide to Heavy Metal; Volume 4; The 2000s (coauthored with David Perri)

2010
Goldmine Standard Catalog of American Records, 1948–1991, 7th edition

2009
Goldmine Record Album Price Guide, 6th edition
Goldmine 45 RPM Price Guide, 7th edition
A Castle Full of Rascals: Deep Purple, '83–'09
Worlds Away: Voivod and the Art of Michel Langevin
Ye Olde Metal: 1978.

2008
Gettin' Tighter: Deep Purple, '68–'76
All Access: The Art of the Backstage Pass
Ye Olde Metal: 1977
Ye Olde Metal: 1976

2007
Judas Priest: Heavy Metal Painkillers
Ye Olde Metal: 1973 to 1975
The Collector's Guide to Heavy Metal: Volume 3; The Nineties
Ye Olde Metal: 1968 to 1972

2006
Run for Cover: The Art of Derek Riggs
Black Sabbath: Doom Let Loose
Dio: Light beyond the Black

2005
The Collector's Guide to Heavy Metal: Volume 2; The Eighties
Rainbow: English Castle Magic
UFO: Shoot Out the Lights
The New Wave of British Heavy Metal Singles

2004
Blue Öyster Cult: Secrets Revealed! (updated and reissued in 2009 with the same title; updated and reissued as *Agents of Fortune: The Blue Öyster Cult Story* in 2016)
Contents under Pressure: 30 Years of Rush at Home & Away
The Top 500 Heavy Metal Albums of All Time

2003
The Collector's Guide to Heavy Metal: Volume 1; The Seventies
The Top 500 Heavy Metal Songs of All Time

2001
Southern Rock Review

2000
Heavy Metal: 20th Century Rock and Roll
The Goldmine Price Guide to Heavy Metal Records

1997
The Collector's Guide to Heavy Metal

1993
Riff Kills Man! 25 Years of Recorded Hard Rock & Heavy Metal

See martinpopoff.com for complete details and ordering information.

Thank you and good night. © Dave McDonald

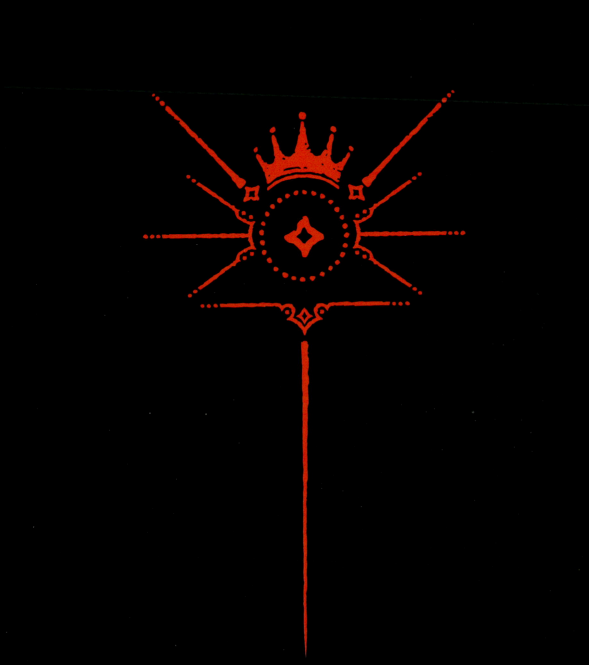

INDEX

In terms of methodology, first, we've exempted the names of Iron Maiden band members (who appear on albums), along with their trusty manager Rod Smallwood, due to the fact that in some cases, sensibly, some of these appear in the book hundreds of times. These have been left in the index, along with the designation "see introductory note."

Second, given that the chapters are both structured and titled primarily by album, these also have been left in the index, and given the designation "see chapter [#]."

Third, we've indexed every Iron Maiden song, but not the solo project songs. Trust that those are nearly completely covered in the chapter about the album they appear on.

Fourth, there are a few additional miscellaneous entries that have been given the "see introductory note" designation for the same reason as above, namely that the high number of times that they are mentioned renders the indexing of each instance somewhat meaningless.

AC/DC, 34, 48, 62, 106, 127, 139, 154, 165, 179, 190, 228, 256, 262, 266, 294, 296, 300, 311, 354
"Aces High," 167, 169, 171, 192, 204, 248, 262, 407, 454, 508
Accident of Birth, see Chapter 14
Adventures of Lord Iffy Boatrace, The, 237
Aerosmith, 256, 288, 303, 408
"Afraid to Shoot Strangers," 262, 264, 267, 314
"Aftermath, The," 307–308
"Age of Innocence," 439, 443–444
Air Raid Records, 358
"Alchemist, The," 352, 498, 512
Alexander, Phil, 400–401, 403
"Alexander the Great," 211–212, 225, 550, 599
Alive in Studio A, see Chapter 12
"All in Your Mind," 243
Anderson, Ian, 113, 322, 390, 403, 440, 514, 519
Andrews, Mark, 587
Andrews, Rob, 177
"Angel and the Gambler, The," 365, 370–371
Angelo, Rob, 20

Angel Witch, 16, 20, 35, 37, 58, 65, 73, 76, 99, 109, 111, 136, 179, 223
"Another Life," 24, 35, 89, 91–92
Anthology, 328, 463
"Apparition, The," 266
Argent, 607
Argus, 10, 118
Arnopp, Jason, 261, 267, 274, 280
Around the World in 66 Days, 518
Art of War, The, 583
A.S.a.P., 209, 230–231, 331, 526
"Assassin, The," 249, 265, 273
Awoken Broken, 526, 528
Aylmer, Chris, 11, 87
Ayreon, 412

Back in Black, 6, 139, 499
"Back in the Village," 170, 338
Balls to Picasso, see Chapter 12
Banger Films, 151, 451, 483, 493–494
Barnyard Studios, 237, 258, 260, 306, 364

INDEX

Barton, Geoff, 17, 32–33, 35–37, 62
Battery Studios, 81, 84, 116, 237, 239, 245, 318
Bayley, Blaze, *see* introductory note
"Bayswater Ain't a Bad Place to Be," 258
BBC, 36, 110, 246, 293, 456, 459, 467, 498, 501, 521
BBC Archives, 427
Beast, The, 100
Beast on the Road, 117, 127, 130
Beast Over Hammersmith, 427, 566
Be-Bop Deluxe, 119, 122, 129
Beckett, 88, 124, 164, 170
Begai, Carl, 329, 435, 445, 453
Begrand, Adrien, 482
Behind the Iron Curtain, 176, 229
Bell, Dick, 150
"Be Quick or Be Dead," 258, 261, 309, 438
Best of Bruce Dickinson, The, *see* Chapter 19
Best of the Beast, 314–315, 365, 428
Best of the B'Sides, 427
Bienstock, Richard, 500, 508, 511
Billboard, 73, 96, 145, 153, 189, 281, 310, 394, 410, 417, 468, 489, 516, 518
Birch, Martin, 10, 29, 84, 92, 112, 116–117, 121, 139, 142, 149, 172, 194, 200, 218, 222, 237, 244, 254, 258, 276, 300, 319, 348, 371, 470, 517, 578
Birch, Paul, 162
Bishop, Andy, 508
"Black Bart Blues," 218
Blackmore, Ritchie, 171, 354, 356, 475, 560, 589
Black Sabbath, 6, 10, 12–16, 18, 31–32, 34, 52, 58, 66, 69, 72–73, 84, 89, 106, 112–113, 118–119, 126, 129, 192, 248, 256, 264, 288, 294, 298, 325, 337, 347, 356, 378, 408, 429, 450–451, 461, 478, 501, 527, 532
Blake, William, 342, 344, 346–347, 349–352

"Blood Brothers," 403–405, 413, 426, 434, 510, 519, 566
"Blood on the World's Hands," 307–309, 372
BMG, 329, 377, 423, 579
Bonham, John, 549, 578, 607
Bon Jovi, 156, 192, 228, 380, 584, 607
Bonutto, Dante, 129–130, 149
Book of Souls, The, *see* Chapter 23
"Book of Souls, The," 549, 566
Book of Souls: Live Chapter, The, *see* Chapter 23
Bosso, Joe, 499
Bradstreet, Tim, 467–468
Brave New World, *see* Chapter 17
"Brave New World," 396, 398, 402, 413, 424, 439, 451
Brave Words & Bloody Knuckles (and *BW&BK*), 38, 193, 313, 320, 345, 364, 381, 383, 385, 410, 435, 446, 486, 537
Bridge House, 24, 26, 28, 34
"Brighter Than a Thousand Suns," 471–472
"Bring Your Daughter… to the Slaughter," 238, 251, 253–254, 262, 455, 606
British Lion, *see* Chapter 22
British Lion, *see* Chapter 22
British Steel, 62, 66, 94
Bromley, Adrian, 359, 361–362
Brown, Arthur, 113, 215, 220, 322, 328, 347, 349, 353
Bruce Dickinson's Friday Rock Show, 456, 501
Bruce Dickinson Wellbeing Network, 253, 285, 290, 320, 349
Budgie, 72, 76, 112, 129, 251, 262
Burke, Ray "Geezer," 459
Burning, The, *see* Chapter 22
"Burning Ambition," 24, 42, 53
Burr, Clive, *see* introductory note
Bushell, Garry, 14, 25, 29, 64, 97

Butler, Geezer, 605
Byford, Biff, 153

Cairns, Paul, 30, 34
Calm Before the Storm, 484
Cameron, Deane, 483
"Can I Play with Madness," 218–219, 221–223, 267, 438, 451, 547
Capitol Records, 96–97, 138, 282, 395
Card, Orson, 216, 218, 224
Carr, Andy, 239
Cart & Horses, 12–13, 27–28, 78
Cash, Johnny, 604
Casillas, Eddie, 288, 334, 338, 342, 349
Castle Music, 291, 292, 340, 394–395
Cathars, 440
"Caught Somewhere in Time," 204, 206, 212
"Chains of Misery," 265
Chapman, Graham, 223
Chapman, Paul, 175
Charge of the Light Brigade, The, 146, 151
"Charlotte the Harlot," 20, 24, 35, 71, 73, 120, 229, 262
Chemical Wedding (film), 336, 347
Chemical Wedding, The (album), *see* Chapter 15
"Childhood's End," 264
Children of Madness, 216, 417
"Children of the Damned," 118–119, 122, 130, 192, 246
Churchill, Winston, 167, 192, 591
"Clairvoyant, The," 225–226, 229, 441
"Clansman, The," 372–374, 404, 426, 440, 514, 599
Classic Albums, 418
Clive Burr Multiple Sclerosis Trust Fund, 420, 423, 451
Club Waterloo, 578
CMC International, 291, 335, 356, 377, 391

Coleridge, Samuel Taylor, 173–174
Collen, Phil, 71, 78, 136
"Coming Home," 510–511
"Communication Breakdown," 15, 254
"Como Estais Amigos," 374
Compass Point Studios, 139, 163, 198, 499, 501, 579
Cox, Jess, 112, 179
Cream, 13
"Cross-Eyed Mary," 151
Crowley, Aleister, 145, 220, 336–337, 347
Cummings, Winston, 190
Curbishley, Bill, 429

Dale, Chris, 290, 321, 324, 328–329
Dale, Dick, 606
Dance of Death, *see* Chapter 18
"Dance of Death," 438, 440, 446, 453, 519
"Darkest Hour," 589, 591
Darkside Films, 508
Dawson, Simon, 535
Dawson, Steve, 155
Day, Paul Mario, 13, 28, 35, 88, 94–95, 138
"Days of Future Past," 581, 587–588
"Death of the Celts," 589, 591, 595
Death on the Road, *see* Chapter 18
"Death or Glory," 542–543, 547, 550, 566
Dee, John, 512, 549
Deep Purple, 8, 10, 12–13, 18, 28, 31, 53, 58, 84, 107, 109, 119, 157, 164, 177, 192, 209, 218, 237–238, 253, 293, 318, 322, 324, 326, 352, 354, 356–357, 359, 361, 377, 380, 547, 604
Def American, 292, 296–297
Def Leppard, 31, 44, 51, 62, 65, 71, 73, 76, 136–137, 165, 179, 192, 228, 300, 450
"Deja-Vu," 210–211
Del Rio, Fabio, 239

Desperado, 230
"Devil Went Down to Georgia, The," 605
Diamond Head, 42, 51–52, 73, 125, 157, 178
Di'Anno, 162–163
Di'Anno, Paul, *see* introductory note
Di'Anno's Battlezone, Paul, 200
Dickinson, Bruce, *see* introductory note
Dickson, Alex, 290, 318, 326
"Die with Your Boots On," 145, 149, 192, 434
"Different World," 468–470, 484, 508
Dio (and Dio, Ronnie James), 66, 84, 106, 112–113, 121, 126, 179, 188, 195, 225, 295, 310, 335, 377, 403, 433–434, 501, 532, 545
Dirty Deeds, 311, 313, 376–377, 381, 412
Dive! Dive! Dive!, 241, 255
"Doctor Doctor," 312
Dodero, Camille, 493
Dome, Malcolm, 52, 326, 409
Donington, 165, 188, 229, 246, 272, 281, 380
"Don't Look to the Eyes of a Stranger," 372, 374
Down Fall the Good Guys, 256, 296
Downing, K. K., 64–65
Dragonforce, 432, 449, 541
"Dream of Mirrors," 404–405, 409, 424
"Drifter," 24, 35, 66, 74, 92–93, 96
Dry, Anthony, 510, 545
"Duellists, The," 170
Dumatray, Henry, 245, 264–265
Dune, 149, 176
Dunn, Sam, 151, 493

Eddie Rips up the World Tour, 449, 451
Eddie's Archive, 427
Ed Force One, 488, 493, 557
"Edge of Darkness, The," 307
Ed Hunter, 366, 368, 387–388, 390–392, 394–395, 407

"Educated Fool, The," 373–374, 439
Edward the Great, 369, 427, 483
"El Dorado," 503–504, 508–510
Elena, Alessandro, 290, 321, 323
Elliott, Paul, 309, 374–375
Emerson, Lake & Palmer, 177, 378, 556
EMI, 18, 44, 46, 50, 53–54, 57–60, 64, 69, 73–74, 77, 81, 87–88, 97, 115, 128, 139, 151, 195, 203, 229, 282, 291, 314, 377, 385, 423, 427, 433, 448, 451, 483, 486, 489, 504, 518, 522
"Empire of the Clouds," 555
Endino, Jack, 318, 323
Enfer, 149, 171, 198, 208–209, 211–212
Entire Population of Hackney, The, 195
En Vivo!, *see* Chapter 21
Epstein, Dmitry, 412, 415, 455
Essential Iron Maiden, The, 450
Ethel the Frog, 58
"Evil That Men Do, The," 223–224, 229, 477, 509
Evil Ways, 15, 124
Ewing, Jerry, 396, 403, 406
Evening with Nicko, An, 519
Eyes Wide Shut, 437

"Face in the Sand," 440, 443
"Fallen Angel, The," 405
Falling Down, 301
Fates Warning, 72, 195, 249
"Fates Warning," 249
"Fear Is the Key," 264, 267
Fear of the Dark, *see* Chapter 10
"Fear of the Dark," 226, 264, 267, 276, 279, 440, 494, 510, 540
Fender, 10, 82, 110, 214, 477
Fighting Back, 200, 216
Final Frontier, The, *see* Chapter 21
First Ten Years, The, 254

"Flash of the Blade," 170
Fleetwood Mac, 354, 537, 604
"Flight of Icarus," 139, 140, 145, 149, 192, 209, 223, 249, 438, 442, 509–510
Flight 666, 391, 483, 488, 493–494, 511
Flying Heavy Metal, 456
Foord, Dan, 526, 528
"For the Greater Good of God," 476
"Fortunes of War," 306–309, 440
Free, 10, 12, 15, 32, 75, 193, 254, 324, 390
Friday Rock Show, The, 42–43
From Here to Eternity, 254
"From Here to Eternity," 73, 262–263, 441
"Fugitive, The," 265
"Futureal," 366, 369, 381, 401
Future Past World Tour, 599

"Gangland," 115, 123
"Gates of Tomorrow," 441
Genesis, 10, 76, 138, 153, 478
"Genghis Khan," 89–90, 98, 115
Gers, Janick, *see* introductory note
"Ghost of the Navigator," 396, 402, 413
Gibson, 14, 110, 212, 477
Gillan, 76, 100, 109, 111, 230, 238, 246, 323, 369, 380, 397, 443
Gillan, Ian, 84, 106, 113, 116, 245, 321, 329, 356, 390, 473, 518, 547, 604
Girlschool, 99–100, 128
Give Me Ed . . . 'til I'm Dead Tour, 432–433, 438, 447
Glockler, Nigel, 154
Golden Earring, 37, 75, 243, 371, 538
Goodall, Ashley, 18, 29, 44, 46, 50, 53, 58–60, 67, 77, 115
Gogmagog, 188–189
Goodman, Mikee, 526–529

Gordon, Andrew, 587
Grammy, 267, 503, 510
Grand Prix, 129, 150
Grant, Melvyn, 261, 366, 506, 508
Grant, Peter, 233, 394, 447
"Great Unknown, The," 542, 548, 566
Great Wall of China, 584
Green, Nigel, 300
Green, Peter, 604
Greenhalgh, Howard, 285, 438, 470
"Green Manalishi," 604
Guillaume Tell Studios, 541, 580–581
Guns N' Roses, 192, 218, 228, 241, 256, 288, 296, 337, 349, 429, 467
Gypsy's Kiss, 10, 13–14, 204

Hagar, Sammy, 11, 41, 113
Halford, 414–415, 418–419, 457
Halford, Rob, 225, 260, 272, 284, 365, 385, 415, 451, 456–458, 608
"Hallowed Be Thy Name," 123–124, 126, 192, 280–281, 434, 439, 467, 516
Hammer Horror, 459, 461, 605
Hammersmith Odeon, 41, 95, 113, 192, 194, 229, 369
Hammill, Peter, 113, 322, 606
Harris, Lauren, 484–485, 487
Harris, Steve, *see* introductory note
Hawkins, David, 530, 535–537
Hawkwind, 106, 328, 605
Head On, 87–88, 109
Heaven and Hell, 66, 84
"Heaven and Hell," 121, 550
"Heaven Can Wait," 204, 207, 212, 229, 279
Heinlein, Robert, 209
"Hell on Earth," 593, 595
Helloween, 195, 229, 292, 299, 313, 354, 376, 381, 432, 446

INDEX

Henderson, Tim, 301, 318, 324, 398, 408–409, 419, 428, 445, 458, 461–462, 483, 503, 517, 529, 542, 544, 549, 552, 557

Hendrix, Jimi, 12–13, 15, 34, 110, 214, 222, 298, 339, 475, 579

Hipgnosis, 56, 240, 321

History of Iron Maiden Part 1: The Early Days, The, 448

History of Iron Maiden Part 2: Live After Death, The, 486

"Hocus Pocus," 41, 484

Hollingsworth, Ray, 24

Holloway, Alan, 379

Holy Diver, 179, 295

"Holy Smoke," 243–244, 248, 253, 262, 265, 273, 438–441

Honey, Matthew, 380

"Hooks in You," 250–251, 262

Hotten, Jon, 237, 241–242

Huxley, Aldous, 399, 402

Hyden, Steven, 553

"I Can't See My Feelings," 262

"Ides of March, The," 87–88, 90

"If Eternity Should Fail," 542, 546, 556, 566, 606

"I Got the Fire," 11, 66, 74, 130, 139, 229, 312

"I Live My Way," 300, 308–309

"I'm a Mover," 11, 254

"Infinite Dreams," 221–222, 229

Infinite Entanglement, 301, 560–561

Ingraham, Dave, 287, 334, 338, 342

"Innocent Exile," 12, 24, 35, 89–90, 101

Intercity Express Tour, 243, 245

In the Name of the Rose, 305

"Invaders," 118–119, 167

"Invasion," 30, 80

Iommi, Tony, 13, 390, 518

Iron Maiden (1970 band), 14

Iron Maiden, see Chapter 1

"Iron Maiden," 24, 30–31, 34–35, 43, 52, 72, 123, 192, 195, 246, 494, 566

"Isle of Avalon," 512

Jeffries, Neil, 254

Jethro Tull, 10–13, 75, 109, 113, 118–119, 151, 215, 482, 514, 519

Johansson, Henrik, 322, 324, 329, 335, 391

Johnson, Robert, 604

Jones, Tom, 200

"Journeyman," 440, 442, 444, 446, 453, 473

"Juanita," 209

"Judas Be My Guide," 265–266

Judas Priest, 6, 18–19, 28–29, 31, 35, 37, 40, 55–56, 62–66, 77, 93, 95–96, 101, 108, 119, 126, 128, 130, 149, 166, 179, 201, 209, 215, 239, 243, 260, 294, 315, 392–393, 405, 428, 450, 457, 556, 587, 608

"Judgement Day," 308–309, 616

"Judgement of Heaven," 307–308

"Justice of the Peace," 300, 308–309

Kay, Jimmy, 11, 20, 23, 27, 49, 71, 131, 292, 373, 579

Kay, Neal, 16, 20, 25, 31–34, 36–40, 44–46, 50–51, 54, 60, 65, 74, 110–11, 180

Kelley, Edward, 512

Kenney, Michael, 212, 306, 449

Kerrang!, 59, 97–99, 112–113, 122, 129, 139, 149, 238, 254–255, 272, 274, 290, 309, 326, 374–375, 463, 507, 510, 537, 583, 585, 595

Killers, see Chapter 2

"Killers," 21, 70, 81, 90–92, 96, 101, 229

Killers, Paul Di'Anno's, 260, 290, 365, 417, 419

"Kill Me Ce Soir," 243

INDEX

King Crimson, 119, 322, 347
"King of Twilight," 169
Kiss, 8, 29, 55, 62–63, 66, 68, 76–79, 96
Kneale, Nigel, 459, 461
Kodo drums, 583–584
Koroneos, George, 368, 374, 377, 387
Kossoff, Paul, 12, 15, 212, 214, 589
Kotzen, Richie, 580

Lafon, Mitch, 445, 447, 526–528
Laing, Rob, 543, 547, 552
Lawson, Dom, 193–194, 469, 471, 476, 486–488, 517, 537
Led Zeppelin, 10, 12–13, 15–18, 28, 31, 34, 52, 58, 75, 100, 109, 139–140, 177, 190, 222, 246, 254, 293, 298, 308, 322, 324, 380, 390, 450
Lee, Tony, 603
"Legacy, The," 466, 478–479
Legacy of the Beast, 569
Leslie, Grahame, 530, 535, 537
Lewis, Alan, 33, 35, 37
Lewis, C. S., 407
Lifeson, Alex, 91, 323, 326
"Lightning Strikes Twice," 372
Lights, Dave, 22–23, 52, 85, 151
Lionheart, 62, 78, 100, 165
Live After Death, see Chapter 6
Live at Donington, see Chapter 11
Live at the Rainbow, 81
Live Fast, Die Fast, 296
Live!!+One, 81
Loneliness of the Long Distance Runner, The, 208
"Loneliness of the Long Distance Runner, The," 208
Lonewolf, 158, 162
Long Beach Arena, 193–194, 345
"Longest Day, The," 473

"Look for the Truth," 306–307, 309
Loonhouse, Rob, 19, 41, 65
"Lord of Light," 477, 482
Lord of the Flies, 305
"Lord of the Flies," 305, 312, 451
"Losfer Words (Big 'Orra)," 170, 176, 192, 195, 440, 549
"Lost in a Lost World," 587
Ludwig (drums), 578
Lynott, Phil, 11, 30, 129, 137

Machine Head, 14, 253
Made in Japan, 12, 359, 361
Maiden England (tour), 520, 540–541
Maiden England, 229–230, 246, 254, 298
Maiden England '88, 522
Maiden Japan, 101
Makin' Magic, 138
Malone, Will, 61–62, 73
Mandrake Project, The, 602, 606–608
Manhattan Project, 472
Man in the Iron Mask, The, 14
"Man of Sorrows, The," 333, 335–338
"Man on the Edge," 300–301, 306, 308–310, 369, 401, 438
"Man Who Would Be King, The," 498, 514, 518
Marquee, The, 20, 38, 66, 75–76, 99, 180, 195, 291, 296–297
Marshall (amplifiers), 126, 214, 302, 474, 588
Martin, Simon, 545
Martin, Vincent, 272, 300, 315
"Massacre," 218
Matter of Touring, A, 483–485
Matthews, Ron, 13
Matter of Life and Death, A, see Chapter 20
MCA, 44, 60
McBrain, Nicko, *see* introductory note

McCoy, John, 109, 111
McFadyen, Scot, 151, 493
McFarlane, Todd, 419
McMurtrie, John, 508
Melody Maker, 11, 23, 32, 59, 97, 214, 239
Menace to Society, 298
"Mercenary, The," 404–405, 424
Mercuriadis, Merck, 467
Metal for Muthas, 9, 38, 44, 46, 48, 50–51, 53–55, 57–62, 64, 75
Metal for Muthas Volume II, 44, 75
Metal-Is, 413
Metallica, 6, 92, 119, 136, 155, 164, 166, 177, 256, 258, 296, 309, 312, 327, 410, 441, 445, 450
Metal 2000, 412, 418
Millar, Robbi, 114, 194
Missionary Position, The, 237
Mistheria, Maestro, 459, 605–606
Monjeaud, Hervé, 299, 446
Monsters of River Rock: My Life as Iron Maiden's Compulsive Angler, 579
Monsters of Rock, 165, 228–229, 272, 282, 367, 381, 418
Montrose, 11, 40, 74–75, 130, 139, 258
"Montségur," 439–440, 442
Moody Blues, 519, 587
Moonchild, 220
"Moonchild," 221, 223, 225, 489
Moore, Alan, 605
Moore, Gary, 15, 76, 129, 165, 339, 589
Moore, Nicky, 111–112, 164
Moore, Tony, 21–22, 24
More, 13, 35, 73, 94–95, 138
Moreno, Dave, 459, 607
"More Tea Vicar," 446
Morricone, Ennio, 605
"Mother of Mercy," 510
"Mother Russia," 251–252

Mötley Crüe, 113, 156, 165, 175, 179, 190, 192, 241, 450, 504
Motörhead, 8, 29, 32, 34, 37–38, 44, 48, 50, 65–66, 78, 223, 293, 313, 354, 377, 412, 429, 433–434, 541
MTV, 97, 175, 275, 285
Murders in the Rue Morgue, The, 89
"Murders in the Rue Morgue," 89, 96, 190, 192
Murray, Dave, *see* introductory note
Music Machine, The, 35–38, 44, 57, 110–111, 180
"My Generation," 312

Nalbandian, Bob, 367, 378, 387
Nektar, 169
"New Frontier," 441, 446
Newhouse, Steve "Loopy," 27, 131, 150
New Musical Express (*NME*), 59, 97, 126
Newton, Steve, 117, 128, 133, 139, 144–145, 169, 174–175
Newton, Tony, 536, 566
Nightmare on Elm Street 5: The Dream Child, A, 238, 251
"Nodding Donkey Blues," 258
Nirvana, 231, 256, 265, 318, 323, 327, 450
Nomad, 415, 485
"Nomad, The," 396, 405–406, 408
"No More Lies," 439, 443–446, 453
No More Lies–Dance of Death Souvenir EP, 444
No Prayer for the Dying, *see* Chapter 9
"No Prayer for the Dying," 248, 262
No Prayer on the Road, 255
Northfield, John, 13
Nugent, Ted, 8, 17, 35–36, 40–41
Number of the Beast, The, *see* Chapter 3
"Number of the Beast, The," 99, 120, 123, 128, 130, 169, 192, 369, 413, 427, 434, 438, 448, 453, 489
Nutz, 16, 58, 61, 154

INDEX

"Oh Well," 604
Olsen, Keith, 284, 286, 288
"Only the Good Die Young," 226
Operation: Mindcrime, 226–228, 279, 295
Osbourne, Ozzy, 44, 76, 112, 165–166, 190, 256, 267, 296, 311, 325, 451
Osbourne, Sharon, 451, 471, 482
"Out of the Shadows," 473–474, 482, 511
"Out of the Silent Planet," 407
Ozzfest, 418, 451, 463, 471, 482

Painkiller, 6, 243
Palmer, Robert, 163, 173
Palmerston, Sean, 434
Paper Money, 11
"Parchment, The," 591, 593, 595
Parents Music Resource Center, 121, 189
"Paschendale," 442–446, 453, 489
"Pass the Jam," 434
Patchett, Dave, 437
Peel, John, 119
Perez, Juan, 459
Phantom Music Management, 484
"Phantom of the Opera," 21, 43, 72, 80, 124, 192, 195, 203
Piece of Mind, see Chapter 4
"Pilgrim, The," 472–473, 482
Poe, Edgar Allan, 89
Point of Entry, 64, 93, 96, 128
Potter, Valerie, 413–414
Powell, Andy, 129
Powell, Cozy, 380, 607
Powerslave, see Chapter 5
"Powerslave," 171–173, 174, 192, 226, 579
Praying Mantis, 16, 20, 36, 40, 51, 58–60, 66, 74, 76, 111, 129, 176, 189, 255
Premier (drums), 519

Primal Rock Rebellion, *see* Chapter 22
Prisoner, The, 171
"Prisoner, The," 115, 119, 129–130, 170, 229, 246, 324
ProTools, 280, 348, 425–426, 436, 460–461, 549, 581, 583
"Prowler," 24, 30, 34–35, 69, 229, 276
Psycho Motel, 169, 273, 298–299, 310, 331, 337, 339–340, 526, 528, 538
"Public Enema Number One," 249, 262
"Purgatory," 24, 35, 92, 98, 117
Puttin' It Straight, 138
Pyromania, 136

Quatermass and the Pit, 459, 461
Queensryche, 72, 166, 176, 195, 216, 226–227, 249, 279, 295, 322, 414, 419, 445
Quest for Fire, 147
"Quest for Fire," 144, 147, 251, 406
Quinn, Paul, 154

Rainbow (band), 19, 23, 41, 84, 106, 128–129, 264, 315, 354, 369
Rainbow (bar), 203, 228, 240
"Rainbow's Gold," 88, 124, 164, 170
Rainbow Theatre, 64, 66, 75, 78, 81, 114
"Rainmaker," 435, 439–440, 444–446, 453
Raising Hell, 279, 298
Rance, Terry, 13
Raven, 75, 153, 358
"Reach Out," 200, 209–210, 518
Reading Rock, 76, 100, 106, 129
Real Dead One, A, see Chapter 11
Real Live One, A, see Chapter 11
Recording Industry Association of America (RIAA), 157, 195, 201, 215, 229, 254
"Red and the Black, The," 543, 548–549, 566, 593

Reesman, Bryan, 490, 493, 504, 512, 514

"Reincarnation of Benjamin Breeg, The," 467, 475, 482

Reinholdsson, Mattias, 253, 268, 320, 324, 347

"Remember Tomorrow," 70–71, 101, 103, 112, 128

Resurrection, 415

"Revelations," 119, 144–145, 147, 149, 172, 192, 220, 434

Riddles, Kevin, 136, 179

Riggs, Derek, 6, 38, 55–56, 66, 74, 81, 85–86, 94–95, 98, 101, 103, 112, 117, 139, 141–142, 151, 166, 171, 191, 202–204, 206, 210, 218–219, 234, 243, 247–248, 252, 254, 261, 277–278, 280, 299, 303, 315, 332–333, 336–337, 399–400, 446, 448, 470, 482, 485

"Rime of the Ancient Mariner, The," 171, 173–174, 192, 211, 225, 402, 442, 489, 543

Ristic, Alex, 272, 345

Rock in Rio, *see* Chapter 17

Rock N Roll Ribs, 558

Roland, 209, 212

Rolling Stones Mobile, The, 237, 253

"Roll Over Vic Vella," 262

R101 (airship), 324, 555

"Rothchild," 24, 88

"Running Free," 21, 42–43, 52–53, 55–57, 70–72, 85, 88, 101, 189–190, 192, 195, 272

"Run Silent Run Deep," 250

"Run to the Hills," 117, 122–123, 192, 195, 223, 237, 294, 423, 438, 453, 489

Rush, 16, 39, 42, 62, 72, 91, 121, 173, 192, 208, 249, 303, 307–308, 318, 322–323, 326–327, 336, 472, 513

Ruskell, Nick, 583

Ruskin Arms, 12, 28, 57, 64, 86, 115, 203

Sabaton, 541, 569

Sampson, Doug, 11–12, 26–27, 30, 38, 40, 42–44, 48, 53

Samson, 11, 16, 20–21, 35, 37, 49–52, 58, 62, 76, 87–88, 99–100, 106, 108–113, 115, 126, 155, 164–165, 214, 238, 240, 326, 355, 357–359

Samson, Paul, 11, 51, 87, 108, 110–11, 164, 214

Sanctuary (companies), 15, 58, 231, 233, 279, 290, 391, 394, 414, 417, 428, 429, 446, 457, 463–464, 467, 470, 484

"Sanctuary," 24, 43, 52, 58, 66, 70, 74, 190, 192, 204, 413

Sarm West Studios, 432, 466

"Satellite 15… The Final Frontier," 504, 508–509

Saupiquet, Nelly, 199

Sawyer, Bob, 20

Saxon, 25, 31, 50–51, 62, 65–66, 96–97, 112–113, 153–155, 157, 164–165, 178–179, 192, 223, 293, 587

Schenker Group, Michael, 106, 129, 157, 175, 250

Schwartz, Paul, 408

Scorpions, 56, 113, 127–129, 166, 179, 192, 251, 286, 356, 450, 604

Scott, Bon, 62, 294–295

Scream for Me Brazil, *see* Chapter 15

Scream for Me Sarajevo, 558

Screaming Lord Sutch, 604–605

Secher, Andy, 147, 153

"Sea of Madness," 205, 207, 212, 550

Senjutsu, *see* Chapter 24

"Senjutsu," 583, 587, 595, 599

Seventh Son (book), 218

Seventh Son of a Seventh Son, *see* Chapter 8

"Seventh Son of a Seventh Son," 225

Seventh Tour of a Seventh Tour, 228–229

"Shadows of the Valley," 542, 550–551

Shakespeare, William, 223, 561

Sharma, Amit, 584

Sharp, Keith, 138, 142, 150, 483

Shepherd, Brian, 46, 54, 60

"Sheriff of Huddersfield," 200, 258

Shirley, Kevin, 7, 396–398, 401–402, 408–409, 425–427, 432, 435–436, 445, 466, 777, 482, 487, 499, 509–510, 541, 547, 566, 571, 580, 587

Shock Tactics, 110, 112

"Sign of the Cross," 304–306, 308–309, 369, 440, 599

Signature Sound, 457, 603

SikTh, 526, 528

Silver and Gold, 230–231

Silver Cloud, 333, 342

Simmons, Gene, 77

Simmons, Sylvie, 222

Skunkworks, see Chapter 14

Skunkworks Live, 328

Skyhooks, 75, 80

Slagel, Brian, 97, 177

Sledgehammer, 38, 58, 76, 109

Slevin, Patrick, 501, 509

Small, Aaron, 519

Smallwood, Rod, *see* introductory note

Smiler, 11–13, 15, 26

Smith, Adrian, *see* introductory note

Smith/Kotzen, 580

Snider, Dee, 176, 189, 230, 448

Somewhere Back in Time: The Best of: 1980-1989, 489

Somewhere Back in Time (tour), 486, 487, 489–490, 493

Somewhere in Time, see Chapter 7

Somewhere on Tour, 199, 211–212, 215

Sooty Show, The, 218

Sound City, 295, 333, 342

Soundgarden, 231, 287, 298, 318, 322–323, 326–327, 348–349, 354

Soundhouse, The, 16–17, 19–20, 32–34, 36, 38–42, 45–46, 65, 111, 180–181

Soundhouse Tapes, The, 9, 30, 38, 40, 43, 49, 62, 64, 314

"Space Station #5," 258

"Space Truckin'," 461

Speed, 20, 106, 108, 110

"Speed of Light," 542, 545, 547–548, 550, 566

Spinefarm Records, 526

Stanley, Paul, 77

"Starblind," 513, 518

Star Wars, 202, 204, 210, 320, 507

State of Mind, 273, 298–299, 339

"Still Life," 146–147, 229

Stone, Steve, 399

Stranger in a Strange Land, 209

"Stranger in a Strange Land," 208–210, 212, 370, 402

"Strange World," 24, 30, 72, 88, 147, 209

"Stratego," 584, 587, 599

Stratocaster, 214, 477

Stratton, Dennis, *see* introductory note

Stuart Crouch Creative, 545

Styx, 17, 34, 39, 46, 72, 106

Sullivan, Dave, 13

"Sun and Steel," 147

Sutherland, Jon, 126, 141–142

"2 A.M.," 308

"2 Minutes to Midnight," 115, 164, 169, 171, 192, 207, 281, 434, 442, 547

12 Wasted Years, 216, 229

"22 Acacia Avenue," 20, 73, 120, 130, 176, 192, 203, 262, 441, 477

38 Special, 128
"Tailgunner," 248, 258, 262, 265, 273, 508
"Talisman, The," 513–514, 517–518
Tarantino, Quentin, 605
Tatler, Brian, 51, 125, 157, 178
Tattooed Millionaire, see Chapter 9
Taylor, Andy, 15, 37, 117, 394, 467
Taylor, Richard, 530, 532, 535–538
"Tears of a Clown," 541, 543, 550
Thatcher, Margaret, 35, 74, 81, 522
"That Girl," 209
"These Colours Don't Run," 470
"Thin Line Between Love and Hate, The," 408
Thin Lizzy, 10, 13, 15–16, 20, 30, 32, 57, 129, 136–137, 192, 218, 225, 239, 335, 339, 354, 356, 469, 473, 533, 535, 551
Thiollay, Pierre, 198
"Thriller," 605
"Thunderburst," 87–88
Thunderstick (Barry Purkis), 21–24, 26, 87–88, 108, 110, 358
"Time Machine, The," 589
Tipton, Glenn, 62
Toad the Wet Sprocket, 36, 58–59, 61, 111
Top of the Pops, 55, 58, 94, 125, 149, 301
Tormé, Bernie, 109, 129, 177, 230, 238
"Total Eclipse," 117, 123
"To Tame a Land," 149, 174, 225
Touchard, Philippe, 171–172
Townshend, Pete, 33, 222
"Transylvania," 24, 35, 43, 72, 276
Travers, Pat, 15, 76, 138, 484
Tribe of Gypsies, 285, 462
Trinifold Group, 428
Trivium, 484, 599
Trooper (beer), 522, 541, 569

"Trooper, The," 81, 145–146, 151, 192, 246, 280, 308, 310, 420, 434, 451, 471, 477
Trust, 93, 99, 127, 130–131, 138, 142, 484
Tsangarides, Chris, 136–137, 239, 241, 243
Tucker, John, 25–26, 37, 42, 60
Tucker, Mick, 65
Turbo, 201, 209, 215, 243
"Twilight Zone," 85, 94
Twisted Sister, 129, 156, 176, 228, 230
Tygers of Pan Tang, 31, 44, 51, 76, 106, 112, 129, 136–137, 153, 165, 179, 239
Tyranny of Souls, see Chapter 19

UFO, 31, 76, 91, 99, 126, 175, 192, 204, 251, 311–312, 371, 450, 459, 531, 533, 535, 538
Ulrey, Jeremy, 555–556
Ulrich, Lars, 97, 177
"Unbeliever, The," 308
Unmasked, 76, 78, 96
Urchin, 15, 20, 26, 76, 80, 195, 209–210, 230

Vance, Tommy, 17, 59, 119
Van der Graaf Generator, 113, 119, 322, 606
Van Halen, 16, 35, 84, 137, 165–166, 179, 304
Van Halen, Alex, 578
Van Halen, Eddie, 15, 579
Van Horn, Jr., Ray, 132, 421, 480
Video Pieces, 151
Virtual XI, see Chapter 16
"Virus," 513–314, 369
Visions of the Beast, 433, 450–451, 508

Wacken Open Air, 489, 504
Wall, Mick, 36, 242, 249, 251, 275, 385–386
Wapram, Terry, 20–21, 26
W.A.S.P., 176, 215, 377

INDEX

"Wasted Years," 200, 205–207, 209–210, 212, 216, 222, 267, 280, 338, 407, 438, 510, 550
"Wasting Love," 264–265, 273, 284
Watchmen, 605–606
Way, Pete, 91, 175, 212
Waysted, 175, 212, 215
"Weekend Warrior," 265–267
Welcome to the World, 339
Wessex Studios, 42
What Does This Button Do?, 566
"When the River Runs Deep," 549
When the Wind Blows, 514
"When the Wild Wind Blows," 498, 514, 518
"When Two Worlds Collide," 369, 372–373
"Where Eagles Dare," 142, 144, 151, 170
Whitesnake, 29, 76, 84, 137, 188, 218, 228
White Spirit, 75, 81, 109, 238, 443
Who, The, 55, 371, 531–532, 535
Wicker Man, The (film), 400
"Wicker Man, The," 395–396, 399–402, 405, 408–409, 413, 423, 434, 455, 508, 510, 519, 522, 545, 547
Wiederhorn, Jon, 499, 501, 507–508, 514
Wigens, Tony, 79, 131
Wilcock, Dennis, 11, 13, 20, 24, 26–27, 73, 88
"Wildest Dreams," 433–435, 438–439, 445–446, 453, 470, 508
Wilding, Phil, 237
Wilkinson, Julie, 545

Wilkinson, Mark, 400, 407, 545, 581
Wishbone Ash, 10, 12–13, 20, 43, 84, 118, 129, 371, 443, 533
Wisseloord Studios, 198
Wolfsbane, 243, 256, 272, 292, 294, 296–297, 307–309, 404, 521, 560
"Women in Uniform," 80–81, 229, 312
Wordsworth, William, 604
World Piece Tour '83, 150–151, 153, 157
World Slavery tour, 164, 175–176, 188–189, 194–196, 215, 254
World's Only Female Tribute to Iron Maiden, 448
World Wide Blitz, 96
"Wrathchild," 21, 24, 34–35, 52, 88–90, 94, 192, 280, 349, 435, 481, 566
"Writing on the Wall, The," 581, 584–585, 589, 599

X Factor, The, see Chapter 13
X Factour, The, 310–314

Yakuza, 583

Z, Roy, 284–287, 290, 329, 331, 333–334, 337–338, 342, 344, 347, 352, 355–357, 361, 385, 397, 454, 456–459, 462, 545, 602–608
Zomba, 81
ZZ Top, 12, 129, 237, 354